PRAISE F[...]

"No one paints a more delicious portrait of Hollywood than Jackie Collins." —*New York Post*

"Jackie Collins knows a thing or two about life in the fast lane . . . [with] her wry sense of humor and spitfire approach." —*Bazaar*

. . . AND HER BLOCKBUSTER BESTSELLERS

The Power Trip

"This sea of extravagant creatures, whose sexual tastes lie on the fringe of raunchy, is abashedly rousing, and what more could one hope for from Collins?"

—*Publishers Weekly*

Poor Little Bitch Girl

"If anyone knows Hollywood, it's Jackie Collins . . . With *Poor Little Bitch Girl* the bestselling author proves she's still got it." —*New York Daily News*

"Jackie Collins is at her seasoned best with this raunchy, retro hot-sheets romance." —*Publishers Weekly*

Also by Jackie Collins

The Santangelo Novels

DOUBLE
LUCKY

TWO BOOKS IN ONE

Drop Dead Beautiful
and
Goddess of Vengeance

Jackie
Collins

St. Martin's Paperbacks

This is a work of fiction. All of the characters, organizations, and events portrayed in these novels are either products of the author's imagination or are used fictitiously.

DOUBLE LUCKY: DROP DEAD BEAUTIFUL copyright © 2007 by Chances, Inc. and GODDESS OF VENGEANCE copyright © 2011 by Chances, Inc.

Excerpt from *The Santangelos* copyright © 2014 by Chances, Inc.

For information address St. Martin's Press, 175 Fifth Avenue, New York, NY 10010.

ISBN: 978-1-250-06829-3

Printed in the United States of America

St. Martin's Paperbacks edition / May 2015

St. Martin's Paperbacks are published by St. Martin's Press, 175 Fifth Avenue, New York, NY 10010.

10 9 8 7 6 5 4 3 2 1

DROP DEAD
BEAUTIFUL

*For my family, who are a constant
source of love and encouragement
And
For my friends, whom I often write about,
only I change the names to protect the
not so innocent!*

PROLOGUE

The house in Pasadena was grand by anyone's standards. Large and imposing. An impressive Colonial mansion that reeked of money, nothing flashy.

Penelope Whitfield-Simmons and her son, Henry, lived in the mansion. Penelope was the widow of the powerful newspaper magnate Logan Whitfield-Simmons, who died at the age of seventy-two from a massive heart attack while out on a fishing trip with his only son. Henry, twenty-two at the time of his father's death, was now thirty, but he still lived at home, because in Logan's will, Henry received nothing until the death of his mother, and Penelope—a healthy seventy—had no intention of going anywhere.

Henry had no drive, no ambition. When he was younger he'd decided he wanted to be an actor. "Acting is for pansies," his father had roared. "Your place is in the newspaper business with me."

Henry had appealed to his mother. "Listen to your father," Penelope had said. "Everyone knows that people in the film business are all drug addicts, sexual deviants, and perverts. Not our kind, dear."

Ha! *Henry had thought. As if she would know.*

Behind their backs he tried his best. He'd secretly taken acting classes and found himself an agent.

One day a fellow student in his acting class mentioned that Alex Woods, the renowned Oscar-winning director, was auditioning young actors for the lead role

opposite the very famous Venus Maria in his new movie,
Seduction.

*Henry was excited. He set about finding out every-
thing he could regarding the upcoming film, even going
so far as to bribe his agent's assistant to get him a copy
of the script. He studied the script religiously, practicing his dialogue and moves in front of a mirror. When
he considered himself fully prepared, he instructed
his agent to get him in for an audition.*

*His agent had looked at him as if he were a mental
case, and informed him that getting an audition for an
Alex Woods film was virtually impossible for an actor
who had no prior experience.*

*Henry came from a world of extreme wealth and
privilege. At an early age he'd learned from his father
that in their world nothing was impossible.*

*With a great deal of manipulating he'd arranged to
get himself in for an audition.*

*The day he arrived for his appointment there were
fifteen other young actors sitting around in the cramped
waiting room. Henry proceeded to stare them down.
They might be good, but Henry was confident that he
was better.*

The Asian girl behind the desk handed him sides.

*Sitting, fidgeting, waiting, he'd imagined his future.
He would land the role, tell his parents, and there would
be nothing they could do about it.*

*He, Henry Whitfield-Simmons, was about to become
a famous movie star, with or without their approval.*

It never happened.

And why not?

Because of one woman.

Her name was Lucky Santangelo.

CHAPTER ONE

Drop Dead Beautiful. The three little words were scrawled on the Cartier card Lucky Santangelo had just opened. Hand-delivered, the note had been brought up to the house in Bel Air by Philippe, her houseman, who'd discovered it in the mailbox at the end of the driveway.

Drop Dead Beautiful. No signature, no return address.

Was it an invitation to an upcoming event too clever for its own good?

Whatever. One quick glance at the card, and Lucky tossed it in the trash.

Lucky Santangelo. A dangerously seductive woman with blacker-than-night eyes, full sensuous lips, a tangle of long jet-black hair, deep olive skin, and a lithe body. Wherever she went, Lucky still brought a room to a standstill, for not only was she wildly beautiful, she was also a powerhouse—a woman to be reckoned with, a force of nature. Street-smart and forever savvy—Lucky Santangelo had it all.

In her past, she'd built hotels in Vegas, owned a major movie studio, and been married three times. She'd also survived much heartache. Her mother, Maria, had been murdered when she was five years old. Her brother, Dario, was shot to death and tossed from a moving car. Then finally her fiancé, Marco, was gunned down in the parking lot of her Vegas hotel.

Eventually Lucky had found out that the man who'd ordered the brutal killings was her godfather, Enzio Bonnatti, a man she had always respected and trusted.

The information devastated her. Filled with vengeance, she'd lured Enzio into a carefully planned trap at his home, and shot him dead with his own gun, claiming that he'd tried to rape her. It was deemed a clear-cut case of self-defense.

Self-defense. *Sure.* She'd made it *look* like Bonnatti had been about to rape her, and the D.A. had bought it all the way. No surprise there. Her father, Gino, had major connections.

The real truth was that she'd shot the son of a bitch because he'd deserved to die, and she'd never regretted doing so. Justice had taken place. *Santangelo* justice.

Don't fuck with a Santangelo—the family motto.

Grabbing her purse from a shelf in the luxurious dressing room, Lucky headed for the door. Everything was large and luxurious in Bel-Air—the privileged enclave of the very rich and famous. The house she and her husband, Lennie, were living in was a short-term rental. Recent storms had wreaked havoc on their home in Malibu and they'd been forced to leave while repairs were being made.

The beach was more her style. Bel-Air was too cut off from real life with its winding hillside streets and enormous mansions hidden behind vast gates and high walls of impenetrable greenery. People existed as if they were living under siege, surrounded by multiple security guards and vicious attack dogs. That way of living was not for her. She enjoyed feeling unprotected and free, which was one of the reasons she'd opted out of running Panther Studios several years earlier.

Being the head of a Hollywood studio was no nine-to-five job. She'd found herself working seventeen-hour days, leaving no time for family and friends. One morning she'd woken up and thought, *That's it, I'm out.* She'd had enough of dealing with ego-inflated stars, nervous-for-their-jobs executives, fast-talking agents, neurotic directors, fat-assed producers, and anyone else who thought they could make it in the movie business—which was most people in L.A.

So she'd quit running Panther, and after producing one movie, *Seduction*, starring Venus Maria, and her new discovery, Billy Melina, she'd sold the studio and gotten out of the film business altogether.

Lennie was in the movie industry. That was enough for one family.

Besides, Lucky had other plans. She was getting back into the hotel business in Vegas—the place where it had all begun for her. Several years ago she'd put together a syndicate of interesting and colorful investors to develop a huge multibillion-dollar complex called the Keys. She'd been working with architects and planners for the last five years, and in less than a month they were about to celebrate the grand opening. Since the hotel project was her baby, she was beyond excited.

"Mom!" Max burst into the dressing room without knocking. Max, her sixteen-year-old wild child. Tall and coltlike with smooth olive skin, green eyes, an unruly tangle of black curls, and a killer bod, Max was a show-stopper. She was also a rebel, playing truant from school on a regular basis.

"Here's the thing," Max announced, bouncing up and down on the balls of her feet. "There's no *way* I can go to Grandpa's party."

"Excuse me?" Lucky questioned, attempting to remain calm.

"Y'see, there's this big blowout for one of Cookie's best friends up in Big Bear," Max blurted, speaking too fast. "A whole crowd of us wanna go, so like I can't let Cookie down."

"You can't, huh?" Lucky said coolly.

"Nope," Max answered, tugging on a stray curl. "Cookie's my best friend an' this is like *essential.*"

"You are *not* missing Gino's birthday," Lucky said firmly. "No way."

Max stared balefully at her mom. "Huh?"

"You heard me," Lucky said, heading for the door.

"I can't believe you'd be this *mean,*" Max complained, trailing behind her.

"Mean?" Lucky sighed. This was major déjà vu. It reminded her of all the times she and Gino had gone head to head, and there were too many to remember.

"*Why* do I have to stay for Gino's stupid party?" Max demanded. "It's not as if he'll *miss* me."

"Of *course* he'll miss you," Lucky insisted, hurrying down the stairs.

"He'll like *so* not," Max grumbled, right behind her.

Lucky turned around, shooting her daughter a warning look. "You're getting on my bad side, so stop it."

"But—"

"*No,* Max," Lucky said, walking out the front door. "I'm not interested, don't want to hear it."

And with those words she got into her red Ferrari and roared off down the driveway.

"*Crap!*" Max shrieked as her mother's car vanished into the distance.

"Whassup?" questioned her younger brother, Gino Junior, rounding the corner from the tennis court.

"Mom sucks!" Max complained, ignoring Gino Junior's two leering friends, both of whom she knew had a total crush on her.

"What she do now?" Gino asked. He was only fifteen, but he was already six feet tall and built like a football player.

"She won't let me get out of Grandpa's lame party. That's *so pathetic.*"

Ignoring her, Gino Junior raced into the house, followed by his two friends, who couldn't take their eyes off her.

"Horny little pricks," she muttered under her breath. "Go jerk off someplace else. Like *Siberia*."

Lucky drove like a race car driver, skillfully weaving in and out of traffic. She turned the CD player on full volume—Usher blasting.

Lately Max's behavior was becoming quite a challenge. Everything seemed to turn into an argument. Lucky sighed. It wasn't easy being a parent, especially when in your head you were hardly any older than your own child.

A frosted and Botoxed blonde in a shiny new Mercedes cut in front of her, causing her to hit the brakes. "Shit, lady!" Lucky yelled. "Whyn't you learn to fuckin' *drive*?"

Not that anyone could hear her, but shouting at other drivers eased the tension, although if Lennie happened to be in the car, it made him crazy. "One of these days someone's gonna get out their car and shoot your ass," he was always warning her.

"Yeah, sure," she would reply. "I *dare* them to."

At which point Lennie would shake his head. In his eyes there was no taming Lucky Santangelo. She walked her own path, and that's exactly the way he liked her.

CHAPTER TWO

Movie star Billy Melina was over six feet tall, tanned, with shaggy, bleached-by-the-sun hair, and a body straight out of an Abercrombie & Fitch catalog. At twenty-eight Billy was in spectacular shape, with sharply defined abs that rippled as the starstruck young girl kneeling in front of him bobbed her head up and down, servicing him with sticky lips and a busy tongue.

"Suck it!" Billy commanded, pressing his hands down on top of her head. "Suck it, suck it *hard!*"

She was doing the best she could. What more did he expect?

"Aarghh . . ." He let out a long, agonized groan. "That's it, sweet thing, that's *it!* I'm coming . . . I'm coming."

The girl attempted to pull away.

"No! No!" Billy yelled, pressing down even harder on the back of her head. "*Swallow* it, suck it all *down.*" He groaned again, then mumbled, "Go, baby. Go. That's it! *Yeeeah!*"

For a moment there was silence while the girl tried to decide if it was now okay to release his massive dick from the confines of her mouth.

He decided for her, pulling away with a sudden jerk, immediately stuffing himself back into his tight white Calvins and pulling up his jeans.

They were standing next to the pool in Billy's Hollywood Hills house—a house that the Realtor had assured him had once been rented by Charlie Sheen. A house that had cost him three million dollars, and who the fuck had ever thought he would be able to afford to buy such a house?

Certainly not his old man, Ed, who'd laughed in his face when Billy had informed him, eight years ago, that he was off to Hollywood to become a famous actor. Certainly not his alcoholic stepmother, Millie, whose parting words had been, "Good riddance, Billy boy. Doncha bother comin' back anytime soon."

He'd shown them, hadn't he? Oh yeah, he'd certainly shown them. He was Billy Melina. Hotshot twenty-something movie star. Yeah—a freakin' *movie star.* He was on a very exclusive list of young actors who had the clout to open a movie. DiCaprio, Depp, Pitt—although Brad wasn't so young anymore. And then there was Billy Melina.

Yeah! Get off on *that,* old Ed and Millie pissface.

The girl, clad in denim cut-offs and a skimpy yellow tank, got off her knees and stood up. "Was that okay?" she asked matter-of-factly, as if she'd just served him an omelette.

"Sweet," he replied, wondering how fast he could get rid of her.

Earlier in the day he'd picked her up at Tower Records on Sunset. When the girl had spotted him, she'd sidled over and requested his autograph. He'd noticed her nipples, pushing to escape her barely-there tank top. Then he'd noticed her legs, long and tanned. Her face was pretty—nothing special, but he was feeling major horny, and since his call to the set was not until three that afternoon, he'd invited her up to his house for lunch and a fast blow job. Not that he'd actually mentioned that a blow job was part of the deal—but they'd both known what would happen.

Quivering with excitement, she'd jumped in her truck

and followed his sleek Maserati up the winding streets to his house, barely keeping up in her beat-up old truck with a broken taillight—a truck similar to the one he'd driven to Hollywood eight years earlier with two hundred bucks in his pocket and no prospects.

"Hey," he suggested as they stood beside the pool. "How about I give you an autographed picture so you can tell your friends you met me?"

"That'd be cool," she said, acting shy—as if his cock hadn't been in her mouth minutes before.

"Wait here," he instructed sternly. "I'll be right back."

When Billy had first arrived in Hollywood, he'd called women "ma'am," and been full of respect and good manners. Stardom had gotten him over *that* particular hump, although he still had a chivalrous streak.

He darted into his house through sliding glass doors, feeling ever so slightly guilty on account of the fact that he had a girlfriend—a gorgeous, famous movie star thirteen years his senior—and if she ever found out that he wasn't exactly Joe-faithful, she'd be well and truly pissed. But hey, a blow job wasn't cheating—everyone knew that. Jeez—President Clinton had declared it wasn't sex on national TV. How could anyone argue with *that*?

Ramona, his Hispanic housekeeper, was singing to herself in the kitchen, quite oblivious to the goings-on out by the pool. Kev, his assistant/best friend from the old days, was on the loose somewhere, running errands or picking up girls. He'd certainly get off on this one.

Billy rifled through the stuff on the coffee table in his den and located a stack of glossy eight-by-tens mixed up with unopened bills, pornographic fan mail, a half-smoked joint, well-thumbed car magazines, and an empty candy box. He grabbed a pen, hurriedly scrawled his signature on the photo, and raced back outside, eager to get her off the premises.

The young girl had divested herself of her cut-offs and tank, and was swimming bare-assed naked in his pool.

Shit! What was he supposed to do now?

"Hey," he said, chewing on his thumbnail.

"Didn't think you'd mind," she responded nonchalantly.

Well, I do, he thought sourly.

"Uh . . . okay," he said, still chewing. "But I gotta take off any minute, so you're gonna hafta haul your hot little ass outta there."

"How about *you* getting in?" she suggested, becoming bolder by the minute. "It's all *warm* an' *wet*, you won't be disappointed."

She flipped onto her back, floating in his azure pool, her small nipples erect and disturbingly tempting.

He contemplated this juicy prize, there for the taking. She had a flat stomach, a huge bush of wiry pubic hair—which he found quite sexy because shaved pussy was all the rage in Hollywood—and those long, sexy legs.

Familiar stirrings down below, even though only moments before he'd experienced an extremely satisfactory orgasm.

What the hell, he'd nail her in the pool, then hustle her out of there before she knew it.

After all, what Venus didn't know . . .

"Where's Billy?" Alex Woods demanded of Maggie, his personal assistant, a tall woman of Native American descent with long black hair scraped back into a ponytail and strong, almost manly features.

They were standing next to a wooded area several miles outside of L.A. shooting Alex's current movie, *Kill*, a violent thriller.

Maggie sensed an outburst coming on. She was well

aware that as a director Alex Woods was an Oscar-winning genius, and yet as a man he could be a nightmare. When things were not to his liking, everyone had to watch out—including her. She often wondered how his Asian lawyer girlfriend, Ling, put up with him.

"He's on his way," she assured him in a calm voice.

"What the fuck is *that* supposed to mean?" Alex snapped, rubbing his hands together. "His call was for three, and it's now three forty-five."

"I know," Maggie said, remaining calm.

"So get in touch with his driver and tell the asshole to put his foot down."

"Billy refused to use his driver," Maggie explained. "He insisted on driving himself."

"What kind of *shit* is that?" Alex screamed, suddenly losing it. "The insurance forbade it. D'you hear me, Maggie? They *forbade* that he drove himself to any of the locations. You *know* that."

"Yes, I do," Maggie responded in a quiet voice, because having worked with Alex for quite a few years, she also knew there was absolutely no point in provoking a screaming match.

"She knows!" Alex yelled, mimicking her. "She fucking *knows*, and yet she does nothing."

Maggie shrugged.

"Shit!" Alex screamed. "Goddamn actors. They should all go fuckin' Tom Cruise themselves out of the business."

"What does *that* mean?"

"Wait a few years," Alex said ominously, "you'll find out."

"No panic," Maggie said, relieved. "Here he comes now."

An Electra Glide fully restored Harley roared into sight, Billy Melina astride in all his glory, black-leathered up to the eyebrows.

Alex strode toward the young actor as Billy jumped off his bike. "You're fucking *late!*" he yelled.

"Traffic," Billy countered, his voice filled with the arrogance of an actor who knows there is no way he can get fired.

"Unprofessional," Alex growled.

"Not my fault, man," Billy said, casually removing his helmet.

"Of course not," Alex drawled sarcastically. "Why would it be *your* fault? Nothing's your fucking fault, is it?"

Maggie quickly attempted to defuse the situation. "Billy," she said. "Come with me. They're waiting for you in the makeup trailer."

"Hey, Mags," Billy said, turning on the charm. "You're lookin' hot. How's about you an' me—"

"Move your punk ass," Alex interrupted.

"Sure, old man," Billy said, grinning.

Infuriated, Alex stomped off toward his crew busy setting up across the street. Old man indeed. There was nothing worse than some two-bit actor with a handful of box-office hits who considered himself the second coming of Steve McQueen.

Fuck all actors. And *definitely* fuck Billy Melina.

Alex had seen them come, and he'd seen them go. At fifty-something he was a veteran producer/writer/director who'd been through the Hollywood wars countless times. He knew all the games, all the shenanigans. He'd seen studio heads ousted at a moment's notice, and a staggering lack of honesty and loyalty. The only studio head Alex had enjoyed working with was Lucky Santangelo when she'd owned and run Panther Studios. They'd had a connection that was more than business, and although Alex had always gone for Asian women, there was something about Lucky that had immediately drawn him in.

Unfortunately, she was married and in love with her husband, although there'd been a moment in time when they *had* gotten together. One crazy, insane night of love and lust when Lennie was gone, and Lucky had thought he was dead. Christ! The memory of that one night in a cheap motel in the middle of nowheresville was always there. It was a night he would never forget.

Lucky had never mentioned their one night together again. He knew that in her mind it was something she preferred to think had not taken place. But it had, and he would always have strong feelings for her. There was nothing he could do about it.

Since that time they'd remained friends, had even produced a very successful movie together, and now he was a major investor in her Vegas hotel project.

Maggie returned from depositing Billy in the makeup trailer.

"Five minutes," Alex growled. "I want that punk kid on the set in five minutes. You got that, Maggie?"

"Yes, Alex, five minutes."

"And no more turning up on his fucking Harley. I want his skinny ass in a *car* with a *driver*. It's in his contract. Make sure he honors it or get on the phone to his agent."

"Yes, Alex."

"Okay. Now let's go make a fuckin' movie."

CHAPTER THREE

Anthony Bonar—formerly Anthony Bonnatti—had it all. A well-appointed luxurious villa twenty-five minutes outside of Mexico City, a duplex penthouse in New York, a vacation home in Acapulco on the bay, and a rambling waterfront estate in Miami. He also had an American wife, Irma, to whom he'd been married for fifteen years; two children—a boy and a girl; two mistresses, his own plane, a helicopter, and a lucrative business. When asked—and not many dared—he would inform them that he was in the import/export business, which wasn't exactly a lie, because running a vast drug empire was exactly that—import from here, export to there.

For the first twelve years of his life Anthony had been raised in Italy by his mother, Mia, a hardworking maid who'd toiled in a beachfront hotel in Naples. The same hotel the Bonnatti family had stayed at on vacation when young Santino Bonnatti was a constantly horny teenager. The same hotel where Santino had knocked twenty-two-year-old Mia up one balmy night while making out with her on the beach under the stars.

After the Bonnatti family checked out and returned to America, Mia had no idea she was pregnant. When she found out, she was unable to summon the courage to get in touch with the family. It wasn't until twelve years later, when she was diagnosed with cancer and given only a few months to live, that she'd contacted the Bonnattis.

A few weeks later Santino's formidable mother, Francesca Bonnatti, flew to Italy to investigate the girl's story. Upon arrival she'd taken one look at young Anthony with his big brown eyes and cocky attitude and realized that Mia was speaking the truth, for Anthony looked nothing like her son, Santino, nor did he resemble his birth mother, Mia. No, Anthony was the mirror image of Francesca. A male version. He was *definitely* a Bonnatti.

Francesca flew her illegitimate grandson back to the States to live with Enzio and herself.

Anthony flourished. He was an exceptionally smart boy who quickly learned to speak English without an accent. Raised on the streets of Naples for the first twelve years of his life by a mother who barely had time for him, he'd learned how to survive on his wits. His grandfather soon took a shine to his ballsy illegitimate grandson. Before long Enzio began taking Anthony on business trips to Colombia and Mexico City, proudly introducing the boy to all his main contacts.

When Santino, outraged that his father had taken such a liking to his so-called son, moved his family and his own business interests—mainly the distribution of pornographic movies and magazines—to California, Enzio wasn't bothered, for Santino was certainly not the son he'd hoped for.

When Enzio was shot, it was sixteen-year-old Anthony who'd comforted Francesca and stayed by her side. Santino and his brother, Carlos, attended the lavish funeral, but neither of them stayed around. *Fuck Santino Bonnatti*, Anthony had thought. *And fuck his fat wife and asshole kids.* He wanted nothing to do with any of them, just as they had wanted nothing to do with him.

After Enzio's death, Francesca encouraged Anthony to put everything Enzio had taught him to good use. He didn't let her down.

Six years later when Santino himself was killed, Anthony hadn't felt one shred of emotion. Why would he? His so-called father had treated him as if he didn't exist, so there was no reason for him to care.

By the time Anthony reached his early twenties, he'd forged major contacts with the biggest drug overlords in Mexico City, Colombia, and Bolivia.

Anthony got off on having money and power, realizing early on how attractive those two things were to women. Plus he was not bad-looking in a darkly brooding way. Unfortunately, though, he was only five feet seven, not as tall as he'd like to be, and his lack of height pissed him off, but it didn't stop him from sleeping his way through most of the models, would-be actresses, and young socialites in New York and Miami.

Francesca was proud of his success, but she was also wary of his playboy ways, so one day she informed him that it was time he found himself a *nice* girl, got married, settled down, and started a family.

A family he would start, but settling down was for old men with nowhere left to go.

After a few months of Francesca's nagging, he decided he'd better do as she suggested and start looking for The One.

It wasn't long before he met Irma at a party in Miami. She was seventeen and he was twenty-four.

He'd taken one look at the well-endowed, pretty teenager and come to the conclusion that she might be the one—*especially* when she confided she was still a virgin.

After obtaining Francesca's approval, Anthony and Irma were married in a church in Mexico City where Anthony was negotiating to buy a large estate outside the city.

Irma—virginal in a white lace dress—made a delightful bride. They honeymooned in Europe, and shortly after their honeymoon Irma became pregnant.

Their son, Eduardo, was born the day before Irma's eighteenth birthday. A year later she gave birth to a girl, Carolina.

Anthony *and* his grandma were satisfied. Irma had delivered the perfect family, and Anthony decided that she should now concentrate all her energy on being a nurturing mother, while *he* continued to build up his business, travel the world, and whore around.

Grandmother Francesca had taught him well. Women, she'd assured him in an authoritative tone when she'd first brought him to America, were either mothers, wives, sisters, or daughters—other than that they were *puttanas*, whores and sluts.

After the birth of his two children, Anthony decided that sex with Irma was over; he didn't care to stick it in the same place his precious children had emerged from.

Although Anthony's main residence was in Mexico City, he also spent plenty of time in Miami and New York, with twice-yearly trips to Colombia and Bolivia. The drug trade he'd fallen into was already making him more money than he'd ever imagined, but in spite of his wealth and good fortune, Anthony was not completely at ease. Francesca expected *him* to be the one to avenge the murder of his grandfather and his piece-of-shit father. And she never let him forget it.

"The Bonnatti name must be avenged," she was always telling him. "You *know* the history only too well."

Oh yeah, he knew the history, and even though he'd legally changed his surname to Bonar, he was a Bonnatti by birth.

Francesca often regaled him with stories of the bad blood between the Bonnattis and the Santangelos. It was a feud that went way back.

According to Francesca, Gino Santangelo and Enzio Bonnatti were once close boyhood pals, going into business together, scoring huge amounts of money. Both teenage sons of immigrants, they'd been quick to seize all the opportunities America had to offer, from running numbers to loan-sharking, gambling, and hijacking trucks loaded with illegal booze. They'd stayed together several years, until Enzio had begun to pursue a different line of business—drugs and prostitution, two areas Gino Santangelo refused to be involved with.

Gino Santangelo must've been some dumb fuck, Anthony often thought. *What kind of man turns his back on making mega bucks?*

Apparently Gino did, because instead of continuing his partnership with Enzio, he'd built hotels in Vegas, legitimizing his business to a degree, and then allowed his daughter, Lucky, to move in and run things.

Although Enzio and Gino had parted on cordial terms, over the years they'd become dire enemies, creating a feud between the two families that had festered and only gotten worse throughout the years.

Frankly, Anthony wasn't interested in vendettas and revenge; that kind of thing was for old-timers, mustache Petes, men of his late grandfather's generation. But he knew Francesca would never quit until he did something about the Santangelos.

The Bonnattis and the Santangelos. Not a match.

CHAPTER FOUR

The Heavenly Spa in Pasadena was the one place Lucky felt that she could truly relax. She and Venus, her closest friend, always made the effort to meet there at least a couple of times a month. It wasn't easy, as they both balanced hectic schedules, but somehow or other they managed it.

Lucky rushed in aware that she was late, still pissed about Max mouthing off, although she couldn't be *too* mad, for at sixteen she'd had exactly the same badass attitude.

Ha! Like mother like daughter. And there wasn't much she could do about it except keep a watchful eye out.

"How's Billy?" she asked once she and Venus were settled in the mud-wrap treatment room while two formidable-looking Russian women slathered thick mud all over their bodies.

"You think I'm crazy, don't you?" Venus sighed, lying back totally naked except for an animal-print thong.

"Hey, whatever turns you on," Lucky remarked, stretching out her leg as one of the large Russian women applied a healthy coating of mud to her well-toned thighs. "If you're still into Billy, that's your prerogative. Believe me, I'm the *last* person to judge anyone—*especially* a major diva like you."

"Major diva, my ass," Venus retorted, laughing.

"Go ahead, deny it," Lucky teased. "Everyone's got your number."

"Look," Venus said, suddenly serious, "I know how fond you were of Cooper—"

"Still am," Lucky interrupted, choosing her words carefully. "Only just 'cause *I* liked him doesn't mean that you had to do time in a marriage that wasn't working."

"*I'm* not the one to blame," Venus said, shifting onto her side. "The man screwed around on me, and if that wasn't enough, Mister Life and Soul of the Party turned into Mister Boring—a man who insisted on being in bed every night by *nine!* I mean, can you imagine?" she added, rolling her eyes.

"Men get that way," Lucky said sagely, enjoying the sensation of the cold mud on her body. "It's on account of a little something called marriage."

"*Lennie's* not like that," Venus pointed out.

"Doesn't mean we haven't had our differences," Lucky retorted.

"Which you've always managed to work out."

"This is true."

"So . . . what did *I* do wrong?"

"Nothing," Lucky said, shrugging. "Except that you became a bigger star than him."

"You think?"

"C'*mon*, Venus, you *know* you did. Shit happens. Egos go trippin'. Cooper has a *giant* ego—surely you noticed?"

"Believe me," Venus said with a secret smile, "that's not all Cooper had. . . ."

"No details," Lucky said, quickly interrupting. "I do *not* get off on details."

"Not that I miss it," Venus mused. "Because I can assure you, Billy is *certainly* a member of the well-hung club. In fact—"

"Goddammit!" Lucky exclaimed. "Didn't I just say no details? Other people's sex lives bore me shitless!"

"Aren't *I* the fortunate one," Venus boasted, laughing. "Got me two in a row."

"Yeah, and let's not forget the other half-dozen in between," Lucky murmured, sotto voce.

"Ha!" Venus said vehemently. "Jealous?"

Lucky raised an eyebrow. "Have you *met* Lennie?"

"Yeah, yeah, I *know,* Lennie is the greatest everything, and you're both ecstatically happy, and neither of you cheats. But I must say, if *Cooper* had turned up with an illegitimate kid, I'm not sure I could've—"

"Don't go there," Lucky said in a warning voice. "Ancient history isn't my thing."

Much as she loved Venus, sometimes the platinumblond superstar overstepped certain boundaries. The truth was that Lennie had fathered a child under extreme circumstances—he'd been kidnapped, trapped in an underground cave in Sicily, and made love to a woman, Claudia, who'd helped him escape. It was a onetime thing, and he'd never seen the woman again until she'd turned up on their doorstep in Malibu with Leonardo, a boy she'd claimed Lennie had fathered.

It was a difficult time to get through, but they'd done so, and when Claudia was killed, Lucky had adopted Leonardo as if he were her own. Somehow it had made their marriage stronger, bonding them even closer.

"So," Lucky said, moving on. "Will you be bringing Billy to Gino's party on Sunday?"

"Why wouldn't I?" Venus said, narrowing her eyes.

"'Cause I had to invite Cooper," Lucky explained. "Y'know how close he is to Lennie."

"Fine with me." Venus sniffed. "I suppose he'll be with that coke-snorting *child* he's been banging."

"You sound bothered," Lucky said.

"Are you *kidding* me? The only thing that bothers me is that he takes her out with Chyna, and that's not right."

"Chyna's a smart kid," Lucky said, thinking about Venus's young daughter. "She can handle it."

"She shouldn't have to," Venus said adamantly. "Cooper's latest girlfriend is a drug- and sex-addicted nineteen-year-old wannabe actress *whore.* What the hell is Cooper *thinking?* He's old enough to be her *grandfather.*"

"Hey, maybe we should hook her up with Billy," Lucky joked. "They're almost the same age."

"Fuck you," Venus drawled.

"I leave that chore to my husband," Lucky murmured dryly.

"For God's sake," Venus said, "I have to take enough shit from the press, don't *you* get on my case."

"It was a bad joke. Sorry."

"Billy might be only twenty-eight, but he's an old soul," Venus felt obliged to explain. "The age difference doesn't bother either of us. The only people who seem to care are the goddamn tabloids—and oh yeah, the nighttime talk-show hosts who make a living ragging on us 'cause their dumb writers can't come up with anything more original."

"Okay, I get it."

"I love Billy, and I *know* he loves me."

"As long as you're sure. I wouldn't want to see you get hurt."

"Why?" Venus said suspiciously. "What've you heard?"

"Nothing."

"You're sure?"

"Positive."

"You'd tell me if you heard anything."

"Stop obsessing."

"I can't help it. Billy gives me chills. I feel as if I'm sixteen!"

Lucky's cell rang. She reached for it and exchanged a few sentences with Lennie, finishing off with, "I miss you—love you. See you later."

"Exactly how long is it since you two have seen each other?" Venus asked, raising an eyebrow. "Fifteen minutes?"

"Not my fault if he's crazy in love," Lucky said, hardly able to wipe the smile off her face because it was true, they were still crazy in love.

"Goddammit!" Venus exclaimed. "You and Lennie make me sick you're so damn *happy*."

"I gotta tell you, when it works, it *really* works," Lucky said. "And believe me, I am *not* complaining."

"Nor should you," Venus sighed. "Everyone knows that Lennie's the greatest."

Lucky nodded and smiled. "And *nobody* knows it better than me."

CHAPTER FIVE

Francesca Bonnatti was a wise and canny woman. She'd observed much in her life, both good and bad. Now, at eighty-four, she was not at all ready to give up her vendetta against the Santangelo family. Sicilian by birth, Francesca had come to America with her parents, a hardworking immigrant couple, when she was eleven. Sent straight to school, Francesca soon found she was the odd one out—the Italian girl with the fancy name who could barely speak English. She applied herself, diligently learning the language, and by the time she was thirteen, she'd succeeded in absorbing herself into the American way of life.

At fifteen she left school and started training as a bookkeeper.

"A bookkeeper is a good job for a girl to have," her father assured her. "With that skill you will always find work."

Fifteen, smart, and quite a beauty—it wasn't long before boys came flocking around.

When she was sixteen she met Enzio Bonnatti, a man eleven years older than her. At the time she was working for a grizzled old accountant who looked after some of Enzio's accounts.

Enzio Bonnatti was tall and dangerous-looking. He was also of Italian origin, which she knew would please her father. The eleven-year age difference would not.

Enzio started visiting the cramped office where she

worked on a regular basis. He always had a pretty girl hanging on to his arm. He got a big kick out of teasing Francesca, showing off as he swaggered around the office.

One day he brought his friend Gino Santangelo with him. Gino was shorter than Enzio, but he was full of charisma, with his thick, black curly hair and intense dark eyes.

Francesca began flirting with Gino to make Enzio jealous. The more she flirted, the more Enzio appeared with different girls. It was a game they both played. Teenage girl and older man. When was he going to ask her out?

Eventually he did, and she started seeing him secretly, not daring to tell her parents.

Enzio was very demanding; a kiss on the cheek did not do it for him. Every time he tried to go further, Francesca demurred, telling him she was a virgin and had no intention of changing that status until she was a married woman.

On her seventeenth birthday she told her parents she'd met a boy who wanted to take her out. She wondered what they would do if they discovered that she was really seeing the notorious Enzio Bonnatti, a man who had quite a reputation in the neighborhood. It would not sit well with her hardworking parents, so to appease them she bribed one of the boys she worked with to pretend to be her date. The boy picked her up at her house, then delivered her to Enzio's apartment. When she arrived, Enzio said, "You gotta look older 'cause we're goin' to a nightclub. I got you a dress, go put it on."

"What kind of dress?" she asked.

"You could call it a fancy dress," he joked. "It fell off the back of a truck."

Enzio wasn't shy about what he did, he never tried to hide it from her, and even though she knew his activities were not exactly legal, she couldn't help enjoying the sense of excitement he brought into her mundane life.

The dress was red and tight. It clung to her teenage curves, emphasizing her breasts and butt, making her appear older than her years. It obviously had a positive effect on Enzio, for later that night he proposed.

She told him she'd think about it. Although she liked Enzio, she'd grown to like his friend, Gino, even more. But Gino never gave her the time of day, which infuriated her. She couldn't understand it. Most men paid her plenty of attention.

One day she asked Gino why he chose to ignore her.

"You're my best friend's girlfriend," he answered. "That's why."

"I'm not his girlfriend," she objected. "Enzio's always running around with other women."

"You're the one he's gonna marry," Gino replied. "You can be sure of that."

"My father won't allow me to marry him."

"Wanna bet?" Gino said. "You'll see."

It frustrated her that Gino never responded to her beauty. She tried on many occasions to get him to change his mind but he was steadfast. His friendship with Enzio came first. Loyalty meant everything to Gino Santangelo.

Without her knowledge, Enzio went to her father and obtained his permission for them to get married. She suspected he either bribed or threatened her father to agree.

They were married two days before her eighteenth birthday. Gino was Enzio's best man.

Now, all these years later, she still thought about Gino and what might have been.

Gino Santangelo was the one she should've married. He was the one who got away.

Now all she could think about was that Gino Santangelo was alive and Enzio was dead—murdered by Gino's bitch daughter.

Retribution was a necessity for the Bonnatti family name, and Anthony had to resolve the situation. The Bonnatti honor was at stake.

For quite a while now Francesca had been muttering about the six-billion-dollar hotel complex in Vegas Lucky Santangelo was building. "You cannot let this happen," she'd informed her grandson over and over. "Gino and Lucky Santangelo tried to take everything from us. Now we take our revenge."

Anthony had many connections in Vegas. If he kept the Keys from opening, it would shut his grandmother up once and for all. After all, if it wasn't for Francesca, he would've had nothing. And since she never stopped insisting that it was time the Santangelo family paid for their sins against the Bonnatti family, it would satisfy her. Anthony had a plan. A deadly plan. Costly and explosive. If it worked out, then Grandma would be one very happy woman indeed.

It was the least he could do.

CHAPTER SIX

Max Santangelo Golden had a secret. A big one. She'd met this boy—well, man really—on the Internet, and every night for the past six weeks they'd exchanged all kinds of information online. His name was Grant and he was twenty-two. From his e-mails he sounded smart and interesting. He lived in San Diego, drove a Jeep, and didn't have a girlfriend. Best of all, he'd posted his picture and he was a hottie—kind of like a younger Brad Pitt. The point was he did not fall into the category of sex-obsessed, lame teenage boy, and that was a major plus, because she was *so* over stupid boys. She wanted a real man, and Grant sounded like he might be the one.

So Max had lied, told him she was eighteen, that she worked for a fashion designer and had recently broken up with her boyfriend—which sounded way cooler than saying she was sixteen and still in high school. Actually, she *had* just broken up with her boyfriend, so that wasn't exactly a lie. She'd broken up with Donny because she'd caught him making out with some bleached-blond skank at Houston's in Century City of all places. He'd said he had to go somewhere with his parents and she'd said she was staying home. But later she'd changed her mind, called up her posse, Harry and Cookie, and the three of them had gone to Houston's for the mind-blowing ribs. And there he was, Donny Leventon—seventeen and a hunk—slobbering all over said skank, who could've been his *mother* she was so old. At least *thirty*. It was *so* utterly gross!

Cookie had spotted him first. "Whoa! Major disaster about to happen!" she'd gasped, nudging Max. "We gotta split like *now!*"

Whereupon Max had taken in the scene and, being her mother's daughter, acted accordingly. Without a moment's hesitation she'd marched over to Donny's table, picked up a glass filled with Coca-Cola and ice, and tossed the contents into his lying scumbag face. Before he could react, she was out of there, Cookie and Harry right behind her.

After what she termed "the Houston Incident," she'd refused to ever speak to him again. The real truth was that Donny had broken her heart—just a tiny bit. He was her first real love, and he'd let her down.

Rejection was not something Max had ever had to deal with before, and it was hard, but eventually, when Donny came begging for her to take him back, she'd given him all the rejection she could muster. Let him see how *he* liked it.

Anyway, the point was Internet Dude had asked her if she wanted to get together, and impulsively she'd said yes.

Two days later he'd announced that he'd hired a cabin up in Big Bear for the following weekend, and she'd promised to meet him there.

This was her move to make Donny sorry he'd ever cheated on her. Not that they'd been having sex, but they *had* been pretty intimate without going all the way. Now she would go all the way with Internet Dude, and *then* she would make sure Donny found out. *That* was the ass-wipe's big punishment.

Donny should've waited, she thought sadly. *I would've given it up—eventually.*

Her plans were all in place, but unfortunately her

crappy mom was putting up roadblocks, which pissed her off, because why *shouldn't* she do exactly as she pleased? Her mom *always* had—everyone knew about Lucky Santangelo and *her* notorious past—so why was *she* expected to be such a little lamb?

She had *no* intention of *not* going to Big Bear and missing out on an exciting experience, but how to pull it off without getting grounded for weeks on end, *that* was the problem.

She wasn't exactly losing sleep over it, because if there was one thing she excelled at, it was solving problems. And with the help of her two best friends—Cookie, a pretty black girl, and Harry, an in-the-closet gay teenager—she'd somehow work it out.

Cookie and Harry were the best, always up to support an adventure, and meeting some hot guy in Big Bear was a *major* adventure. Not that they were going to get to meet him, but they'd back her up all the way. That's what true friends were for.

Later that afternoon, Cookie and Harry came over to lie out by the pool and mull over the situation.

"*I* wanna *meet* your Internet perv," Cookie insisted, swigging from a can of Red Bull. She was a curvaceous girl in a young Janet Jackson kind of way. Chocolate-brown dreadlocks framed her heart-shaped face, and her lips were full and pink. Her father was Gerald M., the forty-nine-year-old smooth-soul-singing icon. Cookie had chosen to live with him in Beverly Hills because her mom was a prescription-drug whore who'd moved over the hill to the Valley with a twenty-five-year-old some-time musician, and Cookie couldn't stand either of them. Her mom and boyfriend cohabited in stoned bliss, while Cookie enjoyed the good life with her famous father.

"Yeah, an' *I* wouldn't mind giving him a blow job," Harry leered, huddling under a huge sun umbrella, hiding from the sun. Harry was skinny and alarmingly pale, with dyed black hair worn spiked, as if he'd recently stuck his finger in a power socket. *His* mogul-type dad worked late hours at the TV network he ran, while his mom, a born-again, spent most evenings at her church or meeting with her pastor, a man Harry was convinced she was sleeping with.

"Bet you both *wish* you were coming with me," Max said, tossing back her long mane of dark curls. "But hey, *I'm* the one that's gonna be screwing him, *that* privilege is *all* mine, so try not to turn into jealous wrecks."

"*If* your mom lets you go," Cookie pointed out, adjusting the top of her bikini.

"I'm workin' on it," Max said confidently, knowing that she was taking off to Big Bear whether Lucky agreed or not.

"I *so* hope this dude's like *not* a *perv*," Cookie offered, wriggling around on her sun lounger, her brief pink bikini showing off every curve.

"And *I* hope he is," Harry said excitably, his skinny body fully covered in a faded black T-shirt and baggy black pants worn half-mast. "'Cause then you can give us all the sicko details when you get back."

"*If* she gets back," Cookie interrupted, rolling her eyes for emphasis. "'Cause he could cut her up into itty-bitty pieces an' bury her under the mountain."

"Thanks for the thought," Max said, biting down on her lower lip. "But hey, I know how to kick ass, so any cutting goin' on will be coming from *me*. Get it?"

"Bad shit happens," Cookie said, nodding wisely. "I read where this woman met this dude on the Internet and he like *strangled* her, 'cause that's what she told him she was into. How psycho is *that*?"

"Grant's cool," Max said airily. "I can tell."

"How?" Cookie demanded.

"I got good instincts."

"You'd better answer your cell at all times 'cause we'll be on red alert," Harry said sternly.

"Should I pick up my cell even when we're doin' it?" Max teased.

"What?" Harry said, his face reddening.

"Don't go getting all prudish on me," Max said, giggling as she reached for a tube of suntan cream. "I gotta do it *sometime*, and Grant's the perfect victim."

"He is?" Cookie asked. "How's that?"

"Well," Max said, "he's like an out-of-towner who can't go around blabbing about me. Oh yeah, an' he's older, so he'll be like an *expert* at it."

"You *go* for it, girl," Cookie said, making a victory sign. "Only try not to get slashed along the way."

"Oh, so now he's a *slasher*," Max drawled, reaching for a bobby pin and piling her hair on top of her head. "Anyone ever mention that your imagination *sucks?*"

"Could be he's straight out of a Wes Craven horrorfest," Harry said, making a spooky face. "Girl alone with strange dude equals she'll like *definitely* get her throat slit."

"It's so *encouraging* to have friends like you two losers," Max said, jumping up and making a running dive into the pool.

She didn't care what anyone said—she was going to Big Bear. No doubt about it.

CHAPTER SEVEN

For some time Irma Bonar had been thinking about taking a lover. At thirty-two, she'd finally decided to do something about her empty life stuck outside Mexico City in an enormous villa surrounded by servants and bodyguards. This was the place her husband, Anthony, had decided she should live, while *he* traveled anywhere he wanted doing God knew what.

Anthony Bonar was a difficult man. Difficult, arrogant, and most of all controlling.

The fact that he no longer wished to have sex with her did not please Irma at all. Over the years she'd gotten used to her husband's ferocious style of lovemaking, and now she could not understand why their once-active sex life had ground to a sudden halt.

Whenever she mentioned it to him, Anthony always managed to come up with a variety of reasons. Reason number one: he had a lesion on his penis and he wasn't sure what it was.

Irma had carefully inspected his limp manhood and found nothing.

"It's there," Anthony had insisted, "an' if you don't wanna catch nothin', you'd better listen t'me for once."

This frightened her off for a while, until one night he'd shoved his supposedly damaged cock into her mouth for a late-night blow job because he'd had a fight with one of his mistresses and the *puttana* had sent him home horny.

After that incident the lesion excuse didn't work anymore, so he'd announced that his doctor had warned him that his testosterone level was dangerously low, and that he had to lay off sex for a while.

Gradually Irma had grown to understand that her dear husband did not wish to have sex with her, and galling as she found it, she was forced to settle for the occasional jump in the dark when *he* felt like it, usually late at night or early in the morning when she was half asleep. Anthony always made sure to pull out before coming. He had no desire to make more babies—two was definitely enough.

Irma did exactly as Anthony expected of her. She concentrated on their children, making sure Carolina and Eduardo received the best of everything. She also absorbed herself in decorating their various homes, although once each place was finished, Anthony sent her back to Mexico, where he insisted she live. Anthony professed to love their home. *If he loves it so much,* Irma often thought, *why doesn't he live here permanently?* He came and went whenever it suited him, while she was stuck there with no friends and no one to talk to.

Anthony did not encourage her to make friends, although *he* certainly entertained an adoring entourage when he deigned to spend time at home. There were several couples he invited over when he was there. One of the women was American, but Anthony had warned Irma not to have any contact with the woman when he wasn't around.

"Why not?" she'd wanted to know.

"'Cause I don't want nobody findin' out nothin' 'bout my business," he'd said. "You'd better keep to yourself, Irma. That's an order."

When the children were old enough, Anthony had decided that they should continue their education in

America. This delighted Irma, because she was desperate to move back to the States.

"*You're* not comin'," Anthony had said, brooking no argument. "You'll stay in Mexico—it's our main home, it's where you should be."

"No," Irma had protested. "Where I *should* be is with our children. They're still young, they need me."

"Forget it," Anthony had answered harshly. "The kids are growin' up. I'm hirin' a housekeeper to take care of 'em, make sure they do their homework an' eat properly. Oh yeah, an' Francesca will be around. They'll come to you for vacations."

Irma was livid. Anthony's witch of a grandma got to live in America while *she* had to stay in Mexico. It wasn't fair. But she knew better than to argue. Anthony had a fierce temper, and early on she'd learned that the wise way was to shy away from his uncontrollable wrath.

Anthony Bonar was not only difficult and controlling, he was a screamer of mammoth proportions. Loud, frequent outbursts were not unusual; he even screamed at his grandmother when the mood took him. The old woman screamed back, giving as good as she got. In a twisted way they both seemed to enjoy their verbal battles.

Irma didn't. She had never gotten used to their upsetting dance over the years.

Once the screaming stopped there were profuse apologies and overly affectionate *I love you*s from both of them.

Irma thought the interaction between the two of them was sick, but she never interfered for fear of repercussions. Irma had learned over the years that it was best to keep quiet.

Sometimes Anthony Bonar thought that if it wasn't for his children he would divorce Irma and marry his outstandingly sexy mistress, Emmanuelle. She was so hot that sometimes he couldn't believe she was his. Twenty years old with a body any red-blooded male would kill for, she was one of the most sought-after models in Miami. Not one of those snooty bitches who strutted the runways, no, Emmanuelle was featured on the covers of *Stuff* and *Maxim*—a popular cover girl with her sexy blond curls and the best fake tits this side of Rio, the city where she was born.

Anthony had met her in a club six months earlier. She'd been snorting coke with a hard-living male movie star who swung both ways. Anthony had taken one look at her and proceeded to move in big-time. Within weeks he'd set her up in an apartment, bought her a new Mercedes, showered her with jewelry and designer clothes.

Anthony got off on collecting beautiful, sexy women, and Emmanuelle was a prize. But as much as he reveled in his power over females, business always came first. Business, followed by his two children, then his grandmother, and trailing way behind was Irma. Truth was he didn't really like his wife; she was boring and a nag—always on his case about moving back to America. Most women would be thrilled to live in a twenty-five-thousand-square-foot home with servants and bodyguards. But not Irma, oh no, not *his* wife. Irma wanted to be near him so she could bug the shit out of him with her constant demands for sex.

Why did she still expect him to fuck her? He'd given her two children. Wasn't that enough? She was a *mother*, for chrissakes; he didn't fuck mothers.

Besides, he had other things on his mind, and making Grandma happy was a number-one priority.

When he'd told Francesca his plans for finally taking action against the Santangelos, her long, thin face had lit up. "At last you have the balls of your grandfather," she'd exclaimed. "You make me a very happy woman, Anthony."

"Whatever I'm doin', it's for you," he'd said. " 'Cause you care so much."

"No!" she'd said sharply. "Not for me. For the Bonnatti *name*. For the Bonnatti *honor*. Your stupid half-brother couldn't do it. Nor could Donatella. Now it is *your* duty to ruin the Santangelo family once and for all."

"Hey, it's gonna happen," he'd promised.

"It better," she'd answered sharply. "You hear me, Anthony? It better."

"What? Ya don't believe me?"

"It's taken you long enough."

"Jesus Christ! I do everythin' for you, an' still you doubt me."

And so the screaming had started. Always the screaming.

Anthony was used to it. In a strange way it was his only true comfort zone.

Sitting outside under a leafy tree in the garden of their house, Irma watched the two gardeners at work. One was an older man, his lined face grizzled from the sun. The other was a much younger man, with a muscled body and brooding features. Irma stared at him, observing his dark, bushy eyebrows, thick lips, and muscular arms. He reminded her of her first boyfriend way back in Omaha when she was a mere fourteen. Andy Francis, a very possessive boy who'd slugged other boys simply for looking at her. *Well,* she thought with a slight smile, *I was the prettiest girl in school*.

Memories of Andy brought back feelings of her first sexual stirrings. Andy's hard little kisses, his fifteen-year-old tongue stuck firmly in her mouth thrusting and twisting. Andy's eager hands exploring under her sweater, unfastening her bra and clumsily fondling her breasts. Andy's frustration when she refused to allow him to go any further.

Irma found that she couldn't stop staring at the younger of the two gardeners. He was new, she'd only seen him a couple of times before.

Suddenly he glanced up and met her gaze. His eyes were full of suspicion, but he didn't look away, and neither did she.

It was a moment that set her thinking. Was this destined to be the man she had an affair with? This lowly Mexican gardener who probably stank of sweat and wine and would handle her roughly, because in his eyes he surely must see her as a beautiful blond *lonely* American princess.

She experienced a shiver of excitement, followed by a moist feeling between her legs.

Oh God, it had been so long since Anthony had touched her. Right now she was suffused with desire.

She couldn't take her eyes off the man, his rippling muscles, his stoic face. Yes, she had to have him. And why shouldn't she? Anthony thought he was so clever with his secretive ways, but she knew about his mistresses—the Italian whore he kept in a penthouse in New York, and the so-called model in Miami. Besides, he'd taken her children from her, and that wasn't right.

She also knew plenty about his business dealings. The drug shipments, the many meetings, his associates in Colombia and Bolivia whom she'd met.

Damn Anthony. He was forcing her to go elsewhere for the sexual satisfaction she craved.

The old gardener turned and began a slow trudge toward the greenhouse. The young gardener stayed where he was.

Irma couldn't stop watching him. After a few moments she acted on impulse and beckoned him over. He headed in her direction, a wary expression on his face.

What am I doing? she thought. *This is crazy.* But her heart was beating so fast she couldn't stop herself.

When the gardener arrived in front of her, she lost all sense of reason and found herself incapable of looking him in the eye.

"*Señora?*" he questioned. His smell wafted in the air, healthy sweat mixed with garlic.

"Uh . . . you're new here, aren't you?" she managed, fanning herself with a magazine. "What's your name?"

"*Perdone, señora,*" he mumbled, rubbing his thigh with a large work-worn hand. "*No hablar Engleesh.*"

"You don't?" she said, startled. Then she thought, *Why would he? He's only a gardener, probably dropped out of school early.*

She studied his lips. They fascinated her, they were so thick and tempting. Then there was the faint stubble on his chin, so manly. And his forearms, strong and muscled.

"Name," she repeated, fanning herself more vigorously. "*Nombre?*"

"Luis," he muttered in a low voice.

"*Gracias,* Luis," she said, dismissing him with a flick of her hand.

He turned and walked away, giving her ample time to study his tight ass in faded jeans.

Abruptly she stood up and headed for the house. If she couldn't have Luis, perhaps she would settle for the handheld neck massager she'd recently purchased. The small piece of machinery certainly wasn't Luis, but the results were always a ten.

Emmanuelle was a girl who liked to party, but Anthony Bonar soon convinced her that the best parties consisted of two people only—although an occasional other girl introduced into the mix did not seem to bother him. Early on in their relationship he'd threatened to fucking kill her if she ever cheated on him. Those were his exact words, and she was almost convinced that he meant it. Almost, not quite, for Emmanuelle was young and got off on enjoying herself. After all, Anthony was not always around. Early on she'd discovered that he had a wife *and* another mistress in New York, so she'd decided that if *he* was getting it elsewhere, why shouldn't she?

So far she'd only cheated on him once with a fellow model. Nobody found out. They'd done it in a dressing room halfway through a photo session. Hot, fast sex standing up.

Anthony *never* did it standing up. He wanted her flat on her back with her ankles around his neck while he pumped away like a machine. In, out. In, out. No technique whatsoever.

She'd soon realized that her new boyfriend was not the greatest lover in the world—although he obviously thought he was. Most men did.

Emmanuelle refused to disillusion him, for she'd met generous men before, but Anthony was in a class by himself and she was partial to luxury goods, especially when they came with a major price tag. This meant that although Anthony Bonar wasn't her usual type, she played him all the way.

In spite of the blond curls and fake tits, Emmanuelle had a head for business, and she knew she had Anthony hot enough to buy her almost anything she wanted. The downside was that he put nothing in her name—not the Mercedes, not the lease on the apartment he'd set her up in, not even the jewelry he'd gifted her with. If she ever left him, it all had to come back to him, he informed her. Or else.

Anthony was big with threats. Emmanuelle didn't like that, but even so she'd decided to stick it out for the time being until she could figure a way to persuade him to start putting things in her name. After all, if he broke up with her, it wasn't fair that she would walk away with nothing. And since he was enjoying the many and varied pleasures of her fabulous body, not to mention her extraordinary oral expertise, he *should* pay, there was no doubt about it.

Emmanuelle knew she was right.

CHAPTER EIGHT

"Baby!" Venus murmured, wrapping her well-toned arms around Billy Melina's neck and kissing him on the lips. "I missed you so much. How'd it go today?"

"Alex Woods is a workaholic freakin' *asshole*," Billy complained, shrugging off his Chrome Hearts leather jacket and flinging it on Venus's oversized bed.

"Everyone knows that," she agreed, kneeling on top of the bed looking sexy in a barely-there black lace teddy. "However, at least he's a *talented* asshole, which so many of them aren't."

Billy was inclined to disagree. It was almost midnight and he was wiped out. He'd had a bitch of a day what with the sex session out by his pool with the girl from Tower Records, then working endless hours on the street faking tough-as-shit choreographed fight scenes. Alex Woods was king of the "Let's go for another take" school of directors, and it drove Billy nuts. How many times was he supposed to get punched in the head and thrown over the hood of a car? Oh sure, he had a stand-in, but Alex insisted that *he* be front and center for most of the action, and when he objected—even a little bit—Alex berated him in front of the entire crew. "Our *actor* doesn't want to get down 'n' dirty," Alex jeered. "Let's get a chair for our fucking actor so he can put his fucking feet up. Wouldn't want to *overwork* him."

At which point Billy had agreed to shoot the scene himself. No stand-in required.

Man, he felt totally shattered. When they'd wrapped for the night, all he'd really wanted to do was go home and soak in his hot tub. Instead he'd been obliged to rush over to Venus's palatial mansion in Beverly Hills, because she'd called him on his cell four times insisting he come by when he was finished, and he didn't want to disappoint her.

"It'll be late," he'd warned.

"I'll be waiting," she'd answered. "Keeping the bed warm for you, baby."

If anyone had told him eight years ago that Venus Maria, one of the most famous women in the world, would be keeping the bed warm for him, he would've laughed like a freakin' loon.

Venus Maria. Platinum-blond superstar. A woman so famous she was now known by only one name: Venus. Everyone knew who she was. They bought her CDs, flocked to her movies, wore the hottest jeans in town with her name emblazoned on the label, sprayed themselves with her latest signature scent, and worshipped at her live stadium performances.

Venus was a freakin' icon. And *he* was her boyfriend. Her much *younger* boyfriend—well, not *that* much younger, thirteen years. And that meant nothing. It wasn't as if he was some snot-nosed boy toy—he was a very successful movie star in his own right. He had a house, plenty of money, and a sizzling career. He didn't *need* Venus's fame to tag on to; he had his own.

Besides, if the situation were reversed and she was thirteen years younger than him, nobody would give a rat's ass. Hollywood was awash with old geezers whose wives and girlfriends were decades younger than them, and nobody said a word. Unfortunately, he and Venus got the treatment. Front page of the tabloids always carrying on about their age difference. Was she going to marry him? Was she pregnant? Were they breaking up? Was she too rich for him? Was he famous enough for her?

At first he'd got off on all the attention, then after a while it started to get to him. He was a star, too; he didn't appreciate all the trash talk he had to endure.

Venus loved him, he knew that. The big question was: Did *he* love *her?* Or did he love everything she represented? The extreme fame and superglamor. The adulation and nonstop fan worship. Sometimes he simply wasn't sure whether it was love or infatuation.

And if he *really* loved her, would he cheat on her the way he had that afternoon?

For a moment he flashed onto the young girl who'd followed him up to his house in her rundown truck with the broken taillight. She'd followed him willingly, and he'd given her exactly what she expected.

Screwing her was a trip. Her lips, so soft and sweet, not to mention the sticky tightness between her legs.

And yet . . . he couldn't help feeling guilty.

Sort of . . . because if he caught Venus screwing another man, he'd go ape shit. Venus was his girlfriend—*his* freakin' girlfriend—and if she played around on him, it would mess with his head big-time.

Not that he was possessive—at least he didn't *think* he was. Venus was the possessive one. She could be bossy, a bit of a control freak, but she could also be supportive and loving, the way she was tonight. Although . . . from the look in her eyes, he knew she expected sex, and man, tonight was not the night. After Alex's brutal workout his body was bruised, wrecked, and beaten.

"Come to bed, baby," she purred. "I'll give you a back rub, you know how you like that."

Yeah, sex was *definitely* on her agenda, and what was he supposed to do about *that?*

Nothing, because a sane man didn't turn down a superstar, not if he wanted to continue being her boyfriend.

"A back rub sounds kinda hot," he mumbled.

"Of *course* it does," she murmured, husky-voiced and ready for action. " 'Cause *I'll* rub you, then *you'll* rub me. . . ."

"That's a plan," he said, pulling off his T-shirt. "Only first I gotta shower."

"Why?" she asked, reaching up and stroking the back of his neck. "Funky works for me."

"How about *skunky* funky?" he said, extracting himself from her touch. "Look at me—I'm in sweat overdrive, babe, an' I got a hunch you won't go for that."

"Okay, take a shower," she sighed. "But hurry up, you *know* how impatient I get."

She wasn't kidding about *that*. Miss *I want it now!* Venus never let up when she had her mind set on something.

"You got it, ma'am," he said, reverting to his former self, the dumb-ass kid who'd hit Hollywood eight years ago thinking all women deserved respect.

How green was *he?*

Green and fortunate, because after several months of bumming around trying to make something happen, working as a waiter and sleeping on a friend's floor, he'd found himself an agent who'd sent him on an interview for an NBC sitcom. He'd scored the part, been in six on-air episodes, and just when he'd imagined himself as the second coming of Matthew Perry, the show was canceled and he was back where he'd started—waiting tables at the Cheesecake Factory in Brentwood.

Two months later he got a call from his agent informing him that Alex Woods wanted to see him. Alex Woods—mega producer/director/writer supreme! Holy shit!

The day of his interview with Alex was forever etched in his mind. He'd walked into an imposing office nervous as a virgin on a date with a porn star. And there she was, standing around as if she had nothing better to do. Venus. *The* freaking Venus. She of the platinum-blond hair, sexy stance, and out-of-this-world bod.

"Hi, Billy," she'd said, as if she actually *knew* him. "Thanks for coming in today. I'm a big fan of your work."

Thanks for coming in! Big fan of his work! Was she freakin' *kidding!* He would've done anything for a meeting with Venus—she was the jerk-off queen of all his fantasies.

Alex Woods was slouched behind a large untidy desk, speaking on the phone. He'd glanced up and waved distractedly in Billy's direction.

"Sit down, Billy," Venus had said, indicating a sprawling couch.

Billy sat. Venus sat.

He'd thought he was freakin' dreaming it was all so surreal.

Later he'd read a scene with her in front of Alex and Lucky Santangelo, another producer on the movie.

He was good; in fact, he was *better* than good—in his mind he'd nailed the part and then some. And why not, with Venus as his inspiration standing opposite him in dangerously low-cut yoga pants and a belly-baring top? Not only was she this freakin' worldwide superstar, she was also surprisingly friendly and nice. She actually treated him like an equal. She actually *talked* to him before he had to read. Who'd've thought?

Two weeks later his agent called with the words every actor yearns to hear. "Congratulations, Billy. You got the part."

He remembered stammering, "I got the *what?*" And then he'd hit the clubs with a few of his buddies—including his closest friend from back home, Kev, whose floor he'd been sleeping on for the past few months. He'd gotten bombed out of his mind and ended up with a forty-year-old Puerto Rican stripper who'd called him Blondie Pie, and given him a mild dose of the clap.

A week later he was on the set of Alex Woods's new movie, *Seduction*, acting opposite Venus. It was the start of his ride. And what a ride it had turned out to be.

Shower over, Billy returned to the bedroom bare-assed naked. Venus gave him an appreciative once-over and beckoned him to join her on the bed.

Fortunately, the Donkey King—the name a former girlfriend had bestowed on his penis—was up and at 'em, at the ready to do whatever his master bade.

"Come here, you crazy sex maniac," Venus crooned.

Yeah, like *she* could talk.

He headed for the bed, and the soft, sexy, comforting warmth of his girlfriend. The same girlfriend he'd cheated on earlier that day.

Shit! Better make it up to her, he thought, quickly forgetting about his bruised and battered body. *Better be ready to rock and roll all night long.*

And while Billy was making out with one of the most famous women in the world, Alex Woods was drinking Jack Daniel's on the rocks at a bikers' hangout somewhere in the mountains off the Pacific Coast Highway. He didn't feel like going home to his architecturally perfect house situated on a prime piece of Broad Beach property.

He didn't feel like staring out at the black ocean or switching on his movie-size TV screen.

He didn't feel like making conversation, or anything else for that matter, with Ling, his Asian girlfriend—a twenty-nine-year-old lawyer with a serene attitude and amazing sexual skills.

What *did* he feel like doing?

He felt like being by himself, getting drunk, and thinking about Lucky Santangelo.

Lucky was always on his mind. Always . . .

So that's exactly what he did.

Tomorrow was another day; he could forget about her then and resume life as he knew it.

Only that never happened. Lucky was his secret obsession, and as long as Lennie was around, he knew it had to stay that way.

CHAPTER NINE

If it wasn't for Lucky Santangelo, Henry Whitfield-Simmons might have been a big star. Or at least that's what *he* believed. He knew he was far superior to Billy Melina, the actor who had stolen his role in the Alex Woods film that Henry had been so sure he was about to get.

Henry considered Billy Melina to be an inferior human being, with no acting ability whatsoever. He'd seen his movies. He'd sneered at his movies. It was a travesty that Billy Melina had been hired in his place, and gone on to become a famous star.

Even though his failed audition had taken place many years previously, Henry brooded about it on a daily basis. He knew for a fact that if it wasn't for Lucky Santangelo, *he*, Henry Whitfield-Simmons, would have been the one up there on the screen with Venus Maria in *Seduction*. Even now, although the day of his audition was eight long years ago, Henry had never forgotten nor forgiven. Lucky Santangelo, a producer on the film, was the one to blame; *she* was the one who hadn't wanted him. He was positive of this because while auditioning, he'd observed Lucky sitting across the table with the casting people, staring at him with her black unfriendly eyes while tapping her fingertips impatiently on the table. Alex Woods wasn't present that day, nor was Venus Maria.

Henry was about to read a second scene when he'd

noticed Lucky signal to the casting people that she'd seen enough. How unspeakably rude!

Henry was justifiably angry, for not only was she rude, Lucky Santangelo had ruined his future. She'd taken his one chance and thrown it away with her careless actions.

Shortly after his failed audition, Henry had been summoned to go on a fishing trip with his father. It was just the two of them on a small fishing boat out on the lake, because Logan Whitfield-Simmons truly believed that getting back to the simple things in life was the best way to bond with his uncooperative and unambitious son, whom he didn't understand at all. Logan never understood anybody who was unproductive and had no work ethic. He was determined to instill some sense into his only son.

"When are you going to join the family business?" he'd asked, bristling for the right answer.

It was a leading question that initially Henry ignored, until eventually it led all the way to a vicious argument.

"You know perfectly well I want to be an actor," Henry had yelled, filled with frustration. "It's my ambition, and *you* can't stop me."

"Can't I?" Logan had answered, his long face grim.

"No!" Henry had shouted. "Not you, not Mother, *nobody.*"

"You'll be an actor over my dead body," Logan had shouted back.

Soon the yelling had escalated into a serious screaming match. Logan was very angry with his useless son, who refused to listen to reason, and Henry had no intention of giving up his dream.

They screamed insults back and forth, until the older man suddenly fell silent. His face paled and he clutched his left arm. "Je . . . sus," he'd managed, before collapsing onto the bottom of the boat. "Get . . . me . . . my . . . pills."

Henry did nothing. He merely sat and watched as his father writhed in agony for at least five minutes before dying of a massive heart attack. Only then had Henry taken the boat back to the landing dock. He wasn't sorry, not at all. It was his father's own fault—he'd caused the fatal heart attack himself by shouting at him.

Logan Whitfield-Simmons's funeral was a heavily attended and somber affair. The Whitfield-Simmonses were a well-known and respected family in Pasadena. In fact, they were a well-known family across America. Logan Whitfield-Simmons was always at the top of *Forbes* magazine's richest people in America list, while Penelope Whitfield-Simmons was lauded on the society pages for her extensive charity work, elegant clothes, and Fortune 400 friends. Great things were expected of Henry, their only son and heir. He fully intended to disappoint.

After his father's funeral Henry felt a certain freedom. Without asking anyone's permission, he borrowed his mother's credit card, went out and purchased an extremely expensive sports car. Two days later he smashed the car up in a head-on collision. Unfortunately for Henry, he emerged from the accident with a broken pelvis and hip, and since his hip never set properly, he was stuck with a permanent limp, putting paid to his dreams of becoming a famous actor.

After his accident Henry rarely left the house. Mostly he stayed in his room watching movies or hunched over his computer.

Penelope was not concerned that her son stayed at home and did nothing; having him around was company for her. "My son, the computer nerd," she would sigh to her friends. "Henry knows more about computers than anyone. He's threatened to teach me one day, although who has the time to understand all that newfangled technology?"

Henry lived a whole other life on the Internet. There were girls to visit, places to go he'd never gone before, naked girls he didn't have to talk to, because Henry had never been good with the opposite sex. Henry Whitfield-Simmons was still a virgin. As far back as he could remember, his mother had always warned him that girls would chase after him because of the family's wealth and position, and that he should always resist their advances. He'd taken note of her wise words, and never had a girlfriend.

One day while surfing the Internet, he'd come upon a site that featured young teenage girls. Somehow he'd managed to enter their private domain, a Web site where they exchanged personal messages and wrote vividly about their thoughts and dreams. Most of their thoughts and dreams concerned boys, which Henry found boring. But he liked looking at the photos the girls posted of themselves. They were pouty and pretty; young, innocent girls playing dress-up with long, flowing hair draped seductively over one eye, and come-on expressions.

Henry was soon addicted. Every night he would sit at his computer checking them out. Until one night he realized there was something very familiar about one of the girls, and when he Googled her, he discovered who she was. The girl was Maria Santangelo Golden, Lucky Santangelo's daughter.

The information astounded and thrilled him.

CHAPTER TEN

Even though Lucky arose at five A.M., ready to work out with her personal trainer—so L.A. (but if she didn't have Cole to kick her butt three days a week, she'd never do it)—there were never enough hours in the day to get everything done, especially as she flew to Vegas twice a week. After a vigorous workout she usually made her East Coast phone calls—business and family. Her son Bobby had recently opened a restaurant/club in New York, and Brigette was busy designing her own jewelry line. Neither of them needed to work, as they were both descendants of Greek billionaire Dimitri Stanislopolous, Lucky's second husband, and had both inherited huge fortunes, although Bobby would not inherit the bulk of his until he hit twenty-five.

Lucky was happy about that. Bobby was smart and extremely good-looking—the burden of such a fortune was bound to influence him. She fervently hoped that in two years' time he'd be able to handle the pitfalls that came with being ultrarich.

Bobby had dropped out of college after a couple of years because he was bored and wanted to get out into the world and do something. Lucky had encouraged him; as far as she was concerned, it was more important to get a street education. Not that opening a club was exactly street, but it *was* an education.

Every few weeks Lucky took a plane into New York

to check things out. Brigette was doing well. She'd given up her once-hot modeling career, and after a series of disastrous affairs and a bad marriage, at thirty-two she finally seemed to have gotten it together.

Brigette was the child of Olympia, Dimitri's daughter who'd died from a drug overdose locked in a hotel room with famous British rock star Flash.

As one of the richest heiresses in the world, she'd always lived her life in the spotlight. Constantly dogged by paparazzi, written about in all the gossip columns, and envied by most mere mortals, not only was Brigette unbelievably rich, she was also a natural blonde with a willowy figure and an extremely pretty face. Brigette was every fortune hunter's dream. Problem was she always managed to attract the wrong men. If there was a bad-boy loser around, send him in Brigette's direction— she seemed to collect them. The last disaster was Carlo Vittorio Vitti, an Italian count who'd managed to turn Brigette onto drugs, married her, then attempted to murder her so he could inherit her enormous fortune.

Ever since that fateful marriage, there'd been a lull, and for the last few years Brigette seemed at peace. All the same, Lucky kept a close eye on her.

Bobby, on the other hand, was Mr. Cool. He had a Kennedy-esque air about him—great looks and charmingly self-deprecating. Girls fell at his feet and he took his pick, working his way through the pack.

"You're my hero," Gino Senior told him every time they got together. "Screw the Stanislopolous bloodline— you're a Santangelo all the way, an' doncha forget it."

Gino, who resided in Palm Springs with his decades-younger wife, Paige, was crazy about all his grandchildren, especially Bobby, who reminded him of his own womanizing youth.

Lucky felt fortunate to have such a great family, but

having a family didn't mean sitting around doing nothing. Money had never been a problem for Lucky—her name said it all, plus she was a savvy businesswoman with all the right instincts. She was totally psyched about getting back into the hotel business. The last hotel she'd built was the Santangelo in Atlantic City—a fine hotel—but Atlantic City wasn't Vegas, so after a few years she'd sold it, garnering almost three times her investment. Now, in Las Vegas, she had created the Keys complex—a hotel casino with luxury apartments. It was her dream hotel, and she couldn't wait for opening night, which was in a few weeks' time.

In the meantime she had Gino's ninety-fifth birthday party to plan. She wanted it to be ultraspecial, so she'd hired a party planner to take care of all the details. Gino would love being the center of his own party; he lived for action. At almost ninety-five he was as active as ever, full of energy and a zest for living.

Gino the Ram was his nickname when he was a teenager running riot on the streets of Brooklyn.

As a kid, Lucky couldn't wait to hear all about Gino in his wild days—clawing his way up from nothing, making his fortune, scoring with dozens of beautiful women, until one day he'd met Maria, and she'd turned out to be the love of his life.

Maria. Lucky's mother. Brutally butchered and left for five-year-old Lucky to discover floating on a raft in the family swimming pool, the blood draining from her lifeless body.

Her mother's death had forced Lucky to be strong and independent. It had taught her how to be alone and to never be scared again.

The violent and unforgettable tragedy had taken away her childhood and all the good memories, but screw it—even after Dario was murdered and then Marco, she'd never allowed herself to get beaten down. Never.

No. Lucky's power was in her strength, and nobody could take that away from her.

Nobody dared.

Early Thursday evening Max bounced into the den where Lucky was busy working on the security list for Gino's party, and Lennie was jotting down random notes on the script of his upcoming movie.

"Hey, Mom," Max said, employing her best conciliatory tone of voice. "I just came up with a totally cool idea."

"Really?" Lucky said, hardly looking up.

"Yes," Max replied. "Y'see, I have the perfect solution."

"You do, huh?" Lucky said skeptically.

Max nodded, full of confidence. "I'll drive to Big Bear *tomorrow,* then come back Sunday morning like *way* in time for Grandpa's party. How's that?"

Lennie glanced up from his script. "You're going to Big Bear?" he said. "I used to love to ski."

"And your lovely daughter doesn't," Lucky said crisply. "Besides, Max, there's no way you can miss dinner tomorrow night. Gino's driving in from Palm Springs, and Bobby and Brigette are coming from New York. It's a big family reunion dinner, and I'm cooking."

Max groaned inwardly. Friday nights Lucky made a point of everyone sitting down for the whole family dinner thing. Why did *she* have to be there? Surely she had enough of Gino Junior and his lech friends all week?

"But Mom—" she began, working it hard.

Lucky shot her daughter a look. Friday nights were important, especially *this* Friday with everyone arriving. She'd planned on taking over the kitchen herself and making the one dish she excelled at: pasta and meatballs with her special sauce. It was Lennie's favorite meal, and preparing it was her favorite therapy. Besides, she'd always encouraged her kids to bring their friends, so why was Max so intent on giving her a hard time?

"You should be here," she said, throwing her daughter another long, steady look. "Everyone wants to see you."

Max frowned. This Friday-night family deal was totally lame, she was so not into it, even though her friends couldn't wait to come over for Friday dinner. "Damn, girl!" Cookie was always informing her. "You actually, like, *have* a family. All I've got is my dad, an' all *he* has is a different big-boobed skank like every other *second*. An' *he* gets to fuck 'em. *I* have to talk to them, so Friday night at your house rocks!"

It infuriated Max that both Cookie and Harry considered Lucky and Lennie the coolest parents ever.

"*You* don't have to live with them," she would often point out. "They're not that easy. My mom can be a total pain. When I got that tattoo on my thigh she went total ape shit."

"I'd swap 'em for mine any day," Harry would always reply. "At least they notice you're alive."

Max had to admit that on the very few occasions she'd seen them, Harry's parents were quite scary. And as for Cookie's dad, Gerald M., he was a major sex addict.

"Everyone will see me on Sunday at the big party," Max said, flashing Lennie a pleading look. "Dad . . ."

"What's the deal?" Lennie asked, finally putting down his script.

"One of Cookie's friends is having a blowout birthday thing Saturday night," Max said, words tripping over each other. "And Mom says I can't go. But if I'm back in time for Grandpa's party . . ." She trailed off, continuing to gaze pleadingly at Lennie, all intense green eyes and innocent expression.

Lennie got the message. "Hey, Lucky," he said. "Whyn't you let her go? What's the big problem?"

"No problem," Lucky responded, suddenly feeling

like the uptight mother figure, a feeling she did not appreciate. "I guess as long as she's back for Gino's party
it's okay."

"I, like, *so* will be," Max dutifully promised, vainly
attempting to subdue her triumphant expression.

"We'll need the number where you're at," Lucky said,
sensing that somehow or other she'd just lost out. It
pissed her off when Lennie overruled her without even
a discussion about what they should do. Parenting was
supposed to be a joint venture—something Lennie
didn't seem to get.

Lennie winked at his willful but quite beguiling
daughter. "Happy now?" he asked.

"Thanks, Dad," she said, giving him a quick hug,
then hurriedly fleeing before Lucky changed her mind.

On the way to her room Max made a mental note that
the next time she wanted anything she should ask while
Lennie was around; he was way easier to deal with than
her mom.

Upstairs she called Cookie. "It's on!" she announced.
"I'm driving up there tomorrow."

"Tomorrow?" Cookie said. "Doesn't that screw up
Friday dinner at your house?"

"Dinner's a no-go," Max explained. "I told them this
thing in Big Bear is for one of your friends, so natch
you'll be coming with me."

"But I won't," Cookie stated blankly.

"*I* know that, and *you* know that, but *they* don't. So
you've got to lay low, an' tell Harry the same."

"*Crap!*"

"What?"

"Missing dinner at your house like major sucks!"

"Oh, I'm so sorry that *my* hot date messes up *your*
weekend," Max drawled sarcastically.

"Okay, I like *get* it," Cookie answered crossly. "No
need to freak out."

"Who's freaking out?"

"You are."

"I am *so* not."

But inside she was, just a tiny bit.

Shutting her cell, she hurried over to her laptop and quickly logged in. "*I'll be in Big Bear Friday afternoon,*" she tapped out. "*Where shall we meet?*"

Within minutes Grant had e-mailed her back. "*Meet me in the Kmart parking lot. Stay in your car. I'll find you.*"

I'll find you! How romantic was *that*?

She rushed to her closet, desperately trying to decide what to wear. Skinny jeans or short skirt? T-shirt or sexy tank? Bra or no bra? Strappy heels or flats?

She finally decided on tight jeans and a layered T-shirt—best to go the casual route, she didn't want to look as if she'd tried too hard.

How tall was he? She'd forgotten to ask.

It didn't matter. This weekend she was doing the deed with her Internet hottie.

Oh yeah! She was doing the deed and there would be no regrets.

Sorry, Donny. You blew it.

"Remember the first time we met?" Lucky murmured later that night as she and Lennie lay in bed.

"You think I could forget?" Lennie responded. "It was Vegas, an' if I recall correctly, *you* tried to rape me."

"You thought I was a hooker," she said indignantly.

"Yeah," he agreed, laughing. "And a *very* expensive one."

"Screw you," she said, pretending to be mad. "I wanted to sleep with you and *you* turned me down."

He raised an eyebrow. "I did?"

"You *know* you did."

"Yeah, well, didn't we make a date for later and *you* failed to show?"

"As if I *would* after the way you treated me."

"*Then* you had me fired," he said, mock-frowning at the memories. "Nice. Very nice. I was out on my ass with nowhere to go but down."

Lucky smiled as she remembered. Lennie had been working stand-up in the lounge of the Magiriano, her hotel. She'd felt restless and lonely and he was there and available, so she'd invited him up to her suite, and when she'd indicated that she expected a lot more than conversation, he'd walked out on her.

"The thing is I'd heard you were such a major *playa*," she teased. "So how come you rejected *me*?"

"'Cause you came on like a guy," he said, reaching over her for a bottle of FIJI Water.

"Something wrong with that?" she said, challenging him with her dark eyes.

"Whyn't you shut up an' c'mere," he said, putting the bottle down.

"Okay, mister," she said, playing along. "Take off your pants and show *me* some action."

"Thought I just did."

"Oh, *my* bad," she said, laughing softly.

"How quickly they forget," he sighed.

"Forget *you*? *Never*," she said teasingly.

"Anyone ever tell you you've got a smart mouth?" he said, throwing her a quizzical look.

And before she could answer, he was pressing his lips down on hers and they were starting all over again.

A long and sexy marriage suited both of them.

CHAPTER ELEVEN

"You're the best," Emmanuelle crooned. "I've never met a man like you before. Oh my *God*, Anthony, you make me so *weak*."

She actually wanted to say *weep*, because sexually Anthony was totally inept. He was under the impression that climbing on top of her and going at it like a randy dog was enough. No foreplay, no words of desire, nothing, *nada*—just an angry hard-on and a fit of manic energy as he pumped away, heading toward his own satisfaction like an express train, not at all concerned about *her* orgasm.

"Yeah, pie-face, you sure are one lucky little girl," Anthony agreed, still vigorously thrusting back and forth.

Even though Anthony was only thirty-nine, Emmanuelle had a sneaking suspicion he took Viagra to make sure he stayed hard. One time she'd discovered a couple of the telltale blue pills in his jacket pocket, and when she'd asked about them, he'd gotten furious and informed her they were for headaches. Some headaches!

Rapidly getting bored with Anthony's lack of skill, Emmanuelle decided to fake it early, hoping it might make him come. She began her own personal ritual, a series of long, drawn-out sighs, followed by cries of "Oh, *Anthony*. Oh yes, yes, *yeeees!* You make me so *wet* and creamy. Oh, *yeeees*, baby, you're the man, the big, big *man*."

She was done, finished.

Not really, but let him think she was.

Contracting her vagina, she squeezed his cock tight.

It did the trick. He hurriedly pulled out and spurted all over her stomach.

Anthony refused to wear a condom; he also refused to come inside her. Emmanuelle knew it was because he didn't want to take the risk of getting her pregnant.

Ha! Like she would want *his* baby. All she wanted from Anthony Bonar was material goods—in *her* name. And the sooner, the better.

Two minutes later Anthony was standing in the shower scrubbing off Emmanuelle's scent. Once the sex was over he had nothing to say to her. Fact is, he had nothing to say to women period. The only woman he'd ever come across worth a dime was his formidable grandmother. Now, there was a woman who gave as good as she got. He admired her, yet at the same time he was more than a little scared of her. Ridiculous really, because Anthony was never scared of anyone or anything, but sometimes Francesca made him feel exactly like the twelve-year-old boy she'd plucked off the streets of Naples and given a life. Some life it was too. He was rich, and in *his* world extremely powerful. He could have more or less anything he wanted, and he did. Yes, he'd come a long way from his impoverished childhood with an Italian mother who'd worked as a maid, and an American father who'd never bothered to acknowledge him.

Now, if he was to satisfy his grandmother, he had to bring the Santangelo family down. And Lucky building the Keys in Vegas had given him the perfect opportunity.

Two days passed before Irma spotted the young gardener again. This time she was determined to take it a step further since a so-called friend had sent her a newspaper clipping of her husband exiting a nightclub in Miami with the piece of white trash he kept stashed in an apartment there.

Anthony had some gall to flaunt his "girlfriends," or "cheap hookers," as Irma thought of them. It infuriated her. Didn't he *give* a damn?

Apparently not.

Well, if *he* didn't care, why should *she?* She'd sleep with the gardener and to hell with her controlling husband. Let him see how *he* liked it when *she* did it back to *him*. Not that he'd ever find out, but *she* would know, and that was enough to satisfy her.

It was late afternoon and the older gardener was nowhere in sight. However, Luis was there, on his knees, tending to the rosebushes.

After a few moments of indecision, Irma approached him. "*Hola*, Luis," she said, fanning herself with a magazine.

Unfortunately, her Spanish language skills were quite limited, although she was well aware that *hola* was a familiar greeting used by friends, and Luis was *not* her friend, he was her employee, or rather Anthony's employee—which would make sleeping with the man a sweet punishment for her cheating husband.

Luis glanced up, startled. "*Señora*," he managed, wiping a slick of sweat from his brow.

She studied his face for a moment, his thick lips and brooding features. He was rough and masculine-looking, so unlike Anthony, who was very much into grooming with the most expensive face creams and hair products, his bathroom shelves crammed full of bottles and potions. Anthony, who plastered his face with fake tan, had his eyebrows plucked professionally, and indulged in a weekly facial.

"Can you please cut some roses for me?" she said.

And when Luis looked up at her blankly, she panto-mimed what she wanted, bending to touch a rose, al-lowing him to get a perfect view of her breasts as the summer shift she had on fell slightly open.

"Ah . . ." Luis said, his eyes lingering, "*Si, señora.*"

Irma experienced a flutter of excitement. Where would they do it when the moment came? Her bedroom? The very same bedroom she shared with Anthony when he honored her with his presence?

Why not?

Or perhaps they would stay outside while there was no one around to spy on them. The guards were on duty at the front of the house, and the old gardener was ob-viously not there.

Her heart began pounding. Merely thinking about making love with this man had her juices flowing.

So intent was Luis on surreptitiously checking out her breasts that he accidentally cut himself on a prickly thorn.

Irma watched intently as a thin line of blood trickled across his wrist.

"Oh, dear," she exclaimed, tentatively touching his forearm. "You're bleeding."

"*Non importante,*" he muttered, quickly standing up.

"Yes," Irma insisted. "It looks bad, Luis. You should come with me." Taking him by the arm, she began lead-ing him toward the house.

Luis's eyes darted around to see if there was anyone watching. He needed this job, and the American woman obviously needed more than her roses clipped.

Irma was past caring. If Anthony was informed of her indiscretions, she didn't give a damn. Her dear husband hadn't touched her in over a year. Luis was about to be her revenge.

*   *   *

The Grill was Anthony's number-one bodyguard. Nobody knew where he had picked up the name, and nobody asked. As a professional bodyguard The Grill didn't need much—his fists were enough to defend himself and his boss, his fists and a complete knowledge of all martial arts. The Grill was from Slovakia. At six feet four, with muscles of steel and a plain, foreboding face with a dangerous scar carving its way across one cheek, he cut a sinister figure. Anthony liked having him around simply for the fear factor—nobody cared to mess with The Grill.

Finished with Emmanuelle for the night, Anthony headed for the airport and his plane.

"We're goin' to Vegas," he informed The Grill.

The Slovakian man barely nodded. Wherever Anthony Bonar went, he followed. He had no life of his own. Anthony Bonar was his destiny.

Checking out his flashy gold Rolex, one of his many watches, Anthony decided to call his Italian girlfriend, Carlita, a raven-haired beauty of twenty-eight. Carlita, a former model, designed overpriced handbags and belts, a business he'd financed. Anthony appreciated a woman with ambition, and Carlita certainly possessed plenty of it. He'd met her at a party two years previously, and stuck with her ever since. She was smarter than Emmanuelle, she knew what was going on in the world.

Carlita's voice mail picked up. He tried her cell and the same thing happened. Goddamn voice mail. Annoyed that he couldn't reach her, Anthony made several business calls before retiring to his private bedroom for the six-hour flight to Vegas. May as well catch some shut-eye. Making love to Emmanuelle was quite exhausting—she was young and energetic, and she expected a peak performance every time.

Naturally he delivered. In bed he was a raging bull. Oh yes, Anthony Bonar had never had any complaints.

That's the way it was. And that's the way it would stay.

Sunlight filtering through the curtains woke Irma. She lay very still for a few moments reliving the events of the previous day.

Luis. One moment he was the gardener, the next—her lover. And *what* a lover. Alternatively rough and gentle, his large hands exploring her most private parts the way Anthony never had, his lips kissing her in places Anthony had never ventured.

And then . . . he'd brought her to a climax, and she'd been overcome with a feeling of ecstasy the likes of which she'd never experienced before.

Anthony had never made her come.

Anthony had never touched her down there except with his penis—a ferocious weapon intent on nothing but its own satisfaction.

Anthony had never really cared.

Irma sat up in bed, her cheeks glowing.

Luis wasn't the answer, but she knew one thing for sure: she had to divorce Anthony.

The time had come to get away from her coldhearted husband, reclaim her children, and finally take responsibility for her own happiness.

CHAPTER TWELVE

Every morning Venus worked out, varying her activities, but making damn sure she did either jogging,
weight training, Pilates, or yoga. Lucky and she used the
same trainer, Cole de Barge, a great-looking black guy
with abs of steel, fine muscle definition, and the one special thing a girl needs from a trainer—a take-charge
attitude. There was no slacking off around Cole.

Venus enjoyed teasing him. "If you weren't gay, I'd
sweep you off to some exotic island and marry you."

Cole simply smiled. He had perfect teeth. In fact he
had perfect everything.

"Do *not* try to get around me," he said, turning stern.
"Today we're takin' a hike in the Canyon, so you'd better
bring your favorite bottled water, an' no complaining."

"But Cole," she protested, feigning a delicate yawn.
"Last night I—"

"Hey, Miss Superstar," he interrupted, "it ain't my
business what you did last night. Your *body* is my business, so move your fine ass an' let's get it on."

That's what she liked about Cole—he took no prisoners. She might be dizzily famous, but if Cole wanted
her up and out, she was there. No arguing with Cole, and
the results were worth it. Besides, Billy had left at some
ungodly hour, and since Chyna, her daughter with Cooper, was away at summer camp, she had nothing else to
do. She was between movies, between recordings, and
between concert tours. It was her time to relax.

"Very well," she said grumpily. "Don't worry that I had no sleep—"

"I'm not worrying."

"Billy spent the night," she explained. "He was coming off a tough day with Alex Woods. It was up to me to console him."

"So that's what they're callin' it now—consoling."

"Oh, get a life!"

"I *got* a life, superstar, an' today it involves pushing you out there. So let's hit it. Now!"

Reluctantly she followed Cole out the front door. Today she really didn't feel like indulging in any physical activity. She was genuinely tired, so why couldn't she have stayed in bed and watched mindless morning TV? Although there was nothing mindless about Matt Lauer on the *Today* show—he was still the hottest talking head on TV.

And thinking of hot . . . last night Billy had excelled himself. She'd always thought her ex-husband—legendary movie star/cocksman Cooper Turner—was the best she'd ever had in bed, but Billy surpassed him. Such enthusiasm, such energy, such a tongue!

If only she wasn't thirteen years older than Billy. It was a major drag. This year she'd be forty-two, and while everyone knew that forty was the new twenty— what did that make Billy? *Twelve?*

He'd assured her he didn't mind, that age was just a number. Yeah, sure, but the tabloids never let either of them forget their age difference, and she knew that it bugged Billy when the late-night comedians made jokes about them. It was all so unfair. When she'd been married to Cooper Turner nobody had said a word about Cooper being twenty years older than her. Talk about a double standard. If she was European would anyone care? European actresses were revered for getting older. American actresses were not. America was a raging youth culture, but along with Madonna and Sharon Stone, she was hanging in there, she *still* looked great, and why not? She worked like a motherfucker to make sure everything stayed in place. Hence her ritual with Cole, whether she felt like it or not.

"I'm right behind you, slave driver," she announced, catching up with Cole as he walked briskly to his car—a new sports Jaguar. "*Very* fancy," she remarked. "Business must be outta the park."

"It's a present," he said.

"From a grateful client?"

"Let's just say he's *very* grateful, but he's not a client."

"Name please."

"You'll get his name when we're married with a weekend house in Aspen and two adopted kids."

"Revealing as usual," Venus said dryly.

"Some of us prefer to keep our private lives private," Cole replied, not eager to discuss his personal life.

"Some of us are *able* to do that," Venus responded tartly, hiding her eyes behind blackout Dolce & Gabbana shades.

"Yeah, an' *some* of us are making millions a year, which is the price they pay for *no* privacy. Sorry, *Miz* Superstar."

"He *always* has to get the last word," she sighed, jumping into the passenger seat.

"That's *right!*" Cole said, getting behind the wheel. "An' now we're off to Franklin Canyon, so get your energy goin', girl, we're takin' an hour-long hike, *no* slackin' off allowed."

Venus slumped back in her seat and groaned. Cole was a hard taskmaster, but that's the way it had to be.

"Orange juice, Meester Billy?" Ramona inquired, invading his bedroom, standing next to his bed and peering down at him, a glass of freshly squeezed juice in one hand.

"Huh?" Billy mumbled, barely opening one eye. He'd staggered home at five A.M., telling Venus he had an early call—which was a lie—then collapsing into his own bed, totally spent. Now his housekeeper was standing over him, and how many times had he told her not to wake him? Didn't she understand that he needed his sleep?

"Jeez," he muttered. "What's the time?"

"Time for you to haul your lazy ass outta the sack," announced Kev—gofer, assistant, driver. Kev was short, with wiry brown hair and a permanently cocky expression. They'd been best friends since meeting in kindergarten at the tender age of five. They'd grown up together, closer than brothers. Kev had taken off for L.A. before Billy with a plan to somehow or other break into movies. It hadn't happened for him, Billy was the one who'd gotten the golden ticket, and once Billy made it, he'd brought Kev along for the ride.

"Get fucked," Billy groaned, reaching under the sheet to scratch his balls.

"It's past twelve," Kev said, opening the blackout blinds, flooding the room with bright sunlight. "You got an interview for that fancy mag *Manhattan Style*. The journo's comin' here at one, an' Janey's on her way over now. She told me to wake your ass, an' remind you this is important shit. It's the cover story, so she says there's no way you can blow it off."

"Crap!" Billy muttered, kicking away the sheets, revealing his naked body and a very impressive piss hard-on.

Ramona seemed oblivious to her employer's lack of clothes and his erect penis. She handed him the glass of juice and left the room.

"Why's Janey coming?" Billy inquired.

"'Cause she's your publicist, an' that's what she does," Kev replied.

"No, what she *does* is charge me a shitload of money to do fuck all," Billy grumbled.

"*You're* in a piss-poor mood."

"So would you be if Alex friggin' Woods had spent the day watching you get the bejesus whacked outta you," Billy complained. "An' how come you didn't make it to the location last night?"

"You never told me you needed me there."

"I gotta tell you everything?" Billy said, finally getting out of bed and making his way into the bathroom.

"You usually do," Kev said, trailing behind him. "If you'd wanted me there you should've said so."

"What am I supposed t'wear?" Billy asked as he finished peeing and headed for the shower.

"Janey said you'd better look hot."

"Janey wouldn't know hot if it hit her in the ass."

Kev chuckled. Ramona reappeared with two plastic dry-cleaning bags. "Meesus Janey say you wear these," she announced, handing the bags to Kev.

"What's a movie star supposed t'do t'get some kind of *privacy*?" Billy grumbled. "My johnson's not a show 'n' tell, so everyone get the fuck OUT!"

Ramona and Kev hurriedly retreated, leaving Billy alone in the bathroom. He stepped into the shower, thinking that perhaps he should call Venus, tell her how great last night was.

Problem was he wasn't feeling it. Anyway, she was probably still asleep, or out with her trainer—the good-looking black guy she swore was gay, although sometimes Billy wasn't so sure. The dude didn't *act* gay. He didn't even *look* gay.

Shit! What if she was screwing her trainer and they were both laughing at him behind his back?

This thought eased his guilt about the girl in the

truck with the broken taillight. If Venus could do it, so could he.

And yet . . . Once again waves of guilt swept over him. Venus wouldn't. She couldn't. Venus was a one-man woman. She'd often confided how much it had hurt her when she'd caught her husband screwing around on her. But hey, that's what guys did—*especially* movie star guys. Surely every woman was aware of that?

He got out of the shower, toweled himself dry, and ripped open the plastic cleaning bags. Black silk pants and a crisp white Armani shirt.

Screw it, he was more comfortable in jeans and an old army shirt stolen from the wardrobe department on one of his movie shoots. Janey would simply have to accept his style or get herself fired.

One of the most important lessons Billy had learned in Hollywood was that nobody was indispensable. They all thought they were, but the sad truth was that everyone was replaceable. Including himself.

"Starbucks," Venus gasped as she and Cole got back in the Jag after a long, grueling mountain hike.

"Is that so you can undo all the good work we just put in?" Cole questioned, throwing her a disapproving look.

"Please! I don't usually beg. But I would *kill* for a caramel low-fat Frappuccino."

"You'll get nailed by the paparazzi," he warned.

"I don't care."

"Okay," Cole said, starting his new Jaguar, a gift from an aging rock star who was trying to persuade Cole to work—and other things—exclusively for him. The Jag was a bribe Cole had accepted as long as there were no strings. He quite liked the guy in a casual way, but he had no intention of hooking up on a permanent basis. He'd done that once, and the memories were not good.

Besides, his sister Natalie, the host of a TV entertainment show, would kill him. She considered all celebrity relationships poison, and she should know, having indulged in a few disastrous ones herself.

There was a line at Starbucks, as usual.

Venus peered out the car window. "*You* go in," she suggested. "You know what I want."

"This goes against everything you *should* be doing," Cole said sternly.

"C'mon, indulge me, babe," Venus crooned.

"Doesn't everyone, *babe*?" he said sarcastically.

Venus giggled. "Yeah, for an old broad I suppose I do get everything I want."

"Including Mr. Melina."

"Ah, Billy," Venus said fondly. "He's such a sweetheart."

"Sure," Cole agreed.

He didn't want to ruin her day, but yesterday he'd spotted Billy leaving Tower Records with a young girl in tow. Hey—maybe she was his sister. Besides, Cole didn't believe in causing trouble. As a trainer of the rich and *infamous* he knew where every body was buried. He also knew he was better off keeping his mouth tightly shut.

"He is, you know," Venus added, as if she was trying to convince herself. "*And*, in case you're wondering about the age thing, Billy is an old soul, he's not like a twenty-something guy. *And* we've been friends for eight years, so it's not as if I don't *know* him."

Cole shrugged. He didn't want to get involved. No good ever came from interfering in other people's love lives.

"We have the same interests," Venus continued. "Lucky thinks we're great together, and he doesn't put up with my b.s. So . . ."

So what? Cole wanted to say. *The dude's a hot young movie star dealing with pussy overload. It's a given he'll cheat. Wise up, Venus, you're too clever to put up with his shit.*

But Cole stayed silent. It simply wasn't his business.

CHAPTER THIRTEEN

"Did you see Max before she left?" Lucky asked, sweeping into Lennie's poolside office early Friday morning.

He was on the phone and waved her away with a dismissive gesture.

"Are you *kidding* me!" she exclaimed. "Don't dismiss me like I'm a fucking fruit fly!"

"Hang on a minute," Lennie said into the phone. Choking back laughter, he pressed down hold. "Fruit fly? A fucking *fruit* fly?"

Grinning, Lucky said, "Sometimes I have to come up with something original to get your attention."

"I'm talking to the studio."

"Fuck 'em," she said, perching on the edge of his desk. "Have you seen Max?"

"Nope."

"Her car's gone, and she didn't leave a number."

"Call her cell," Lennie said, returning to his phone call.

Hmmm . . . Lucky thought, getting up and heading for the kitchen. *As if I don't have enough on my mind without Max sneaking off.*

Although what did it matter? Lennie was right: she could reach Max on her cell at any time.

Yes, but Max should have come and said good-bye. She'd wanted to make absolutely sure her wild little daughter was back in time for Gino's party. Right now unreliable was Max's middle name.

Sixteen. Some age! She remembered it well. At sixteen you thought you were invincible, you thought you owned the world, you thought you could do anything and get away with it, you thought your parents were moronic idiots.

Yeah. Sixteen. Fun memories. Until Gino had married her off to Craven "the lox" Richmond, and she'd been too young and too foolish to realize she could've said no.

Ah well . . . She had no intention of marrying Max off, but she did plan on keeping a closer eye on her. After Gino's party, after the launch of the Keys, she would spend some quality time with her daughter. She had to convince Max that not cutting school was important for getting into the right college. And even though *she'd* made it without a formal education, she wanted Max to experience all the advantages.

Philippe approached. The very precise Philippe had come with the house, and although Lucky often found his manner to be too formal, she put up with him because he was a stickler for making sure the house ran smoothly. Now, with houseguests arriving, Gino's upcoming party, and the opening of her hotel in Vegas, she was grateful to have Philippe and his organizational skills. At least she knew he was there ready and willing to take care of everything.

"Mrs. Golden," he said stiffly.

"Yes, Philippe?" she answered briskly.

"There is another hand delivery for you," he said, passing her an ecru envelope.

She ripped open the envelope and inside was a Cartier card with the same scrawled message—*Drop Dead Beautiful.*

What kind of an invite is this? she thought. *Quite stupid if it doesn't include a save-the-date.*

"Did you see who left it?" she asked, opening the fridge and reaching for a can of 7UP.

"No, Mrs. Golden. It was in the mailbox with the rest of the mail. But I can assure you it was hand-delivered."

Drop Dead Beautiful. Sounded like a movie or maybe the opening of a happening new club. Hollywood publicists were getting much too inventive.

The phone rang, taking her mind off the latest note. Sticking it under a pile of cookbooks, she took the call. It was Alex Woods.

"Lucky," he said. "We haven't spoken in a while. Thought I'd check in."

"Alex, what's going on?" she said, always pleased to hear from him even though she knew he still harbored a mild crush.

"I'm shooting my movie."

"I know that," she said, taking a swig of 7UP from the can. "How's it going?"

"Great. How's our hotel progressing?"

"We're on schedule. I have a fantastic team in place, and we'll be opening on time. You'll be there of course."

"Wouldn't miss it. When I invest money I want to see the results."

"Oh, you will. The Keys is going to rule Vegas, I can promise you that."

"Everything you do always works out, so I'm confident this'll be another moneymaking triumph."

"Enough with the compliments—Lennie tells me the two of you have been trading missed calls."

"*You* know what it's like when you're at the end of a shoot, no time for anything."

"Ah yes, I remember it well," she said, momentarily nostalgic for her producing days.

"We should develop another movie together."

"Oh sure," she said sarcastically. "I can do that—in my spare time."

"We'd have a blast, just like before."

"How's Billy working out?" she asked, quickly changing the subject.

"I hate goddamn actors," Alex said vehemently. "Once they make it, they're out of control."

"I know you do, but you wouldn't be able to do your job without 'em," Lucky said, wondering what Billy was up to now.

"Ever heard of animated flicks?" Alex said.

"Yeah," she said, laughing. "I can just imagine an animated Alex Woods movie. Cute little rabbits and adorable farm creatures beating the crap outta each other with machetes! Blood and severed limbs everywhere!"

"Ah . . . she knows me so well," he said dryly.

"Oh yes, Alex, I do."

"Any chance of lunch anytime soon?"

"Thought you were busy shooting."

"I am. But maybe you'll visit the set one day. I'll have them set up lunch in my trailer."

"You, me, and Lennie?"

"Just you and me was what I had in mind."

"It's good I don't take you seriously."

"Why's that?"

"'Cause then I'd have to tell Lennie you were hitting on me, forcing him to kick your ass."

"Sounds dramatic. But I was always under the impression that *you* had the balls in the family."

"Low blow, Alex."

"Just telling it the way I see it."

"Lennie has plenty of balls, believe me."

There was a short silence while she tried to figure out what was on his mind. Every so often he made an attempt to get together without Lennie. She always laughed him out of it. She was very fond of Alex as a friend, and that's the way she wanted to keep it. Yes, she'd slept with him once and once only, but it was long ago and it didn't really count, because at the time she'd thought Lennie was gone forever. It was obviously a night Alex had never forgotten.

"You're coming to Gino's party on Sunday?" she asked, breaking the silence.

"Wouldn't miss it," Alex replied.

"Bringing Ling I hope."

"Should I?"

"*Why* are you asking *me?* She's *your* girlfriend. Isn't it about time you made it legal?"

"Gotta go," he said abruptly. "See you Sunday." And he hung up.

That's right, Alex, let's not get anywhere near your personal life, Lucky thought. She wished he'd find that special someone, because even though he'd been living with Ling for a couple of years, she obviously wasn't it.

There were times Lucky found it uncomfortable between her and Alex—especially as she'd never told Lennie about their one-night stand. The truth was she wanted Alex and Lennie to remain friends, but if Lennie ever found out . . .

It was all too complicated, she refused to think about it. There were too many other things to deal with, and right now making Gino's party perfect was number one on her agenda.

CHAPTER FOURTEEN

Friday morning Brigette and Bobby Stanislopolous met at a private airport in New York, ready to board the Stanislopolous plane to Los Angeles. Neither of them used the plane much; it was the company jet and usually flew members of the Stanislopolous board and chief executives around Europe. However, it was at their disposal whenever they needed it.

When they met up at the airport, Brigette realized she hadn't seen Bobby in almost a year. "Look at you," she exclaimed, genuinely pleased to see him. "Handsome!"

Bobby was indeed handsome. Like Lucky he was tall, with olive skin, jet-black hair, and intense black eyes. Like his late father, Dimitri, he had a Greek nose, strong chin, and dominant personality. He was a hybrid—half Santangelo, half Stanislopolous.

"Is that any way to talk to your uncle?" he teased, checking out his devastatingly pretty niece.

"Oh, sorry, *Uncle* Bobby," Brigette said with a flicker of a smile. She was naturally blond and cover-girl pretty. "I hear your club is doing great," she added. "Good for you."

"Yeah," Bobby replied, nodding his head. "We got written up in *New York* magazine last month. How come I've never seen you there?"

"I finished with the club scene after I finished with modeling," she said. "It's not for me. Too many needy people on the prowl."

"You gotta be my guest one night," Bobby said, full of enthusiasm at the thought of showing off his gorgeous niece. "I'll look after you. We'll have fun, that's a promise."

"Thank you, *Uncle* Bobby," she answered, smiling. "I shall look forward to that."

Wow! She's such a babe, Bobby thought. *What a waste. I know a dozen guys who'd give their left nut for a shot at her. And if we weren't related . . .*

"Is the plane ready for boarding?" she asked.

"All set," he said, scooping up her Fendi overnight bag and throwing it over his shoulder.

"Then let's go," Brigette said, standing up.

"You got it," he said, taking her arm.

Together they headed for the plane.

Meanwhile, Gino Senior sat in the front passenger seat of his new Cadillac, while Paige, his wife of twenty years, drove. For an old broad Paige still had it going on, or at least Gino thought so. He couldn't have asked for a more spirited, loyal, always-there-for-him wife. And attractive too, with her flaming red hair and pocket Venus figure. Even in her seventies Paige still cut a swath. He'd made a smart choice when he'd dumped his third wife, the frosty Susan Martino, and married her best friend, Paige. There'd been a few bumps along the way—nobody was perfect. He'd never forget walking in on the two women in bed together. But that was ancient news, and who was he to make judgments? After all, his past was hardly blameless.

Ah . . . So many women, so many memories . . .

Now he was old. Frigging *old*. And it didn't seem possible when in his head he was still maybe forty years of age. Christ! Looking in the mirror and seeing an old face peering back at him was not something that thrilled him. Better than the alternative, though; he was a true survivor and let no one forget it. He'd outlived them all—Enzio Bonnatti, Pinky Banana, Jake the Boy—all the old crew. He'd weathered jail, a heart attack, the death of a child, a couple of assassination attempts, the murder of his beloved first wife. Jeez! And a thousand other things.

In two days he was about to be ninety-frigging-five, and it wasn't so bad, apart from the fact that his body was falling to pieces. His knees were gone, arthritis had claimed his hands, his back hurt, his eyes were fading fast, and worst of all, he couldn't get it up anymore. Not that he had any desire to, sex was off the agenda—had been for a couple of years. Gino the Ram was no more. He'd had a good run, and he didn't regret one step of the way, although he did feel sorry for Paige—she must miss the action. Not that she complained; Paige would never do that.

"Can't wait t'see the kids," he said, settling back. "This should be some weekend."

"Fasten your seat belt," Paige said, sounding quite bossy. "If we have an accident, you could go through the windshield."

"Big friggin' deal," Gino replied, indulging in a vigorous coughing fit. "I'm gonna be ninety-five, woman. Ya think a goddamn seat belt's gonna save me?"

"Be sensible, Gino."

"Now, when's *that* gonna happen?" he said, shooting her a quizzical look.

"What time is everyone getting here?" Lennie asked, wandering into the den, where Lucky was busy making notes.

"Brigette and Bobby should be here at four," she said, putting down her pen and stretching her arms above her head. "And Gino and Paige are arriving around the same time."

"Full house this weekend," Lennie remarked.

"Gino wanted to stay in a hotel, but I told him he has to stay here."

"Maybe he likes hotels," Lennie said, walking over to her and starting to massage her shoulders.

"Hey, maybe *I* want him here," Lucky retorted.

"That's 'cause you're Miss Control Freak."

"I am certainly not," she objected.

"Y'know," Lennie mused, "if anyone had told me you'd turn into Earth Mother, I would've laughed in their face."

"You would, huh?" she said, turning her head.

"Lucky Santangelo Golden, former wild one—Earth Mother supreme."

"What *are* you talking about now?"

"Take a count. Three kids—well, four if you count Leonardo. One father. A stepmother. A goddaughter. A husband—"

"That would be *you*," she said, starting to smile.

"Yeah, me," he said, smiling back. "And we'll all be in the same house this weekend, getting ready for Gino's big one. And if I know you, you'll be watching out for everyone. Like I said—Earth Mother supreme."

"Who'd've thunk?" she said ruefully. "Me. The original independent woman. But I wouldn't have it any other way. Would you?"

"No, sweetheart, not for a minute. You make my life complete."

"I do?"

"Y'know," he added thoughtfully, "we've been through a hell of a lot together."

"Now, ain't *that* the truth," she said, getting up.

"So . . . I want to thank you, Mrs. Golden. And if you come over here, I'll show you how."

"Hmm . . ." she said, smiling. "Might I remind you it's the middle of the day?"

"No shit?"

"And I have a thousand things to do."

"So I suppose a blow job's outta the question?" he said, only half serious.

"Lennie!" she exclaimed, taking a step back.

"I know, I know," he said, ruefully. "It's the middle of the day. But hey, I can remember the time when—"

"When *what?*"

"You know what."

"Okay, *husband*," she said, impulsively grabbing his hand. "I think you need to come with me."

"Huh?"

"With me," she said firmly. "That's an order."

"And where are you taking me?" he asked, playing along.

"Somewhere we can lock the door. How's that for a plan?"

He grinned. "Now, *that's* the girl I married."

"You'd better believe it!"

And out on the highway Max drove too fast, just like her mother.

Today she was into rap. Loud, throbbing, ear-splitting rap played mega volume in her car—the amazing BMW sports car her parents had bought her for her sixteenth birthday. Lucky had been against her getting a sports car, but Lennie had soon persuaded her. Lennie had to be the coolest, most laid-back dad in the world. He could talk Lucky into anything—which was why Max realized she should have gone to Lennie in the first place instead of asking Lucky if she could go to Big Bear.

But hey—whatever. Here she was sitting in her BMW on her way to Big Bear heading for an adventure. No problemo. No *way*. This was major exciting!

Giggling to herself, she turned the volume even higher.

Internet guy, here I come. I hope you're good and ready!

CHAPTER FIFTEEN

"I shall be going away this weekend," Henry informed his mother. He was standing in the imposing front hallway of the Pasadena mansion wearing khaki pants and a mud-brown shirt. His prematurely thinning hair was plastered down, and he carried a large canvas hold-all. Henry was not handsome, nor was he ugly—he was merely quite ordinary-looking with no distinguishing features.

Penelope was shocked and at the same time secretly pleased, because much as she tolerated having Henry around, she realized that it was not exactly healthy for him to never leave the house, especially for a boy of his age—man really, for Henry was almost thirty.

"Where are you going?" she inquired.

"To visit friends," he answered vaguely.

Friends? Henry didn't have any friends, at least none that she knew of.

"How long will you be gone?" she asked, adjusting a tall vase of tulips perched on an antique table.

"It depends," he said evasively.

"Have you met a girl?" she asked. "Because if you have, I wish to meet her before you even *think* of getting involved. Remember what I have always told you about girls, Henry. When they look at you, all they see is dollar signs. You are a Whitfield-Simmons, and do not ever forget it."

As if he could. She'd drilled it into him since he was

six. He was a Whitfield-Simmons, and one day he would inherit the Whitfield-Simmons fortune.

"Maybe," he replied, refusing to look her in the eye. "I'll phone you, Mother, and let you know when I'll be back."

"Very well, Henry, I certainly hope you have a pleasant time."

"I think I will," he said, limping toward the door. "As a matter of fact, I'm sure I will."

"Look after yourself, dear," Penelope said, her attention drifting back to the tulips, which seemed in dire need of fresh water.

"I always do," Henry muttered, aware that his mother was no longer listening to him.

He exited the house and stood for a few minutes in the circular driveway.

Markus, his mother's chauffeur, appeared. "Can I help you, Mr. Henry?" Markus asked. He was black and subservient, and had been with the Whitfield-Simmons family since before Henry was born. Shades of *Driving Miss Daisy*, Henry thought. He knew plenty about movies, because apart from his time spent hunched over his computer, he was a movie buff, fascinated by old movies, and especially horror classics such as *The Texas Chainsaw Massacre*, and every one of the Freddy films.

"No help needed, thank you, Markus," he said. "I shall be away for the weekend."

Markus's bushy eyebrows shot up. "That's nice, Mr. Henry, a nice change for you."

"Yes, it is," Henry agreed.

"What car will you be wanting to take?" Markus inquired.

"Mother's Bentley."

"Oh, no, Mr. Henry," Markus said, looking dismayed and beginning to sweat. "Mrs. Penelope won't allow that. She's given me strict orders—"

"I understand, Markus. I was merely joking."

"Yes, Mr. Henry, I knew that," Markus said, thoroughly relieved. "You was joking with me."

"I'll take the Volvo."

"Certainly, Mr. Henry, I'll bring it round to the front."

"That's okay, I'll get it myself."

"If you're sure . . ."

"I'm sure."

Henry walked around the side of the house where the cars were lined up in a row of garages. There was his mother's shiny royal blue Bentley, also a pristine black Cadillac she used when she considered the Bentley too flashy to take on one of her charity jaunts downtown, and next to the Cadillac, a gray Mercedes SUV for shopping trips.

The dark brown Volvo lurked in a corner spot. It was the car out-of-town guests used when they came to stay, and sometimes Markus was allowed to take it out. Ever since his accident Henry had not wanted a car of his own; there was no point since he wasn't going anywhere.

But today he was. Oh yes, today he was off on a mission, and he had to admit that getting out of the house was quite exhilarating.

Opening the trunk of the Volvo, he carefully placed his canvas holdall inside. It contained everything he needed for a very interesting weekend indeed.

CHAPTER SIXTEEN

Vegas and Anthony Bonar were a good match. *What's not to like?* Anthony thought whenever he visited the desert city. *Gambling, spectacular shows, fine restaurants, and beautiful women—plenty of hot, sexy, ready-to-do-anything babes.*

Not that he was looking, he had enough to deal with juggling Emmanuelle and Carlita—Irma didn't count. But even though he wasn't on the hunt, Vegas was Vegas, and if some ready-to-rock piece of ass took his fancy, why turn it down? Viagra meant never having to say you were too tired.

He didn't need the damn blue pills, but after trying Viagra a couple of times he'd become addicted to the major hard-on that never quit. Emmanuelle and Carlita did not object, in fact quite the opposite—the two of them begged him for more. *Insatiable bitches*, he thought with a self-satisfied smirk.

The first woman he'd ever screwed was a whore plying her trade on the streets of Naples. It had happened a few weeks before his twelfth birthday and he was already ragingly horny. The whore had beckoned him into an alley—snatched his money, which he'd stolen from his mother's purse, and screwed him standing up. Fast and furious, that was the way she'd liked it. He'd realized then and there that was the way *all* women liked it.

He'd never changed his sexual style. Fuck 'em hard and fuck 'em long. The story of his success with women.

Renee Falcon Esposito, joint owner of the Cavendish Hotel, had sent a limousine to the airport. Renee and he went way back to the days she was married to Oscar Esposito, the Colombian billionaire politician, a man who'd met his fate by being tossed from a moving plane after trying to pull a double cross on an extremely powerful and vengeful drug lord. Since Anthony had been banging Renee on the side, she'd immediately turned to him for help. He'd never revealed to her that he was part of the plot to get rid of Oscar, but he *had* helped her flee Colombia with the money she'd inherited from her deceased husband—not to mention several safe-deposit boxes stuffed with illegal cash, which he'd persuaded her she had to split with him.

He'd moved Renee back to her hometown, Las Vegas, where she'd eventually hooked up with another mega-bucks female, Susie Rae Young, the widow of famous country singer Cyrus Rae Young. The two of them had formed a life partnership *and* built their dream hotel in which Anthony had declared himself a silent partner.

That was over ten years ago, and business was excellent, so Renee had not taken much convincing that the Keys was a direct threat and could pull away many of their best customers. Anthony insisted they had to do something drastic to stop the Keys from opening. He'd come up with an idea of how to do this. It was a costly plan, but it would be totally effective. Anthony had agreed to pay half of the million bucks it would cost them to have an expert blow up the complex—one building at a time. He had no intention of paying his half. Let Renee foot the entire bill. She owed him.

The hotel limo was waiting on the tarmac alongside his plane. The driver was a tall Swedish blonde dressed in black leather from her knee-high boots to the jaunty cap sitting on top of her head.

"Welcome back to Vegas, Mr. Bonar," she said in a throaty, accented voice. "I will be your driver while you are here."

He barely glanced in her direction.

"My name is Britt," she continued, handing him a small silver cell phone. "All my numbers are programmed in. I'm on duty twenty-four hours a day. Call whenever you need me, I'm at your disposal."

Anthony tossed the phone to The Grill, a move not lost on the blonde, who pretended not to notice.

"Straight to the hotel, Mr. Bonar?" she inquired, holding open the door.

"Yeah," he said, climbing in the back. "An' no conversation."

The Cavendish was a small—by Vegas standards—boutique membership-only luxury hotel catering to extreme high rollers, sports and movie stars, plus high-powered moguls and executives. Very few of the general public were allowed in. The gambling was exclusive, as was the hotel, which had a reputation for supplying all services a guest required. "The best of everything" was the hotel's motto, and that included any known drug, and the highest-priced call girls in the city. Renee ran a tight operation, with major security all around.

Renee herself was standing in the cool marble lobby of her hotel waiting to greet him. Every time he saw her, Anthony couldn't help marveling at the woman's transformation. When he'd first met her, Renee had been Oscar Esposito's American trophy wife, a curvaceous former showgirl with teased blond hair, long legs, and large breasts. Definitely fuckable. Definitely a babe. Now she weighed well over two hundred pounds, wore her hair in a severely cropped dark brown bob, and her implants were long gone. Renee was a different woman. A tough dyke who'd carved a niche for herself in Vegas as a canny businesswoman with a life partner who was even richer than her. All she and Anthony had between them now was business, and that's the way it suited both of them.

"Anthony," Renee greeted. "My favorite bad boy."

"Renee," Anthony responded. "My favorite dyke."

Renee had stones, an admirable quality in a woman, although Anthony wasn't too sure about the lesbian thing. Surely she missed cock?

"Smooth flight?" Renee inquired.

"Not bad," Anthony replied, his eyes flicking around the lobby, checking things out.

"I've put you in Bungalow One. I thought we'd meet for dinner, Susie's excited to see you."

"I ain't here to socialize, Renee," he reminded her gruffly. "I'm here to make certain everythin's in place."

"I can assure you it is," Renee replied, irritated that he would doubt her. "You told me to hire Tucker Bond, and I did. We're paying for the best, Anthony. Half up front, and the rest when the job is done."

"I don't want no fuckups," Anthony growled.

"I don't allow for fuckups," Renee responded.

"Yeah?"

"I'm as concerned as you are," she said, annoyed that Anthony had a way of speaking down to her that she did not appreciate.

Once Anthony was settled into the luxurious bungalow with its own private swimming pool and a bar stocked with the finest brands of liquor and wine, he placed another call to Carlita.

This time his sexy Italian mistress picked up.

"Where the fuck ya bin?" he demanded, drumming his fingers impatiently on the table.

She made up some excuse about visiting a sick relative.

"So sick ya couldn't pick up ya fuckin' cell?" Anthony said, frowning.

Once again Carlita had an answer, telling him that her phone had a low battery or some such shit.

He said nothing. He was pleasant, affectionate even, although he had a strong gut feeling that the douche bag was cheating on him.

As soon as he put the phone down, he called one of his minions in New York and issued an order to have Carlita followed. "Whatever she's doin', I wanna know 'bout it," he instructed. "An' if you find her doin' anythin' she shouldn't, get me photos, proof. Do whatever you gotta do t'bring me the goods."

If she was innocent of screwing around on him, nothing lost.

And if the *puttana* was guilty . . .

Well, if she was guilty, it was her funeral.

Irma's second session with Luis was all she had hoped for and more. It was late afternoon, she'd sent the housekeeper out, the old gardener was still away, and the guards were stationed at the front of the house with Anthony's two ferocious Dobermans.

"I need you to look at my indoor plants. Follow me," she'd informed Luis, who still hadn't understood a word she'd said, although he'd certainly understood what "Follow me" meant.

As soon as they'd reached the privacy of her bedroom, she'd locked the door behind them. Luis hadn't hesitated. He'd ripped the clothes from her body with feverish haste, then he'd begun divesting his own garments as fast as he could get them off.

Words were not spoken.

Words were not needed.

Once she was naked, he'd leaned her back against the wall, spread-eagling her legs.

Propped against the wall with her legs apart, she'd felt exposed, vulnerable, and unbelievably sexually excited.

Luis had stroked her nipples, fingered her crotch, then dropped to his knees and started going down on her, his tongue forcing its way through her wiry bush of pubic hair, darting into her most secret place—a place Anthony had *never* visited with his tongue.

After a few minutes of indescribable ecstasy, she'd shuddered to an earth-shattering climax, moaning with passion as Luis stood up. He'd then gathered her into his strong arms and carried her over to the bed, whereupon he'd laid her down, once more spread her legs, and mounted her, slowly and surely moving back and forth inside her.

Words were still not spoken.

Words were still not needed.

For once, Irma had been totally satisfied.

Being married to a corrupt politician had taught Renee the ways of the world—the world that Anthony and his business associates inhabited. She knew how to please the men she had to deal with, and not in a sexual way. Renee had turned herself into one of the boys—a tough broad who ran a tight operation and could dole out punishment with the best of them.

A few months after opening the Cavendish, Renee had caught one of her dealers cheating. Two days later his bullet-riddled body had turned up in a used-car lot. Renee had wanted his body to be found. The message was clear enough: *Don't think you can fuck with me simply because I'm a woman.*

The message worked until an L.A.-based madam decided to have a few of her best girls work the high rollers at the Cavendish. The madam moved them in big-time under the guise of actresses and models, but Renee soon caught on. She had invitations printed inviting half a dozen of the girls to a very exclusive lingerie party given by a Saudi prince. She also put the word out that each girl who attended would receive a large cash bonus.

Saudi prince and *cash bonus* were the four key words. The girls arrived wearing nothing much at all. At the door of the penthouse suite where the party was to take place, they were relieved of their purses as a security measure.

While the girls—clad in nothing more than revealing underwear—waited in the plush suite for the Arab prince to appear, Renee had her people visit all their rooms and gather together every item of the girls' expensive clothes and accessories. When this was done, Renee supervised a huge bonfire in the parking lot, and the girls were herded together and forced to watch as everything they'd arrived in Vegas with was burned—including the contents of their purses.

After the bonfire ceremony they were driven into the desert and left there half naked with no money, no airline tickets, no cell phones—nothing.

Somehow or other they all made it back to L.A. And sure enough, their madam got the message.

Nobody sued.

Nobody came back.

Point made.

Since that time Renee had dealt with several other employees who had caused her trouble. She was relentless when it came to protecting her territory, which was why she'd agreed with Anthony when he'd come up with his plan to destroy the Keys. He was right, the new hotel complex was a direct threat to the Cavendish, especially as the building was so close. The Keys would be targeting all of the Cavendish's best customers, and as the building progressed, Renee was just as determined as Anthony to do something about it.

Anthony had come up with the idea of hiring Tucker

Bond to take care of their problem, and Renee had put it together, speaking to the man herself.

It was an expensive undertaking, but Anthony was splitting the cost, and he'd assured her it would be worth it to get rid of their direct competition.

The Keys project opening in Vegas was bad business for everyone. That's all there was to it.

CHAPTER SEVENTEEN

"Billy Melina," the female journalist singsonged in a raspy voice. "Billy Melina in the flesh."

Florence Harbinger was fiftyish, fat, and frumpy with a digital recorder clutched in one hand and a verging-on-sarcastic attitude.

Instinctively Billy knew he'd have to work hard to win this one over. Female journalists. A breed unto themselves. They needed care and attention, otherwise they'd destroy you in print. Billy had learned the hard way.

Rule number one: Compliment.

Rule number two: Flirt.

Rule number three: Ask about their family.

Rule number four: More flirting and make it stick.

Florence Harbinger had a reputation. She ate actors for breakfast and spit 'em out all over the pages of the high-profile magazine she worked for. And because the magazine was so high profile, every publicist in town was hot to get their star clients on the cover, and getting the cover meant sitting down with the lovely Florence. Billy was *so* not into it.

Where was Janey when he needed her? His so-called publicist was a total flake. If she didn't put in an appearance in the next five minutes, he was definitely firing her skinny ass.

"Billy, Billy, Billy," Florence repeated, chanting his name. "So tell me, dear, how's it working out with you and the older woman? Is it difficult? Are we having fun? Or do you think being with the multitalented Venus diminishes *your* fame?"

Oh yeah, this was going to be a bumpy ride. Grin and flirt with the dried-up old hag who probably hadn't gotten laid in years. Give her a taste of the old hick-seed charm he'd possessed when he'd first hit Hollywood.

"You know, Florence," he said, speaking slowly, "I never thought of that." As he spoke he gave her the famous Billy Melina blue-eyed stare. Kev called it the "panties off" stare, hard for any female young or old to resist. "By the way, have you lost weight? You're lookin' *very* good," Billy continued.

Florence was too old and seasoned to fall for it completely, but her attitude toward him noticeably softened, and by the time Janey arrived, the interview was well on course.

Janey, a sallow-faced girl with wispy yellow hair and an out-of-control overbite, allowed the interview to run over, which infuriated Billy. How many times had he told her that if a journalist couldn't get what they wanted in an hour, it was over?

Billy was incensed, trapped, and pissed off. This wasn't right. He was talking too much and probably saying things he shouldn't, and dumb Janey was hanging in the kitchen with Kev as if he, Billy, was perfectly fine with *two freaking hours* of interrogation. SHIT!

Finally his cell rang and he took the opportunity to make a quick escape. "Gotta take this," he informed Florence, who looked like she was all set for another two hours of scintillating conversation. "I'll be right back."

He raced into the kitchen and blasted Janey, who managed to look forlorn and hard-done-by—as if *he* was the one at fault.

"Two minutes," he hissed. "Two more freakin' minutes, then you come in and break it up."

"HELLOOO." Whoever was on his cell was yelling for attention.

"Sorry," he said, realizing it was Venus.

"*What* is going on?" Venus wanted to know.

"Oh, hey, it's nothing," he said vaguely. "I'll tell you later."

"Why not now?"

"Uh . . . I gotta call you back."

"Why? What are you doing?"

Another interrogator. What was it with women and their questions?

"I'm in the middle of an interview, so I'll—"

"Who with?"

"Some magazine."

"*What* magazine?"

"Really, babe, I gotta call you back."

"Fine," she said in her best *You're an asshole* and *I hate you* voice. "You do that."

Oh crap. Now he had Venus on his case and that wasn't a good thing.

"Billy," Florence called out from the living room. "Where are you, dear? I need to verify a couple of facts."

He was *not* having a great day.

Venus clicked off her cell and frowned. What was up with Billy? He wasn't himself, he was edgy, and—dare she even think it?—distant.

Oh God, he was distant. Did that mean he was having second thoughts about their relationship? Did distant mean he was looking for an out?

This was ridiculous. They'd been together almost a year, and as far as she was concerned they were blissfully happy. Well . . . about as blissfully happy as two movie stars can be considering their every move was dogged by the paparazzi, not to mention the false rumors that appeared in print or on the Internet every single day. She couldn't count how many times she was supposedly pregnant, or how many times they'd secretly gotten married, or how many times they'd broken up. All lies. All hurtful. All damaging to their relationship.

Venus sighed as she realized she'd done something extremely foolish. She'd fallen in love with Billy, and how dumb was *that?* Now she was experiencing all the pangs of teenage rejection, because surely if he didn't have time to talk to her—that was rejection?

Dammit! Love was a pain in the ass. Love made you weak and vulnerable and open to getting hurt. This was not her M.O. at all. Venus was strong and invincible and an icon. That's why her fans loved her so much. Now she'd gone and fallen in love with a boy—not a man like Cooper, a boy—a movie star boy who however hard he worked would never be as famous as she was.

Or as rich.

And yet . . . it didn't matter to her, she was cool with it.

But if he rejected her, dumped her . . .

No, it simply couldn't happen.

Stop being needy, she told herself. *Everything's fine. Billy loves you. He tells you all the time.*

Billy Melina. Who would've ever thought *he'd* be the one when he'd walked into Alex Woods's office eight years ago? She certainly hadn't. All she'd seen then was an apprehensive, fidgety twenty-year-old boy who, when he'd read a scene with her, had exhibited a fierce and endearing talent.

She'd kind of steered him through his first important role, and he'd given a dynamic performance, launching a highly successful career.

They'd become friends. She was married to Cooper and had a small child. Billy was on the road to stardom with a pretty new girl on his arm—or in his bed—every other day. Occasionally they spoke on the phone, or ran into each other at big events such as superagent Ed Limato's Oscar party or one of the endless award ceremonies.

When Billy made the cover of *People* magazine as "The Sexiest Man Alive," she'd sent him a life-sized inflatable doll with a funny note attached. And when she'd won two Emmys, a People's Choice Award, and three Grammys all in one year, he'd sent her a Harry Winston diamond star pendant with a sweet letter praising her achievements.

After that they'd started meeting for lunch on a regular basis. She'd teased him about his parade of nubile girlfriends; he'd listened when she'd found herself confiding her marital woes.

He was understanding and an excellent listener.

When she finally left Cooper, Billy was there to hold her hand and help her through it.

One memorable night their friendship developed into a full-blown love affair. She hadn't planned it, hadn't wanted it, but somehow it was inevitable.

The gossip rags went into overdrive. Venus and Billy Melina—what a tabloid-headline-making duo! It was all too irresistible.

Now they'd been together almost a year, but she wasn't sure how it was going. She knew she should be happy—Billy hadn't said anything or done anything that would make her feel otherwise—but deep down she had a nagging feeling that something was amiss, and one of the keys of Venus's huge success had been to always follow her instincts.

What were her instincts telling her now?

She wasn't sure. She didn't know.

But hey, she had to believe it would all work out in the end. Everything always did.

* * *

"You drink too much," Ling scolded.

"What now?" Alex Woods said, emerging from the shower, knotting a towel around his waist.

"Last night you came home drunk," Ling continued in a sanctimonious tone. "And you were driving, Alex, that's extremely stupid. If you had been stopped and Breathalyzed, it could have turned out very badly."

Was his exquisitely beautiful Asian lawyer girlfriend calling him stupid?

No. It wasn't possible.

Or was it? Because if it was, it was time for her to go. Nobody called Alex Woods stupid and got away with it. If she was working on one of his movies, he would fire her ass. But she wasn't working on his movie, she was living in his architecturally modern beach house, sharing his oversized water bed, and sometimes driving his Porsche. Plenty of perks. More than enough. And he did not need criticism coming out of her perfectly formed mouth. Oh no. Her mouth was for other purposes.

"What if you'd been arrested?" Ling droned on. "Then what, Alex? Headlines you do not care for. Publicity you hate."

"Spoken like a true lawyer," he said, dropping his towel.

"I'm sorry if you do not like to hear the truth," Ling said, all pissy-faced. "But it is only for your own good."

Yeah. Sure.

"Did you have your gun on you, Alex?" Ling continued. "Because I continually remind you that you do not have a license to carry a firearm, and were you stopped and the gun was found, that would constitute a far greater problem."

"Okay, okay," he said impatiently. "I'm listening. Next time I go on a bender I'll leave my gun at home. Does that make you happy?"

"Yes, Alex, that makes me happy. Although why you need a gun at all—"

"I get threats, Ling," he said, reaching for his pants and pulling them on. "How many times I gotta tell you?"

Over the years he'd grown to realize that there wasn't a woman in existence who knew when to shut the fuck up. Except perhaps Lucky Santangelo. When it came to Lucky, she could talk all night and he'd listen to every word. But then, Lucky was unique, a one-of-a-kind woman who possessed the three B's in abundance— Brains, Beauty, and Balls.

Thinking about Lucky made him smile.

"Why are you smiling, Alex, it is not funny," Ling scolded, as if she were speaking to a naughty child.

"Give it a rest," he said. "I don't *want* to hear it and I don't *have* to hear it, so shut the fuck up."

"Do not speak to me like that," Ling said, tilting her chin.

Oh Jesus. She wasn't his *wife*, why was she lecturing him as if she were?

He stared at his five-feet-two-inches-tall girlfriend with the slim, toned body and ridiculously large fake tits—too big for her slender shape. Her tits had always bothered him. What was she thinking when she'd had them done? *I want to be a lawyer, but maybe I'll moonlight as a stripper on the side*?

It didn't make sense.

"I have a major fucking hangover," he said, feeling the throb in his head. "So I suggest we drop this conversation before you get yourself in trouble."

"Very well, Alex," she said, tight-lipped. "But I tell you only because I care."

"I'm sure you do," he sighed.

End of dialogue.

Cut.

Print.

CHAPTER EIGHTEEN

Hugging her father felt so damn good. Gino the survivor, a real character. Lately Lucky had come to the conclusion that the older she got, the more she understood him. Now she realized why he'd married her off at sixteen. He'd thought he was protecting her, saving her from her wild ways, and his mind was set that way because he'd been raised during a time when women were not considered smart, independent human beings; women were considered soft and obedient, they were supposed to get married, have kids, and shut the fuck up.

Wow! What a shocker she must have been to him—a girl who craved freedom and power; a girl who was sexually free; a girl who did things her way and turned out to be exactly like Daddy.

The two of them could laugh about it now, for Lucky considered Gino to be not just her father, but also her best friend. She loved hearing him reminisce about the early days when he was living on the streets of New York struggling to make a buck. He often spoke about the time he was involved with the very elegant and very married Clementine Duke, the nightclub he opened way back, his long stretch in prison, and the excitement and challenge of building his first hotel in Vegas.

Oh yes, Gino had stories like nobody else.

Her kids adored him and he them. Gino Junior called him Mister Cool, and Bobby had always looked up to him. Max—not so much. "He's like *major old,*" Max always grumbled whenever Gino visited, as if being old was a bad thing. "Why do I have to kiss him every time I see him? He smells of fish, like a decrepit trout."

"Your grandfather believes in taking a lot of vitamins," Lucky had explained. "Sometimes they leave an odor."

"It's utterly *gross!*" Max would complain.

Perhaps it's just as well that Max is not here for dinner, Lucky thought, ushering Gino and Paige upstairs to their room. She gave Gino another hug, and left them to unpack.

Downstairs Lennie was about to get to work on his script. "Good thing we made out before they got here," he remarked.

"Glad you're pleased."

"And it wasn't just sex, it was fantastic sex, an' not even make-up sex!"

"You're such a romantic."

"I try."

"Try harder," Lucky quipped.

A short while later Bobby and Brigette arrived.

Is it possible that this tall handsome guy is my son? Lucky thought proudly. *Wow, I must've done something right.*

"Where's Max?" Bobby asked, exchanging a series of playful punches with Gino Junior, who was excited to see his big brother.

"She went to a party up in Big Bear," Lucky explained. "She'll be back in time for Gino's celebration."

"*Great,*" Bobby complained, pulling a face. "I come into town and she takes off. I gotta have a serious talk with that girl."

"I wish somebody would," Lucky muttered.

"What does *that* mean?"

"It means she's exactly like her mom was when Lucky was her age," Lennie interjected.

"Who's exactly like their mom?" Brigette asked, entering the house, followed by a red-faced driver attempting to balance several large Fendi bags.

"There you are," Lennie said, grabbing her in a bear hug. "How's my girl?"

Brigette smiled. She had special feelings for Lennie, who'd once been married to her mother, Olympia. Lennie had always treated her with kindness, unlike so many other people she'd had to deal with. "I'm doing okay, Lennie."

"You look fantastic," he said, thinking how fresh and pretty she was for a girl who'd been through so much.

"Max is on the missing list," Bobby announced. "She took off to some party," he added, shaking his head as if he couldn't quite believe that his half-sister hadn't stayed around to greet him. "How about that? Wait till I get hold of her, she's in for major punishment."

"You can phone her later," Lucky said. "Lay a guilt trip on her, especially as she left without saying goodbye this morning."

"*Bad* little girl," Bobby said. "Hey, Mom, you're looking as beautiful as ever."

"Thanks, Bobby, you always know what to say."

"Don't thank me, thank the good genes you got from your old man. Is Gino here yet? Can't wait to see him."

"They arrived ten minutes ago, they're settling in."

"We could've all stayed at a hotel," Bobby said. "Wouldn't that've been easier for you?"

"Not at all," Lucky replied. "In case you haven't noticed, this house is huge—there's plenty of room for everyone. Besides, us all being here together is kind of nice. We should make the most of it."

"How soon do you get your Malibu house back?"

"Another couple of months. But it's not so bad, 'cause Lennie's going to be shooting his movie in Canada, and I'll be spending most of my time in Vegas."

"Oh yeah!" Bobby said enthusiastically. "The Keys. Can we talk about me opening a club there?"

"We already have a club, Bobby. You know that."

"Yeah, but you don't have *my* club. It's taken off big-time."

"I'll keep you in mind if we decide to open another one. Maybe sometime in the future if you're really serious."

"It's great to have connections," Bobby muttered. "Gets me exactly nowhere."

"Who's coming tonight?" Brigette asked.

"Family only," Lucky replied. "I'm cooking pasta, so you'd all better be ravenously hungry, or else."

"Did you invite Venus?" Bobby ventured.

"Still got a crush?" Lennie interjected with a sly grin. "'Cause if you do, I hear she's into younger men."

"Be quiet," Lucky said, trying not to smile. "Bobby never had a crush, did you?"

"No *way*," Bobby said, a touch too emphatically.

"She'll be at the party Sunday," Lucky offered. "You can catch up then."

"The Santangelo clan," Brigette said with a sunny smile. "I'm so glad I'm part of it."

"And we're glad to have you," Lucky said warmly.

"Yeah," Lennie agreed. "Especially without some deadbeat trailing along behind you."

"Hey, don't be so hard on her," Bobby objected. "That's my niece you're talking to, and she's one hot number."

"Thanks, Uncle," Brigette said, still smiling. "You're not so bad yourself."

"Okay," Lucky said. "Why don't I take you upstairs to your rooms, and you can unpack?"

"Great idea," Bobby said. "Then later we'll talk about my future club in your hotel. It's not like I come cheap, y'know, you'll have to pay for the privilege."

"Really?" Lucky drawled. "Can't wait to negotiate with you, Bobby. I'm sure you're a regular hard-ass."

"I want to be around for *that* meeting," Lennie said, joining in.

"I'll make sure you are," Bobby said, full of confidence.

"Yes, Lennie," Lucky said. "You can take notes, see who wins."

"I think I already know the answer to that one," Lennie said, grinning.

"Don't be so sure," Bobby responded. "I'm a Santangelo crossed with a Stanislopolous. That means you can never count me out."

Big Bear was unfamiliar territory to Max. She drove around getting lost, stopping to ask directions to Kmart, which turned out to be on the main street.

All of a sudden she was nervous. How would she recognize Grant? How would he recognize her? Had she mentioned what car she was driving? She must have told him she had a BMW—then again, maybe she hadn't.

Crap! This was nerve-racking, and she was not feeling as cool about it as she'd thought she would. What if she hated him? What if he was a major jerk? Or even worse—a major perv like Cookie had suggested he might be?

Oh great! This could end up being a no-win situation.

Desperate to find a bathroom and dying of thirst, she parked her car, hurriedly glanced around the parking lot, and went inside the store thinking that maybe Grant was already there, looking for her.

She spotted a lanky-looking guy in a Lakers sweatshirt and faded Levi's lounging near the check-out. He didn't seem to be buying anything, and even though he looked nothing like the photo Grant had posted, she wondered if it could possibly be him. After walking by him a couple of times she finally swooped in for an approach. "You wouldn't be Grant, would you?" she asked, giving him the green-eyed stare that most boys seemed to find irresistible—most boys except Donny, the cheater, and he'd turned out to be the biggest asswipe ever.

The lounger checked her out. He saw an incredibly pretty girl with clouds of dark curls and a killer bod. "That a new pickup line?" he said, looking her up and down.

"Excuse me?" she said, frowning.

"You trying to pick me up?" he repeated, groping in his Levi's for a stick of gum.

"No," she said defensively. "If I was *trying* to pick you up, you'd know it."

"Would I?" he said, peeling off the gum wrapper.

"Bet on it," she answered, using one of her mom's favorite sayings.

Crumpling the wrapper, he tossed it on the ground. "I'm not Grant," he said. "Who is he anyway?"

"My friend."

"Some friend," he said derisively. "You're not even sure what the dude looks like."

She shrugged, attempting to appear casual. "I wondered if you were him, that's all."

"I'm not."

"*Okay*," she said, irritated. "I so get it."

"Right."

"Yes, right."

Boys! They were like *such* a major pain. This one couldn't have been more than eighteen, so he obviously wasn't Grant, although she had to admit he was a real hottie, even if he *was* wearing a Lakers sweatshirt and she was a Clippers fan.

She wandered off, trying to remember whether Grant had said she should wait in her car or not. After a few minutes she glanced at her watch. It was almost one. Crap! Why hadn't they fixed a time? She'd snuck out of the house early in case Lucky changed her mind, and now here she was wandering around a dumb-ass Kmart wasting precious time, because all they had together was two days.

Hmm . . . two days with a perfect stranger.

And what if he wasn't perfect? What if he was some looney dork she hated on sight?

Oh no, that couldn't happen, she'd informed Cookie and Harry she was going to have sex with her Internet dude. But what if she *hated* him?

Grant was twenty-two. She'd told him she was eighteen. He'd probably expect her to be experienced—especially as she'd said she'd recently broken up with her boyfriend. It was one thing communicating with someone via the Internet, but actually meeting them was way different.

Oh double crap! This was turning out to be *so* not such a clever idea. She'd embarked on this adventure full of bravado. Now all that bravado was beginning to crumble.

Maybe she should make a run for it and drive home before Grant appeared.

But how could she? Losing face with Cookie and Harry was *definitely* not on her agenda.

She had to go through with it and that, unfortunately, was that.

CHAPTER NINETEEN

Getting bored easily was a state of mind, and Anthony Bonar often found himself in that state of mind. He craved action at all times, and after a long meeting with Renee he did not feel like sitting alone with her and Susie for dinner. Susie was a pain in the ass. There was something about her he didn't like and he had a strong hunch the feeling was mutual. He needed some excitement. He was in the mood for a one-night stand—a girl who was sexier than Emmanuelle and more exciting than Carlita. His two mistresses were adequate, but occasionally he desired a new body to play with. Tonight he decided that body should be black.

His requirements were specific. She had to be a knockout, in her twenties, not a whore, and smart.

He informed Renee of his requirements. She nodded, as if finding such a girl was no problem.

He retired to his suite, took a nap, and when he awoke there was a message from Renee that she'd found just the girl for him.

Renee never disappointed.

He joined Renee and Susie for dinner in one of the hotel's restaurants. Susie was a fragile blonde in her forties with birdlike features and a slight facial tic. Her famous country singer husband, Cyrus, had choked to death on a chicken bone six months after their wedding, which was fortunate for Susie, who'd always preferred female company. A year after Cyrus's demise she'd met

Renee and true love had bloomed. Anthony was uneasy in their company—the whole dyke thing disturbed him.

The girl Renee had set him up with was half Ethiopian and half Portuguese. She was twenty-nine, six feet tall, and striking in a regal ethnic way. Her name was Tasmin, and according to Renee, she was not a whore, although Anthony wasn't too sure about that. He trusted Renee—but not completely. How had she come up with this exotic creature on such short notice if the girl wasn't a professional?

"Where'd you dig this one up?" he asked Renee when, after dinner, Tasmin excused herself and went off to the ladies' room.

"You said you wanted smart," Renee replied, sipping a hefty brandy. "She's a bank manager, works at the bank I use."

"You gotta be shittin' me," Anthony spluttered.

"Would I do that to you?" Renee said calmly. "She's very astute and a genius with numbers. I'd love to steal her away to work for me."

"Oh, no no *no!*" interrupted Susie. "I'm not having *her* around you all day."

"Surely you trust me, Susie?" Renee asked.

"Not with *her*," Susie answered, pouting.

"C'mon, sweetie, don't be like that," Renee said, putting her arm around her girlfriend's shoulders. "You *know* you can trust me."

"I do?" Susie responded, batting her eyelashes. "Perhaps you should try to convince me."

"Christ!" Anthony complained. "Can't you two dykes give it a rest?"

"So *sorry* if we've offended your macho sensibilities," Renee said bitingly as Tasmin returned to the table.

Anthony decided he'd been social for long enough. He leaned toward Tasmin, placing his hand over hers.

"Tas, baby," he said, as if they were the oldest of friends. "I hear ya good with numbers. Wanna count how many steps it takes t'get to my suite?"

Regal, ethnic Tasmin turned out to be a freak in the bedroom. Anthony had expected hot, but this one was a total fucking maniac, and strong with it. She practically *raped* him.

He was taken by surprise. They arrived in his suite, he opened a bottle of champagne, and suddenly, like a wild tiger, Tasmin sprung into action, ripping off her clothes, grabbing his pants and pulling them down, fastening her mouth on him until he was so hard he thought he might explode.

Then she pushed him—with a great deal of unexpected strength—onto the bed, leapt aboard, and straddled him, going at it like an athlete on the way to the finishing line.

He was too shocked to object. This was a whole new experience for a man who was always on top and always in charge. And come to think of it, it wasn't a bad experience at that. Tasmin certainly knew what she was doing—that is, until she produced a set of gold-plated handcuffs from her purse and attempted to fasten them around his wrists.

"What the fuck ya doin'?" he demanded, hurriedly rolling away from her.

"Relax," she said calmly. "I can promise you'll enjoy the experience. Surely you've tried it before?"

"Not me, honey," he growled. "Enough is enough."

Tasmin was a woman of few words. "Handcuff *me*, then," she ordered. "Handcuff me to the bed and go down on me."

"What?" Anthony spluttered. He was an Italian American macho man with standards, there was no way he'd go down on a woman, that was *their* job, oral sex was all about the woman giving the *man* pleasure. Who did this douche bag think she was dealing with?

"If that's what you're lookin' for, you're outta luck, honey," he said, thinking it was time he got rid of her.

"Why?" she asked boldly. "The taste of pussy frighten you?"

This one was definitely trying his patience. He'd fucked her—or rather, she'd fucked him. Now he wanted her out.

"This little party is over," he said, getting up, walking to the bathroom door and reaching for a bathrobe.

"You think?" Tasmin said, squatting on the bed—all erect nipples and satiny milk chocolate skin.

"I know."

She laughed.

Was she laughing at him?

Would she dare?

"Somethin' funny?" he snarled, giving her a cold-eyed glare.

"You," she replied, coolly swinging her handcuffs back and forth as she knelt on the bed.

"Me, huh?" he said, a slow anger beginning to build within him. "I'm funny, huh?"

"You so-called macho guys from New York and Miami, you're all the same when it comes to sex. Scared little Mommys' boys. Mustn't get too down 'n' dirty. Mustn't do bad things or Mommy will spank your little bottom."

Was she talking to *him*, Anthony Bonar? Was this smart-mouthed *puttana* disrespecting *him?*

Hadn't Renee told her who he was? Hadn't Renee warned her to treat him nice?

"Get the fuck out," he said, his voice hard.

"My pleasure, Mr. Nothing," she answered. "I'll go, and you can run on back to Mommy, I'm sure she's waiting for you."

Something snapped. Something bad. He'd had a long day and he didn't need this shit.

Without thinking about the consequences, he went for her, slapping her across the face with the back of his hand, his pinky ring cutting open her cheek.

"You dumb cunt, nobody talks t'me like that," he shouted. "Now GET OUT."

Tasmin had some moves of her own. She'd taken self-defense classes and did not take kindly to being assaulted. She made a fatal mistake. She slapped him back.

That a woman would dare to attack him was beyond his comprehension. The last person who'd physically attacked him had ended up in a ditch with his throat slit.

She must be insane, he thought as he whacked her across the face again, getting blood on the sleeve of his bathrobe.

She was angry too. She fought back, leaping upon him until the two of them fell on the bed, wrestling for the power position.

This woman was one strong motherfucker; she almost had him pinned down.

Bringing his knee up he jammed it into her stomach, grabbed a handful of her hair, and sharply jerked her head back, snapping her neck.

"You fucking *bitch!*" he screamed. "You think you can talk to me like that an' get away with it? You get the fuck outta here *now*." And he shoved her away from him with all his strength.

She fell onto the floor next to the bed.

Muttering to himself, he went into the bathroom. "You better be outta here by the time I come out," he yelled over his shoulder.

Shrugging off the bathrobe, he stepped into the shower and stood under the cold stinging water, reaching for the soap and thoroughly lathering his cock and balls.

What if she had AIDS? He hadn't used a condom, she hadn't given him time to even think about using one.

JESUS CHRIST! Wait until he got hold of Renee and told her about this. She should be more careful about who she recommended, he was getting too old for this shit. He had Emmanuelle, and Carlita, and he had a wife sitting on her fat ass in Mexico City. So what did he need other whores for? And although Renee had assured him that this one *wasn't* a whore, she'd certainly acted like one.

Now that he got to thinking about it, she was even worse than a whore. She was supposed to be so smart and intelligent, but in his mind he decided she was nothing but a cheap nympho slut with a bad attitude.

After toweling off, he went back into the bedroom and was surprised to see that she was still there. He couldn't believe it: there she was, lying on the floor exactly where he'd left her.

"I thought I told you to get out," he said harshly.

She didn't reply.

He walked over to her and prodded her in the stomach with the tip of his foot.

She didn't move.

He prodded her again.

Goddammit! Slowly realization dawned.

The bitch had gone and died on him.

CHAPTER TWENTY

"I was thinking we could go out for a quiet dinner, just the two of us," Venus suggested to Billy when he finally called her back.

"Sounds like a plan. Where d'you wanna go?"

"You choose."

"No," he countered, "*you* pick a place. We always end up going where you want anyway."

"That's not true," she said quickly.

"Yes it is."

"No, Billy, it's not."

There was a short silence while they both decided whether they wanted this to turn into a fight or not.

Venus decided not. "How about the Ivy?" she said.

"Paparazzi frenzy," he groaned, not relishing the thought of being chased down the street by a crazed pack of jackal-like photographers intent on getting the worst photos.

"Spago?"

"Not feeling it tonight."

"Where, then?"

"Dunno. Surprise me."

She put down the phone, annoyed. Billy was the man in the relationship; why did *she* have to make all the decisions? Surely *he* was supposed to surprise *her?* Her former husband, the legendary cocksman Cooper Turner, had spent half of their marriage surprising her, until one memorable day *she'd* surprised him banging her stand-in while he was visiting the set of one of her movies.

Cooper had suffered from that well-known male affliction, the zipper problem. What a disappointment he'd turned out to be.

That was one of the things she liked about Billy: he didn't have the zipper problem. Oh yes, when they were out and about at various events and he was surrounded by beautiful, sexy women, he looked, but as far as she knew, he never took it any further. Nor did she for that matter, and she had plenty of opportunities. There were always hunky backup dancers around, hot male costars, horny producers and directors—they were all within her radar, but she was never tempted.

Venus was a one-man woman, and right now Billy was her man.

"*What* sounds like a plan?" Kev asked, wandering into the kitchen.

"You listening in on my phone conversations?" Billy responded, shoving his cell phone into the back pocket of his jeans.

"If it's a private deal, you'll tell me to bug off," Kev said, helping himself to a cold beer from the fridge.

"Dinner with Venus, that's the plan."

"Didn't you say you wanted to stay home tonight and watch the game on that frickin' giant-screen TV you had delivered yesterday?"

"Yeah, that was the original plan," Billy said, stifling a yawn. "But now Venus wants to go out to dinner."

"How come?"

"Waddya mean, how come?" Billy said, frowning. "She's my girlfriend, for chrissakes. Gotta do what the girlfriend wants."

"How come?" Kev repeated.

"What's *up* with you? Stop repeatin' yourself like a freakin' parrot."

"Nothin's up with me."

"There's something on your mind."

"Maybe."

"Spit it out, asshole."

"It's just that it gets on my tits seein' it, that's all," Kev blurted.

"Seeing *what?*" Billy asked, exasperated.

"Y'know, seein' you turning into one of those pussy-whipped dudes," Kev said, taking a swig of beer from the can, then wiping his mouth with the back of his hand.

"Me?" Billy said, outraged. "Pussy-whipped? You gotta be jerking me off."

"Venus calls, you cancel everything an' run. It's all wrong."

"So I'm missing the game, big freakin' deal," Billy said, walking into the living room.

"'S not the point," Kev said, following him. "Guys gotta be in charge, otherwise girls trample all over 'em."

"Since when did *you* become an expert on relationships?" Billy said, flopping down on the couch.

"I know what I see."

"Screw you, Kev. I *am* in charge."

"Yeah?" Kev said disbelievingly.

"Yeah," Billy responded, wishing Kev would shut his big mouth.

"Then if you're in charge, why doncha stay home an' watch the game? Y'know it's what you wanna do."

"No, Kev, it's what *you* wanna do."

"Not me," Kev said, shrugging. "I got a date. But if I *did* want to see the game, I'd cancel her ass so fast she wouldn't know what hit her."

"You would, huh?"

"'Course."

"Then do it."

"Do what?"

"Cancel her. I'll do the same."

"Yeah?"

"Pussy-whipped, my ass," Billy muttered.

"You really want me to cancel my hot date?" Kev said, not quite sure he believed him.

Billy threw him a long, cool stare. "Do I look like I'm lyin'?"

First Venus tried on a slinky black Dolce & Gabbana dress, then she decided it was way too fancy for a casual dinner with her boyfriend. Jeans were more Billy's style, tight low-slung jeans worn with high boots and a plain white tee. She put the outfit together and paraded in front of the mirror, immediately realizing it was too casual—more suitable for lunch at the beach. She'd had her assistant book a table at Giorgio's, and although the Italian restaurant was near the ocean, it wasn't beach style. Last time she'd been there she'd run into Tom Hanks, Charlie Dollar, and Steven Spielberg, so she had to look her best. That was one of the major setbacks of being a star: everyone was ready to criticize.

How was she looking? they all wanted to know. Old? Fat? Lifted? Botoxed? If she looked good she got accused of all of the above. And if she looked like crap she was accused of letting herself go.

It was a no-win situation. The perils of being a superstar.

She finally decided on black matador pants, suede boots, a red cashmere shell, and a short black Armani jacket. Casual but chic. Sexy but not over the top. Billy would like it.

Her cell rang. Private line. Billy.

"Hey," he said.

"Hey," she responded.

"Uh . . . would you be mad if we didn't go out to-night?"

"What?" she said, shocked that he was obviously about to cancel.

"I'm still kinda beat up from that session with Alex, an' I just got an early call for tomorrow, so . . ." He trailed off, waiting for her to say something.

She summoned her pride and put on an okay voice, although inside she was seething. "Fine," she said, and then because she couldn't help herself she added, "Do you want me to come over?" *Oh God! How needy!*

"That's okay," he said. "I'm gonna get an early night, catch up on sleep."

"Then I guess we'll talk later?" she said, realizing that begging him to call back was even more needy.

"You got it, babe."

She put down the phone and let out a primal scream. "Son of a *bitch!*" she yelled. "How dare you treat me like this! How fucking dare you!"

And then a little voice in her head whispered, *He's treating you like this because you're allowing him to. Cut your losses and end it while you can.*

But she didn't want to end it.

She was in love, and how sad was *that?*

CHAPTER TWENTY-ONE

The Volvo broke down in the middle of nowhere. The engine spluttered and after a few moments the car shuddered to a halting stop.

Henry was nonplussed—he didn't know what to do. First he checked the gas gauge. Almost a full tank. Next he got out of the car and inspected the tires. They were all in good shape. Gingerly he popped the hood to take a look. Not that he knew what he was searching for, the mechanics of how a car ran had never interested him.

Damn! This was not the way he'd planned it. After a smooth and uneventful drive he was supposed to arrive in Big Bear, find the girl, and take her to the old family cabin nobody had used since his father died. Nobody except him. Over the last month he'd made two daytime trips there. Best to be prepared, and once they reached the cabin he certainly was. After that it was anyone's guess what would happen.

This was an exploratory trip to meet her, find out more information about her mother, and decide how best to pay back Lucky Santangelo for depriving him of the career he should've had—the career Billy Melina had stolen from him.

Now this unexpected setback.

He reached for his cell to summon the Automobile Club roadside assistance.

His phone flashed a *No Service* message.

Henry kicked the side of his car. He was filled with a burning sense of frustration.

It was fast becoming apparent that he was stranded and there was absolutely nothing he could do about it.

By three P.M. Max was thoroughly fed up. She'd explored the Kmart aisle by aisle, perused countless magazines, bought a couple of CDs, lingered by the makeup shelves, and now she was seriously thinking of getting in her car and driving back to L.A. because what was the point of being stuck in Big Bear with nothing to do and no Internet guy in sight?

How stupid they both were, she and Grant. They had not fixed an exact time and they had not exchanged cell phone numbers, so how were they supposed to communicate?

She tried to recall their last exchange of words. *Meet me in the Kmart parking lot*, he'd written. *Stay in your car, I'll find you.*

Like exactly *how* was he supposed to find her when he probably didn't even remember what car she was driving?

Dumb! Dumb! Dumb!

He'd mentioned that he drove a Jeep, and she'd told him she would be arriving in Big Bear in the afternoon. Maybe he wasn't expecting her until four or five, and that's why he hadn't appeared yet.

She wandered outside and ran straight into Mister Hottie—the dude in the Lakers sweatshirt.

"Whoa!" he said, coming to a stop. "Still lookin' for Grant?"

"Do you *know* Grant?" she asked suspiciously.

"No. But he's gotta be some kinda dumb-ass if he's standing *you* up."

"Who said he's standing me up?" she demanded, green eyes flashing.

"Gimme a break. He's not here, is he? So the dude's gotta be a loser."

"No way," she said, jutting out her chin. "He'll be here soon."

"Where'd you hook up with him anyway?"

"We met on the Internet," she blurted. "We're supposed to get together today. It's my fault—I must've messed up on the time."

"Are you tellin' me you don't even *know* this loser?"

"Yes, I know him," she answered defensively.

"Seems like you don't."

"Yes, I *do*," she said, checking out Mister Hottie for the second time that day. He was annoyingly argumentative, with dazzling blue eyes and an appealing cleft in the middle of his chin. Tall too, and major cute.

Once again she wished he was Grant. But no such luck, he obviously wasn't.

"So," he said, squinting at her. "While you're waiting for loser of the year, wanna go get an ice cream?"

"Ice cream!" she exclaimed. "What are you, *eight?*"

He threw back his head and laughed, giving her a chance to admire his very white teeth. "Never too old for ice cream," he said, "an' you look like you could swallow something sweet."

Was he talking dirty to her? She wasn't sure, boys were always coming out with stuff that sounded vaguely rude.

"I suppose I wouldn't mind a coffee," she said guardedly, realizing that she hadn't eaten all day, and coffee was hardly going to do it. She required a big, fat, juicy burger and a double-thick shake.

"I'll buy you a coffee if you tell me your name," he said, kicking a stray leaf into the gutter.

"Max," she said, still sizing him up. "What's yours?"

"Ace," he replied, still checking her out.

"That's an odd name."

"An' Max isn't?" he said, rubbing his chin.

"Max is a perfectly normal name," she said tartly.

"For a guy."

"Well, here's the thing," she confessed. "I used to be Maria. Changed it to Max when I was nine."

"How come?"

"Who wants to be reminded of *The Sound of Music* every time they hear their name? Not me. Changed it, and refused to answer if anyone called me anything else."

"Your parents have anythin' to say 'bout that?"

"They got the message."

"So even at nine you had it goin' on."

She giggled. "I guess."

He started to walk. "There's a Starbucks down the street," he said. "I'll buy you that coffee."

"Cool," she said, following him because she had nothing better to do. Besides, there was something likable about him, and it wasn't just that he was hot. He had a quirky attitude and plenty of confidence. In a way he reminded her of herself.

Hmm . . . maybe she should dump Mr. Internet and stick with this one.

She wondered if he had a girlfriend, if he was out of school, and what he was doing hanging around Kmart all day.

He walked fast on long legs, and she had to hop and skip to keep up. "You like the Lakers?" she asked.

"Somebody gave me the shirt. I'm not into following teams."

"You're not?" she said, slightly breathless.

"It's a fat waste of time unless I'm playing."

"What *do* you play?"

"Soccer."

"Are you brilliant?"

"When I want t'be."

"When's that?"

"Jeez," he said, shaking his head. "You sure ask a shitload of questions."

"Oh, like *you* don't," she responded.

"Here's a question for you," he said, stopping for a moment. "How old are you?"

"Eighteen," she lied. "How about you?"

"Nineteen."

"So you're out of school?"

"You too, right?"

"Oh yeah," she said, adding another lie while staring at the cleft in his chin, wondering what it would be like to kiss him.

"I'm guessing you don't live around here," he said, starting to walk again.

"Do you?" she countered.

"Why d'you answer a question with another question?" he said, looking perplexed.

"'Cause I'm naturally curious."

"*Nosy* is the word you're searchin' for."

"How rude!"

"No, honest."

"What are you doing anyway? I know why *I'm* hanging around. How about you?"

He stopped again, turning to face her. "You see that bank over there?" he said matter-of-factly.

She glanced across the street. "Yes."

"Well . . . here's the deal," he said, taking a long beat. "I'm plannin' on robbing it."

"This is what I like t'do," Gino announced, clearing his throat. "Haul my ass outta bed real late, take an afternoon nap, watch a coupla those cop shows on TV, suck down a few inches of Jack, have a fine meal with my old lady, an' hit the sack nice 'n' early."

"It's all about your bed," Lucky observed.

"Yeah, kiddo, an' when you're ninety somethin' it'll be all 'bout yours."

She smiled. "There's a bottle of Jack Daniel's in your room. And guess what? I'm cooking dinner myself—pasta and meatballs, your favorite."

"What a girl!" he exclaimed, grinning. "If only your mother had lived to see how you turned out."

Inexplicably her eyes filled with tears. She wasn't a crier, but how often did she get a one-on-one with Gino, and how often did he talk about her mom? Practically never. She'd always figured it was too upsetting for him to reminisce about Maria, but since *he* was the one who'd brought it up, maybe now was the time to pursue it.

"I guess you've never stopped missing her," she said softly.

"I miss her every single day," he sighed. "My Maria was the best. Y'know, kiddo, I still think about her all the time."

"So do I," Lucky murmured. "I remember her skin, it was so smooth, and she always smelled like rose petals."

"That she did," Gino said, nodding.

"Every night she would read to me and Dario. She loved this English author—Enid Blyton—and she'd read these crazy stories about a magic faraway tree with special powers and strange lands at the top of the tree where you could run around doing anything."

"Gave you ideas, huh?" Gino chuckled.

"Mama always told me girls can do anything."

"An' boy, did you follow her advice!"

"I was five when she was murdered," Lucky said sadly. "Only five . . . but I've never forgotten her."

"I know, sweetheart, I know . . ." he said, opening his arms.

Suddenly she found herself nestling close to the man she'd spent so many years feuding with, and now he was old—although he was still sharp. But she knew that one of these days in the not-so-distant future she'd have to say good-bye, and it broke her heart.

Gino Junior came barging into the room, interrupting their moment of closeness. "When's dinner?" he asked. "Let's go, Mom, I'm starving."

Lucky broke away from her father and composed herself. "You're not starving," she admonished. "And since I'm heading for the kitchen, I could do with some help."

"Mom . . ." Gino Junior groaned.

"You can learn to roll meatballs the Italian way. You'll enjoy it, trust me."

"Grandpa . . ." Gino Junior said, appealing to his grandfather to save him.

Gino Senior obliged. "Give the kid a break," he rasped. "Paige'll help you. She's always bin pretty adept at rollin' balls."

Lucky shook her head and tried not to smile. Gino was an original, no doubt about that.

Henry waved down a truck and slipped the driver a hundred bucks to find out what was wrong with his car.

He'd been attempting to wave cars down for two hours, and this was the first driver who'd stopped. Henry hadn't given him much choice, he'd practically flung himself in front of the oncoming truck.

After the driver had finished bitching and complaining about Henry forcing him to pull up so abruptly, Henry had handed him the hundred-dollar bill, and the truck driver had done a full inspection. Finding nothing mechanical, he'd eventually discovered that the gas gauge was faulty—stuck on half-full, while the gas tank was actually empty.

"You're outta gas," the truck driver announced, scratching his hairy belly under an I DIG FAT CHICKS T-shirt.

Henry frowned. Damn Markus. The man was lazy. Surely he must have known the gas gauge was faulty? After all, it was his *job* to know.

Henry glared at the truck driver as if *he* was to blame. "What am I supposed to do?" he whined.

"For another hundred I can fix ya up with a can of gas," the truck driver offered. "My emergency supply."

Well aware he was being taken advantage of, Henry agreed. He had no choice.

CHAPTER TWENTY-TWO

Anthony and Renee stood over Tasmin's lifeless body, both of them gazing down at the naked girl, Renee in disbelief and shock, Anthony full of anger that this had happened.

"You broke her neck," Renee stated.

"She fuckin' attacked me," Anthony responded. "For a moment there I thought she was gonna pull a piece on me."

"The woman is naked, and *you* thought she had a gun?" Renee said, shaking her head in disgust.

"What the *fuck* was I supposed t'do?" he said, impatient to get the hell out of Vegas and far away from this situation, which was bugging the shit out of him. "Jesus *Christ*, Renee, this is *your* fuckin' fault, you set me up with her."

"You kill a girl and it's *my* fault," Renee said, stoney-faced.

"You'd better arrange to dispose of the body," Anthony said flatly. "No way can I be involved in this."

"Damn you, Anthony," Renee said, her voice rising. "This isn't some bimbo we're talking about. This is a respectable woman with a high-powered job and a kid at home. How am I supposed to cover *this* up? You're in big trouble, Anthony."

He turned to her, his eyes like two pieces of cold steel. "*I'm* in trouble? You think *I'm* responsible for this shit?"

"If you're not, who is?"

"She acted like a fuckin' lunatic," he said, starting to yell. "An' she ended up gettin' what she deserved."

"Sure," Renee muttered, "and you're just an innocent party."

"What's your fuckin' problem?" he shouted, his face darkening.

"You were too rough with her, any fool can see that."

"You gotta be fuckin' *shittin'* me!" he exploded. "The broad was a sex freak."

"You're a big boy, you could've handled yourself without killing her."

"Let me tell you somethin', Renee," Anthony said, outraged that he was being forced to explain himself. "She wanted me to lick her fuckin' pussy. Ya think there's any way in hell I'd lower myself an' do that shit?"

"Going down on a woman is a normal sex act," Renee said, hating the very sight of him.

"Maybe to you," he spat. "But there's nothin' fuckin' normal 'bout you."

"Is that why you broke her neck—because of some macho Italian code of ethics?"

"How many times I gotta tell ya?—she fuckin' attacked me for no reason," he said harshly, wondering why he was bothering to continue this conversation. "I hadda defend myself, she's six feet tall an' strong as a fuckin' horse. You take care of it, Renee, like I took care of you when you had to get outta Colombia in a hurry. Remember?"

Yes, she remembered all right. He'd helped her leave, and he'd also helped himself to half the cash Oscar had stashed. Then when she and Susie had put together the money to build the Cavendish, he'd declared himself a silent partner. No paperwork involved, simply a monthly payout in cash.

"I take care of this and we're even," Renee said flatly. "Score settled."

"What the fuck *you* so uptight about?" he demanded.

"Tasmin was a smart, beautiful woman. Look what you've done to her. Don't you have any remorse?"

"For chrissakes!" he roared. "She was nothin' but a crazy freak."

"Your idea of a freak and mine differ," Renee snapped.

"I bet," he sneered. "You'd feast on pussy all day long if you had your way."

"Nice," Renee said coldly. "Real nice."

"Don't you forget who helped you when you needed it," he warned. "Take care of this mess, use your most trusted people. I'm gettin' outta here—deal with it."

Anthony left the problem of Tasmin's lifeless body with Renee and took off. He had no feelings of guilt. Renee owed him and now it was payback time.

The Grill drove him to the airport in one of the hotel's cars. Even though he still had things to take care of in Vegas, he knew this wasn't the time to linger. Best to distance himself and get out quickly.

Once he was safely on his plane and it had taken off for New York, he called his wife.

"What's goin' on?" he said gruffly.

"Where are you, Anthony?" Irma asked. "When will you be home?"

"I'll let you know." A long beat. "You miss me?"

Irma was shocked; it was so unlike her husband to ask her such a question. "Yes," she said stiffly, hesitating for only a second or two.

He decided she didn't sound like she meant it, and after he hung up, he got to wondering what Irma did all day. The kids were in Miami with their nanny and Francesca; the house in Mexico City was taken care of by his coterie of servants; so how *did* Irma keep herself occupied?

She probably went shopping, spent his money, and indulged in massages and manicures. Womanly pastimes, that's all she was capable of.

For a moment he felt sorry for her. At least she was a normal woman who'd never requested any depraved sexual acts from him. Goddammit, she was his wife, she'd better not.

Next he phoned Emmanuelle. "What's goin' on, sweet-ass?" he asked, thinking of her undulating sun-kissed body and luscious lips, and wondering why he'd gone elsewhere when Emmanuelle was always available.

"I just finished shooting the cover for *Crude Oil* magazine," Emmanuelle said excitedly. "Isn't that the *best!*"

"Yeah?" he questioned, not so sure he liked her posing for magazine covers where every asshole on the street could ogle her spectacular body. "What didja wear?"

"*Veree* short Daisy Dukes and kind of a skimpy bra," she said, her voice low and seductive. "*Veree* sexy. You'll *love* the photos."

"You'd better not love the photographer," Anthony warned. "It better be a woman."

"No, honey bunch," Emmanuelle cooed, purposely pissing him off because she got a kick out of making him jealous. "It was a super-sexy Latin *man*."

"Don't fuck with me, Emmanuelle," Anthony growled. "I ain't in the mood."

He put the phone down and thought briefly about Carlita before calling his man in New York. "Any news?"

"Too soon, boss. Nothin' to report."

Could it be that he was wrong about Carlita?

Maybe.

Maybe not.

Now he had to think about what he was going to tell Francesca. She'd expect to hear that everything was in line to sabotage the opening of Lucky Santangelo's hotel, only in view of what had taken place he wasn't so sure about Renee. She was pissed because he'd accidentally killed some freaky bitch, and even worse—she'd refused to admit that it was all her fault for putting them together in the first place.

Too fuckin' bad. She'd better get over it and fast, because once the body was taken care of he would be back in Vegas calling *all* the shots.

And that's exactly the way it should be.

After speaking to her husband, Irma experienced a moment of sheer panic. Did Anthony suspect something? Did Anthony *know?*

She assured herself that she was being paranoid—there was no chance of Anthony suspecting anything. How could he? She was beyond discreet, never bringing Luis in the house when any of the servants were around, always making sure to lock the bedroom door so no one could accidentally intrude.

The only way for Anthony to find out would be if he walked in on them, and that could never happen because Anthony always informed her in advance when he was coming home. He did this because he expected her to have everything ready for him. He insisted that the kitchen was fully stocked with all his favorite foods; his two Dobermans had to be sent to the vet to be bathed and groomed; plus he expected her to put together a series of fancy dinner parties for his friends.

Well, Anthony called them friends. Irma called them a bunch of suck-up freeloaders who laughed at Anthony's jokes and sat around watching him admiringly whenever he decided to entertain them with his not-so-brilliant karaoke skills. Karaoke was his favorite way of amusing himself, but only as long as he had an adoring audience fawning all over him.

No, Anthony would *never* surprise her. He wanted everyone on alert when *he* came home.

She walked to the window and glanced outside.

Luis was busy working on the grounds.

Immediately she experienced a rush of excitement. Just looking at the man made her heart beat faster.

Luis was her savior.

Luis made every day worth living.

Later she would invite him up to the house.

She could hardly wait.

When Anthony was eleven and more or less existing on the streets of Naples, he'd stabbed a man. He wasn't sure whether he'd killed the man or not, but he'd certainly experienced an overpowering rush of adrenaline—especially when he'd bent over the fallen man and extracted his wallet from his jacket pocket.

Stuffing the wallet down his pants, Anthony had raced off down the street like a deer. *Run fast, never let 'em catch you*, that was his motto.

Most of the time he hung out with a gang of kids who all came from one-parent families. They watched out for each other, sometimes robbing tourists and other unsuspecting civilians. Anthony led the pack; even at such a young age he was a born leader.

Arriving in America at the age of twelve, and spending time with his grandfather, Anthony had soon realized that in America anything was possible. Enzio Bonnatti had taught him a lot, and he was sad when the old man got himself shot, but he was happy Enzio had shown him a way of living that brought great rewards.

Although Tasmin's death was accidental—and nobody could prove otherwise—Anthony had no regrets. She'd been asking for it with her kinky requests.

His only problem was Renee. The old dyke better not give him any shit, because if she did, he had ways of dealing with her.

Nobody fucked with Anthony Bonar and got away with it. And if Renee was smart, she'd definitely keep that in mind.

CHAPTER
TWENTY-THREE

"What's up?" Venus asked over the phone.

"What's up is I'm knee-deep in ground beef, tomato sauce, bread crumbs, and garlic," Lucky answered, cradling the phone under her chin.

"You are? Why's that?"

"'Cause I'm making my famous Italian-style meatballs. Remember I told you I'm cooking a big blowout dinner for Gino and everyone? They're all here, the entire family, and I'm loving every second of playing Mama. How's that for a switch?"

"Can I come over?"

"I thought you and Billy were all set for a romantic night on the town?" Lucky said, squeezing a tube of tomato paste into the bowl.

"We were," Venus said, trying to sound like she didn't care. "That is until Billy bailed on me, and now I really need to talk."

"You do?" Lucky said, because family dinner and Venus pouring her heart out was not a perfect combination.

However, she rallied, because Venus was her best friend and she knew if the situation were reversed Venus would be there for her.

"Sure, come on over," she said warmly. "Gino would love to see you, and Bobby's gonna be thrilled."

"*Little* Bobby?"

"Not so little anymore," Lucky pointed out. "And hands *off*. Remember who he is."

"Oh sure," Venus said with a dry chuckle. "Like I'm about to make a move on your son. I don't think so."

"I don't think so either, so let's keep it that way."

"Yes, *ma'am*."

"And don't dress up, it's super casual, and bring your appetite."

"Any more instructions?"

"Nope, that's it for now."

"Okay, I've got it. Hands off Bobby. Skanky old jeans. Enormous passion for meatballs."

Lucky laughed. "We'll talk, but it'll have to be later, okay?"

"Sounds like a plan," Venus said, then after a long beat she added, "It's just that I don't think I can be alone tonight."

"I understand."

Venus put down the phone. She felt as if she was thirteen and her big high-school crush was crapping all over her. Why, oh why, had she allowed herself to fall in love with Billy? They hadn't even been together a year and he was pulling away, she sensed it, and it was driving her nuts.

Well, screw him, she thought, attempting to pull herself together. She was Venus Maria, superstar. She would *never* let him see her crumble, however much it hurt.

"This is freakin' great!" Billy exclaimed, lounging on the couch in his underwear and a T-shirt in front of his new big-screen high-definition TV, munching popcorn and scratching his crotch.

"Told ya," Kevin boasted. "You can pick your nose, hang a fart, change channels, do whatever the fuck ya want. An' no little lady gettin' on your case."

"It rocks."

"Sure it does. And . . ." Kev paused for a moment before continuing. "If ya start feelin' horny later, I got a number I can call that'll send a coupla girls over to do anything your dick desires. No questions asked."

"Hookers?"

"Highly paid young ladies."

Billy hesitated, then: "I'm not into paying for it, Kev. That's not my bag."

"I know that, an' everyone knows you don't have to. But sometimes it's the convenient way. They come. They go. No hassles."

"Look, just 'cause I'm takin' a night off doesn't mean Venus and me are through. We're very much together."

"Yeah, I get it. But sometimes banging a girl you paid for can be a kick."

"Thanks, but I'm not into cheating."

Kev shrugged. "Whatever swings your balls."

For a moment Billy flashed on the girl he'd picked up at Tower Records. He felt guilty, but the good news was that no one knew, and he wasn't about to tell. The girl was a one-off, a lack of judgment on his part.

He redirected his attention to the TV, stuffed his face with a handful of popcorn, and settled back to enjoy the game.

Venus liked to drive herself whenever she could dodge the paparazzi who lurked outside her gates day and night waiting for her to emerge. A few months ago she'd come up with the perfect escape plan, eliciting the help of a friendly neighbor—a stoned record producer who'd allowed her to build an illegal underground tunnel into his garage, where she kept a dark blue Phaeton with blacked-out windows. Whenever she didn't feel like being followed she used the tunnel and took out the anonymous

Phaeton, zooming past the hapless paparazzi who had no clue that it was her in the car.

Tonight she hurried through her escape tunnel, got in the car, and revved up the Phaeton—her low-key luxury vehicle. Outsmarting the paparazzi gave her a big charge. Fuck 'em. Oh sure, they had a job to do, but did they have to do it 24/7? It made her especially mad when Chyna was with her, and they stuck cameras in her child's face.

Cooper didn't seem to care. He was always allowing himself to be photographed with his cute and somewhat precocious little daughter. There they were in *People* and *Us* strolling down Rodeo eating ice cream, sitting courtside at the Lakers game, picking up shells on the beach in Malibu. Recently he'd added Mandy—his teenage girlfriend—to his family outings. Mandy was a publicity-crazy nineteen-year-old wannabe singer/actress/model, and Venus did not want her daughter being around the girl.

"It's not healthy for Chyna to be exposed to so much media," she'd complained to Cooper, carefully not mentioning Mandy's name.

"Look who's talking," Cooper had responded. "You're *queen* of the media, running around all over town with your young stud. Were you banging him when we were together?"

"No, Cooper—*you* were the one out getting laid. Remember?"

Another nasty verbal battle had then taken place, which was exactly what Venus didn't want. There was nothing worse for Chyna than having to watch her divorced parents fight.

At least their daughter was safely away at summer camp, and according to her e-mails and phone calls, she was having a fantastic time.

* * *

"Shit!" Billy exclaimed.

"What?" Kev responded.

"I think I got a problem."

Kev burped and loped into the kitchen to fetch another beer.

Billy rolled off the couch and followed him. "Aren't you listening to me?" he said, scratching his crotch. "You're supposed to listen to me."

"I'm listening," Kev said, popping the top off a bottle of imported Carlsberg. "You got a freakin' problem. Spit it out."

"Like *you* care."

Kev took a swig of beer before giving his full attention to his best friend and employer. "Spill. What's the problem?"

"I think," Billy said, vigorously scratching away, "I got me a case of the freakin' crabs."

CHAPTER
TWENTY-FOUR

"You're joking, aren't you?" Max said, staring at Ace wide-eyed.

"What do *you* think?" he answered with a sly grin.

"I think you're putting me on," she said, struggling to remain cool in the face of his confession.

"Why's that?" he asked, staring her down.

" 'Cause if you *were* planning on robbing a bank for real," she said, narrowing her eyes, "there's no way you'd tell me."

"Why not?" he said, shrugging. "It's not as if there's anything you can do about it."

"I could go to the cops," she answered boldly.

"An' tell 'em *what*?" he said, full of bravado.

"That . . . y'know . . ." She trailed off, aware that if she went to the cops she'd probably sound like a crazy person. And why *would* she go to the cops anyway? It wasn't her business what he planned to do.

"Yeah, go on," he said, encouraging her.

"You're like eff-ing with me," she said.

"If that's what you think."

She didn't know what to think. But at least he was keeping her occupied until Internet Guy put in an appearance—that's if the jerk ever showed up.

They were standing outside Starbucks, and Ace made a move to go inside.

Max stood her ground. "I've decided I don't want a

coffee," she said petulantly. "I'm incredibly hungry. I need like real food."

"Am I stopping you from eating?" he said, giving her a quizzical look.

"Y'know what?" she said boldly. "There's no need to sweat it, I can buy my own burger. All you have to do is point me in the direction of someplace that serves food, then go rob your bank."

"Oh, Miss Cool," he said, grinning, "doesn't give a fast crap."

"It's not as if I believe you," she said, tossing back her long hair.

"Nobody said you had to," he answered. "An' by the way, how long you planning on waitin' around for your loser friend? 'Cause it looks t'me like he's a no-show."

"He'll be here," she said stubbornly.

"I sure hope so—otherwise it seems *I'm* stuck with you."

"Wow!" she said, green eyes flashing danger. "You certainly have a high opinion of yourself."

"How's that?"

"What makes you think you're *stuck* with me? I'm getting something to eat, then driving back to L.A."

"You can't do that," he said, straight-faced.

"Why not?"

"'Cause I might wanna use your car as my getaway vehicle. Y'know, after I rob the bank an' all."

"*Whaaat?*"

"Hey—idea," he said, laughing. "Maybe you could be my getaway *driver.*"

"You're looney-tunes," she said, shaking her head in exasperation.

"You're not exactly sane," he countered.

"*Excuse* me?" she said, thinking that although she hardly knew him, she was beginning to like him. A lot.

"Picking up some whacked-out loser on the Internet,"

he continued. "Whaddya gonna *do* with him if he does appear?"

"You don't want to know," she said in what she hoped was a mysterious tone.

"I get it," Ace said, "you're gonna make out with this dude."

"None of your business."

"I'm guessin'. Boyfriend dumps you, an' this is your way of gettin' back at him. Am I on the right track?"

Max glared at him, deciding she didn't like him after all. How dare he be such a smart-ass. And how dare he figure out exactly what she was up to.

The dinner was great; everyone cleaned their plates. Lucky caught Lennie's eye across the table and he winked at her, assuring her that the family reunion was progressing smoothly. Lennie was her rock, always there, always positive.

Gino sat at the head of the table flanked by Venus on one side and Brigette on the other. Gino might be almost ninety-five, but he could still appreciate a beautiful woman, and Venus and Brigette were the cream.

Bobby was on the other side of Venus, then Lucky, and next to her sat her half-brother, Steven, his wife, Lina—the vivacious English ex-supermodel—and their exquisite little daughter, Carioca. Paige was next to Carioca, then Gino Junior and Lennie.

The family were all present except for Leonardo, who was at the same summer camp as Chyna, and Max—who Lucky realized had not bothered to check in. Two black marks against Max. First one for leaving without saying good-bye. Second one for not calling.

Lucky decided that when her daughter got back—and it had better be in time for Gino's party—they were due for a major sit-down.

"I'd like to propose a toast," Gino said, tapping the

side of his wineglass with a fork. The table fell silent.
"My daughter," he continued, "is not only beautiful,
smart, an' one hell of a wife an' mother—she could get
herself a job in an Italian restaurant any day. These friggin' meatballs." He kissed the tips of his fingers and
made a sucking noise. "*Bellissimo! Fantastico!*" He
raised his glass, and his dark eyes met Lucky's. "To my
daughter. Always remember, kiddo, girls can do anything. An' I do mean you."

Lucky felt a sudden rush of emotion. For Gino to be
so open with his feelings—especially in front of
everyone—was not an everyday occurrence.

"Uh . . . thanks, Gino," she managed, then lightening
up she added, "Didn't know my meatballs would have
such an effect."

There was much laughter, then Bobby raised his glass
to toast his grandfather. Soon everyone was adding comments and having fun.

Lucky looked around the table and felt fortunate to
be part of such an interesting and sometime loving family. They were all individuals, but tonight everyone
seemed to fit.

Later the family gathered in the large living room,
catching up. Steven was talking away to Gino. Brigette
and Lina, who'd once modeled together, were exchanging horror stories from their past. Carioca fell asleep
with her head on Paige's knee, while Lennie, Bobby, and
Gino Junior went outside onto the terrace and started up
a challenging game of table tennis.

Finally Lucky had a chance to talk to Venus, who'd
been quiet all night, which was so unlike her.

"What's up?" Lucky asked, pouring her friend a li-
queur glass of limoncello, Venus's favorite after-dinner
drink.

"Instinct. A feeling," Venus replied, gesturing vaguely.
"Nothing concrete."

"Instinct about *what*?"

"Billy, of course," Venus sighed.

"I thought the two of you were blissfully happy—what with his big cock and old soul."

"Don't remind me," Venus said, rolling her eyes.

"Well, c'mon, what happened?" Lucky pressed. "Did you have a fight?"

"No, nothing like that."

"Then *what*?"

"Like I said, instinct."

"That's not enough for me to comment on," Lucky said, pouring herself a shot of limoncello. "You've got to give me more than that."

"Okay," Venus said patiently. "Here's the deal. We were supposed to go out tonight, have a quiet dinner together, then just as I was getting dressed, he called to cancel."

"What did he say?"

"He told me he was tired, and that Alex had given him an early call for tomorrow. That's it."

"Hey, if he has an early call, it's understandable, right?"

"I guess," Venus said unsurely. "But then I offered to come over to his place, and he said no."

"That's understandable too. Would you want someone coming over when you've got an early call? You of all people should know what it's like."

"I'm getting the distinct impression you're on his side," Venus said irritably.

"No way," Lucky responded. "But I get it."

"I wish I did," Venus said, downing her limoncello in one swift gulp.

"You've got to give him space," Lucky said, willing her friend to snap out of the ridiculous girly funk she was obviously in. This wasn't like the Venus she knew.

"Why's that?"

"'Cause if you don't, he's gonna feel crowded. And if you understand anything about men, they're all shit-scared of any hint of commitment. That's when they run. You know, 'It's not you, it's me,' and all that crap they come out with."

"I think I know why he's acting like this," Venus mused. "It's all this press stuff that never stops. Morons writing trash about us, delving into our innermost thoughts. We need to get away to some unreachable is-land."

"Nowhere's unreachable today," Lucky pointed out. "They'll follow you with their long-range lenses and there'll be even more photos."

"I'm just . . . I dunno," Venus said, gesturing help-lessly. "I guess I'm depressed."

"Billy cancels one dinner and you're depressed," Lucky said. "This isn't like you, Venus. Where's the kick-ass girl I used to know?"

"It's not just him backing out of one dinner. He's pull-ing away, I can feel it."

"Oh, for God's sake, you're not a kid," Lucky snapped, fast running out of sympathy. "Why don't you *ask* him what's going on?"

"'Cause if I ask, he might say he doesn't want to be with me anymore. Then what?"

"Then you'll hook up with somebody else," Lucky said patiently.

"It's not that easy."

"You've never had a problem before."

"I know, but this time I've done something really foolish."

"C'mon, let's hear it, what now?"

"I've gone and fallen in love."

Finally Henry made it to Big Bear. He drove directly to the Kmart parking lot, got out of his car, and looked around. He seemed to remember that Max said she drove a BMW, but he couldn't recall if she'd mentioned what color it was. He knew he'd recognize her once he saw her, because she'd posted her picture and he had a copy in his wallet. She resembled a very young version of Lucky Santangelo, the woman who'd stolen his future.

Oh yes, he was about to make sure that Lucky's daughter paid dearly for her mother's mistake.

He limped into the store cursing his bad leg, for there were times he yearned to move faster. He'd been dealt a bad hand, although not quite as bad as his dearly departed father.

He moved slowly, checking out the aisles one by one, realizing that they hadn't fixed a time, and since it was now late afternoon, would she have waited for him to arrive?

Why not? he reasoned. After all, she'd come all this way.

A large black woman brushed against him. He hissed an insult under his breath.

The woman heard him and stopped abruptly. "*What* you say?" she demanded, several wobbly chins quivering with indignation. "What you *damn* say?"

"I wasn't talking to you," he muttered.

"You'd better watch your mouth," she snorted, marching away.

Watch his mouth? All he'd said was, "Don't touch me, you fat bag of lard."

He hated being out amongst the common people; it was beneath him. He was Henry Whitfield-Simmons, a special man, a privileged man. He could not abide crowds—they made him feel insecure. Not that the Kmart store was crowded. There were very few people walking around, and that was good.

So where was she? Max Maria Santangelo Golden. Where the hell was she?

He limped to the front of the store and stood outside, his eyes scanning the street.

She was there, somewhere. He knew it.

Now all he had to do was find her.

CHAPTER TWENTY-FIVE

Halfway to New York, Anthony changed his mind. "Tell the pilot to reroute, we're flying to Miami," he informed The Grill.

The big man didn't argue—even though they'd been in Miami less than twenty-four hours earlier. Whatever Anthony Bonar wanted, he got.

The Grill informed the pilot of their change in destination. The pilot, who had a wife and two kids waiting in New York, was disgruntled. He carried on about air-traffic control and landing permission.

The Grill told him to work it out.

Anthony owned a luxurious waterfront home in Miami where his two teenage kids lived with their English nanny, while Francesca resided on the property in a guesthouse he'd had specially built to her specifications. Emmanuelle lived nearby in a magnificent Ocean Drive penthouse—*his* penthouse, because he'd never put anything in her name. If Emmanuelle ever decided to leave him, she left with nothing. He was no fool. He'd even made Irma sign a postmarriage prenuptial giving her practically nothing should they ever divorce—which was unlikely, because having a wife was excellent insurance as far as protecting himself from other women.

Anthony never did anything without thinking about it first. He was smart that way; his grandfather had taught him well. "When it comes to women, ya gotta use your head," Enzio had often lectured. "Your dick is for fuckin' 'em, an' your head is for fuckin' 'em in a different way. Don't never forget that."

For a brief moment Anthony thought about Tasmin. He hoped that by this time Renee had disposed of the girl way out in the desert, buried where nobody would find her. The authorities could add her name to the hundreds of people who went missing every day in America. She was a bank manager, for chrissakes. Who gave a damn? It wasn't like he'd fucked a movie star and snapped her neck.

Renee was upset with him, but that wouldn't last. She was smart enough not to piss him off. And if she was *really* smart, she'd never mention Tasmin again. It was over, done with, there was no going back.

By the time his plane landed in Miami, it was late morning. He had a choice: Should he go to his home, or should he go straight to Emmanuelle's apartment? He decided to surprise Emmanuelle.

His number-one mistress lived in a white Art Deco building right in the middle of Ocean Drive. The doorman knew him. Unbeknownst to Emmanuelle, Anthony paid both the night and day porters to give him a full report of her activities.

The day porter, a Hispanic man with bad teeth and an unruly mass of frizzy hair, greeted him with an ingratiating leer. "Señor Bonar, eez pleasure to see you back so soon."

"Anything to report?" Anthony said, not in the mood for pleasantries.

"Nothing, *señor*, all is quiet." The day porter lowered his voice to a conspiratorial whisper. "She's had no visitors. I watch. I see."

Anthony gave a curt nod and moved away from the man who never failed to annoy him. He stepped into the elevator with The Grill right behind him. He always kept The Grill in close proximity since he never knew what dangers were lurking. His connections were varied, and sometimes not so trustworthy. He also had to be on the alert for undercover cops who often attempted to infiltrate his business. Fortunately, he had a nose for smelling them out, and when he did, he either added them to his extensive payroll, or their careers turned out to be short-lived.

He entered Emmanuelle's apartment with his key and discovered her asleep in the bedroom, naked beneath peach-colored satin sheets. Emmanuelle was a true diva in training—she went for all the trimmings: satin sheets, sumptuous cushions, and huge fur throws. It always surprised Anthony that she was able to sleep on the slick satin sheets, because whenever *he* lay down on them, he had the distinct sensation that his ass was about to slide right off the bed. Damn sheets! But if they made her happy . . .

Stripping off his clothes, he dumped them on the floor before climbing into bed beside her. No Viagra today, with Emmanuelle he didn't always need it.

Smoothing his hand over her bare ass, he began sliding his fingers into the crack.

"Honey bunch, it's you," she murmured, rapidly waking up. "What're you doing here?"

"I'm back," he announced, as if she wasn't already aware of his presence.

"You only just left," she said, yawning. "Are you checking up on me?"

"I check up on you all the time," he said with a smug smile. "Only you don't know it."

"You do?" she responded, thinking to herself, *I might look like a bimbo, but I'm well aware he pays people to watch me. I would never be dumb enough to bring a guy here for that reason. I'd go to their place or we'd check into a hotel.*

It was actually quite fortunate she was back in her

own bed, because the previous night she'd gone out dancing and a couple of smokin' guys had definitely caught her attention. She'd flirted a lot, been tempted, then decided she was too tired from her photo shoot to do anything about it, so she'd come home. Alone. Thank God! Because here was Anthony, back again, and she hadn't been expecting him for another couple of weeks.

"How come you're back so soon?" she asked, her delicate fingers fluttering over his chest, twirling his coarse black chest hairs around her fingers. She knew he liked it when she touched him there.

"Must've missed you," he said, his hand diving between her legs.

"Oooh," she murmured, wriggling away from him. "Baby's gotta take a shower."

"You don't wanna do that," he said. "'Cause I wanna fuck you just the way you are."

Back in Las Vegas, Renee Falcon was crazed with fury—a cold, hard, hopeless fury she knew she had to keep to herself, because what else could she do? Anthony Bonar had come into town, she'd fixed him up with a date, and he'd left her with a dead body that he expected *her* to dispose of.

He'd given her no choice. She couldn't report him to the cops, and she certainly couldn't allow a body to be discovered on the premises of her hotel.

She'd known Tasmin from her dealings with the bank, and although they were not exactly friends—more casual acquaintances—she'd always liked her. Tasmin was smart, a hard worker, and the mother of a ten-year-old boy. She was also—according to rumors—a swinger. So Renee had thought that fixing her up with Anthony might work for both of them. Now this horrible tragedy.

Jesus Christ! It wasn't as if Tasmin was some out-of-town runaway whose body could be disposed of and nobody would ask any questions. There'd be plenty of questions about Tasmin.

Renee was acutely aware that they'd all been seen together at the hotel restaurant, which meant there were probably witnesses who would have observed Tasmin leaving with Anthony.

Damn Anthony Bonar. Underneath the relentless grooming and five-thousand-dollar suits lurked a murderous blackmailing chauvinist greedy thug. Yes, that's what he was. A dangerous killer with absolutely no conscience.

Renee realized she'd have to pay a great many people off to make this go away. And would Anthony recompense her? No. He was a cheap motherfucker on top of everything else. He was supposed to pay half of Tucker Bond's astronomical fee, and so far, every time she asked him for it, he stonewalled her. Maybe she should cancel the whole damn thing.

Right now she had to concentrate on the task at hand. Job number one was disposing of the body—a costly undertaking, but one she could make happen. After the body was gone she had to arrange for the room to be thoroughly cleaned, the sheets disposed of, fingerprints removed from everything. As far as anyone was concerned, Anthony had not spent any time at the hotel. He'd flown in for a meeting, had dinner, and left immediately after.

Yes, that was it. Tasmin had driven away from the hotel and that was the last anybody had seen of her.

Fortunately, Renee had surrounded herself with employees she could trust—that is, as long as they were well compensated.

By the time she'd taken care of everything, she was worn out and still very angry.

Susie was half asleep when she finally got back to their house.

"Where have you been?" Susie asked, removing her powder-pink sleep mask. "Anthony calls and you go running. What did he *want*? That man is so classless and dumb, it's beyond me why we have to entertain him every time he comes to town. Isn't it enough that he takes money from us every month?"

"Don't ever let him hear you call him dumb," Renee said, shrugging off her jacket. "You should know better than that."

"For God's sake," Susie complained, pouting. "We don't *need* someone like him in our lives. I hated dinner, I hated that you acted as his pimp. Surely he can find his own girls?"

"Listen, Susie," Renee said, sitting down on the edge of the bed, her face grim. "Something bad happened. I can't tell you what it is because I don't want you involved, but I *can* tell you that we won't be seeing Tasmin again."

"Why?" Susie said tartly. "Has she run off with Anthony?"

"Please—no questions," Renee said wearily. "And if the police come around asking anything, all you know is that we had dinner with Anthony, he was *not* staying here, and Tasmin was not his date. That's it. Nothing more."

"What *is* going on?" Susie asked, sitting up in bed.

"Tasmin was dining with us," Renee continued. "Anthony just happened to join us. It's important. Do you understand?"

"No, I don't," Susie said, looking alarmed.

"I've told you enough," Renee sighed.

Susie put her hand on her partner's arm. "Renee, whatever it is, it's *you* who mustn't get involved. You have to distance yourself from that horrible man."

"I already *am* involved," Renee answered, wearily

shaking her head. "There's nothing I can do about it, Susie, so please leave it alone."

"Hey, kids," Anthony said, entering his house and greeting his two teenage children.

Fourteen-year-old Eduardo was on his way out. He attempted to push past his father mumbling that he'd see him later.

"Where ya goin'?" Anthony demanded, grabbing his son's arm. "Why ya runnin' out on me?"

"He has basketball practice, Mr. Bonar," their English nanny announced. "His friend's father is picking him up."

"Okay, so go," Anthony said, releasing Eduardo. "Have a ball. Shoot one for me."

Thirteen-year-old Carolina was sitting cross-legged on the couch watching a dating game on MTV. Next to her perched Dee Dee, her bubble-gum-chewing best friend.

"Anybody need money?" Anthony offered. Oh yes, he knew how to attract his pretty daughter's attention.

Carolina didn't disappoint him. Jumping off the couch, she flung her arms around his neck. "*Please*, Papa," she cooed. "My credit card is over the limit, and Dee Dee and me want to go to the mall, so we need *plenty*. I have to buy a new outfit for the school dance and lots of other stuff."

"You girls *always* need money," Anthony said, smiling expansively at his daughter and her friend. Carolina was blond and cute and in his eyes could do no wrong. She was as pretty as Irma had been when he'd first met her, and that was saying something.

Eduardo was another case, surly and not quite the son Anthony had hoped for. All Eduardo wanted to do was play sports. He wasn't even interested in girls, and he certainly wasn't interested in learning about the family business, which in the long run was probably wise, because Eduardo did not exhibit any sign of the Bonnatti balls.

Fishing in his back pocket, Anthony handed Carolina a fistload of hundred-dollar bills. She grabbed them out of his hands with an excited "*Whoopee!* Thanks, Papa."

Their English nanny, an older woman with iron gray hair, worn in a no-nonsense bun, and a fierce expression, didn't say a word, although her disapproving look indicated more than words.

Anthony took no notice. Like he gave a shit what some uptight English twat thought.

"Gimme a big kiss, Princess," he said, hugging his daughter again.

Carolina kissed him full on the lips.

He chuckled, and smacked her lightly on the ass. "No talkin' to boys at the mall. No talkin' to boys period. You're too young. Understand me?"

"Yes, Papa," she said obediently.

"I mean it," he said sternly. "I'm the only boy you can talk to. Ain't that so, Princess?"

"I know, Papa," Carolina said, rolling her eyes.

"Okay," he said, giving her another brisk pat on the ass. "I'm gonna look in on my grandma. Wanna come with?"

"I saw her yesterday," Carolina replied, counting out her money while giggling with her friend.

"You're sure?"

"Very sure, Papa."

"I'll take a shower first. You remember what I told you."

Upstairs in his bedroom, he stripped off his clothes yet again. He hadn't showered at Emmanuelle's; as soon as he'd fucked her, he'd wanted out. But now, once again he had an urge to get her smell off him.

After a quick shower, he marched naked into his bedroom, clicked on the large-screen TV, and sat on the end of the bed. The bedroom was modern and masculine—all brown leather and chrome furniture, with touches of orange cushions and throws here and there. He had to admit that Irma had done an excellent job of decorating the Miami mansion. It had taken her several months and plenty of money. Once she was finished he'd sent her back to Mexico City, he didn't want her hanging around in Miami. It was better that they didn't live in the same city. A nonstop diet of Irma could drive a man loco. The kids didn't seem to miss her—truth was they barely mentioned her.

Flicking through the channels and finding nothing to attract his attention apart from an endless offering of mind-numbing soaps, he dressed and headed for Francesca's. His grandmother would want to know everything. She always did.

He'd only tell her what he thought she should know, and that was it.

He certainly wasn't telling her about Tasmin. She'd have plenty to say about *that*.

Too much information could sometimes be a bad thing. The less she knew, the better.

CHAPTER TWENTY-SIX

Max was just about to get into her car when she heard a voice behind her.

"You must be Max," the voice said.

"Huh?" she gasped, turning around, totally startled. A man was standing there. He was at least thirty, not very tall, slight of build, with thinning hair and a weaselly face. He was carrying a large canvas hold-all. "How do you know who I am?" she asked suspiciously.

"I recognized you from your photo."

"What photo?" she said, glancing quickly around the car park. It was dusk, the light fading fast, and unfortunately there was no one else in sight.

"The one you posted on the Internet," he said, taking a moment to study her face. So very pretty. So very young. Full, pouty lips and innocent green eyes. The clouds of black curly hair reminded him that she was a younger version of her mother. Lucky Santangelo—the woman who'd ruined his life, the woman who'd taken away his moment of triumph and handed it to Billy Melina. "I'm Grant," he said, unable to take his eyes off her.

"*You're* Grant?" she questioned, hardly able to conceal her surprise, because he looked nothing like the photo he'd posted. He was way older and way creepy. Ugh!

"I'm late because my car ran out of gas," he explained, shuffling awkwardly from one foot to the other. "Sorry about that, but at least I'm here now."

"Uh . . . you're like *very* late," she pointed out, wishing she hadn't blown Ace off with a casual "Go rob your bank. See ya." She could sure use him now.

"You can leave your car," Weasel Face said. "We'll take mine."

This must be a joke. There was no way she was getting into a car with this guy—he was hardly the Internet dude of her dreams. Cookie must've had a premonition—this dude was most likely a serial killer who planned on chopping her up and eating her for his dinner. He was a definite creep. Ha-ha! The joke was on her.

"I enjoyed your e-mails," he continued in a conversational tone. "We have so much in common."

"We do?" she gulped, glancing quickly around the car park.

"Yes, we do," he said, moving closer and placing his hand on her arm, a move that totally freaked her out. "It seems we both enjoy the same things."

Oh crap! If she kicked him in the balls, would it give her enough time to jump in her car and take off?

"You don't look like your picture," she said accusingly. "That photo wasn't you, was it?"

His grip tightened on her arm. Her stomach experienced some kind of crazy cartwheel, this was not a good scene.

Then all of a sudden, like some kind of Superman, Ace appeared out of nowhere. "Hey, little cous'," he said, stepping between them, forcing Henry to let go of her arm. "Is this the dude we were waitin' for?"

Wow! Ace was no slouch in the "getting it" department. She was impressed.

"Who's this?" Henry said, glaring at Ace, a ferocious scowl covering his face.

"This . . . uh . . . this is my cousin Ace," she said, thinking fast. "He uh . . . drove me here today."

"He came *with* you?" Henry said, his thin lips tightening. "Why?"

"'Cause, uh . . . my mom didn't want me meeting someone I didn't know by myself," she said, biting into her lower lip.

Henry was silent for a moment, digesting this new information. He was extremely upset that she was with a male companion, even if the boy *was* her cousin. This was a complication he had not expected.

"You'll be fine with me," Henry said, attempting to recover his composure. "Your cousin can go home."

"You're not listenin', man," Ace said, still standing between them. "Max's mom asked me to stay with her. We're like on this weekend trip together. So, uh . . . you got a plan?"

"I've hired a cabin," Henry said, furious that this boy would dare to interfere.

"Like for the three of us?" Ace asked, exchanging a quick glance with Max.

"I was not aware there were going to be three of us," Henry said stiffly.

"Hey, look," Ace said. "Max's mother doesn't want her staying over anyway, so we kinda thought we'd say hello, then take off." He threw Max a meaningful look. "Right?"

"Yes," she said, thinking how fortunate it was that she'd bumped into Ace, and what a relief that he was there to extract her from such a weird and uncomfortable situation. Not because he was the greatest protector in the world—because according to him he was a would-be bank robber—but having him around was certainly better than nothing. "We have to get back to L.A. My mom's giving a family dinner."

"But we made an arrangement," Henry said, a muscle in his cheek twitching. "A firm arrangement."

"Not so firm," Max said quickly. "And if I'd had your cell number, I would've called and told you I wouldn't be able to stay."

Henry glared at her. Pretty as she was, she was not behaving in the way he had expected.

Wow! Max thought. This was turning out to be even more of an adventure than she'd anticipated. She would have major stories to tell Cookie and Harry when she got back.

"I was expecting to spend the weekend with you," Henry said, still glaring. "I organized everything. I hired a cabin, bought supplies. This was supposed to be our time to get to know each other."

Eeww! Max thought. *This guy takes creepy to new heights.*

"Sorry, dude," Ace said, cracking his knuckles. "It's not as if you *know* Max."

"I *do* know her," Henry corrected, a slow rage beginning to build inside him. "And she knows me. We have—"

"Hey," Max interrupted. "That's not true. It's not like I exactly *know* you. I mean, it's not as if we ever *met* or anything."

"Listen, we gotta go," Ace said, nudging Max in the ribs. "Gimme the keys, Max, I'll drive."

"Sure," she said, handing Ace her car keys, quite excited at the thought of a fast getaway from this creepo freak.

And then everything happened very quickly, although later, when she looked back, Max decided it was more like a slow-motion sequence from a movie than an actual real-life event.

Grant produced a gun. Just like that he pulled it out of his pocket and pointed it straight at the two of them.

"Get in the car," he said, his voice flat and devoid of

any emotion. "You first," he said, waving the gun in Ace's face. "Behind the wheel. One wrong move and I blow this pretty little girl's head off. Do you understand me?"

Yes. Ace understood him.

CHAPTER
TWENTY-SEVEN

Saturday morning Lucky was awakened by an early-morning phone call from Mooney Sharp, the general contractor in charge of everything to do with the Keys. The call came through on her private phone, a line she had asked Mooney to use only in emergencies.

"What's going on, Mooney?" she asked, struggling to wake up.

"You gotta get yourself up here, Lucky," Mooney informed her.

"Why's that?"

"The cosigner from the bank hasn't turned up. We usually do the check signing every Friday afternoon, but she was busy last night, asked if we could postpone to this morning. I said sure. Now she's not here."

"Where is she?"

"Called her house—the babysitter said she never made it home last night. I guess she must've gotten laid or somethin'."

"What's this got to do with me, Mooney?"

"There's checks gotta be signed today. I need a cosigner—an' you're it."

"Why am *I* it?" she asked irritably.

" 'Cause I haven't been able to reach anyone else."

"Great!"

"I was thinkin' you could fly in for a couple of hours."

"Jeez, Mooney, this is not an easy weekend for me. I'm throwing a big party tomorrow for Gino."

"This is urgent, Lucky. Some of the contractors don't get their checks today, they'll walk. We can't afford for that to happen, not at this final stage."

"Fine," Lucky said, making a quick decision. "I'll be there as soon as I can."

Lennie was still asleep. Lucky leaned toward him. "Hey, sleepyhead, wake up," she said, nudging his shoulder.

"It's too early," he groaned.

"Gotta go, they need me in Vegas," she said briskly. "Thought I might score a good-bye kiss."

He opened one eye. "You're going today?"

"Yup. I gotta cosign checks."

"Why d'*you* have to do it?"

"Don't even ask."

"Jesus, Lucky—"

"I know," she interrupted. "But I'll only be gone a few hours, and I was hoping you'd hold it together here. That's unless you feel like coming with me."

"No, I don't feel like coming with you," he said, stretching out his arms. "Rome, maybe. Paris, yes. Vegas—no way."

"So you'll entertain Gino, Paige, and the others?"

"Me?"

"Yes, you, and they'll be erecting the party tent today, plus the caterers will be setting up, but Philippe will take care of that side of things. You're in charge of family."

"Gee, thanks," he said, pushing his hand through his hair. "Just how I wanna spend my weekend when I should be working on my script."

"Please, Lennie," she cajoled. "It's not often I ask you to do something for me."

"You're *always* asking me," he said, reaching out for her.

"I am?" she said softly, falling into his arms.

"Yes, you are," he teased, pulling her close for a long, slow kiss.

"You'd better let me go or I'll never get out of here," she murmured.

"So stay."

"You know I can't," she said, wishing she could.

"Okay, okay," he said, releasing her from his arms. "Go make your trip. I'll hold it together here."

"And please call Max. I left a message on her cell yesterday and she never called back. I'm so pissed, but I don't have time to get involved in a fight. That's why *you* should call her, make sure she's back in time for the party."

"Yes, *ma'am*," he mocked. "Anything else?"

"You're the best and I love you," she said, kissing him.

"Keep on tellin' me that an' we'll live happily ever after."

"Oh, we will," she promised, kissing him again.

Downstairs in the kitchen Brigette and Bobby were sitting at the counter drinking coffee.

"How come you two are up?" Lucky asked.

"We're operating on a different time zone," Bobby reminded her. "Three hours ahead."

"I have to fly to Vegas today," Lucky said, pouring a cup of coffee for herself.

"Can I come too?" Bobby asked. "Haven't been to Vegas since I was a kid."

"If you want to."

"Definitely. Can't wait to see what kind of a club you've put together. I'll be your adviser."

"Gee, thanks Bobby," Lucky said caustically, "just what I need."

"Hey, I do have one of the hottest clubs in New York, as I keep on telling you."

"I know," she said patiently. "You do keep on telling me, don't you?"

"You've been there, you've seen for yourself."

"It's great."

"So?"

"So, as I am constantly reminding you, you weren't in the club biz when I put together this complex. Who knew you wanted to run clubs? Certainly not me."

"If you're all flying to Vegas," Brigette said brightly, "can I come too?"

"Yeah!" Bobby said enthusiastically. "We can make a day of it. Blackjack, twenty-one, craps—maybe time for a quick dive into a strip club somewhere along the way. A lap dance will suit me just *fine!*"

"Absolutely not!" Brigette said, starting to laugh. "I'm thinking shopping."

"What?" Bobby said, straight-faced. "You're not into lap dances?"

"You can both come," Lucky decided. "As long as you remember this is a fast trip—no time for gambling, strip clubs, *or* shopping."

"C'mon, Mom," Bobby said, winking at Brigette. "A little lap dance never did anyone any harm."

Ignoring her son, Lucky headed for the door. "Be ready in one hour. Do *not* keep me waiting."

On their way out Lucky left Gino a note.

I know you understand—Vegas calls.
We'll be back in time for dinner.

If anybody understood business it was Gino.

As they were getting in the limo to take them to the airport, Philippe hurried over to the window and handed her an envelope. She opened it in the car.

"Who's that from?" Bobby wanted to know.

"I keep on getting these cards dropped off at the

house," Lucky said, tapping the card on her knees. "All they say is 'Drop Dead Beautiful.'"

"That's weird," Brigette said.

Bobby grabbed the card from her and inspected it. "You shown this to anyone?" he asked.

"Why would I? It's probably an invitation to an event, and eventually I'll find out what it's for."

"How many of these have you gotten?"

"Um . . . maybe this is the third one."

"Where are the other two?"

"Guess I must've thrown them away."

"And they were all put in the mailbox?"

"What are you, a district attorney?" Lucky joked.

"Seriously, Mom," Bobby said, "we should have someone check out the security cameras, get a look at who's delivering them."

"Why are you so concerned?"

"'Cause you never know."

"Never know *what?*" Lucky asked, amused that Bobby was taking some frivolous invite so seriously.

"You must have enemies, y'know, people from your past."

Lucky wondered exactly how much Bobby knew about her past. Too much from the sound of him.

"What *are* you talking about?" she said lightly. "I do not have any enemies."

"Your son Googled you," Brigette said, joining in. "He knows plenty about both of us."

"I grew *up* knowing about our family," Bobby said. "I didn't have to Google anyone. And hey, Mom, you think I don't *remember* what happened to me and Brigette when we were kids? That whole kidnapping thing which you refuse to talk about."

"I never talk about it, Bobby, because bringing it up is bad karma. It all happened a long time ago, so leave it alone."

"I was *molested*, Mom, in case you've forgotten. I was five years old and molested by some crazy old mobster. You think I can forget that?"

"I don't expect you to forget it," Lucky said carefully. "But we've all moved on."

"Yes, Bobby," Brigette said. "If *I* can move on after what happened, so can you."

"Hey," Bobby said. "Without you, Brig, I probably wouldn't even be here. You were the one who shot the old pervert. I'll never forget you picking up that gun and—"

"Enough," Brigette interrupted, her blue eyes clouding over. "Now *I'm* the one who doesn't want to start taking a trip down memory lane."

"Okay, I get it," Bobby said. "Sorry I brought it up."

Mooney Sharp met them at the airport. A big man in his late fifties, Mooney was over six feet, with a halo of bushy red hair, matching eyebrows, and a huge gut. His favored outfit was cowboy boots, pressed jeans, and a low-slung belt with an enormous silver buckle—all the better to exhibit his massive stomach. At seventeen all his front teeth had gotten knocked out in a bar fight, and now his party trick was to remove his row of yellowing false teeth and horrify everyone with a manic toothless grin.

"Hey, Mooney," Lucky said. "As you can see, I'm here. Happy?"

"Morning, boss," Mooney answered, tipping his well-worn Stetson. "Lookin' great as usual."

"Compliments are going to get you nowhere," Lucky said. "I had to leave all my houseguests and jump on a plane, not my favorite way to spend Saturday morning."

"Sorry, Lucky, like I told you, I couldn't reach anyone else with signing privileges, an' this *is* an emergency."

"It better be."

"Oh, it is. We're in the final stages, wouldn't want anything holding us up."

"You remember my son, Bobby, don't you?"

"Sure do," Mooney said, giving Bobby a hearty handshake. "You was just a little tyke last time I saw you."

"And this is Brigette, my godchild."

"See you made it a family party," Mooney remarked, escorting them to his mud-splattered SUV. "I'm big on family. Trouble is I never get to see 'em."

"How come?"

"'Cause I'm busy workin' for you twenty-four-seven," he said with a hearty guffaw.

"Wanna quit?" Lucky asked jokingly, sitting up front.

"If I quit, I die," Mooney said, getting behind the wheel.

In the backseat Bobby leaned across to Brigette who was sitting beside him. "Sorry about earlier," he said. "Y'know, bringing up the whole kidnapping deal. I didn't mean to—it kinda slipped out."

"That's okay, Bobby," she said quietly. "It's just bad memories."

"I'm sure."

"It was my fault for getting us into it in the first place," she continued. "I was so young and naive, and you were just a helpless little kid. I knew I had to do something to protect you, and the gun was right there."

"You did the right thing, Brig. You saved us both."

"Y'know, Bobby," she said thoughtfully. "Maybe we *should* talk about it. I saw a shrink. You never did."

"No, shrinks aren't my style. I've moved on—it's the way to go."

"Okay," Brigette said, her pretty face serious. "But any time you feel the need . . ."

"Thanks. If I ever do, I'll call you."

The moment they hit the Strip, Lucky turned her

head, feeling the old familiar surge of adrenaline. "Well," she said, "we're back in Vegas."

"I think I love it," Bobby said enthusiastically. "Gambling and girls—my two favorite things. Maybe I should build my own hotel—blow you out of the water!"

"You're a Santangelo, all right," Lucky said, smiling.

"Yeah," he agreed with a sly grin. "A Santangelo loaded with Stanislopolous money. Pretty cool combination, huh, Mom?"

For a moment she thought she was talking to Gino, which made her smile even more.

"Yes, Bobby," she said. "Pretty damn cool."

CHAPTER
TWENTY-EIGHT

Lying is never a good thing. Lying always has a way of coming back and kicking you in the ass, or so Billy discovered. He'd lied to Venus, told her he had an early call. The truth was that he didn't have to work again until Monday, so when Venus called him on his cell Saturday morning, he was still happily asleep.

"Mmm . . . yeah?" he mumbled.

"Billy?" she said, sounding surprised. "Are you asleep?"

Without thinking, he said, "Uh, yeah, somethin' wrong with that?"

"You told me you had an early call," she said accusingly.

"Shit . . . yeah, um . . . that got canceled."

"It did?" she said coldly. "What time was it canceled?"

"Uh, sometime last night. Late. Kev took the call. I was, uh, trying to get to sleep early, like I told you."

"You never called me last night," she sighed. "You promised you'd call before you went to bed." Oh God! Was that a needy whine she detected in her voice?

"Sorry, V," he said. "I was watching the game, must've passed out in front of the TV 'cause I don't remember anything till I woke up at three an' hauled myself into bed."

"I see," she said, hating the way she sounded, like an uptight schoolmarm questioning a badly behaved student. Lucky was right—this was so unlike her, she had to get it together.

"How're you doing?" he ventured, well aware that she was way pissed at him.

"I'm doing great, Billy, if you care."

"What does *that* mean?"

"It means that I don't know what's going on between us, and I think it's time we sat down and talked."

Oh shit, he thought. *She wants to have the "We need to talk" conversation.* When women wanted *that* conversation, it was always a no-win situation.

"Whatever," he said vaguely.

"Don't you think we should?" she persisted. "Surely you sense that something's going on between us?"

"Like what?" he said, following the "I'm just a dumb guy, what do I know?" tactic.

"We shouldn't discuss it over the phone."

"You wanna come by?" he suggested, immediately wishing he hadn't.

"If you'd like me to," she said cautiously.

"Why wouldn't I? I'm not working today. I got a free pass."

"Okay, I'll be over soon."

Billy put down the phone and groaned. His crotch was still itching like crazy, even though last night he'd sent Kev out to the drugstore to buy some special cream to kill the little fuckers. Kev had questioned him into the ground about where he'd gotten them from. But he'd stayed firm, and come out with the old toilet-seat story.

Of course, he knew where he'd gotten them. It must've been from the girl he'd picked up at Tower Records. She'd infected him, dirty little groupie.

More important—what if he'd passed on the disgusting bugs to Venus? How the hell could he explain *that*?

Hey, Miss Superstar Girlfriend. I might have given you a dose of the crabs. How about we discuss it?

Running his hand through his hair, he got out of bed. "Kev!" he yelled. "Where the frig are you?"

Then he remembered that Kev had gone home last night after bringing him the medication from the drugstore. Rubbing it into his crotch was a laugh a minute, and even worse, it didn't seem to be working.

Devoid of clothes, he made his way into the kitchen. Ramona did not come in on Saturday or Sunday. He'd decided privacy was on the top of his hit list for the weekends; he didn't want his housekeeper hanging around. Besides, she needed time off too.

Removing a carton of orange juice from the fridge, he drank straight from the carton and burped. Ah, yes— not being polite was one of the advantages of living alone. Discovering a California Pizza box in the fridge, he opened it and devoured half a cold barbecue chicken pizza. It tasted great, better than cereal any day, and he had to build up his strength: Venus was in the "We've got to talk" mode, so he'd better be prepared.

It suddenly occurred to him: Was breaking up on her mind? Is that where they were heading?

Yeah, probably. It was time. He was so over being referred to as Venus's boy toy. Goddammit, he was a big star in his own right, he didn't have to put up with that crap any longer.

If they *did* decide to break up, he had to make sure that Venus knew it wasn't anything she'd done. She was an amazing woman, and yeah, he loved her in his own way. But he needed to be free of all the garbage that went along with being Miz Superstar's boyfriend.

Problem was he didn't have the balls to come right out and tell her, so he was hoping *she'd* be the one who'd break up with him.

Yes, that would be very convenient.

Or would it?

* * *

Venus was mad as she listened to herself turning into the kind of woman she couldn't stand. The kind of woman who hung around waiting for the phone to ring, holding her breath for some guy to validate her very existence.

Billy Melina had her hooked, and she hated it. She, who was usually so in control, was now out of control because of a man. *Billy* was calling all the shots, and *fuck him!*

Lucky was right. If Billy wanted out, she should be the one to move on, get out first. Why allow *him* the pleasure of doing it?

Oh God, I'll miss him, she thought. *Those abs, that face, that beautiful dick. My Billy. My gorgeous guy. I can't help it. I love him.*

What would people say? Would they think he'd dumped her because she was an older woman? Or would she be able to spin it and announce that *she'd* dumped *him*?

Yeah, that was it. She'd tell her friends that she'd let him go because he was too young and immature, and he wanted to move in. The press would go to town on that one.

Statement from her publicist to the hungry media:

> *Billy Melina is a wonderful and spiritual man and we'll always be close friends. Unfortunately, the timing is not right for either of us.*

She thought about who she might start seeing next. There were always opportunities, always men panting to go out with her. There was the black TV entertainment reporter with the dazzling smile and flirtatious manner. There was the successful movie producer who was constantly inviting her out. There was the Bad Boy movie star—one of Billy's main rivals—who kept on phoning to inquire whether she'd gotten rid of Billy yet. And then there were the fans—legions of them. Only she'd never date a fan; too risky.

What was she going to do? She wasn't ready to break up with Billy. She didn't want to, she was perfectly happy, *he* was the one causing waves.

Oh God! The thought of dating again. No! No! No! It was too horrific to even contemplate.

The first date, the first kiss, the first fuck. A *nightmare*. Not to mention the dumb conversations that had to take place.

Where do you live?

What's your star sign?

You like dogs or cats?

Sushi or steak?

Missionary or tantric?

No. She was not allowing Billy to break up with her. No way.

The paparazzi were lying in wait outside Billy's house.

Don't they have anything better to do? Venus thought, ducking her head and driving past. She didn't want them to see her in the Phaeton, it was her secret getaway car, and if they saw her in it, her clever ruse would be over.

She called Billy on her cell. "What shall I do?" she wailed.

Oh, great! She'd gone from needy girlfriend to helpless one. Dammit! If she didn't get it together soon, she'd be forced to slit her wrists.

"Uh . . . drive home, I'll come pick you up," Billy suggested. "Or maybe we should hang out at your place."

She didn't want him at her house. If he was there, he could leave whenever he felt like it, and that gave *him* the power position. Today that position was going to be strictly hers.

"Not to worry," she said. "I know exactly what to do. See you soon."

Hitting the gas pedal, she raced down the hill and along Sunset until she reached the Beverly Hills Hotel, where she gave her car to the parking valet and asked him to call her a cab. The parking valet, a would-be actor, was in awe. Especially when she slipped him a fifty-dollar tip.

Ten minutes later she was paying off the cabdriver outside Billy's house, while the assembled paparazzi launched into a photo-taking frenzy. They were not shy about yelling out questions:

"How come you're in a cab?"

"When are you and Billy getting married?"

"Any babies in your future?"

"Over here, Venus, gimme that dazzling smile."

Ignoring them, and a gaggle of girl fans hovering near the bushes, she rang the doorbell. Billy had never offered to give her a key, and since she hardly ever came to his house, she'd never asked for one.

On the other hand, he had the code to get into *her* house, so maybe she *should* have a key.

Billy came to the door himself, causing the girl fans to dissolve into moans and shrieks of ecstatic joy, and the paparazzi to blind everyone with their continuous flashbulbs.

Billy grabbed her by the arm, yanking her inside, slamming the door behind them.

"Jesus, Billy, isn't it time you put up gates?" she said, trying to catch her breath. "It's a circus out there."

"You think I should?" Billy asked, managing to sound as if he'd just ambled into Hollywood straight off the farm.

"Of course you should. And not for my sake. You're famous. You need protection. What if one of those crazy fans had a gun?"

"Oh, c'*mon*, don't go gettin' all dramatic on me."

"I suppose you've never heard of Rebecca Schaeffer or John Lennon?"

"Who's Rebecca Schaeffer?"

"It doesn't matter, Billy," she sighed. "What does matter is that it's essential you get security gates put up around your house. Why don't you have what's-his-name arrange it?"

He knew exactly who she meant by "what's-his-name." Kev. She had a thing about Kev. Early on in their relationship she'd pronounced that Kev was a hanger-on and incompetent. She was always trying to persuade him to hire a "real assistant."

Well, too bad. Apart from being his gofer, Kev was his best friend from way back. Besides, the underlying reason she wanted Kev gone was that she considered him a bad influence.

"I'll think about it," he mumbled, trailing her into his living room, hoping he'd remembered to hide Kev's latest stash of porno tapes that he insisted on bringing over.

She zeroed in on his coffee table, picking up photos of girls in various stages of undress. "Who are these?" she asked.

"Fans," he said sheepishly. "They send me this crap all the time."

"To your house?"

"Some. Or the studio forwards them over."

"Are you telling me you don't have anyone organizing your fan club?"

Man, she was in a pissy mood, bossy too. "Uh . . . when I'm on a movie the production office hires someone to take care of it," he said.

"Billy, we've got to get you organized. This is ridiculous."

"Yeah, I guess," he said lamely.

"So," she said, moving a pile of newspapers and

magazines out of the way before sitting down on the couch. "Where's your housekeeper today?"

"Jeez, Venus, relax, we're here by ourselves. We don't need a bunch of people looking after us, do we?"

Realizing she was being picky, she shut up. If he wanted to live in a state of disarray, it was his problem.

"Actually you're right," she said, performing a catlike stretch. "It's kind of nice not having anyone around except us."

"You see?" he said triumphantly. "No one to spy on us, check out what we're doing. We can walk around naked if we feel like it."

"Or swim naked in the pool," she said, glancing out the full-length glass doors to the inviting pool. "I haven't done that since I bought my first house."

He immediately flashed onto the girl who'd given him crabs. She'd been naked in his pool. Oh shit! Did the little buggers swim?

His crotch itched at the memory. He scratched himself vigorously, silently cursing.

"What's the matter?" Venus asked.

Should he tell her? Well, at least he'd better make up a cover story in case he'd infected her.

"Got a slight problem," he said sheepishly.

"What problem?"

"One of the stuntmen on the movie had crabs. *My* stunt double, believe it or not. Wardrobe got our pants mixed up, and since I was going commando—"

"No!"

"Sorry, babe. I only just found out. Hope I haven't passed them on to you. I've got the cream to treat 'em . . ."

"I don't believe this!"

"Yeah. I know. I could kill the son of a bitch."

"So *that's* why you've been in such a strange mood."

Whew! He was off the hook. All she was worried about was his mood.

"Uh . . . yeah . . . guess so."

"You should've told me before."

"I should've?"

"Well, yes. It's unfortunate, but these things happen."

"They do?"

"Oh Billy, you're such a baby," she said affectionately.
If he'd had a hard-on, it would've deflated on the spot.

CHAPTER TWENTY-NINE

After spending time with Francesca and assuring her that everything was on track to bring down the Keys and the Santangelo family once and for all, Anthony realized there was nothing for him to do in Miami. Sure, he had Emmanuelle, and he had his kids, but he'd been neglecting business, and since the crux of his business operations was in Mexico City he decided he should get back.

He instructed The Grill to have the plane ready. "We're going to Mexico City," he informed him.

The Grill nodded, a man of few words, always ready to move at a moment's notice.

Anthony had promised to take Emmanuelle out to dinner, but he didn't bother informing her that he would not be doing so. Emmanuelle getting all dressed up and sitting around waiting for him gave him a sense of extreme power and control. Women needed to be controlled at all times, and any man who didn't realize that was a foolish man indeed.

The thing with Tasmin had disturbed him, and even though it was Tasmin's own fault, Renee's reaction had put a damper on his weekend. Fuck Renee Falcon. How dare she criticize him. It wasn't as if he'd experienced a rush of adrenaline knowing that he'd accidentally killed a woman. Now, if Tasmin had been a man . . .

He called Renee on his way to the airport.

"Everything taken care of?" he said roughly.

"What do *you* think?" she replied, sounding distant and cold.

Lesbian *bitch!* When she'd dealt with the Vegas business it was time to set her straight and let her know who was boss.

Give a woman too much power and it always came back to bite you in the ass.

Sometimes Irma felt as if she was living in a prison—a luxurious, magnificent prison, but a prison all the same. Oh yes, the house was grand, the grounds lush and green, there were servants to do anything she wished.

She had everything anyone could possibly ask for, and yet there were guards at the gates.

Anthony had informed her that he employed the guards to protect them from kidnappers and robbers. But she knew the real truth. Her husband was a drug dealer—and as such he had to surround himself with all the protection he could pay for.

When she'd first met Anthony, he'd told her he was in the import/export business, and that's what she'd always tried to convince herself was the truth. But she'd always known it wasn't so. Anthony was a major dealer, that was a plain and simple fact. She'd met several of the men he did business with when he'd taken her to Colombia to attend a drug lord's daughter's wedding. And she'd witnessed many meetings at the house, and mysterious helicopter arrivals late at night.

Now that Luis had made her feel desirable and confident again, thoughts of leaving Anthony were constantly on her mind. She could not communicate this to Luis, but what did it matter? She wasn't planning on running off with him, although sometimes she daydreamed it might be possible.

Every night she tossed restlessly in bed, her mind racing in many different directions, thinking about what to do. She had a lot of burning questions. Since she had no money of her own, no bank account, no savings, how would she survive without Anthony to support her? Anthony had never allowed her to have her own checking account; he gave her a fistful of charge cards and cash whenever she asked. His office in Mexico City paid all the bills.

She had her clothes and jewelry, but what about her children? Could she simply abandon them?

It really didn't make any difference because she wasn't allowed to see them anyway, not unless Anthony said so.

I need a lawyer, she thought. *And not a Mexican lawyer who will automatically be on Anthony's side—an American lawyer. I have to get away from this place I am imprisoned in. My life is seeping away and I am kept here like a caged animal.*

She wondered what Anthony would do if she asked him for a divorce.

Silly question—she knew exactly what he'd do. He'd go berserk, he'd start screaming the way he screamed at his grandmother, he'd refuse to believe that she wanted to leave him. Anthony had a very high opinion of himself, especially sexually. Not that he'd touched her in almost a year, but he still regarded himself as King Stud.

Being Mrs. Anthony Bonar was a huge burden to carry around, and the time had come to shed that burden.

Luis was the perfect lover for her. He was young and available, and conveniently he was allowed on the property at all times, since he was one of the estate's gardeners. Who would ever suspect him? Who would ever guess that she had personal knowledge of the rippling muscles beneath his workshirt, that he was built like an Adonis, that his kisses were so sweet and tender? Who would ever suspect that she would fall in lust with this man?

Most of the staff had Saturday off, unless Anthony was in residence. Only Marta, the cook, remained, and she was half deaf anyway. As usual the guards were stationed at the front of the house with the dogs, and the old gardener never came in on weekends—there was only Luis.

Irma glanced out the window, making sure he was there, before taking a leisurely bath, then putting on a simple white dress. She felt like being virginal today. Virginal, so Luis could rip the dress from her body. She knew that once her bedroom door was locked, the lowly gardener turned into a sensuous animal, and frankly she couldn't wait.

After putting on the white dress, she dabbed perfume behind her ears, between her breasts, and on her thighs. Then she hurried downstairs, making a detour through the kitchen.

Marta was sitting in front of the kitchen TV engrossed in a dramatic Spanish telenovella with the sound turned up.

"Marta," Irma said, startling the woman. "I won't be needing anything else today. I'm on a diet, so no dinner for me. You can go home now."

"*Gracias, señora*," Marta said, quickly standing up and gathering her purse before Señora Bonar changed her mind.

"Enjoy your weekend," Irma said, walking outside into the garden.

Luis spotted her and quickly looked away. He never indicated anything intimate between them; it was only in the privacy of her bedroom that he became this erotic and sensual creature.

"Luis," she said, approaching him in a formal manner. "I'd like you to come look at my houseplants."

She kept up this charade because she never knew who might be watching them. There were many cameras on

the property, so it was possible they could be observed
without them knowing.

"*Sí, señora,*" Luis said, keeping his eyes fixed firmly
on the ground.

"I'll see you in the house," she said.

He didn't understand the words she was speaking, but
he did understand exactly what she meant.

She turned and headed back toward the house.

He waited a few minutes, then casually made his own
way across the lawn and into the big house.

Luis always got a thrill entering the cool tiled hallway
with the massive chandeliers hanging from the fifty-foot
ceiling. It was such a magnificent mansion, so different
from the squalid two-bedroom house he lived in with
his sickly mother, three argumentative sisters, and
pregnant wife. Obviously Señora Bonar was unaware
that he had a wife, and he was not about to tell her. Not
that he could, since he didn't speak her language.

He climbed the marble staircase two steps at a time.
How fortunate was he? He had a job, a frustrated American woman who wanted sex every day, and a wife at
home who would shortly give birth to his first son.

Irma's bedroom door was open. He walked in, closing and locking the door behind him.

Irma was lying on the bed in her white virginal dress,
waiting for him.

Luis didn't hesitate, he hurriedly unzipped his pants
and fell on top of her. He was hot and horny and he took
her fast.

Irma was dismayed—fast sex reminded her of Anthony. She expected Luis to take his time like he usually did.

"Luis," she objected, making a vain attempt to push
him off her, "what are you doing? Slow down."

"*Qué?*" he muttered. But it was too late—he'd already come.

Irma was disappointed and a little angry. If she wanted fast sex with someone rough, she would hardly have chosen Luis.

She got off the bed and stalked into her bathroom, near tears.

Luis could tell she was upset, so he followed her.

"No, Luis," she said, shaking her head. "Not like that, never like that."

"*Ah, cara*," he said, and very slowly he moved toward her and began peeling down the straps of her white dress, exposing her full breasts.

"No, Luis," she repeated, holding up her hand. "No more."

Ignoring her, he started touching her nipples with the tips of his fingers. Fondling, squeezing, then bending his mouth down and sucking, kissing . . .

She was immediately filled with a fierce and overwhelming desire for this man.

Oh yes, Luis knew how to turn her on. They might not speak the same language, but he certainly knew how to fulfill every one of her fantasies.

CHAPTER THIRTY

It was morning, Max knew that. She knew because she could hear birds singing outside the small room she was locked inside. The one window in the room was boarded up, but light filtered through the cracks.

Her head ached, her shoulders hurt, her stomach rumbled, and she had a desperate need to pee. She'd slept fitfully, experiencing hideous nightmares about Cookie's predictions that Internet Dude could turn out to be some kind of maniac serial killer. Was this person who'd held a gun on them and brought them to the cabin a serial killer? Were her worst nightmares about to come true?

She was lying on a hard bed, her left ankle chained to the sturdy wooden leg of the bed. Ace was nowhere in sight.

Pulling her thoughts together, she started going over the events of yesterday in her head. The drive to Big Bear, the waiting around for her Internet guy to show, hooking up with Ace, and finally the weasel-faced stranger approaching her and telling her he was Grant, although he looked nothing like the picture he'd posted. What a liar! What a creep!

Fortunately, Ace had reappeared all set to rescue her, but the man had pulled a gun on them, then forced them both into her car. He'd made Ace drive while he'd sat in the back next to her.

She was horrified at what was happening. Then she'd

started thinking that maybe it was a hoax, some kind of weirdo TV show that Cookie and Harry had set up.

But no, they wouldn't be so nuts.

I'm not frightened, she'd told herself. *I refuse to be scared.*

But when the man had leaned over and forced a blindfold around her eyes, she'd finally felt the cold grip of fear.

"Where're we headin'?" Ace had asked at one point.

"Be quiet and drive," Grant had replied in a low, even voice. "Follow my instructions and do not say another word."

"You'll never get away with this," Ace had muttered.

"That's for me to decide."

Scrunched in the backseat, she'd stayed as far away from the Internet Freak as possible, managing somehow or other to remain calm. She'd thought about her mom. What would Lucky do?

Oh man, Lucky would probably kick his ass big-time. Her mom was known for taking no prisoners, and although they had their differences, under it all Max really admired her.

They must have driven for at least half an hour before finally stopping. When the car came to a halt, Internet Freak had ripped the blindfold from her eyes, and she'd seen that they were parked outside a cabin in a heavily wooded and seemingly remote area.

"Both of you—get out of the car," he'd ordered.

Ace had slid out of the driver's seat and stationed himself next to the car.

"And you," he'd said to Max. "Tie his hands behind his back."

"With what?" she'd answered, staring him down, letting him know she wasn't intimidated, not her.

"Use your blindfold for now."

She'd tied Ace's hands, making the knot as loose as possible.

"Stay cool," Ace had whispered when she was close to him. "We'll get out of this."

"I know," she'd whispered back.

"Tighter," Internet Freak had said, watching her closely.

She'd redone the knot, her heart beating fast, her mind reliving every horror movie she'd ever seen. Those kinds of films were always set in some backwoods area, and there was always a teen couple who inevitably ended up dead on arrival. Oh, great! Was that their destiny?

"What do you want?" she'd asked, turning to face him. "Money? 'Cause my mom will pay you."

"Your mom," Internet Freak had sneered. "I don't want your mom's money, I have plenty of my own."

"Then what *do* you want?" she'd asked, keeping her voice firm.

"I'll tell you when I'm ready to tell you," he'd said. "And stop asking questions."

He'd then instructed Ace to get in the trunk of the car. When Ace objected, he'd threatened to shoot her, so Ace had complied.

After that was done he'd commanded her to enter the house. Once inside he'd shoved her into the small room and manacled her ankle to the leg of the bed. Then he'd left her there without saying another word.

Now it was morning and she had no idea what was going on.

Where was Ace? Was he all right?

Where was Internet Freak? What were his intentions?

He'd taken away her purse with her cell phone, but surely by this time someone would've called her and realized she was missing? Her mom, Cookie, Harry—they'd all been so adamant she had to check in.

The room smelled musty, as if it hadn't been used in

years. Her eyes ached to match her relentless headache. She was desperately hungry and thirsty.

After a few minutes of getting acclimatized, she half fell off the bed, attempting to drag it toward the window.

The bed was too heavy, it wouldn't budge.

She reached down to her ankle. It was beginning to chafe and swell.

"Hey!" she yelled loudly, refusing to panic. "Anyone out there? Anyone at all?"

There was no response.

CHAPTER THIRTY-ONE

Giving Brigette and Bobby a tour of the Keys was a thrill for Lucky. She flew to Vegas every week, so nothing was new to her, but seeing the enormous development through Brigette's and Bobby's eyes was exciting, and they seemed fully impressed, as so they should be. Even if she said so herself, the Keys was awesome.

"This is probably the best hotel I've created," she said proudly. "What do you think?"

"Oh my God," Brigette gasped. "It's amazing. I want to buy one of those apartments today! They're incredible."

"Yes, and I'm happy to say they're nearly all presold, although I think there might be a couple of penthouses still available."

"We'll take 'em," Bobby quipped. "I'll buy one, Brig can have the other."

"I thought you were going to build your own hotel, Bobby," Lucky said, teasing him.

"Maybe I will," he answered. "Put you out of business."

"So that's your ambition, is it?" she asked, hands on hips. "To put your poor old mom out of business?"

"Poor old Mom, my ass!"

They grinned at each other, shadowboxing.

She'd given them the grand tour, making their way through an army of workmen finishing up various areas. Finally they'd reached the private rooftop nightclub where the final touch-ups were taking place.

"Well?" she asked both of them. "Opinions please."

"It's okay," Bobby said, surveying the premises with a critical eye. "I could've done better for you."

"Really," she said coolly, making it more of a statement than a question.

"It's . . . y'know, nothing special."

"Nothing special!" she exclaimed. "Are you kidding me? How about the illuminated staircase? The one-hundred-and-eighty-degree view over the Strip? The indoor fountains? The VIP rooms? The paintings—all originals I might add."

"That's not what makes a great club, Mom. A really cool club is all about the vibe."

"And what vibe would that be?"

"The people, the mix—now, *that's* what makes a club a happening place."

"And what makes you think we won't attract the right people?"

He shrugged.

"Hey, Bobby," she said lightly. "I *do* have major connections. I've built hotels before, I ran Panther Studios, Lennie is one of the most respected directors in Hollywood, so between us we know just about everyone."

"You gotta get 'em young," Bobby explained. "It's all about the youth culture. Hot sexy girls in hot sexy outfits. Rich dudes with their Ferraris and cool dude attitudes. All under thirty-five and horny."

"Thanks, Bobby. Are you trying to make me feel old?"

"You? You'll *never* be old. Look at you, you're the best-looking mom *I've* ever seen."

"And you've seen a lot of them, have you?"

"I get around," Bobby said, laughing.

"Let's get positive here. What's your favorite part of the hotel?"

"The different decors on each floor are amazing,"

Brigette said. "And I love the way the main swimming pool is built so that it's half underground. It's pretty cool that people can swim right into an underground grotto."

"Yeah, that's hot," Bobby agreed. "But you've still gotta make it exciting—like stage a topless wet thong competition, stuff like that."

"Very classy, Bobby," Lucky said dryly. "May I suggest you save that kind of stunt for *your* hotel?"

"How about *guys* in thongs?" Brigette suggested, winking at Lucky. "I'd judge that one!"

"I'm glad to see you're heading back to the real world," Lucky said. "Isn't this better than locking yourself up in your New York apartment and never going out?"

"I guess," Brigette said, quite enjoying herself.

"The golf course is pretty spectacular," Bobby said.

"And great shops," Brigette added. "Gucci, Cartier, Chanel—excellent choices."

Lucky nodded. "The Keys will have the premier shopping mall in Vegas. This is just the beginning."

"Gotta give you props," Bobby said. "When you do it, you *really* do it."

"So I've been told," Lucky said, smiling. "Now, if you two want to go off and play for a couple of hours, I have to sit with Mooney and take care of business. We'll meet back here at three."

"Sounds like a plan," Bobby said. "Come on, Brig, we got us a sexy lap dance waiting."

"Bobby!" Brigette objected. "I told you—no lap dances."

"You know you want it."

"I do not," she said indignantly.

"You gotta stop fighting your impulses," he said, grinning at her.

"For God's sake," Brigette said, breaking out in a smile in spite of herself. "Will you give it a rest?"

"*What?*" Bobby said innocently.

"You know what," she said, linking her arm through his.

The two of them left Lucky surveying her latest kingdom. She wished she'd thought of bringing Gino with them today—it would've been the perfect opportunity for her to give him the grand tour. He and Paige were coming to the big opening ceremony, but that was a major event; she would have preferred giving him a private look.

Her thoughts turned to his party. Thank God she had Philippe on the case. Today he'd be coping with the caterers, the company erecting the huge outdoor tent, the flower deliveries, and security. Everything had to be ready for Gino's party—she wanted it to be the most special day of his extremely eventful life.

She called Lennie to make sure everything was on schedule.

"It's a madhouse here," he complained.

"Where's Gino?"

"Junior's playing tennis. Senior's watching college football on TV."

"Did you call Max?"

"Left a message on her cell."

"And she hasn't called you back?"

"Not yet."

"That kid—"

"Don't go getting excited, I'll talk to her. How's everything there?"

"I'm signing checks and heading right home."

"That's very good news, sweetheart, 'cause I miss you."

CHAPTER THIRTY-TWO

Breaking up was not on the agenda after all. Venus was thoroughly relieved; all her worries that Billy was cooling off had turned out to be nothing but a dumb case of the crabs. Like who hadn't experienced *them?*

After Billy confided his problem, she led him into the bathroom, made him drop his pants, sat him on the side of the tub, picked up his razor, and shaved his pubic area clean as an eight-year-old boy's.

"There! All fixed," she announced. "Now we have matching Brazilians!"

They both broke up laughing.

"Come on," Billy said, grabbing a fresh pair of Levi's. "I'm taking you out to lunch."

"What about the paparazzi?"

"Fuck 'em. We're going to the beach."

Soon Venus was perched on the back of his motorcycle, arms clasped firmly around his waist, a crash helmet covering her platinum curls, a dozen paparazzi in hot pursuit.

They didn't notice. They were both up for an adventure. Things were definitely getting better.

When Alex Woods was working, he was content. Making movies was his sole reason for getting up in the morning. Not only did he write and direct all his own films, but he sometimes produced, usually with a partner. His best producing partner had been Lucky. They'd worked together so well, a perfect fit. No hassles, no use-less fights about the budget, everything was cool with Lucky. *Seduction* was one of his favorite movies. It had made Billy Melina into a star, while Venus had given the best performance of her career.

After they wrapped production, Alex was shattered when Lucky informed him she'd decided not to produce any more movies. He'd argued with her, tried to convince her, but she was adamant.

Lucky was a challenging woman, always pursuing new ideas, always doing exactly what she felt like doing whenever she had the urge. Now she was back in the hotel business in Vegas, and he was a major investor in the Keys. He wasn't worried about his money—with Lucky in charge it was all good. Besides, he enjoyed spending time in Vegas. It was a kick-ass city with plenty going on. There were times when he jumped on a plane, flew to Vegas, gambled for a couple of hours, then made it back to L.A. before midnight. It was relaxing—the perfect quick getaway for a workaholic.

He felt like doing just that on Saturday when he awoke fighting a massive hangover. He had no desire to bring Ling along—her nagging about his drinking turned him off. Who did she think she was, giving her opinion on whether he should drink or not? If she didn't like it, she should pack up and leave.

The truth was he couldn't care less *what* she did. They'd been living together for almost two years—it was long enough. Besides, having a woman living in his house was not an appealing situation. Women were always trying to add feminine touches. Who needed fresh flowers and a fridge full of food? He ate out most of the time—it wasn't his style to indulge in housekeeping.

Without telling Ling, he left his house, drove to the airport, and hopped a plane to Vegas. As long as he had his laptop with him he could work, gamble, maybe get laid if he felt like it, then fly home. He needed the quick break—then he'd resume work on Monday feeling refreshed. Working with Billy Melina was a pain—stardom had gone to the kid's head, not to mention his sure-to-be-disastrous affair with Venus. Alex liked actors to do exactly what he told them to do. Billy wasn't pliable anymore—he had ideas of his own. It pissed Alex off.

The plane was late taking off, and packed. Alex didn't care, he'd never lusted after things like private planes or two-hundred-foot yachts. Cars were his deal—he owned several. Three classic Ferraris, a Porsche, and a vintage Bentley. Ling had taken over driving his Porsche, which didn't thrill him. When she'd first moved in she'd had her own car, but when the lease expired she'd started driving his Porsche. It annoyed him, but he wasn't about to buy her a car. Generosity was not high on his list of things to do for the woman in his life.

In Vegas he usually stayed at the Cavendish. They always took care of him, and the owner, Renee Falcon, was quite a colorful character.

After checking in, he took a cab over to the Keys to take a look at how things were progressing. He'd visited several times during construction, and the place was unbelievable. Lucky had the touch, but that was no surprise since Lucky always did things with class and style.

The Keys complex was surrounded by high-security fences with guards stationed at key points.

Alex flashed his pass at one of the guards. "Mooney around?" he asked.

"He's up in the main communication offices meeting with Ms. Santangelo."

Had he heard right? Was Lucky in town? She hadn't mentioned she was flying in. This was very welcome news indeed.

He strode across the property, past the two huge swimming pools, past the private poker rooms, through the casino, and upstairs to the main office. Everywhere he looked people were busy working toward getting ready for the grand opening.

Since the office door was ajar, he walked right in.

"Mr. Woods," Mooney said, standing up, "this *is* a surprise."

Lucky was sitting in front of a big circular console surrounded by dozens of in-house TV monitors. "Alex," she exclaimed. "What are *you* doing here?"

"The question is, what are *you* doing here?" he responded, happy to see her.

"Check signing," Mooney explained. "Couldn't find anyone else."

"Now this I don't get," Alex said, perplexed. "Lucky Santangelo has to fly to Vegas to sign checks. Are you kidding me?"

"You know how hands-on I am," she said. "There are only four people who can countersign with Mooney, and I happen to be one of them. The other three weren't available, so here I am."

"My friend the control freak," Alex said, shaking his head. "You never fail to amaze me."

"Well, it takes one to know one," she said, grinning. "And how come *you're* here?"

"Working with that asshole Billy Melina, I found myself in desperate need of some R 'n' R."

"Is Billy being difficult?"

"You know what it's like with actors—give 'em a taste of success an' they think they walk on water."

"I never imagined Billy would go that route."

"He has. They all do."

"Lennie never did."

"Lennie's an exception."

"So . . . Billy Melina drove you to Vegas. Hmm . . ."

"Not exactly. I figured that while I'm in town, I'd check out my investment."

"Don't trust me, huh?" Lucky said.

"You're the only one I do trust," Alex responded, quite seriously.

"That's nice," she said, keeping it light.

"Aren't you supposed to be throwing a party tomorrow?"

"This is true, which is why I'm flying back to L.A. this afternoon."

"You here by yourself?" he asked, wondering if Lennie was about to appear and ruin everything.

"Bobby and Brigette came along for the ride."

"Where are they?"

"I'm not sure," she said vaguely. "I think they went off to get a lap dance or something. Perhaps you should join them."

"Lap dances aren't my scene."

"Really?"

"Yes, really."

They exchanged a long slow look.

Sometimes, Lucky thought, if it weren't for Lennie . . .

Lunch at Geoffrey's, a restaurant perched on a cliff overlooking the Pacific Ocean, was suitably romantic. Venus devoured a huge dish of lobster and shrimp. She held hands with Billy across the table and wondered why she'd been feeling so insecure. Everything was perfect. A perfect morning, followed by an exhilarating ride on his motorcycle all the way to the beach, clinging to his back as he broke a few speed records while attempting to ditch the pursuing paparazzi. And now lunch.

She felt as if she was sixteen and in love for the first time. There was certainly something to be said for the joys of a younger man. She tried to imagine Cooper on a bike flying through the mountains at eighty miles an hour. That would never happen. Cooper was into drivers and limos and bodyguards. Cooper lived the life of a big star to the hilt. She'd heard a rumor lately that he was even thinking of stepping into the political arena. Hmm . . . lots of luck with *his* reputation.

Now that things were back on track with Billy, she could start concentrating on her career again. The following month she was in the recording studio laying down final tracks for her upcoming CD, due to be released the same week her fifteen-city concert tour began. After that she had two movies lined up, the launch of her new fragrance, and a line of upmarket sports clothes. Plus she'd promised Lucky that she would make a surprise appearance at the opening of the Keys. Which meant that somewhere along the way she would have to fit in rehearsals with her backup dancers and, since it was a new theater, a serious sound check at the Keys venue.

"You're off on a mind trip," Billy remarked, leaning across the table. "Where you at?"

"Right now I'm here with you," she said affectionately. "I'm thinking how great it would be if we could get to do this every weekend."

"You'd soon be bored."

"No I wouldn't."

An overbearing woman in a lilac pantsuit interrupted them by storming the table and thrusting a slip of paper under Billy's nose.

"My daughter'll never forgive me if I don't ask you to do this," she gushed. "My daughter simply adores you, thinks you're wonderful. Would you mind signing? Oh my! This'll make her year."

Billy graciously scrawled his signature on the slip of paper, then passed it over to Venus.

The woman started to object—that is, until she

recognized Venus, whereupon she launched into fan overdrive.

Venus signed, not so graciously, and told Billy to get the check.

Somehow or other the spell of being two almost normal people out on a lunch date was broken.

Still . . . it was nice while it lasted.

CHAPTER THIRTY-THREE

The offices Anthony Bonar kept in Mexico City were merely a front. Beneath the facade of a thriving import/export business most of his dealings in the drug trade took place.

He entered his private office, nodding at a couple of trusted associates he'd summoned from his plane. It was time to make sure everything was on track—shipments, deliveries, cash payments.

Privacy and secrecy were of paramount importance to Anthony—every morning he had a surveillance expert sweep his office for bugging devices. In his business it was imperative to always be careful and alert. One mistake and it could all be over.

His office was spacious, the focal point being an oversized partners desk. In front of the desk stood a big leather couch along with several matching chairs. A fully stocked bar was over in the corner, while one wall consisted of floor-to-ceiling bookcases. This wall featured a concealed door that led into an inner office where Anthony took care of private business. A sophisticated entry code scanned his fingerprints before the concealed door would open, and he was the only person with access. He kept three safes in his second office, all of them stuffed with cash. There was also a private exit to the street should he ever have to get out fast.

After a couple of hours going over the latest business

transactions with his associates, he instructed The Grill to bring the car around. It was time to go home.

"You want I call Mrs. Bonar, tell her you're coming?" The Grill inquired.

"No," Anthony said. "I'll surprise her."

This was a first. Usually he told Irma well in advance when he was coming, but since he planned on only staying overnight he didn't bother. Tomorrow they'd move on to their Acapulco home. He felt like taking a break— the unpleasant experience in Vegas still had him on edge.

Irma would be pleased to see him, especially when he told her they were going to Acapulco, and as an extra surprise he was flying in the children.

On the drive to his house he called the Miami mansion and spoke to the nanny. "Pack everyone up, you're all comin' to Acapulco," he informed her. "My secretary's gonna contact you with flight details. Be there tomorrow."

"The children will not be very happy about this, Mr. Bonar," sniffed the nanny. "They have arrangements with their friends."

"Cancel whatever *arrangements* they got. Tell 'em to bring their friends if it'll keep 'em happy. Make it happen, Nanny, or get your uptight ass fired."

Irma glanced at the bedside clock, noting that it was almost five. Luis was asleep beside her, sprawled across the bed. Since the gardeners' hours were eight until four, she realized that she had to get him out of there before the guards became suspicious. It was one thing Luis being there all day, but all night? She didn't think so. Too risky.

Gently she leaned over and stroked his muscled back. "You have to go," she whispered. "It's getting late."

"*Qué?*" he muttered, turning over and stretching.

"You have to go, Luis," she repeated. "Get up."

"*Ah, sí,* Missus Bonar," he said, leaning on one elbow. "*Veree* good."

"You're starting to speak English," she exclaimed.

"Engleesh," he repeated, a shy smile spreading across his craggy face.

She put her hand against his cheek. "I'm going to teach you a word every time we're together," she promised. "Love. Can you say love?"

"Love," he repeated, rolling off the bed.

She watched him as he picked up his clothes and began pulling on his worn jeans and frayed work shirt. He was certainly what her sister back in Omaha would call a hunk.

She moved close to him, placed her arms around his neck, and impulsively kissed him. "*Adiós,* Luis," she said softly. "*Mañana?*"

"Tomorrow," he agreed, nodding his head.

It pleased her that he'd obviously been trying to learn a few words of English; it proved that he cared. She wished he could spend the night, but how could she outthink the guards? It was impossible. If Luis stayed, they'd know.

Once he left she was faced with a long lonely night by herself. What did Anthony imagine she got up to? He refused to allow her any friends, nor could she entertain when he wasn't in residence.

Well, she was *definitely* entertaining the thought of leaving him, and *that* was one reality he couldn't stop.

Luis lingered in the vast marble hallway on his way out. To think that all this belonged to one man, the house, the grounds, the woman . . .

Ah, the woman. Señor Bonar might own a lot of things, but he sure as hell did not own the woman.

Luis experienced a moment of sheer satisfaction as

he let himself out the front door. The woman was his whenever he wanted her. That was a fact.

He walked around to the back of the house and climbed into his battered truck, then he drove toward the entrance gates of the Bonar mansion.

As he drew his truck up to the wrought-iron gates, one of the guards stepped forward and waved him to stop.

Cursing under his breath, Luis recognized Cesar, the guard, the sometime boyfriend of his slutty sister, Lucia. Luis disliked Cesar intensely.

"Hello, Luis," the man said in Spanish. "What's goin' on?"

Luis shrugged and told him that nothing much was going on.

"You're working late today," Cesar said, consulting his watch. "It's past five."

"I had things to do," Luis said.

"What things?" Cesar asked.

"Things in the house for Señora Bonar," Luis said evasively.

"You seem to be spending a lot of time in the house," Cesar said.

"When Señora Bonar wants something, it is my job to take care of it."

"I'm sure," Cesar sneered.

Luis held his temper in check. Was Cesar insinuating something?

"How's your lovely wife?" Cesar asked.

"Very well," Luis replied.

"Give her my regards. Tell her I drop by for supper one night, your sister asks me all the time."

"You'd be very welcome," Luis lied, experiencing a sick feeling in the pit of his stomach. Maybe he was taking too many risks spending so much time in the house with Señora Bonar. But then again, why shouldn't he? There was nobody around to stop him.

"Can you open the gate?" he said.

"You know who's on their way home?" Cesar said, in no hurry to do anything.

"Who?" Luis asked, impatient to get out.

"Señor Bonar."

"*Sí?*"

"Ah," Cesar said, stroking his small black mustache, "here comes his car now."

A sleek silver Mercedes drove into view.

"Pull over, allow him to pass," Cesar ordered Luis in his most officious security guard voice.

Luis did so, staring out of his window at the approaching car. He'd never seen Señor Bonar; all the months he'd worked at the house the master had never appeared.

As the heavy gates opened, Anthony rolled down the back window of his Mercedes, glanced over at Luis, still behind the wheel of his truck, and signaled the guard.

"Who's that?" he snapped, forever suspicious.

"One of the gardeners, Señor Bonar," Cesar replied, standing at attention. "He's leaving now."

"Any problems here?" Anthony inquired.

"No problems, *señor.*"

"Keep it that way."

Anthony took another look at Luis. Their eyes met for a fleeting second.

Luis experienced a full-body shiver of sheer dread. Anthony Bonar had the coldest eyes he'd ever seen.

CHAPTER THIRTY-FOUR

Things were not progressing the way Henry had planned. He'd wanted the girl, not the girl plus one. And the plus one could present problems he'd never even considered.

After locking Maria—or Max, as she was known—into the secure room, he'd had to decide what to do about her so-called cousin. He'd felt a strong urge to shoot him and bury him out in the woods. But that would be wrong, wouldn't it? And Henry had no intention of ending up in jail punished for a crime he'd never meant to commit. So he'd left him in the trunk of Max's car for a while, then later he'd driven to the outhouse in the back of the cabin, and once there he'd opened the trunk. He had not expected the cousin to hurl himself at him screaming expletives, almost knocking him to the ground.

Not quite. Henry recovered quickly, held on to his gun, and waved it in the boy's face. That shut him up.

Henry had never realized before how powerful the threat of shooting someone could be. The gun came from his father's collection. It was not too small, not too big, perfect for threatening purposes. He was quite familiar with guns, for when he was twelve his father had taken him on a hunting trip with several of his rich cronies. They'd flown to Canada on a private plane, then gone on an all-out killing expedition in the wilderness where his father had forced him to shoot wild boar and any other animal that moved. Henry had hated the experience, he'd hated firing the gun, then dealing with the blood and guts of the dead and wounded animals, but at least he'd learned how to handle a gun.

Once he had her cousin securely locked in the windowless outhouse with the solid oak door, he had not felt like starting his relationship with Maria. Yes, Maria—he did not care for the name Max, it was a most unsuitable name for a pretty young girl to adopt as her own. And she *was* pretty. Oh yes, she was very pretty indeed. Prettier than her mother, who had more of an exotic look about her. Maria's face was softer, her lips fuller, and she had the most exquisite emerald green eyes he'd ever seen.

Henry had expected none of this—he'd anticipated that the girl would be a bitch like her mother. The surprise was that this girl could never be a bitch, he'd immediately sensed that she was very special indeed.

He knew he should go to her, assure her that everything would be all right, but somehow he couldn't bring himself to do so. Best to let things lie until the morning. Best not to rush her.

Besides, now that he had her in his power, he was strangely nervous. He wanted her to like him, and he realized that locking her up was not a good start.

He had to think of ways to change the circumstances of their first meeting. Ways to make her like him.

Saturday morning Henry heard her yelling. He was the only one to hear her, for when his father had built the out-of-the-way log cabin, he'd bought up all the surrounding land, guaranteeing complete privacy for miles around.

After his father's unfortunate death, nobody had visited the cabin except him. Henry had a feeling that somehow or other everyone had forgotten it existed, which was fine with him because when his mother passed on it would be his anyway, and he'd been thinking that maybe he'd sell the Pasadena mansion and move to the cabin where nobody could bother him.

It occurred to him that if he was able to gain Maria's trust and convince her what a witch Lucky Santangelo was, perhaps she would come with him—willingly the next time.

Things could have been so different if she hadn't brought her cousin with her. Damn him! This was an inconvenience he hadn't expected. If the cousin hadn't been present she would have come with him quietly, exactly as they'd planned. Hadn't they corresponded nicely on the Internet? Didn't she know plenty about him? The fact that he didn't look like the photo he'd posted meant nothing—she would have soon gotten used to him. He'd posted a photo of an obscure model, knowing if he'd put up a photo of himself she probably wouldn't have come.

Henry was aware that he was not the best-looking man in the world. However, that did not mean he wasn't a talented and accomplished actor, unlike Billy Melina, who was nothing but a pretty boy with no substance.

Henry hated Billy Melina, just as he hated Lucky Santangelo. But he didn't hate Maria. Oh no, one look into those hypnotizing emerald green eyes and he didn't hate Maria. Quite the reverse in fact.

During the night he'd taken Maria's car and driven back to Big Bear, where he'd left it in the Kmart parking lot. Before doing so he'd wiped it clean of prints, feeling like a criminal, which was stupid since he was certainly no criminal. He'd also taken her laptop, which he'd discovered under the passenger seat. After that he'd driven his Volvo back to the cabin and unloaded the supplies he'd stocked up with on his way to Big Bear before the car had run out of gas.

He'd filled the fridge with food, lit a fire, and made the place as comfortable as possible. Then he'd gone to sleep on the foldaway bed in the main room. Now it was morning and he could hear Maria yelling to be let out.

The anticipation of seeing her again filled him with excitement. What would she say to him this morning? How would she feel? She was probably hungry and thirsty, so before unlocking the bedroom door where she was held captive, he prepared a tray with something for her to eat. A dish of cut-up fruit, a glass of orange juice, and two pieces of wheat toast. He wished he'd thought of bringing flowers, even a single rose would've been a nice touch.

When he opened the door he found her sitting on the floor, her ankle still manacled to the leg of the sturdy bed. He immediately noticed her ankle was red and swollen and he felt bad.

"Who *are* you?" she shouted, glaring at him, her expression wild and furious. "What the hell do you want with me? I *hate* you, you freak! Let me out of here!"

He was shocked. He hadn't expected her to hate him. His feelings were hurt.

"I thought you might be hungry," he said, carefully placing the tray on the end of the bed, determined to stay polite in spite of her nasty attitude. "Do you like fruit?"

"What am I supposed to do, grovel and thank you?" she yelled, shooting him another furious look. "I need to use the bathroom."

"I can't let you do that unless you promise to behave," he said, wishing she would stop shouting.

"If you don't let me go to the bathroom," she threatened, "I'll pee all over the floor."

He didn't appreciate vulgarity, it wasn't right. But he had to remember that she'd been raised by Lucky Santangelo, so she obviously didn't know any better.

"I'm trusting you," he said, reaching in his pocket for the key to the shackle on her ankle.

"Trusting me?" she shouted. "Are you out of your fucking *mind*?"

Now she was using foul language, another habit she'd probably picked up from her mother.

He bent down and unlocked the shackle.

She stood up, quite unsteady. He took her arm and led her to the small bathroom his father had added on when he'd found the outhouse was not to his liking.

"Well," she demanded when they reached the bathroom, "are you going to stand there *watching* me? Is that how you get your sick kicks?"

"I'll wait outside," he said stiffly.

She slammed the door in his face and he heard running water.

This was not the way he had planned things at all. His original plan was very clear. They would come to the cabin together, spend a pleasant time talking about all the things they'd e-mailed to each other, and he would have found out plenty about her mother. Only then would he have decided what his next move would be. The way things were turning out was a completely different scenario.

He wasn't happy, and yet he wasn't exactly sad. The girl was his. They were alone together. She was in his power, and Henry had never had anyone in his power before. It felt quite invigorating.

Then he remembered her cousin locked in the outhouse. What was he supposed to do about him? He couldn't let him starve to death.

Perhaps he should drug him, but he hadn't brought any drugs. Who'd have thought it would come to this?

Kill him, a little voice whispered in his head. *It's the only way.*

* * *

Desperately trying not to panic, Max checked out the bathroom. There was a rusty old tub, a shallow sink, and a wooden toilet. That was it. High up was one tiny window, too small to wriggle through.

This was a crazy situation, completely insane. She'd actually been abducted! Was she dreaming? Was this some kind of out-of-control nightmare? If it was, she hoped she'd wake up soon.

Once again she wondered if Cookie and Harry had anything to do with this. Then she thought no, it was impossible.

Gingerly she climbed on top of the wooden toilet making a vain attempt to pry open the tiny window.

It wouldn't shift, the window was totally jammed.

"Crap," she muttered, jumping down, running the tap, and quickly peeing.

He knocked on the door. "Are you coming out?" he asked.

"I'm never coming out, you pervert," she yelled back, pulling up her jeans.

"Then I shall have to come in," he said, opening the door and walking in. "I should look at your ankle," he said. "Is it sore?"

"You're only going to manacle me again, so why bother?" she said, tossing back her long dark hair.

"Not if you make me a promise that you won't go anywhere," he replied, marveling at her beauty.

"You put a fucking *leg iron* on me," she said accusingly. "How could you do that?"

"Kindly control your language, young lady," he said, thinking how pleasant it would be if she would only stop swearing.

"I ain't no lady, mister," she answered, staring at him defiantly. "And you ain't no gentleman."

Taking her arm he led her back into the bedroom.

"Do you *realize* what you're doing?" she said, her

voice rising. "You've *kidnapped* me, forced me to come here with you at gunpoint. That's a federal offense, mister, and when they catch you they'll lock you up and throw away the key."

"They'll never catch me," Henry said confidently, quite enjoying this exchange of words.

"Where's Ace?" she demanded, changing tactics. "What have you done with my cousin?"

"He's perfectly safe," Henry said, once more shackling her ankle to the leg of the bed.

"How do I know that?"

"Because I'm telling you."

"Ha! Big deal. I bet my family is looking for me *and* him, so you'd better let us go, otherwise you're gonna be in *major* fucking trouble."

"You're a very pretty girl with a very dirty mouth," Henry remarked, pursing his thin lips. "Your mother should wash it out with soap."

"What're you, from another century?" she said scornfully.

He didn't like the fact that she was so aggressively verbal. Surely she could sense that he wasn't about to hurt her?

Surely she knew they were destined to be together?

CHAPTER THIRTY-FIVE

After an hour of sitting at the roulette table Brigette was up several thousand dollars. There was nothing like a winning streak to make a girl smile. Bobby kept running off to the crap table, then coming back to check on how she was doing.

"Roulette's an idiot's game—how come you're winning?" he asked, hovering over her shoulder.

"I know," she said, blue eyes gleaming. "I keep on putting a stack of chips on eleven, and can you believe it's come up three times!"

"Way to go, Brig."

"Oh, *yes*."

"Didn't realize you were such a gambler."

"I'm not."

"You could've fooled me."

"Do you mind?" she said, placing more chips across the table. "You're disturbing my concentration."

"Don't go losing it all."

"No intention of doing that."

"And don't pick up any guys," he added, observing that quite a few men lurking around the table had their eyes on her. It was a given. She was undeniably hot.

"Why not, Bobby?" she asked innocently, as if she were totally unaware of the kind of attention she was attracting.

"'Cause *I'm* the one who's watching out for you today—after all, I *am* your big, bad uncle."

216 JACKIE COLLINS

"Surely you mean my *little* uncle," she contradicted, grinning at him. "Let's not forget you're nine years younger than me, Bobby."

"Okay, so I'm your little uncle who's keeping a close eye on his smokin' niece."

"Shh . . . you're messing with my luck," she said, busily placing even more chips around the table.

The wheel started spinning. Once again her number came up. She let out a whoop of delight.

"Wow!" Bobby whispered in her ear. "A few thousand dollars certainly turns *you* on."

"You're right," she said, excitedly scooping in her winning stack of chips. "'Cause this is *my* money, Bobby. I didn't inherit it from anybody. Made it all myself."

"How about cashing in and we go get a drink?"

"I'd sooner have something to eat."

"We can do that too," he said. "Go on, Brig, make a move before you lose it all back."

"If you insist," she sighed, reluctantly pushing her stacks of chips back toward the croupier.

"I was thinking I could take you for a pizza at Spago," Alex suggested, willing her to say yes, because how often did he get a chance to be alone with Lucky?

"Is that what you were thinking?" Lucky said, shuffling through a pile of change orders from various contractors.

"You're finished signing, aren't you?"

"I guess, but there's other things I should go over," she answered vaguely.

"*Now?*"

"Well . . ." she said, hesitating for a moment. "I suppose I *could* do everything on Monday when I come back."

"Go eat," Mooney encouraged, letting out a discreet

burp. "Have fun while you're here. Go toss a few coins in a slot machine."

"Do I *look* like a slot machine kind of girl?" Lucky said dryly.

Mooney roared with laughter.

"Okay, Alex," Lucky said. "I can always find time for a pizza." She turned to Mooney. "Why don't you take a break and come with us?"

"Gonna pass," Mooney said. "Too much to do, but I'll drive you over."

Ten minutes later Mooney dropped them off at Caesars, where they made their way to the outside patio at Spago.

"This is a quite a coincidence," Lucky said after they were seated. "Both of us in Vegas at the same time." She took a long beat before adding, "You wouldn't be stalking me, would you, Alex?"

"Sure," he answered, quite amused. "I'm stalking you, Lucky. Got nothing better to do with my time."

"Sending me notes too?"

"Notes?"

" 'Drop Dead Beautiful.' "

"What the hell are you talking about?"

"I've been getting a series of notes delivered to my house. Could be an invitation to something, but Bobby thinks I should have someone look into it."

"Wanna tell me about it?"

"I just did."

A young waiter came over, handed them both menus, and took their drink orders.

"What exactly do the notes say?" Alex asked, after ordering a Bloody Mary.

"That's it," Lucky said. "Short and simple—'Drop Dead Beautiful.' "

"Sounds like a movie. In fact, I think there *was* a movie with that title."

"The thing that's a bit odd is that the notes are hand-delivered to my house," Lucky said, picking up a glass of water and taking a sip.

"What does your security guard say?"

"I gave up guards a couple of years ago. Didn't want to live like that, nor do I want my children thinking they have to be protected."

"No?"

"*Definitely* no. I've hired security for Gino's party, but other than that I want to be able to get in my car and go places without being followed and watched."

"Y'know, Lucky," Alex said thoughtfully, "you have a big reputation and a ton of money. You *should* have security."

"Don't need it, Alex."

"Okay," he said, picking up the menu. "Let's talk pizza. What you got in mind?"

"I'm thinking smoked salmon," she said, relieved he was dropping it.

"I'm thinking I'll join you," he said, snapping his fingers for their waiter.

After they'd ordered, Lucky sat back and took a long look at Alex. He was aging well—in fact, he looked better now in his late fifties than ever. He was super smart, very attractive, and extraordinarily talented. She wondered why no woman had been able to lure him into marriage.

"Where's Ling?" she asked casually.

"Ling doesn't fly well," he responded.

"You know, Alex," she said, fingering the rim of her water glass, "you should get married. You need a woman to look after you."

"Yeah," he answered, giving her a look. "And who do you think that woman should be?"

"Haven't given it any thought," she said offhandedly.

"Apparently you have."

"No."

"No?" he said disbelievingly.

"I do have a few things on my mind other than your marital status," she said, fishing her sunglasses out of her purse and putting them on.

"Yeah," Alex drawled sarcastically. "It's bright in here, isn't it?"

"Fuck you," Lucky responded, trying not to smile, because she had to admit that Alex knew her so well. He even knew that whenever she felt uncomfortable she hid behind her shades.

"Anytime," he said, half smiling. "All you have to do is name a time and a place."

"Oh, shut up," she said, finally laughing.

"And she finds me an object of amusement," he said dryly.

The waiter delivered their drinks to the table—a Bloody Mary for Alex, Perrier for Lucky.

"This is nice," Alex said, picking up his drink.

"What's nice?"

"You and me sitting here enjoying some time together, just the two of us."

"This is hardly a date," Lucky pointed out. "So don't try making it into one. We're good friends who happened to run into each other."

"Good friends who are never alone anymore."

"Any*more*, Alex?" Lucky said, raising an eyebrow.

"When we were making *Seduction* we had plenty of alone time," Alex reminded her. "I remember it well."

"Sure," Lucky said lightly. "Us and a crew of hundreds."

"I guess you're choosing to forget all the time we spent in the editing rooms?"

"Why do you think I wasn't prepared to make another movie with you?" she said flippantly.

"Don't be like that."

"Like *what?*"

"Like you don't feel that there's anything between us."

"Alex," Lucky said impatiently. "I've told you this before, there can't be anything between us."

"Because of Lennie?"

"I love Lennie, you *know* that. How many times do I have to tell you?"

He sighed. "There's something I've always wanted to say to you."

"Please don't," she said, drumming her fingers on the table. "I don't want to hear it."

"I'm going to."

"No, Alex, you're not," she said firmly.

Before he could reply, Bobby and Brigette strolled into view.

Lucky immediately waved them over to the table, delighted to create a distraction.

"Alex," Brigette exclaimed, flushed from her recent win. "Haven't seen *you* in ages."

"It's been a long time," Alex agreed, standing up. "And look at you, Bobby, I hear you're running the hottest club in New York."

"Tell my mom," Bobby said wryly. "I'm not sure she believes me."

"Sit down, join us," Lucky said quickly. "We're about to have smoked salmon pizza."

"Delicious!" Brigette exclaimed. "I'm starving!"

"Then we shall order two more," Lucky said, signaling their waiter.

Alex threw her a look. "Of all the joints in Vegas they had to pick this one," he murmured ruefully. "Timing's everything, huh?"

Lucky nodded. "It sure is."

And once again they exchanged an oh-so-intimate smile.

CHAPTER THIRTY-SIX

When Internet Freak returned later that day with a tray of food and a bottle of water, Max was ready for him. She'd had all afternoon to think about what she was going to say.

"You should know that I'm only sixteen," she announced, making a desperate attempt to let the creep know how young she was. Maybe, just maybe, it might convince him to release her. "When I told you I was eighteen," she continued, "I was lying. And another thing, I never mentioned to my mom that I was meeting some strange guy, and when she finds out I'm missing, she'll major *freak*!"

"But you're not missing," Henry said patiently. "You're here with me. You're perfectly safe."

Unexpected tears filled her eyes. This dude was a looney and she couldn't take much more of this insane situation. "I'm *not* safe," she shouted, forcing her tears to go away. "I'm your fucking *prisoner*. You've kept me locked up here since last night. YOU'VE GOT TO LET ME GO!"

"Eventually," Henry said, quite composed.

Eventually. What did *that* mean?

Gotta stay strong, she told herself. *It's not smart to show weakness.* Ever since she was a little girl, Lucky had drilled into her that girls can do anything. Lucky's mantras: *Be strong. Kick ass when necessary. Never give in.*

Well, there was no way she was giving in to this creepo loser with his weaselly face and psycho lifeless eyes.

Taking a deep breath, she glared angrily at her captor. "Where's Ace?" she demanded. "Why are you keeping us apart?"

"That is not your concern," he said.

"Yes it *is*," she argued, still glaring at him. "Where is he?"

"I sent him away."

"No you didn't."

"Yes I did."

It suddenly occurred to her that Ace and Internet Freak might be in cahoots. It was very possible that Ace was part of the plan and *that's* why he wasn't around. Of course. It was all so obvious. He'd sent Ace to soften her up and then pounced. How stupid was she to fall for it?

She shivered uncontrollably.

"Are you cold?" Henry asked, sounding concerned.

"I'm uncomfortable," she complained. "You'd better undo this thing on my ankle 'cause it really hurts."

"If I do, you'll try to run. But I should warn you that there is nowhere to run to. We are in an isolated spot surrounded by woods, and you would be very foolish to attempt to leave."

"I won't run," she lied.

"Can I trust you?"

"Do I look like an idiot?"

He produced the key and undid the shackle.

She rubbed her ankle, which was blistered and red. "I need disinfectant," she said. "I can barely walk."

"I'll see what I have," he said, leaving the room, locking the sturdy door behind him.

Immediately after he was gone, she jumped off the bed and made it to the window. It was boarded up with strips of plywood on the outside. A quick exploration of the room did not give up anything that looked even remotely useful.

Crap! She'd been hoping for something—anything that she could use as a weapon when he returned. Smash him over the head and run. He wasn't holding his gun, and he looked like a weakling with his gimpy leg and scrawny build. She was sure she could take him.

Yes. She didn't need a weapon. She was strong, she'd taken self-defense classes.

Her plan was to catch him off guard, kick him hard in the balls—and run like hell.

CHAPTER
THIRTY-SEVEN

The villa in Acapulco was Anthony's favorite home. He'd designed every detail of the three-story waterfront villa himself, from the Italian marble bathrooms (six) to the sunken black-bottomed infinity swimming pool overlooking Acapulco Bay.

The grounds consisted of a magnificent landscape of coconut trees, giant palms, and fragrant walls of many different colors of bougainvillea. There were several areas for dining alfresco. Anthony's favorite part of the outdoor design was an all-glass elevator that descended from the top floor of the house to the lower-level entertainment area. He'd been inspired by the movie *Scarface*.

Another feature Anthony was particularly pleased with was his own personal boat dock and heliport, where a select few of his business acquaintances could come and go without the outside world checking on their activities. It was a very convenient way of conducting business.

Anthony kept a full staff in residence, including Manuel and Rosa Sousa, a married couple who ran the estate when he was not there. Rosa was a magnificent cook, while Manuel oversaw everything else. They had worked for Anthony since he'd built the villa ten years previously.

One day Emmanuelle had seen pictures of the villa and begged him to take her there. "It's so beautiful," she'd sighed longingly. "And very *sexy*. We could make love in every room." A seductive pause. "Maybe even in the elevator. What do you think, honeybun? Will you take me there?"

He'd thought it was quite an appealing idea, but he had yet to invite her. It was one thing entertaining his mistresses in other cities, but to bring them into one of his homes . . . maybe not. Even Anthony observed *some* boundaries.

Irma had been startled to see him, even more startled when he'd informed her they were flying to Acapulco the following morning.

"Why didn't you let me know you were coming?" she'd asked. "Nobody is prepared."

"What? You don't like surprises?" he'd responded, fondling his two large dogs, and deciding that his wife looked as if she'd lost weight. Not that Irma was ever fat—quite the contrary—but she was looking particularly sleek and attractive. Hardly Emmanuelle-style attractive, nor Carlita, but for the mother of two children, she wasn't bad.

That night he'd given her the pleasure of blowing him, and the next morning they were on their way to Acapulco, accompanied by two other couples he didn't mind spending time with. Fanta and Emilio Guerra were rich Mexicans in the clothing business. And Innes and Ralph Masters were Americans who lived in Mexico City. The two men greatly admired Anthony, while their wives lusted after him. It amused Anthony the way the two couples glorified him. They laughed at his jokes, took full advantage of his generous hospitality, and clapped at his singing prowess.

All in all they were an adoring entourage, and who didn't enjoy being adored?

Irma shuddered when she realized how close she'd come to getting caught. God! What if Anthony had walked in on her and Luis? It was scary and unthinkable. She'd had a narrow escape, and it had shaken her, made her think about the risks she was taking.

Anthony turning up unannounced was most unusual—in fact, she could not recall it ever happening before. There were always the calls to warn her of his imminent arrival, and then much activity would take place in the house as everything was cleaned and scrubbed to a spotless finish, the dogs were groomed, the friends were alerted, and by the time Anthony arrived, everything was in place.

This time not only had he arrived home unexpectedly, but he'd announced that they were leaving for Acapulco the next day. Irma had no wish to go to Acapulco with her husband, but she could hardly say no, especially when he informed her that the children were meeting them there. At least that was some kind of consolation.

Later that night, lying in bed, he'd started pawing her for a few seconds before pushing her head down until it was on a level with his penis. She knew what he wanted, and she was forced to oblige, for the consequences of *not* doing what Anthony wanted were not pretty. So she'd shut her eyes and pretended it was Luis she was servicing, and somehow or other she'd managed to get through it.

In the morning they'd boarded the plane with his friends in tow.

Under different circumstances she might have quite liked Fanta and Innes—they seemed to be pleasant enough women. But circumstances were such that all they did was buzz around Anthony, hanging on to his every word.

Ralph Masters was a lecherous creep. Whenever Anthony's attention was elsewhere, Ralph managed to make suggestive remarks toward Irma—remarks she would never dare repeat to Anthony. Emilio Guerra, on the other hand, chose to totally ignore her, treating her as if she didn't exist. As far as Emilio was concerned, she was just a wife, and therefore hardly worth his attention.

The plane ride was excruciating. Champagne and caviar flowed, while Anthony's sycophants agreed with everything he said.

It wasn't where Irma wanted to be. She'd allowed her thoughts to drift, wondering how Luis would feel when he came to work and found she wasn't there. Someone would probably mention that the master of the house had arrived home, and Señora and Señor Bonar had left for the Acapulco house.

She'd asked Anthony how long they would be staying in Acapulco. "What does it matter?" he'd said. "We stay as long as I wanna stay."

That was Anthony Bonar. He never told anyone what he was doing from one day to the next.

Anthony's two large Dobermans traveled on the plane with them. The dogs always made Irma nervous, so much so that when Anthony was not in residence she insisted that they stay outside with the guards. When he was home, Anthony allowed them to sleep on the bed, and it terrified her, but when she complained, her husband simply laughed at her fears.

The Acapulco villa was Anthony's domain. The couple who worked for him, Manuel and Rosa, kissed his ass big-time.

Upon their arrival Anthony picked Rosa up and swung her around for the benefit of his friends. She was a short woman, and quite plump. Placing a fake smile on her face she tolerated the manhandling, but Irma sensed she loathed the way Anthony treated her.

"How's my Rosa, huh?" he'd crowed, pinching her cheek with a not-too-gentle touch. "Rosa's worked for me ten years, but I could fire her tomorrow, huh, Rosa? Would I do that? No, 'cause you're the best little cook in the whole of Acapulco."

Anthony was showing off in front of his friends, flexing his control.

"Okay, Manuel," he'd said. "Get your lazy ass to the airport, go meet my kids. They're coming. It's good, huh?"

Yes, Irma thought, *it's very good.* At least she would get to see her children.

And back in Las Vegas, an investigation was about to take place concerning Tasmin Garland's disappearance. Her babysitter reported to the police that Tasmin had not returned home on Friday night. Her ex-husband, a croupier at one of the hotels, followed the babysitter's concerns by filing a missing-persons report. He was about to get remarried, and much as he loved his son, he did not plan on having the boy live with him.

Where was Tasmin Garland? Forty-eight hours had passed since she was last seen; it was question time. Diane Franklin, a tenacious, twice-divorced black detective in her mid-forties, was assigned the case.

After talking to the babysitter and the ex-husband, the next person she had on her list to question was Renee Falcon.

CHAPTER THIRTY-EIGHT

Playing with Billy on his home turf was a revelation for Venus. Instead of staying in her fortresslike mansion, where she felt safe away from the adulation of her rabid fans, she and Billy were out and about. First the ride on his motorcycle, which she'd never done before, then the delightful lunch at Geoffrey's, and after that they'd stopped at the Cross Creek shopping center in Malibu, where she'd purchased a shady sun hat, a pair of black-out sunglasses, and a nondescript track suit.

"Disguise time," he'd informed her.

"I have plenty of disguises at home," she'd assured him.

"I know, but you're not at home, are you?"

"We'll never fool the paparazzi, they're out in droves."

"Trust me," Billy had said, grinning. "I got a plan."

Carrying her purchases, she'd hopped on the back of his bike and they'd taken off again.

There was something very sexy about riding on the back of a motorcycle. It had to do with contact—the way her breasts felt pressed up against his back, the wind in her face, the warmth of his body. She'd held on tightly as they'd sped down the Pacific Coast Highway, several paparazzi still in hot pursuit.

"Why can't they leave us alone?" she'd breathed in his ear.

" 'Cause they got a job to do, an' *my* job is losing

'em," he'd answered, before making an illegal U-turn and roaring off in the opposite direction.

Venus couldn't help laughing. It was highly dangerous but unbelievably exciting—it made her realize just how much she'd been missing out on the fun side of life.

Being married to Cooper could do that to a girl. Cooper Turner, legendary movie star, legendary cocksman, and very boring when one was married to him. That's why their marriage had failed, because Cooper had forgotten how to have fun. He'd turned into the reformed playboy. Marriage had changed him, but it hadn't changed her. She'd always had a rebellious streak, and just because she was a few years older than Billy, it didn't mean that he couldn't bring it out in her.

"I think you've lost the paparazzi," she said breathlessly. "I think they're history."

"You just gotta have the moves," Billy boasted, making a sharp left turn toward Paradise Cove. "I want you to go to the ladies' room an' put on your disguise."

"That's a bit pointless, isn't it, since everyone will still recognize you?"

"Not unless I want 'em to," Billy said. "I got the kinda face that blends in."

"No you don't," she said, laughing.

"Yes, I do," he insisted.

"How about the woman who came up to you in Geoffrey's? It wasn't *me* she recognized, it was *you*."

"I have that effect on women," he joked. "If they look me in the eyes, they got me."

"You can be such a punk."

"Think so?"

"Apparently Alex does."

"How do *you* know *that*?"

"'Cause he complained about you to Lucky."

"Oh, that's great. What did he say?"

"He thinks all your success has gone to your head."

"Maybe Alex should move with the times," Billy said irritably. "I'm not about to be his puppet an' jump every time he tells me to. I have my own ideas. I'm gonna direct one of these days."

"I'm sure you will."

"I *know* I will."

The rest of the day was equally blissful. They'd walked along the beach holding hands, fooled around on the sand, and paddled in the surf. It had been a long time since she'd felt so totally carefree—that is, until the paparazzi discovered them again, and then it was over.

On the ride home she said, "I think I'll stay at your house tonight."

"That'll be a first," Billy shouted, roaring down the fast lane. "You've never wanted to stay there before."

"Tonight I do," she answered, hugging him even tighter.

Arriving back at Billy's, they discovered Kev stretched out on the couch with a bottle of beer in one hand and a carton of popcorn in the other. He was busy watching motor racing on TV.

"Venus," he exclaimed, abruptly sitting up and brushing popcorn off his jeans.

"Kev," she responded. "How's it hangin'?"

"No complaints," he said, hurriedly getting off the couch.

Billy threw him a look. Kev was no slouch in the getting-the-hint department. "Guess we won't be watchin' the game tonight," he said.

"That's right," Billy replied.

"*Okay*," Kev said, sliding toward the door. "Think I'll be movin' on."

"See ya, dude," Billy said. "Come to the location Monday."

"I'll do that," Kev replied, and then he was gone.

"Doesn't it bother you, him coming and going as he pleases?" Venus asked once Kev had left.

"'Course not," Billy said, grabbing a handful of pop-corn. "Kev's like my brother."

"We could be making love, and he could walk right in on us."

"Lucky him."

"Seriously, Billy."

"Stop bitchin' and come over here, babe," Billy said affectionately, dropping down onto the still warm couch and holding out his arms.

So she did, and everything was great.

Sunday morning they awoke late, read the papers, and lounged around the house. Billy put on college football, while Venus attempted to make scrambled eggs in the kitchen. She hadn't cooked in a while, and they turned out mushy, but at least she'd tried.

"Do we *have* to go to that party tonight?" Billy asked, trying to pretend he was enjoying the eggs. "I'm not in a party mood, and I have a real early call tomorrow."

"Yes, we have to go," Venus said. "It's for Lucky's father, and since she's my best friend, I can't *not* go. Anyway, Gino's a great character."

"He is?"

"You've met him, haven't you?"

"I might've, but that would've bin a few years ago when we were making *Seduction*."

"Then tonight you'll see him again," she said, stand-ing up and ruffling his hair. "Here's a thought—how about developing a movie about Gino's life? It would make quite a story. Way back his nickname was Gino the Ram—seems he was quite a stud in his day."

"Would I get to play Gino?" Billy asked, stifling a yawn.

"Are you five-foot-eight, dark-haired, and an Italian American?" Venus said, smiling.

"No, but I'm a stud, aren't I?"

"Oh, yes!"

"Well . . ."

"Billy, this party is important to me. Don't give me a hard time."

"Okay, babe, we'll go."

She hugged him. "That's my Billy."

Later, when it was time for her to go home and get ready for the party, she'd called a cab, taken it to the Beverly Hills Hotel, then waited five minutes before coming out and getting in her car.

Fooling the paparazzi was a full-time job.

Ling wasn't talking to Alex, and he didn't give a shit. She was annoyed that he'd gone to Vegas without her. It didn't seem to matter that he'd come back the same night—she was in full nagging mode.

"You know, Ling, I don't need this," he said, giving her a warning look as he walked into his study overlooking the ocean. "I got work to do."

"I don't need it either," she responded, following him. "You're very cold toward me, Alex. You never pay any attention to me. I sit in your house all day—"

"Don't give me that," he interrupted. "You're a lawyer. You go to work."

"And then I come home and cook dinner and you're never here. You show up anytime you want, usually drunk."

"Then why do you stay?"

"Because"—her voice quavered—"I love you, Alex."

Love. The *L* word. Christ! What had he done to deserve this?

"I'm sorry, Ling," he said, not really sorry at all. "This isn't working out for me."

"And don't think I don't know why," Ling said spitefully. "It's because of Lucky, isn't it? Every time you see her you're like a different person. You turn into a puppy dog. If you had a tail it would wag."

"Quit saying such ridiculous crap," he said, sitting down in front of his computer.

"I can see it, and I'm sure everyone else can too," Ling insisted. "*Especially* Lennie."

"You're full of it."

"Look in the mirror, Alex. Look in the mirror and see a man who's in love with another man's wife."

"What do you want from me, Ling?" he said, losing his temper. "I'm not about to marry you. I'm not about to commit to a long-term relationship. *What* the fuck do you want from me?"

"Nothing," she said sulkily.

"Okay, now we've established that, are you staying or going?"

"I'll stay," she said. "Because I know you'll realize in time that I *am* the right woman for you."

Why was it so damned difficult getting a woman to leave?

CHAPTER THIRTY-NINE

Sunday morning Internet Freak unlocked the door and entered the room where Max had spent a second miserable night with her ankle shackled to the leg of the bed.

Her clever plan of instant freedom had not worked. Yesterday, when he'd returned with a bottle of disinfectant, she'd been all primed and ready to kick him in the balls and make a swift run for it. Unfortunately he'd turned out to be stronger than she'd thought. The moment she'd attempted to jump him, he'd grabbed her arms in a steel lock behind her back, and forced her onto the bed.

She was shocked at his strength. Shocked and horrified. Was he going to rape her? Was that why he'd kidnapped her?

But no, he didn't attempt that. He'd shackled her ankle again, informed her he was most disappointed that she was not to be trusted, and stormed out of the room, not returning until now.

"Call your mother and leave a message," he said, thrusting her cell phone into her hands.

"What'm I supposed to say?" she muttered, glaring at him.

"Tell her you're with friends and you've decided to stay longer."

"You must be like super *crazy!*" she yelled, still desperately trying to bury her fear. "I keep on telling you—my mom's expecting me home today for a big party. If I don't get there she'll have *everyone* out looking for me, and believe me, when she finds out what you've done, you'll be *major* sorry. Nobody messes with my mom. Nobody. She *kills* people who do."

Henry shoved the phone into her hands. "Do it," he said. "People keep leaving you messages wondering why you're not calling them back."

"My friends have probably gone to the cops already," she said, sure that Cookie and Harry must be freaking out because they hadn't heard from her.

"Why would they do that?"

"'Cause you're holding me here, a prisoner."

"They don't know that."

"Oh yes they *do!* You're screwed, mister."

"That's why you'll make a call, to put everyone's mind at rest," he said, determined to ignore her rudeness because he was sure that deep down she couldn't possibly mean it.

"I'm hungry," she said. "Give me something to eat and I'll make the call."

"You will?"

"Yes," she said sulkily, thinking that perhaps there was a way to convey that she was in serious trouble.

Henry nodded and shuffled his feet. His original plan had been to get back at Lucky Santangelo, but plans change, and now he wanted to make Maria see just how good he could be for her. Why not? He had plenty of money, or at least he would have when his mother died, which hopefully might be soon. He was not a gambler or a cheat. He was a nice guy. A regular guy. He was the same person she'd corresponded with online and liked enough to meet.

The truth was he was enamored with this girl. Right now she was all that mattered to him, and given more time he was certain he could convince her to like him back.

"I'll get you something to eat," he said. "Then you'll make the call?"

She nodded.

He left the room thinking that his immediate problem was what to do about Ace. Since locking him in the outhouse, he had not ventured back. He was hoping that when he finally opened the door the boy would be in too weak a state to attack him.

How long could someone live without food and water?

It wouldn't be his fault if Ace expired in there. That would not be murder. That would just be unfortunate.

CHAPTER FORTY

"She's sixteen," Lucky pointed out. "Sixteen, Lennie. She should have *some* sense of responsibility."

"How responsible were you at sixteen?" Lennie questioned.

Sometimes Lennie drove her crazy with his laid-back attitude. "I was fucking *married* for chrissakes," she pointed out. "It's Sunday, and there's absolutely *no* excuse for her not returning our calls. You've left two messages. I've left three. She ran out of here without saying good-bye, and I don't mind telling you I'm major pissed."

"No? Really?" he said in a lightly mocking tone. "Whyn't you tell me how you *really* feel?"

"Don't do this, Lennie," she warned, flashing him a deadly look. "Do not piss me off even more."

"Listen," he said encouragingly. "Max will be home in time for Gino's party, so try and hold off the big mother/daughter fight until tomorrow."

"What fight?" Bobby asked, bouncing into the room.

"Your little sister," Lucky said.

"Yeah, what about my little sister?"

"We haven't been able to reach her," Lucky said, fuming. "And if she doesn't get home in time for Gino's party, that's *it*—she's grounded for the rest of the year."

"I'm kinda pissed at her too," Bobby remarked. "I was looking forward to us hanging out. Max is *the* best."

"She's not the best at all," Lucky said sharply. "She's a brat."

"No way, Mom."

"She is, Bobby," Lucky insisted. "You don't have to live with her. Everything I say she turns into an argument."

"I know I keep repeating myself," Lennie said. "But face it, Lucky, she's *exactly* like you were at her age. The kid's a rebel, does things her way. You should understand that better than anyone."

"Oh God," Lucky said, shaking her head. "You two, one look at a pretty face and that's it, you both turn to mush."

"Yeah, Mom," Bobby said. "That's why we've always done exactly what *you* want us to do. And talking about that—what *do* you want us to do today? There's people everywhere, so is there anything I can do to help with the party?"

"Yes—stay out of the way."

"Is that it?"

"I don't know, Bobby, I'm so mad right now."

"I could take everyone out to lunch."

"Great idea. Take them to the Hotel Bel-Air and get a table on the patio. Gino will like that."

"Here's a thought," Lennie said.

"What?" Lucky sighed.

"If you're so upset with Max, call her girlfriend Cookie, the one she was going to Big Bear with. When she answers, have her put Max on."

"Are you saying that Max is *purposely* avoiding speaking to us?" Lucky said, frowning.

"You know your daughter, she's not into lectures."

"I don't have Cookie's phone number."

"Isn't her father that soul singer, Gerald M.?" Bobby inquired. "I can get you his number from our computer at the club—everybody who's anybody's listed. One call and the number's yours."

"Do it," Lucky said. "Before I run out of patience."

"When you speak to Max, no fighting," Lennie said. "Just make sure she'll be back in time for the party."

"Any other instructions?" Lucky asked, shooting him an "I do not appreciate being told what to do" look.

"Y'know, on second thought, *I* should be the one to call Cookie," Lennie decided. "Go get the number, Bobby."

"Like I don't have enough with the hotel opening and the party for Gino," Lucky grumbled as Bobby left the room. "This is a joke. I'm wiped out."

"Who was it that insisted on flying to Vegas yesterday?" Lennie said. "I think that might've been you. You should've had Mooney bring *you* the checks."

"There was a whole stack of them."

"What happened to the woman from the bank who was supposed to cosign?"

"Who the fuck knows?—Mooney's trying to locate her. I refuse to deal with that bank again. I instructed Mooney to switch our accounts."

"That's pretty harsh, isn't it?"

"No. If the woman can't be bothered to cosign the checks, I refuse to keep someone so unreliable around. We're a huge account, she should be more responsible."

Bobby returned with Gerald M.'s private number.

Lucky started to punch the number into her cell phone. Lennie grabbed it from her. "I said *I'll* do it."

The phone rang. Finally somebody picked up. "Gerald?"

"Who's askin'?"

"Lennie Golden, Max's dad."

"Great t'hear from you, Lennie," Gerald said, sounding stoned. "How ya doin', man?"

"Not bad," Lennie responded. "I need Cookie's cell phone number."

"How's that?"

"The girls are in Big Bear and Max is having a problem with her phone, so we thought we'd reach her on Cookie's."

"Yeah, yeah," Gerald M. said. "Cookie can give it to you herself, she's standing right here."

"She is?" Lennie said.

"Cookie," Gerald M. called out. "Baby girl, get over here."

Lennie turned to Lucky. "Cookie's in L.A.," he said. "She's coming to the phone."

"You've *got* to be kidding me," Lucky said, snatching the phone out of his hand. "Cookie?"

"Oh, uh, hi, Mrs. Golden."

"Where are you?"

"I'm, uh, at my dad's house."

"I thought you were going to a party in Big Bear with Max."

"Uh, y-yes," Cookie stammered. "Well, um . . . I was like *there*, but then I had to get back early."

"Didn't you and Max drive up to Big Bear together?"

"No, we, um . . . took separate cars, so, uh . . . that's why I'm like home, 'cause I had my own car."

"Cookie," Lucky said, smelling trouble, "what *is* going on?"

"Nothing, Mrs. Golden," Cookie said, brimming with fake innocence.

"Whose party was it?" Lucky demanded.

"Um, this friend of mine. Like she's this girl I know."

"Give me the house phone number."

"The party was on Saturday, it's way over."

"I understand that, but I'd like to speak to your friend's mother."

"You can't do that, they've flown back to Aspen."

"Back to Aspen," Lucky repeated. "Y'know, Cookie, do me a favor, get your ass in your car and drive over here. I need to talk to you face-to-face."

"But Mrs. Golden—"

"Cookie, this is not up for discussion. Do it, and do it now."

CHAPTER FORTY-ONE

On the way over to the Santangelo/Golden house, Cookie frantically punched out Harry's number. He finally answered after three attempts.

"Where have you *been*?" she screeched. "I'm in major crap city."

"With my dad," Harry answered. "We're on a TV set. The reception on my phone sucks."

"Did you reach Max yet?"

"No. I've left messages."

"So have I," Cookie said. "And listen to this—I've been summoned to her house by Lucky."

"*Whaaat?*"

"Yeah, she tracked me down, and now I like have to go to her house and explain where Max is."

"This is bad," Harry said. "What are you going to say?"

"I dunno," Cookie said. "I mean, Lucky's gonna ask me all these questions about where the party was an' like who the people were an' was Max staying there. What *am* I gonna *say*?"

"Don't sweat it," Harry said, annoyingly unconcerned. "It's Sunday, Max'll be back soon."

"I hope so," Cookie wailed. "'Cause truthfully I'm kinda freaked that she hasn't answered our calls."

"Me too."

"She goes off with some Internet asshole an' we hear nothing. It's like too *weird*."

"Maybe you'd better tell her mom."

"Maybe *you'd* better meet me at her house an' we'll tell her together."

"Can't," Harry said flatly. "I'm in Pasadena."

"Awesome, Harry, you're a big freakin' help," Cookie complained, pulling her car up behind a row of party trucks. "Okay, I'm here now," she said, parking her Corvette, jumping out and making her way to the front door.

Gino Junior was sitting on the steps with an acne-encrusted friend. "What're *you* doing here?" he asked.

"Yeah, what're you doing here?" his friend echoed.

The two boys were checking her out. Gino Junior and his friends were always doing that, horny little jerk-offs.

"Max isn't back yet," Gino Junior offered. "She's gonna be in *way* shit with Mom when she gets here."

"Where is your mom?" Cookie asked, agitatedly twirling her sunglasses and wondering what she was going to say to Lucky.

"In the kitchen," Gino Junior said. "Screaming at everyone."

"See ya," Cookie said.

"Yeah," Gino Junior said. "At the party. It's gonna be full of old farts, so let's sneak off somewhere an' kill a bottle of vodka."

"Grow up, Gino," she said over her shoulder, making her way into the house and through to the kitchen.

Lucky was talking to the caterers, waving her arms in the air. It did not look like she was in a pleasant mood. As soon as she saw Cookie she stopped, marched over to her, took her arm, and steered her out of the room. "Come with me," she said, black eyes flashing danger signals.

"Uh, Lucky, uh . . . nice to see you too," Cookie stammered.

"Don't give me that 'nice to see you' crap," Lucky

snapped, narrowing her eyes. "I was your age once, I do know what goes on. Has Max got some boy she's meeting? Is that it?"

"Uh . . . I told you, they—"

"Enough with the bullshit, I want the truth," Lucky said, maneuvering Cookie into her study where she slammed the door shut. "Now sit down and tell me *exactly* what's going on. You didn't go to Big Bear with her, did you?"

"I, uh, yeah . . ."

"I'm telling you, Cookie," Lucky warned, "this is no joke, so don't fucking lie."

"Mrs. Golden—"

"And don't start calling me Mrs. Golden. You've always called me Lucky before, so stop with the innocent friend act 'cause I'm not buying it. Let's get it clear here—I want to know where Max is, and when she's coming home."

"Well . . ." Cookie stammered. "I . . . I tried calling her a few times. I—"

"We've all tried calling her," Lucky interrupted. "And since she's not answering her phone, I suggest you quit stalling and start giving me information."

"Max . . . uh . . . she met this guy," Cookie blurted, because she realized they were at a point where she was forced to tell a few semitruths, and if Max didn't like it, that was her problem because she should've checked in instead of leaving everyone hanging.

"What guy?" Lucky asked through clenched teeth.

"He's like this really cool guy," Cookie lied. "And Max . . . uh . . . wanted to spend time with him."

"'Spend time with him,'" Lucky repeated, raising an eyebrow. "What exactly does *that* mean?"

"She, uh . . . wanted to, uh, I dunno," Cookie mumbled, trailing off.

"And you're her alibi, right?"

Cookie slumped back in the chair, feeling out of her depth. "There's no way I can rat Max out. You'll have to ask her yourself."

"If she was here, I'd love to ask her," Lucky said coldly. "So since she's not, it's up to you to tell me who the boy is, and what's his phone number?"

"I don't know much," Cookie said, blinking rapidly, wondering why *she* was the one getting all the shit. "She kind of hooked up with him on the Internet."

"Are you *serious?*"

"They've been, y'know, like e-mailing for a while. And, um, like I mentioned before, he's a really cool guy."

"You've met him, have you?"

"Uh . . . no."

"Has Max met him?"

"She has now."

"Oh my God! Save me from stupid fucking girls!" Lucky exploded. "Jesus Christ! You're telling me Max went to Big Bear to meet up with a guy she found on the Internet, and now we can't reach her, and *you* think that's okay?"

"Max can look after herself," Cookie muttered.

Lucky shook her head. This was the worst news she'd heard in a long time.

"What's his name?" she demanded.

"Uh . . . I dunno," Cookie mumbled.

"You must know."

"It's uh, like Grant, yeah—that's it. Grant."

"Grant who?"

"Max never said."

"Perfect!"

An hour later Lucky and Lennie were still trying to figure out what to do. Max had taken her laptop with her, so it wasn't as if they could find out anything there. And a brief search of her room revealed nothing. If it wasn't for the party, Lucky would've jumped in her car and driven to Big Bear herself, although she was sure that by this time Max was on her way home. And boy, when Max finally got home she was in for a major lecture.

Lucky had to admit that Lennie was right: in a way she understood Max's rebellious behavior. At sixteen Lucky had been the original wild one, she'd taken off for weeks at a time before Gino had managed to track her down. But that was then and this was now, and the world was a far more dangerous place.

Max was a smart kid, but unfortunately she thought she knew it all. She was also a beauty in a heartbreakingly young way, and that could get her in big trouble.

Lucky couldn't help thinking back to Lennie's kidnapping ordeal. And the time Santino Bonnatti had abducted Brigette and Bobby when they were both so young.

Surely the nightmare couldn't be happening all over again?

No. It was impossible. Any minute now Max would come walking through the door.

CHAPTER FORTY-TWO

Roasted pig was one of Anthony's favorite meals. He got a big kick out of seeing the succulent animal—head and all—right in the center of his buffet table. Rosa didn't disappoint. Sunday brunch she delivered a baby roasted pig with the traditional apple stuffed firmly in its mouth.

"*Eeww!* Gross, Papa," Carolina complained, skipping away from the buffet table.

Anthony chased his daughter, caught her, and pinched her bottom. "It's a tasty treat, Princess," he assured her. "You're gonna love it."

"No, Papa, I won't love it," she protested, scampering back to her table where she was sitting with two girlfriends who'd flown to Acapulco with her. Eduardo was also at the table, but he'd elected to come alone. The adults were at their own table, where in addition to the Guerras and the Masterses, Anthony had invited half a dozen other friends who lived locally.

Irma sat stiffly among them, daydreaming about Luis and the quite exceptional sex they'd experienced together. She couldn't get the young, muscled gardener out of her head. Her thoughts drifted to his tongue between her legs, and his fingertips moving so expertly over her nipples.

"What *you* thinking about, little lady?" Ralph Masters asked, edging nearer, his meaty hand drifting onto her thigh under the cover of the fiesta-style tablecloth.

"Excuse me?" Irma replied, quickly brushing his unwelcome hand away.

"Did you and my friend do it last night?" Ralph whispered in her ear with a salacious leer.

"Ralph, please do not talk to me like that," she said, shifting in her chair. "It's most inappropriate."

Ralph licked his fleshy lips. He was a big man with small eyes and dyed black hair that resembled a bad wig—although it wasn't. Innes, a woman twenty years his junior, was his third wife.

"Don't be like that, I meant it as a compliment," he said in a low voice. "When a woman's getting the right kind of action I can always tell. My specialty is the tongue." Suggestively he flicked his tongue at her. "Most men aren't into oral, but I'm an expert."

"Good for you," Irma said, turning her back on Ralph and concentrating on the Mexican businessman sitting on her other side.

Anthony was in his element. Entertaining an admiring group of friends was his favorite way of relaxing, especially with his children present. Carolina was such a ripe little peach, if he wasn't her father he would pluck her for himself. Thirteen and sweet as pie. Woe betide any boy who came sniffing around Carolina. Anthony would make sure she stayed a virgin until she was twenty-one, then he would personally select a match for her—a male who lived up to his expectations in every way. He beamed at the thought of watching Carolina develop into a young woman, although come to think of it, she was already quite well developed. She had breasts and a cute little ass, she probably even had her period. He reminded himself to ask Nanny.

Eduardo had not brought any friends with him. He was a surly boy with nothing to say for himself. What a disappointment he'd turned out to be, but fortunately Carolina made up for her taciturn brother.

After a long and leisurely lunch, Anthony regaled his guests with several off-color jokes, then out came the karaoke equipment, set up by Manuel.

"Anyone for a song?" Anthony asked, puffing on an expensive Cuban cigar.

"Anthony, please, you sing for us," begged Fanta Guerra, a comely Latina woman with huge breasts and shoulder-length honey blond curls.

"Yes, Anthony," Innes, Ralph's American wife, said, puckering her silicone-enhanced lips. "We've missed you so."

Irma was well aware that both women would make love to her husband given half a chance. She didn't care; they were welcome to him. Now that she was mentally prepared to move on, she felt a lot stronger.

Anthony took his position near the karaoke machine, microphone in hand. "And what am I singing for you lovely people tonight?" he asked.

"Oh please, sing 'My Way,' " pleaded Fanta.

Innes, not to be outdone, gushed, "I love it too. You sing it so well, Anthony. You sing it better than Sinatra."

Their husbands chuckled, while Anthony basked in the praise, and the other guests clapped enthusiastically as they settled into chairs set out in a semicircle.

"So," Anthony said, playing with the microphone, "what does my little Carolina want to hear?"

Little Carolina didn't want to hear anything. Little Carolina wanted to run off to a disco with her friends, but she knew that her papa would never allow her to do that. "Whatever you want to sing, Papa," she said demurely.

"I'm singin' 'My Way.' After that you an' I gonna perform a duet."

"No, Papa! Please, no!" she squeaked.

"Yes, Princess, the two of us will make beautiful music," Anthony said, oblivious to her embarrassment.

Irma had not had a chance to interact with her children. The sad thing was they treated her like a distant relative—it seemed that Anthony and Francesca had managed to completely alienate them. Irma was sad because it wasn't as if Carolina and Eduardo didn't love her. Truth was they hardly knew her.

Anthony lifted the mike and began singing. He didn't have a bad voice, but it was hardly in the Sinatra category.

As he crooned, giving the song his all, he moved amongst his guests, leaning down to serenade and caress the women, a lascivious twinkle in his eye.

He should have been an entertainer, Irma thought. *Instead of a drug lord, a controller, a son of a bitch.*

Soon she wouldn't have to put up with him any longer.

Soon she was moving on.

CHAPTER FORTY-THREE

Henry was filled with excitement and a sense of freedom coupled with power, although he was shocked that Maria had tried to escape. She obviously did not appreciate all the trouble he'd gone to.

After her failed attack on him he'd been forced to shackle her ankle once more. He hadn't wanted to, but in view of her behavior it was necessary.

At least he'd persuaded her to call her mother, which was a wise move, because it wouldn't do to have Lucky out searching for her daughter. Not that she'd ever find her. They were isolated and perfectly safe where they were.

Muttering under his breath, he made his way around the back of the cabin to the outhouse where he'd imprisoned Ace approximately thirty-six hours earlier.

He'd been putting it off, but he'd known that eventually he'd have to do *something*.

It infuriated him that this boy had come along and interfered with his plans. Without him, everything could've been so clean and simple. Now he had to deal with the situation, and he had no clear idea of how to manage it.

A voice kept screaming in his head:
Shoot him.
Bury him in the woods.
It's the only way.
But that would be murder, wouldn't it?

Not if the boy is already dead.

Standing outside the door of Ace's prison, he strained to hear if there was any movement inside.

Not a sound. Total silence.

This was good. This meant he wouldn't have to deal with the cousin. This meant that he didn't have to open the door if he chose not to. He was out of the Pasadena mausoleum and living an adventure. He was not shut in his room watching endless horror movies and pornographic images on his computer. He was the star of his own movie, and this was one role Billy Melina could *never* steal from him.

AN ADVENTURE
Starring
HENRY WHITFIELD-SIMMONS
and
MARIA GOLDEN

It should be a love story.

It *would* be a love story.

Now that the cousin was taken care of, he would make it happen.

CHAPTER FORTY-FOUR

The enormous white tent set up on the grounds of Lucky and Lennie's Bel-Air house was an impressive structure, no expense spared. The tent was ablaze with hundreds of twinkling fairy lights, crystal chandeliers, and garlands of white calla lilies winding around Roman columns. Exotic orchid arrangements were the magnificent centerpieces on each table, along with musk-scented candles in tall sterling-silver holders. The theme was white and silver from the long flowing tablecloths to the pristine place settings.

Before reaching the tent where dinner was to be served, guests gathered around the two Art Deco bars, one on each end of the shimmering blue pool. Sensual Brazilian music played over loudspeakers, while attractive waiters and waitresses circulated holding aloft trays of champagne, wine, and sparkling water.

Venus and Billy were amongst the first to arrive. Bobby was playing host for his mother who was still upstairs dressing. He raced over to Venus, his former boyhood crush, and greeted her with an enthusiastic kiss on both cheeks. "You are looking spectacular," he said admiringly.

"Doesn't she," Billy agreed, claiming possession.

"You know Bobby, Lucky's son," Venus said, introducing the two men.

"Oh yeah, you're the dude with the club in New York, right?" Billy said.

"A *hot* club in New York plus a billion dollars when he hits twenty-five," Venus added, smiling. "And you *know* how I like young men. You'd better watch out, Billy."

"Hey, baby," Billy said, taking her arm. "*I'm* the *only* young man in your life, an' don't you forget it."

"As if I could," she said, hugging him.

"I had a crush on her when I was twelve," Bobby admitted. "Posters on my wall, CDs on my mind, the whole ten yards."

"Didn't we all," Billy said with a knowing grin. "I can remember—"

"Hey!" Venus objected. "You're making me feel as if I'm ninety years old!"

Bobby lifted a glass of champagne from a passing waiter and surveyed the arriving guests.

"Got a hunch I'm not gonna be getting much action here tonight," he said. "It's like couples' city. I knew I should've imported a date."

"Sorry, bro," Billy said, holding on to Venus. "But this one is definitely taken."

"I can see that."

"There's Gino," Venus said, gesturing across the pool. "C'mon, Billy, let's go say hello."

"For an old guy, he looks pretty damn great," Billy said, squinting.

"Yeah," Bobby agreed. "For an old geezer, Gino is amazing."

"Y'know," Venus ventured, "Billy and I were thinking of maybe developing a movie about his life."

"No shit?" Bobby said, looking interested. "Have you run it by Lucky?"

"Not yet, but wouldn't it make an incredible movie?"

"It sure would," Bobby said. "Gino stories are legendary in our family. When I was growing up, Uncle Costa had tales to tell nobody would believe."

"Maybe we should sign Uncle Costa up as creative consultant," Billy suggested. "Is he here tonight?"

"If he is it's a miracle," Bobby said with a wry grin. "Costa's long gone. If he was still around he'd be about a hundred years old."

"Oh," Venus murmured dryly as they all headed toward Gino. "The same age as me!"

Gino was delighted to see everyone. All dressed up in a pinstriped suit, white shirt, and red tie, he did not look anywhere near ninety-five—he was still an impressive-looking man with all his own teeth, a healthy head of gray hair, and a ribald sense of humor. He sat in a chair next to the bar, holding court.

"An' here she comes," he exclaimed as soon as he spotted Venus. "Lucky's hot little friend. How ya doin', kiddo?"

"I'm doing great, Gino," Venus responded, bending down and kissing him on both cheeks. "Even better for seeing you."

"Always noticed you was a sexy-lookin' broad," Gino said, clearing his throat. "Ah . . . if only I was a coupla years younger, what I wouldn't do to you!"

Everyone laughed. Venus introduced Billy.

"Paige," Gino said, grabbing his wife's arm. "Y'see this kid, he's a big friggin' movie star. We saw him in somethin' last week, am I right?"

"Indeed we did," Paige agreed.

"Yeah, you played a psycho killer. Nice job, kid, you got it down."

"Tell that to Alex Woods," Billy said, still smarting from Venus's earlier comments about Alex's opinion of him. "Anyone seen him around?"

Venus gave Billy a sharp nudge in the ribs. "Now don't get all wound up over nothing," she cautioned. "I shouldn't've told you what he said."

"Well, you did, babe, an' now I'm pissed."

A few minutes later Lucky made her entrance wearing a red column of a Valentino dress that set off her smooth olive skin and unruly cascades of jet black hair. She wore diamond hoops in her ears and a stack of antique diamond bracelets up both arms. As usual she looked incredible.

Lennie was by her side. He'd been trying to calm her down about Max all afternoon. The good news was that they'd recently received a message from their daughter on Lucky's cell phone, which had made her feel better, although she was still furious at her errant daughter. "I'm gonna bust her too-smart-for-her-own-good ass when she finally makes it home," she'd threatened, after listening to Max's message a third time.

The message was Max saying, "Mom, sorry to miss Granddad's party. I'll be home tomorrow. Love ya."

Hmm . . . *love ya*. That wasn't Max's usual greeting, and she always called Gino by his name, never Granddad. Lucky had her misgivings. What the hell was Max up to now? And how come Cookie didn't know anything?

Glancing around at the clusters of guests, Lucky noticed Cookie over in a corner with Max's other friend, Harry. The two of them looked like they were in deep conversation. Distracted, she waved a quick greeting at everyone, said, "I'll be right back," and hurried over to Cookie and Harry.

"Did you hear from Max?" was her first question.

"No," Cookie answered, wishing Lucky would stay out of her face. Why was *she* the one getting all the flak? "Did you?"

"She left a message on my cell," Lucky said. "I'm wondering why she didn't call on the main line."

"So like what did she *say*?" Cookie asked, most put out that Max hadn't called her, she'd left enough frantic messages.

"Just that she's coming home tomorrow."

"Tomorrow?" Harry questioned.

"I'm mad as hell," Lucky said. "And you two—what were you thinking, letting her go off to Big Bear to meet a stranger? I thought you were her friends."

"You know what Max is like," Cookie said, shrugging. "We couldn't stop her even if we wanted to. Max does things her way."

"I understand that," Lucky said coldly. "But did you have to encourage her?"

"We're real sorry, Mrs. Golden," Harry muttered.

"Don't call me Mrs. Golden," Lucky snapped. "It makes me feel ancient. You know my name—use it."

"You're like *so* right," Cookie said, biting her lower lip. "We should've tried to stop her."

"Yeah," Harry agreed, his black hair spiked higher than ever.

"Thing is, I *did* tell her," Cookie said, getting into it. "I like *so* warned her that the Internet dude could turn out to be a pervert freako who could chop her up into little pieces." Harry shot her a warning look. "Uh . . . just joking," she finished lamely.

Shaking her head, Lucky walked back to join Venus and Billy. "You look fantastic," she said to Venus, still distracted. "And Billy—always a star."

"Oh, just what I need," Venus muttered. "Here comes Cooper." And as she finished saying it, Cooper strolled over with his very young girlfriend, Mandy, whom Billy seemed to know.

"Hey, Mandy!" Billy exclaimed, giving her a friendly hug. "How ya doin'?"

"Billy!" Mandy squealed. "You're here! How fab! I thought it would be all old people!"

Venus gave Cooper a cool look. "Hello," she said.

"Good evening, Venus," he replied.

"I see you went trolling outside the school yard for a

date," she said, indicating Mandy, who was all over
Billy.

"You too," Cooper said, glancing at Billy. "Must run
in the family, huh?"

"Alex, you drive like a maniac," Ling complained, sitting stiffly in the passenger seat.

"I drive the way I've always driven," Alex replied,
maneuvering his Porsche into a line of cars waiting to
enter the Bel-Air driveway of Lucky's house. "Never had
an accident."

"Your driving makes me nervous."

"Then shut your eyes."

"Why can't you be nice to me?"

"I *am* nice to you," he said. "You live in my house,
isn't that being nice to you?"

"Is it because of your mother that you're the way you
are?"

"I have no problem with my mother," he said, reaching for a cigarette.

"I think you're wrong. Your mother is a *very* domi-
neering woman."

"No she's not," he said shortly, lighting up. "And do
not discuss my mother, she's off limits. Try to remember you're a lawyer, not a shrink."

"That's right," Ling said, holding tightly on to her
clutch purse resting on her knees. "I'm a divorce lawyer, so I know plenty about relationships."

"Good," Alex said, exhaling smoke. "'Cause I'm not
planning on getting married, which means you won't
have to represent me."

"I represent women, only women," Ling said.

"Of course you do," Alex said, taking another drag
on his cigarette. "When the fuck is this line of cars getting to the goddamn house?"

Ling gazed out of the window and hoped that maybe

tonight she would meet somebody more to her liking than Alex Woods. He was an extraordinarily talented man, but he treated her with no respect, and that wasn't right. But then again, as she'd recently confessed, she was in love with him, which made things complicated.

Soon they reached the front of the line where parking valets jumped forward to take the Porsche.

Alex got out and strode into the house. Ling tagged along behind him, finding it difficult to keep up in her ultrahigh heels.

Waiters holding trays of champagne were circulating. Alex grabbed a glass and downed it quickly. "Let's go find the bar," he said. "I need a proper drink."

"Please don't drink too much," Ling begged.

"For God's sake, quit with the nagging."

Venus loved being out with Billy, especially amongst her peers. She knew they made an amazing couple—he didn't look too young and she didn't look too old. They looked like contemporaries. She also liked that he was getting plenty of attention as well as her. Billy was an excellent actor, and a well-respected one too. It wasn't like she was out with some boy toy; Billy had his own high profile.

Holding on to his arm, she proudly introduced him to people he hadn't met before, enjoying the compliments bestowed upon him.

Billy was enjoying himself too, although his crotch itched like crazy. Venus might have gotten rid of his crabs, but the stubble burn from her shaving skills was driving him nuts.

"Gotta go to the men's room, babe," he said, slipping away from her.

As he walked toward the house, a tray-carrying waitress stepped in front of him, blocking his way.

"Billy?" she said.

He gave her a puzzled look. "Do I know you?"

"You should know me," she retorted. "It was you who gave me the crabs."

Holy shit! It was the waif from Tower Records. Miss Broken Taillight herself. And here she was all neat and clean in a waitress uniform with her hair piled on top of her head, looking quite respectable.

"What do you mean, *I* gave *you* crabs?" he said, outraged. "I got them from *you*."

"You certainly did not!" she replied, equally outraged. "You were the one who had them."

Jesus! He motioned her over to the side of the room. "People can hear," he said, keeping his voice low. "Don't talk to me about this here."

"When *should* I talk to you?" she retorted. "You gave me crabs and I had to spend a ton of money I didn't have visiting the doctor and finding out what it was. You're disgusting!"

"Hey," he said, scowling, "you didn't get them from me 'cause the only person I sleep with is my girlfriend."

"Really?" she said. "Then what does that make me? A one-afternoon stand?"

"I didn't mean that," he said, steering her over to a quieter corner. "What I meant was that when we did it, I was broken up with my girlfriend."

"Is Venus your girlfriend?"

"Yes," he admitted.

"And you hooked up with me? Wow! I'm flattered. I hope you didn't give *her* crabs too."

"Jesus Christ," he muttered, "will you shut the frig up? What do you want from me?"

"I want you to remember me when you see me. We had sex, I went down on you. Doesn't that mean anything to you, Mister Big Movie Star?"

"What we had was a short encounter."

"An encounter?" she said incredulously. "Should I

have gotten your autograph on my ass? If I remember correctly, all you offered me was a signed photo."

"What are you after? Money?"

"I'm an actress, not a hooker," she said huffily. "Give me a part in your movie and I'll shut up. Otherwise I'm telling Venus what a bad boy you've been. Okay?"

No. It wasn't okay at all. But what could he do?

Hurriedly he gave her his cell phone number. In the distance he saw Venus approaching.

"Get lost," he said, desperate to make a quick escape. "You got a deal, call me tomorrow. Now get the frig away from me."

CHAPTER FORTY-FIVE

Max wondered how long the freak was going to keep her prisoner. It disturbed her that he hadn't covered his face. She knew what he looked like, which meant if she ever got out she would be able to identify him. And that wasn't good, because in all the movies she'd ever seen involving a kidnapping, the kidnappers kept their faces covered—because if they didn't, it meant they were planning to kill their victim.

Man, this was bad. This wasn't a game.

And yet there was something about Internet Freak that gave her hope. He obviously wasn't your usual run-of-the-mill criminal. He kept on looking at her with what she could only describe as a lovesick expression—like ugh! It was as if he wanted to be her boyfriend.

Maybe she should stop yelling at him and play up that angle, find out what he was really after, 'cause it didn't seem to be money.

When he returned late in the afternoon she was all prepared with her new attitude.

"I think we got off to a bad start," she ventured.

"Excuse me?" he responded, startled that she was speaking to him without yelling.

"Well, you *are* the same guy I was communicating with via e-mail, yes?"

He nodded unsurely.

"Then what went wrong?"

"Wrong?" he repeated blankly.

"I mean the whole thing with the gun," she continued. "And this shackling me to the bed like some kind of animal. I thought we were friends."

"But we are," he said anxiously. "Friends, yes, we are certainly friends."

"Friends don't point guns at people and *kidnap* them."

"I didn't mean to. But the circumstances . . . your cousin . . . I wasn't expecting him. You said you'd come alone. I was prepared for us to spend the weekend together, just the two of us."

His words got her wondering about Ace. Could it be that they *weren't* in cahoots, and if not, what had he done with him?

"Where is Ace, Grant?" she asked, speaking slowly.

It was the first time she'd used his name. It galled her to do so because all she really wanted to do was kick him in the balls and run—which hadn't worked out so well earlier in the day.

"I told you," he said, clenching his teeth. "I let Ace go."

She knew he was lying, because why would he let Ace go? There was no way.

"Can you undo this thing around my ankle? It really hurts," she said, summoning up a tear or two for his benefit.

"Last time—"

"Forget about last time, Grant," she said, keeping her voice low and soothing. "I learned my lesson and this time I'll behave. I promise."

She watched him closely. His expression weakened, and she knew she was about to get a lot further by being nice.

He produced the key, undid the shackle, fetched her disinfectant and cotton swabs for her ankle, then allowed her into the living room where he fixed her a bowl of canned tomato soup. Wow! Why hadn't she thought of being nice before?

They talked. Or rather *he* talked while she managed to check out her surroundings, taking in every detail. She noticed there was a chain and a double lock on the front door, and no bars on the window in the combination kitchen/living room where they were sitting. In the kitchen section she spotted a knife stand and a collection of pots and pans. In the living room she noticed that he'd set up his rollaway bed under the window.

His voice droned on, horribly monotonous. He told her he was an award-winning actor, and had received many accolades.

"Would I have seen you in anything?" she asked, not believing him for a minute.

"Did you see the film *Seduction*?" he asked, nervously cracking his knuckles, thrilled that he was getting a chance to impress her with his achievements.

Of course she'd seen *Seduction*—her mom had produced the movie. She remembered visiting the set when she was just a little kid. She sure as hell didn't remember him.

"Were you in it?" she asked.

"I should've been," he said, his tone suddenly changing, becoming sharp and angry.

"Then why weren't you?" she asked, putting down her soup spoon.

"Because of—" He stopped abruptly.

Now that they were getting along so nicely, he didn't care to bring up her bitch mother.

Later, when they were really close, he'd tell her the real story.

Later, when he'd convinced her they should stay together forever.

CHAPTER FORTY-SIX

Sunday night Anthony decided to throw another party. Even though it was a last-minute decision, he expected it to happen in spite of the fact that Rosa and Manuel had worked their asses off getting the roasted-pig lunch together at such short notice.

"My little Carolina's gonna be fourteen in two weeks' time, so tonight we celebrate," Anthony informed his guests. "Right, Fanta? Right, Innes?" The two women nodded enthusiastically. "C'mere, Rosa," he bellowed, summoning his cook.

Rosa appeared, wiping her hands on her apron. She was exhausted, and it showed on her heavily lined face.

"Rosa!" Anthony exclaimed, grabbing her in an overpowering bear hug. "You go make two of those chocolate cakes I like, an' a lemon birthday cake for Carolina. An' I think we have lamb tonight, an' chicken, an' those potatoes you cook so well. We have another feast," he crowed, pinching her cheek with his thumb and forefinger. "You see this woman?" he boasted to his cronies. "She would do anything for me. Anything! Correct, Rosa?"

"*Sí, señor*," Rosa muttered, enduring the humiliation of a pinched cheek.

"An' if she doesn't—I fire her ass. *Sí*, Rosa?" he said, roaring with laughter. "What you waitin' for, woman?" he added, smacking her on the ass. "Go make the cakes, oh yeah, an' some of those almond cookies you're famous for. Move it!" he added, giving her one final whack on her ass before sending her on her way.

"*Sí, señor*," Rosa said, wondering how he expected her to have time to organize a dinner party *and* bake. The man was loco, but she and Manuel needed their jobs, and when Anthony wasn't in residence things were quite peaceful.

"She loves me," she heard him braying to his lunch guests. "I'm tellin' you, she loves me to death!"

Irma sat quietly watching Anthony strut and show off, plotting and planning her imminent escape. She knew that her husband kept cash in all his main homes, and taking some of his stash would hardly be considered stealing. After all, she was his wife, and if they lived in America half of everything he had would be legally hers.

She knew the combination of the bedroom safe in their house in Mexico City. Several months ago they'd arrived home from a big black-tie event late at night. Anthony was drunk—he'd flung his emerald cuff links and hundred-thousand-dollar diamond-encrusted watch at her and told her to put them in his safe. She'd asked him for the combination, and in his drunken state he'd given it to her.

She'd opened his safe, and was shocked to see bundles of cash piled high. After putting his watch and cuff links away, she'd written down the safe's combination and hidden it.

Yes, she was more than entitled to anything she cared to take.

Much to Luis's fury, Cesar decided to take Lucia up on her invitation to dinner. He arrived unexpectedly late Sunday afternoon, carrying a wilted bunch of flowers and a bottle of cheap sangria.

Lucia greeted him as if she was receiving a visit from

the king of Spain. Lucia was desperate to get married
and as far away as possible from the overcrowded family situation. She'd dated Cesar on and off for a year, and
even though she'd given him what she considered memorable sex, he was not close to making any kind of permanent commitment. Cesar appearing at their house
was an encouraging sign.

"Look who's here," she bragged to her two sisters and
wheelchair-bound mother. "Doesn't Cesar look handsome?"

Luis was dismayed to see him. He was not sure what
Cesar knew about him and Señora Bonar—if anything.
But it still made him uncomfortable that Cesar was in
his house, making himself at home.

Ana Cristina, Luis's seven-months-pregnant wife,
followed her sister-in-law's lead and greeted Cesar as if
he were royalty. Everyone was impressed with his job.
"Security guard" had a special ring to it. They all hoped
he'd marry Lucia or at least take her off to live with him.
Their tiny house was so full, and with Ana Cristina and
Luis's baby due soon, Lucia's absence would be a god-
send.

Luis, the only man in the house with four women,
reluctantly offered Cesar a bottle of beer.

Cesar patted Ana Cristina's swollen belly. "Do we
know what we're having?" he asked, his hand lingering
a little too long on his wife's stomach for Luis's liking.

"A boy," Ana Cristina replied, shyly lowering her
eyes.

"A boy! Congratulations!" Cesar exclaimed.

"It's a blessing," Ana Cristina murmured.

"Indeed it is," Lucia said, hanging on to Cesar's arm
while fluttering her overmascaraed eyelashes. "Babies
are always such a blessing, aren't they, Cesar?"

Cesar didn't reply. "Let's sit outside," he said to Luis.
"Enjoy our beers, watch the world pass by."

There was nothing Luis would like less.

"Sure, Cesar," he said.

The two men stepped outside onto the patch of sparse sun-dried grass and sat down on two mismatched plastic lawn chairs.

After a few moments of silence Cesar leaned over to Luis and muttered, "I want in."

"Excuse me?" Luis said.

"I want in," Cesar repeated.

"In what?" Luis said, twisting his beer bottle.

"Do not act as if you don't know what I'm talking about."

"I don't," Luis replied.

"You idiot!" Cesar said, becoming agitated. "I want in with the American woman. I want to sample some of that juicy American pussy you've been dipping into. And if you don't arrange it, Luis, not only do I tell your fat wife, but I tell Señor Bonar too. Do we understand each other, *amigo?*"

CHAPTER FORTY-SEVEN

Eventually the party moved outside to the tent where dinner was to be served. An eight-piece Cuban band played on a platform next to a circular dance floor, while a voluptuous Latina woman seductively crooned "Bésame Mucho."

Lucky was trying her best to enjoy herself, but she still couldn't get over her anger at Max for not arriving home in time for the party, especially since she'd emphasized how important it was to her.

"You gotta calm down, sweetheart," Lennie said, attempting to soothe her bad mood. "You can't walk around with a pissed-off expression. This is Gino's big night—don't let Max ruin it for you."

"Nobody knows better than me what a special night this is," Lucky said, steaming. "But Lennie, I'm *so* mad at her. How could she do this to us? We have no clue where she is, or even *who* she's with. It's crazy."

"I know," he agreed.

"Trust me," Lucky said, her black eyes flashing major danger signals, "when that child gets back she is *so* grounded. I'm not allowing her out of the house. She can say good-bye to her phone *and* her car."

"We'll get into it when she comes home."

"Yes we will," Lucky said fiercely. "And you'll get into it with me, 'cause you're not playing good cop while I'm the bad one. This is something we're handling together. Her behavior is freakin' beyond."

"You got it, Lucky," he said, still trying to calm her. "Now, let's try to relax and show Gino a good time."

"*What* is going on with you?" Venus asked Billy, cornering him on the way to their table. "First I see you talking to one of the waitresses, and the next thing I know, you're all over Cooper's girlfriend like you're long-lost buddies."

"Mandy was in one of my movies," he explained. "She's a sweet kid."

"Really?" Venus said archly. "What did she play, the child?"

"She's nineteen, babe," he said, his mind still on his unfortunate encounter with Miss Broken Taillight.

"Oh wow, nineteen," Venus said sarcastically. "Just about young enough for Cooper."

"Bitchy! Bitchy!" Billy said, baiting her.

"Doesn't she get that she's fucking her *grandfather*?" Venus snapped.

"You wouldn't be jealous, would you?" Billy said, grinning.

"Me? Of course not, but a little more attention in my direction might be nice."

"You can't always be the center of attention," Billy teased. "Is Miz Superstar feeling neglected?"

"*Excuse* me?"

"You heard."

"Don't be ridiculous."

"You're the one who's carrying on about nothing."

"Stop chasing after my ex-husband's underage girlfriend and *I'll* stop carrying on."

"Who's chasing? I'm being polite."

"Your idea of being polite and mine obviously differ," she said, hating herself for sounding like a jealous shrew.

"C'mon, babe," he said, turning on the Billy Melina charm, "lighten up."

"Don't tell *me* to lighten up when you're the one doing all the chasing."

"Do you seriously think I'd do that?"

"You're sure talking to her a lot." *Oh God, Venus, stop it already!*

"Mandy doesn't know anyone here."

"And since when did that become *your* problem?"

"We'd better go sit down," he said, leading her to the table next to Gino and Lucky's.

Venus took a quick peek at the place cards. Billy was seated next to her, and on her other side was Alex. Charlie Dollar was already sitting across from them with *his* date, another juvenile delinquent.

What was it with these fifty- and sixty-something men who thought that the only date worth having was a twenty-something Twinkie? They probably imagined it made them look like a big sexy stud, when all it actually did was make them look older and kind of pathetic. Without Viagra they'd all be singing the blues.

"Hi, Charlie," Venus said, waving at her old friend.

"There's my Venus," Charlie drawled with a jaunty wink. "Queen of the tasty treats."

Charlie Dollar was a huge movie star, a stoned icon for his generation. A superlative actor and quite a man about town; whatever he did, it always involved a little bit of magic. Even at sixty-something he still managed to snag any girl who took his fancy. Slightly balding with a paunch and a maniacal grin, Charlie was up there with Nicholson and Pacino as one of the all-time movie greats.

"Say hello to Bubbles," Charlie said. "She's my latest project."

"Hi, Bubbles," Venus said, waving at his very young date, wondering if she was a stripper. Who else would walk around with a name like Bubbles? Oh yes, Michael Jackson's monkey.

"Ohmi*god*!" Bubbles trilled in total awe, flapping her hands. "I'm so thrilled and honored to meet you. I grew up watching you on TV and listening to your music. My daddy is your biggest fan!"

Christ! What *was* this? Make-Venus-feel-old night?

"Thanks, dear," Venus said, about to sit down. Before she could do so, strong arms grabbed her from behind. "Good evening, gorgeous. I'll be watching everything you put in your mouth tonight, an' that *includes* food."

"Who *is* this?" she asked, struggling to turn around.

"Your main man."

She spun around and there was Cole, her trainer. He was with Rich Morrison, a fifty-something billionaire English rock star, who favored white suits and an abundance of expensive jewelry. Rich was considered an icon, having been in the business for twenty-five years, and having scored numerous awards and more gold records than Elton John.

Cole, a black beauty, and Rich, all in white, made quite a couple.

So this is the giver of Cole's new Jag, Venus thought. She was delighted to see her old friend Rich. She'd had no idea he was Cole's latest admirer, but it made perfect sense because Cole was a black Adonis *and* smart— and those were the two qualities Rich coveted above all else.

At the next table Lucky was trying to get her people seated. Gino was at the head of the table with Paige on one side and Steven's wife, Lina, on the other.

Lina, a beautiful black supermodel, was full of personality—she lit up any room. Next to her sat her daughter, Carioca, then Gino Junior, with Lennie next to him. Lucky had Bobby on her right, then Brigette and Steven. It was the family table; the only person missing was Max.

At least Gino seems to be enjoying himself, Lucky

thought. *Ninety-five years old and forever a party animal.*

She wondered how he really felt. Pretty old, no doubt, but still holding up.

Glancing over at the table next to her, she observed Venus and Billy indulging in some kind of verbal battle, while Alex was nursing a half-full glass of Scotch, and Ling didn't appear to be too happy. It was definitely time for Alex to settle down with the right girl and take himself off the market.

Was Ling the right girl? Probably not.

Lucky knew that Alex still harbored a big crush on her. She'd thought that by this time it would've faded—but no, Alex was forever hopeful.

At the last moment the party planner had switched tables, and somehow or other Cooper and his girlfriend had ended up at Venus's table, which had not been Lucky's intention. She hoped Venus wasn't too mad.

"Lucky," Steven said. "This is a wonderful evening."

"Thanks, Steven," she said. "I wanted it to be special for Gino. I mean, how often is he going to be ninety-five?"

"Take a look at him," Steven said, beaming. "The old man is in his element."

"I know." Lucky nodded. "Surrounded by beautiful women and feeling no pain. The story of his life."

"Where's Max?"

"Oh, you know Max," Lucky said vaguely. "She's off running around with her friends. Teenage girls, what can I tell you? Hopefully she'll make it later."

"I was thinking of flying up to Vegas with you next weekend," Steven said. "Thought I'd take a look at everything before the grand opening."

"I'd love that."

Lucky appreciated having Steven in her life. A half-brother was so much better than no brother at all, and since Dario had been so brutally murdered it was great having found someone she could look up to. Steven was the result of Gino's one-night affair many years ago with a black woman, Carrie. It had taken Gino a while to accept the fact that he'd fathered a black son who had not appeared in his life until he was an adult, but once Steven had shown up, Gino had rallied and eventually accepted Steven into the family.

Steven was an extremely successful lawyer. Several years previously his wife had been shot and killed in a carjacking, and sometime later he'd married Lina. They seemed to be very happy together, in spite of Lina's somewhat wild past.

After dinner was served Gino stood up and prepared to make a speech. The room hushed. Someone handed Gino a microphone—he held it gingerly.

"First time I had one of these things stuck in my face," he joked. "Plenty of guns, never one of these." Pause for laughter. "Y'know," he continued, "never thought I'd make it to ninety-five friggin' years old. It's a miracle I'm still around, an' I plan on stayin' around a lot longer for my family. My unbelievable ballsy daughter, Lucky. My son, Steven, who came into my life late and made it even better. My grandkids, I love 'em all. Then there's my wife, Paige, she's the woman who keeps an eye on my drinkin', gamblin', an' womanizing." Another big laugh from the crowd. "Paige is kinda like a prison guard," Gino continued, warming up. "An' believe me, I've crossed paths with a few of *them* in my time. Anyway, I wanna thank you all for comin' out tonight, for supportin' me and my family. An' a special toast to Lucky for makin' this party for me. So drink up an' have a good old time, 'cause me—I can't wait t'hit the dance floor."

Lennie gave Lucky a nudge. "Your turn."

"I'm not good at speaking in public," she protested.

"Do your best, sweetheart, I know you can."

"Guess I've got no choice," she said, taking a long deep breath before standing up and tapping the side of her glass until the room was silent again. A tentful of expectant eyes turned toward her. She hated being in the spotlight; keeping a low profile was much more to her liking.

"Uh, thanks, Gino," she began. "Your speech was beautiful, and this is quite an occasion." Her eyes met Lennie's. He nodded encouragingly. Taking another deep breath, she continued speaking. "So . . . y'know, ever since I was a little girl Gino never allowed me to call him Daddy, I have no idea why. Then I got to thinking it was because of the parade of women coming in and out of our house, and he didn't want some little kid running in yelling, 'Daddy! Daddy! Daddy!'" Everyone laughed. "Well . . . after that I got used to calling him Gino, and I got used to his ways. Hey, you all know Gino, I had no choice." More laughter. "Anyway, growing up with Gino was a major pain in the ass, so to compensate I decided to become an even *bigger* pain in the ass than him. But anyone who knows us realizes that we finally got together and made our peace, and since that time Gino has been everything to me. I can't even begin to tell everybody how great he is, and I'm so *happy* that he's hitting ninety-five. Wow! Some freakin' landmark! So Gino," she said, tilting her champagne glass toward him. "I toast you and everything about you." A long slow beat. "Oh yes, and thanks . . . Daddy . . . I love you, I really do. Happy birthday!"

Glasses were raised and champagne was drunk.

Lucky sat down.

"Perfect," Lennie murmured in her ear. "You're a talented woman."

"It wasn't that good," she said modestly. "Just some hokey speech I came up with at the last minute."

"It was from your heart," Lennie assured her. "That's all that matters."

"You think?"

"I know," he said, taking her hand and squeezing it tightly. "God, I love you."

"Right back atcha!" she said, reaching up to touch his cheek.

"Let's blow this party and go make out."

"Now?"

"*Right* now. You and me in the guest bathroom. How about it? Just like old times, huh?"

"Lennie . . ." she began.

"*What?*" he said, giving her the look she could never resist.

"Nothing," she said, standing up. "So c'mon, move it, Mr. Golden, or are you all talk?"

"That's my Lucky," he said, grinning.

"Oh *yes*, mother of your children and sex maniac!" she said, pulling him to his feet. "That's your Lucky."

Laughing together they left the tent.

Nursing his fourth—or was it fifth?—tumbler of Scotch, Alex watched them go. Lucky. *His* Lucky. Without her existence things could have been so simple. But with her around nothing was simple, and nothing was ever enough. Not the endless women, the expensive possessions, his successful career. Three fucking Oscars, and he'd give them up tomorrow for just one night with Lucky. She was his ultimate woman, and yet she belonged to Lennie. And what could he do about that?

Nothing.

Exactly nothing. And the pain of not having her never left him.

"Alex," Billy said, breaking into his thoughts.

"What?" Alex growled.

"I heard tell you think success has gone to my head?" Billy said, taking a belligerent stance.

"Huh?" Alex questioned, standing up. He hated it when punk actors got in his face—this wasn't the first time.

"Yeah, you told Lucky an' she told Venus, who told me," Billy said, determined to force a confrontation.

"What the fuck is this, grade school?" Alex spluttered.

"No. Reality," Billy said. "I'm not that green kid you put in his first movie. It's time you gave me some respect."

"Respect!" Alex chortled. "You'll get my respect when you do somethin' to deserve it."

Billy's handsome face darkened. "What?"

"You heard."

"Fuck you, Alex," Billy said in a loud voice. "You're yesterday's news, an old guy who's losin' it. So whyn't you wake up an' smell the retirement hittin' you smack in the face."

Alex took a step forward and spewed a litany of insults. "You dumb, no-talent, ass-kissin', fuckin' boy toy prick. You—"

Before Alex could utter one more insult, Billy hit him square on the jaw. Pow! A direct shot that took Alex by surprise, but not enough to stop him from retaliating. As a Vietnam vet, Alex had a few moves of his own, and he came back at Billy with a vengeance. Suddenly it was on, a full-out fistfight.

Venus, who'd been deep in conversation with Cole and Rich, jumped to attention. "Oh *my God!*" she screeched. "Somebody stop them!"

And Gino, sitting at the next table, looked on admiringly. "Now *this* is what I call a *party!*" he crowed to Paige. "Trust my Lucky to come up with the right friggin' mix! This is the best damn party of the year!"

CHAPTER FORTY-EIGHT

Max was asleep, once more locked in her prison, when she thought she heard a scratching sound coming from the outside of the boarded-up window.

The sound awoke her instantly. She quickly sat up, got off the bed, and padded toward the window, her heart beating fast. She'd persuaded the freak to keep the shackle off her ankle—the sense of freedom it gave her was quite liberating.

"Anyone there?" she whispered, attempting to peer out, but all she could see was pitch blackness.

"It's Ace," a voice whispered back. "Is that you, Max? You in there?"

Relief flooded her whole being. Ace had come to rescue her. Thank God!

"Yes, it's me," she answered excitedly. "I'm locked up here."

"I'm gonna try getting you out," he promised.

"How?"

"Who knows?" he said in a low voice. "Where's the freak?"

"I think he's asleep, but he's right next door so you'd better be quiet."

"I'm gonna attempt to pry the boards off the window."

"What if he wakes up?" she asked, panicking. "He's got a gun."

"I know, but we're better off gettin' outta here."

"God, Ace, where have you *been*?" she cried.

"He had me locked up, I only just managed to break out. Okay, here goes," he said, tearing at the boards with his bare hands. "Wish us luck."

Almost two nail-biting hours later he'd made enough space for Max to squeeze through. Once she managed to force her head and shoulders out, he dragged her the rest of the way, scraping the side of her body from thigh to chest. She bit her lip trying not to cry out with pain.

It was still night and the blackness was oppressive. She couldn't see a thing as Ace quickly hugged her. "Let's go," he said, his voice full of urgency.

"Where to?" she asked, shivering uncontrollably.

"Anywhere away from here."

He grabbed her hand and they began to run.

Running, breathing, running, breathing, Max thought her lungs were about to explode, but Ace wouldn't allow her to stop, even though they were running in total darkness. She kept tripping and falling as they made their way through what appeared to be a heavily wooded area.

"Shouldn't we try to find the road?" she gasped.

"No," Ace said. "When he discovers we're gone, that's exactly where he'll start looking."

"But if we stay in the woods, we'll be totally lost," she said, experiencing a sick feeling in the pit of her stomach. "Neither of us knows where we are, and he told me this area is completely deserted, nowhere near anything or anybody."

"Don't sweat it," he said, keeping a firm grip on her arm, supporting her when she stumbled.

"I tried to escape," she said, breathing hard. "Kicked him in the balls, it didn't have much effect."

"That's 'cause he hasn't got any," Ace said, stopping for a moment and bending over. "Jesus! I am *so* fucking hungry."

"What? He didn't serve you three-course meals?" she said, squatting on the ground.

"Glad you've still got your sense of humor."

"Trying to keep my spirits up," she said, shivering. "Where were you anyway?"

"Locked in a stinking outhouse. He dumped me in there and never came back. I could've starved to death."

"You haven't had anything to eat or drink all week-end?"

"Nope. Sweet that I took a survival course in school."

"You did?"

"Yeah, we had to survive in the desert on practically nothing for six days."

"Wow!"

"This time I had a coupla packs of gum in my pocket, must've given me enough strength to dig my way out. There was a john over a hole in the ground. That's where I dug. It took me long enough, but I made it."

"Does he still think you're in there?"

"Guess so," he said, pulling her up. "C'mon, we gotta keep movin'."

"But I'm so cold and hungry," she said, still shivering.

"Tell me about it," he said as they began stumbling through the woods again, Max desperately trying to forget the pain she was in with her side and her ankle. "Y'know," she muttered. "He told me he let you go, so I immediately started thinking you were part of it, that he'd sent you to lure me into his trap."

"I might be a bank robber," Ace quipped, "but that doesn't mean I'd get involved in a kidnapping plot."

"He sounded so cool, I thought meeting him would be an adventure."

"One hell of an adventure this turned out to be. You realize we could've both got shot."

"You don't have to draw me a map."

"Listen, Max, I'm not that much older than you, but

there's no way you should go running off with strange dudes. He's probably one of those sick pedophiles."

"I'm hardly a child," she said, tripping over a branch and almost falling. "Ow!"

He caught her by the arm. "What's up?"

"It's just that I scraped my side coming out the window, it really hurts."

"You think *that's* bad, wait till you see my hands."

"What's wrong with them?"

"I told you, I had to dig myself out of that place. Then I had to tear those wooden boards off your window. My freakin' hands are nothing but splinters and blood."

"Can I do anything?"

"Just keep moving, we can't afford to stop."

"But I'm tired."

"Max!" he said forcefully. "Suck it up."

"Okay, okay," she answered breathlessly. "But what if he finds us?"

"He's not going to."

"Then if *he* can't find us," she reasoned, "nobody else can."

"We're gonna get out of here," Ace assured her, "so stop with the whining."

"I'm *not* whining."

"You could've fooled me."

CHAPTER FORTY-NINE

Monday morning Renee Falcon received a call from a detective. She wasn't surprised—she'd known it was only a matter of time before she was tagged as one of the last people to see Tasmin Garland before her mysterious disappearance. Only it wasn't so mysterious to Renee; she'd had to pay a lot of people big bonuses to make sure they kept their mouths shut. And unfortunately that made her an accessory to murder, thanks to Anthony Bonar.

In retrospect, Renee wished she'd called the cops and busted Anthony's stinking ass. Unfortunately, she was unable to do so on account of the fact that he had too much information about her past, and if she'd given him up, he would've spilled buckets about the money she'd gotten out of Colombia and shifted to Vegas illegally, and the murdered croupier whose body was buried out in the desert, and the amount of drugs she'd purchased for her hotel guests' pleasure over the years.

Damn Anthony Bonar. She wasn't above putting out a hit on him. What a joy it would be to get rid of him once and for all. Good riddance to a misogynous murderous fuckhead.

She agreed to meet the detective in the coffee shop at the Cavendish. Arriving early, she settled into her usual corner booth, ordered coffee, and picked up a newspaper.

When Detective Diane Franklin walked in, Renee

was surprised. "I wasn't expecting a woman," she said, checking out the black detective, attractive in a no-nonsense way.

"Who did you think you were speaking to on the phone, a secretary?" Diane said, noting that Renee Falcon was an overweight woman with a masculine-style haircut and mannish attire.

"I imagined Detective Franklin was a man."

"As you can see, I'm not," Diane said, sliding into the booth. "I'm a black woman and proud of it."

"I didn't say anything about you being black," Renee said.

"That's all right, I'm sure you noticed."

The two women sized each other up like a couple of heavyweight boxers about to enter the ring.

Shit! Renee thought. *We're off to a fine start.*

Hmm . . . Diane thought. *This one is not going to be easy.*

"Coffee?" Renee inquired.

Diane nodded.

Renee summoned one of the waitresses.

"As I mentioned on the phone," Diane said, "I'm here about Tasmin Garland's disappearance."

"Tasmin has disappeared?" Renee said, managing a look of surprise. "Are you sure?"

"Mrs. Garland hasn't been seen for forty-eight hours, therefore we're starting an investigation," Diane said, producing a weathered notebook from her purse and laying it on the table. "She left a ten-year-old son, an ex-husband, and an excellent job. I understand that the night she vanished she was coming to have dinner with you at your hotel. According to her babysitter, you had told her you were fixing her up with a date."

"No, that's not right at all," Renee said, taking a sip of coffee. "There was no date involved."

"Mrs. Garland seemed to think that's why you had

invited her to dinner," Diane said, her eyes watching Renee's face. "She definitely told the babysitter she was meeting a date."

"Nonsense," Renee said briskly. "A friend of mine was in town and he happened to join us for dinner. He's a married man, there was absolutely no date involved."

"You're sure about that?" Diane asked, tapping her pen on the table.

"Perfectly sure. I don't understand why Tasmin would have been under that impression."

"Who was your friend?" Diane asked.

"What friend?"

"The one that Tasmin was under the impression she was being set up with?"

"An out-of-town business acquaintance."

"His name?"

"Does it matter?"

"Yes."

Renee hesitated for a moment. She couldn't lie—too many people had seen Anthony sitting at their table. Besides, she had to act as if she had nothing to hide.

"Anthony Bonar," she said at last.

"What business are you in with Mr. Bonar?"

"He's not really a business acquaintance," Renee said, quickly changing her story. "More of a longtime friend."

"So," Diane said, scribbling in her notebook. "A business acquaintance or longtime friend? Which is it?"

"Longtime friend," Renee replied.

"And where does Mr. Bonar reside?"

"He travels a lot."

"Is he based in Vegas?"

"No."

"I'll need contact numbers."

"Why?"

"Because I'll need to speak to him."

"Very well. My assistant will have to deal with that."

More scribbling before the next question. "Was it just the three of you at dinner? Yourself, Mrs. Garland, and Mr. Bonar?"

"No," Renee said, reluctant to drag Susie into it, but aware that she had no choice. "My significant other was with us."

"And who is that?"

"My partner, Susie Rae Young."

"Any relation to . . . ?"

"Yes," Renee said abruptly. "She's his widow."

"I see." A long beat. "Changed paths, did she?"

"I hardly think that's any of your business."

"You never know when you're investigating a case what details might turn out to be relevant."

"All I can tell you is that Tasmin came to dinner," Renee said. "Then left around ten-thirty, eleven o'clock. That's the last time I saw her. So . . . if there's nothing else, I have a very busy day ahead of me."

Diane had no intention of going anywhere, not until all her questions were answered to her satisfaction.

"You do business with her at the bank, is that correct?" she asked, pen poised.

"I have done so."

"Was everything satisfactory?"

"Of course."

"Of course?" Diane said. "Sometimes people are dissatisfied with their bank managers. You weren't. Everything was copacetic?"

"Yes."

"How was her mood during dinner?"

"Her mood?"

"Was she upbeat? Depressed? Was she in the frame of mind where you thought she could get in her car, drive off, and never be seen again?"

"She seemed to be happy enough, we had a very pleasant dinner."

"And the conversation was about?"

"How the hell am I supposed to remember what we talked about?"

"Movies? Politics? Family? Perhaps she mentioned her ex-husband?"

"I do not recall."

"Very well, Mrs. Falcon. If you have anything else that you consider helpful you can call me on my direct line." She handed Renee a printed card. "And you don't mind me asking a few questions around the hotel, do you?"

"As long as you don't disturb my guests."

"I'll also have to speak with Mrs. Rae Young as soon as possible."

"There's no need for you to do that," Renee said quickly. "I've told you everything you need to know."

"I understand, but it's my job to interview everyone."

"How time-consuming," Renee said acidly.

"It is," Diane replied, closing her notebook. "But it's prudent to be as thorough as possible. When can I interview Mrs. Rae Young?"

"I'll have to ask her."

"I'd prefer direct contact. Where can I reach her?"

"I'm not sure where she is today."

"A phone number will do."

Reluctantly Renee gave her Susie's number, and abruptly concluded the meeting by standing up.

"I have an extremely busy day ahead of me," she repeated.

"Thank you for your time," Diane said, also getting up from the table.

"Let me know when she turns up," Renee said.

"*If* she does," Diane said.

"I'm sure she will," Renee said, heading for the entrance to the coffee shop.

Diane watched her go. She'd seen plenty during her seventeen years on the force, especially working in Vegas, but in all the years she'd worked there, she'd never met anyone quite like Renee Falcon. The woman was a force. Big and brash. Gay and proud of it. Forceful and overbearing. With something to hide.

Diane Franklin had a nose for secrets, and Renee Falcon was definitely harboring a secret. Diane would bet her career on it.

CHAPTER FIFTY

Alternately running and walking, Max managed to keep on her feet, although she was about ready to give up. She was cold and hungry and everything hurt. Eventually, after what seemed like hours, Ace allowed them to take a rest.

She collapsed under a tree, hugging her knees to her chin, trying to control her shivering.

"What happened to your phone?" he asked.

"He took it. Where's yours?"

"What do you think?"

"I can't tell my mom what happened," she said, worrying about Lucky's reaction.

"Why not?"

"She'd go totally crazy if she knew I let myself get kidnapped."

"You didn't *let* yourself do anything, it was one of those insane things," he said, putting his arm around her and pulling her close. "I'm not coming on to you," he assured her. "I'm keeping us both warm. Body heat, y'know?"

His arms around her felt good, she had no objections. "How about *your* parents?" she asked, snuggling close.

"Don't have any—they died in a plane crash. I live with my older brother. He's a fireman."

"Your brother's a fireman?"

"What did I just say?"

"Sorry, that's one of my bad habits, repeating things."

"You have bad habits?" he teased.

"Shut up."

"I will if you will."

"I don't think I can go much farther," she said. "My ankle's hurting so badly."

"What's up with your ankle? I thought it was your side that hurt."

"He shackled my ankle to the bed, it's all blistered and bleeding."

"Jeez! What a sicko."

"He kept me like that for two days until I finally persuaded him to take it off. Thank God I did, otherwise I'd never have been able to reach the window and get out."

"Sorry this had to happen to you, Max," he said.

"No," she replied. "*I'm* sorry I dragged *you* into this mess, 'cause—y'know . . ."

"What?" he said, squeezing her hand.

"Nothing," she murmured, thinking how incredibly close she felt to this boy she hardly knew. This boy in the Lakers sweatshirt with the cleft in his chin. This boy who'd saved her.

Henry didn't often dream, but when he did his dreams were always extremely vivid and graphic. In this particular dream Maria was stroking his forehead and telling him she loved him. He could see her face, so young and serene and innocent, her intense green eyes staring into his, melting into his as if they were one. Then she climbed on top of him and very slowly began to unzip his pants.

He reached for her breasts to feel them, touch them . . .

And he climaxed in his sleep, which awoke him.

He lay there for a minute, disoriented and perfectly satisfied. He might be a virgin, but that didn't mean he

DROP DEAD BEAUTIFUL 291

did not experience the most earth-shattering orgasms. Usually they were brought on by a trio of girls he visited on the Internet. This time it was different. This time it was real.

After a while he consulted his watch. Five A.M. Monday morning, and only just beginning to get light outside. Maria was asleep in the bedroom. His Maria, so near, so dear.

Yesterday she'd begun to thaw toward him. He'd talked and she'd listened. He'd removed the shackle from her ankle because he'd finally felt he could trust her. She must've sensed—like he did—that it was the beginning of the rest of their lives together. The beginning of paradise.

Feeling exceptionally happy and content, he got out of bed and padded to the bathroom, stopping to listen outside her door as he passed.

Soon he would be in that bed with her. Oh yes, very soon.

But he had no intention of pushing her. As far as he was concerned she could take all the time she needed.

"Let me take a look at your hands," Max said as soon as it started getting light.

Ace held out his hands for her to inspect. They were blistered and covered in scratches, his fingernails broken and torn.

"Do they hurt?" she asked, gently touching them.

"'S okay," he said. "I'll live."

"You want to see my ankle?" she offered.

"It's not number one on my list of things to do, but if you insist," he said, taking a quick peek. "Man, what an asshole!"

"Like you said, he's a sicko."

"At least we got away."

"Thanks to you," she said, looking around and observing nothing but long grass and tall trees. "How long do you think we've been running?"

"I dunno, my watch broke."

"He took mine."

"Do I stink?" Ace asked, sniffing his sweatshirt.

"I'm not exactly Miss Clean, so I wouldn't know."

"No, seriously, do I? I was locked in that place forever. I had to dig through God knows how much crap to get out."

"You're not exactly smelling like a rose, but neither am I."

"She's so sweet."

"No, I'm not," she said, thinking that sweet was hardly the way she wanted him to view her.

"Man," he said, standing up and stretching. "You wanna know what I'm imagining?"

"What?"

"One big fat juicy burger, with fries, and a can of cold beer. Did he feed you?"

"Fruit and cereal, soup and bread. He had a fridge full of stuff."

"That means he was prepared," Ace said thoughtfully. "He must've had it all planned."

"He was definitely expecting me to go off with him for the weekend." She hesitated for a moment. "This might sound weird, but I think he has kind of a crush on me."

"Sure," Ace said disbelievingly. "That must be why he shackled your ankle and held a gun to your head. Some big crush."

"He sounded so cool in his e-mails," Max mused. "I guess he totally faked me out. I feel like *such* a moron. If my mom finds out, she'll kill me."

"So you're telling me that you get kidnapped, manage to make a daring escape, and your mom's gonna kill you?"

"You don't know her."

"Don't think I want to."

"Anyway, I've made up my mind that if we get out of this, I'm not telling her. If she finds out the truth she'll never let me out of the house again."

"Some dragon lady."

"I'll tell her I had a flat tire, got carjacked and dumped off in the woods."

"*That's* a better story than the truth?"

"Maybe."

"Be quiet a minute," he said, standing very still. "I can hear a car, we must be near a road."

"Really?" she said excitedly.

"Yeah, this way," he said, pulling her up. "Let's go hitch a ride."

"Looking like this?" she said, stumbling. "Nobody's going to stop for us."

"Here's the deal—I estimate we're about twenty-five miles outside town, so we need to get a ride. Otherwise we're screwed, he'll catch up with us for sure. When we hit the road, stay by the side so we can see if it's him coming. I saw his car outside the cabin, he must've taken yours back and made a swap."

"Do you think my car's in the Kmart parking lot?"

"If it is we'd better get to it before he does."

"I'm so cold," she said, shivering uncontrollably. "I think I've had it."

"No flaking out on me now, Max. You'll have plenty of time to collapse when we're safe. Right now you gotta move it. I promise you—we're almost there."

CHAPTER FIFTY-ONE

"I never want to do that again," Lucky groaned, reaching for a bottle of water on her bedside table.

"What're you never gonna do again?" Lennie asked, rolling over in bed and placing his hand on her thigh. "The sex? The party? The fight?"

"We missed the fight," she pointed out. "And stop being facetious, I'm in no frame of mind to deal with your sarcasm."

"You're not?" he said, stroking her leg.

"No, Lennie," she said, removing his hand. "I have a bitch of a headache, even my eyes hurt."

"It's not a headache, sweetheart, it's a hangover. You were drinking champagne."

"Don't remind me. Champagne *always* gives me a mother of a headache. Why did you let me drink it?"

"Why did *I* let you?" he said, amused. "When have I ever stopped you from doing anything?"

"That's true," she admitted. "Still . . . I'm sorry we missed the fight," she added, stifling a yawn.

"I'm not. Had more fun making out in the bathroom with you. Now, that's *my* idea of a party."

"I guess I'd better get up," she said, sliding out of bed and heading for the bathroom. "Can you call downstairs and check if Max is back?"

Lennie buzzed Philippe in the kitchen and asked the question.

"She's not back," he called out. "Everyone else is assembling for breakfast."

"Son of a *bitch!*" Lucky exclaimed, emerging from the bathroom. "I'm supposed to fly back to Vegas today, but there's no way I can go until I look her in the eye and tell her *exactly* how I feel about her missing Gino's birthday."

"Go to Vegas. I'll deal with Max."

"Lennie, when it comes to our daughter you're a softie and she knows it."

"Listen," he said. "You've got a hotel to open. You can't let Max distract you."

"It's hardly a distraction, more an act of war," she said, pulling on black workout pants and a long-sleeved Nike T-shirt. "Plus I'm worried about her."

"You are?"

"Why do you think she called Gino Granddad on her message?"

"Who knows?" Lennie said, tying his robe. "Could be she was feeling guilty about missing his party."

"I'm starting to have a bad feeling about things."

"What things?"

"We can't reach our daughter. We have no idea who she's with. The whole situation is giving me negative vibes, and you're totally calm about it."

"She's on her way home, Lucky."

"And what if she's *not*? What if she's run off to Vegas and gotten married?"

"Are you serious?"

"I wouldn't put doing something totally crazy past her. Who knows *what* she's capable of?"

"Yeah, but married? Our Max? In Vegas? Forget about it."

"I hope I'm wrong, but my instincts tell me we shouldn't be hanging around waiting for her to show. We should be doing something."

"Such as?"

"Looking for her, Lennie. How about that?"

"And where do you suggest we start?"

"I wish I knew, but I don't, so I'm calling Cookie. She might remember something she's not telling us."

"What about your trip?"

"Vegas will have to wait."

"I think Billy's adorable," Brigette said, helping herself to a plate of scrambled eggs and bacon from the buffet Philippe had set up in the breakfast room. "And Alex is nothing but a big old bully."

"Hey," Bobby said, drinking a large cup of black coffee, "are you forgetting it was Billy who took the first shot? What was Alex supposed to do, just stand there?"

"He didn't have to pound Billy into the ground," Brigette retorted, sitting down at the table.

"Got a little crush, have we?" Bobby said, teasing her. "If Venus finds out—"

"Oh, yes," Brigette said quickly. "And talking of crushes, I couldn't help noticing that you were all over Venus like a cheap suit!"

"Nothing cheap about me," Bobby responded, cracking a grin. "And isn't she a bit *old* for me?"

"You know what they say, *Uncle*—a woman in her forties is in her sexual prime, and a man in his twenties has it all going on. So . . . get her to dump Billy and the two of you can swing from the chandeliers!"

"C'mon, Brig," he objected, "she's my *mother's* best friend."

"All the better," Brigette said crisply. "That way you can keep it in the family."

"Man, you've got a mouth on you," Bobby said, shaking his head. "From Little Miss Shy to the mouth that roared!"

"I wasn't always sweet little Brigette, sitting in my

apartment quiet as a church mouse," she said. "No, there was a time I was out there being used and abused by a series of assholes."

"Hey, listen, whatever turns you on."

"But that's exactly the point, it *didn't* turn me on. The last one almost killed me. Left me to die in some ramshackle farmhouse outside of Rome, pregnant. I lost the baby and practically bled to death."

"I guess an experience like that would turn anyone into a shut-in."

"Thank God for Lucky, she was the one who saved me. Without her intervention who knows what would've happened."

"That's my mom," Bobby said, going over to the buffet table and helping himself to a bagel. "She's pretty adept at saving people."

"You're so fortunate having her as your mother," Brigette sighed.

"An' don't I know it," Bobby agreed, sitting down next to her.

"Anyway," Brigette said. "I enjoyed coming to L.A. with you, and last night was a fun party. Seeing all my old friends was quite a kick. Did you know that Lina and I used to model together?"

"Wow!" Bobby exclaimed, whistling admiringly. "The two of you must have been some hot combination."

"We were," she said, smiling at the memories. "Between us we ruled L.A., New York, Milan, Paris."

"I bet you did."

"Good times while they lasted."

"Hey, Brig, here's an idea," he said, chewing on his bagel. "When we get back to New York, you should start hanging out with me. I've decided to make it my mission to find you a guy who's not an asshole."

"No thanks, Bobby."

"Why not?"

"'Cause I'm perfectly content being man-free," she said firmly. "One of these days you'll learn. Love is a tough road, and believe me, the highs are not worth the lows."

"*Very* philosophical."

"I try."

"And so pretty while she's trying," he said, making major eye contact.

"If you weren't my uncle, I'd think you were flirting," Brigette said, half smiling.

"Who, *me?*"

"You're a dog, Bobby. The kind of guy I would've been attracted to before I learned better."

"That's insulting," he said, not insulted at all.

"How many girls did you sleep with and not call back last year?"

"Hey," he objected.

"I thought so," she said triumphantly. "You're a dog."

"Who's a dog?" Lucky asked, entering the room.

"Your son."

"That's okay," Lucky said, pouring herself a glass of freshly squeezed orange juice. "He's twenty-three, he's entitled to enjoy himself."

"Not if he treats women badly."

"Who said I treat women badly?" Bobby spluttered. "I take 'em out to dinner, buy 'em presents—"

"Sleep with them, then run like thunder," Brigette said, finishing the sentence for him.

"Nice opinion you have of me," Bobby said cheerfully.

"Took me years to figure out men," Brigette said. "I think I've finally got it down."

"So cynical for one so young," Lucky said, sitting at the table.

"Yes," Brigette agreed, quite enjoying the banter. "And you, Lucky, better than anyone, know why."

"That's true," Lucky said.

Philippe entered the breakfast room looking quite flustered for once.

"Everything all right?" Lucky asked.

"There's twenty men dismantling the tent," Philippe said. "May I suggest everyone stays out of their way until they're finished?"

"Why? Is someone in their way?" Lucky asked.

"Gino Junior and his friends."

"I'll talk to him, Philippe."

"Thank you, Mrs. Golden. Oh, and this was in the mailbox," he added, handing her the now-familiar envelope.

"What's that?" Bobby said, pouncing.

"Just another one of those stupid invitations," she said, tearing it open.

Bobby grabbed it from her. The same three words were scrawled on the card: *Drop Dead Beautiful.*

"We need to get someone on this," he said.

"No we don't," Lucky said.

"At least put in extra security cameras by the mailbox so we can see who's delivering the envelopes."

"Okay, if it'll make you happy I'll have Philippe arrange it."

"*I'll* tell him."

"That's fine."

Satisfied, Bobby poured himself another cup of coffee. "Max back yet?" he asked. "Be nice to see her before we take off."

"She'll be back today," Lucky said, not prepared to share her daughter's bad behavior with everyone.

"Thought she was coming back for Gino's party," Bobby said.

"So did I. But you know Max . . ."

"Yeah, *right.*"

"What time are you leaving?"

"Around two. Thought I'd hang out with Gino before he heads off to Palm Springs. He told me he's taken up golf."

"Gino? Golf?" Lennie said, strolling into the room and heading straight for the coffee. "Now, *that* I'd like to see."

"I wouldn't," Lucky said. "The thought of Gino on a golf course with a bunch of old-fart buddies hitting a ball around is *not* the Gino I know and love."

"Ha!" Bobby said. "You'd like him to be all Brando-like, sitting in a room handing out favors to the neighborhood peasants!"

"You have a brilliant imagination, Bobby," Lucky said coolly.

"Didn't Gino used to—"

"Okay," Lucky said as Gino Junior came in with two of his friends. "That's enough."

"But Mom—"

"Enough, I said. And you," she added, talking to Gino Junior, "leave the people dismantling the tent alone, they've got a job to do."

"We were only goofing around, Mom."

"Then don't. Okay?"

Since when had she become the mother figure? The disciplinarian?

Well . . . having kids did that to a person.

She couldn't wait to get back to Vegas and her hotel. Right now that's where she belonged.

They were opening in two weeks and she *had* to be there, *wanted* to be there.

As soon as she tracked down Max she'd be on her way.

CHAPTER FIFTY-TWO

After making himself a cup of tea, Henry returned to his rollaway bed, where he attempted to go back to sleep and summon up the magnificent and magical dream he'd experienced earlier.

Ah . . . Maria. All over him. So young and innocent. Maria, his dream girl.

The title he'd bestowed on her excited him, making him more anxious than ever to see her.

Once more he got out of bed, wondering if it was too early to wake her. Today he would fix her a proper breakfast, eggs and bacon with toast and strawberry jam.

Yes, he decided, she would like that, unless she didn't eat bacon. Perhaps she was a vegetarian. He needed to know more about her. He needed to know everything about her.

He wondered what his mother would have to say on the day he brought Maria home. He rehearsed the scene in his head, imagining the look of surprise on Penelope's face.

"Good morning, Mother."

"Good morning, dear."

"I would like you to meet Maria, the girl I'm going to marry."

"She's very pretty, dear. And she looks smart too. Are you sure she's not too pretty and smart for you?"

Dammit! That was not the way the scene was supposed

to go. Penelope Whitfield-Simmons even controlled his daydreams with her caustic remarks.

Ever since he could remember, his mother had put him down, belittled him, treated him with no respect. She'd never told him he was clever or handsome or any of the things a son wants to hear from his mother. She'd never hugged him or kissed him. It simply wasn't fair.

He steamed about his mother for a moment or two, then realized she wasn't there to annoy him with her nasty spiteful remarks. He was on his own, free to do whatever he wished.

And he wished to see Maria.

He got out of bed, dressed, and carefully began to prepare his loved one her breakfast.

"You got your car keys?" Ace asked.

"What do you think?" Max snapped back. She knew she shouldn't be taking her bad mood out on Ace, since he'd basically saved her, but she couldn't help herself.

They were sitting in the back of a battered Chevrolet Impala driven by an elderly man with his redheaded thirteen-year-old grandson in the passenger seat beside him.

Fortunately, the old man couldn't see that well, so at the behest of his grandson, who'd spotted Max in her torn jeans and tight tank top standing by the side of the road, he'd stopped for them and was giving them a ride into town.

Max slumped against the seat in the back. She was exhausted, everything hurt, and she was scared of going home. She was certain that if Lucky ever found out the truth, she'd ground her forever. She'd missed Gino's big party, and in Lucky's eyes there would be no excuse for that, especially as she'd faithfully promised to be there. Her life was about to turn into pure crap.

"It's okay if you don't have keys," Ace said. "I can hot-wire it."

The thirteen-year-old swiveled his head, staring at Max's boobs, his teenage lust bursting out all over. "You know how to hot-wire a car?" he asked, still staring at Max's chest. "Awesome!"

"He knows," Max answered, indicating Ace. "He robs banks, hot-wires cars, he's a regular man of all trades."

"Awesome!" the boy repeated.

Ace took a swig from the water bottle the old man had offered, then passed it to Max. She took a couple of gulps. Now that they were almost safe, her nerves were beginning to kick in. What was she going to tell Lucky? Definitely not the truth, it was too stupid and humiliating, plus Lucky would never let her forget it.

She decided to go with the carjacked story. That was her safest bet.

"You happen to have a phone?" Ace asked the kid.

"I wish," the boy said. "Grandpa thinks cell phones rot the brain."

"Who do you want to phone?" Max asked, shooting Ace a sideways glance. He was still a major hottie, in spite of his bedraggled appearance.

"My brother."

"You're not going to tell him, are you?"

"Not if you don't want me to."

"No, I don't."

"So we're just gonna let that freak get away with it?"

"What freak?" the boy asked.

"Nobody you ever wanna meet," Ace said.

The old man, hunched over the wheel, launched into a nasty coughing fit. The boy took the water bottle back from Max and handed it to his grandfather. The car swerved on the dusty road as the old man drank.

"How about I drive?" Ace suggested, leaning forward. "You look like you could use a break."

The old man acquiesced. He was tired and his arthritis was playing up, his hands bent and misshapen. "Wouldn't mind that a bit, son," he said, clicking his teeth. "You got a license?"

"Yes, sir," Ace replied politely.

The old man pulled the car over. Ace got out. The boy slithered over the passenger seat and into the back next to Max.

She shied away—he reminded her of Gino Junior's friends with their horny eyes and leering stares. The old man settled into the front passenger seat while Ace got behind the wheel.

"How long before we reach Big Bear?" Max asked.

" 'Bout half an hour," the old man said, and promptly fell asleep.

CHAPTER FIFTY-THREE

"A detective will be calling you," Renee informed Anthony over the phone.

"What the fuck you talkin' 'bout?" Anthony replied, a ferocious scowl covering his face.

"Detective Franklin from Vegas. She might even send someone to interview you if she's not satisfied with your answers, so I suggest you try and repeat exactly what I've already told her."

"You must be fuckin' shittin' me?" Anthony exploded. "You gave the cops my name?"

"I *had* to, you were sitting at the table with us for over two hours, everyone from the busboys to the guests in the hotel saw you. I can't pretend you weren't there."

"Why the fuck not?" he said, marveling at Renee's stupidity.

"I've had to pay a lot of people off, but the entire hotel—impossible."

"I don't fuckin' get it," Anthony raged. "That's the dumbest move you've ever made."

"No," Renee said sharply. "My dumbest move was aiding and abetting you. I should've called the cops."

"Don't even think about it," he said, his voice cold. "You know what would've happened to you if you'd made a foolish move like that."

"Are you threatening me, Anthony?"

"Of course not," he said, backing down. "But what the fuck am I supposed to say to this detective?"

"Tell her you're a friend of Susie and mine, we had dinner, and that's it."

"Jesus *Christ!*" he snarled. "Who needs this shit?"

"I know," Renee said. "I'm not thrilled myself. I've got a detective snooping around my hotel questioning people—how do you think I like that? I haven't given her your number yet. What number should I tell her?"

"Here's the deal," Anthony said, still pissed off. "I'll call her."

"That won't fly."

"How d'*you* know?"

"Because I do."

"Jesus Christ, Renee! You're a fuckin' moron! Give her my cell, not any of my business numbers."

Renee controlled her own temper. Anthony was the fucking moron and she was starting to think of ways to get him out of her life permanently.

"When will you be back here?" she asked.

"In time for the big event. Everything still in place? No fuckups?"

"Apart from cops crawling all over my hotel, everything's on track."

"You can handle it."

Of course she could handle it. Who did Anthony Bonar think he was, issuing orders as if she were some lowly employee there to do his bidding? Fuck him.

"Right now Tasmin is listed as missing," she said.

"An' there's no way they can come up with more, ain't that so?"

"Yes, Anthony," she said through clenched teeth.

"Your people were thorough?"

"Yes," she said, knowing he was making sure she'd arranged to have Tasmin's body buried where nobody would ever find it, that is, unless *she* pointed them in the right direction. "Everything's taken care of," she added.

"It better be," he said, slamming down the phone. "Son of a *bitch!*" he yelled, furious that he had to deal with this shit.

"What's the matter, Papa?" Carolina asked, entering the room wearing a skimpy yellow bikini and flowered flip-flops.

"Nothing, Princess, it's business," he said, distracted.

"What business exactly are you in?" Carolina asked, biting into an apple.

"Import/export, you know that," he replied, noticing that the bikini she had on was showing too much skin. She was thirteen, for chrissakes, what moron allowed her to buy a bikini more suited for a Victoria's Secret model?

"Yes, Papa, but *what* do you import?" Carolina persisted. "One of my friends asked me the other day, and I didn't know what to say."

"I import all kinda things, Princess. I buy items from China, ship 'em to America, then they get sold in the stores."

"Oooh," Carolina said, taking another bite of her apple. "Can I go to one of the stores and buy stuff?"

"There's nothing you'd like," he said, wondering where this sudden interest in his business was coming from. "It's all cheap crap, not your style."

"Why do you sell crap?"

"'Cause it makes me big bucks."

"I lika big bucks," Carolina said, giggling.

"Ain't ya got some kinda cover-up?" Anthony asked. "You're too young to be walkin' around with everythin' hangin' out."

"Maybe one day *I'll* go into business," Carolina mused, ignoring his criticism.

"No import/export for you," he said sharply. "When you're old enough Papa's gonna find you a nice boy to settle down with so you can give me lotsa grandkids."

"What if I don't *want* to get married, Papa?" Carolina said, pulling a face. "Boys suck."

"Some of 'em do an' some of 'em don't. One day you'll change your mind."

"Why would I do that, Papa?" she asked, her pretty face a picture of innocence.

"Enough with the questions," he said impatiently. "An' go put somethin' on over that bikini."

Carolina looked dismayed.

"Sorry, Princess," he said quickly. "Didn't mean to get on your case. C'mon back over here an' give your papa a big, fat hug."

She ran over to him. He squeezed her a little too tightly. "What you doin' today?"

"We're having lunch at the beach club, then we might go water-skiing."

He enjoyed the fact that he had kids who got to do all the things he'd never had the opportunity of doing when he was growing up. They snow-skied, water-skied, played tennis, rode horses. He was proud that he'd been able to give them so much.

"Where's your mom?" he asked.

"Dunno," Carolina replied.

"Go find her, tell her I wanna see her."

"When are we leaving here, Papa?"

"You know I never make plans ahead. I'm a 'feel it, do it' kinda guy."

"My friends need to know 'cause they have to tell their parents."

"When do you *wanna* leave?"

"Whenever you do."

"Okay, I'll let you know."

"Thanks, Papa," Carolina said, skipping from the room.

His mind was still on the phone call from Renee. He

couldn't even relax in peace without being bothered by the Vegas incident.

It was over.

Done with.

Why was Renee behaving like such a stupid bitch?

"Papa wants to see you," Carolina said, approaching Irma, who was lying out by the infinity pool soaking up the hot Acapulco sun.

"What does he want?"

"How should *I* know?" Carolina said somewhat rudely.

Irma didn't bother telling her daughter off. She'd relinquished all responsibility. Anthony was in charge now—Carolina was all his.

"Tell him I'll be right there."

"I'm not a *message* service," Carolina said, ruder by the minute. "Tell him yourself."

What a lovely young lady *she* was turning into. Good luck, Anthony.

Irma got up from her lounger and made her way toward the villa. When she got there she found Anthony sitting on one of the outdoor patios smoking an oversized cigar, his two dogs lying at his feet.

"You wanted me?" she said.

"Yeah," he answered, blowing acrid smoke in her direction. "What's up with you?"

"What's up with me?" she repeated. "I'm not sure what you mean."

"I mean, what the fuck's up with you," he said, scowling. "You're acting like a zombie, all zoned out like nothin's gettin' through to you. You on Prozac or one of those antidepressant pills?"

"Why would I be on antidepressant pills?" she said, veering toward being sarcastic. "You've taken my children, left me in a foreign country with no friends. Surely I'd have no reason to be depressed?"

"You got homes all over the fuckin' place, money to shop your ass off, an' now you're complainin'—is that what I'm hearin'?"

"You can hear what you want to," Irma said, feeling quite bold. "I don't care anymore."

"You'd better stop this shit," Anthony raged. "I work like a maniac to keep my family happy, an' this is the thanks I get? A miserable wife who barely fuckin' functions."

"Oh, I function," she said, wishing she could tell him how well she functioned when Luis was in her bedroom going down on her with a passion she'd never felt from her husband.

"Yeah, in Chanel an' Louis Vuitton with my credit card in your hand you function like a fuckin' machine."

"Is that all?" Irma said calmly. "Can I go now?"

Anthony had been straining for a fight, and Irma wasn't giving him one. What the fuck was she on?

"Don't think you're goin' anywhere," he said. "I—" Before he could continue, his cell phone rang. He snapped it open. "Yes?" he barked.

"Mr. Bonar?" a female voice said.

"Who wants t'know?" he said suspiciously.

"This is Detective Franklin from Las Vegas. I'd like to ask you a few questions about Tasmin Garland."

"Hold on a minute." He turned to Irma, waving her away. "Business, gotta take this."

"Permission to leave granted," Irma murmured, infuriating Anthony even more.

He waited until she was out of sight before taking the call. "Yes?" he said, pacing.

"Were you fixed up on a blind date with Mrs. Tasmin Garland last Friday night?"

"Huh?"

"I've spoken to Renee Falcon. I believe you, Mrs. Rae Young, and Mrs. Garland had dinner Friday night at the Cavendish Hotel. Is that correct?"

"Why you askin'?"

"Because Mrs. Garland is missing. She hasn't been seen since that dinner."

"I hardly know her."

"You dined with her, Mr. Bonar. She informed her babysitter that she was being fixed up on a blind date, and since you were the only man present . . ."

"That means shit. I was sittin' there with a coupla muff divers, didn't even catch the other broad's name."

"I see. Well . . . perhaps you can recall the conversation, the mood of the evening."

"Sorry," he said abruptly. "Had a steak, talked business with Renee, an' left town."

"Unexpectedly?"

"Huh?"

"Unexpectedly, Mr. Bonar?"

"No."

"Your pilot says otherwise."

She'd talked to his fucking pilot! This was unbelievable!

"My pilot knows nothin'," he said, a sharp edge to his voice. "I tell him what t'do when *I* decide t'do it."

"I see. And you decided to leave Vegas at midnight. Unexpectedly."

"It wasn't so unexpected. I knew I was going."

"Apparently your pilot didn't. He thought you were staying overnight."

"I don't pay my pilots to think. I pay 'em to get me from A to B."

"I understand."

"Yeah."

"I want to make certain I get this right. You're saying that after the dinner was finished, you never saw Mrs. Garland again, is that correct?"

"'S right. So if ya got nothin' else . . ."

"Thank you, Mr. Bonar. Any further questions, I'll call this number."

"Yeah, do that," he said, clicking his phone shut.

Goddammit! Fucking dumb questions.

He summoned The Grill. "Call the main office," he said. "I need 'em to change my cell phone number, an' get me a new pilot—tell 'em to fire the one I got now. Make sure the new one starts pronto, 'cause we're leavin' for Miami tomorrow."

CHAPTER FIFTY-FOUR

The boy in the back of the Chevrolet was chattering to Max about music, telling her who he liked and who he didn't. The old man was snoring. Max lapsed into silence, trying not to think about how much her side and ankle hurt her.

Ace, with one scratched-up hand on the steering wheel, was wondering if there was anything to eat in the car—a chocolate bar, chewing gum, anything. He leaned over to take a look in the glove department, and as he did so the old man woke up.

"What you nosin' around for?" the old man said, his voice quavering. "We got no money. We're hardworkin' farmers. If you're gonna rob us, it ain't your day, sonny boy."

"Not planning on robbing you, sir," Ace said. "I was seeing if you had anything to eat."

"All you hadda do was ask," the old man grumbled. "We got a half-eaten ham sandwich if that's any use to you."

A half-eaten ham sandwich sounded like bliss. "Uh . . . thanks," Ace gulped, overcome by the thought of food.

"Give him the sandwich, boy," the old man ordered his grandson.

"But Gramps," the boy whined. "I was gonna have that later."

"Can't you see these people are hungry?" he said,

throwing Ace a suspicious look. "What you two young-uns doin' out on the road so early anyway?"

"Thought I told you," Ace said. "Our car broke down."

"A likely story the mess you're in. I've heard every story from here to Florida," the old man said. "A likely story. Give him the sandwich."

Reluctantly the boy rummaged in his backpack and produced a brown paper bag. "Here," he said, thrusting the bag at Max, his eyes fixed firmly on her breasts.

She opened the bag, took out the sandwich, and passed it forward to Ace. "You have it," she said.

"We'll split it," he answered.

"No, I'm okay. Really. It's all yours."

Ace devoured the sandwich in three quick bites.

"That's the best-tasting thing ever," he said. "Thanks."

The grandfather had fallen asleep again, and the boy was continuing his music conversation. "I got my own radio," he boasted. "Gramps won't get me one of them boom boxes like I want, he says we can't afford it. I'll get it one of these days soon as I start workin'."

Max made a mental note to find out where these people lived and send this boy a CD player. If it wasn't for them, they would still be standing on the road hoping that Internet Freak wasn't going to find them and stick a gun in their faces.

She wondered what was going on at home. As soon as she got near a phone, she'd call Cookie and find out before driving back to L.A.

Hopefully when they arrived at the parking lot her car would be there, Ace would start it for her, and she'd drive back to L.A. as quickly as possible.

What a nightmare this past weekend had been.

What a story to tell Cookie and Harry!

She couldn't wait.

* * *

It was a clear day, crisp, cold, and quite invigorating. Henry decided to go outside into the garden and pick some flowers to put on the tray before he took it in to Maria for her breakfast. He was determined to find something pretty to put on her tray.

Making his way around the side of the house, he was startled to see several boards lying on the ground. He couldn't imagine where they'd come from. Then it dawned on him that they'd been wrenched from Maria's window.

For a moment he didn't understand what was happening. It was impossible for her to escape, and yet . . .

Frantically he ran over to the window and peered in. There was no Maria lying in the bed. No Maria in the room. No Maria!

Rage swept over him, a stark cold rage that enveloped his entire body.

Where was she? How had she escaped?

He ran to the outhouse, finding that the big wooden door was still intact. Rushing back into the cabin, he got his gun and the key to the outhouse, then he went back outside and tentatively unlocked the door.

Instead of the body he'd been hoping to see, there was a gaping hole in the ground leading to a tunnel where the cousin had obviously managed to burrow his way out.

Black fury roared in his head. How had this happened? Even more important, how long had they been gone?

He raced back into the cabin, grabbed his car keys, ran out to his car, jumped in, and set off.

Nobody was taking Maria away from him now. Nobody.

The old man was snoring loudly.

"Mind if I put the radio on?" Ace asked.

"I don't care," the boy answered. "Gramps listens to them country stations, but I like rock and roll."

"Who's your fave?" Max asked.

"Rolling Stones, they're good."

"You're too young to know anything about the Stones," Max said, turning her head to look out the back window.

"You too," the boy said. "How old *are* you?"

"I'm—" She was just about to lie, but then she thought, what's the point? "Sixteen," she said. "And you?"

"Gonna be fourteen in a month."

"You're both too young to know who the Rolling Stones are," Ace remarked.

"I am so not," Max objected. "I'm into all kinds of music. Rap, soul, alternative rock."

"The Stones must be as old as this kid's grandfather," Ace said, feeling a lot stronger since eating the half sandwich.

"Thing is they're still rockin'," Max pointed out. "Saw their last concert in L.A. They rule!"

"I've got a record of Mick Jagger singing 'Satisfaction,'" the boy boasted.

"Wow!" Max said, giving him a little slack. "You're smarter than you look."

"You bein' rude?" the boy asked, scratching his head.

"Just eff-ing with you," Max teased.

"Now, now, kids," Ace said from the driver's seat. "And I do mean kids," he added pointedly.

"What?" Max said.

"Sixteen, huh?"

"Shut *up* and put on the radio," she said, embarrassed because she'd originally told him she was eighteen, and now he'd caught her in a lie.

He reached over and switched on the radio. Music filled the car—a twangy female moaning about lost love and a husband who'd dumped her with six kids and no money.

Glancing in the rearview mirror, Ace noticed a car coming up fast behind them. He drew over to the side to let it pass.

Then he saw that it wasn't just any car. It was the Volvo he'd seen outside the cabin, and if he wasn't mistaken, sitting behind the wheel was Internet Freak in hot pursuit.

"Shit!" he exclaimed.

"What?" Max asked, leaning forward.

"Believe me, you don't wanna know."

CHAPTER FIFTY-FIVE

They'd argued all the way home. Venus was furious with Billy for getting in a fight with Alex—a fight that had ended only when Steven and Bobby managed to separate the two men. But not before Billy had received a black eye and Alex a split lip.

When they'd finally arrived at her house, Billy had informed her he wouldn't be staying the night due to his early call to the set the next morning. "Speak to you tomorrow," he'd said, barely kissing her on the cheek.

"Fine," she'd said, and stormed inside, angry and frustrated. Billy's childish behavior reflected on her. She was sure it would get reported in the tabloids or on some scurrilous gossip Web site, and once more she would be the brunt of every late-night talk-show host's jokes.

She'd spent the rest of the evening alone in her bedroom, seething.

By the time Cole arrived early Monday morning for their workout session, she was ready to explode.

"You're lookin' angry," Cole remarked. "Beautiful but angry. Think we'll do the gym today, get out some of that aggression."

"Wouldn't *you* be angry if you were in my position?" she demanded. "I'm sleeping with an idiot!"

"My philosophy is never take responsibility for somebody else's bad behavior," Cole said, flexing his arms as they made their way across the courtyard to Venus's fully equipped home gym.

"It's not fair," she complained. "I'll get all the blame for this, y'know."

"How come?" Cole asked, adjusting the weight level on one of the many pieces of Cybex gym equipment.

"Because it'll be in the papers that *I* instigated the fight. They'll say that Alex Woods and Billy Melina were fighting over me. I can see it now: 'Venus's Boy Toy Springs to Her Defense,' something like that. They make up this shit all the time."

"Honey, Billy doesn't get called a boy toy anymore. He's a movie star in his own right."

"Yes, Cole, *I* know that and *you* know that, but it's more fun for the tabloids to give him a label. You know how they get off giving celebrities demeaning nicknames."

"You've got a point, but we're not gonna dwell on it. Now let's get your ass on the treadmill."

"No treadmill today, I don't feel like it."

"Exercise helps."

"It does?"

"You betcha."

"I'm just pissed, you know."

"I understand," Cole said soothingly. "But you can't let it get to you."

"Nice, huh? I can see it now, the two of them working together today. Billy with his black eye and Alex with his split lip. It'll be a fun day on the set."

"I think it's cool they're working together," Cole said. "They'll be forced to interact, then it'll all be history. You'll be the only one thinkin' about it."

"I suppose it *is* my fault," she admitted.

"An' why's that?"

" 'Cause I'm the one who told Billy that Alex said something negative about him to Lucky, and no good ever comes from repeating gossip."

"Okay, that's a positive—you learned a lesson."

"Did you bring me a Starbucks?"

"Do I look like I'm carrying Starbucks?"

"I'll send somebody out to get us two Mocha Frappuccinos—what do you think?"

"I think you're putting off getting on the treadmill. We'll add boxing today, get out all that aggression."

"Not yet. Let's talk about you for a change, I'm bored with me. Tell me about you and Rich. I'm impressed."

"What're you impressed about?" Cole said with a casual shrug. "Rich is a nice guy."

"He's not just a guy, Cole, he's an icon."

"I get off on mixing with icons. Why d'you think I'm with you every morning?"

"Hmm . . . so now that you've got a super-affluent sugar boyfriend—"

"Listen to you, madam, taggin' *me* with a nickname."

"Okay, I shouldn't have said that. I'll try again. Uh, now that you've got this very famous rock star boyfriend, you really don't have to keep working, do you?"

"I train people because I *like* doing it," Cole explained. "Why do *you* keep performing? You've got enough money socked away to stop anytime you want."

"'Cause I love it."

"Then concentrate on what you do an' stop bitchin' about your boyfriend. Career first—weren't you the one who taught me that?"

"You're right," she said, finally jumping on the treadmill in a better frame of mind. "Career first. Assholes second."

"Well," Cole said with a jaunty grin, "let's not get carried away."

"It's all over the freakin' news," Kev announced.

"What is?" Billy asked. He was sitting in his trailer at the location, waiting to be called to the set. Kev had arrived with the newspapers, a stack of mail, and a Thermos of decent coffee.

"This fight you had last night," Kev said, dumping a pile of fan mail on a side table. "I wanna hear all about it."

"Jesus!" Billy complained, not in the mood to discuss it with Kev. "You can't do anything in this town without it getting out."

"You actually *hit* Alex Woods?" Kev said. "Punched him in the freakin' face?"

"Take a look at my eye, Kev," Billy said evenly. "*He* hit *me*."

"Can't see anything," Kev said, squinting at him.

"That's 'cause they covered it in the makeup trailer, but I have a mother of a black eye underneath all this crap."

"Who threw the first one, bro?"

"It might've been me."

"Shit!" Kev said, slapping his palms together. "Wish I'd been there to see it. What did Venus say?"

"She's major pissed."

"I bet. You know how she likes to protect her image."

"*I'm* not her fucking image," Billy exploded. "How come you say dumb crap like that?"

"'Cause one minute you're tellin' me you're a free man watchin' football an' hittin' the clubs, and the next you're Mr. Freakin' Boy Toy."

"Fuck you, Kev. Don't ever call me that."

"I'm only repeating what they're saying on TV. Turn on channel eleven, Jillian and Dorothy are all over it."

Billy frowned. He had an important scene that morning and he wasn't sure how things would turn out when he and Alex came face-to-face. Was he supposed to apologize?

No, why should he? Alex was as much to blame as he was. Alex was the one running around behind his back mouthing shit. *He* was the one who deserved an apology, not Alex Woods.

He had other things on his mind too. The girl who'd given him crabs, who according to her *hadn't* given him crabs. She was threatening to tell Venus if he didn't score her an acting gig on his movie. And how was he supposed to do that now? Alex would not be exactly open to granting him any favors.

There was a knock on the trailer door.

"Who is it?" he called out.

"Maggie."

"What's up, Mags?" Billy said, throwing open the door, thinking that maybe she could help.

Maggie climbed the steps. "There's press hanging around everywhere," she informed them. "Alex is not happy."

"Uh, yeah?" Billy said, wondering what her point was.

"Not the press that was supposed to be here today, press that decided to show up uninvited."

"I wonder why," Kev chortled, quite enjoying the latest drama.

Billy threw him a dirty look.

"They want your take on the fight, Billy. How about making a comment?"

"It wasn't a fight, Mags, it was a minor altercation."

"Alex has already put out a statement."

"What'd he say?"

"That it was a misunderstanding and the two of you are the best of friends."

"I'll make the same statement, then."

"That's what I wanted to hear," Maggie said. "The less you say, the better. The movie is what's important."

"Yeah, I know."

"And regarding your . . . altercation, on my advice, Alex has forgotten about it. I suggest you do the same."

"Wish I had a woman like you in *my* life, Mags."

"You do," she said crisply. "You've got Venus. She's quite a woman."

"Yeah, right."

Maggie turned to leave.

"Hey, Mags," Billy said, stopping her at the door and turning on the baby blues so she could melt right into them.

"Yes, Billy?"

"Uh . . . there's this girl," he said, keeping it vague. "She's a friend of a friend, and, uh . . . I kinda promised I'd get her a bit in the movie. Nothing big, like a walk-on."

"A walk-on," Maggie repeated, raising a cynical eyebrow.

"That's it."

"Billy, you know what Alex is like. He sees every face, casts every role big and small."

"You can swing it, Mags."

"What's her name?" Maggie sighed.

"I'll let you know."

After a vigorous workout Venus got on the phone to Lucky.

"Hey," she said. "Great party."

"Thanks," Lucky said.

"Apart from that, I called to tell you how sorry I am about Billy getting out of line. It was so uncalled for."

"That's okay," Lucky said. "It made Gino's night."

"Seriously?"

"Oh yes, there's nothing that turns Gino on like a good fight."

"Billy's sorry it happened too," Venus said quickly, apologizing for her boyfriend, who apparently didn't give a shit.

"It's forgotten."

"Hardly. The press is all over me. They're outside my house in droves waiting for Billy to comment, and he's not even here."

"Where is he?"

"Out on location with Alex," she said, laughing derisively. "That should be a press-worthy scene."

"I would imagine so."

"Y'know, Lucky, I think the time has finally come for me to move on."

"Again?"

"This time I mean it. Oh, and when I do—please, I beg you—make sure I *never* hook up with an actor again. Too much baggage."

"Whatever," Lucky said, her mind elsewhere.

"What's up with you?" Venus questioned. "You sound out of it."

"Max is still not home and I'm mad as hell. Right now I'm on my way out to talk to Cookie again. These kids share secrets—I've got a hunch our little Cookie knows more than she's saying. . . ."

"Anything I can do?"

"Thanks for the offer, but no."

"Well . . . if you think of anything . . ."

"You'll be the first."

"I should hope so."

After speaking to Lucky, Venus realized it was time she got it together. Billy was taking up too much time and energy. Because of him, she was neglecting her career, and her career was what she *should* be concentrating on, not a man. Even worse—a younger man. And on top of everything else—an actor!

What was she thinking? Falling in love was a bitch. Getting over it was even worse.

But she would do it. No more making excuses for Billy's behavior. No more putting herself out for him. He had to grow up and take some responsibility.

And just as she was thinking about ending their affair, he called, apologized profusely, and told her he'd make it up to her and that he'd been thinking about her all day.

She melted.

Damn! She was still in love.

Why not?

"Who's this girl you wanna get on the movie?" Kev was desperate to know.

"A friend of a friend," Billy answered evasively.

"What friend?"

"Fuck off with your questions."

"How's your crabs?"

"What?"

"You heard."

The trouble with best friends was that they usually found out stuff, and Kev knew him too well for him to keep up the lie.

"Okay," he admitted. "It was a mistake, a one-off."

"Tell me everything," Kev begged, agog with interest. "And don't leave out *any* of the dirty details."

CHAPTER FIFTY-SIX

Ace hit the accelerator, and the Chevrolet shot forward.

"What's up?" Max asked, alarmed.

"It's him," Ace said.

"Who?" the boy asked, wriggling around on his seat.

"Nobody," Max replied, looking out the back window and seeing the Volvo in close pursuit. Her stomach did a somersault and she felt like she was about to throw up. How could this be happening, just when she'd thought they were safe?

"Don't worry," Ace said, pressing his foot down hard. "There's nothing he can do."

Oh, yes there is, Max thought. *He can shoot our asses.*

She glanced quickly at the boy. "What's your name?" she asked.

"Jed," he said. "Why we speeding? Gramps don't like goin' fast, sez it uses up too much gas."

"Gramps is asleep," Max pointed out. "So what he doesn't know . . ."

"Think I'd better wake him," Jed said, looking worried.

"No," Max said quickly. "Don't do that. We're playing a game with a friend, it's no big deal."

Jed climbed up on his knees and peered out the back window. "If this person's your friend, how come you ain't drivin' with 'im?"

"'Cause it's complicated," Max replied as Ace put his foot to the floorboard and the Chevrolet hit its limit.

Her heart was pounding—they were still in the middle of nowhere.

WHAT IF INTERNET FREAK CAUGHT THEM?

He spotted them immediately and gave chase.

So incensed was Henry that he could barely see straight. Not only was he angry, he was also deeply disappointed, he'd had such high hopes for himself and Maria. And now she was running away from him, and it was so wrong.

The problem was her cousin. He should've shot the cousin when he'd had the chance.

Pow! A bullet through the heart.

Good-bye, cousin.

Good-bye, problem.

A muscle in his cheek twitched uncontrollably as he chased the old Chevrolet down the deserted road. Eventually they'd reach the main highway, so it was imperative he stopped them before they got there.

But how? He was not a very experienced driver, he had no idea how to run another car off the road, because if he did, that's exactly what he'd do. Besides, he couldn't take a chance of hurting Maria. It wasn't *her* fault she'd run, it was all to do with the cousin.

Henry was filled with hate against the cousin, just as he was filled with hate against Lucky Santangelo and Billy Melina. They were all unworthy, all three of them.

Only Maria was pure. His Maria.

Somehow or other he had to save her.

"Can't you go any faster?" Max yelled.

"We're going as fast as we can," Ace yelled back.

"I'm gonna wake Gramps," Jed whined.

"No you're *not*," Max snapped, thinking it was a miracle that the old man was still asleep.

"You people are weird," Jed sniveled.

"We're not weird, we're like having fun," Max said, trying to convince him that nothing much was going on.

"This ain't *my* idea of fun," Jed said. "I wanna wake Gramps."

"No!" Max said sharply. "Let him sleep."

"But I—"

"Tell you what," Max said, trying to keep it together. "When I get back to L.A., I'm sending you a CD player and all the Stones CDs. What do you think?"

"You'd do that?" Jed said, his face lighting up.

"Yes. I swear," she answered, saying a silent prayer that Internet Freak was not going to catch them.

Ace swerved the car, narrowly missing a coyote that suddenly appeared in the middle of the road.

Max could see he was sweating, but she had to admit he was doing a great job of getting them away from the Volvo, which seemed to be slowing down. She was trying to remain calm for the sake of the kid, but it wasn't easy, since her heart was pounding so hard she thought it might burst right out of her skin.

"When?" Jed asked.

"When what?"

"When I gonna get me one of them CD things?"

"Soon," she said. "Like that's a faithful promise."

Henry hit the coyote full on. The animal rose up in the air and came thumping down on the hood of the car with a sickening thud, blood trickling down the windshield.

Henry pressed his foot down on the brake and promptly lost control. The Volvo veered across the road, finally shuddering to a stop in a ditch.

Henry hit his head on the windshield, and then there was nothing but silence.

CHAPTER FIFTY-SEVEN

Lucky drove over to Cookie's house all set to catch her off guard. This time she was determined to find out more information. Enough fudging around from Cookie—there was only so much pretending she could get away with. Cookie *had* to know *something* and Lucky was going to find out what that something was.

Once she'd driven through the impenetrable gates and high-tech security cameras—a way of life in Bel-Air and Beverly Hills—Gerald M. himself opened the massive front door. Barefoot and attractive in an "I am a big star and don't you forget it" kind of way, Gerald ushered her in. "Hey, Lucky, you gotta come out to my studio," he enthused, fiddling with a large diamond cross hanging on a diamond-studded gold chain around his neck. "I laid down a track yesterday that's gonna blow your ass from here to the Bahamas!"

Somewhere in the background a beautiful Latina girl clad in a barely-there bikini flitted from one room to another. Gerald M. ignored her.

"Actually, I came by to see Cookie," Lucky said.

"Some party last night," Gerald continued. "You stage that fight thing or what?"

"Sure I did, Gerald," she said patiently. "It was all staged, couldn't you tell?"

"Genius, baby!" he chortled.

"Thanks," she said, fast becoming impatient. This

was not a social call, she wanted action. "Is Cookie around?"

"Still sleepin' it off."

"Do you mind if I go upstairs?"

"Sure," he said, fingering his cross. "Then you gotta come by my studio out by the pool."

"I'll do that," she said, heading for the ornate staircase.

"First door on the right," Gerald called out as a petite blonde emerged from the kitchen drinking Diet Coke from the can.

First door on the right was locked. Lucky knocked loudly several times, until eventually a bleary-eyed Cookie opened up. She was clad in an oversized Snoop Dogg T-shirt and nothing else.

"Mrs. Go— I mean, Lucky!" Cookie exclaimed. "What're *you* doin' here?"

Lucky glanced pointedly at her watch. "It's almost noon and no daughter, so I thought you and I should have a little talk. Can I come in?"

"Uh . . . sure," Cookie said, reluctantly backing up to allow Lucky access to her darkened bedroom.

The room reeked of pot and incense and the walls were painted dark brown. Curled up in a sleeping bag on the floor was a male figure.

"Am I disturbing something?" Lucky inquired, black eyes glittering with impatience.

"No, course not," Cookie said, poking the male figure with her foot. "It's only Harry. He sleeps over when it's late."

"Too far to drive to Brentwood," Lucky said dryly.

"Too wasted," Cookie giggled.

Great, Lucky thought. *And these two are Max's best friends.*

"So," she said as Harry surfaced, spiky black hair standing on end, "I need more information about Max."

Cookie rubbed her eyes. "I wish we like *knew* more," she ventured. "But honestly, we don't."

"Come *on*, Cookie. I understand what it's like to be sixteen—loyalty to your friends and all that. Only this is getting serious. I have to speak to Max, and I have to speak to her today."

Cookie gave her nothing, and by the time Lucky got back to the house, she was steaming. Paige was outside the house supervising Gino Junior, who was loading their luggage into the car.

"What happened?" she asked. "I thought Gino was all set for a round of golf. Why are you leaving so soon?"

"Gino has decided we should beat the traffic," Paige explained. "And who am I to fight with your father? He's the worst backseat driver in the world, so I try to avoid all the nagging I can."

"You're a smart lady, Paige."

"Living with Gino, I have to be."

"Hey, Mom," Gino Junior said, almost dropping a heavy Vuitton bag. "Granddad says I can go stay. Is that okay with you?"

"If you promise to behave yourself," Lucky said. Gino Junior always had a good time with his grandfather, and that suited her fine since she'd be spending so much time in Vegas.

Gino emerged from the house. "You're back, kiddo," he said. "I wondered where you were."

"Yes, Gino, I'm back, and I'm looking forward to seeing you in Vegas."

"Can't wait! We'll be there. The party was the greatest, kiddo. Now come over here an' give an old man a hug."

She hugged her father, told Gino Junior to behave himself, and instructed Paige to drive carefully.

Once they'd left, she went into the house and looked for Lennie. He was sitting in front of his computer.

"Any new info?" he asked.

"Cookie's stonewalling me," she said, shaking her head. "Says she's sure Max is okay. As if *she* would know. She and Harry are lying around in her room totally stoned."

"What do you want to do?"

"I guess we'll wait until four, then if we haven't heard from her, I'm reporting her missing."

"Isn't that kind of drastic?" Lennie said. "She called yesterday and left a message that she'd be home today. I'm thinking that would hardly put her on the missing list."

"And what if she's not home today?" Lucky demanded, getting more anxious and frustrated by the minute.

"We'll deal with that *if* it happens. And believe me, sweetheart, it won't, she'll be back today."

"I'm glad *you're* so sure."

"I am. Everything's gonna work out."

Sometimes Lennie drove her crazy with his laid-back attitude. Here she was hanging around L.A. waiting for Max, when she should be in Vegas meeting with the heads of all the different departments. The Keys was due to open in two weeks and that's exactly where she should be right now. She had so much to do it was ridiculous. But no. Max was screwing up all her plans, and there was nothing she could do about it except sit and worry that her daughter was okay.

CHAPTER FIFTY-EIGHT

Once they'd lost Internet Freak, it didn't take long before everyone realized the old man wasn't merely asleep, there was something seriously wrong. He'd slumped forward in his seat, and when Jed tried to wake him, he'd failed to respond.

Jed immediately began to panic. Max attempted to calm him. "Has your grandpa been sick?" she asked.

"He takes pills," Jed said, wiping his nose with the back of his hand.

Max shook the old man's shoulders. No reaction. "I think he might be unconscious," she whispered to Ace.

"Okay, we're almost at Big Bear," Ace said, his eyes fixed firmly on the road ahead. "Keep it together and find out where they live."

Jed mumbled that they lived way back where they'd come from. According to him, they were on their way to visit the old man's sister. Unfortunately, he didn't know her exact address, although he knew that she lived somewhere in Big Bear.

"This sucks," Ace muttered.

Jed looked as if he was about to cry.

Max squeezed his hand. "Your grandpa's going to be okay," she assured him.

"You shouldn't've been driving so fast," he muttered. "That's what did it."

"No, it didn't," she argued. "Going fast had like

nothing to do with it. Your grandpa might have, I dunno, some kind of heart condition."

"He sleeps a lot," Jed admitted.

"How old is he?"

"Eighty-three."

"Well, *my* grandfather's a whole lot older than that," she said encouragingly. "And he's *really* healthy, so chances are your gramps will be kicking around for years."

Finally they reached a gas station. Ace hurriedly jumped out of the car and rushed to a pay phone.

"Are you calling your brother?" Max asked, putting her head out the window.

"Yes," Ace replied. "He'll figure out where we should take him. The old man needs a doctor right away."

She thought it was pretty cool the way he was taking charge. She imagined how different it might've been if only *he* had turned out to be her Internet guy. Oh yes, they would have gone off and spent a fantastic weekend together, most likely fallen in love and lived happily ever after.

Instead of which . . . what a nightmare!

Ace's brother, Hart, met them in Big Bear. He was taller and older than Ace. He leaned in the car, checked on the old man, then instructed his brother to follow his truck to a nearby clinic where he'd arranged to have an orderly waiting outside with a wheelchair.

At the clinic, the three men managed to get the old man into the chair. Then Hart had to leave for work, so Ace suggested they stay around to see if they could help. Max agreed it was the least they could do.

Once inside the clinic a doctor took over, leaving them in the waiting area while he whisked the old man off.

Max hurried to the ladies' room where she attempted to clean herself up. Staring in the mirror she realized what a lucky escape they'd had. Internet Freak could have done anything to them. He'd had them trapped, or so he'd thought. Ace escaping was pretty darn brave. He could've got himself shot, but he hadn't been scared, he'd stayed around to rescue her like some kind of superhero. Without him doing that . . .

She shuddered. She didn't want to think about what might have happened.

When she got back, Ace went off to the men's room.

She sat down next to Jed, who looked at her forlornly. "Is my gramps gonna be okay?" he asked.

"Sure he is," she replied cheerfully. "Do you live with him?"

He nodded his head.

"Where's your parents?" she asked curiously.

He shrugged. "Don't have none."

"How come?"

"My mom ran off when I was three. Dad went after her. At least that's what Gramps told me."

"Do you know if they're still alive?"

He shrugged again. "Dunno."

Ace came back with a couple of chocolate bars and sodas he'd gotten from the vending machine. Max grabbed a chocolate bar, peeled off the wrapper, and stuffed it in her mouth. "*Sooo* good," she sighed.

After a while the doctor returned and informed them that the old man's condition was not as serious as they'd thought. Apparently he suffered from narcolepsy and had fallen into an extremely deep sleep.

"You can come in and see him now," the doctor said. "He's awake and doing fine."

They all trooped into a room where the old man was sitting in an armchair. "What happened?" he asked, looking quite alert. "Why'd you bring me here?"

"You shouldn't be driving with your condition," the doctor scolded. "Especially long distances."

"Who, me? I'm strong as iron," the old man retaliated. "An' I *gotta* drive, it's my living. Besides, Jed here's gonna learn soon enough—ain't ya, son?"

"You had me worried, Gramps."

"Nonsense. I took a little nap an' you all panicked. Kids today!"

"Well, now that you're okay," Ace said, "we gotta get going. So, uh . . . thanks for the ride."

"Jed," Max said, "I'll send you that CD player. I promise I won't forget."

"What player?" Gramps asked grumpily.

"She's buyin' me a CD player, Gramps," Jed said excitedly. "She's sendin' it to me."

"We'll see about that," the old man huffed. "We've never bin acceptin' of nobody's charity."

"Write down your address," Max said, taking a piece of paper from the table.

Jed looked pleadingly at his grandfather, who reluctantly nodded that it was okay.

Jed scribbled on the piece of paper and handed it to her. "You're nice," he said shyly. "And you're pretty."

"Thanks," she said, almost blushing.

"S'long, everyone," Ace said. "We're on our way."

They left the old man and the boy at the clinic and began to walk the fifteen minutes to Kmart.

"I'm keeping my fingers crossed that my car's there," Max said, walking fast to keep up with him. "What do *you* think?"

"I think this is one weekend neither of us will ever forget," he said, shooting her a long look.

"What did you tell your brother about being gone all weekend?"

"That I was with my girlfriend."

"You've got a girlfriend?" she said, feeling horribly disappointed.

"Yeah," he answered casually. "Didn't I mention her?"

"No, you didn't."

"Sometimes I spend the weekends at her place. He doesn't care what I do, he's a brother, not a parent. Big difference."

She was silent, thinking, *Is this it? When I find my car do I just say good-bye to Ace and that's it?*

"Uh, is there a way I can, y'know, thank you for rescuing me this weekend?" she said, biting down hard on her bottom lip. "Are you on e-mail?"

"Very funny," he said wryly. "You wanna start with *me* now? One Internet Freak wasn't enough?"

"No, seriously," she said, breaking a smile. "What's your e-mail?"

"I'm not into e-mail."

"You're not?"

"Who's got the time?"

"You have plenty of time. The day I ran into you, you were lurking around doing exactly nothing."

"That's 'cause I kinda had a fight with my girlfriend."

"You did?"

"Yeah, she works at Kmart. I hooked up with you to make her jealous."

"So the whole bank robbery thing—"

"It was a story," he admitted.

"I knew that," she said quickly.

"No you didn't."

"Yes I did."

"Okay, and *I* knew you weren't eighteen," he said, squinting at her. "Why'd you lie?"

"It wasn't a lie."

"It was blatant."

"I'll be seventeen soon enough."

"When's your birthday?"

"In about eight months!"

"You're too much," he said, laughing. "And I don't have e-mail. But," he added casually, "maybe I'll call you sometime."

"No you won't," she said, thinking, *No he won't.*

"Yeah, I will."

"Instead of calling, come visit me in L.A.," she answered boldly, stopping for a minute to catch her breath.

"With my girlfriend?" he countered.

"If you want."

They exchanged a long look.

"We could double-date," she added, starting to walk again. "You and her, me and *my* boyfriend."

"Thought you said you broke up with your boyfriend?"

"I was lying. This weekend was all about making him jealous." A long beat. "You know what *that's* like, don't you?"

"Are you trying to one-up me?" he said, grinning.

"Maybe," she replied, thinking how hot he was with the smile and the great white teeth and the appealing cleft in his chin.

"Hey," he said nonchalantly, "the kid was right."

"About what?"

"You *are* pretty."

She held her breath for a moment. *Pretty . . . hmm . . .* And she looked like crap—they both did. Apparently he didn't think so.

"Uh, you should see me when I try," she said, going for flippant.

"Guess I'll havta raincheck that."

They exchanged another look.

Five more minutes and they reached the Kmart parking lot. "Wow!" Max said, quickening her pace. "I think I see my car. How exciting is *this*?"

"Let's hope he hasn't left a bomb under the hood," Ace said.

"Oh, great!" she groaned. "Make me feel secure."

"You're always secure, aren't you? You're that kind of girl."

"How can you say that? You hardly know me."

"Oh, I know you."

"Good, 'cause that means you trust me, and I'll need money for emergencies 'cause the Freak took my wallet with everything in it."

"Rescuing you isn't enough," he grumbled, digging in the back pocket of his jeans. "Now she wants my money."

"I'll pay you back, I promise."

"You'd better," he said, handing her two crumpled ten-dollar bills. "That's all I've got."

"Thanks," she said, taking the bills.

"Y'know," he said thoughtfully, "I still think we should tell the cops. The dude's a predator, he threatened us with a gun. And if I hadn't gotten out . . . who knows what would've happened to us."

"No!" she said sharply. "We have to walk away. We're safe, that's all that matters."

"You're just scared your mom's gonna be mad at you."

"So?"

"Okay. If that's what you want. But don't forget he's got all your shit. Laptop, credit cards, phone."

"It can all be replaced."

"Whatever."

A few minutes later he'd hot-wired her car, given her a stern warning not to stop until she got to her destination, and said good-bye.

Sitting behind the wheel of her car with the engine running, she was reluctant to take off. Was it her imagination, or had she and Ace developed a real bond? They'd shared a frightening experience and got through it together. Somehow or other she didn't want to leave. But of course, she knew she had to.

Forget about Ace, she told herself. *He's taken. He doesn't even live in L.A. So forget about him.*

"Okay, bye again," she said, leaning out her window and waving.

"Try not to get in any more trouble," he said. "'Cause next time I might not be around to rescue you."

And then it was over and she was on her way home.

CHAPTER FIFTY-NINE

Irma was dispatched back to Mexico City by commercial jet while Anthony traveled in luxury on his private plane accompanied by his children, their friends, and the nanny.

Standing in the airport with her luggage, Irma was happy to be parting company with her husband. She was returning to her house, her lover, and she was now ready to cement plans for her future.

Spending a long weekend in Acapulco with Anthony and her children had made it a lot easier for her to make a final decision. As she'd watched her family at play she'd realized she had nothing in common with any of them anymore. It was time to get back to the real world, and living in the real world meant leaving the house in Mexico City. First she would help herself to money from Anthony's safe, enabling her to open her own personal bank account, then she'd decide when to go and what to take with her.

Unfortunately, Luis could not be part of her plans. He was a big temptation, but since he didn't speak English, running off with him would be impossible. Sometimes, in her fantasies, she'd daydreamed about the two of them disappearing to Bali or some other exotic island, but it was merely a fantasy.

She smiled to herself thinking that she was still a young, vibrant woman, and there were plenty of men out there. All she had to decide was where she would go.

New York was out of the question, so was Miami, but lately she'd been having thoughts about Los Angeles. She certainly entertained no thought of going home to her parents in Omaha—that would be admitting defeat. Besides, her parents were completely self-absorbed, they'd never asked her for anything. They'd no doubt be horrified were she to turn up on their doorstep.

On the flight from Acapulco to Mexico City, she found herself sitting next to an American businessman. He was about forty with prematurely graying hair and a pleasant smile. He wasted no time in starting a conversation.

"I'm traveling to Mexico City on business," he informed her. "How about you?"

"I live there," she replied, folding her hands on her lap. "Or rather my soon-to-be ex-husband does." She paused for a moment. "Actually," she continued, savoring every word, "I'm shortly moving to Los Angeles."

Saying it out loud gave her a thrill.

"You are?" he said, rummaging in his pocket. "Then I should give you my card because L.A. is where I live."

"How interesting," she answered boldly. "Perhaps you can tell me all about the city."

He proceeded to do so, and by the time the plane landed they were old friends.

"You wouldn't happen to be free for dinner tonight?" he asked as they waited for their luggage. "Here I am, a lonely American all by himself in Mexico City, and here you are—a beautiful American woman about to get a divorce. It seems like fate, doesn't it?"

"It certainly does," she replied, twisting her wedding band on her finger.

"Well," he said, pressing for an answer. "Are we on?"

"Yes," she replied after a few moments' indecision. "I'd very much like to have dinner with you."

"Excellent. I'm at the Presidente InterContinental Hotel. Seven-thirty suit you? We could meet in the bar."

Why not? she thought. She had a lover at home and an attractive man to take her to dinner.

Anthony kept two mistresses. It was her time now.

Back in Miami, Anthony didn't bother going home—he called Emmanuelle from the airport.

"Where are you?" he asked, none too pleased. "I tried the apartment, you're not there."

"That's 'cause I'm in the middle of a photo shoot," she explained, speaking on her cell while her Puerto Rican hairstylist fussed with her long hair extensions.

"I'm here," he said. "An' I wanna see you."

"I won't be finished for a couple of hours."

"What is it with you an' fuckin' photo sessions?" he growled. "How come you wanna be on the cover of every fuckin' magazine in town?"

"They pay me the big bucks, Daddy," she said soothingly. "And get me mucho attention."

"*I* pay you big bucks, an' *I* give you *plenty* of attention," he responded. "An' don't call me Daddy."

"But, honey," she purred, "you never put anything in my name and that hurts my feelings."

Feelings? She had feelings? This was a big surprise.

"I'm young," she continued. "I have to make my own money 'cause if we break up, baby doesn't want to find herself out on the street with nothing."

He was silent for a moment, considering what she'd said. Christ! Women and money. Was that all they ever thought about?

"Where's the studio?" he asked.

She told him.

"I'll come by, check you out."

"No, poopsie, you'll be bored," she said quickly,

thinking there was nothing she'd like less than Anthony barging into one of her photo shoots. "You know how you like being the center of attention," she added. "You'll hate sitting on the sidelines."

"I wanna see you at work," he said stubbornly.

"Okay," she sighed, realizing he was giving her no choice. "If that's how you really want to spend your day."

"No, what I *really* wanna do is fuck your brains out," he said, flashing on her luscious body.

"Later, honey," she promised.

"You're makin' me wait?" he said incredulously.

"Only a few hours," she murmured, ending the conversation.

Only a few hours. Ha! Emmanuelle was letting her so-called career as a half-naked cover girl go to her head. She'd better start realizing that the car and the apartment and the clothes were perks that went along with making *him* happy, and he wasn't happy when he had to wait.

Anthony Bonar did not wait for any woman.

They waited for him.

Flushed with her success on the plane, Irma arrived back at her house and was surprised when the guard at the gate stepped out of his cubicle and stopped her driver.

"Yes?" she said, opening the back window of the car. It was unusual for the guards to communicate with her in any way. They usually spoke only to Anthony.

"Ah, Señora Bonar," the guard said, leaning one hand against the top of the car while bending his head to speak to her. "I was wondering about the dogs. Are they following behind with Señor Bonar?"

"No, the dogs are still in Acapulco," she said, shrinking back from his garlic breath. "Mr. Bonar took the plane to Miami."

"I see," the guard said, not moving.

"Is that all?" Irma asked, eager to get up to the house.

"*Sí*, Señora Bonar," he said, still not moving. "I am Cesar," he added with a lascivious leer. "And might I say you look very lovely today."

Abruptly she closed the car window and Cesar backed away. Was it appropriate for one of their guards to be complimenting her? Maybe she was giving off vibes today, what with the man on the plane, and now the guard throwing compliments her way.

Marta, the cook, greeted her in the front hall. "I hear you have many parties in Acapulco, *señora*. I speak with my cousin, Rosa, she tell me lot of parties, much work, too much work."

"I'm sure it was," Irma said, not about to get into a discussion about Rosa's workload. "Are the gardeners here today?"

"*Sí, señora*, they both outside."

"The dogs are still in Acapulco so you don't have to worry about feeding them. I'm sure you're thrilled about that."

"*Sí, señora.*"

"I see no reason why you can't take the rest of the day off."

"Is okay, *señora*, I fix you dinner tonight."

"No, it's not necessary. I shall be dining out."

"Out, *señora?*" Marta said, raising her eyebrows. Everyone knew Irma never left the house at night unless the master was in town.

"Yes, that's right," Irma said quickly. "You may go home early."

"*Sí, señora.*"

Irma hurried upstairs and went straight to her bedroom window. She immediately saw that the old gardener was bent over the rosebushes working diligently, but she couldn't spot Luis.

She was desperate to see him, yet in a way she knew it was a bad idea, because getting too attached was a mistake.

And yet . . . the moment she thought about him she was filled with a flurry of sexual longing.

Hmm . . . she thought. *There's nothing to prevent me from having sex with Luis in the afternoon, and dinner with a perfect stranger in the evening.*

Absolutely nothing.

And that's exactly what she intended to do.

CHAPTER SIXTY

"Hi, Max," Gerald M. said, opening up the front door of his mansion, munching a tuna sandwich. Standing behind him was a statuesque blonde of indeterminate age. Bland and beautiful with overly full lips, she wore pink shorts, a tankini top, and a blank expression. Gerald M. did not bother introducing her. "Lucky was here looking for you earlier," he said, taking another bite of his sandwich.

"She was?" Max said, out of breath and totally relieved that she'd made it all the way back to L.A. without any mishaps. Thanks to Ace, the nightmare was behind her.

"Yeah. You'd better give her a call, she seemed kinda frantic. She was gonna come out to my studio an' listen to my music. She never made it. Tell her she's gotta come back, she's gotta hear the latest tracks I'm layin' down."

"I'll do that," Max said, wishing he wasn't in such a talkative mood. "Is Cookie around?"

"My little girl's feelin' kinda fragile today—came down for coffee, an' went straight back up to her room."

"She did?"

"Yeah, it was some party last night, you missed out. Where were you?"

"Uh, I kinda got hung up."

"Yeah, well you don't look so good. You want a sandwich? A Coke? Anything?"

"No thanks. I'll run up and see Cookie if you don't mind."

"No problem. Go ahead. An' tell my baby girl I'll be in the studio. You kids should come on out, take a listen."

"We will," she said, bounding up the stairs to Cookie's room and hammering on the door.

"Go away," Cookie mumbled. "I'm tryin' to sleep."

"It's me, Max."

Within seconds Cookie had opened up, still clad in nothing more than an oversized man's T. "Where've you *been*, you freak!" she exclaimed.

"It isn't *me* who's the freak, it's the Internet maniac I hooked up with."

"*Oh . . . my . . . God!*" Cookie said, pulling her into the room, slamming the door shut, and locking it again. "What happened? Tell me everything! We haven't stopped callin' you all weekend, Lucky's freakin' furious! She's questioned me like a billion times!"

"What did you tell her?"

"Nothin' much."

Harry, sitting on the floor smoking a joint, joined the conversation. "You promised to check in," he said accusingly. "Why didn't you?"

"Would've if I could've," Max replied, flopping onto the bed, wondering if she should call Ace to let him know she'd made it.

"What happened to you, girl?" Cookie said. "You look like crap."

"This is the story I'm telling my mom," Max said, finally feeling safe and secure. "I was carjacked, okay?"

"Carjacked!" Harry yelled, expelling a mouthful of smoke. "Whoa!"

"Not really," Max explained. "But that's what I'm telling Lucky."

"So all this time you were getting it on with Internet

Guy, right?" Cookie said, sitting cross-legged on her bed, fresh cornrows framing her expressive face.

"No," Max corrected, pausing for effect. "The real story is I was freaking *kidnapped*."

"*What?*" Harry said, dragging on his joint. "Like by an ax murderer?"

"As if I'd still be here if it was an ax murderer," Max said scornfully. "However, people, know this—it was *way* bad. You can't even imagine how bad."

"Seriously, you like got *kidnapped?*" Cookie said, her eyes widening.

"Yeah, an' then I like got rescued by this hottie who was kidnapped with me," Max said, once again thinking about Ace.

"Huh?" Harry said, blowing smoke throughout the room. He was totally stoned.

"It's a long story," Max sighed. "I hurt my ankle and my sides are all scratched up and—"

"Man!" Cookie exclaimed, jumping off the bed. "Are you makin' all this up?"

"No way," Max said vehemently. "We were kidnapped at gunpoint and held hostage."

"For money?" Cookie asked, her eyes growing wider by the minute.

"Not for money."

"Then *what*?"

"I dunno. It was all so weird."

"How about getting laid?" Cookie questioned. "Did you do it? Was it totally great?"

"Aren't you listening?" Max said, noticing that both her friends were stoned. "I got *kidnapped*, not *laid*."

"You'd better call Lucky," Cookie said. "She's *major* uptight."

"I will, but I should clean up first. Can I shower? And borrow clothes?"

"Sure," Cookie said. "But then I wanna hear *everything*. There's no way you can zoom in here, drop that you were kidnapped, an' not give out details."

"I will, after I've done something about my ankle," Max said, rolling up the leg of her jeans.

"Eew!" Cookie exclaimed, taking a peek. "That's gnarly. How'd you do it?"

"Internet Freak chained my foot to a bed."

"This is *so* like a scene from a horror movie," Harry said, spiked hair standing on end.

"No movie," Max said gravely. "Truth."

"Whyn't you call Lucky before you shower?" Cookie suggested. "Get that over with. She's crazy mad, apparently she was supposed to go to Vegas today, canceled 'cause you were on the missing list."

"Oh shit!"

" 'Oh shit' is right."

"Lend me your phone."

"Where's yours?"

"It's with my credit cards, money, and laptop. Internet Freak took everything."

"That sucks," Cookie said, handing her phone over. Max finally got up the nerve to call Lucky.

"Uh, hi, Mom," she ventured when Lucky picked up. "It's me, Max."

There was a long, ominous silence, until finally Lucky said, "Where exactly are you?"

"Long story," Max said cheerfully. "I'll be home in an hour, tell you everything then."

"You're in L.A.?"

"Uh . . . I'm kinda on my way. Y'see, the thing is I got kind of carjacked."

"Carjacked," Lucky repeated disbelievingly.

"Yeah, so, um—"

"Not another word," Lucky said, her voice icy. "Get your ass home, go straight up to your room, and stay

there until I get back from Vegas, where I should've
been five hours ago. Do that, and don't even think about
leaving the house. You're grounded. Understand?"

"But, Mom," Max wailed. "That's so unfair. It wasn't
my fault."

"It never is," Lucky said, clicking off.

"Man!" Max complained, making a face. "She just
told me I'm grounded."

"Surprise, surprise," Cookie said, yawning. "You
promised her you'd be home for Gino's party an' you
bailed. What did you expect? Oh yeah, and for your information, the party was like a *total* blast. You missed
an awesome fight an' everything."

"You got any disinfectant and bandages?" Max asked,
not interested in hearing about the party she'd missed.
"And I'd kill for something to eat, I'm major starving."

"Here," Harry said, groping in his pants pocket and
tossing her a pack of M&M's. "Knock yourself out."

"*You* can deal with her," Lucky steamed, clicking off her
cell phone. "Believe me—she's all yours."

"I've got a production meeting at four," Lennie said,
glancing at his watch. "I take it she's on her way home."

"Thank God—yes! And I *have* to get my ass to Vegas, so now that I know she's safe, I'm leaving ASAP.
It's all down to you."

"What's her story anyway?"

"Some bullshit about getting carjacked, which I do not
believe for one single minute, and you shouldn't either."

"That's our Max—she's inventive."

"She sure is."

"What time will you be back?"

"Who knows? There's so much to deal with. We open
in less than two weeks and Mooney says it's crazy. I
might have to stay over a couple of days. Are you sure
you can handle everything here?"

"'And once again his beautiful wife runs off, while he is left in charge of their delinquent daughter.'"

"*Please*, sweetheart."

"Yeah, yeah. Go look after your other baby."

"Now, about Max—"

"You don't have to tell me—she's grounded."

"I mean it, Lennie, do *not* weaken, I'm depending on you."

"Surely you trust me?"

"When it comes to little Miss Green Eyes, *no*."

"That's 'cause I can't help it, she reminds me of you."

"Should I take that as a compliment?" she asked wryly.

"Max is beautiful, wild, and full of adventure. That's you, Lucky, so yeah, take it as a compliment and don't be too hard on the kid."

"Man," Lucky said, shaking her head. "She's got your number big time. Just remember: grounded—G-R- . . ."

"I *know*. Now get moving. You've got a hotel to open."

It was such a relief to only have to face Lennie, since Lucky wasn't home. It made things way easier. Whew! Her dad was so laid-back and cool and most of all *understanding*. He bought the carjacked story, didn't question her too much, and had one of his assistants arrange to get her a new phone, cancel her credit cards, replace her driver's license, and he even produced a duplicate set of car keys. Lennie was the *best*!

If only Lucky could be so understanding. But no. Lucky would immediately know she was lying. Lucky had a bullshit detector a mile long.

"Sorry, but you're grounded, sweetie," Lennie informed her. "I gotta go to a meeting, so make sure you stay around the house."

"I get carjacked, robbed, and *I'm* grounded," Max protested.

"Your mom's orders."

"Since when did you take orders from *her?*"

"Watch it, Max. Don't screw with my good will."

She went upstairs, lay on her bed, and thought about Ace. She'd told Cookie and Harry about him, but neither of them really got it, they were more interested in puffing weed and listening to details about Internet Freak. *Ugh!* Every time she thought of the creep she got the chills.

Now that her ordeal was over and she was safely home, it all seemed so surreal, as if she had dreamed it. Only her ankle—already healing—and her scratched sides reminded her that it was indeed real. The Internet Freak—whoever he was—had been a definite psycho, and once again she realized how very fortunate they were to have escaped.

Ace had wanted them to go to the police and report him, but she simply couldn't face doing that. If Lucky ever discovered how stupid she'd been, she'd *never* live it down. Lucky expected everyone to be strong and invincible, just like she was.

Yes. Carjacked was the way to go. She'd told Lennie a story and she was sticking to it. Carjacked, managed to outwit the would-be carjackers, and somehow or other gotten stuck in the woods—which is why she hadn't made it back for Gino's party.

It was the best she could come up with.

CHAPTER SIXTY-ONE

Fortunately, they were out on location and not confined to a studio, so Billy felt that it wasn't necessary to confront Alex. Apologizing to the director was not an option—he was adamant about that.

There were extra security guards to control the paparazzi, and several cops doing duty on crowd control.

Billy lounged in his chair on the street way behind the camera, long legs stretched out in front of him.

"She called you yet?" Kev asked, wandering over.

"Who?" Billy said, although he knew exactly who Kev meant.

"The ho who gave you the crabs," Kev said, chewing on a carrot stick.

"Stop mentioning the crabs," Billy said irritably. "According to her, she didn't give 'em to me."

"Then who did?"

"How the frig do I know?"

"Maybe you got 'em from Venus," Kev said slyly.

"Get a life, Kev."

"You never know."

"Venus is dead-on faithful."

"For sure?"

"Yes," Billy said. "Disappointed?"

"I suppose she's gotta be, hasn't she?"

"How's that?"

"You're her young stud. She wouldn't want to piss you off, not until she's through with the ride."

"How many times I gotta tell you to quit with the stud jokes?"

"Seems t'me you an' Venus can't last that long anyway. It's not as if you're gonna walk down the freakin' aisle. I mean, have you considered the fact that when you're forty she'll be fifty-three?"

"Is this what you do all day, Kev, sit around thinking up this crap?" Billy said, yawning. "Stay outta my business, okay?"

"Your business *is* my business," Kev said, still chewing on his carrot stick. "You pay me to be your main man."

"Yeah, an' my main man is not gettin' paid to bug the shit outta me."

"Okay, okay," Kev said, throwing up his hands. "I like Venus, but even *you* gotta admit you're not exactly a perfect match."

"Listen to the expert," Billy said. "I'm having a good time, that's all that matters."

Unfortunately, Kev was envious of his relationship with Venus. Before Venus, they'd spent their nights cruising the clubs, picking up girls, bringing them back to the house, and experiencing a slam-dunk party every night. Then Billy had hooked up with Venus, and as far as Kev was concerned, the fun times were history.

Billy still wasn't sure how long it would last between him and his superstar girlfriend. This boy toy crap was getting older every day.

Later his cell phone rang and it was Miss Broken Taillight. He didn't know her name, so when she said, "Hi, this is Ali," he had no idea who he was speaking to.

"Yeah," he said. "Can I help you?"

"Yes, you can help me," she answered, sounding uptight. "I'm the girl who was up at your house last week. Remember me? The one who sucked your cock. You made me a promise and I'm calling to collect."

"Collect?" he said. "That's an odd way of putting it, makes you sound like a bookie."

"You made me a promise," she repeated. "And I made *you* one back. I won't spill to your girlfriend, and you'll swing me a part in your movie."

"I will, huh?"

"That was our deal."

"Then you'd better drive down to the set," he said, telling her where to come. "I'll figure something out."

"You'd better."

Ignoring her implied threat, he said, "When you get here, ask for Kev. Do *not* let on you know me. You're dealing with my friend Kev on this."

"Oh," she said huffily. "So now I'm not good enough to know you, is that it? Why can't I be your out-of-town cousin or something?"

"It's not an option. There's press everywhere, an' I can't be seen talking to you."

"Why?"

" 'Cause we'll end up in *People* or *Us*. Like I said— deal with Kev."

"You're such a prick."

"Thanks. I love you too," he said, snapping his phone shut. He called Kev over and filled him in.

"What's she like?" Kev asked, sounding a little too interested.

"Young, pretty, skillful, and hands off."

"Why? You savin' her for a repeat performance?"

Before he could answer, he was finally called to the set. He couldn't prove it, but he was sure that Alex had changed the shooting schedule so that he was forced to sit around all morning even though his call was six A.M.

The scene he was about to shoot was with a fellow actor, a black ex–football player who was over six feet four and built like the proverbial brick house.

Billy knew he was about to get a beating whether he

wanted one or not. Shooting this scene would be Alex's way of getting back at him.

Fuck it! He'd take it like a man. How bad could it be? The crew were all watching; the other actor seemed like a reasonable guy. The only sadist on the set was Alex Woods.

He was right. Alex demanded seventeen takes, and in each take he had to get punched on the jaw, and even though they were supposed to be fake punches, Alex wanted it to look real—so guess what, he got pounded.

It was bad enough that he had a black eye; once they were through, his jaw felt as if he'd been struck a series of blows with a sledgehammer.

"I'm going back to my trailer," he told the assistant assigned to him when Alex was finally satisfied.

"I'll escort you," said the girl. She was overweight and enthusiastic, and any time she could spend with Billy Melina was a bonus.

There was quite a crowd of people on the street straining to see stars. They all wanted to get a peek at Billy. The cops were doing a good job of keeping them back.

His trailer was parked on a side street. The female assistant chattered nonstop about what a thrill it was working with him, and how wonderful he was in the scene, how she'd seen all his movies, how she'd only been working on this particular one for a month and it was the best moment of her life meeting him.

Assistant/fan. Great! Just what he didn't need.

He tuned her out, not in the mood to listen.

"Thanks, hon," he said when they reached his trailer.

He climbed the steps, all ready to collapse on his couch, flung open the door, and there was Miss Broken Taillight giving Kev a blow job.

CHAPTER SIXTY-TWO

Emmanuelle was posing, showing off in a string bikini that left little to the imagination. She lounged against a tropical background in the studio, Cuban music blasting over the loudspeakers, a wiry photographer dancing around behind his camera.

Anthony was embarrassed for her. She shouldn't be half naked in front of a studio full of people, it wasn't right. He could see her nipples straining against the thin material of her tiny top, the curve of her snatch through the bikini bottom.

In spite of himself, he began to get hard. Goddammit! If he was hard, so were all the other men in the studio—unless they were gay. Emmanuelle always assured him that all the men she worked with were gay, but looking around he wasn't so sure.

The Grill was hovering somewhere behind him. He didn't want the big lug ogling his girlfriend's private parts—it infuriated him.

"Go wait in the car," he ordered.

"You sure, boss?"

"Yeah, I'm fuckin' sure," he replied, scowling.

Emmanuelle hadn't spotted him yet, she was too busy posing, flinging her long legs this way and that, bringing her arms up, seductively touching her breasts, playing to the camera as if it were his dick.

Jesus Christ! Enough already!

He stepped up beside the guy with the camera. "Hey!" he yelled at Emmanuelle. "Over here, sugar."

Emmanuelle barely stopped posing. Putting a finger to her lips, she murmured, "Shush, honey, I'm in the middle."

"The middle of what?" he said.

"In the middle of my shoot," she answered, pouting.

"'Scuse me, we're working here," the photographer said, taking an aggressive stance.

Anthony turned on him, his face dark as thunder. "Ya think I'm fuckin' blind?" he snarled. "I can see that. You're shootin' my fuckin' girlfriend."

"Okay, man," the photographer said, hurriedly backing off. "But do you think you can give us some space here? We'll be ready to break in twenty minutes, then she's all yours."

"Fuck you," Anthony said. "If I wanna talk to my girlfriend, I'll talk to her now."

Emmanuelle jumped up and ran forward, breasts jiggling. "That's okay, Rodriguez," she said, coming between them. "It might be a good idea if we break early."

The photographer glared at her, while the makeup and hair people started gossiping among themselves, shooting Anthony looks as if to say, "Who *is* this thug?"

Taking Anthony's arm, Emmanuelle steered him into her dressing room. "Honey," she said. "You can't pull me out of a shoot like this, it's not fair."

"Is this what you call work?" he snorted. "Look at you—ya got no fuckin' clothes on."

"You know what I do, poopsie," she purred. "You *love* seeing my photos when they're on the cover of a magazine."

"There's only one thing I love," he said, reaching forward and pinching her left nipple.

"What, honey?" she said, trying not to wince because he was hurting her.

He kicked the door shut. "I love it when you suck my fuckin' dick," he said, unzipping his pants.

"Not here, baby," she objected. "Everybody's outside, I can't do it here."

"Oh, yes you can," he said, pressing down on her shoulders. "Now get on your knees an' show me your *real* talent."

Unable to lure Luis up to her bedroom, Irma was disappointed. After showering and changing clothes she'd gone out to the garden where Luis was busy mowing the lawn. When she'd approached him and asked him to come into the house he'd shaken his head, indicating the older gardener who was working nearby.

"It's okay," she'd said, giving him a meaningful look. "I need you to come see my houseplants."

"No, *señora*," he'd replied, vigorously shaking his head, refusing to look her in the eye. "No today."

She couldn't believe he was turning her down. But then, perhaps he was merely being careful, or perhaps he was upset that she'd gone to Acapulco with her husband. After a while she'd given up, and gone back into the house.

Now she watched him from the window. She watched him until he left at four o'clock.

Later she ordered a car and driver to take her to the hotel in town. Using her husband's driver would be a mistake, the man probably reported everything to Anthony, and that would be a disaster. Better to be safe than sorry.

Cesar stopped Luis at the gate as the younger man attempted to drive out.

"Well," Cesar said, licking his thick lips in anticipation, "when do I get a taste of American pussy?"

"I don't know what you're talking about," Luis replied in Spanish. "You are imagining things, Cesar."

"I am imagining nothing," Cesar responded. "You think everyone doesn't know what's going on? I want a piece, Luis, otherwise I tell Señor Bonar, and I tell your wife."

"You wouldn't dare tell Señor Bonar."

"You imagine you know me, Luis, but you don't," Cesar said. "Either I fuck that American ass, or your fun and games are over."

"You're crazy," Luis said, refusing to play Cesar's sick game.

"No," Cesar fired back. "*You're* the crazy one, because if you do *not* arrange what I want, your life will be over, my friend."

During the drive into the center of the city, Irma attempted to compose herself, although her thoughts kept on drifting back to Luis. Why hadn't he come into the house? It was frustrating. Three days away from him and she found herself yearning for his touch.

Am I in love? she thought.

No. Lust. Pure and simple lust.

Her companion from the plane, Oliver Stanton, was waiting at the hotel bar nursing a tumbler of Scotch. As soon as he saw her approaching he jumped to his feet. "You look lovely," he said.

"Thank you," she replied, noting he was tall and well built, although not as well built as Luis.

The name Oliver had a nice ring to it. She decided that she and Oliver would date when she arrived in Los Angeles. She and Oliver might even become a couple.

She wondered what he did. During their conversation on the plane she had not thought of finding out, or maybe she'd forgotten to ask him as she'd been so busy talking about herself and her early days as a beauty queen, so much so that she hadn't given him a chance to talk about himself. It didn't matter, she'd draw him out at dinner.

"I thought we'd eat in the restaurant here," he said. "I checked it out, seems perfect."

"Fine with me," she said, nodding.

They made pleasant conversation over dinner. She enjoyed her food and drank several glasses of red wine. Glancing around the restaurant, she felt like a human being for a change, not Anthony Bonar's wife relegated to the background. Her future stretched before her, and she was ready to embrace it.

They lingered over dessert, until eventually Oliver leaned across the table, took her hand, and said, "How about coming up to my room for a nightcap?"

She was thankful she'd thought of removing her wedding ring as she considered the possibility. She was not naive—she knew exactly what Oliver had in mind. And why not? She was about to be a free woman, and Luis had rejected her—which she did *not* appreciate, and even now Anthony was probably bedding down his Miami bimbo.

"Yes," she murmured, the wine loosening her inhibitions. "I think I'd like that."

"Good," he said, signing the check.

Once they were in the elevator on their way up to his room, Oliver moved in close and kissed her, a dry kiss, unlike Luis's passionate tongue kisses, but it got her juices flowing all the same, and when they reached his room she was ready, and so was he.

He pushed her back on the bed, lifted her skirt, and pulled down her panties. Then he gave her head for approximately one minute, reached up and fondled her breasts for another minute, then unzipped his pants, put on a condom, and was inside her within seconds.

She lay there thinking about Luis, and how he worshipped her body, how he spent time kissing every inch of her body, how different his touch was.

When Oliver climaxed, she didn't.

"That was very, very nice," he announced, rolling off her. "You're quite a woman. Did you—"

"Yes," she lied, searching for the right word. "It was wonderful."

"Now we can enjoy our nightcap," he said, getting up and going over to the minibar. "Brandy? Liquor? What's your pleasure?"

"Do you have wine?" she asked, adjusting her clothes and getting off the bed.

"Anything m'lady wants," he said, opening a half-size bottle of red wine and a miniature bottle of brandy.

She sat at a small corner table as he handed her a wineglass and pulled up another chair. Then he toasted her and told her once again that she was quite a woman.

She didn't feel like quite a woman, she felt empty inside, and it occurred to her that sleeping around was not a very satisfying way to go.

Five minutes of conversation, she'd drink her wine and make a graceful exit. "So, Oliver," she said, remembering that she still had not asked him what he did, "what business are you in?"

"You'll never guess," he said, smiling at her.

"I think I will," she replied, trying not to stare at his crooked front tooth, which she'd never really noticed before. "Let me see, you're a lawyer."

"Wrong."

"A doctor?"

"No," he said, still smiling.

"Then you're right—I'm unable to guess."

"I don't tell everybody what I do because it's a little daunting for some people," he said, lowering his voice.

"Hmm . . . sounds intriguing," she said, playing with the stem of her wineglass.

"Some people would say it is, and some people would

say it isn't." He paused for a moment. "I'm in the drug enforcement business."

"Excuse me?" she said, startled.

"Yes, I'm a drug enforcement agent," he said, obviously proud of his job. "Y'know, we're the ones who chase down the bad guys and throw 'em in jail."

"You do?" she gasped.

"Are you aware that Acapulco is the drug capital of Mexico?" he said, all businesslike.

Was this some kind of cruel joke? Her first date, and he turned out to be a drug enforcement agent.

"I, uh, I need to use the bathroom," she said faintly.

"I'll be waiting," he said, giving her another steady smile.

She got up and almost ran to the bathroom, desperately trying to control her sense of panic.

Oliver Stanton was a drug enforcement agent.

Her husband was a drug lord.

This situation was totally out of control.

CHAPTER SIXTY-THREE

Throwing herself back into rehearsing for the one-night show to celebrate the opening of the Keys was therapy for Venus. She had every intention of putting on a spectacular show for her friend. After all, Lucky had worked so hard planning and building a magnificent hotel complex in the desert, and Venus, who had never played Vegas, was doing it as a big favor. However, favor or not, she'd decided it had to be the best one-nighter she'd ever put on.

It was quite satisfying getting back to rehearsing with her backup dancers and singers, her director and musical arranger. Spending time with Billy was fun, but climbing up on her pedestal was just as much fun in a different way. Sometimes it was hard for her to realize just how famous she'd become. She'd made it all the way from nothing, now here she was—Venus—known worldwide by only one name, like Madonna or Cher. It was quite an achievement.

During a break she checked her cell and saw that Billy had called twice. He'd also text-messaged her once again saying how sorry he was.

His apologies were sweet, but a bit late in the day. Why hadn't he been sorry last night on the way home? *He's too young for you*, she told herself. *This older woman/younger man crap is just that—crap.*

She should be with an older, wiser man—not quite

as old as Cooper, maybe somebody around her own age. Yes, a George Clooney.

Although the thought of losing Billy filled her with sadness.

It wasn't time. Not yet.

"Jesus Christ!" Billy exclaimed.

"Oh man!" Kev yelled, reaching an orgasm at exactly the same moment as Billy barged in.

Ali jumped up and ran into the bathroom. They could both hear her spitting into the sink.

"Charming," Billy said, disgusted. "What did I tell you, Kev? What the fuck did I say? I told you hands off, remember?"

"She came on to me," Kev said somewhat sheepishly. "I'm hardly gonna turn it down."

"What do you mean, she came on to you? What did she do? Unzip your pants and whip it out?"

"More or less."

"Ah, jeez!"

Ali emerged from the bathroom wiping her mouth with a crumpled Kleenex. "I thought that's what you wanted me to do," she said sulkily. "I thought that's the only way he'd give me a part."

"*He's* not the one giving you the freakin' part," Billy said, exasperated. "He's gonna talk to the director's assistant, who'll try an' fit you in a scene."

"I didn't know that."

"Learn it," Billy said sharply. "Running around this town giving everyone b.j.'s won't get you shit."

"That's what Marilyn Monroe did."

"Yeah, a hundred years ago. Girls don't have to do that anymore."

"Oh, yes they do," she argued. "How do you think I got that waitressing gig at the party the other night? I had to blow the caterer."

"Jeez," Billy said, shaking his head. "Look, I think I've arranged for you to get a walk-on in the next scene, but you'll have to behave yourself. Don't go offering b.j.'s to everyone who asks."

"Nice trailer," she said, flinty eyes checking everything out. "It's bigger than where I live."

"Where *do* you live?" Kev asked, obviously in deep lust, and not at all embarrassed at getting caught with his zipper down.

"Hollywood," she answered vaguely. "In a room with a coupla other people."

"You a runaway?" Billy asked, inexplicably feeling sorry for her.

"What makes you think *that*?" she said, giving him a wary look.

"Just a thought. How old are you, anyway?"

"Old enough," she replied, full of false bravado.

"You got money?" he asked, remembering what it felt like arriving in L.A. with exactly nothing.

"I told you," she said. "I don't want your money. What I want is a part in your movie. I wanna get discovered."

The great Hollywood mantra: *I wanna get discovered.*

"Okay," he said, wondering if Venus had ever uttered those same words when she was young and broke and desperately trying to make it in a town crammed with hopefuls. "Kev'll take you to meet Maggie, the director's personal assistant. She'll see you get a walk-on, an' you'll get paid too. You've got a SAG card, right?"

"Yes," she said proudly.

"That's something."

"I need to get a line," she added.

"Got a feeling Mags can't pull *that* off," Billy said, thinking, *No way!* "Alex's scripts are written in stone, all speaking parts are cast way before he starts shooting."

"I want a line," Ali repeated, her pointed face setting into a stubborn expression. "Otherwise—"

"Okay, stop trying to blackmail me," Billy said. "It doesn't make you look good."

"I'm not here to look good," she said, glaring at him.

"I'll see what I can do."

This was getting ridiculous. What had happened to his simple life before stardom? Before Venus. Before Alex Woods. Although he couldn't really blame Venus and Alex—they'd discovered him. Truth was he owed Alex a lot, and if the director would stop bad-mouthing him all over town there was a good chance they could be friends again.

As for Kev, well, he'd deal with him later.

To add to the joys of the day, Janey, his publicist, knocked on the trailer door and came charging in.

"Hello? Are you on lunch break?" she trilled. "I'm here to remind you that you've got an interview to finish, Billy. With Florence Harbinger. She's here and she's waiting. Can I bring her in?"

Oh, shit! It was one of those days.

Venus was sweating, which was exactly the way she liked it when getting back into one of her vigorous dance routines.

Her dancers were young and energetic and thrilled to be back in business. They gave their all to her hit song "Tornado." She loved the feeling of camaraderie it gave her working with her dancers again. They were an enthusiastic mixed-ethnic group with unbridled stamina and a whole lot of energy. They inspired her to do even better. Soon she'd be going out on tour again, and this was a nice way to ease back into the rigors of the road.

During a break she took a call from her daughter, Chyna, who seemed to be having a great time at summer camp. After camp, Chyna was off on a European vacation with her father, and she was very excited about that. Venus missed her cute little girl, but as long as Chyna was having fun, it was okay. There was another text message from Billy on her phone offering to cook his famous chili for her that night.

Hmm . . . Billy was definitely trying to make amends for losing it with Alex. And so he should.

Okay, she'd go along with it. Why not? Billy was obviously here to stay.

For now.

"Pete," Maggie said to the first assistant director. "There's a girl Billy would like you to place somewhere in the next scene."

"Is she an extra?" Pete asked, chewing on a wad of tobacco.

"She is now," Maggie said. "Our star is asking for a favor, and we don't want to turn him down, do we? After all, he just had the crap beaten out of him."

"Does Alex know about this?" Pete inquired, still chewing.

"Alex trusts *you* when it comes to extras," Maggie said. "You'll know exactly where to place her."

"Okay, but what if he asks me?"

"Why would he do that? She's a slip of a girl, he won't even notice her."

"Are we talking about the same guy? Alex notices it when the camera operator drops a fart!"

"You can swing it, Pete. Have her walking past a car or something."

"Whatever you want, Maggie."

"You're a doll, Pete."

Maggie was very popular on the set. She was the buffer between Alex and his crew. Alex Woods was known for his uncontrollable temper and furious outbursts, and

Maggie was the only one who could always be relied on to calm him down.

She hurried back to Billy's trailer and told him the good news.

"How about giving her a line?" Billy suggested.

"Now you're asking the impossible," Maggie said. "I got her into the scene, be satisfied."

"She wants a line," Billy said.

"I don't think I can manage that."

"You can manage anything, Mags."

"No I can't, Billy, I wish I could."

"All right, get her in the scene and see how it goes."

"Where is she?"

"Outside with Kev smoking a cigarette."

"Don't allow them to smoke in your trailer, huh?"

"That's right."

"Who is this girl, anyway?" Maggie asked.

"A friend of a friend from back home," Billy said vaguely. "I'm trying to do a favor."

"Sure," Maggie said, not believing him for a moment. "Are you going to lunch now?"

"Gonna eat in the trailer an' nurse my bruises. Gotta do a second interview with Florence Harbinger for *Manhattan Style*."

"Do *not* talk about the fight between you and Alex," Maggie warned. "Not even off the record."

"You think she's heard about it?"

"Everybody's heard, and according to my spies, it'll be all over *ET* tonight."

"How do people find out these things?"

"A waiter. A parking valet. A paid snitch."

"Great!"

"Okay," Maggie said. "I'll take your girl over to the wardrobe department and—"

"She's not my girl," Billy interrupted, irritated that

Maggie would think she was. "Her name's Ali, and she's not my girl."

"Merely a term of speech."

"She's a friend of a friend."

"I know. You told me," Maggie said patiently, used to dealing with actors and their requests, especially when it came to getting random girls walk-ons. "Have a pleasant lunch, and watch what you say—*especially* about Alex."

Maggie left, and Billy sat on his couch texting Venus while preparing himself for the onslaught of Florence.

Five minutes later the journalist swept into his trailer smelling of lavender and booze, a most disturbing combination. "Billy," she gushed. "Such a pleasure to see you again." An obvious lowering of the voice. "Tell me," she almost whispered, as if they were about to share an important secret. "How's everything with you and Venus? Still going strong?"

"I saw you a few days ago, Florence," he said, flashing the charming smile, the one he pulled out whenever it suited him. "Nothing's changed since then. We're very happy together. It all works."

"Really? Even the age difference?"

"We never notice it—only other people do."

"Well," Florence said, disappointed she wasn't scoring a scoop, "if anything *does* change, promise me I'll be the first to know."

"With bells on, Flo."

"Now," Florence said, switching on her digital tape recorder, "I understand you've not talked about this much, but when are the two of you planning on getting married?"

"You know what, Florence?" he said, choosing his words carefully. "Venus and I both have commitment phobias, so marriage will not be happening any time soon. That a good enough answer?"

"I'll have to get a quote from Venus on that," Florence said, groping in her purse for a lozenge.

"You should."

"Let me see. What *didn't* I ask you last time?"

Oh shit! He was so right. It was *definitely* going to be one of those days.

CHAPTER SIXTY-FOUR

After spending several frantic days in Vegas, Lucky flew back to L.A. feeling a lot calmer as far as Max was concerned. Her daughter was home, safe, and when she thought about it—as Lennie kept on telling her—that's all that really mattered.

"Don't even bother getting into it with her," Lennie warned over the phone. "She knows she crossed the line and she's sorry."

"So that's it?" Lucky said, perplexed. "*She's* sorry and I'm not supposed to mention anything?"

"What's the point?" Lennie counseled. "You're not about to gain anything by fighting with her."

After thinking it over, she was inclined to agree. There was so much else going on that getting into a long, drawn-out battle with her daughter seemed redundant. The timing was all wrong.

The Keys was almost ready to open, and for the next ten days she would be consumed by details, and making sure everything went smoothly. She had meetings set with everyone from her general manager to the head of the gambling casino and all the other heads of various operations—security, catering, entertainment, and many other departments. Each person mattered. Each one of them had to be ready to perform at the top of their game. Lucky had plans for the Keys to outshine every other hotel on the Strip, and when Lucky wanted something, she usually got it.

She was psyching herself up for another major event. Gino's ninety-fifth birthday party would be nothing compared to the grand opening of the Keys.

There were so many details to take care of, not the least making sure that all her guests flying in for the event would be comfortable. An entire floor of the hotel was reserved for family and friends. Bobby and Brigette were returning from New York with a planeload of New York–based celebrities. Gino and Paige would be coming from Palm Springs. Steven's wife, Lina, the ex-supermodel, was putting on a lingerie fashion show to rival anything Victoria's Secret had to offer. Charlie Dollar was bringing a group of L.A. luminaries via private plane. Venus would be making a special one-night appearance.

And then there was Alex Woods, who since the party had taken to calling her on a daily basis to complain about Billy and Ling and anyone else he could think of.

Alex had issues. And she didn't have time to deal with them, especially as he ended every conversation with, "So . . . when are you leaving Lennie?"

He thought it was funny. She thought it was not. Alex needed to get himself a woman he could respect and forge a real relationship with. It was patently obvious that Ling was on her way out.

Back in L.A. Lucky finally sat down with Max, who informed her she was major sorry about missing Gino's party, and how could she make it up to him, and it would never happen again, and she couldn't help getting robbed and carjacked, but at least she'd held on to her car, so that was good, wasn't it?

None of it made any sense to Lucky. But instead of staying mad, she gave her daughter a stern lecture about not using the Internet to meet strangers and left it at that.

Lennie added his ten cents. "Your mom's got a lot going on," he said. "We both do, so we're forgetting about your little trip, and you'd better make sure it never happens again."

Oh man, she was sure. She was also furious that Cookie had blabbed about her meeting a guy over the Internet. Was nothing sacred?

The next day Lucky prepared to fly back to Vegas.

"I'm thinking of staying until we open," she told Lennie before she left. "It's kind of insane flying back and forth. Gino Junior's having a great time in Palm Springs, and you're here to watch Max."

"Sure," Lennie said. "I'll try to fly in next weekend."

"That'd be perfect."

"Perfect, huh?" he said, giving her a lazy smile.

"Yes, you and me in Vegas. We can relive the first time we met."

"Oh, like the time you fired me, right?"

"Ah, but this time instead of firing you, we make mad passionate love. We christen the penthouse."

"I like it already," he said, still smiling.

"Oh!" Lucky exclaimed. "We're forgetting about Max. This is not the best time to leave her alone."

"I could bring her with?" Lennie suggested.

"Definitely not. Don't worry, I'll think of something."

Wow! Max thought, thoroughly relieved after her face-to-face with her mom. *I got off lightly.*

She knew for sure that Lucky would go totally nuts if she ever found out the real story of what had happened to her. There was no way Lucky would allow Internet Freak to get away with it—she'd track him down and punish him big time. Truth was the creep deserved to be punished, but who could find him now? She'd tried to see if his e-mail address was still in use on the house computer, but just as she'd thought, it was gone. Internet Freak had vanished.

It disturbed her that he'd taken her laptop with all her

personal stuff on it. He was probably jerking off over her pictures—that's what freaks did, didn't they?

Lucky had arranged for Leonardo's nanny, Greta, to come back from her vacation early so there would be someone other than Philippe to watch Max when Lennie took off. Max didn't mind; staying around the house for a few days was no great hardship, especially after what she'd been through.

Before Lennie left for the weekend, she tentatively approached him while he was working on the script of his upcoming movie.

"Hi, Dad," she said, hovering beside the computer.

"What can I do for you?" he said, distracted.

"I was wondering, uh . . . am I still grounded?" she asked, going for the innocent approach.

"For a couple more days," he answered vaguely, too busy with his script to take much notice.

"So . . . can I like go out to the drugstore and stuff?"

"Sure. But come right home after."

Lennie's so easy, she thought. *I can get away with anything when it comes to my dad.*

Lately, all she could think about was driving back to Big Bear to see Ace. She wanted to pay him the money she'd borrowed. And she wanted to buy him a new watch since it was her fault the one he had got broken. She also had to buy the kid—Jed—a CD player and send it to him.

She'd called Ace a couple of times on his home phone, and both times she'd gotten an answering machine. Since she'd left the number of her new cell phone and he hadn't called back, it was frustrating. Didn't he care to find out if she was okay after their harrowing ordeal?

Then she thought that maybe he was too busy with his girlfriend, Miss Kmart, and she started wondering if the girl was pretty, and if they were having sex.

Hmm . . . he probably had sex with plenty of girls. He was nineteen and too hot for his own good.

One thing she knew for sure: she had to see him again, even if he *did* have a girlfriend.

Lennie made it to Vegas for the weekend, and Lucky couldn't have been happier, even though they were surrounded by total chaos as everyone got ready for the grand opening. The residential part of the complex was finished, every detail down to fully stocked luxury state-of-the-art kitchens and closed-circuit TV in every room.

"This is ours," Lucky announced, giving Lennie a tour of the penthouse she'd had built to her specifications. "It's got one bedroom—*our* bedroom, 'cause this apartment is a no-kid zone, a special place where we can spend time alone."

"You're too much!" he exclaimed, checking out the huge terrace and amazing view—the city sprawled out like a mosaic of twinkling lights.

"I know," she responded. "And don't you love it."

"I love *you*."

"Come," she said, taking his hand. "I want to show you the rest of the apartment."

"The bedroom?" he said.

"No," she said laughing. "First, your room."

"My room? What's that?"

"Somewhere you can create while I keep a watch on the hotel," she said, flinging open the door to a wood-paneled den set up with a big-screen TV, a sophisticated computer editing console, a state-of-the-art sound system, and all of his former movies and scripts leather-bound and stacked high.

"You're an amazing woman, Lucky Santangelo," he said, checking everything out. "How'd you find the time to organize all this?"

"Because," she said, smiling, "it's for you, and I always have time for you. . . ."

Ever since Max had gotten back, Cookie and Harry were behaving like major assholes. All they wanted to do was lock themselves in Cookie's room and sit around getting stoned. She was away a few days and suddenly both her best friends had turned into major potheads. Drugs didn't tempt her—she'd tried coke once, hated it, and smoking pot made her sleepy and desperate for chocolate.

At the age of twelve her mother had given her a strong lecture about drugs, and it had obviously stuck. "Only morons and losers enjoy getting high," Lucky had informed her. "If you want to go through life in a daze, then start taking drugs, but if you're smart, you'll soon realize it gets you nowhere fast, so don't fall for that peer pressure crap. And don't smoke nicotine either. I've been an on-and-off smoker all my life and I hate it. It's a filthy habit, but I can't seem to quit for any length of time. So do not start and you won't find yourself in that pathetic position."

The thing that Max really admired about Lucky was that she wasn't really like a mother figure. Sure, she could be stern at times, but she was very up on everything going on in the world and totally open about sex and stuff. At fourteen Lucky had handed her a pack of condoms and said, "You won't be needing these for a couple of years, but when you do, make sure you use 'em. You're a smart girl. You'll decide when the time is right."

Max had already decided.

The time was right and her potential victim was Ace.

All she had to do was get him to call her back.

CHAPTER SIXTY-FIVE

Henry Whitfield-Simmons drove back to Pasadena in a simmering state of frustration and anger. After hitting the coyote and running the Volvo off the road, not only had he lost sight of the car with Maria inside, but the front tire of the Volvo was damaged, forcing him to change it himself. Since he was no mechanic, the mountain road was deserted, and there was nobody around to help him, it ended up taking him hours.

By the time he'd managed to make it to Big Bear, it was much later. He drove into town wary of getting caught in a trap. It was quite possible the two of them could have gone to the cops.

No, he'd immediately corrected himself. *Not the two of them. Maria wouldn't do that—her cousin would.*

Her cousin was a son of a bitch. *He* was the one who'd persuaded Maria to leave. He'd obviously forced her to do so, and she'd left because he'd given her no choice. Maria had wanted to stay with him, he was sure of it. They'd just started getting to know each other and things were going well between them.

Damn the cousin. Damn him to hell.

After checking out the parking lot and discovering her car was gone, Henry had driven back to Pasadena in a white-hot rage thinking about Maria all the way.

He'd arrived at the mausoleum late in the afternoon to find that his mother was in the middle of one of her charity tea parties. Dozens of women were wandering around the mansion in their ridiculous hats and expensive outfits. On top of everything else, Penelope decided to humiliate him. "Here comes Henry, my little computer nerd," she'd informed anyone who would listen as he'd attempted to slink upstairs unnoticed. "Did you have a pleasant time, dear? Did you meet any suitable girls?"

Why did she do this to him, when all he'd wanted to do was escape to his room where he could log on to Maria's laptop and find out even more about her?

That was almost two weeks ago, and after checking out Maria's e-mail, he'd discovered that Lucky Santangelo was opening a new hotel in Las Vegas, the Keys.

Naturally Maria would be there. So would Lucky, Billy Melina, even Alex Woods.

Henry checked out the Keys online and discovered that there was a grand opening party planned. Tickets were expensive, but that was no problem.

Ah . . . this would be his opportunity to reconnect with Maria. And this time he'd be better prepared to take her away forever.

Nobody was coming between him and Maria again. The two of them were destined to be together.

And that was exactly the way it should be.

CHAPTER SIXTY-SIX

Anthony was not happy. Over the last week he'd fielded three calls from Detective Franklin in Vegas.

He called up Renee to complain.

"There's nothing I can do," Renee said, stoic as usual. She was experiencing her own problems regarding Detective Franklin. The woman was like a bulldog hanging on to a bone with her incessant questions. And Susie was on her case too.

"What *did* happen to Tasmin?" Susie kept on asking. "And why can't I say she left with Anthony?"

"Because you can't. If you do, it will make *me* out to be a liar."

"So where *is* Tasmin?"

"Nobody knows."

This answer did not satisfy Susie, who every so often continued to question her.

"Whaddya mean, nothin'?" Anthony demanded over the phone. "Why's she still callin' me? Askin' the same dumb questions."

"Tasmin's ex-husband is kicking up a big stink about her being missing, apparently he has connections in the police department," Renee explained. "I've been questioned three times, the detective has talked to Susie twice, and half the hotel staff have been interrogated."

"Pay the bitch off," Anthony growled. "Offer her fifty thousand in cash. She'll go for it."

"No, she won't."

"Give it a try, Renee. Money talks."

"It'll look wrong if I even attempt to pay her off. She'll take it as a sign we have something to hide," Renee said, impatient to get him off the phone.

"You think I give a shit?" Anthony responded. "Get the cunt off my fuckin' case, that's all I care about."

Renee hung up the phone. She'd had it with Anthony Bonar. After Tasmin's brutal murder she was done.

There had to be a way to get him out of their life once and for all.

And then it occurred to her. There was.

Anthony had been on his plane on and off for the past ten days, flying back and forth between New York, Miami, and Mexico City, with a crucial twenty-four-hour business trip to Colombia thrown in. Anthony always felt like a peasant whenever he visited the ruling drug lords in Colombia. Those men lived like kings in their huge mansions three times the size of his, with an army of guards on call and dozens of servants. But he couldn't complain—he was not exactly suffering.

In New York he'd received a report that Carlita was not cheating on him. He was so pleased that he'd invested another two hundred thousand in her business. Then he'd spent a pleasant couple of days with his elegant Italian mistress visiting all his favorite New York restaurants and clubs. Carlita was a class act; he was definitely keeping her around.

Back in Miami, Emmanuelle was as demanding as ever. Her latest request was that she wanted him to take her on a vacation. "Please, honey," she'd begged. "You never take me anywhere."

"Where you wanna go?" he'd asked.

"Europe," she'd replied, all excited at the prospect. "Paris, London, and Rome."

One thing about Emmanuelle, she always went for the best.

"Tell you what," he'd said. "You'll come with me to Vegas. There's a big hotel opening, it's gonna be quite a scene."

"But sugar pie—"

"Vegas or nothin'," he'd said flatly. "Your choice."

Shortly after he'd invited Emmanuelle, Francesca informed him that she expected to go with him to Vegas.

"You can't fly," he'd said, determined to put his grandmother off. "The doc told you no traveling with your heart condition, ya gotta take it easy."

"My heart is strong enough to witness the downfall of the Santangelo family," Francesca had replied. "I'm coming with you to Vegas."

Stubborn old woman. What could he do? He'd finally decided to take Francesca *and* Emmanuelle. Francesca was a woman of the world, she'd understand that a man had to have a mistress as well as a wife—it was the traditional Italian way. Although he suspected Francesca would have preferred Carlita to Emmanuelle.

Problems, always problems. But first he had to spend a couple of days in Mexico City attending to business.

After sleeping with the drug enforcement agent, Irma suffered a panic attack. She couldn't help wondering if Oliver Stanton had known who she was, and by sleeping with her was he attempting to garner information about her husband?

The situation forced her to rethink her plans. She sat at home and worried about what she'd done. And to make things worse, Luis was still refusing to come into the house, which she couldn't understand.

She finally instructed Marta to tell Luis to meet her in the bedroom to check out her houseplants.

"I keep on asking him," she informed Marta. "It

seems he doesn't understand me. And my orchids need special attention."

Marta nodded, her face revealing nothing. "*Sí, señora*," she said, wondering if Señora Bonar was aware that several members of the staff suspected that she and Luis might be having sex. If they were, it wasn't right. Marta knew Luis's family; she also knew his pregnant wife. But Marta was not one to gossip, and she couldn't say exactly what was going on behind closed doors, although Señora Bonar was giving her an awful lot of time off whenever Luis entered the house.

Ten minutes later the old gardener knocked on Irma's bedroom door.

When she saw who it was, she was angry. Luis not coming when she'd specifically requested him was most disrespectful.

Gritting her teeth, she showed the old gardener the bedroom plants and her precious orchids.

The grizzled old man spoke very little English. "*Orquidea* no need much water," he informed her.

"Thank you," she said, tight-lipped.

"*Gracias, señora. Orquídea buenas.*"

Later she went down to the kitchen, cornered Marta, and asked her why Luis hadn't come to tend to her plants when she'd specifically requested his presence. She realized she was treading on dangerous territory, but she was determined to find out anyway.

"Luis go home early," Marta explained, busying herself at the sink.

"Why was that?"

"His wife, she expect baby soon," Marta said, wiping her hands on her apron.

"His *wife?*" Irma said, barely able to conceal her surprise. "I wasn't aware that Luis was married."

"*Sí, señora.*"

Now she was really upset. Luis was married with a

pregnant wife and he hadn't told her. This was unbeliev-able.

And yet . . . she still yearned for his touch. She still had a burning desire to feel his naked body up against hers.

Several days later Anthony arrived home, insisting on the usual round of parties at the house. Irma endured more evenings of too much rich food, endless karaoke, and adoring sycophants.

After a few days he got bored as usual, and informed her he was leaving for Las Vegas on yet another busi-ness trip. She wasn't sorry to see him go.

A few days before Anthony was due to leave for the opening of the Keys, one of the guards from his house appeared at his office and badgered his assistant, tell-ing her that he had to see Señor Bonar regarding a mat-ter of great urgency.

His assistant asked what it was in reference to. The guard replied that it was of utmost importance that he speak to Señor Bonar personally.

"Send him in," Anthony said, puffing on a large cigar.

The man entered his office and planted himself in front of his desk. Anthony did not invite him to sit.

"Whaddya want?" he snapped. "Make it quick."

"I am Cesar," the guard said. "I have worked for you two years, Señor Bonar. I come here to tell you some-thing of a delicate nature."

"Spit it out," Anthony growled, leaning back in his leather chair.

"My circumstances are such that I need to buy a new car," Cesar said, his greedy eyes darting around the office.

Was this son of a bitch *blackmailing* him? Informa-tion in return for a car. Anthony couldn't believe the stones on this guy. It was outrageous.

"What information you got that gets you a fuckin' car?" he snarled.

"Private information, Señor Bonar," Cesar said, standing up ramrod straight. "Information you would not want to go any further."

"I wouldn't, huh?" Anthony said, expelling a stream of acrid smoke in Cesar's direction.

"No, *señor*."

"Okay, we'll do it this way. You tell me what's on your mind, an' if it's worth anything I'll give you cash. An' if it's bullshit, you get nothin'. That fair enough for you?"

"*Sí, señor*."

"Okay, let's hear what you got."

Cesar glanced toward the door. "It is sensitive, Señor Bonar."

"Speak!"

"I regretfully tell you, *señor*, that a person who should be trustworthy is not," Cesar said, clearing his throat. "This man is taking advantage of your wife."

"What the fuck you sayin'?" Anthony said, sitting bolt upright.

"There is a man working on your estate, *señor*, who is doing bad things with your wife."

"Whaddya mean, bad things?" Anthony said, a muscle twitching beneath his left eye. "Is he raping her? Takin' money from her? What the fuck d'you mean?"

"This man enters your house when you are not there. He stays many hours. He spends time in your bedroom with the *señora*."

"Who is this person?" Anthony demanded, his eyes cold as steel.

"One of your gardeners, *señor*." Cesar paused, experiencing a moment of deep satisfaction before continuing. "His name is Luis."

"You sure about this?" Anthony said, staring him down.

"*Sí, señor.*"

"Absolutely fuckin' *sure*?"

"*Sí, señor,*" Cesar said, blinking rapidly several times.

Anthony unlocked his desk drawer, took out a wad of cash, and threw it at Cesar. "Take this and get the fuck outta my office. An' if you open your mouth to anyone 'bout this—anyone at all—I cut out your fuckin' tongue with a buzz saw. Get it?"

"*Sí, señor.*" Cesar said, backing out of the office.

The moment he left, Anthony began pacing. This couldn't be true, could it? This couldn't be possible that Irma, his *wife*, and a gardener on his estate were having sex. In *his* house. On *his* bed.

Some other man fucking his wife.

It was unthinkable.

And yet . . . this stupid guard had come to him with the information, and why would the man lie? Why would he put himself in jeopardy?

Anthony thought back to Acapulco and the change in Irma. She was insolent, withdrawn, and looks-wise she was glowing.

Yes! It was true! The bitch was getting fucked! And not by him.

After simmering for a while, Anthony summoned The Grill into his office.

"This is what I want you t'do," he said, issuing instructions. "An' make sure ya take care of it immediately."

Several hours after Anthony left the house, he called Irma from his office and informed her he was sending his car for her, and that she was to meet him in the city for lunch.

Lunch? In the city? She'd thought he was on his way to Vegas.

"I'm not sure . . ." she began.

"There's somebody I want you to meet," he said.

"Who?"

"A business acquaintance. The car'll be there shortly."

Irma was ready when the car arrived. She was also apprehensive that somehow or other Anthony might have found out about Oliver. Over the past two weeks she'd received several calls from her dinner date, none of which she'd returned.

What if Oliver called while she was with Anthony? What if she bumped into him in the city?

This was not an ideal situation. Her nerves were on edge, and for now her plans were on hold.

Sitting behind his ornate desk, Anthony put down his phone and stared off into space. Who would have thought that his wife would betray him? Carlita? Yes. Irma? No.

Soon he would know for sure. And once he did, Irma would be punished in a way that would hurt her more than she could possibly imagine.

Nobody cheated on Anthony Bonar and got away with it. Nobody.

CHAPTER SIXTY-SEVEN

Max came up with what she considered to be a brilliant idea. Once again she ran it by Lennie, who was so into his upcoming movie he would've said yes to anything.

"Uh . . . there's this boy," she informed him. "And when I got carjacked he kind of helped me. So . . ." She hesitated for a moment before continuing. "I was, uh, thinking I could return the favor by inviting him to the Keys opening."

"What did Lucky say?" Lennie asked, barely looking up from his computer.

"She said yes."

"Okay. Go ahead, invite him."

Later she phoned Lucky in Vegas and had the same conversation. Lucky was so into the opening of her hotel she would've said yes to anything. Well—almost anything.

"What did Lennie say?" Lucky asked.

"He said yes," Max replied, cheerfully lying.

"Then I don't see why not."

How cool was this? She'd wrangled an invite for Ace to attend the opening, and she was determined he'd accept. They'd been speaking on the phone regularly since he'd finally called her back. She'd been delighted to hear from him, ridiculously so. And was it her imagination, or did he sound equally pleased to hear from her?

Yes, he did. She was sure of it.

Since they'd reconnected they'd been talking every

day. He never mentioned his girlfriend. She never mentioned her nonexistent boyfriend. They talked about everything from their ordeal to music to movies to books. In fact, they talked nonstop.

She found out he was working as a ski instructor and saving up to one day open his own ski shop.

"No college?" she'd asked.

"The most successful people in America never went to college," he'd informed her. "And one of these days I'm gonna have a chain of ski shops in every resort in America."

He was ambitious, and so interesting and different from all the rich kids she'd grown up with. But best of all, he was so *hot!* And she couldn't stop thinking about him.

Things seemed comparatively calm on the Venus/Billy front. She was busy with her various projects, plus rehearsing for Vegas. And he was busy finishing up on Alex's movie.

They both decided that for the Vegas trip they would drive up on Venus's tour bus as opposed to flying. Billy's movie wrapped the day before they were due to leave, and Venus opted out of attending the wrap party. "You'll be bonding with the crew, and saying your goodbyes," she pointed out. "It's better I don't come."

"If you're sure," Billy said. "'Cause you know I'd love to have you there."

"No, you go. If you feel like it, you can drop by my house later."

"Sounds like an invite I can't refuse."

"I appreciate a man who can't refuse me," she purred.

Ever since the fight with Alex, Billy had been on his best behavior. Venus honestly felt they were right back on track. It was a satisfying feeling.

* * *

Billy and Kev went together to the wrap party on sound stage 3. The place was jammed with crew members and their significant others, most of whom were desperate to get their picture taken with Billy. He obliged, until after about twenty minutes he was startled to see Miss Broken Taillight—alias Ali—flittering around in her cutoff denims and skimpy tank top, long sexy legs tanned and appealing.

"What's *she* doin' here?" he muttered to Kev, who looked a bit sheepish and mumbled something about inviting her. "Why'd you do that?" Billy asked.

" 'Cause she's a sweet kid," Kev said, heading for the bar.

"Yeah, and she gives a sweet blow job, right?" Billy remarked, following him.

"Nothing wrong with that," Kev said, requesting a beer. "*You* didn't seem to object."

"I don't wanna see her around," Billy lectured. "If Venus had come with me tonight, it would've been awkward."

"Why?" Kev said, handing Billy a bottle of imported beer. "She's not gonna run up to Venus and say, 'Oh, I screwed your boyfriend,' is she?"

"I don't know, *you* tell me," Billy said pointedly.

"Did you hear that Alex gave her a line?"

"How'd *that* happen?" Billy said, swigging beer.

"Guess Maggie worked her magic."

"At least it gets her off my case," Billy grumbled, still not happy.

"There's somethin' I've been meaning to tell you," Kev began, looking embarrassed.

"What now?" Billy sighed.

"I'm kinda into her," Kev admitted. "Like I'm thinking of taking her to the party in Vegas."

"You fuckin' nuts?" Billy said, frowning.

"No, I kinda *promised* I'd take her."

"Jeez, Kev!"

"She lives in a rat hole in Hollywood with two gay guys and another girl. I feel sorry for her. I was over there the other night—the place is a pit."

"What's *that* got t'do with anything?"

"Have a little heart. She's trying hard to make it, workin' any job she can. It's that same old story—she comes from a broken home, took the bus to L.A. to get away from her stepdad, and ended up livin' on the street until she hooked up with friends."

"So now you're the knight with a permanent hard-on who's gonna save her. Right?"

"Maybe."

"Of all the girls in L.A. you had to pick this one," Billy said, shaking his head. "What's wrong with you?"

"Anyway," Kev said, "thought I should give you a heads-up."

"That's big of you, Kev."

"Oh yeah, an' I made her swear she'll never mention anything to Venus about gettin' it on with you."

"She'd better not, 'cause if she does, your ass is freakin' fired."

"No worries," Kev said confidently.

"I know I shouldn't be the one saying this, but my hotel is *amazing*," Lucky raved to Venus over the phone. "Totally amazing and perfect and great. Better than I could possibly have imagined. Gino will *love* it."

"I'm happy for you," Venus said. "Can't wait to get there and check it out for myself."

"We have a luxurious penthouse suite ready for you and Billy with its own pool and an incredible view of the Strip. Massage therapists are on alert, and anything else you want. Put in your requests now."

"I'll ask Billy. Maybe a pool table."

"Already in your suite."

"A Jacuzzi."

"Both inside and out."

"How about a stripper pole?"

"Done!"

"I'm joking."

They both laughed.

"I'm so pleased you're coming up the night before, so is Lennie," Lucky said. "We'll have a great dinner, just the four of us. I've been testing all the restaurants. The food is sensational, world-class chefs everywhere I turn."

"Billy and I are driving up, which means I'm not sure what time we'll get there."

"Driving, huh?"

"We're using my tour bus—thought it might be fun."

"Hmm . . . five or six hours on a bus. Doesn't sound like fun to me. Are you sure I can't send a plane for you?"

"No thanks. I can assure you—five or six hours on my bus with Billy is gonna *rock!*"

"Okay, so travel safely, I'll be thinking of you."

Lucky put down the phone and surveyed her kingdom from the window of her penthouse. It was true. Everything about the Keys was looking awesome, and the hotel section was already running like a smoothly oiled machine. Her general manager was a real pro; so were the dozen or so undermanagers.

Since she'd planned and built two hotels before, she was well aware of what mistakes to avoid. Organization was the name of the game, especially for opening night, and especially with planeloads of celebrities flying in, and a ton of press waiting to cover the event.

It was going to be *the* most special and spectacular night Vegas had ever seen.

She couldn't wait.

CHAPTER SIXTY-EIGHT

During the car ride to Anthony's office Irma's mind was darting in many different directions. What did he want with her? Was it possible that he'd found out about Oliver?

One never knew with Anthony. He'd become so adept at completely ignoring her existence that being summoned to his office was quite alarming. When had Anthony ever been interested in her opinion of his business acquaintances?

He greeted her with an affectionate hug.

"Where are we going for lunch?" she asked. "And who is it that you want me to meet?"

"That was just my way of gettin' you here," he said. "Is it a crime to wanna have lunch with my wife for a change?"

"Of course not," she stammered, completely thrown.

He took her to the most expensive restaurant in the city for lunch, and all through the meal he was overly attentive toward her.

Something was definitely going on. She felt uncomfortable and horribly guilty about her one night with Oliver Stanton.

"Is everything all right?" she asked when they were almost finished.

"Why wouldn't it be?" he countered, tapping his fingers on the table.

"I thought you were leaving for Las Vegas, and then you call me for lunch."

"You had something else to do?" he questioned, staring her down.

"Not at all," she answered, lowering her eyes.

"I've bin thinkin' that I should spend more time with you."

"Do you mean traveling?" she said hesitantly.

"Yeah, why not? We got the place in Miami, the apartment in New York—there's no reason you can't come with me sometimes."

"I thought you wanted me to stay in the house here," she said, picking at her dessert.

"It might not be such a bad idea for you to spend more time with the kids. Eduardo's a surly little bastard, an' Carolina's growin' up fast. Could be she needs a mother around."

Was there a light at the end of the tunnel? Had she picked the wrong time to leave him? Could it be that Anthony was actually softening?

After they left the restaurant, he led her down the street to a jewelry store, greeted the owner, whom he knew, and instructed her to pick out a gift for herself. "Choose anythin' you want," he said, lighting up a cigar. "Anythin' you think you deserve."

"It's not my birthday, Anthony," she murmured.

"I know that, but I feel like bein' generous. I can spoil my own wife, can't I?"

Was he sick? Did he have a brain tumor?

She stood in front of trays of lavish jewelry, finally picking out a modest gold bracelet.

"Nah," Anthony said, vigorously shaking his head. "You wanna get somethin' with diamonds. You're my wife—you gotta have the best."

The jeweler produced another tray, this time filled with diamond jewelry.

"Did I mention I'm thinkin' of taking you to Vegas?" Anthony said.

"You are?" she said, startled.

"Yeah, there's a big hotel opening. You might get a kick outta bein' there. It ain't healthy you bein' by yourself all the time. Go ahead, choose somethin' flashy, 'cause I wanna show you off." He picked up a pair of flawless yellow diamond drop earrings. "How 'bout these?" he suggested.

"They're *very* expensive," she demurred.

"My wife deserves expensive," he said expansively. "Try 'em on."

She did so. They were quite incredible.

"You like 'em, they're yours," he said.

Anthony was like a changed man. Irma was perplexed, but at the same time secretly pleased because this was the man she'd always hoped he was. Attentive, generous, kind.

She settled on the earrings. The jeweler had them gift wrapped, then Anthony escorted her to the car and instructed the driver to take her home.

"I'm leavin' for Vegas now," he said. "If I think you'll like it, I'll send for you. Okay, sugar?"

Sugar? He was calling her sugar? Wasn't that a term of endearment strictly reserved for his mistresses? She was confused.

"Take good care of this little lady," Anthony said, speaking to his driver. "She's precious cargo. She's my wife."

Once he'd put Irma in the car, Anthony returned to his office. The Grill was waiting for him.

"You do it?" Anthony asked, his expression stony.

"All taken care of, boss."

"Give it twenty-four hours, then get it outta there."

"Yes, boss."

*   *   *

Irma arrived back at the house clutching her gift-wrapped earrings, which she knew had cost over a hundred thousand dollars. She felt quite light-headed.

When they were first married, Anthony had bought her a few pieces of jewelry, but over the past several years he'd not given her so much as a birthday present. Was he trying to make up for it now?

She went up to her room, immediately heading over to the window to see what Luis was doing. He was present; the old gardener was not.

Maybe she should see him one more time. And after that she could be the faithful wife, because if Anthony was changing, she could do the same and allow him one more chance.

But still . . . Luis was a big temptation, and she didn't like that he'd rejected her. She craved one more opportunity to be in his arms. Just one more time. . . .

She hurried downstairs and out to the garden. "Luis," she said, walking right up to him, "come with me."

He shook his head, wary eyes darting this way and that.

"Now!" she said firmly. "I'm your boss, come with me."

He didn't understand her words, but he certainly understood her tone of voice. Putting down his rake, he followed her into the house and up the staircase to her bedroom.

She locked the door and turned to face him. "Luis," she said, "what *is* going on with you?"

"'Scuse, *señora*?" he muttered, wishing he was somewhere else.

"Do not call me *señora*," she said sharply. "My name is Irma, you know that."

"*Sí* . . . Irma."

"Why didn't you tell me you were married and your wife is pregnant?"

He shrugged. He understood two words—*pregnant* and *wife*. The American woman knew, but still she'd invited him into her bedroom, so she must not care. The sex with her was so different from the sex with his wife, and Cesar had not mentioned a word lately, so perhaps it was safe to make love to her one last time. It was obviously what she wanted, and even though she was pretending to be angry, her eyes were filled with anticipation and her cheeks were flushed.

He could not resist. If they did it one more time, how would Cesar ever find out? Besides, Cesar was not on duty today, and the *señora* was looking extremely beautiful, unlike his wife who was so big with child that she refused to allow him anywhere near her.

He reached forward and placed his hand on her breast. She did not object. Immediately he felt himself becoming hard.

Next he began undoing the buttons on her blouse, before unhooking the clip at the front of her bra, exposing her small but perfect breasts with the extended nipples.

"Oh, Luis," she sighed, throwing her head back as his fingers lightly brushed the tips of her nipples, before he brought his lips down to slowly suck on them.

"Luis," she sighed again.

Sweeping her up in his arms, he carried her to the bed and proceeded to make tender love to her, promising himself that it would be the last time.

And while she lay back on the bed enjoying his steady kisses and soft caresses, Irma promised herself that this would be the very last time.

CHAPTER SIXTY-NINE

"I have to make a trip, Mother," Henry said to Penelope, not interested in explaining himself, but realizing that at the present time he had no choice. "I might be gone for quite some time, and I will be needing a substantial amount of money."

"I gave you two hundred dollars last week," Penelope said, arching an imperious eyebrow. "Why would you need more?"

"I know, Mother, but that is not enough."

"Enough for what, Henry?" Penelope said, brushing an imaginary speck off her pristine linen skirt. "We are not a family who fritters money away."

"One day I'll inherit everything," Henry pointed out. "Therefore I do not understand why I cannot have some of it now?"

"Because you are not a responsible person," Penelope snapped. "No, you are not responsible at all."

"Responsible for what, Mother?" he asked, controlling the rage he felt toward this woman who would not give him what was rightfully his—or at least it would be when she was dead.

Dead. The word had a satisfying ring to it. . . .

"You are not responsible for anything, Henry," Penelope said, sniffing her disapproval. "Look at you—you've made nothing of yourself. You sit in your room in front of your computer all day long. It pains me that you have never shown any interest in joining your father's business. We're both on the board of directors and you've never so much as bothered to attend one meeting."

"Father's business doesn't interest me," he muttered.

"What *does* interest you, Henry? I would be intrigued to know."

"Acting, Mother. I wanted to be an actor, but neither you nor Father encouraged me to follow my dream."

"Your dream!" Penelope scoffed. "How ridiculous! Actors have to be handsome with a personality. Look in the mirror, Henry—with your face you had no chance of succeeding, none at all. *That's* the reason we discouraged you."

"I *am* talented, Mother," he said, knowing full well it was impossible to convince her.

"At what, Henry? Sitting alone in your room? You've never brought a girl home, you are not involved in any social or charity activities." She paused, giving him a penetrating stare. "Are you gay, Henry?"

He found the word *gay* coming out of his mother's pursed lips quite disturbing.

"No, Mother," he answered, swallowing his rage at the way she spoke to him. "I am not gay. And you will be pleased to know that recently I met a girl I like."

"Well, that's news," Penelope said, her long thin face expressing surprise. "Do I know her? Is she from a good family?"

"She's from an . . . interesting family."

"Affluent?"

"Yes, Mother."

"Of our stature and social standing?"

"Yes, Mother. Therefore I wish to treat her in a proper fashion." He paused for a long moment, allowing her to digest the information. "She has an event coming up I need to attend."

"What kind of event?"

"She's an architect, she's designed an apartment

building in Nevada, and I wish to go there for the opening. I cannot make the trip unless I have money, otherwise her father will conclude that I am not a suitable match for her."

"How much money are you requesting, Henry?"

"Fifty thousand dollars."

"Surely you jest?" Penelope said, unamused.

"I do not jest, Mother. One day it will all be mine, as I keep on reminding you."

"Unless I decide to change my will," Penelope said.

Henry experienced a cold chill. Why would his mother say such a thing? Why would she even think it?

"It is imperative I impress this girl," he said, choking back a response to her comment.

"Impress her?"

"I'm considering buying her an engagement ring."

"Nonsense!"

"Excuse me?"

"An engagement is out of the question until I have met this girl and her family. You must bring them here before I even think about granting my approval."

"Very well, Mother," he said, his voice constricted. "You'll arrange for the money?"

"No, Henry, I'll arrange for *five* thousand dollars, which is a great deal of money. One stipulation: you cannot buy this girl a ring, not until I have met and approved of her. Only then will we discuss the purchase of a ring."

"Yes, Mother," he said, thinking that five thousand was a paltry amount, and he needed more to look after Maria, to take her away where nobody could find them. What he needed was his entire inheritance.

He stared at his mother, loathing her. Penelope Whitfield-Simmons was a tightfisted, mean woman, and he hated her with a deep and lasting passion. She'd never shown him any motherly love, never cared about him like a mother should. All she'd ever done was deride him in front of her friends and told him how useless and untalented and ugly he was.

It occurred to him that if she wasn't around, everything would be his and his days of begging would be over.

Now she was talking about changing her will, and that wasn't right.

He had to do something about it. And he had to do something about it fast.

Dead . . . The word had an interesting ring to it.

CHAPTER SEVENTY

Apart from Philippe, who spent most of his days cleaning silver and taking care of the house, and Greta, Leonardo's nanny, Max had the Bel-Air house to herself. Greta, who'd been summoned back from her vacation to keep an eye on Max, was a certified TV addict who spent her days glued to daytime soaps and her nights glued to prime time. Max considered neither of them a problem, and since she figured she wasn't grounded anymore, she acted accordingly. It was great when both her parents were too busy to notice what she was up to. She wished it was always this way.

After talking her dad into allowing her to invite Ace, then getting Lucky to agree, she'd been told by Lennie that there were rooms booked for her and her friends at the Keys. "Your mom says you and Cookie can share a room, while Harry can bunk in with your new friend."

"His name's Ace, Dad," she'd said, thinking what a bonus! She hadn't been sure if Lucky would even want her at the opening considering her absence from Gino's party. But not only was she invited, she could bring friends!

Ace was driving to L.A. in his brother's truck, staying the night in Bel-Air, and the next day they'd head for Vegas.

Max warned Cookie and Harry that they had to be on their best behavior when they met him. "You can't be like lying around totally stoned," she said. "I have no clue if he's into that, and since I'm not, don't even mention getting high."

"What's the plan for later?" Cookie asked as they sat beside the pool.

"I was thinking dinner first," Max said, "then maybe a club."

"My I.D. is like *so* fake," Cookie complained, rubbing suntan lotion on her stomach. "Besides, all the bouncers know me now, I can't get in anywhere."

"I know a club we can hit," Harry said, sheltering his skinny white body under an umbrella. "Hundred bucks at the door an' no problem—doesn't matter how old we are."

"Perfect," Max said, thinking she couldn't wait to show off L.A. to Ace. He'd told her he'd never been there before, which was kind of crazy.

"What's he like?" Cookie wanted to know.

"A major babe," Max said, thinking she couldn't wait for her friends to meet him.

"As cute as Donny?" Cookie asked.

"Donny sucks," Max said, dismissing her ex. "I'm so over that loser."

"About time," Cookie said, dangling her feet in the pool.

They decided on an Italian restaurant for dinner, then the underground club Harry knew about.

"Harry," Max ordered. "You pick up the check at both places 'cause I'm not sure if Ace has much money. I'll pay you back our share. And whatever you do, don't let him split it with you. Okay?"

"How do I know you'll pay me back?" Harry said, being difficult.

"Oh, pul—*eaze!*"

"She's in love," Cookie giggled. "Our girl's got a major crush."

"No way," Max said, blushing.

"Yeah, way," Cookie teased. "What you gonna wear?"

"Haven't thought about it."

"Liar!"

"I am *so* not!"

"Are you doin' the deed?" Harry asked. "I mean, you'll be all alone in your house."

"Not alone. Greta's here, and Philippe."

"Your house is so big you can get away with anything," Cookie said.

"Yeah," Harry agreed.

"Is Mister New Dude gonna stay in your room tonight?" Cookie asked.

"His name is Ace, and he's got a girlfriend."

"Sure, but he's leaving her and driving to L.A. to see *you*," Cookie pointed out.

"He knows I'm only sixteen. I had to tell him."

"I don't get it," Cookie said. "Is sixteen considered underage?"

"Dunno," Max said, shrugging. "But it doesn't matter."

"He might not wanna do it if he thinks you're underage," Harry said, throwing in his opinion.

"I think fifteen's underage," Cookie said. "Sixteen's a go."

"You're wrong," Harry said. "The age of sexual consent is eighteen in California."

"Whatever," Max said, pretending she hadn't really thought about it, although the truth was that's *all* she could think about.

To have sex with Ace or not to have sex with Ace—that was the question.

They decided to drive up to Vegas in Harry's new SUV early the next morning. It had a souped-up engine and he was desperate to take it on a long drive.

"I guess it'll be okay with Ace," Max said.

"Why are you so bothered by what *he* thinks?" Harry

asked. "It's totally unlike you to care. *You* should be telling *him* what we're gonna do."

"You don't understand," Max said. "He's not the kind of guy I tell what to do."

"What kind of guy *is* he?" Cookie questioned, adjusting her Dolce & Gabbana sunglasses.

"Cool," Max replied with a dreamy smile. "Amazingly cool."

CHAPTER SEVENTY-ONE

Waiting for Lennie to join her in Vegas, Lucky could hardly believe that in less than twenty-four hours she would be opening her third hotel in the shimmering city. The Keys was a more exciting project than any of the others. It was bigger and better and more extravagant—a true oasis of calm and beauty in a city known for its sometimes flashy showmanship. The Keys was not another theme hotel pretending to be Venice or Paris or Rome. It was simply there, making a statement. White and stylish—modern architecture combined with old-fashioned warmth and luxury. Even the casino was different, lighter and more welcoming, with a friendly lineup of pit bosses, dealers, croupiers, and attractive casino hosts of both sexes. The grounds were lush and lovely, filled with exotic plants and flowers. There were three swimming pools—one for adults, one for children, and one for the in-betweens. All of them surrounded by swaying palm trees. The children's pool backed up against a glass-enclosed aquarium where exotic fish proliferated. The adults' pool featured a fully stocked bar. And the in-between pool supplied underwater iPods and a choice of sounds.

Lucky realized she could happily move into her penthouse permanently. She didn't miss L.A. at all, and if it wasn't for Max, Gino Junior, and Leonardo, she would take up residence in a flash. But having kids tied a person down, and until they all went off to college, she and

Lennie were stuck in one place. Well, not really stuck—soon their Malibu house would be finished and they could move out of stuffy Bel-Air and back to the beach, which they both loved. But she also loved Vegas. There was something about the place—it reminded her of Gino and the early days. Oh God! So many memories. Building the Magiriano and the problems involved—graft, union walkouts, and threats—but she'd built one hell of a hotel. And Marco—oh Marco, how she'd loved him, and when he'd been shot and killed, Vegas had lost its thrill. But now she was back and the Keys was all hers. And now she had Lennie, her husband, her rock. Yes, Vegas was still an exciting city with so much going on.

Venus called to announce that they'd just arrived and that they were totally impressed with everything.

"Our suite is beyond gorgeous," she enthused. "How clever are *you*?"

"Look who's calling *me* clever," Lucky responded, looking forward to showing off her new hotel to her best friend. "Was the drive up fun?"

"Oh yes," Venus said, sounding like she really meant it. "We spent most of it in my bed! Gives a whole new meaning to the mile-high club. Guess we just started the mile-long club!"

"You're incorrigible," Lucky said, laughing.

"Hey, when you've got a young lover, you gotta keep him occupied."

"Seems you do."

"Oh, news flash," Venus announced. "Alex and Billy are on speaking terms, there'll be no more fights."

"That's a relief. I hate it when two grown men beat the shit out of each other."

"Me too. It's the last thing any of us need."

"Okay, so settle in," Lucky said. "Then I thought we'd have drinks at our place around eight. I'll send someone to escort you."

"Are we on the same floor as you?"

"No. You're in one of the hotel penthouses, we're in the apartments."

"Drinks at eight sounds perfect, and after dinner Billy wants to gamble."

"Not at my hotel. I'd feel bad if he lost. Besides, the casino doesn't officially open until tomorrow night."

"Okay, then where?"

"How about dinner here, then we'll go over to the Cavendish? Nothing like checking out the competition."

"No rivalry amongst hotel owners?"

"Not as far as I'm concerned."

Later Lennie arrived, they took a shower, made love, then lay on the bed staring up at the skylight she'd designed above the bed with blackout blinds that could be closed at the press of a button. The blinds were open, revealing a startling expanse of sky and stars. It was beautiful and romantic.

"Man," Lennie observed. "I gotta admit, when you do something . . ."

"You'd better stop telling me that," Lucky said, smiling. "It'll go to my head, and I'll become impossible."

"Not you, sweetheart. When's Gino arriving?"

"Everybody's coming in the morning."

"Excited?"

"Of course I am."

"What time's the party tomorrow?"

"The reception starts at six, then everyone heads to the theater for Lina's event, followed by Venus's show. After that it's outside for the fireworks display. Did I tell you I was able to get these silver fantasy fireworks from Italy? They are *so* fucking beautiful."

"*You're* so fucking beautiful," Lennie said, stroking her hair. "Man, did I luck out finding you."

"Right back atcha."

* * *

Billy and Venus showed up on time.

"Oh my God!" Venus said, checking everything out. "This place is amazing! I need to buy me a penthouse immediately. It's too damn fabulous. What do you think, Billy?"

"It's pretty great," he agreed, wandering around from room to room, especially loving Lennie's den. "You want me to buy one of these apartments for you?"

"How's your career going?" she teased.

"Very funny."

"I've got a great idea," Venus said. "Let's buy an apartment together, put both our names on it."

"Not good," Lennie said, handing out martinis.

"Why not?" Venus asked, blond and stunning in a simple Roberto Cavalli short silver dress.

"He's right," Lucky agreed, equally stunning in a soft black leather pantsuit that fit her like a second skin. "If the two of you ever split up, who gets the apartment?"

"That would be one hell of a fight," Lennie remarked.

"Thanks, my friends," Venus said, bristling slightly. "What makes you think we're going to split up?"

"I can solve this," Billy said, quickly jumping in. "Either *I* buy it, or *she* does, or *I* buy it for her."

"Maybe I should mention there are only two penthouses left," Lucky said. "Brigette's thinking of buying one, and Bobby's got his eye on the other."

"I'm your best friend," Venus pointed out. "I should get first dibs."

"I've been telling you about them forever," Lucky reminded her. "If you'd come in at the construction stage, you could've had the shell designed exactly to your specifications."

"I didn't realize they were this fabulous."

"Anyway, the two available penthouses are not quite finished, so whoever gets them can choose their own kitchens, bathrooms—"

"Tell you what," Billy said magnanimously. "I'll buy it for Venus as a present."

"Nice gesture, Billy," Lucky said. "But I think I should tell you that the asking price is twelve million dollars."

"Holy shit!" he exclaimed. "Are you *kidding* me?"

"Totally serious."

"Guess I'm not getting a present," Venus said ruefully. "My boyfriend is a cheapo."

"Come *on*," Billy said. "Even *you* have to admit that's freakin' outrageous."

"*How* much did you make on your last movie?" Venus asked, winking at Lucky.

"Not enough," he said, thinking that she couldn't possibly be serious.

"Now, now, you two," Lucky said. "No fighting over millions, it's time for dinner. Let's go."

CHAPTER
SEVENTY-TWO

After Luis left, Irma slept peacefully. She was no longer concerned about Oliver Stanton. Sleeping with him had been a mistake, but now he'd stopped calling and gone away. She was sure it was pure coincidence that they'd sat next to each other on the plane, that she'd ended up having dinner with him, and that he'd turned out to be a drug enforcement agent. She regretted it, but at the time she'd thought she was leaving Anthony. The new Anthony was certainly worth giving another chance to. He was acting like a different man, and she was impressed.

She wondered what had happened to change him. Being thoughtful and generous was so unlike Anthony. Maybe his mistresses had started to misbehave, and he'd remembered he had a wife at home. That could explain it.

Anyway, they were merely mistresses, while *she* was Mrs. Anthony Bonar. That had to mean something, and it obviously did, because *she* was the one getting the diamond earrings.

Idly she wondered if she could persuade him to vary his lovemaking technique. Anthony was so rough, and now, for the first time, she understood what making love could be like.

Luis was an accomplished lover, but he was also an uneducated man with a pregnant wife, so she'd definitely decided not to continue their sexual tryst. Last night was the final time. It was memorable and now it was over.

She'd slept with her new diamond earrings on the bedside table, and the first thing she did when she woke up in the morning was to admire them. They were simply the most beautiful pieces of jewelry she'd ever possessed.

Marta brought her breakfast on a tray.

"What a lovely day it is today, Marta," she said, smiling at the woman.

Marta nodded, her face surly. She'd seen the *señora* bringing Luis into the house the previous day. She'd seen him follow her up the stairs into her bedroom, then she'd seen him depart several hours later. It wasn't right. Should she warn his wife? But if she did, Luis would be out of a job and she knew his family did not have much money.

One thing she *did* know, and that was, as the Bonars' housekeeper, the safest thing was to keep her mouth shut.

However, she couldn't help confiding in her cousin, Rosa, the Bonars' cook in Acapulco.

"What the *señora* does is nothing," Rosa spat. "Señor Bonar has mistresses everywhere. It is good she does it back to him."

"Luis is a nice boy," Marta insisted. "I know the family, his wife is pregnant."

"So what?" Rosa responded. "If I was sleeping with a man other than my husband, I'd choose someone young too."

"And *married?*" Marta said disapprovingly.

"You can't blame the woman. Señor Bonar is a pig—he ignores his wife and manhandles me. I'm forced to accept the way he humiliates me in front of his friends. He often threatens to fire me, then he thinks it's so funny. I loathe him."

"Why don't you quit?" Marta asked.

"Why don't *you?*" Rosa responded.

They both knew that neither of them could afford to.

Unaware of the heated conversation going on downstairs, Irma glanced at the morning paper, ate her scrambled eggs and toast, and finally got out of bed. Had Marta noticed the diamond earrings lying on her bedside table? She probably should have put them away; tempting the staff was not wise.

Excited at the thought of Anthony taking her to Las Vegas, she realized he had not taken her anywhere in years. This could be a new beginning. A second honeymoon.

She went into the bathroom and ran a bath.

When Anthony phoned her later she wasn't surprised. She'd been expecting to hear from him.

"My earrings are beautiful," she said. "I can't wait to wear them."

"I haven't left yet," Anthony said. "I'm still here."

"You are? Why?"

"There was a problem with my plane. Didn't wanna bother you, so I spent the night at a hotel."

"You should've come home," she said, thinking of the consequences if he'd discovered her in bed with Luis. It did not bear thinking about.

"We'll have lunch again before I leave," he said. "I'll take you back to the same jewelry store, buy you somethin' else. Wouldja like that?"

"If you're sure."

"I'm gonna send the car for you."

"What about Las Vegas?" she asked hopefully. "Am I still going with you? I can pack and be ready to go with you today."

"Not a bad idea," he said. "Do that. Don't bring much with you—only a small bag."

"But if it's a big opening, surely I'll need a gown?"

"You'll pick up whatever you want in Vegas. An' don't forget t'bring your earrings."

"As if I'd forget."

"See you later," he said, hanging up the phone and calling for The Grill.

"Yes, boss?"

"Go get it now," he ordered. "An' make sure the car bringin' my wife is delayed on the way here."

"Yes, boss."

"Make it fast."

"Yes, boss," the big man said, his wide face impassive.

Anthony rubbed his eyes and thought about what he'd do if the evidence was incriminating.

Someone would end up dead.

That he knew for sure.

CHAPTER
SEVENTY-THREE

The funeral of Penelope Whitfield-Simmons was a somber affair. It took place in Pasadena and there were almost a hundred mourners gathered at the graveside. Front and center was Penelope's only son and heir, Henry Whitfield-Simmons.

Henry stood with his head bowed. Later he maintained the same desolate expression as people lined up to offer him their condolences. He recognized most of the women—they were his mother's friends, the pack of vicious gossips she'd surrounded herself with. The same women who'd either laughed at him or ignored him. It was different now that he was about to inherit the Whitfield-Simmons fortune.

"I'm so sorry, dear," one of the women said, gripping his arm with a clawlike hand. "What will you do?"

I will be very happy, he thought. *Very happy and very rich.*

"I'll manage," he said, adding a forlorn, "We'll all miss her so much."

"I know, dear," another woman said, patting his shoulder as if he were a pet dog. "Your mother was so fond of you, Henry. She talked about you all the time."

"She did?" he said, not believing her for a minute.

"Yes," the woman continued. "She was worried that you'd never find the right girl. I was delighted when she phoned me last week and told me that you had indeed met somebody."

"She was right," Henry said. "I have."

"That's wonderful news. The right girl will help you get over this sad occasion. Penelope wanted nothing more than to see you happily married, and perhaps one day have children of your own."

"It'll happen," Henry said, imagining what a beautiful baby he and Maria would produce. "If we have a daughter, we'll call her Penelope."

"Such a precious sentiment," the woman sighed.

Henry nodded. *Yes it is.*

There was a formal reception back at the mansion. It seemed to Henry that most of the people who attended wanted nothing more than to drink and eat and gossip amongst themselves. They were certainly not there to mourn Penelope Whitfield-Simmons, and although some of them mentioned her in passing, it was more of a social occasion.

"She was so young," one woman said. "To think that the poor dear simply went to sleep one night and failed to wake up the next morning."

"Yes," Henry said. "According to the doctor, her heart stopped beating."

"It's so sad," the woman said. "But at least it was a peaceful ending."

His mother's lawyer was there, a heavyset man wearing a suit and horn-rimmed glasses.

"We have a lot to talk about, young man," the lawyer said, approaching him in a blustery fashion.

"We certainly do," Henry replied, getting right to the point. "I understand that I am the sole beneficiary."

"Your mother told you that?"

"She certainly did. We discussed everything, especially my upcoming trip."

"You're going away?"

"Yes. I have an important trip to make that I cannot postpone. I'll be leaving at the end of the week. My mother was arranging for a substantial amount of cash for me to take. Since I *am* the sole heir, I'm sure you will see that it is taken care of before things are officially settled."

"How much did your mother promise?" the lawyer asked.

"One hundred thousand dollars," Henry said calmly. "And also please have your office arrange a black American Express card for me. I'll need it while I'm traveling."

"Where will you be going, Henry?"

"Europe. In the meantime I've decided to put the house on the market, so perhaps you can take care of that too."

"You're putting your mother's house on the market?" the lawyer said, expressing surprise. "Surely you should think about this for a while."

"I do not need to. My mother and I discussed it many times. She didn't want me living here by myself surrounded by memories. She was adamant that when she died I must sell the house."

"How long will you be gone?"

"I'm not sure, but I'll be in touch. And I wish to have the money and the credit card before the end of the week."

The house was delightfully peaceful when everybody finally left and he was alone. The live-in couple retired to their apartment above the garage, while Markus went home at night.

Before Markus left, Henry had informed him that he would shortly be going on a trip. "Prepare the Bentley," he'd ordered.

"Mrs. Whitfield-Simmons's Bentley?" Markus had said, acting as if she were still alive and likely to object.

"The Bentley is mine now, Markus, so make sure it's gassed up and ready, because last time I took the Volvo it ran out of gas. That was your fault. Isn't your job to see that each one of the cars are fully gassed at all times?"

Markus had shied away from Henry Whitfield-Simmons, who seemed to have developed a new aggressive personality overnight. "Yes, Mr. Henry," he'd muttered.

"Then if you wish to keep your job, make certain it's done."

Alone in the house, Henry wandered around, realizing that the only part of the house he was really familiar with was his own room. Now he could go where he wanted, touch whatever he felt like touching. As a child the only words he remembered his mother saying over and over were, "Don't touch that, Henry, you're so clumsy, you'll break it."

Now he could break anything he felt like, because everything was his.

He sat in Penelope Whitfield-Simmons's bedroom and read her obituary in the *Times*. Then he carefully cut it out and placed it in his wallet.

Penelope Whitfield-Simmons was dead.

It was her own fault.

CHAPTER
SEVENTY-FOUR

"Jeez," Ace whistled. "You didn't warn me that you lived in a freaking palace."

"This is just a rental place," Max said casually, greeting him at the door. "Our real home's in Malibu."

"A rental?" he said, shaking his head in wonderment. "More like a hotel. I've never seen anything like it."

"Now that you're here, come on in," she said, taking his arm, trying to conceal her excitement at seeing him.

"I dunno why I said yes to this," he mused.

"Oh, *I* do," she said teasingly. "You were *desperate* to see me again. You couldn't *wait!*"

"You're a cocky little thing, aren't you?" he said, a slow grin spreading across his face.

"So I've been told," she replied, leading him into the grand entry hall.

"I feel like I'm in the lobby of a Hilton," he said, gazing around.

"Mom would *love* to hear that," she said, laughing.

"Is the dragon lady around?"

"She'd freak if she heard you calling her that. And no, she's safely in Vegas awaiting our presence."

"Does that mean I get to meet her?"

"Of course," she said, still holding on to his arm. "C'mon, let's go upstairs, I'll show you your room."

"I have a room?" he said, raising his eyebrows. "I thought the whole point of my coming here was that we were heading straight to Vegas."

"We're leaving first thing in the morning," she assured him. "Tonight you get to see L.A."

"It wasn't what we planned, Max."

"Plans change, and Harry's got a new SUV, so—"

"Who's Harry?" he interrupted.

"I told you about Harry, he's my gay friend. You don't mind that he's gay, do you?"

"Why would *I* mind?"

"Just thought I'd fill you in."

"You think he'll try to jump me?"

"Sure," she joked. "*Scared?*"

"Shaking," he deadpanned.

"My other friend, Cookie, is meeting us later with Harry," she said, opening the door to the guest room.

"Is she gay too?"

"No. Now *stop* it," she said, laughing again.

"Am I supposed to sleep here?" he said, throwing his duffel bag on the floor. "It's bigger than my entire house."

"It's not *that* big. By the way, did you bring a tuxedo?"

"Do I look like the kinda dude who *has* a tuxedo?" he said, giving her a quizzical look.

"No," she said, hardly able to take her eyes off him. "But I told you the opening was like, black tie, didn't I?"

"How do *I* know what black tie means? I brought a suit and I brought a tie. Sorry—neither of them are black."

"We could rent you a tuxedo," she suggested.

"No thanks."

"Why not?"

"The penguin look doesn't suit me."

"Are you hungry?" she asked.

"Kinda," he replied.

"Let's go down to the kitchen then."

He followed her downstairs where she asked Philippe

to make them a sandwich. Then she led him out to the pool.

"This place is like something out of a movie," he marveled. "It's so big."

"Our house in Malibu is much nicer. I love the ocean, don't you?"

Philippe brought them out toasted-cheese-and-tomato sandwiches and a selection of soft drinks.

"You really live the cushy life, don't you?" Ace said.

"Uh, how's your girlfriend?" She couldn't stop herself from asking.

He threw her a penetrating look. "If I was still with her, do you think I'd be here?"

"You mean you broke up?" she said, attempting to sound casual, but desperate to find out everything.

"You got it."

"What happened?"

"She dumped me."

"*She* dumped *you?*"

"Yeah."

"Why'd she do that?"

"'Cause I was supposed to meet her the night we got kidnapped, and when I never turned up she was pissed, so she went off with one of my friends."

"Wow! That's not nice."

"This is even not nicer—they both got drunk and got it on. When I found out, it was my turn to be pissed, so I guess you could say we kinda dumped each other. End of story."

She was dying to ask him a ton more questions, but then she figured it wouldn't be cool if she showed too much interest.

"What's going on with you an' your boyfriend?" he asked, springing open a can of Coke.

"Uh . . . we broke up," she mumbled.

"Who did the dumping?"

"Who do you think?"

"You?"

"I caught him out with another girl, so I said good-bye."

"We're some pair."

"*Are* we a pair?" she asked hopefully.

"No, we're two people who just got caught up in a bad scene and now we're friends."

"Sure we are."

"Hey, Max, I'm not forgetting how old you are, so don't go reading anything into this trip."

"What's my age got to do with anything?" she said, irritated.

"You're sixteen, Max. I'm here as your friend an' that's all."

"Ooh," she said with an exaggerated eye roll. "And there was little old me thinking you came to ravish my teenage body."

"I came 'cause I needed to get away," he said, quite serious.

"Not to see me?"

"To see you too. Oh yeah," he added, lightening up, "an' to get that twenty bucks you owe me."

"Like I'd forget," she said, digging in her jeans pocket and handing him a couple of crumpled tens. "See, I had it all ready for you."

"I was kidding."

"It's your money, take it."

Later they met up with Cookie and Harry at the Cheesecake Factory in Beverly Hills.

Cookie took one look at Ace and liked what she saw. "Definite babe magnet," she mouthed to Max behind his back.

"Ace just broke up with his girlfriend," Max announced as they sat down.

"That's convenient," Harry said, paler than ever. "Now you two can get it on."

Max threw him a furious look.

"My dad's taking a plane up to Vegas tomorrow, so if we don't feel like driving, we can fly with him," Cookie said, ordering a Diet Coke. "Anyone wanna do that?"

"I thought we were testing out my new car," Harry interjected. "Got a few records I wanna break."

"What do *you* feel like doing?" Max asked, turning to Ace.

"You people are unbelievable," he said, wondering what he was doing hanging out with this bunch of rich kids with whom he had nothing in common. "Planes, new cars—I'm not used to this."

"Yeah, well, since you and Max are hooking up, you'd better get used to it," Harry said, picking up the menu.

"Nobody's hooking up," Max replied, glaring at him. What was wrong with Harry? He was behaving like a dick.

"That's right," Ace said. "We're just friends."

"Really?" Cookie said disbelievingly.

"I guess Max told you what happened to us?" Ace said. "It was some screwed-up experience."

"Yeah, like *major* spooky," Cookie said. "I warned her about weirdos online, but Max never listens to anyone."

"Please don't talk about me as if I'm not here," Max said quickly.

"I was all for going to the cops," Ace said. "She wouldn't let me."

"Good boy," Harry sneered. "You'll find it pays to be obedient around our Max, she's a total control freak."

"Shut *up*, Harry," Max warned. "What's up with you?"

"Nothing," he answered sulkily.

"Max told us you were kinda like a superhero," Cookie said. "Y'know, rescuing her, getting her outta there."

"I did what I had to," Ace said modestly, while Harry made a face and pretended to throw up.

During the course of the dinner, Max discovered several things about Ace. He did not smoke, he did not do drugs, and he went to church with his brother every Sunday. He was so unlike most of the boys she knew, and she was fast becoming totally crazy about him. By the time they'd finished eating and had made their way to the club Harry was so sure they'd get into, she was feeling quite dizzy, and not in a bad way.

Harry circumvented the line outside the club and marched up to the burly doorman, who was unimpressed—especially when Harry started yelling and waving hundred-dollar bills around. It made no difference. Underage was underage, and they couldn't get in.

"This is bullshit," Ace said, grabbing Max's arm. "Let's split."

"Sure," she said, nudging Cookie, who got the message and dragged Harry away from the entrance to the club and back to his car.

"I'll drive," Ace said.

"No way," Harry objected, swaying slightly.

"You're stoned," Ace accused.

"No way," Harry repeated, glaring at him.

Crap! Max thought. *So this is why Harry is acting like such a prick. Ace is right. He's totally stoned.*

"Hey," Ace said forcefully. "Either *I* drive or we're getting a cab."

"Go ahead," Harry said belligerently, spiky black hair standing on end.

"Cool it, Harry," Cookie said, stepping between them. "Let Ace drive. What's your problem?"

"It's *my* car and I'm driving it," Harry shouted. "So you can all go fuck off."

"He's not usually like this," Max whispered to Ace. "I don't know what's up with him."

"Listen," Ace said. "He's your friend, and I'm sorry, but neither of us are getting in a car with him."

"What about Cookie?"

"She shouldn't drive with him either. Tell her."

"Cookie, come with us," Max said.

"I'll stick with Harry," Cookie decided. "He's not *that* stoned. You two take off, we'll see you in the morning."

"I'm so sorry about Harry," Max said as she and Ace walked off down Hollywood Boulevard.

"Those two are your best friends?" he said.

"They're normally great, but lately they're into this whole getting-stoned mind trip. It's not *my* idea of a fun time."

"Glad to hear it. I went through that phase when I was sixteen, but I didn't drive. Truth is I didn't have a car."

"My mom thinks doing drugs is totally uncool. That's one thing we agree on."

He took her hand as a couple of suspicious-looking guys walked toward them.

"I'm really glad you're here," she said, loving the way her hand felt in his.

"I'm not getting in a car with Harry tomorrow," he said. "We'll take my brother's truck."

"Really?"

"Your friend is on a roll, Max. I don't want to be around when he crashes and burns."

"Isn't that like rather dramatic?" she said, looking up at him.

"Maybe, but it's what happens."

"Harry's going through a tough time. His dad is some kind of mogul, and his mom's a born-again. They went through a bad divorce, plus he's stuck in the closet, so he's major screwed up. Cookie, Harry, and me have been best friends since we were like five years old."

"I understand, an' I'm not being difficult, but you don't wanna get in a car with somebody when they're high."

"Okay, we'll take your truck, and they can either go in Cookie's dad's plane or drive."

"Who's Cookie's dad?"

"He's a famous soul singer. Gerald M. You heard of him?"

"Nope."

"You really do live in the boondocks, don't you?"

"You sound like a Beverly Hills brat when you say things like that."

"Well, I'm not," she said defensively. "You should meet my grandfather, he's a real character, he built hotels in Vegas way back. He's ninety-five now. My parents were way pissed I missed his party."

"Your parents sound interesting."

"My dad's the greatest. He started out as a comedian, then he became a movie star, now he writes and directs movies."

"I know, I looked him up on my brother's computer."

"Oh, so you *do* have e-mail at your house. How come you didn't tell me?"

"Max," he said, giving her another one of his penetrating looks. "There's a lot I haven't told you."

"Like what?"

"Like one of these days—if we stay friends—you'll find out."

CHAPTER SEVENTY-FIVE

The Grill was a speed demon. It would have taken a normal person an hour to get to the house and back, but The Grill managed to make it in half the time.

He entered Anthony's office and handed him the small hidden camera that he'd installed in the master bedroom at his boss's house the day before.

"You arranged for the car bringing my wife here to be delayed?" Anthony asked.

The Grill nodded.

"Get out," Anthony ordered. "And tell my secretary nobody's to disturb me."

"Yes, boss," The Grill said as he left the office.

Anthony connected the small spy camera to the TV before switching it on. He wasn't sure what he was about to see, but whatever it was it would either validate what Cesar had told him, or it would make the man out to be a liar, in which case Cesar would be severely punished before his ass was fired.

Working the remote, Anthony sped through the scenes of the empty bedroom, stopping when Irma appeared. He observed her enter the room and walk straight over to the window.

What was she doing at the window? He couldn't tell.

She looked out of the window for a few minutes before turning around and leaving the room.

He fast-forwarded again until she returned. Only this

time she was not alone—this time there was a man with her.

Anthony's back stiffened as the man followed Irma into their bedroom. Then the bitch locked the door, she locked the fuckin' door!

Anthony sat very still watching intently as his wife began talking to the man, saying something Anthony couldn't hear. He adjusted the sound and rewound to make sure he missed nothing.

"Luis," Irma said, "what is going on with you?"

"'Scuse, *señora*," the man muttered.

"Don't call me *señora*," Irma said. "My name is Irma. You know that."

"*Sí*, Irma," the man said.

Anthony pressed Pause and rewound again, just to make sure he was catching every word.

"Why didn't you tell me you were married and your wife was pregnant?" Irma said as the tape continued.

The man shrugged and looked away. But then to Anthony's fury, the son of a bitch turned toward her, and in a most familiar fashion placed his fuckin' hand on her right breast.

Anthony leaned forward, hardly believing his own eyes. That Irma would *dare* to do this was beyond his comprehension.

Within seconds the man began undoing the buttons on her blouse. Next he unhooked the clip on the front of her bra, exposing her breasts.

Anthony attempted to keep his breathing even, but the anger that was building inside him was getting ready to explode.

"Oh, Luis," Irma sighed, throwing her head back in abandon.

The man, or Luis, as that was obviously the bastard's name, lightly brushed her nipples with his fingertips before bringing his lips down to suck on them.

She did *not* object. *His wife did not object!*

"Son of a mothafuckin' *bitch!*" Anthony screamed, his face reddening. "Cheating fuckin' WHORE!"

Irma sighed the name "Luis" again before the prick swept her up in his arms and carried her over to the bed where he proceeded to make love to her.

ANOTHER MAN WAS FUCKING HIS WIFE. ANTHONY BONAR'S WIFE! AND THE CUNT WAS ENJOYING IT!

Anthony could feel the bile rising in his throat. This was the woman he'd married, the woman he'd given his name to, the *mother* of his children.

This woman was nothing but a prostitute, a douche bag, an unfaithful cheating CUNT.

Abruptly Anthony switched off the TV and summoned The Grill.

The big man entered his office and stood at attention.

"I have a job for you to take care of," Anthony instructed. "A job that needs to be executed immediately."

The driver took Irma to the same restaurant where she and Anthony had lunched the day before. She was not happy because the driver had insisted on making several stops along the way, claiming he was running errands for Señor Bonar. After the third stop she complained bitterly that she would be late for lunch and Señor Bonar would be very angry if she was late.

The driver shrugged and informed her that he was only following Señor Bonar's orders.

Irma decided she would tell Anthony she did not wish to use this particular driver again—he was insolent.

When she finally arrived at the restaurant Anthony was not there, even though she was at least twenty minutes late. She requested a glass of wine and looked at the menu, then after fifteen minutes she called for the head waiter and asked if Señor Bonar had left a message for her.

"No, *señora*," the man said. "Perhaps you would care to order?"

No, she wouldn't care to order, not until Anthony got there.

Another ten minutes passed and she wasn't sure what to do. She requested a phone and connected with Anthony at his office.

"Where are you?" she said. "I've been sitting here for over half an hour."

"Something came up," he said.

"Will you be here soon?"

"Go ahead and order."

"Without you?"

"I'll try to make it. Otherwise come to the office when you're finished."

"But I hate sitting alone in a restaurant," she complained. "It's uncomfortable. I feel awkward."

"Sometimes we gotta do things we don't want to. This is one of them."

He did not sound as friendly as he had the day before, but she understood that when Anthony was immersed in business he became distant.

"Am I still coming to Vegas?" she asked, hoping that he hadn't changed his mind.

"Wouldn't want you to miss out, would I?"

"I'll go ahead and order. Should I get something for you in case you make it?"

"It's unlikely," he said. "Take your time, I'll be at my office waitin' for you."

"Can I bring you anything at all?"

"Funny thing," he said slowly. "Seems like I lost my appetite."

She ordered a salad and another glass of wine. She lingered over the wine. Anthony did not appear.

After a while she asked for the check, paid it, and was on her way out of the restaurant when who should she run into but Oliver Stanton.

"Irma," he said, stopping and blocking her path.

"Oliver," she replied, thanking God that Anthony wasn't with her.

"I called you," Oliver said, giving her a hurt look. "More than once, and you haven't returned my calls."

"I know," she answered, trying to come up with a reasonable excuse. "I've been very busy."

"Was it something I said? Did? Because I was under the impression that we really hit it off."

"No, no, Oliver, our evening together was most enjoyable."

"But you never called me back."

"I will," she said quickly. "I've got your number."

"Is that a promise?"

"Yes," she said, hesitating for a moment. "It's just that things have changed since we were together."

"They have?"

"I can't explain right now," she said, eager to get away from him. "I'll call you later."

She hurried from the restaurant without looking back. The driver was waiting by the car.

"Señor Bonar's office," she said, getting in the car. "And this time no stops along the way."

"Sí, señora."

She reached in her purse, took out her compact, and applied powder and lip gloss. Running into Oliver Stanton was quite a surprise. What if Anthony had been with her? How would she have explained it?

Anthony's suite of offices was on the top floor of the building. His assistant was not at her desk and there seemed to be nobody else around, so Irma made her way to his office.

Anthony was sitting behind his desk smoking an expensive cigar.

"I thought you were so busy," she scolded. "I didn't enjoy lunching by myself. Sitting alone in a restaurant is embarrassing."

"Embarrassing, huh?" he said, puffing away on his cigar.

"Is everything all right?" she asked. "Are the children okay?"

"Why wouldn't they be?"

"It's simply that you seem so different from yesterday."

"Different. In what way?"

"I don't know, Anthony. Yesterday I thought that things were getting better between us. Now you're acting toward me as if—"

"As if what, Irma?"

"As if I've done something wrong."

"Have you?" he asked, blowing smoke in her direction.

"Have I what?"

"Done something wrong."

"Of course not," she said, adding, "I'm so looking forward to Vegas."

"Yeah, I'm kinda lookin' forward to it myself," he said. "But first there's a few things I gotta take care of, so whyn't you sit down 'cause I got somethin' t'show you."

"What do you want to show me, Anthony?" she asked, sitting on a leather chair, folding her hands neatly on her lap.

"A movie," he said mildly.

"A movie?"

"Yeah. It's not exactly a love story, more a kinda porno."

"Anthony," she said sternly, "you know I do not en-joy porno films."

"I believe you mentioned that when we were first married. Only things change, don't they?"

"No, Anthony," she said primly. "I refuse to watch porno. I find it demeaning to women."

"You might get a kick outta watchin' this one, 'cause it stars someone you know."

"Who?" she asked, immediately thinking that per-haps it was one of his entourage's wives. Wouldn't *that* be something.

"Sit back, Irma, an' enjoy the show. I gotta hunch you're gonna find it more than interesting."

THE KEYS

CHAPTER SEVENTY-SIX

"Good morning," Lucky said, kissing her husband on the lips.

"Man," Lennie groaned, waking up with a lazy smile on his face. "So cheerful for a dawn wake-up."

"It's six A.M., the sun is shining, and today's my big day."

"Yeah, an' last night was my big night trading shots of tequila with your friend Billy. Why'd you let me do it?"

"I seem to recall us having the same conversation when I overdid the champagne at Gino's party. Wasn't it me saying to you, 'Why'd you let me drink champagne?' And you saying to me, 'When have I ever stopped you from doing anything?' "

"She has a memory too."

"She sure does. So I suggest that you haul your lazy ass out of bed and come with me."

"Where're we going?"

"Who knows? I've got this urge to walk around my hotel and take it all in before chaos."

"Chaos, huh?"

"I guess I'm experiencing that feeling you get just before the opening of one of your movies."

"Extreme stomach cramps and a desperate need to hide?"

"No," she said, laughing. "Excitement. Pure unadulterated excitement."

Lennie looked at his wife, marveling at how beautiful she was. Lucky Santangelo. Mother of his children. Powerhouse. Businesswoman. Tough. Vulnerable. Wildly sexy. His true partner in every way.

What a woman!

"Let's go," he said, jumping out of bed.

"You're naked," she pointed out. "Put your pants on."

"First time you've asked me to do that," he said, grinning.

"Don't piss around with me today, Lennie, 'cause nothing you do is going to upset me."

"Okay, then I won't bother putting on pants."

"Ha ha! This is *not* a nudist camp—pants on and let's hit it. Okay, lover?"

"Okay, wife."

Venus was up early too, in spite of the fact that they'd all ended up at the Cavendish and gambled until three A.M. Billy had been on a winning streak, which had put him in an excellent mood.

"I had no idea you were such a big gambler," Venus had said. "Vegas agrees with you."

"When I win it does," Billy had said. "Last time I was here was for a bachelor party, had a wild time."

"I bet you *did*, what with all the strip clubs, not to mention the convenient whorehouses."

"Baby," he'd said, laughing, "if there's one thing I've *never* had to do, that's pay for it."

Now it was morning and she was ready to rehearse. "How are you going to occupy yourself today?" she asked.

"Don't worry about me. I'll find something to do."

"Yeah, if I know you, you'll be heading back to the tables to lose it all."

"Don't knock it. Besides, there's nothing else to do in Vegas."

"Yes, there is," she said crisply. "Shopping."

"Shopping is a girls' thing."

"Since when? You love to shop."

"Not today. Anyway, Kev's arriving this morning, he'll keep me company."

"Is he coming by himself?"

"Uh, no," Billy said, dreading the moment he might have to introduce Venus to Ali. "Think he's bringing one of his girls."

"You make him sound like a pimp."

"He wishes."

"Well," Venus said, preparing to leave, "if you need me, I'll be at rehearsal. I should be back around three. Then I plan on having a full-body massage and taking it easy until my makeup and hair people arrive at four."

"Got it, babe."

"Oh yes, and if you feel like buying me that apartment, go right ahead."

"Never knew you were a comedienne too."

"Thanks, darling," she drawled. "A girl's got to try."

Renee Falcon was always up early, unlike Susie who most days lazed in bed until noon. Renee didn't mind, she genuinely loved her partner. Susie was all the things she wasn't—soft and loving and kind and quite astute in her own way.

The previous night Renee had found to be quite disturbing. Her casino floor manager—always on celebrity alert—had called and informed her that Billy Melina and Venus were in the house. Naturally she'd gone into the casino to personally welcome them to the Cavendish. She had not been expecting to find Lucky Santangelo and Lennie Golden with them. She'd never met Lucky, nor had she wanted to in view of what was to take place the following day.

"We're about to be neighbors," Lucky had said with

a warm smile. "Anytime you want to come over to the Keys, you'll be my guest. Call first—if I'm around, I'll make sure to give you a personal tour."

Renee was surprised to note that not only was Lucky Santangelo a true beauty—stunning, with her slim figure, wild profusion of jet-black curls, and penetrating dark eyes—she was friendly too. This was a shock after all the vitriolic things Anthony had said about the Santangelo family, Lucky in particular. He'd called her a bitch and a cunt and a murderer. And he'd given Renee the impression there was no more evil woman on earth. Obviously he was lying, or Lucky was the best actress in the world.

Later Susie had joined her in the casino and then they'd all ended up in the lounge having drinks together. Susie had also liked Lucky, and she'd especially enjoyed talking to Lennie, who she soon discovered had once worked with her deceased husband on a movie.

"I'm inviting you both to our opening tomorrow," Lucky had said before they all left. "There's a reception on the terrace at six, followed by a lingerie show, then Venus's special appearance. I'd be delighted for you both to be my guests."

"We accept," Susie had said with a happy nod.

Renee considered Anthony's reaction had he witnessed this cozy little scene. He would've thrown one of his explosive temper tantrums. But who cared about Anthony? Ever since Tasmin's murder, Renee fervently wished she could sever all connections with him. Yes, the Keys would be competition, but what Anthony had persuaded her to put in place was extraordinarily drastic and now she was starting to regret it. Thank God Susie knew nothing, for she'd put an immediate stop to it.

Lately Renee had spent too much of her time keeping Detective Franklin at bay. The detective had a nose for details, and kept on returning to the hotel with more and more questions. She seemed very interested in speaking to Anthony in person.

Renee managed to stonewall her.

"You're wasting both our time," she'd said. "I've answered all your questions more than once. You've spoken to Mr. Bonar on the phone. I don't understand why you keep coming back."

"Because this is where the trail ends," Detective Franklin had answered. "Doesn't it concern you that after Tasmin spent the evening with you and your guests in *your* restaurant at *this* hotel she was never seen again?"

Renee had shrugged. "Sorry, but I can't help you."

Secretly she wished she could, for her thoughts often turned to Tasmin's body buried in the desert where nobody would ever find it, unless she guided them in the right direction. Then she thought about what a smart and beautiful woman Tasmin had been, and how unnecessary her murder was. A true waste of a decent human being who happened to enjoy sex—and thanks to Renee, had gotten herself fixed up with the wrong one-night stand.

Deep down Renee felt responsible. Even though Anthony Bonar had helped her flee Colombia and set her up in Vegas, she wished she'd never set eyes on the murderous son of a bitch. He was a danger to himself and everyone around him.

Too late now. Or was it? Anthony was heading to Vegas and he expected action.

Sitting next to Ace in the passenger seat of his truck on their way to Vegas, Max felt content—a feeling she wasn't used to. Last night they'd stayed up late, talking. Unfortunately for her *just* talking, because she'd desperately wanted him to kiss her, willed him to do so, but he hadn't. Around midnight he'd said, "I'm gonna catch some sleep, we should try to leave early in the morning."

She'd gone to bed vaguely disappointed, only to be awoken at three A.M. by a call from a hysterical Cookie, who'd informed her that Harry had crashed his SUV, totally wrecked it, failed a sobriety test, and subsequently been arrested.

"But he wasn't drunk," Max had said, struggling to wake up.

"By that time he was," Cookie admitted. "After you left, we bribed our way into another club where Harry made it his mission to see how many vodka martinis he could chug. You know Harry when he's on a roll."

"Weren't you *supposed* to be watching out for him?"

"Since when did *I* turn into like a *nursemaid*?" Cookie grumbled. "Y'know, *I* was in the car too. I could've been killed."

"Are you hurt?"

"A few bruises, nothing major."

"That's good."

"Harry's dad was *way* mad—like *totally* pissed. He sent his big-time lawyer to bail number-one son out, so now Harry's grounded, can't come to Vegas."

"How about you?"

"I figure I'll hitch a ride on my dad's plane an' see you there."

"Sounds like a plan," Max had said, contemplating whether she should wake Ace, but deciding against it. The next morning she'd filled him in over breakfast.

"That's one screwed-up dude," Ace had said, not at all surprised. "He was an accident waiting to happen."

"Guess you were right about not getting in the car with him."

"It's called instincts," he'd replied. "Always gotta follow 'em."

Now they were on their way to Vegas, and as far as she was concerned everything was cool, *especially* as Ace had broken up with his girlfriend. What a bonus!

She stole a sideways glance at him. He was *so* damn handsome, and that cleft in his chin . . . wow!

Donny, once her reason for getting up in the morning, had faded to a distant memory.

Maybe tonight she'd get that kiss she'd been waiting for.

A girl could hope, couldn't she?

And on the same highway, several hours ahead of them, Henry Whitfield-Simmons drove his mother's sleek royal blue Bentley, estimating that he should be arriving in Las Vegas in less than an hour.

He hummed softly to himself. Everything had turned out exactly as he'd predicted. His mother's lawyer had been wary about not getting on his bad side. The man was a trustee of the estate, and as such he would be making himself a hefty percentage of billions of dollars, so his main desire was to keep Henry happy. He'd come up with the credit card and cash Henry had requested.

Once Henry had the black American Express card in his possession, he'd driven straight to the Beverly Hills Neiman Marcus and purchased an entire new wardrobe of clothes, all the better to impress Maria. Not that he felt she was the type of girl attracted by appearances, but it was only polite to look smart for her.

Now he was in the Bentley on his way to Vegas to claim his rightful prize.

And his prize was Maria.

He knew that once he convinced her it was the right thing to do, she would be happy that he'd come to take her away from the life she was forced to lead with Lucky Santangelo as her mother.

Very happy indeed.

CHAPTER
SEVENTY-SEVEN

Irma could not stop shaking—she was in shock—and nobody aboard Anthony's plane cared as it winged its way toward Las Vegas. Not Francesca, her husband's witch of a grandmother, who sat next to her grandson drinking endless cups of black coffee and chain-smoking. Not The Grill, Anthony's giant psycho body-guard with the blank glassy eyes and expressionless face. Not Emmanuelle, her husband's blond mistress who kept on shooting her filthy looks as she thumbed through a selection of trashy magazines. And certainly not Anthony himself. Her vicious husband. Her worst nightmare.

Yesterday's events were etched into her brain forever. How could she forget the horror of what Anthony had put her through.

It had all started with the movie. . . .

She'd watched in disbelief as her image had appeared on the screen. Her words. Her gestures. Luis.

Anthony had *everything* on film. Luis touching her, undressing her, making love to her.

Oh God! Every moment of her last assignation was captured in excruciating detail.

She'd watched and cringed and begged Anthony to stop the film. But no, he was having none of it.

"Shut the fuck up, you whore!" he'd screamed at her. "Keep on watchin' that motherfucker's cock rammin' into *my* wife, the *mother* of *my* kids."

There was a moment when she'd tried to get up and run from his office, desperate to escape the fury she had no doubt would erupt. But as soon as she'd attempted to do so, Anthony had violently slammed her back into the chair, where she'd stayed, watching, until Luis got off the bed, tenderly kissed her, put on his clothes, and left the bedroom.

At last it was over. The TV screen went blank, and there was an ominous silence.

"I'm sorry," she'd begun, choking over the words.

"You'll be a lot sorrier than this," he'd warned. "Where'd ya get the balls to cheat on *me*, Anthony Bonar? You fuckin' *puttana whore*."

"Anthony," she'd pleaded, hoping that somehow or other she could make him understand. "There was a reason I did it. You haven't touched me in years. I was—"

"Shut the fuck up," he'd ordered. "Do not say one more fuckin' *word*."

She'd sat in silence and shame, until the door to his office opened and in walked The Grill.

The big man was not alone; he was dragging Luis with him. *Her* Luis. Her lover, so badly beaten he could barely stand. Both his eyes were blackened, his nose looked like it was broken, his lips were puffed up and split, and there was blood all over his shirt.

Their eyes met for a brief second. "Oh God!" she'd moaned. "What have you done to him, Anthony? It wasn't his fault, it was mine, all mine. *I* seduced *him*. If you have to punish anyone, punish me."

"You," Anthony spat. "Why would I punish *you*? Your punishment is watchin' what happens to your fuckin' boyfriend."

"He's not my boyfriend!" she'd screamed hysterically. "You've done enough. Look at him—he's beaten to a pulp."

"You think I give a shit? You think I'd allow someone

who *works* for *me* to run around sayin' he's fuckin' my wife? You think *that's* the kinda man you're married to? I got news for you, *bitch*. Nobody fucks Anthony Bonar's wife and gets away with it."

The shaking had started then and it hadn't stopped since.

"You got a choice," Anthony had said, staring her down. "An' I'm gonna let you decide, Irma, my dear wife, my favorite *cunt*. His cock or his balls—whaddya wanna cut off?"

"Anthony, don't do this," she'd pleaded.

"I'm givin' you a fuckin' choice, which is kinda big of me," he'd crowed, fully pleased with himself. "Cock or balls? You pick."

"You're insane," she'd moaned.

"Insane? Me? Listen, whore, *I'm* not the one who's bin screwin' another man's wife. This asswipe's the insane one."

"No," she'd said, desperately trying to keep it together and fight back. "*You're* the one who has mistresses everywhere. Three, four, I don't know how many women you sleep with. What was I *supposed* to do?"

"I got a suggestion," he'd said. "Whyn't you fuck the gardener? How's that?"

"If you do anything more to him, I'll go to the police," she'd gasped.

"You'd do that, wouldja? You'd go to the cops 'cause your husband caught ya fuckin' another man." He'd shaken his head as if he couldn't believe she'd come out with something so dumb. "This is Mexico, whore. In this town they'd give me a fuckin' medal for beatin' up this prick."

"It's not just a beating, Anthony, you're threatening more."

"You bet your cheatin' ass I am. Now make up your fuckin' mind. What's it gonna be? Balls or cock?"

"I swear I *will* go to the police, Anthony," she'd said, panicking. "You can't stop me."

"Do that, an' I promise you you'll never see your kids again. Or your mother, or your father, 'cause I'll have somebody go to their house an' burn it to the ground. You got no fuckin' clue who you're messin' with, do you?"

The rest of it was a blur. She remembered the knife, she remembered Anthony putting it in her hand. She remembered lifting her arm and attempting to stab him. He'd laughed, snatched it away from her, and handed it to The Grill.

Above all she remembered the expression on Luis's face. Pure terror.

She could still hear his screams.

Later she'd been bundled into a car and taken to the airport where she'd been put on the plane by The Grill. Anthony had boarded the plane after her, and they'd flown to Miami, where he'd picked up his grandmother and his blond mistress.

"You say one fuckin' word to anyone and you're a dead woman, along with your parents," he'd warned her.

She sat on the plane, dazed, shaking, and numb.

There was nothing she could do about it. Not one damn thing.

CHAPTER
SEVENTY-EIGHT

By the afternoon most of the invited guests had arrived and the Keys was buzzing with activity.

Lucky was running around, greeting family, making sure they were all taken care of, dropping by Venus's rehearsal, and—the best moment of the day—giving Gino a personal tour.

The old man was impressed. "You did it, kiddo," he said, full of pride. "This place is somethin', an' you made it all happen by yourself."

"With a little help from my investors—including you," she said modestly. "Learned everything I know from you."

"You learned it well."

"I had to, didn't I? You'd've kicked my ass if I hadn't."

"You got that right," he said nodding. "You make me proud, kiddo, you did everythin' for this family a son would've done."

"Ha!" she said, pouncing triumphantly. "I *knew* you wanted a boy when you had me."

"Whatever I wanted, you turned out to be a winner. Couldn't've done better than you."

"Dario would've been a winner if he'd had the chance," she said softly.

"Yes he would," Gino agreed, shaking his head as his thoughts turned to the man who'd arranged for the murder of his son. "That dirty bastard Enzio Bonnatti, that two-timing motherfucker—'scuse my French. An' you,

Lucky, you took care of him like a true Santangelo. You're my daughter all right, a Santangelo all the way."

"An eye for an eye," Lucky said, pushing back her long dark hair. "That's what you taught me, and that's the way I've always lived. Don't fuck with me and I won't fuck with you. *Capice?*"

"My daughter. My goddamn pride," Gino said, cracking a grin. "I came to America over eighty years ago, it's the greatest country on earth. In America you can achieve any dream you want."

"I know," she murmured. "You did it all, Gino. Everything."

"I certainly did. I got you, Lucky," he said, becoming more prideful by the minute. "I got grandchildren, a wife I love, an' loyal friends. I got it all, an' y'know what, kiddo, if I died tomorrow, I'd die a happy man. All you gotta do is look at me."

"I am looking, Gino," she said softly. "And I like what I see."

"Y'can call me Daddy if you want, you've earned the right."

"Oh, really?" she said, raising a skeptical eyebrow. "*Finally?*"

"Go ahead," he said with a magnanimous shrug. "I'm givin' you permission."

"Gee, thanks, Gino. But it's a little late for me to revert to calling you Daddy."

"It is?"

Now it was her turn to grin. "Bet on it, old man."

Just as Venus had predicted, Billy hit the Strip and went gambling, successfully losing back all his winnings from the night before. Since he was by himself—Kev had not yet turned up—he was constantly hassled by adoring fans, until he was finally forced to return to the Keys, where everybody seemed to be somebody, so it was no problem sitting out by the pool without being bothered. The hotel did not open to the general public for another week, so the only guests were VIPs, and civilians willing to pay fifteen hundred bucks for a ticket to Venus's one-night show.

He felt kind of psyched that his girlfriend was the hottest ticket in town. If he could only get over the feeling of coming across as second best in her company, they could be very happy together. Venus might be a superstar, but she was *his* superstar, and he was beginning to realize that in spite of everything, he genuinely loved her. He also regretted cheating on her; it was such a dumb thing to do. A stupid move he could only blame on his youth.

By four o'clock Kev had still not shown up and Billy was starting to worry. Kev was driving his Maserati, and Kev was kind of a reckless driver, so he began imagining all kinds of bizarre accidents.

At four-thirty Kev finally called.

"Where the hell *are* you?" Billy demanded, accepting a piña colada from a statuesque poolside waitress. "This is the kind of event I need you at to run protection."

"Protection?" Kev snorted. "What am I, a friggin' bodyguard?"

"Yeah, you're supposed t'do everything for me, Kev. That's our deal. I pay, you do."

"Nice," Kev said disgustedly. "What happened to friendship?"

"C'mon, you know you should be here, so once again—where are you?"

"The truth?"

"No, lie to me."

"You're gonna get mad . . ."

"Why's that, Kev?" Billy said, thoroughly fed up with Kev's antics. "'Cause if you tell me you smashed up my

Maserati, I'll get so freakin' mad you won't even know what hit you."

"Your precious car's fine. In fact, we're in it now."

"Who's we?"

"Ali and me," Kev said, his voice muffled.

"You brought Ali, huh?"

"Yeah, an' before you go off on a rant, here's the news of the day. We, uh . . . we got married."

"You did *what*?" Billy exploded, almost spilling his drink.

"Married. Hitched. Ain't that something?"

"Oh jeez!" Billy exclaimed. "You really are a piece of work."

"How much money did you invest in this hotel?" Ling asked Alex as they checked in.

"Enough," he replied, signing his name on the register.

"And how long before your investment pays off?"

"With Lucky in charge, not too long," he answered, irritated that she felt free to question him.

"Lucky, Lucky, Lucky," Ling muttered. "You're obsessed with that woman."

"Stop with the bitching," Alex groaned. "Otherwise I'll be sorry I brought you along."

"I'm your girlfriend, Alex," Ling said. "Of course I should be with you."

"Then quit making me crazy."

"Easy. If *you* quit lusting after Lucky Santangelo."

"Oh, for God's sake!" he muttered.

"This way, Mr. Woods," said a helpful manager. "I'll be escorting you to your suite."

"I was thinkin' I could go play tennis, Mom," Gino Junior said.

"Go ahead," Lucky said, delighted that her youngest

son showed such a passion for sports. Lennie insisted it kept him out of trouble, and Lucky often wished that Max was into sports—it would probably make things a lot less explosive.

"D'you think Bobby'll play?" Gino Junior wanted to know.

"Go ask him. There's eight courts and a championship pro just waiting."

"I will. And, oh yeah, your hotel rocks, Mom."

"Yes?"

"Totally."

Yes, she thought, *my hotel rocks. And why not? I put my heart and soul into it.*

Gino Junior ran off just as she got a call from Max informing her they were minutes away. Lucky wanted to check out this new friend of Max's, so she headed for the front of the hotel to greet them.

After Venus finished rehearsing she returned to the penthouse suite where she was not thrilled to find Kev, some young girl, and Billy, all drinking champagne. Exactly what she *didn't* need.

She'd never really discussed it with Billy, but she considered Kev to be a bad influence. She and Billy's best friend had never warmed to each other—they'd always kept their distance—and she was certain that Kev put her down behind her back. Before she and Billy had become a couple, Kev was always talking about the parade of gorgeous girls Billy had had, and the amazing events, clubs, and parties the two of them had attended on a nightly basis. Obviously Kev did not appreciate her putting a stop to all the partying. Now *she* did not appreciate him lounging around in their suite swigging champagne with a young blonde.

"What's going on?" she asked, shooting Billy a look. "Are we celebrating something?"

"Hi, babe," Billy said, getting up and giving her a hug. "'S'matter of fact, we are."

"We are?" she said coolly.

"Yeah, um, this is Ali. Kev and Ali just got married."

"Wow!" Venus said, quite surprised. "And how long have you known this young lady, Kev?"

"We go way back," Kev said, a bit sheepishly.

"Actually," Ali said, quickly joining in, "we only met a couple of weeks ago, but Kev's so great, I feel as if I've known him forever."

"Yeah," Kev agreed. "Getting married was a spur-of-the-moment thing. Y'know, bein' in Vegas an' all. I said, 'Let's do it,' an' Ali was way into it."

"How nice," Venus said. "Congratulations to the two of you. I guess that's what the champagne is all about."

"Have a glass," Billy said.

"Not right now," she answered, shooting Billy another look.

"Kev, you should go find your room," Billy said, catching Venus's disapproving vibe. "We'll get together later and celebrate properly."

"Sure," Kev said, getting the hint. "C'mon, Ali, we gotta go."

Ali was busy staring at Venus, which totally alarmed Billy. Was she about to say something incriminating, such as, "I fucked your boyfriend. Oh yes, and I went down on him too"?

No, she wouldn't do that.

Or would she?

"Okay, guys," Billy said, hustling them out the door. "Later."

And somewhere in Vegas, Tucker Bond was busy putting everything in place. Two days earlier he'd driven his large truck into the city and settled himself and his two-woman crew at a convenient motel.

Tucker was a heavyset man in his late forties with weather-beaten skin, sunken eyes, and a thrice-broken nose. Australian by birth, Tucker had lived in America for more than thirty years, although he'd never lost his strong Australian accent. Tucker was a man for hire, and over the years he'd developed quite a reputation for getting things done. Anything.

Tucker didn't care what he did or who he did it for, as long as the price was right.

Destroying the Keys was costing someone a million bucks. Tucker had already made sure the job would take place without a hitch.

Paying for Tucker Bond meant getting the best. Whatever the client wanted, he made sure it happened.

Tucker Bond never failed to deliver.

CHAPTER
SEVENTY-NINE

"Hi, Mom," Max said, leaping out of Ace's truck, long dark hair flying, green eyes sparkling.

"Hey, Max," Lucky said warmly. She'd made up her mind to put Max's bad behavior behind her and try for a stress-free weekend.

"Uh . . . this is Ace," Max said, hanging tightly on to his arm, her multiple gold bracelets jangling.

"Nice to meet you, Ace," Lucky said, immediately realizing that her daughter was suffering from a major crush. And why not? Ace was tall and lanky with an almost surfer-dude look. He had mesmerizing blue eyes that almost matched his light blue denim work shirt, and an appealing cleft in his chin. He was also older than Max by several years. Lucky had to stop herself from asking exactly *how* old he was.

"Your grandfather really wants to see you," she said. "And don't forget to wish him a happy birthday."

"Like I would forget," Max said a tad scornfully.

"Oh, yes," Lucky added, "and you'd better apologize for not being at his party. You'll find him in the Santangelo Lounge."

"The *what?*" Max asked, stifling a giggle.

"Don't start with me, Max," Lucky said, walking them into the lobby of the hotel. "It's called the Santangelo Lounge in honor of Gino."

"Of course it is," Max said, shooting Ace a quick look.

"You can go check in at the front desk first," Lucky said. "Everything's arranged. Max, you're sharing a room with Cookie, and Ace, you're in with Harry."

"Thanks, Mrs. Golden," Ace said. He was shell-shocked by Max's mom—a stone-cold fox—not to mention the opulence of the hotel.

"The reception starts at six on the main terrace," Lucky said. "Try not to be late."

"Do we get a tour of the hotel?" Max asked, not bothering to mention that Harry wouldn't be coming. "It looks totally awesome!"

"Go find Bobby," Lucky said. "He'll show you around."

"Oh great! He's here!" Max exclaimed, turning to Ace. "Bobby's my older brother," she continued, excited by the thought of seeing him. "Bobby's *major* cool, you'll *so* like him."

"Yes, you will," Lucky said. "Bobby's a trip."

"Where's Dad?" Max asked.

"Playing golf with Charlie Dollar."

"I want to see him."

"You will," Lucky said. "So . . . I have a million things to do. Are you two all set?"

"Uh, thanks, Mrs. Golden," Ace said again, trying hard not to stare, for Lucky was not what he'd expected at all. "It's an honor to be here."

At least he's polite, Lucky thought. *And he seems like a nice enough kid, although they all do until they have your daughter half undressed in the back of a parked car. And Max is only sixteen. A wild little sixteen-year-old with a mind of her own and a major rebellious streak.*

Hmm . . . polite and hot. Her teenage daughter was in heaven.

"How long have Kev and that girl really known each other?" Venus asked once Kev and Ali had left.

"I'm sure they go way back," Billy said, keeping it as ambiguous as possible. "You know Kev, he's always hanging with a different girl."

"Yes, I do know Kev. That's why I find it so surprising he should get married. Where exactly did he meet this one?"

"Dunno," Billy said vaguely. "She might've been an extra on the movie."

"Hmm . . ." Venus sighed, rapidly losing interest. "I don't know about you, but I'm exhausted." She flopped onto the couch, stretching languorously. "Although I do have to admit it's quite invigorating getting back into the swing of things. My backup dancers are full of amazing energy, and so they should be, considering they're all ten years younger than me."

"Ten?" Billy teased.

"Okay, *twenty* years younger than me," she admitted, laughing. "God, that makes me feel so *old*."

"You? Old? *Never*," Billy said gallantly. "I'm gonna be thirty in two years—guess that'll be *my* time to feel old."

"It's different for men."

"No it's not."

"You're right. Why'd I say such a stupid sexist thing? Me—who's never bought in to that Hollywood bullshit. It's not different for men at all. Women can screw from thirteen to a hundred and thirteen. Men have the problem of getting it up, only now they've got Viagra to do it for them."

"Never tried Viagra."

"Oh, baby, believe me, you don't need to."

He yawned, relieved that Kev and his new bride were long gone. "How about we take a little siesta?" he suggested.

"How about I can't. My makeup and hair people will be here any minute."

"Tell 'em to come later. You don't need to spend *that* much time getting ready."

"Lucky wants us to go drop by the reception—we can't let her down—and later the place will be jammed with press and camera crews, so yes, I've got to get all glammed up."

"Whatever you do, you're always the sexiest woman in the room, glammed up or not."

"I am?"

"You know it, babe."

"So," she said, basking in his compliments. "What did *you* end up doing today?"

"Craps. Poker. Blackjack."

"My own Mister Predictable. Did you lose it all back?"

"What do *you* think?" he said, grinning.

"Yes."

"Easy come, easy go, an' tonight I'll be a winner again."

"Oh, Billy," she sighed. "What *am* I going to do with you?"

"Follow me into the bedroom, my sexy little superstar, and allow me to show you."

"I'm right behind you," she said, jumping up.

"So," Max said as they walked around the edge of the main swimming pool after spending time with Gino, Bobby, Brigette, and the rest of the family. "What's your take?"

"On what?" Ace replied.

"Everything. The hotel. My mom. My granddad. And especially Bobby."

"I think you've all led a charmed life of money and privilege."

That was not the answer she'd wanted to hear. She refused to be viewed as a spoiled rich kid with famous affluent parents and rich relatives. She was her own person. Max. And more than anything she wanted Ace to see that.

"Charmed life—not so much," she said defensively.

"C'mon, Max," he said, giving her a quizzical look.

"What?" she said. "You think it's *easy* having parents who've achieved so many things?"

"Better than having no parents at all," he pointed out.

"You've got me there," she said, realizing how tough it must have been for him losing his mom and dad.

"Lucky doesn't seem like a dragon lady," he observed. "If you want my opinion I think we should've told her about the kidnapping thing."

"Why's that?"

"'Cause it was bad, Max," he said, frowning. "The freak had a gun. He had *you* chained like a dog, and me locked up. What if he's still out there trying to do it to somebody else?"

"You don't understand," she said, agitated. "Lucky would've blamed *me*. She'd think I was weak and unable to look after myself."

"No she wouldn't."

"You met her for five minutes," Max said sharply. "That doesn't mean you *know* her."

"Okay, okay," he said, realizing he'd hit a sensitive spot. "I get it."

"No you *don't*," she said sulkily. "You've fallen under Lucky's spell. Everyone does. Whenever I'm around her it's like I become invisible."

"In *your* mind."

"Whatever. She's so clever and beautiful and smart. It's crap trying to live up to all of that."

"Hey, Max," he said, stopping and taking hold of her shoulders. "You got *any* idea how hot you are?"

"Me?" she said, staring into his blue eyes.

"No," he deadpanned. "That girl over there."

"I'm so hot that you didn't even kiss me last night," she said, regretting the words as soon as they left her mouth. She probably sounded like dork of the month.

"You're sixteen," he pointed out.

"So was Lucky when she got married the first time."

"Get over it, you're not in a competition with your mom."

"Says who?" she said, moving away from him and sitting on the end of a lounger.

"Says me," he said, squatting down next to her.

"Do y'know why I tried to hook up with that freak from the Internet?" she said, gazing at the ripples in the pool.

"Go ahead, surprise me."

"It's 'cause I wanted to show my ex-boyfriend that he lost out."

"And how were you going to do that?"

"My plan was to sleep with the creep—although when I decided that's what I'd do I thought I was like meeting up with this totally interesting smart dude. Then psycho man appears. Ugh! Gross!"

"So you're a—"

"Virgin. Yes! I admit it," she said, blushing. "How lame is that?"

"Shows you're selective."

"More like retarded," she mumbled.

"Not retarded, Max, cute."

"Cute!" she exclaimed in horror. "I hate that word, it's totally . . ."

"What?"

"I dunno, but I'll think of something."

"Yeah," he said, starting to grin. "You'll think of something, you always do."

Henry Whitfield-Simmons checked into a luxury bungalow at the Cavendish under a false name. Lord Grant was the name he'd chosen. It had a ring to it, suggesting that he could indeed be an English Lord.

He'd changed the plates on Penelope's Bentley, and he was paying for everything with cash.

Being anonymous was quite freeing. Nobody knew who he was or anything about him, and that suited him just fine. All they knew was that he tipped lavishly, wore the best Brioni had to offer, and drove a Bentley.

It was enough.

CHAPTER EIGHTY

Anthony demanded two premier bungalows, which infuriated Renee because she had not realized he would be arriving with an entourage. He turned up with his wife, grandmother, mistress, assistant, and bodyguard. Damn him. The hotel was overbooked as it was, and she'd reserved him his usual suite. But no, that wasn't good enough, he wanted two of the best bungalows, forcing her to move a couple of high rollers who threatened never to return.

"I had to throw people out to accommodate you," she complained. "You're a pain in the ass, Anthony."

"You have no idea," he responded.

Yes I do, she wanted to say. But she kept her silence because she knew it would be foolish to speak her mind. Instead she went back to her house on the hotel grounds and bitched to Susie about Anthony's arrival.

"Why is he here?" Susie was curious to know.

"I presume to spend leisure time with his grandmother," Renee said, not revealing the true purpose of Anthony's visit. The less Susie knew, the better. Susie would not understand why certain things had to be done, and if she ever found out she'd try to put a stop to it. Susie did not approve of anything illegal. To say she was naive was an understatement—she honestly believed that Tasmin had disappeared all on her own and that Anthony had nothing to do with it, although she still asked the occasional question.

"Anthony has a grandmother that he actually takes around with him?" Susie asked, her eyes widening.

"He's very Italian when it comes to family," Renee explained. "His wife is with him too."

"Anthony has a wife?"

"Yes, Susie. He has a wife *and* a grandmother. He didn't just crawl out of a hole in the ground."

"You could've fooled me."

"Here's the kicker," Renee said. "His bimbo mistress is also along for the ride."

"Oh my goodness," Susie exclaimed. "How does *that* work? Do you think they're having a threesome?"

"Hardly," Renee said. "The wife looks shell-shocked while the mistress is all perky and ready to party."

"Not with you, I hope," Susie said, her jealous streak surfacing at the slightest provocation.

"Of course not with me," Renee assured her insecure partner.

God! If Susie ever found out she'd once slept with Anthony, her life wouldn't be worth living.

"You know," Susie said thoughtfully, "I've been thinking about it, and although I know you're unsure, the Keys opening next door to us is a bonus."

"Excuse me?" Renee said. "Why do you think that?"

"I know you imagine it'll take business away from us," Susie said. "But you're wrong. The Keys being so near to us will enhance our hotel. You'll see. It's all about synergy. We're the two classiest hotels on the Strip, and it'll all work out. I'm happy they're opening, and I also think Lucky can be a good friend to us."

Susie was right. Susie was always right.

Renee's mind began ticking. Yes, now she was sure she had to get Anthony Bonar out of their lives once and for all.

*   *   *

Irma was in turmoil. How was she supposed to make sense of the situation she found herself in? It was all so unbelievably horrifying.

Her husband was a cruel and repugnant man, a vindictive inhuman monster. The very thought of what he'd done to Luis would haunt her forever, and worst of all, *she* was responsible, for it was she who'd lured Luis into her bedroom the first time, and if she hadn't done so, none of this would have happened.

Yes, the sad truth was that she was to blame.

Now she was trapped with Anthony, who'd informed her that she was not allowed to speak to anyone or go anywhere without his permission. "You're gonna do exactly what I say," he'd told her. "An' doncha open your fuckin' mouth to anyone, or your parents gonna feel the heat. Understand what I'm sayin'?"

Yes, she understood, and she had no doubt his threats were authentic. After the things she'd witnessed she was genuinely frightened. Anthony was not a bluffer—her psychotic husband was capable of anything. He'd proved that.

"Tonight we're goin' to a party, so go buy a dress an' be prepared t'look like you're enjoyin' yourself," Anthony announced, strolling into the bedroom where he'd made sure she was a prisoner. He'd instructed The Grill to remove the phones and make certain any doors leading outside were locked. There was no escape.

"How can I go shopping?" she cried out. "After everything you've done, how can you expect me to do that?"

"Who gives a shit?" he snarled. "'S long as you're ready at six. Buy a decent dress, an' wear your new earrings."

She was forced to visit the shopping mall with The Grill, who stood guard outside a fitting room while she reluctantly chose a plain black dress to wear.

It was all so surreal. Here she was in Las Vegas buying a dress, while back in Mexico City her lover had no doubt bled to death.

Poor Luis. Poor dear, sweet Luis. She remembered his gentle touch and suddenly she was overcome with grief. She sank to the floor of the fitting room and began quietly weeping.

After a while she pulled herself together. Above all else, Anthony had to be punished for his sins.

There must be a way, and she was determined to find it.

After arranging invitations to the opening reception at the Keys, Anthony had gone ahead and bought tickets for the concert event, although he wasn't sure if he'd stay around that long. Emmanuelle had informed him she was desperate to see Venus perform. Little did she know that there would be a lot more to observe than an aging blond singer, although the real action would take place to coincide with the fireworks display.

He decided to stay long enough to watch the fun begin, then he'd gather his entourage and get the hell out. A timely exit was one of the advantages of having his own plane.

According to Renee, everything was in place, and by God, she'd better be right. He was expecting results. They were spending a million bucks to make sure the Keys burned to the ground. Tucker Bond was expensive, but according to his reputation he never failed.

Destroying the Keys and making Grandma happy was worth every dollar. Anthony did not regret one red cent.

Not that he planned on paying Renee back—it was *her* responsibility. She could whistle for him to come up with his half.

* * *

Emmanuelle danced happily around the bungalow, quite taken with the Elton John–style white piano, indoor Jacuzzi, and luxury furnishings. Boarding the plane in Miami, she'd been startled to notice Anthony's wife huddled in one of the seats. "What's *she* doing here?" she'd whispered to Anthony, thinking that if he planned on a cozy threesome, she was a definite no.

"Take no notice of Irma," Anthony had said. "We got an understanding. Ignore her."

So Emmanuelle had done exactly that, playing up to Anthony's grandmother, who was quite a colorful character with her nonstop smoking, incessant coffee drinking, and raspy voice.

As soon as Francesca spotted Emmanuelle, she'd taken Anthony to one side. "Why you do this?" she'd demanded, spoiling for an argument. "Why both women here?"

"One's my wife, one's my mistress," Anthony had explained. "That's the Italian way, right, Grandma?"

"You leave those two together, they'll tear each other to pieces," Francesca had muttered.

"I promise you Irma's gonna do nothin'. She knows t'keep her mouth shut an' stay in her place."

"You and Irma fighting?" Francesca demanded, narrowing her eyes.

"No fight."

"You bloody sure, Anthony?"

"Would I lie to you?"

Detective Franklin had cultivated quite a few spies at the Cavendish, and it wasn't long before one of them reported that Anthony Bonar was back in town. This was the news she'd been waiting for. She got in her car and drove straight to the hotel.

For the past few days she'd been contemplating a trip to Miami, where it seemed Anthony Bonar spent most of his time. Now that he was actually back in Vegas he'd saved her the trouble. She had more than a strong hunch that Anthony Bonar knew a lot more about Tasmin's disappearance than he was saying. And Detective Franklin was famous around the department for hunches that usually paid off.

She'd checked Anthony Bonar out. He'd been arrested once many years ago when he was a teenager on a possession-of-drugs charge. A lawyer had sprung him within twenty-four hours, and he'd managed to stay out of jail ever since, although he'd certainly been investigated many times. He was known to be involved in major drug trade activities, but the FBI had never been able to find enough evidence to put him away.

"I'm here to see Mr. Bonar," she informed the desk clerk at reception.

"Do you have an appointment?" the clerk asked.

"No, I do not," Diane Franklin said, flashing her badge. "But somehow I imagine this is appointment enough."

"I'll let him know you're on your way."

Tucker Bond worked with two assistants, both female, both adept at whatever job he assigned them. He'd found that women were easier to control than men, and attractive women blended in. They were also a great deal more trustworthy and loyal.

These two had worked for him for more than ten years. They did whatever he told them to do, and no arguments. On this job he was paying them a hundred grand each. Not bad for a few hours' work.

Not bad at all.

"Fuck!" Anthony steamed. The last thing he needed was a small-town detective questioning him about Tasmin Garland. He'd answered a shitload of questions over the phone, so what was this about, and why hadn't Renee warned him?

Bitch! They were all bitches. Especially his cheating whore wife, whose fate he had all planned. Watching her boyfriend lose his manhood in front of her was not punishment enough. Oh no. He had more delights in store for her.

Tonight she'd be humiliated.

Tomorrow she'd be shipped off to Bolivia where he'd made arrangements for her to be placed in a facility that craved blond American whores. She'd asked for it. Any woman who screwed another man in the marital bed was asking for it.

If Irma wanted to fuck around, who was he to stop her?

Detective Franklin was full of more dumb questions. Anthony resented her intrusion into his life. Bad enough he had to deal with a detective, but a black female one at that. Shit! What was the fuckin' world coming to?

He answered her questions fast and hustled her out in record time.

The bitch would never get anything on *him*.

CHAPTER EIGHTY-ONE

The opening of the Keys was a much coveted event. Celebrities were jetting in from all over the world, delighted that they'd been invited. Lucky Santangelo and Lennie Golden were a power couple with friends across the globe, and everyone wanted to be there to help them celebrate.

The world press were also assembling. Journalists, camera crews, photographers. *ET*, *Access Hollywood*, *Extra*, *E! News*—they were all there to cover the event.

Security was a top priority—every member of the press had to display a laminated name tag and a red-carpet pass.

Henry Whitfield-Simmons had acquired both. With money, anything was possible.

Detective Franklin returned to the precinct more convinced than ever that Anthony Bonar had something to do with Tasmin's disappearance. Now that she'd actually met the man face-to-face he struck her as a lying scumbag in an expensive suit. She'd come across his type before. Anthony Bonar was the kind of man who imagined money could buy him anything and anybody. He was involved with Tasmin's disappearance, she would bet her life on it. And as for Renee Falcon, she knew a lot more than she was saying, that was for sure. Her girlfriend had given her away. Her girlfriend had more or less accused Anthony of having something to do with Tasmin's disappearance.

The way Diane Franklin saw it, Renee had fixed Anthony Bonar up on a date with Tasmin and something had gone horribly wrong.

But what? That was the big question.

"What do you think?" Lucky asked, emerging from her dressing room in a floor-length scarlet Versace backless gown, Jimmy Choo stilettos, diamond earrings, and Neil Lane black-and-white Art Deco diamond bracelets decorating both wrists.

Lennie whistled as he checked out his wife. "I swear I've never seen you look so staggeringly beautiful," he exclaimed. "You're incredible."

"I mean what do you think of my dress?" she said modestly.

"It's not the dress I'm concerned with, it's the body underneath."

"Lennie!" she said, smiling. "Be serious."

"The dress is a smash."

"Not too revealing?" she asked, twirling for him.

"If I had my way you'd be hidden under a burka. I don't enjoy other men ogling my woman."

"I'm your woman, am I?" she teased.

"Now and forever."

"Good, 'cause that's the way I like it."

"Can I fix you a drink?" he asked.

"How about a martini?" she said, walking out onto the spacious terrace overlooking the sparkling lights of the city.

"Coming right up."

As she stood gazing out at the spectacular view, her thoughts drifted back to the opening of the Magiriano, her first Vegas hotel. This time it was better, because this time she had Lennie and her family beside her.

It was exciting. More exciting than owning and running a major movie studio. More exciting than all the other businesses she'd been involved with.

Yes. The Keys was her ultimate prize.

She often wondered why she felt such close ties to Vegas, although deep down she knew why. It was the place it had all begun for her when she'd taken over from Gino and finished building the Magiriano. It was the place where she'd become a woman of substance, a woman capable of doing anything.

Now here she was, opening her dream hotel, and everything was perfect.

Well . . . almost . . .

Something was bothering her. Something that she'd dismissed over the past few weeks as a frivolous invitation to a party or event. Bobby had been concerned, and maybe rightfully so, because over the last twenty-four hours she'd received two more handwritten hand-delivered notes, similar to the ones she'd received in L.A. Only now, instead of saying *Drop Dead Beautiful*, the word *Beautiful* had been replaced with *Bitch*.

Drop Dead Bitch. And the word *Bitch* was scrawled in what looked like blood.

This was no invitation. This was a threat.

And since Lucky was not the kind of woman to be intimidated, she'd decided to deal with it after the opening.

Nothing was about to spoil her night of triumph.

Emmanuelle appeared in the living room of their bungalow wearing a shiny gold sequin number, short to show off her legs, low-cut to show off her tits, and dipping at the back to show off the beginning of her ass crack. Her blond hair was piled high, and her lips were pouty and full. Francesca informed Anthony in a hoarse stage whisper that his mistress resembled a street hooker.

Anthony didn't care, Francesca had no idea what girls looked like today, and as far as he was concerned, Emmanuelle was every man's walking wet dream, a cover-girl fantasy in the flesh.

"Irma!" Anthony yelled, prowling around the living room. "Get your ass out here."

Irma appeared from the bedroom. She was twelve years older than Emmanuelle and tonight she looked it. Though she'd once been a glowing beauty queen, Anthony had managed to turn her into a tense and unhappy woman wearing a black dress and the diamond drop earrings he'd insisted she put on.

She refused to even glance at Emmanuelle, which suited Emmanuelle, because she'd already decided that the only way to deal with the wife situation was to ignore her. If Anthony was playing games it was all right with her, as long as *she* wasn't involved.

"Take off your earrings," Anthony commanded his wife. "Take 'em off an' give 'em to Emmanuelle."

Irma stared at her husband, unbridled hatred in her eyes.

"Take 'em off," Anthony repeated, "before I rip 'em off your fuckin' ears."

Irma reached up and removed her diamond drop earrings.

"Give 'em to Emmanuelle," Anthony instructed, enjoying this little scene. "They're hers now."

"You think I care?" Irma said, through clenched teeth. "You think I give a damn?"

"Shut the fuck up an' hand 'em over," Anthony said, annoyed that she still had some fight left in her.

Irma took off the earrings and threw them on the floor, infuriating Anthony even more.

He jumped forward and slapped his wife across the face, his pinky ring cutting into the delicate skin on her cheek, drawing blood.

Fortunately, Francesca chose that moment to walk back into the room. Her flinty eyes took in the scene, and she began screaming at her grandson in Italian.

Anthony glared at her, but he backed off and walked over to the bar where he poured himself a hefty tumbler of Scotch.

Emmanuelle picked up the earrings from the floor—she wasn't allowing *them* to go to waste—while Irma retreated to the bedroom.

Anthony downed his drink and stared at his blond mistress as she put on the earrings and paraded in front of him.

On Emmanuelle they looked fake. Stupid, fake baubles, like her stupid, fake tits.

Sometimes everything wasn't enough.

"Can you believe she put Ace on a different floor?" Max complained. "It's like she *totally* doesn't trust me."

"Wise woman, your mom," Cookie said, rolling her eyes as they both stood in front of the bathroom mirror applying gloss and mascara and gold shimmer and all other kinds of makeup enhancements, readying themselves for the night ahead.

"Whose side are you on, anyway?" Max asked, smudging black eyeliner to give her eyes a smoky look.

"I'm on the side of anyone who can find me a hottie of my own tonight," Cookie replied, picking up the curling tongs and attacking her hair.

"There should be plenty around," Max remarked. "She's got most of young Hollywood putting in an appearance. I took a peek at the list."

"You did?" Cookie said, trying not to appear too excited. "Any sexy young Will Smiths on it? He's *sooo* hot for an old dude."

"Not my type."

"Course he isn't," Cookie grumbled. "You've got

your own personal hottie stashed in a room he's *not* sharing with Harry. Man, you're gonna have a wicked time!"

"I can only hope," Max said, applying blusher. "Thing is, I'm not so sure he's into me, he kinda thinks I'm too young."

"You gotta *play* it, girl," Cookie advised. "You know how to do that, don't you?"

"Kinda. Sorta."

Cookie piled on the lip gloss. "What did Lucky say about him?"

Max shrugged. "Dunno. She was all over the place."

The phone rang and Max picked up.

"Miss Golden, this is the front desk."

"Yes?"

"Your cousin requested that you meet him outside the spa in fifteen minutes."

"My cousin?" Max said, frowning.

"That is correct, Miss Golden."

"Oh, my cousin!" she said, giggling as she put the phone down.

"What's going on?" Cookie asked.

"It's Ace," Max said, a grin spreading across her face. "Y'see, Internet Freak thought that Ace was my cousin, so now Ace is into the game. He wants me to meet him outside the spa."

"I thought we were all going to the party together."

"Is it okay if we see you there? You don't mind, do you?"

"Why would I mind?" Cookie said sarcastically. "I'm totally psyched walking in by myself."

"Not to worry, we'll get there before you," Max said, excited at the thought of seeing Ace. "Quick, pass me the tongs, I've got to get downstairs pronto!"

"Okay, go have fun."

"I will," Max said, pulling on her favorite Seven jeans

and a slinky red silk tank. "Do I look hot?" she questioned, staring at herself in the mirror.

"Sizzling!"

"Really?" she said unsurely.

"Go get him, girl. It's time."

Detective Franklin was still sitting at her desk thinking about her meeting with Anthony Bonar when a male colleague dumped a package on her desk.

"This came addressed to you," he said.

"What is it, a bomb?" she joked.

There was a running gag at the precinct that anytime an unidentified package appeared, it had to be a bomb.

"No chance. It's kinda soft."

"Hmm . . . like you were last night on your hot date," Detective Franklin said.

The other detectives in the room roared with laughter.

"Who's opening it?" she asked.

"Your turn," the male detective said.

"Am I the only one with stones around here?" she asked, ripping open the package.

"You said it," the guys chorused.

The package contained a bloodstained white bathrobe from the Cavendish Hotel. Pinned to it was a crude hand-drawn map, and a piece of paper with cut-out letters from a newspaper spelling out TASMIN and ANTHONY BONAR.

"Someone get this to the lab immediately and have tests done right away," Detective Franklin said, adrenaline coursing. "Blood, semen, hair, and anything else they can come up with. I think we got us a body and a killer. Let's go!"

CHAPTER EIGHTY-TWO

"How come *I* didn't get to meet Max's latest victim?" Lennie asked as their private elevator descended to the terrace level.

"Because," Lucky replied, holding tightly on to his hand, "you were out on the golf course having a great time with Charlie Dollar when they arrived."

"Is this the boy Max was in Big Bear with?"

"Apparently so. According to her, he saved her ass from a gang of carjackers—or so she says. Personally, I think she came across him online, met up with him in Big Bear, and fell in first love."

"First love?" Lennie questioned.

"Oh, you know. Or maybe you don't—you're not a girl."

"Gee, you noticed!" he drawled.

"Anyway, first love is special," Lucky said, matter-of-factly. "It's all-consuming and usually involves rejection. My opinion is that this boy isn't as into Max as she is into him. He's older and killer handsome, so he'll break her heart, forcing her to realize that all men aren't perfect, and that'll prepare her for the reality of life, so it's all good."

"Jeez!" Lennie whistled. "My wife the cynic."

"It's called training."

"And who trained *you?*"

"I had to learn all by myself."

"You're a hard woman."

She reached up and softly caressed his cheek. "Did I tell you how handsome you look in your tux?"

"No. You take me for granted."

"Lennie," she chided, "you are the one man I will *never* take for granted."

"Promise?"

"Bet on it."

Lord Grant, aka Henry Whitfield-Simmons, left the Cavendish and drove his Bentley to the Keys. He had passes for the reception and tickets for the lingerie show and concert. Tickets he had no intention of using, for by the time the show started, he and Maria would be busy getting reacquainted.

"We should get married, Alex," Ling said, surprising him in the shower.

"You're not bringing *that* up again," Alex responded as his beautiful naked Asian girlfriend with the straight pubic hair and inappropriate fake tits sunk to her knees and began doing things to him he could never resist.

He leaned back against the side of the shower as Ling went to work. She was an excellent lawyer, but her real talent lay in her delicate tongue—a tongue that could perform feats resulting in extraordinary sexual pleasure.

"Jesus, honey," he groaned, giving himself up to the moment. "I don't want to be late . . ."

Oh no, Ling thought, *mustn't be late for Lucky. That would never do. Lucky always has to come first. Lucky! Lucky! Lucky!* She was so sick and tired of his obsession.

Soon she had his full attention as she employed her talents to their best advantage. Ling had learned at a very young age how to bring a man to the brink of orgasm and then take him back, just a tad, so that by the time he actually came, it was an orgasm of mammoth proportions.

Alex knew nothing of her early life in China where she'd been raised in a house of ill repute, before managing to escape at the age of fourteen, thanks to a married American businessman fifty years her senior. The man had brought her to America, set her up in an apartment, and financed her education. In return she'd given him the best sex of his life.

He'd died ten years ago a happy man. She'd gone on to pass the bar and become an extremely accomplished divorce lawyer at one of L.A.'s most prestigious law firms.

Meeting Alex Woods was the finest moment of her life. She admired his blazing talent and unbridled masculinity—she'd always been a big fan of his films.

Shortly after moving in with him she'd decided she wanted to marry him, but Alex was forever resistant, in spite of her unusual sexual prowess.

Over the two years they'd been together she'd convinced herself that Lucky Santangelo Golden was the reason for his reluctance to make the ultimate commitment. Without Lucky, there would be no problem.

In Ling's eyes Alex Woods harbored an obsessive love for Lucky Santangelo Golden that was not healthy. It was up to her to do something about it.

Tonight she might get the opportunity to do just that.

The grand terrace of the Keys was the perfect setting for a party: creamy limestone floors and towering Italian marble columns, giant urns filled with a profusion of purple bougainvillea, and thousands of white candles in silver holders.

As Lucky entered, still holding Lennie's arm, the sight of everything took her breath away. She felt an enormous surge of adrenaline as she looked around, realizing that all the hard work of putting this project together had been worth it. Five years ago she'd had an idea. Now, here it was—the Keys. Her hotel. Her palace. She was queen of her kingdom.

"Amazing!" Lennie whispered in her ear before they were separated and she was swept up in a sea of people congratulating her. She went with the flow, accepting the many compliments coming her way, graciously kissing cheeks and shaking hands. It was a whirlwind of activity, and no press. The press were not allowed into the reception—they were stationed outside on the red carpet, which would serve as a pathway to the lingerie show and Venus's appearance.

Lucky had an army of people working for her, and they were all doing a fantastic job. From the P.R.'s to the caterers, security, and management, everyone was in top form, making sure there wasn't a glitch in sight. Spotting Gino, she attempted to make her way toward him, but before she could get very far, Alex blocked her path. "Hey, you," he said. "I see you got yourself quite a turnout. Shame you're not popular."

"We're in business," she said, smiling. "Now I'll have to concentrate on paying back all my investors in record time. Think there's a chance?"

"No hurry on my account," he said, leaning in.

She took a step back just as Ling appeared, sleek in a white Valentino suit.

"Don't *you* look lovely," Lucky said to the Asian woman. "How come you're still hanging around with this old fart?"

Ling lacked a sense of humor, especially when it came to Alex. "Good evening, Lucky," she said, her expression tight and unfriendly. "Please do not call Alex names. He may look like he gets the joke, but I can assure you he doesn't. Later, *I'm* the one who has to deal with his bad mood."

"Now *wait* a minute—" Alex objected.

"Hey, hey, hey, here's my Lucky lady," Charlie Dollar,

movie icon supreme, drawled, sweeping in between them. "Got a big fat boner this joint's gonna make it."

"Charlie!" Lucky exclaimed, relieved to move away from Ling's icy demeanor. "I'm so glad you could come."

"Wouldn't miss a Lucky Santangelo event," Charlie said, Cheshire cat grin firmly in place. "Gotta tell ya, nobody does it better."

"Thanks, Charlie, that means a lot coming from you."

"Gotta give props where props are due," he said, stoned eyes checking out the possibilities.

"You are *the* most supportive friend, and I love you for it," Lucky said, kissing him on the cheek.

"Calm down, chickadee, don't go gettin' all sentimental on me. I cry at the sight of emotion."

Charlie always made her smile. "I'll try not to," she said.

"Just came from the lingerie rehearsal. Wowee! Hot bods in Technicolor action. Excellent move not bringin' a date."

"I'm sure you'll have fun tonight, Charlie."

"Don't I always?" he said, another enormous grin crossing his weathered face.

"Oh yes," she agreed. "Got no doubts on *that* score."

Finally she made it over to Gino, who was surrounded by family and friends.

"I'm feelin' the excitement, kiddo," Gino rasped. "You got yourself another hit!"

"I hope so."

"I *know* so."

Anthony Bonar wore Armani. Emmanuelle wore Tramp of the Day. Irma wore a dazed expression. Francesca wore a faded black dress and an embroidered shawl. The Grill wore an ill-fitting suit and a threatening expression.

As a group they stood out.

Irma could not understand why Anthony was doing this to her. Surely he would prefer *not* to see her? Yet he was keeping her close, with The Grill always hovering.

The image of Luis being mutilated refused to go away—it was constant. She could see his face, hear his agonizing screams, while she'd been forced to sit there watching helplessly as her lover was butchered.

Anthony was evil, and the second the opportunity arose she was running.

It didn't matter that she had no money and nowhere to run to. Anything was better than staying with Anthony Bonar. He was a true monster.

Susie wanted to attend the reception at the Keys. Renee wasn't so sure it was a good idea to go, but Susie was insistent, so they went.

The first person they bumped into was Anthony Bonar, swaggering around with his trampy-looking girlfriend in tow, while his wife and grandmother trailed behind him with the hulking bodyguard he was never without.

"What the fuck you two doin' here?" was his opening comment.

"Why shouldn't we be here, Anthony?" Susie replied, speaking up for once, because usually in Anthony's presence she never said a word.

"Renee knows why," Anthony said. "It don't look right."

"Nonsense!" Susie replied. "This hotel opening next to us will be excellent for business."

"Are you fuckin' stupid?" Anthony growled.

"As far as I'm concerned," Susie retaliated, "there's only one stupid person around here."

Renee quickly jumped between them. Since when

had Susie decided to take on Anthony Bonar? That was *her* job.

"Susie, dear," she said. "Can you do me a favor and go talk to the mayor? He's over there. I'll join you in a minute."

Susie threw Anthony a baleful look and walked away.

"Dumb cunt," Anthony muttered.

"Excuse me?" Renee said.

"Dumb cunt," Anthony repeated.

"That's my partner you're talking about."

"Yeah. I know. She's dumb an' she's a cunt."

Renee stared at the man she'd had so many dealings with over the years. The man who'd bled money from her hotel and given nothing back. The man who'd always made her feel that she owed him everything. The man who'd murdered a woman and showed nothing but a cold indifference.

Payback was a bitch. A bitch Anthony Bonar was about to meet head-on.

CHAPTER EIGHTY-THREE

"I want to go over to Gino Santangelo, see if he remembers me," Francesca said, pulling on Anthony's sleeve. She'd spotted her old love across the terrace and was all set on facing him.

"Are you fuckin' *crazy?*" Anthony responded. "You're not doin' any such thing."

"*Sí*, Anthony," Francesca replied, a stubborn gleam in her faded eyes. "You and me, we go over *now.*"

"Aren't you listening to me?" Anthony said, raising his voice. "Read my fuckin' lips: No fuckin' way."

"Don't you tell *me* what to do, Anthony," Francesca raged, pointing a bony be-ringed finger at him. "*I'm* the one took you out of Italy, gave you a life, a business. *You* don't tell *me* what to do, *I* tell *you.*"

"Jesus Christ, Grandma."

"Come," she said authoritatively.

"Keep an eye on these two," he muttered to The Grill. "Don't let either of them outta your sight, understand?"

"Yes, boss."

"And you," he said to his mistress. "Stay put."

"Sure, honey," Emmanuelle purred, although she had no intention of doing so. She was in heaven—she'd never seen so many stars gathered in one place. She already had her eye on Charlie Dollar. Oh yes, Charlie Dollar might be ancient, but he was still raging hot in a Jack Nicholson kind of way. And to Emmanuelle he was a sizzling superstar. She'd seen every movie he'd ever made and she considered herself his biggest fan.

Tonight Emmanuelle was determined to score a piece of Mr. Dollar. Absolutely determined.

"Wow!" Billy said, looking around. "This is quite a star-studded event. Even *I'm* impressed."

"I told you," Venus replied. "Lucky sure knows how to pull 'em out."

"Yeah, and the fact that you're performing later has a little something to do with it too," Billy pointed out.

"Yes?"

"Yeah, baby," Billy said, feeling exceptionally close to her. "Face it—you're an icon, a living legend."

"I'm glad you said 'living,' " she joked.

"You're living, you're breathing, you're beautiful, and I've been thinking—"

"I know," she said teasingly. "You've been thinking that you can't wait to get back to the crap tables as soon as possible. How well I know you!"

"That wasn't what I was thinking at all."

"Hmm . . . let me see. You want to throw Kev a day-of-the-wedding bachelor party with strippers and lap dancers and—"

"Wrong," he interrupted.

"Okay, I'm stumped. What *were* you thinking?"

"I was thinking if Kev can do it, why can't we?"

"Excuse me?"

"You an' me, babe. Why don't *we* get married?"

She took a deep breath. *This* was a surprise. "You're not serious?"

"Your divorce is final, right?" he said, thinking that he was expecting a more enthusiastic response.

"Yes."

"Then there's nothing to stop us."

"Nothing to stop us from doing what?"

"You know, getting married."

"Oh, *wow!* You really are serious, aren't you?"

"Yes, Venus, I am. We've been together almost a year, and I've got a strong vibe we should give it a shot. Whaddya say?"

Before she could say anything at all, Bobby and Brigette descended on them.

"Some party, huh?" Bobby said. "Fantastic turnout. Looking forward to your show, Venus. Hope you're planning to sing all my favorites."

"I'll try, but you'll have to tell me what they are," she replied, still trying to process Billy's sudden desire to get married.

"You got three hours?" Bobby said. "'Cause if you have, I'll tell you. By the way, you look spectacular, as always. Billy, I hope you realize you're one *very* fortunate guy."

"Don't I know it," Billy agreed.

"Y'know," Bobby continued, "when I was twelve—"

"Stop it!" Brigette interrupted. "Venus is not interested in hearing about your teenage fantasies."

"They were hot," Bobby assured her. "Very, very hot!"

"Quiet!" Brigette scolded.

"Uh, Billy," Venus said, turning to her boyfriend. "Remember that question you asked me?"

"*The* question?" he said, gulping down a glass of champagne.

"Well," she said slowly, "I've been considering my answer."

"You have?" he said, swapping glasses with a passing waiter.

"Yes," she said, smiling. "I have."

"And?" he said, nervous as hell, for what if she said no? If she rejected him he'd be gutted, his ego would take a giant nosedive. Christ! He'd actually proposed.

"My answer is . . . yes," she said, putting him out of his misery.

"It is?" A huge grin spread across his face. "You're sure?"

"I couldn't be more sure."

"What's up with you two?" Bobby asked curiously. "Something you want to share?"

"Maybe we'll all meet up later," Billy said, keeping it casual. "We'll share then."

"Suits me," Bobby said. "I'll be hitting the tables right after the show."

"So will I," Brigette said, joining in. "What's the point of having all this money if I can't lose it!"

"You're my kind of heiress," Billy quipped, still feeling nervous but in a kind of ecstatic way. She'd said yes! Venus had said yes! He was marrying a superstar!

No. Big correction. He was marrying the woman he loved.

"Is that an offer?" Brigette joked. "'Cause I'm available."

"*Now* she tells me," Billy said, still grinning.

"Venus, is he making me an offer?" Brigette asked, all big blue eyes and innocent expression.

Venus smiled. "Right now I truly suspect that it's highly unlikely."

"I'm going back to the suite before the show," Alex said. "Forgot my watch."

"I'll come with you," Ling said.

"You don't have to."

"I want to."

"No, you go ahead, save our seats."

"But Alex—"

"Ling. I am perfectly capable of going to the suite by myself."

"Very well," she said, giving him the pissy look he couldn't stand.

"Where's Lucky?" he asked.

"Why?" Ling sniped. "You wish *her* to go with you?"

"Oh, for chrissakes!" he snapped. "Get over this thing you have against Lucky. I merely need to ask her how the fuck I get out of here without doing that red-carpet press shit."

"I'm sure someone else can help you with that," Ling said. "It doesn't *always* have to be Lucky." She paused, glared at him, then added, "Or maybe it does."

"Piss off, Ling," he said, stalking away from her.

"Gino Santangelo," Francesca crowed, wrinkling her forehead. "So many years, so much time. Surely you remember me?"

Peering at the old woman, Gino realized there was something vaguely familiar about her. "Sorry . . ." he muttered. "You're gonna havta remind me."

"Francesca Bonnatti," she said, tilting her chin. "And this my grandson Anthony Bonar."

Gino felt the hairs on the back of his neck stand up. Of course, Enzio's wife, and now widow. What the hell was *she* doing at the opening of Lucky's hotel? And he'd never heard of Enzio having a grandson named Anthony.

Why was Francesca here? And even more important—what did she want?

"Long time, Gino," she said, her eyes vindictive and glittering with hate. "Long time—much water under the bridge, *sí*?"

He had nothing to say to her.

"And your daughter, Lucky, she the one built this hotel, *sí*?"

Gino's mind started racing. His onetime partner and Lucky's godfather, Enzio Bonnatti, had arranged for the murder of his wife and son, and in retaliation Lucky had shot Enzio.

Francesca and he were both well aware of these past events. They were two families pitched against each other forever. Two endless vendettas. The Santangelos and the Bonnattis. They hated each other.

Now Francesca was standing in front of him as if nothing had happened in their dark and ominous past.

"You and me," Francesca mused. "We go back *molti* years, Gino."

"What do you want?" he said guardedly. "What are you doing here?"

"I come to see."

"See what?"

"To see the end of the Santangelos," Francesca said with a hoarse cackle. "You and your family are cursed—*maledetto*. This hotel is *maledetto*. May the ghost of—"

"Grandma, we gotta go," Anthony interrupted, pulling her by the arm, refusing to even look at Gino.

Gino's black eyes checked out Anthony Bonar. The man was not good news, he sensed it immediately. Gino had always possessed dead-on instincts when it came to summing people up, and this one was a bad human being, he had no doubt of it.

What the hell are the two of them doing here? he thought for the second time.

Whatever the reason, it wasn't good.

He should warn Lucky. Francesca Bonnatti and Anthony Bonar were unwelcome guests. It was obvious that as far as the Bonnattis were concerned, the Bonnatti/Santangelo vendetta was still very much alive.

CHAPTER EIGHTY-FOUR

"Hi," Ace said as Cookie opened the door to their room.

"Hey," Cookie responded.

"Uh, is she around?" Ace asked, hovering in the doorway.

"Is who around?" Cookie asked, thinking that Max had found herself a *real* hottie, this dude was majorly *handsome*.

"The queen of England," Ace deadpanned.

"Oh, you must mean Max."

"Yeah, that's exactly who I mean. I was supposed to pick her up and here I am. I put on a white shirt for the occasion. I feel like an idiot. Does it look okay?"

"It's totally happenin', dude, but I thought you were meeting her outside the spa."

"Why would I be meeting her there? I arranged to pick her up here."

"You left a message half an hour ago that she should meet you outside the spa," Cookie said, wondering how he liked the skimpy purple dress she'd decided to wear.

"I didn't leave a message," Ace said.

"Yeah, the guy at the desk called and said her cousin wanted her to meet him."

"Did you say 'cousin'?" he said, getting concerned.

"Yeah. Max explained that you were playing some game pretending to be her cousin."

"Fuck!"

"Wassamatter?"

"This is bad," he said. "It could be that maniac."

"*What* maniac?" Cookie asked, her eyes widening.

"The dude who kidnapped her in Big Bear."

"*Whaaat?*"

"Yeah," he said urgently. "Let's go. We gotta find her before he does."

"I have to talk to you," Venus said, cornering Lucky. "Alone. Now."

Excusing herself from Cole and his rock star boyfriend, Lucky concentrated on Venus. "What's on your mind?" she asked. "What's with the 'alone' and 'now' bit?"

"We're getting married," Venus confided, somewhat breathlessly.

"*Excuse* me?" Lucky responded with a look of surprise. "Did I just hear you say the M word? I mean, isn't that the word you swore you'd never use again after Cooper?"

"Yup," Venus confessed. "You're right. But Billy finally asked me."

"I don't believe this!" Lucky exclaimed.

"Believe it," Venus responded.

"Is it what you want?" Lucky asked.

"I think so."

"You *think* so?" Lucky said, shaking her head. "You'd better be sure."

"Well, I've said yes, so it's too late to *not* be sure."

"Man!" Lucky grumbled. "Like I don't have enough going on, now I've got a wedding to plan. When we get back we'll—"

"No!" Venus interrupted. "You don't understand. We're doing it tonight, after the concert. So if you're planning anything, you'd better do it fast!"

* * *

"Mr. Dollar," Emmanuelle said, sidling close to the famous movie star, thrusting out her considerable assets. "I'm your biggest fan."

Charlie Dollar checked the young blonde out. She was certainly succulent, and he was certainly into succulent. Young too. Yes, this one was just his type.

"Hi, there, chickadee," he said. "What's your name?"

"Emmanuelle," she answered, reaching up to touch one of her recently acquired diamond earrings.

"Oh," Charlie said with a knowing chuckle. "Like one of those dirty movies from the seventies."

"I don't know what you're talking about."

"You wouldn't. Too young. Are you even legal?"

"I'm twenty, and I've been on sixteen magazine covers," she boasted.

"No shit?"

"Sixteen covers," she said proudly. "But I bet you've been on more than that."

"Well, little lady," he drawled, "I'm mucho older than twenty."

"I just wanted to say how much I admire you," she gushed.

"That's very smart, young lady," he said, scratching his stubbled chin.

"I'm here with somebody tonight," Emmanuelle continued. "But I was wondering if you'd give me your number so that when I come to L.A. I can call you."

"You're with somebody tonight, huh?" he said, peering at her over the tops of his tinted shades.

"That's right."

"A guy?"

"I'm not a *lesbian*, Mr. Dollar," she said coyly.

"Shame."

"Excuse me?" she said, toying with her necklace nestled cozily in her cleavage.

"Uh . . . nothin'. Where's your boyfriend?"

"Somewhere around. I'm sure he'll find me in a minute."

"*Then* what's he gonna do, beat my ass?"

"He might," she giggled. "He *is* kind of the jealous type."

"Why is it that you jailbait little hussies always manage to target Charlie?" he complained. "You got any clue how many times I've had one of you poptarts come on to me, an' then some asshole boyfriend or husband appears ready to beat the shit outta me?"

"No," she said, fluttering her eyelashes.

"It happens, sugar-tits, so here's my suggestion—take your pretty little ass an' go peddle the goods elsewhere."

He walked away, leaving Emmanuelle nonplussed.

Irma and The Grill standing nearby observed the entire scene.

Irma felt a tiny frisson of satisfaction. Anthony was going to get what he deserved from this one.

"I should leave," Venus sighed, holding Billy's hand. "I need time by myself before my show. I have kind of a ritual I put myself through."

"I understand that you want to be alone," Billy said, "but you're not changing your mind, are you? You wouldn't do that to me, would you?"

"Now why would you think that?" she said softly. "I'm as excited as you are."

"Just checking," he said with a nervous laugh. "I mean, I know it's sudden and all, but we're doing the right thing—I'm sure of it."

"So am I, baby, otherwise I wouldn't've said yes."

"Okay," he said, taking a deep breath. "After the show we're gonna do it, an' we're not telling anyone except Lucky and Lennie, right?"

"Lucky's promised to get it all organized. All she's

asked is that we wait until after the fireworks display. Then we show up at the chapel, and *voilà*!"

"Sounds perfect."

"What about Kev?"

"What *about* him?"

"He's your best friend. Surely he'll be hurt if he's not included."

"Since when did you care about *Kev's* feelings?" Billy said, thinking that the last person he planned on telling was Kev—who'd immediately share the news with Ali, and Ali was the kind of girl who would most likely alert the media and maybe even sell her story about her afternoon of sex in the pool with Billy Melina, movie star.

Oh shit! Why had he ever banged her? Shit! Shit! Shit!

"I don't hate Kev," Venus explained. "I think he always resented me for taking you away from him."

"You're wrong, babe."

"No I'm not. So here's what I think we should do."

"What?"

"Make a new start and invite him."

"No!" Billy said sharply. "He didn't invite *me* to *his* wedding."

"Don't be so petty," she chided. "That's not like you, Billy."

"I do not want him there, baby. Okay?"

"Whatever you say."

"Hey, I kinda like it when you're subservient."

"And I like you," she said, reaching up to touch his cheek. "I like you so much I'm even marrying you."

"That's right, we're getting married, babe, so I think you can use the L word."

The spa was located in a separate building near the main swimming pool at the back of the hotel. The setting was

idyllic—fountains and exotic fish ponds surrounded by
lush greenery and tall palms. Since the spa did not open
until the following day, and with everyone's attention focused on the reception and concert, the area around the
spa was quite deserted.

Max, who'd thoroughly explored the hotel earlier
with Ace, raced to meet him. She felt comfortable and
excited in his company. Once again she marveled at how
different he was from the kids she'd grown up with in
Malibu and Beverly Hills, her so-called peers—all with
rich, famous, or powerful parents. Cookie and Harry
were the only two she'd bonded with. They were different, and so was Ace—he didn't have that rich-kid vibe,
he was genuine and nice and most of all HOT!

Just thinking about him made her shiver with the anticipation of seeing him. Was it possible to have a relationship with someone who didn't live in L.A.?

Yes! Yes! Yes! They could drive to see each other on
alternate weekends. One weekend she'd go to Big Bear,
the next he'd drive to L.A. It was a workable situation.

Then it occurred to her that she was getting way
ahead of herself, since Ace hadn't even kissed her.
Hmm . . . she definitely had to do something about *that*.

And just as she was thinking he was late, a figure began walking toward her, and to her utmost horror she
realized it was the Internet Freak himself.

For a moment she froze. Then she turned to run.

"Wait!" he yelled, leaping toward her. "Maria, wait!
It's me. I've come back for you. Please wait!"

Reaching in her purse for a Kleenex, Irma discovered
that she still had Oliver Stanton's card. She stared at it
for a moment, studying the numbers. What if she called
him? And in exchange for information about Anthony's
drug dealings asked him to rescue her? It was a thought.
A very welcome thought.

She had plenty of information about Anthony's drug activities. He'd taken her to Colombia on more than one occasion, and she knew some of the names of the people he dealt with. She'd also witnessed many of his late-night business transactions in Acapulco.

Yes, she knew more than enough. But how to get to a phone, that was the problem.

"I need to use the bathroom," she informed The Grill.

"You wait," the big man said, glowering.

"I can't wait," she said sharply. "I need to go now."

"No!"

"Yes!"

Reluctantly The Grill escorted her to the ladies' room, where he stationed himself outside.

The moment she got inside the restroom, she quickly looked around to see who else was in there.

A redheaded woman was standing at the sink washing her hands.

"Excuse me," Irma said, approaching her. "Would you happen to have a cell phone I can use? I left mine at home and it's kind of urgent."

"I don't, dear," the woman said, drying her hands. "Damn thing wouldn't fit in my purse. My friend might have one, though."

"Where's your friend?"

"Making a tinkle."

Irma stared at the closed stall door, willing the woman's friend to emerge.

"Are you all right?" the redheaded woman asked. "You look awfully pale."

No, I am not all right. Earlier today I watched my husband cut off my lover's balls in front of me. And now my insane husband is threatening to kill me and my parents.

"I'm fine, thank you," she managed. "But I do need to make this call, it's very urgent."

"We should go outside," the woman suggested. "I'm sure my husband has his phone."

Before she could think of an excuse, the other woman, a petite brunette, emerged from one of the stalls.

"Ah, Doreen," the redhead said. "Do you have your phone on you?"

"Yes, why?" Doreen asked.

"I promised this lady she could use it. She has to make a quick call."

"The battery might be low," Doreen said, reaching into her purse. "I'm always forgetting to charge it." She handed Irma a pink sequined phone.

Irma pulled out Oliver's card and squinted at the numbers again. Office. Home. Cell.

She chose cell and quickly punched out the number, moving away from the two women who were now chatting about the reception and how much they were enjoying it.

Her hands were trembling, any moment now Anthony might return and come busting in.

She misdialed, tried again, and finally the number rang.

Please God, let Oliver pick up.

Please God, let him answer.

"Hello?"

"Oliver," she gasped. "It's Irma. I need your help."

CHAPTER EIGHTY-FIVE

The reception was winding down. A series of assistant P.R.'s were attempting to usher the most famous guests to the red carpet pathway where they would be photographed and interviewed by the many photographers and TV crews as they made their way to the lingerie show.

Lucky was swamped, what with everyone attempting to speak to her, members of her staff giving her a series of updates, Gino trying to attract her attention, and now a wedding to get together in a matter of hours.

She elicited the help of Mooney, who knew everyone in Vegas, to arrange the wedding chapel and keep everything quiet. If the news of Venus and Billy's impending nuptials got out to the press, it would be chaos.

Next she spoke to her catering and entertainment directors about organizing a small, extremely exclusive private reception in her penthouse later that night.

"A very close friend of mine is getting married," she informed them, revealing no names. "It has to be special."

They assured her it would be. Everyone who worked with Lucky loved her—she had a way of inspiring great loyalty and enthusiasm.

"Have you seen Max?" she asked Lennie when he appeared to accompany her down the red carpet.

"No," he said, shaking his head. "And I was looking forward to meeting the new boyfriend."

"Don't say 'boyfriend' around her, she'll kill you."

"Something wrong with 'boyfriend'?"

"She wouldn't like it."

"Then I won't say it."

"That's wise."

"Gino's waving at you."

"I know. Let's try to get over to him. I can't seem to make a move without a dozen people attempting to stop me."

"In that case, grab hold of my arm and hang on. Smile a lot, I'll get you there."

"You're so macho."

"And handsome, right?" he quipped. "Isn't that why you married me?"

"Oh yes!" she said, laughing as he propelled her through the crowd until they reached Gino.

"What's up?" she asked her father.

"Somethin's not right," Gino replied, rubbing the scar on his cheek.

"Not enough ice in your drink?" she said flippantly. "Music too loud? *What?*"

Gino's face was serious. "Enzio Bonnatti's widow is here with a supposed grandson," he said. "I don't like it, Lucky, they're up to somethin', an' you'd better find out what it is. She had a crazy hostile look in her eyes. Kept on muttering about the hotel being cursed. They're here for some kind of revenge—you can bet on it."

When Anthony came back with an angry Francesca lagging behind him, he was perplexed to find Irma missing.

"Where the fuck is she?" he demanded of The Grill.

"In the ladies' room," the big man muttered.

"What the fuck you let her go there for?"

"She told me she had to go."

"Jesus Christ!" Anthony steamed, walking over to the

door of the ladies' room. "Irma!" he yelled. "Get your ass out here."

Irma came out immediately.

He glared at her. "I told you not to go anywhere. When I tell you somethin', you'd better fuckin' listen."

She refused to look at him.

"Where's Emmanuelle?" he demanded, turning back to The Grill.

"Over there, boss," The Grill said.

Anthony observed Emmanuelle talking to a man. He'd told both women to stay next to The Grill, not to go running around all over the place. Amazing wasn't it, that he had to control everything?

Taking hold of Irma, he pulled her over to Emmanuelle, who was in midsentence. Anthony grabbed Emmanuelle's arm, yanking her away from the man.

"That was so rude," Emmanuelle objected, her cheeks flushed. "That man is a *very* important producer. He told me I should be in movies."

"I don't give a shit who he is," Anthony snapped. "When I tell you to stay somewhere, you stay there. Got it?"

Irma met the girl's eyes.

Emmanuelle stared back at her defiantly before turning to Anthony and saying, "You shouldn't speak to me like that. I'm not your wife."

Anthony controlled an overwhelming impulse to slap her across the face. Emmanuelle was getting too lippy for her own good. It was time to do something to put her in her place.

"Are you sure your heart can take this?" Lucky teased Gino as she escorted him to the front row of the lingerie show.

"Think I'll survive, kiddo."

"Oh yes, I almost forgot," she said, smiling. "Your nickname used to be Gino the Ram, right?"

Gino's mind was elsewhere. "What didja do 'bout the Bonnattis?" he said, frowning. "Didja get 'em outta here?"

"Not yet. There's press everywhere, it wouldn't be smart to cause an incident."

"Whaddya think they're doing here?" he mused.

"They're probably just checking the place out."

"You don't know Francesca like I know that witch," Gino said, still worrying. "She had balls when she was married to Enzio, big brass balls. I'll never forget her sittin' in the courtroom when you were on trial for Santino's murder. She sat there every day, glaring at you, vowing revenge. You don't remember?"

"That whole trial is a blur."

"*I* remember it, kiddo. They're here for a goddamn reason. I can smell it."

"You're wrong, Gino. All that stuff happened so long ago."

"Listen to me, Lucky: she's Sicilian. It don't matter how long ago shit happened, Sicilians never forget an' they never forgive. Have your security people watch 'em, okay?"

"I'll do that. Where are they anyway?"

"Last time I saw 'em they were at the reception."

"I'm leaving you here, but I'll be back. The show's starting in five minutes. I only hope you survive it!"

"Oh, he'll survive it all right," Paige said, leaning forward. "He'll love every minute of it. He might be ninety-five, but believe me, he's still breathing."

Alex did not care how adept Ling was in the bedroom—it was over, her constant jealous bitching about Lucky had finally taken its toll. When they got back to L.A. he was definitely telling her to move out. He'd sooner be by himself than stuck with a woman who really didn't understand him at all. Ling should be with somebody who enjoyed getting the shit nagged out of him.

Besides, he had his movie to edit, no time for Ling. Being in the editing room seventeen hours a day was relationship enough.

Upstairs in their suite, he conducted a search for his watch. It was a special gold Patek Philippe watch given to him by Lucky at the end of the movie they'd produced together. Lucky had inscribed on the back, *I'll always remember our time together. Lucky.*

It was an ambiguous inscription that could mean anything. He chose to think it meant their one night together long ago. Only realistically he knew it didn't. Because of Lennie. Because Lucky was not a cheater, she was a woman of principle. It was one of the things he loved most about her.

It occurred to him that maybe Ling had hidden the watch somewhere. He wouldn't put it past her—once she'd read the inscription, she'd gotten very uptight, claiming the watch was too flashy for him to wear. Flashy! It was a Patek Philippe, for Christ's sake.

He knew the real reason she hated it. It was a gift from Lucky, and that was enough to set her off.

He was getting more livid by the minute, convinced Ling had stashed it away. Unzipping her suitcase he started rooting around, finding no watch, but coming up with an envelope that he took out and opened. Inside were several Cartier cards, and on each card were written the words *Drop Dead Bitch.* The word *Bitch* looked as if it had been scrawled in blood.

What the hell was *this* all about?

Then he remembered Lucky over lunch in Vegas telling him about the odd notes she'd been receiving.

Jesus *Christ!* Had Ling been sending Lucky hate

mail? He couldn't believe it. What kind of psycho was his live-in girlfriend turning out to be?

This was most definitely a reason to get rid of her permanently.

The woman's body buried out in the desert, wrapped in plastic like a shroud, was dug up and taken back to the city where she was immediately identified by her former husband.

Tasmin Garland. Murder victim.

And Detective Franklin had no doubt who did it.

CHAPTER EIGHTY-SIX

Before Max could run too far, Henry caught up with her, tackling her to the ground, where he pinned her with a steel-like grip on both her arms, his body half over hers.

For a man with a gimpy leg he could sure move fast, and he was surprisingly strong.

"What do you want with me?" she shouted, determined not to give in to this creep again whether he had a gun or not. She was Lucky Santangelo's daughter and she realized she'd better start fighting back. *Girls can do anything*—Lucky had taught her that ever since she could remember. It was time for action.

"Maria," he crooned, his disgusting breath in her face. "Why are you trying to run away from me when surely you have realized by now that we belong together?"

She lay very still on the damp ground. It was patently obvious he was a total whacko, and how best to get herself out of this situation? She had to think fast.

"What's your name?" she managed. "Your real name."

"Lord Grant," he said grandly.

"Lord Grant," she repeated.

"Yes. And I came here today for *you*, to take *you* to a place where people will leave us alone."

"What people?"

"Lucky Santangelo," he said, his voice full of animosity. "That woman is not a fit woman to be your mother, she will do nothing but corrupt you. God has sent *me* to save you, Maria."

How did God get into this? Was this guy a Jesus freak on top of everything else?

"Do you *know* Lucky?" she asked, trying to move out from under him.

"Yes, I know Lucky," he said, spitting venom. "Lucky Santangelo ruined my life. However, out of bad comes good, and now I have you."

She shifted on the ground, thinking that at least she finally knew why he was targeting her. This whacko had some kind of grudge against her mom, and somehow or other she'd been dragged into it.

Where was Ace when she needed him?

Before the lingerie show started, Renee excused herself from Susie and went off to make a phone call. She reached Tucker Bond on the designated number he'd given her to be used only in emergencies.

"I'm calling it off," she said.

"You're doin' *what?*"

"Stopping the action."

There was a long silence. Tucker was used to clients changing their minds, but not at the last moment, not when everything was set up and ready to go.

"Can you do it?" Renee asked.

"I can do anything," Tucker replied. "S'long as I get paid. In full."

"I understand," Renee said. "Our financial arrangement still stands. You'll get your final payment."

"Oh yes, I will."

"Then we're agreed? It's off."

"You're the client."

Emmanuelle was in her element sitting amongst an audience dotted with famous people. They were all waiting to view the lingerie show, and she was proud to be one of them.

Anthony had shoved his way into front-row seats. He was confident they had plenty of time before anything happened. The destruction of the Keys would not take place until after Venus's concert, when everyone was outside for the fireworks display. How fitting that everything Lucky Santangelo had worked so hard for would go up in smoke.

He'd sent his grandmother back to the Cavendish with The Grill to watch over her. She'd claimed she wasn't feeling well, but he wasn't sure he believed her. She was putting it on because she was pissed at him for dragging her away from Gino Santangelo. To make him feel bad she'd begun muttering about heart palpitations.

"Stay with her," he'd instructed The Grill. "If you think she needs it, call a doctor. I'll be back soon."

He hadn't wanted to miss out on humiliating his wife even further. How galling it must be for her having to walk around with him and his sexy mistress. How mortifying and degrading and fuck the cunt! He didn't care. It was over between him and Irma. Tomorrow she'd be history, and if Emmanuelle kept on talking to other men, she'd be history too.

"We're going in the wrong direction," Ace said. "The spa isn't this way."

"I'm sure it is," Cookie argued. "I passed it earlier."

"No!" he said urgently. "It's at the *back* of the hotel. Come on, move it."

"Uh . . . if this freak had a gun last time, don't you think we should maybe like call security?" Cookie ventured, trying to keep up with him.

"Good thinking," he said, realizing she was scared. "You go inside the hotel and alert security, I'll find Max. And hurry up."

* * *

Lucky had no idea who to look for. Gino had said Francesca Bonnatti and her grandson were trouble, but where the hell were they?

Hundreds of people were at the lingerie show. How was she supposed to pick them out?

Her eyes scanned the rows of guests, but she couldn't spot an old woman dressed all in black. On the contrary, everyone seemed to be young and beautiful. Such a glamorous turnout!

She spotted Renee Falcon and Susie.

"Hi," she said, going over to them. "I'm so glad you could make it."

"We wouldn't dream of missing out," Susie said. "Only I'm putting a blindfold on this one during the show."

"*Puleaze!*" Renee said, feeling delightfully relaxed.

For once she'd done the right thing, and it was a good feeling.

Ling was sitting in a front-row seat alongside the cat-walk. Alex made it back just before the lingerie show started.

"What took you so long?" Ling asked as a couple of hovering photographers spotted Alex and to his annoyance began snapping his picture.

"I was catching up on some reading," he said, sliding into his seat. "Interesting stuff, take a look." He dove into his jacket pocket and passed Ling one of the Cartier cards.

Her face remained impassive as she glanced at it. "Have you been going through my things?" she asked in an accusatory tone.

"I was searching for my watch, and look what I came up with," he said. "Care to comment?"

"Going through someone else's belongings is low,"

Ling said, refusing to address the issue of the Cartier card with *Drop Dead Bitch* scrawled on it. "I would never go through your things."

"Have you been sending these cards to Lucky?" Alex demanded. "Have you been *threatening* her?"

"Shush," Ling said, "the show is starting."

And indeed it was, as a parade of models, each one more statuesque and gorgeous than the last one, began stalking down the runway wearing nothing much at all except a plethora of hair extensions, five-inch heels, and "I am so much better than you" disdainful expressions.

"You've got to let me stand up, I promise I won't run," Max said, determined that this time there was no way she was becoming a victim.

"It doesn't make any difference," Henry replied. "Because wherever you run to I will find you. We are destined to be together, Maria, and I will make you very happy and content. I wish you would believe me."

"Yeah, I get it," she said as he moved off her, allowing her to stand up. This creep was definitely psycho city. Nutty as a loon. "So . . . uh . . . the reason you think we should be together is because of my mom—something she did to you—right?"

"Lucky Santangelo took my chance of stardom and handed it to Billy Melina," Henry said, spewing his anger and frustration. "But it doesn't matter now, because God works in a mysterious fashion, and because of what Lucky did to me, it has brought *us* together, and that is a magical and wonderful thing."

"Oh sure, wonderful," she muttered sarcastically, brushing off her clothes. "Especially when you've got to throw me on the ground to tell me this."

"I hope I didn't hurt you," he said with a solicitous expression. "I had no intention of doing so."

"I'm okay," she answered, wondering if it was wise

to make another run for it. Did he have his gun with him? That was the question. He was lunatic enough to shoot her in the back if she tried to escape again, so instead she decided to humor him. "Uh . . . what's your plan this time?" she asked. "We're not going to that gross cabin of yours, are we?"

"My mother recently passed on," he said, not sounding at all upset. "Unfortunate for her. Fortunate for us."

As he spoke, Max spotted Ace stealthily approaching from behind where the freak couldn't see him.

Oh, wow! Ace never disappointed.

Taking a deep breath she kept him talking. "Why is it fortunate for us?" she asked, feigning interest.

"Because I am an extremely affluent man," Henry informed her. "I inherited everything, and now I have more than enough money for us to go anywhere and do anything we wish. Nobody can stop us," he boasted. "Not even Lucky Santangelo. This time *I* am in control."

"That's incredible," she said, her heart pounding as she watched Ace edging closer by the second. "Tell me more."

"Oh, I will. I have so much more to tell you, Maria. I—"

Before he could finish the sentence, Ace pounced, knocking him to the ground.

Henry let out a primal scream of pure fury, rolled over, and sprang to his feet. Whereupon he and Ace became embroiled in a fight while Max raced to get help.

This time she wasn't letting him get away with it.

Oh no, she was a Santangelo—this time she was going to nail his ass.

CHAPTER EIGHTY-SEVEN

Irma sat extremely still, her hands clasped on her lap. She was on one side of Anthony, Emmanuelle on the other.

The Grill was back at the other hotel with Francesca and Anthony was busy ogling the models.

What could he do to her if she got up and walked out? He couldn't cause a scene, the place was too packed. He couldn't stop her. In fact, there was nothing he could do.

Yes, exactly nothing, except have her parents murdered and their home burned to the ground, and after he'd arranged that, come after her with a vengeance.

She was trapped with this despicable man, unless Oliver came through for her. She'd spoken to him briefly, managed to tell him what she'd witnessed regarding Luis, and he'd promised to get in touch with the police in Mexico City to see if they could track anything.

She'd told him where she was and then offered him information in return for her rescue, but before he could reply, the battery on the cell had given out. Then she'd heard Anthony yelling for her outside the ladies' room, and she'd quickly handed the phone back to the woman she'd borrowed it from and hurried outside.

Now she was being forced to watch a lingerie show with her psychotic husband and his tramp mistress.

* * *

The models paraded down the runway, strutting their
goods, twirling and turning in the briefest of teddies and
sexy little numbers, the music blaring. Every man in the
place was mesmerized—every man except Alex, who
couldn't give a rat's ass about a parade of half-naked models. He was more interested in finding out what Ling had in
mind sending Lucky a series of sick notes. How *dare* she.

"Give me your purse," he said, trying to jerk it away
from her. "I want to see how many of these pathetic
notes you've got hidden away."

"No!" Ling responded, making him all the more anxious to take a look. "I will not."

"Oh, yes you will."

"Stop bullying me, Alex."

"When you start telling me what the hell you hoped
to achieve."

As Max raced for help, she ran into Cookie and two
beefy security guards.

"Quick!" she gasped. "Hurry! I think he's got a gun."

"Who's got a gun, miss?" asked one of the security
guards, pulling out his own weapon.

"The freak who tried to kidnap me," she said, starting
to run back in the direction of the spa.

"Kidnap you?" the other guard said disbelievingly.

"This is Lucky Santangelo's daughter," Cookie interjected. "So unless you're all planning on getting fired,
let's move it, guys."

Both guards began to run, and within moments they
arrived outside the spa to find Ace and Henry wrestling
on the ground trading punches.

Security guard number one trained his weapon on
them. "Quit it, *now!*" he commanded, as Ace got in one
last punch, a satisfactory blow to the freak's jaw.

And then it was over.

Henry stood up. "This boy jumped me," he blustered. "The two of them were trying to rob me."

And while he was speaking, Max mustered all her strength and kicked him in the balls.

"That's for everything," she said as he crumpled to the ground. "And my name is Max. M-A-X. Don't ever forget it."

"Enjoy the show," Anthony whispered in Irma's ear. " 'Cause tomorrow I'm sendin' you to a place where the only show's gonna be *you*."

Irma stared at her vile husband. "You're a blood-thirsty monster, you know that?" she said, loathing him with a hatred she had not thought herself capable of. "You took away a man's life for doing something *you* do every day. You're no better than a savage."

"Tomorrow," Anthony taunted as a six-foot blonde in revealing leopard-print lingerie sashayed past on the runway, "I'm sendin' you to a place where you'll get to fuck ten men a day. An' you're gonna get off on it, Irma, 'cause you're a born fuckin' whore."

Before she could process what he was saying, a big commotion started happening with the people sitting on the other side of her—an Asian woman and her male companion.

The scuffle was over the woman's purse, which the man was attempting to wrest from her grasp.

Suddenly a gun fell out of the purse onto the ground.

Without thinking clearly, Irma bent down and quickly picked it up.

She held it for a moment, the image of Luis being tortured flashing before her eyes. Then she turned to Anthony, who started to say, "What the fuck—"

Raw fear flicked across his face as she raised the gun

and pointed it straight at him. He knew what she was about to do before she knew it herself.

Quite calmly she flicked off the safety catch, and shot her husband right between the eyes.

Anthony Bonnatti died within seconds.

At last Irma was truly free.

EPILOGUE
Six Months Later

Detective Franklin got her man. Only he happened to be dead at the time—shot in the face by his distraught wife, whom he'd forced to watch the torture and murder of one of his employees.

Detective Franklin didn't know who'd sent her the bloodstained bathrobe and a map leading to Tasmin Garland's body, although she had her suspicions.

What she *did* know was that it was a good thing. Anthony Bonar was guilty. Dead or alive.

Oliver Stanton almost got his man too. But his man was dead on arrival. By the time he arrived in Las Vegas, Anthony Bonar was lying on a slab in the police morgue.

Unfortunate for Oliver, because he'd finally gotten the one break he'd been hoping for regarding the man he'd been tracking for two long and tedious years.

And now it didn't matter. Now all his hard work was for nothing.

Francesca Bonnatti expired within moments of her grandson being shot. She was lying on her bed in the bungalow at the Cavendish, and she went peacefully with a satisfied smile on her face.

Anthony had been with her since he was twelve. She was not allowing him to go anywhere without her.

* * *

Emmanuelle returned to Miami, but since nothing was in her name, she was forced to relinquish her car and vacate her apartment. Her jewelry she kept—she wasn't giving *that* up.

She called the producer she'd met at the Keys party, and he offered her a job in L.A. Little did she know he was the biggest producer of porn on the West Coast.

Emmanuelle was determined to become a star—one way or the other.

Carlita stayed in New York. She was a savvy businesswoman, and everything Anthony Bonar had invested in her design business was all hers. She gave The Grill a job as her head of security. He was eternally grateful.

Carlita was a woman who knew how to look after herself.

Irma Bonar was arrested and charged with murder. After all the evidence was reviewed and the lawyers got together with the D.A., the charge was eventually reduced to manslaughter. Luis's mutilated body had been discovered buried under the rubble of a building site in Mexico City, along with a security guard from the Bonar estate. The security guard's name was Cesar.

Irma was given three years' probation.

As soon as she was able, she presented the house outside Mexico City to Luis's family as a gift, then she signed over the Acapulco villa to Rosa and Manuel.

Irma knew that both gestures of generosity and kindness would have driven Anthony insane. The thought comforted her.

She put the rest of Anthony's fortune into trusts for her children, and bought herself a house in Omaha, near her parents. She moved there with Carolina and Eduardo, both of whom objected furiously.

She didn't care, she knew they'd soon settle into a normal life. And so would she.

Needless to say, Alex Woods and Ling did not stay together. His fury about the notes she'd been sending to Lucky was palpable. And what the hell had she been doing with his unlicensed gun in her purse? That was not easy to explain.

He'd always known Ling was envious of the strong bond he shared with Lucky, but it was too bizarre to imagine she'd been planning to *shoot* her.

No way. Not even Ling was *that* crazy.

Ling moved out and he was happy about it. No more nagging, no more flowers in his house or a fridge full of food.

Once more he was a free soul, and that's the way he liked it.

Nothing could change the way he felt about Lucky. She was his friend. She would always be his friend.

And while Lennie was around, that's the way it had to stay.

To Renee's surprise, Susie was right, and the Keys opening next door to the Cavendish turned out to be excellent for business. Receipts at the Cavendish were up twenty percent on the year before.

Renee did not mourn Anthony Bonar. He'd got what he'd been asking for. After all, one bad turn deserves another.

Renee vowed to clean up her act and be more like Susie. Good karma was important.

So far it seemed to be working.

Venus married Billy back in L.A. several weeks after the drama at the Keys. They both decided their wedding should not take place on the same night as a violent shooting.

Two days before their wedding, Kev got his marriage annulled. Ali was not exactly a girl to settle down with. Neither Venus nor Billy was surprised.

Billy bought Venus an eight-carat diamond ring, and she bought him a two-hundred-thousand-dollar Ferrari he'd been coveting.

Together they purchased the last available penthouse at the Keys.

Billy got off on being married to Venus—he'd never felt so complete.

Venus loved being married to Billy—he was funny and loving and, most of all, he was hers.

The age difference didn't matter to either of them. Like Lucky and Lennie, they both finally felt they'd found their soulmate.

The tabloids existed in a state of ecstasy. Now that their favorite twosome were married, they could speculate about when the divorce would take place. Or even better—when would Venus get pregnant?

The headlines never stopped.

Gino returned to Palm Springs with Paige. Funny how things worked out. He'd sensed that Anthony Bonar was trouble, but he'd never imagined he'd get shot by his own wife.

The Bonnatti family had never had much luck. Too bad. Or not.

At ninety-five Gino felt fortunate to be a survivor. Getting old was a bitch, but it was better than the alternative.

The Santangelo-Golden family declined to press charges against Henry Whitfield-Simmons. Both Lucky and Lennie decided that Max had endured enough, and they did not want to see her dragged through court testifying against him.

So Henry was released, and he drove back to the Pasadena mansion where he was promptly arrested for the murder of his mother. An autopsy, which he had not realized had taken place, had revealed that Penelope Whitfield-Simmons had been suffocated to death. The prime suspect was Henry. Proving that he'd done it was not difficult.

Max confessed everything to her parents. They weren't mad, they were concerned and relieved.

"Family is everything," Lucky told her. "And even though you didn't tell us the truth, we still love you very very much. But if anything like this *ever* happens again and you don't tell us, that's it, you'll be grounded forever!"

Max loved her mom. Lucky was tough, but she always came through when it mattered.

Ace stayed around. He wasn't mad about the L.A. lifestyle, but as he said to Max, "You need me to watch out for you, so I guess I'm gonna have to spend more time here."

"Cool with me," she'd said, trying not to sound too happy about it.

And finally she got the kiss she'd been hoping for.

Yes. It was worth the wait.

Lucky and Lennie continued their life of married bliss. Even when they were apart, it felt as if they were together.

Lennie went off and made his movie in Canada. Lucky spent several days a week in Vegas overseeing the Keys, which was an enormous success.

She spoke to Bobby almost every day, and he assured her he was keeping in touch with Brigette—in fact, he'd introduced her to one of his friends and they seemed to be getting involved.

The club business was booming.

"I'm opening in L.A.," he warned Lucky. "So you'd better watch out, I'm getting closer every day!"

"I'm shaking!" she joked.

Finally the family house in Malibu was ready to move back into. Lucky and Lennie drove there together.

Lucky Santangelo and Lennie Golden. Two of a kind.

GODDESS
OF
VENGEANCE

*This one is for all my fans and loyal
readers around the world.
On Twitter, Facebook, my Web site—
you all rock!
Keep on reading . . .*

CHAPTER ONE

It was early evening and the garden restaurant was only half full. The patrons were trying to play it cool, because after all, this was L.A. and stars abounded. However, most of them couldn't resist an occasional surreptitious glance over at Venus, the platinum-blond, world-famous superstar, as she picked at a chopped vegetable salad.

Sitting at the table with her was Lucky Santangelo, a dark-haired beauty who'd experienced her own share of controversial headlines and scandals over the years. Lucky, the former owner and head of Panther Studios, was a businesswoman supreme who currently owned the luxurious hotel, casino, and apartment complex The Keys in Las Vegas.

The two of them made a formidable couple. In Hollywood, where looks were everything, Venus and Lucky ruled. Venus with her in-your-face blondness, startling blue eyes, and toned and muscled shape. And Lucky—a dangerously seductive woman with blacker-than-night eyes, deep olive skin, sensuous full lips, a tangle of long jet hair, and a lithe body.

"I'm beginning to think you're a sex addict," Lucky said lightly, smiling at her close friend.

"*Excuse* me," Venus retorted, raising a perfectly arched and penciled eyebrow. "Last week you called me a cougar, and *now* I'm a sex addict. *Seriously,* Lucky?"

Pushing back her mane of unruly black curls, Lucky

grinned. "Yeah. I'm so wrong," she drawled sarcastically. "It wasn't *you* who slept with your twenty-two-year-old costar last week, and it wasn't *you* who screwed your sixty-year-old director two days later."

"Oh *please*," Venus said, dismissively waving her hand in the air. "I'm getting a divorce. What do you expect me to do, join a convent?"

"That might be a touch extreme," Lucky said, smiling as she thought about Venus wreaking havoc in a convent. "But anyway, I'm sure you know what you're doing."

"You bet your fine ass I do," Venus answered vehemently. "Billy is all over the Internet and the magazines with that juvenile skank he's supposedly hooked up with. Just like Cooper before him." She paused for a long thoughtful moment. "Another cheating rat. I sure know how to pick 'em."

"You certainly do," Lucky agreed, thinking that Cooper Turner, Venus's husband before Billy Melina, was a whole different ball game. Cooper was a much older movie star with a Warren Beatty–style track record, and everyone had known that Cooper would eventually cheat. Billy—not so much. Even though Billy was thirteen years younger than Venus, he'd seemed thrilled to be with her. And why not? Like Madonna, Venus was a true original with legions of fans worldwide.

"I cannot believe Billy turned out to be such a loser," Venus said, determined to verbally trash her soon-to-be ex.

"Hardly a loser," Lucky couldn't help pointing out. "His current movie has grossed over a hundred million. Not too shabby."

"Yeah, yeah, rub it in," Venus snapped irritably. "Billy's career is on fire, but I can assure you that as a man he turned out to be a big waste of space." She narrowed her eyes. "And what's up with *you* today? Shouldn't you be agreeing with me, not regaling me with his box office?"

"Hey—don't say I didn't warn you about marrying a much younger man," Lucky responded.

"Billy isn't *that* much younger," Venus insisted. "Anyway, it's sure working for Demi and Ashton. Besides, I thought you liked him."

"I did," Lucky said carefully. "I mean I still do. Only, marrying a younger guy . . . it's kind of a given that they're bound to cheat."

"Oh thanks!" Venus said, frowning. "When did *you* turn into Ms. Cynical and a Half?"

"Not cynical, merely practical."

"Says you," Venus snorted.

"You know I tell it like it is," Lucky said, picking up her wineglass and taking a sip.

"Oh yes, we all know that about you. Nothing's off-limits."

"I believe in the truth."

"And I guess it works for you."

Lucky regarded her brilliant friend, and wondered why any man who was fortunate enough to be with Venus would ever *want* to stray. Venus had it all—beauty, brains, and talent.

"Exactly why *are* you divorcing Billy?" she asked.

"'Cause he—"

"Cheated!" They finished the sentence together, then broke up laughing.

"Well," Venus said sagely, "it was fun while it lasted. Eighteen months together and six months married. Now I'm almost free again, and believe me, it's not such a bad thing. I enjoy being on my own. Living with Billy was like doing time in a frat house. It's such a pleasure that I don't have to pick up dirty socks and underwear from the floor, there are no endless midnight snacks everywhere, *and* I get full control of the remote."

"Surely you always had that."

"Actually, I didn't. You know me—when I wasn't

working, I was busy playing wifey to the hilt, and you can see where it got me."

"Free to fuck your costar, *and* your director," Lucky pointed out. "Not so bad."

Venus gave a wicked smile. "I know. Shame we just finished shooting."

"You should fly to Vegas this weekend," Lucky suggested. "It'll take your mind off all things Billy."

"What's going on in Vegas—apart from your fantastic hotel?"

"A board meeting of all my investors. And since you were one of the first, it would be great if you showed your face. Everyone would really love it. And—even better—I've decided to throw an eighteenth birthday party for Max, although the brat is driving me crazy. She's still carrying on about moving to New York."

"I cannot believe that Max is about to be eighteen. Little Maria, all grown up."

"Tell me about it." Lucky sighed. "Time goes too fast."

"You do realize that now there's no way you can stop her from doing anything she wants?"

"Unfortunately, I understand that," Lucky said, nodding. "And if I know my Max, she'll take full advantage."

"Hey—*you* were married at sixteen," Venus said brightly. "So maybe she'll turn out to be street-smart like you."

"Married *off* you mean, by dear daddy Gino," Lucky said, shaking her head as if she still couldn't quite believe that Gino had forced her into a marriage she didn't want. "Can you imagine that Gino thought he was protecting me from my wild ways? What a joke *that* turned out to be!"

"How come you didn't fight it?"

"I was sixteen," Lucky said, remembering the overwhelming rush of helplessness and dread she'd felt on her wedding day. "I guess I considered myself powerless to say no."

"C'mon, Lucky, it didn't do you any harm," Venus said. "Just look at everything you've accomplished. You've built hotels, run a movie studio, had three kids, *and* you're married to Mister Amazing. Admit it, you're a goddamn superwoman!"

"No," Lucky answered after a thoughtful pause. "I'm a woman who took chances every inch of the way. I had to fight for my independence. Believe me, it wasn't easy."

"Right," Venus said. "And that's exactly why you and I understand each other so well. We both know that being a strong, successful woman in this town can be a lonely and difficult path."

"Agreed," Lucky said. "You gotta kick ass like a guy, *and* get called a bitch for your trouble."

"Ain't *that* the truth," Venus said, nodding vigorously.

"But you know something?" Lucky added. "I know who I am—and I wouldn't have it any other way."

"Me too!"

"I think we should drink to invincible women," Lucky said, raising her glass.

"You got it, sister," Venus murmured.

They clinked glasses and smiled at each other.

"I've been meaning to ask you," Lucky said. "Who's getting the apartment at The Keys, you or Billy?"

"Me, of course," Venus answered firmly. "I've already told my lawyer there's no way I'm giving it up. It's mine. Billy can go piss in the wind to get his hands on *that* piece of real estate."

"Glad to hear it. In this world you gotta claim what's yours."

"Hell, yes. The apartment is in *your* hotel, and you're *my* friend, so screw Billy."

"Right on!" Lucky said, nodding her agreement.

After coffee and more conversation—mostly about what an asshole Billy was—Lucky signaled for the check.

A young waiter who'd been watching them all night edged toward their table and presented it to her. Lucky threw down her black American Express card.

"I guess that means it's your turn," Venus said, removing a small gold compact from her oversized Chanel tote and inspecting her flawless image. She knew there'd be a pack of paparazzi waiting for her exit, and there was nothing they liked better than catching a celebrity looking like crap. She wasn't about to give them that pleasure.

The waiter hovered and cleared his throat. Although he was nervous, he saw an opportunity and he was seizing it—even if it meant getting fired should the manager catch him bothering a guest.

"Excuse me, Miz uh . . . Venus?" he ventured, stammering slightly. "I've, uh, written a script that is *so* right for you. I was, uh, hoping you might find time to read it."

Venus threw him a look—the famous cool-as-an-iced-martini look—her blue eyes raking him over.

Oh no, Lucky thought. *Here we go. The diva is on the loose.*

Venus didn't disappoint. "Do I *look* like an agent?" she purred. "*Really?*"

The waiter blanched, quickly picked up Lucky's credit card and the check, and slunk off.

"Poor guy," Lucky said sympathetically. "He was merely taking a shot."

"Well, let him take a shot elsewhere," Venus said grandly. "I can't stand being harassed when I'm trying to relax."

"Oh my God—you can be such a queen bitch!" Lucky admonished. "Wouldn't want to get on *your* wrong side."

"So be it," Venus said with a wry smile. "Shall we go?"

Seventeen-year-old Max Santangelo Golden could somehow or other wrangle her way into any club she wanted. Fake ID? No problem. Lavish tips to the doormen? No problem. Cultivating a friendship with one of the promoters? No problem.

"When it comes to getting in anywhere, I rule!" Max often boasted.

Her two closest friends, Cookie, the chocolate-skinned daughter of soul icon Gerald M., and Harry, the gay son of a TV network honcho, agreed with her. Ace, her on-again, off-again boyfriend, was not so pleased. The L.A. club scene failed to enthrall him. He wasn't into drinking, drugging, and spotting out-of-control celebrities. But Max loved every minute. Not that she drank much or did drugs, but she did get off on people-watching and dancing on tables. Music was her special thrill—especially rap and unknown British groups with wasted-looking lead singers. Oh yes, she was totally into lean and mean. Ace was way hot and sexy, but sometimes Max considered him too nice a dude, and she often craved a more edgy relationship. Besides, Ace didn't live in L.A., so he wasn't always around when she wanted to do something with him.

"Where're we goin' tonight?" Cookie asked as she sat cross-legged on her messy bed, picking at her green nail polish.

"There's a rave for some old rock group at the House of Blues," Harry said, speaking up. "S'pose we could crash if you're up for it."

Harry was the palest boy known to man, pallid-faced and skinny, with gelled and spiked hair dyed a ruthless black. It was only recently that he'd emerged from the closet, although Max and Cookie had always known and totally accepted that he was gay. He had yet to come out to his controlling father, who would probably disown him.

"No can stand the House of Blues," Max opined, her brilliant green eyes flashing disapproval. "It's always full of major wannabes. Besides, we'll never make it into the Foundation Room."

"Why not?" Cookie inquired, leaning over and reaching for a can of 7-UP balanced precariously on the edge of a table.

"Yeah, why not?" Harry repeated. "Thought you could get in anywhere."

"Anywhere I *want* to," Max answered pointedly, tossing back clouds of wavy black hair. "Who needs the freaking Foundation Room? It's always full of ancient rockers gulping down handfuls of Viagra. *So* not cool."

Cookie let forth a manic giggle. "I bet my dad takes Viagra," she said, swigging 7-UP from the can. "Bet he pops those little blue pills by the dozen."

"All old guys do," Harry said with a knowing smirk. "They can't get it up without 'em."

"Gross-out!" Cookie squealed. "Don't wanna think of my dad with a boner!"

Max decided that sometimes Cookie and Harry could be too much of a good thing. The three of them had grown up together, attended the same school, and shared some interesting, sometimes frightening, experiences, but in a way she felt she'd outgrown them. As soon as she was eighteen, she planned on making a break for New York and freedom. Not that her parents weren't great, but the two of them were a lot to live up to. Lucky, who'd achieved absolutely everything she'd ever wanted. And Lennie, a multitalented writer/director who helmed all his own independent movies. Max was tired of being referred to as their daughter. Fed up with the pressure it put on her to do something spectacular with her life.

Her big brother, Bobby, was her role model. Bobby had escaped and made his own way. He was definitely her inspiration—she adored him. Although now he had a permanent girlfriend, Denver Jones, and as much as she reluctantly admired Denver, a Deputy DA, she missed having Bobby all to herself when he was in L.A.

"Got it," Max said at last. "Whyn't we hit the Chateau for dinner? There's always something going on there."

"'S long as I don't bump into my old man," Cookie said, wrinkling her nose. "He's got himself another dumbass girlfriend, an' I think she stays at the Chateau when she's in town."

"What's the deal with this one?" Max asked.

"English, complete with uptight accent and a bug up her ever-so-tight British ass," Cookie said, making a disgusted face. "She thinks she's like the second coming of Keira Knightley. As *if.*"

"Your old man sure covers the waterfront," Harry remarked, pulling up the collar of his long, Goth-like coat.

"Tell me about it," Cookie said with a weary sigh. "I've had more almost-stepmoms than you've had filthy thoughts about Chace Crawford!"

"Okay, okay," Max said, interrupting them. She was into making fast decisions, not screwing around and vacillating about what to do. "We could check out a new club that opened a couple of weeks ago. River. I'm sure we can get in."

"Let's do it," Cookie said, fiddling with the chocolate-brown dreadlocks that framed her exceptionally pretty face.

"D'you think Chace Crawford'll be there?" Harry asked hopefully.

Max threw him a look. "Calm down," she said. "Surely you know Chace Crawford is *so* into girls."

"That's what they all say," Harry muttered. "But I know better."

"Lucky has invited us to Vegas next weekend," Bobby Santangelo Stanislopoulos said, stretching his six-foot-three frame on Denver Jones's shabby-chic couch. "She's planning a party for my sister Max's eighteenth birthday, one of her big family events."

Denver regarded her boyfriend of several months with slight trepidation. Oh, man, the longish black hair, dark eyes, Greek nose, and strong jawline got her every time. If only he weren't so damn handsome. If only she hadn't harbored a crush on him since high school. If only he weren't such a fantastic lover, with all the right moves.

"Your mom intimidates me," she said at last, stroking the belly of her dog, Amy Winehouse, who lay on her back making happy sounds. Amy was a mixed breed that Denver and her ex, Josh, had found wandering on Venice Beach. They'd named the dog Amy Winehouse because of her low, throaty growl. Plus, the fabulous Miz Winehouse was one of Denver's favorite singers.

Bobby laughed. He had a fantastic laugh. Naturally. "C'*mon*," he chided. "I'm sure Lucky thinks you're the greatest thing that ever happened to me."

Denver raised an eyebrow. " 'Thing'?" she said coolly.

"Y'know what I mean."

"The problem is," Denver said, desperately searching for a suitable excuse, "I'm moving over to the drug unit next week, so there's a ton of stuff I feel I should research."

"You'll bring your laptop; that way you can do all the research you want. It's a forty-eight-hour trip, sweetheart. I'm calling for the plane."

She hated it when Bobby said things like "I'm calling for the plane." It was so elitist, so exactly who she wasn't. Some girls might get off on all the luxury, but private planes, lavish parties, and hanging with Bobby's illustrious family was not for her. Plus, she wasn't that fond of Vegas, and she hadn't told Bobby, but she hated spending time at his ultra-happening club, Mood. She especially hated the way women fawned all over him and flirted outrageously, ignoring her as if she didn't even exist.

The truth was, she loved Bobby. But she didn't love the trappings that came with him.

Bobby stretched again and yawned. "Whaddya say?"

"I say I'll think about it."

"Sounds good," he said, reaching up to pull her down on the couch beside him.

She acquiesced. It was early evening and they had no plans, so what was wrong with relaxing for the moment?

They'd been seeing each other on and off for the past three months. The on was when Bobby was in L.A. The off was when he had to spend time at his two clubs: Mood in Vegas, and Mood in New York. The on was the best of times. The off was missing him and wondering what he was doing, and trying to have some decent phone sex, which left them both in a hysterical state of laughter.

Neither of them had uttered the L word. Although they *had* conducted the talk about being exclusive.

Both of them were wary about getting too involved. Secretly they couldn't wait. But playing it semicool seemed to be the name of the game they were currently into.

Bobby began stroking her hair. Denver felt good about her hair; it was long and thick, chestnut brown with natural golden highlights. She knew that her hair was one of her best features, along with her widely spaced hazel eyes and full lips. If she lived in any other big city, she'd be considered a ten. In L.A. she felt she barely made it as a seven.

She was wrong.

Bobby's hands moved down to her breasts, and with a quick move under her T-shirt, he released her bra and began playing with her nipples. Oh yes, unusual for a woman in L.A., her breasts were actually real.

Sighing with anticipation, she leaned into him. It made no difference that they'd already made love in the morning. Desire was desire, and they were both in the mood.

Sometimes she couldn't help wondering how long it would last. Her previous serious boyfriend, Josh, had been a pretty decent lover for the first six months of their three-year relationship, then after that it was a total slump.

"What're you thinking?" Bobby whispered in her ear, giving her a little tongue action at the same time.

"That's such a girly question," she murmured, fiddling with the zipper on his jeans.

"You calling me a girl?" he asked, mock serious.

"You do have *some* female tendencies," she teased.

"Like *what?*" he responded, challenging her to come up with something.

"Oh," she said vaguely, dragging his jeans down, delighted to find that he wasn't wearing underwear. "You have soft lips . . ."

"All the better to kiss you with." And with one swift movement, he flipped her so she was trapped beneath him. "Soft lips and a hard cock," he joked. "How female is *that?*"

"Bobby!" she exclaimed.

Then the banter stopped and the passion began. He had a way of making love to her that forced her to lose every inhibition she'd ever possessed. One moment he was slowly caressing her, the next he was all hard-driving action. The combination drove her nuts. She wanted more and more and more . . .

When it was over, they were spent, wrapped up in each other's arms, sleepy and content.

Denver often wished that those precious times would last forever. Just the two of them. No outside world to interfere.

But the outside world was a big presence, and they both lived in it. Tomorrow Bobby was driving to Vegas before flying to New York for a few meetings. And she had her job, which right now was especially exciting and challenging since she was transferring to the drug unit. Once more they would be separated.

The good news was that she loved her job. It was grueling work, but the end results were incredibly rewarding. She was so glad she'd changed tracks. From working at a high-powered law firm as a defense attorney, she'd scored a job as a Deputy DA, prosecuting people, and she was thrilled with the switch. Why defend the probably guilty (one of her high-profile cases was a movie star who'd arranged his wife's murder, then walked; he was the catalyst for her change of plan) when she could be doing meaningful work—such as putting the bad guys behind bars? How rewarding to go after the dregs who distributed drugs and got kids hooked at an early age. Talk about job satisfaction!

"Hey," Bobby said, "wanna catch a movie and grab a pizza?"

Yes, that's exactly what she wanted to do. Normal activities with her man.

If only things could stay that way.

CHAPTER TWO

Prince Armand Mohamed Jordan rarely used his full title, only when he visited the country of his birth, Akramshar, a small but wealthy Middle Eastern country located somewhere between Syria and Lebanon.

As a naturalized American, and a mega-successful businessman, he felt it more prudent to keep his title to himself, deciding it wasn't business-savvy to advertise his heritage.

Most of the people he dealt with knew him only as Armand Jordan, a sometimes ruthless and extremely powerful man who expected everything to go his way and usually got his wish. None of his business associates was aware that his father was King Emir Amin Mohamed Jordan, a man who ruled his small oil-rich country with a stern fist. A man with six current wives and sixteen children.

Armand was suspicious of friendship. The only person he trusted was Fouad Khan, the right-hand man whom he'd imported from Akramshar many years previously. Fouad knew all of Armand's secrets and kept them to himself. He was Armand's sounding board and confidant, always there to do his bidding.

Fortunately or unfortunately for Armand, he was the king's ninth son, and therefore considered not at all important. So when his American mother—Peggy, a former Las Vegas dancer—had begged to take her son back to America when he was eight, the king had offered no objections. King Emir was bored with the leggy American redhead and her strident accent. Happy to see her go. And much as Peggy had enjoyed the adventure of living in a harem and being lavished with expensive gifts, enough was enough, and she knew it was time to return to civilization. At twenty-six, she had the rest of her life ahead of her, and she planned to live it. The king's only request was that the boy be returned every September to Akramshar so that young Armand could celebrate the king's birthday—the most important day of the year in Akramshar.

Peggy complied. The cash payoff she received was compensation enough for her to do anything the king required.

So Peggy and her son relocated to New York, and Armand soon adapted to the American way of life. It didn't take him long to love everything about America. The endless TV shows full of fun and adventure, the violent action-packed movies, the loud, vibrant music, and the girls. Ah yes, especially the girls; they were far more forward than the girls in Akramshar.

Every September his mother dutifully put him on a plane back to Akramshar, and for several weeks he played the role of a young prince, mingling with the half brothers and sisters he barely knew anymore. They failed to get along.

The juxtaposition of his two lives was exciting. It made him feel special, different from the other kids who attended his private school in Manhattan. He was a prince, and they were nothing. He felt superior to all of them.

When he was thirteen, on one of his yearly visits to Akramshar, his father had taken him aside and informed him it was time he became a man. Immediately, one of the king's minions had ushered him into a room where two prostitutes lounged on a bed waiting for the young prince.

The following experience with the two older women left an indelible impression on Armand. Although he'd fooled around with girls at school, this encounter was quite different. The prostitutes—one Russian, one Dutch—were in their twenties and heavily made up. They wore sexy lingerie and high-heeled shoes, and they introduced him to a variety of sexual acts, some of which he enjoyed, some of which disgusted him. When they felt he was fully initiated, they informed him that all sexual acts should be paid for. Not that they were asking him for money—the king's people had already taken care of them—it was simply something they thought he should be aware of. "Women have to be paid for sex," they said, exchanging amused glances. They were words of wisdom he never forgot.

When he emerged several hours later, his older brothers jeered and laughed at him. He'd ended up fighting one of them, and had gotten a broken nose for his trouble. He hated his siblings. They were all jealous of him because he was different.

His mother remarried a month after his eighteenth birthday. This time Peggy chose wisely: she married Sidney Dunn, a very successful investment banker twenty-five years her senior.

Armand respected Sidney. He felt he could learn a lot from the old man, and learn he did. He chose to get a business degree, and Sidney was always there with his wise counsel.

On Armand's twenty-first birthday, the king summoned him to Akramshar for a special visit. Armand went—reluctantly, for surely once a year was enough. However, it turned out to be a memorable trip, because the king's closest adviser informed Armand that in the future the king might—from time to time—need him to take care of various business transactions in America.

Armand, eager to please his father, agreed. And as a twenty-first birthday gift, the king presented him with a check for a million dollars, money he immediately put to good use. On Sidney's advice, he invested in a parcel of derelict buildings in Queens, which a year later he turned into several apartment complexes, eventually selling them and tripling his initial investment.

After that there was no stopping him. He formed Jordan Developments and began buying up properties, renovating them, and selling them for a large profit. He was also taking care of business for his father, who needed large sums of money legitimized. Apart from Jordan Developments, he formed several subsidiary companies, including an import/export business that he had nothing to do with except in name. By the time he reached the age of thirty, he was acquiring hotels and apartment houses up and down the East Coast.

On his yearly visit to Akramshar, his father looked on him kindly and beamed with pride. "You are the son I can be proud of," the king boasted. "You are smart, and clever, and trustworthy. You are the son who one day should be inheriting my kingdom."

These words did not sit well with his half brothers, who now regarded him with suspicion and, even more, hatred.

But one thing puzzled the king. "Why have you never married?" he demanded. "At your age it is tradition that a man should have many wives and children."

Armand shrugged. To him, a relationship was a distraction he didn't need. His sexual desires were fully met by a series of call girls who serviced his every whim whenever he picked up the phone and summoned them. Women were inferior human beings, something his father had taught him at a very early age. "Females are merely vessels to be used for gratifying one's sexual urges and bearing children," the king had informed him. "Never trust them. And never give them your heart."

His father was right. Women would do anything for money—absolutely anything. And they were stupid creatures too.

A year after his father questioned his marital status, he'd arrived in Akramshar for the usual birthday celebrations, and the king had immediately whisked him off to one of his private palaces. Once there, the king had announced that Armand's birthday gift to him would be to marry the daughter of a close family friend with whom the king conducted business. "You'll have no responsibilities," the king had assured him. "Your wife will stay here and, God willing, bear your offspring. This is my desire for you, my dear son. This is my gift."

The girl was fifteen and a beauty. Her name was Soraya.

Later that day there was a lavish wedding ceremony, and that night Armand deflowered the innocent Soraya. She was trembling and scared, which didn't faze him because he had no intention of going against his father's wishes. Her nervousness was not his problem. She was there to do his bidding, and that was that. He rode her hard, ignoring her startled cries of pain. She was merely a vessel for him to fill, and that was the extent of her usefulness.

A week after his wedding ceremony he flew back to America.

Upon returning to Akramshar one year later, he was surprised to discover that he had a son. Eleven years later he had fathered three more children, all girls, which didn't particularly please him, but it made the king happy.

In his mind he regarded Soraya and her brood as his

fantasy family. They lived in a place called Akramshar. A place where women were docile and obedient and did as they were told. A place where men ruled.

He lived in a Park Avenue penthouse in New York, where money was his aphrodisiac and women were his paid playthings. The two worlds only came together in September, when the king celebrated his birthday. And that was as it should be.

Now Armand was forty-two and becoming restless. He'd conquered the East Coast, and he desired more. His latest plans were to cement a firm position in Las Vegas, a city he'd spent some time in. He was an avid gambler, and the call girls in Vegas were raunchy and used to fulfilling any request, however decadent. Besides, he had family ties in Vegas. His mother had danced at Caesars Palace, and the king had spotted her there and whisked her back to Akramshar. Family ties had to mean something.

His people had done a financial analysis of most of the big hotels. While Steve Wynn's empire was intriguing and lucrative, and the Palms, the Four Seasons, and the Harrah's hotel groups were a possibility, the hotel complex he'd finally decided he had to have was The Keys.

Yes, The Keys was perfect. A magnificent structure built to extremely high standards less than two years previously. Not Vegas flashy, but incredibly luxurious and classy. A stunning casino. World-class restaurants and stores. Exquisite gardens, and park-like grounds. A magnificent apartment complex. Multiple swimming pools. Two spas. A man-made lake. A lush golf course. And then there was the hotel itself.

The Keys was it for Armand.

He wanted it, and therefore he would have it.

CHAPTER THREE

By the time she drove her distinctive red Ferrari down Pico and along P.C.H. to Malibu, Lucky had forgotten about Venus and her man-related issues. Her mind was more focused on Max and her imminent departure. Lucky was wise enough to realize that there was no holding her smart, gorgeous, green-eyed daughter back. Max was going out on her own whether Lucky and Lennie liked it or not. And the truth was, Lucky didn't like it, but there was nothing she could do. As everyone was quick to point out, she herself had been running wild at sixteen. After she ditched her strict Swiss boarding school and took off to the South of France, Gino had tracked her down and hurriedly married her off to the irritating and boring Craven Richmond—Senator Peter Richmond's son. Craven was a weak loser whom she hadn't loved, and even worse, had no respect for. But she'd refused to be trapped. She'd bided her time, and when Gino left the country on a tax exile, she'd broken all ties with the Richmond family and swiftly moved in to take over Gino's lucrative hotel business. She'd succeeded, gotten a divorce, and never looked back.

Now Max was ready to fly, but did her only daughter possess the street smarts to survive all the sharks who'd be circling such a major catch? And if Max chose to move to New York, how was Lucky supposed to protect her?

"You're not," Lennie had informed her, always the

voice of reason. "You gotta let Max go. She's ready to make her own mistakes and learn from them."

Even Gino agreed. "Let her loose, kid," he'd said. "She'll find her feet just like you did."

So be it.

Even though it was past midnight, Max was not home.

Determined not to worry, Lucky picked up the phone and called Lennie, who was on location in Utah. They talked for a while; he soothed her fears about Max, told her not to obsess and that he'd see her in Vegas for the birthday party.

Lucky decided that for once she'd listen.

One big Vegas party, coming up. And after that she'd send Max on her way with her blessing and hope that everything worked out.

"Frankie?" Max yelled, making a wild dash toward the guy emerging from a Grand Sport convertible Corvette. "Is it really you?"

Frankie Romano stopped mid-stride, slowly lowering his mirrored Ray-Bans—an unnecessary accessory because it was dark out. The shades were merely an affectation.

"Jesus!" he exclaimed, after scrutinizing her up and down. "Little Max?"

"Not so little anymore," she answered boldly, remembering the last time she'd seen her brother's friend, the irascible Frankie Romano. He was thinner than she remembered, but his outfit was cool—all leather, retro shades covering his eyes, his dark hair pulled back into a tight ponytail. Very L.A.

She gestured toward the entrance of the new club, where a restless gathering of girls dressed to seduce and a rowdy bunch of guys hoping to get laid attempted to talk their way past three burly security doormen. "Can you get me and my friends in?" she asked, throwing Frankie a winning smile.

"Hey," Frankie said, with a nod of his head, "if I can't, nobody can. Follow me."

Max grabbed Cookie's and Harry's arms, and without hesitation, they marched in behind Frankie.

The doorman gave Frankie a respectful salute.

"Wow!" Max exclaimed, suitably impressed. "They're acting as if you own the place or something."

"I do," Frankie boasted, although not truthfully. "It's mine, all mine."

Max widened her eyes. The last she'd heard of Frankie, he'd been dumped by Annabelle Maestro, his longtime girlfriend, and was looking for a job. Now he claimed to own this happening new L.A. club. She wondered if Bobby was aware of it, because as far as she could recall, the two of them had fallen out due to Frankie's over-the-top drug habit. Too bad. She'd always sort of liked Frankie in a weird way, even though he'd tried to letch after her when she was sixteen and staying with Bobby in New York.

"Does Bobby know you're in the club business?" she asked as Frankie guided them straight to a booth.

"You think Bobby has dibs on running clubs?" Frankie responded, his left eye twitching beneath his shades. "I was deejaying before he ever got into the whole club scene. I would've given him a chance to invest in River, but we've been out of touch. His loss."

"Guess he missed out," Max said vaguely, checking out the club, which resembled a poor rip-off of Mood.

"Since your brother hooked up with that lawyer bitch, you gotta know he's totally pussy-whipped," Frankie said gruffly. "She's got his balls in a clench. Came between us big time."

"I thought it was—"

"What?" Frankie said, shooting her a sharp look.

"Nothing," she mumbled, biting down on her bottom lip. Bobby had told her that Frankie's addiction to coke was not something he could deal with anymore, especially since Denver was a Deputy DA.

"So . . . little Max, all grown up," Frankie said, moving close, his thigh pressing up against her leg. "Haven't seen you in a while. How've you been?"

"Amazing," Max replied, edging away because the last thing she needed was Frankie coming on to her.

"You're looking hot," he continued. "Smokin' hot."

"Thanks," she said, feeling uncomfortable. Was he stoned? Probably.

"Wow!" Cookie exclaimed. "This place is totally bangin'."

Frankie turned his attention to her. "You like?" he said. "I designed the place myself." Another lie.

"We like," Cookie answered, nudging Harry while wondering how old Frankie was, and if he was too old for her. "Can we score a drink?"

"You got it," Frankie said, snapping his fingers, grabbing the attention of a half-naked waitress with long talonlike nails and a fixed smile. "You all have your fake ID's on you, I hope."

"Wouldn't be without them," Cookie replied, licking her generous lips and fluttering her purple-tipped eyelashes.

"That's what I like to hear," Frankie said, thinking that this one might be young, but she was certainly ready.

And what the hell? Young was his flavor of the night.

Pizza and a movie turned out to be sushi at Matsuhisa, a favorite of Denver's.

"I love this restaurant," she said, helping herself to a California roll.

"Why do you think I chose it?" Bobby said, reaching for her hand across the table.

"'Cause you wanted to surprise me?"

"Ah, but she's so smart," he said, dazzling her with one of his special smiles.

"And she's dressed for pizza and a movie," Denver said ruefully.

"*And* she looks gorgeous," he assured her.

"Thanks, Bobby," she said, taking a sip of warm sake.

"For what?"

"For always making me feel good."

"That's easy."

"It is?"

"You *know* it is."

"Don't *you* always know the right thing to say."

"Speaking of the right thing—you *are* coming to Vegas with me next weekend for Max's party, yes?"

"I . . . I'm going to try," she said, still hesitant.

"Whaddya mean, try?"

"Well . . . y'know, work . . ."

"I told you," he said insistently, "we'll go Friday, come back Sunday. You won't miss a thing."

"You have to understand, Bobby, transferring to the drug unit is kind of a big deal. I want to be fully prepared."

"Like I said, you'll bring your laptop. We'll have plenty of downtime."

"Can I think about it?" she asked tentatively.

"She'll think about it," he said, exasperated. "Have I ever told you you're one stubborn woman?"

"Simply because I don't say yes to you all the time . . ."

"No, you don't, do you?" he said, giving her a long, intent look. "Is that why I like you?"

"Hmm," she said thoughtfully. "I guess you're used to women saying yes at all times."

Bobby started to laugh. "What *women* did you have in mind?"

"Remember high school? You and M.J. had it all going on. Girls falling out of trees."

"Oh c'mon, Denver," he said with a quizzical expression. "Now we're reverting to high school? How come you're remembering that now?"

"'Cause watching Mister Football Star score was the main entertainment of the day."

"Then aren't I glad it's all behind me, an' now I've got you."

"Really?" she teased. "You've got me, have you?"

"Don't I?" he said, grinning. "We've been together *how* long?"

"I dunno," she said, knowing exactly how long. "Three months, maybe."

Bobby shook his head. "'Maybe,' she says! You're supposed to tell me to the minute."

"I am, huh?"

"Yes, you am."

They smiled at each other, savoring the moment.

One of the reasons she enjoyed spending time with Bobby was because they always had so much to talk about. He often regaled her with stories about his deceased father's family, who all resided in Greece, apart from his niece, Brigette. Brigette lived in New York and had once been a top model. Along with Bobby, Brigette had inherited most of the Stanislopoulos fortune. Although he was uncomfortable talking about money, Bobby had informed her that he'd chosen not to touch his inheritance, preferring to make his own money from the success of his clubs.

She admired him for his desire to make it on his own. Only occasionally did he indulge in any kind of extravagance—such as using the Stanislopoulos plane.

Sometimes she told him stories about *her* family, a

family he still hadn't met. She was reticent about introducing him to her political activist mother and maverick lawyer father. Not to mention her three brothers. They'd all been very fond of her ex, Josh, and she didn't think she should add Bobby into the mix until she was sure they'd stay together for longer than a few months.

Bobby laughed about it. "Not good enough to meet your family, huh?" he teased.

"You will," she assured him.

And yes, one day she would definitely bring him to meet them. But not yet. It was too soon.

"Bobby!" an exceptionally pretty model type exclaimed, stopping by their table. "Oh my *God!* I haven't seen you since Graydon's party in New York. How *are* you? What are you doing in L.A.?"

"Uh . . . hey," Bobby managed. He didn't have a clue who she was, and he didn't much care. "Do you two know each other?" he said, gesturing toward Denver.

The girl threw Denver a cursory glance, then proceeded to ignore her. "We must get together," she purred, leaning toward Bobby. "I miss you. Call me, I'm at the Mondrian."

Then she tottered off on her six-inch heels, looking pleased with herself.

"Nice," Denver remarked.

"I swear I don't know who she is," Bobby insisted.

"That's okay," Denver said, determined not to throw a jealous fit over nothing. "I have exes too."

"She's not an ex," he said firmly. "No idea w*ho* she is."

"It doesn't matter, Bobby."

"No, it doesn't," he agreed. "All that matters is that I'm sitting here with you."

The thing about Bobby Santangelo Stanislopoulos was that he always knew the right thing to say.

* * *

Max was ready to go, and so was Harry, but Cookie was putting up a fight. "I wanna stay," she said stubbornly. "Frankie'll look out for me."

"You can't stay," Max argued. "We're in Harry's car."

"I'll get a ride," Cookie said.

"Oh, like who you gonna get a ride from?" Max snapped.

Cookie shrugged. "I'm sure Frankie'll drive me home."

"For shit's sake!" Max exclaimed. "Don't you know that all Frankie wants is to get into your pants?"

"So?" answered Cookie with a slightly tipsy smile. "Is that such a bad thing?"

They were arguing in the booth several mojitos later. Frankie was off meeting and greeting, playing the genial host, and Max wasn't feeling it. She wanted out. So did Harry.

"We can't leave you here by yourself," Max said, looking to Harry for some support.

"I told you, Frankie'll look after me," Cookie said, leaning back in the booth.

"Frankie's a cokehead, an' he's old," Harry sneered. "You don't wanna hit that."

"He's *so* not old, an' he's hot," Cookie insisted. "You two better get the fuck outta here, 'cause *I'm* stayin'."

Max decided not to argue. She knew what Frankie was like, and if Cookie was intent on taking that road, there was nothing she could do about it. Cookie was hardly a virgin; she'd been around Hollywood all her young life.

"Whatever you do, don't screw him," Max warned. "He's not someone you wanna hang with. Believe me, I *know*."

"Thanks for the advice," Cookie responded sarcastically. "I'll call you guys later."

"You do that," Max said, checking her watch. It was

already two A.M. "An' don't do anything you'll regret," she added.

"Good-bye." Cookie giggled. "Shift your asses outta here."

Max grabbed Harry's arm. "You cool to drive?" He nodded. "Then let's go."

Sometimes one had to quit on an argument one wasn't about to win, something her dad, Lennie, had taught her when she was five.

She'd learned a lot from both her parents, and there were times she appreciated their wisdom. But still, she couldn't wait to get out on her own.

CHAPTER FOUR

Freedom suited Billy Melina just fine. Being married to a superstar was a major kick for about fifteen minutes, but after a few months of everyone worshipping at her feet, the thrill was gone. *He* was a huge movie star, but when he was out with Venus, nobody gave a crap. This was not a big ego booster. Oh no, not at all.

When Billy wasn't with Venus, the attention came fast and furious. Girls galore. Fans everywhere. Respect from agents, managers, and lawyers who realized his potential. After all, he had only just hit thirty; his entire career lay ahead of him, and his latest release was already breaking box office records.

Billy was over six feet tall, with bleached-by-the-sun hair and a surfer's tan all over his ripped and taut body. Abs were his thing. He worked out two hours a day to make sure they were rippling perfection. He liked seeing himself in the magazines under the heading BEST BODY ON THE BEACH. Eat your heart out, Matthew McConaughey. Go crap yourself, The Situation. Billy Melina was King of the Abs. And with his upcoming divorce from the Queen of the Divas, he—along with his soon-to-be ex—was currently on the cover of every magazine.

Covers were satisfying. Covers validated his existence. Covers gave him a positive vibe.

So did blow jobs. There was nothing like a polished blow job to put a smile on his face. Lately, now that he was free, his big kick was picking up some random girl, taking her back to his rented house, and having her blow him out by the pool. There was something about strange lips enclosing his cock, with the shimmering blue of the swimming pool in the background and the sun beating down on his body, that really got him off.

Venus was under the impression that he'd hooked up with his recent costar Willow Price—a bodacious young blonde with pillowy lips and a burgeoning career. But that was not the case. Willow was good to be seen with at parties and award shows, but they were in no way involved. Willow preferred her sex served lesbian-style, and he was not attracted to her, so being seen together suited them both.

Feeling horny, Billy hopped on his Harley and set off on a hunt.

It didn't take him long to find exactly what he was looking for. The girl he spotted was walking along Melrose wearing a denim skirt that barely covered c-level, a skimpy tee with *I Like It Fast and Sweet* emblazoned across the front, and wedge-heeled sandals.

"Yo," he greeted her, pulling up alongside her on his bike. "Didn't I see you last night at Soho House?"

She stopped, checked him out, recognized him, and couldn't believe her luck. Twenty minutes later she was in front of him, on her knees beside his pool, servicing him as best she could.

When it was done, he called her a cab and sent her on her way.

Billy never had any trouble finding girls.

Breakfast in Malibu was Lucky's favorite time of day. She loved to sit out on the deck overlooking the ocean with a glass of fresh orange juice and a dish of cut-up papayas, figs, and mangos. Since she was an early riser, always up before the rest of her family, she took advan-

tage of the solitude. Early morning was her time for
making plans, deciding what she wanted to do next.
Right now everything about The Keys satisfied her.
Even Gino was impressed with what she had managed
to achieve. She'd built the ultimate prize, the most magnificent complex in Vegas, encompassing everything
from a major casino to a one-of-a-kind hotel and luxury condominiums. "Put in a racetrack an' you're all
set," Gino had joked.

She'd smiled. Not such a bad idea. But then Gino always thought big.

She decided that her next project would be persuad-
ing Lennie to take a well-deserved break. He was such
a workaholic, skipping from one movie to the next. They
had a fantastic marriage, but spending more time together would not be a bad thing. There were days and
nights she really missed him.

Her cell rang. It was her New York attorney, Jeffrey
Lonsdale.

"Yes, Jeffrey, what's up?" she asked, wondering why
he was calling her so early.

"Have you been putting out the word that you want
to sell The Keys?" Jeffrey inquired.

"*What?*" she said, frowning. "Why would you say
that?"

"Because I keep getting calls from a man representing Jordan Developments. He claims you're prepared to sell, and that Jordan Developments is ready
to buy."

"That's total bullshit," Lucky said. "And who the hell
is Jordan Developments?"

"A big real estate company. I'm looking into it. Just
needed to make sure."

"Jeffrey," Lucky said patiently, "surely you know
that if I were prepared to sell, you would be the first to
know."

"Of course. But Fouad Khan, the Jordan Developments representative, seemed very sure and very persistent."

"Well, tell Mr. Khan to go persist elsewhere. The Keys is not for sale. Not now or ever."

"Message received loud and clear."

"Glad to hear it."

"I must say, Lucky, I thought it had to be a joke. Everyone knows you put your heart and soul into building that complex, so I was certain there was no chance you'd be putting it on the market."

"You got that right."

"I'm glad we've cleared that up."

"We have."

"Then enjoy your day."

"You too, Jeffrey."

"Unfortunately, it's raining in New York."

"Sorry to tell you, but it's brilliant sunshine here," she said, gazing out at the vast expanse of blue ocean.

"Ah, Lucky, you always know how to stick it to me."

"You're the lawyer," she said, smiling. "You should be used to people sticking it to you."

"Trust *you* to point that out."

"You're flying to Vegas for the board meeting on Friday, you'll get plenty of sunshine then."

"In a boardroom?" Jeffrey said dryly.

"Stay the weekend," Lucky suggested. "I'm throwing a birthday party for Max. It'll be fun."

"Maybe."

"Not maybe, Jeffrey. Say yes. Bring your wife."

"We're getting a divorce."

"Then bring your girlfriend."

"I don't have one."

"Okay, okay, enough about your love life. But if you do decide to stay over, let my assistant know. He'll take excellent care of you."

She clicked off the phone, thinking what a crazy way to start the day.

The Keys was her ultimate achievement. She would never sell. Never.

Bobby got up early and left the apartment before Denver was awake. He had an important meeting in Vegas with Russian investors who, according to his partner, M.J., were ready to close on a deal to put up all the money for branches of Mood in Miami and L.A. He'd decided to personally show them the star that was Mood, Las Vegas. The Russians were not easy to deal with, but they were the ones with the money to do things the way he wanted. After finishing with the Russians, he had more meetings in New York, then after that he'd hop a plane and be back in time to pick up Denver and take her for a romantic Vegas weekend.

He was getting in way deep with Denver. The more time he spent with her, the better he liked her. She was so damn normal, and smarter than any girl he'd been with. *And* she was beautiful—inside and out. There was an incandescent quality about her that he couldn't get enough of.

He wanted her to spend more time with Lucky, so that the two of them could get to know each other. It was important to him that his mom approve of the girl he was becoming serious about. Not that he'd told Lucky anything; it was up to her to discover how great Denver was, and the birthday party weekend would be the perfect time.

The next step he planned was buying a house in L.A. where they could live together. Denver's apartment was too small for him. He needed more space. He'd brought the subject up a couple of times, whereupon she'd informed him that it was too soon to think of living together.

"But sweetheart, I live here when I'm in L.A.," he'd pointed out.

"No, you *stay* here," she'd corrected. "That's not the same as living together."

Man, she could be difficult. Most girls would go nuts if he offered to buy a house for them. But part of Denver's charm was that she was not most girls, and that was another thing he loved about her.

Flooring his new silver Lamborghini Murciélago LP 640, he blasted Jay-Z and headed for Vegas.

"I fail to understand your problem," Denver's best friend, Carolyn, said, rocking the stroller next to her in the garden of her small West Hollywood house, situated behind Pavilions supermarket on a quiet street. "Bobby is a fantastic guy, and it's blatantly obvious he's wild about you."

"You think?" Denver said, sipping from a mug of coffee.

"I *know*," Carolyn responded, pushing back a lock of honey-blond hair. "He's great, and he's been so nice to me."

"Why wouldn't he be?" Denver said, placing her coffee mug on a rickety outdoor table. "Let's not forget you were caught in a terrifying situation. Kidnapped, taken hostage, and pregnant . . ."

"Then along came you and Bobby like the cavalry— rescuing my sorry ass," Carolyn said, making light of what had been a very perilous situation.

"Couldn't have done it without Bobby," Denver said. "He was a big help."

"Without the two of you . . ." Carolyn trailed off, trying not to think about the ordeal she'd survived. Working in Washington as an assistant to the very married Senator Gregory Stoneman, she'd become involved in a torrid affair with him. Just like most married men, the senator had promised to leave his wife, but of course he'd had no intention of doing so. And when Carolyn had informed him that she was pregnant, he'd panicked, and set up her kidnapping in the hope that she would lose the baby. Thank God for Denver and Bobby; they'd found her just in time.

After spending a few days in a hospital recovering, she'd fled Washington to L.A. She gave birth to her baby—a boy she'd named Andy—and vowed that she would never speak to Senator Stoneman again. Not that he was exactly running after her; she hadn't heard a word since she'd left. And she didn't care. Andy was all hers. She would never allow Gregory anywhere near her son.

"My problem is Bobby's mom," Denver ventured, anxious to vent her feelings. "She's so . . . well, how can I describe her?"

"Go ahead and try," Carolyn said briskly.

"For a start, she's drop-dead beautiful," Denver began, attempting to paint an accurate portrait of the incredible Lucky Santangelo. "I mean, she's tall, olive-skinned, with incredible dark eyes and hair. She's an absolute knockout in a very earthy Italian way."

"What's so bad about that?" Carolyn remarked. "She certainly passed on the good genes to Bobby."

"She's also extremely accomplished," Denver continued, wondering how she could possibly live up to the force of nature that was Lucky Santangelo. "She builds her own hotels, once ran a major movie studio. She gave birth to three children, and if that isn't enough, she's an insane cook, does everything herself, and has a long-lasting and apparently very happy marriage to Lennie Golden."

"The movie star?"

"He was. Now he writes and directs extremely successful independent movies."

"Sounds as if *Bobby* has a lot to live up to."

"Lennie's not his father," Denver explained, picking up her coffee mug. "I thought I told you—his father is a deceased Greek billionaire ship owner. Hence the company plane whenever Bobby wants it. Something else to intimidate me."

"Stop it, Denver," Carolyn said firmly. "Nothing should intimidate you."

"So," Denver said, grimacing, "Bobby's mom is perfect and I'm not."

"Oh my *God!*" Carolyn said, throwing up her hands in exasperation. "Will you listen to yourself?"

"What?" Denver said, aggravated that Carolyn wasn't getting it.

"You're incredible, Denver. You have a terrific career doing something meaningful. You're young, smart, and beautiful, *and* you have a great boyfriend." Carolyn paused for a moment, then added, "It's a given that your cooking skills are nil. But I've got a strong suspicion Bobby is not with you for your culinary assets."

Denver couldn't help laughing. "I'm not beautiful, and I'm not so young anymore, but I *am* smart," she admitted.

"Oh yeah," Carolyn said. "Twenty-seven is *really* getting up there. And let me correct you—your beauty is not magazine perfect, it's warm and natural, made all the better 'cause you damn well have no clue how great-looking you are."

"Thanks, but you should see the girls that hang out in Bobby's club. Not to mention the ones that come up to him when we're out. They're all over him."

"What do you care? He's with you, isn't he?"

"I guess . . ."

"She guesses," Carolyn exclaimed, rolling her eyes. "The man is crazy for you; everyone knows it. And about those random girls? Let me take a shot—size zero 'cause they never eat. Huge boobs—fake. Huge lips—fake. High cheekbones—fake. And—"

"Stop!" Denver said, breaking into laughter. "They're in the entertainment business; they have to look their best."

"Bull!" Carolyn exclaimed. "And don't take this personally, but I'm changing the subject to *me*."

"Good," Denver responded. "What's up with you?"

"I've decided to become gay," Carolyn announced.

Denver choked on her coffee. "What?" she spluttered. "You can't just *decide* to become gay. It's something you're either into or you're not."

"I'm into it," Carolyn said matter-of-factly. "Met this lovely woman at yoga. She's invited me out on a date. So guess what? I'm going."

"Why would you do that?"

"Because I'm off men forever. First I was with Matt, who cheated on me. Then Gregory, who turned out to be a lying, despicable piece of crap. I've had it with the male sex—I don't want anything to do with them anymore. Not so hard to understand, right?"

"Well . . ." Denver began, but before she could say anything else, Andy began to cry, and glancing at her watch, she realized that if she didn't get a move on, she'd be late for work.

"Then you think I should go to Vegas?" she asked, grabbing her car keys and hurrying toward the door.

"Damn right you should," Carolyn said, reaching down to pick up her son.

"Okay, I'll do it," Denver said, deciding that she definitely would. "And you have fun with . . . uh . . . who?"

"Vanessa," Carolyn said, smiling. "And yes, I promise I will."

Groping for her cell while still asleep was nothing new for Max. "What?" she mumbled into her BlackBerry.

"Guess where *I* am?" came the whispered reply.

"Cookie?"

"Yes, it's me," Cookie giggled. "Little ole me."

Max opened one eye. "Where are you?" she asked, although she had a horrible suspicion that she already knew the answer.

"Guess!"

"Don't wanna guess," Max said irritably, kicking off her duvet. "Where the fuck are you?"

"I'm in Frankie's bed, and it was *amazing!*" Cookie sighed. "Like, totally random, amazing sex!"

"Crap!" Max exclaimed, sitting up. "You didn't screw him, did you?"

"Course I did," Cookie said with a triumphant giggle.

"*Oh my God!*" Max scolded. "You're not supposed to screw someone like Frankie."

"Why not?"

"'Cause you're just not. He's way too sketchy, *and* a total druggie."

"But it was *soooo* great," Cookie enthused. "Wanna hear the sex-drenched details?"

"No thank you," Max said primly. "I'd rather not."

"You're no fun," Cookie complained. "I'm gonna hav'ta call Harry. He's *so* into details."

"Do that."

Jeez! Frankie Romano, Bobby's former drug-addict best friend, and Cookie. This was not welcome news. And it was all her fault because she should never have left Cookie at the club. Frankie was a certified lowlife who'd been running call girls with his previous girlfriend, Annabelle Maestro. He'd use Cookie, cast her aside, and the fallout would be a total pain. She'd have to listen to Cookie moan and groan for weeks on end.

What a bummer! Why had she gone and hooked them up with Frankie simply to get into his stupid club? She should've known better.

Grabbing an oversized T-shirt, she fell out of bed, wondering what she could do to rectify the situation.

Unfortunately, nothing came to mind.

Bobby was all business as he pulled into the private parking sector of The Keys. M.J., who was not only his business partner but also his closest confidant, came strolling over to greet him. They exchanged a macho hug.

M.J. was African American and handsome, although slightly short. He was married to Cassie, a young singer with big ambitions. They'd gotten married in Vegas on a whim, and now, just under a year later, Cassie was pregnant. M.J., who'd moved to Vegas from New York to oversee the launch of Mood, was delighted. Cassie was not. At almost nineteen, she wanted a career, not a baby. M.J.'s affluent parents—his father was a renowned neurosurgeon and his mother a former opera singer— were perched on the sidelines, waiting to see what happened next. Cassie was not the girl they'd envisioned for their only son, nor was a career opening nightclubs, however successful they might be.

M.J. didn't care. He was crazy about his young wife, but now with a baby on the way, there was a catch, something he couldn't wait to discuss with Bobby.

"Great wheels!" M.J. exclaimed, checking out Bobby's Lamborghini.

Bobby nodded. "Yeah—since I've been spending so much time on the West Coast, I decided I needed to buy me a car. It can get up to two hundred eleven miles per hour, man. It's insane, and I love every minute of it. Denver doesn't."

"No shit," M.J. said, walking around the car, giving it a full inspection. "I wonder why."

"Thinks it's too flashy and fast."

"Well, bro, low-key it ain't."

They laughed and exchanged an enthusiastic fist pump.

"How *is* your low-key girlfriend?" M.J. asked as they entered the enormous glass-enclosed lobby. "Still putting away bad guys?"

"Denver's great," Bobby said. "She's a special kind of girl."

"I'm gettin' you feel that way. I've never seen you so caught up."

"What can I tell you?" Bobby said with a big grin. "The woman makes me happy."

"And that, my man, is all that matters."

"Right on!"

"An' talking of happy," M.J. said, "I got some news of my own."

"Wanna tell me?"

"Cassie's pregnant."

"Jeez, M.J. You ready for that?"

"Ready as I'll ever be."

"Told your parents yet?"

"Haven't got around to it, but I will."

"You'd better."

"Don't think I don't know it."

"They'll be happy for you."

"Yeah?"

"Sure they will. Now let's go kick some investor butt. And later we gotta get together an' celebrate."

CHAPTER FIVE

Once Armand Jordan decided he wanted something, there was no going back, whether it be a woman, an unobtainable painting, a special delicacy, a one-of-a-kind car, or a building. Nobody ever said no to Armand, and if they did, he merely upped the price.

Usually he favored high-class call girls—hookers had tricks that other women did not possess. Little tricks. Dirty tricks. Filthy things a man can only dream about.

Once in a while he came across a woman who was *not* for sale. This did not faze Armand, for they all had a price. And sometimes it wasn't monetary.

On occasion it intrigued him to discover what that price might be. It was a game he played for his own enjoyment, and when Armand played, he played to win.

His latest conquest was Nona Constantine, the wife of Martin Constantine, one of his rivals in the real-estate business, a man some considered to be almost as powerful as Armand.

How wrong they were!

Nona was exactly the kind of challenge he craved. Married, with a young child, she was a former beauty queen from Slovakia, with high cheekbones and slanted eyes. Her husband doted on her, but Armand's canny instinct allowed him to guess that ever since she'd given birth, Martin was not fucking her the way a woman yearned to be fucked.

Armand worked on her slowly, and since they moved

in the same New York social circles—art gallery open-
ings, charity events, small dinner parties—it was quite
easy to get close to her. Especially as he always had a
girl on his arm. Only *he* knew that his so-called "dates"
were bought and paid for. That way they never gave him
any trouble or made any demands. His unbreakable rule
was never to use the same girl twice.

New York hostesses considered Armand Jordan a
huge catch; they were always trying to fix him up. But
he eluded their attempts. He was attractive in a slightly
mysterious way, with a neat black mustache, thick eyebrows framing brooding eyes, and an impeccable dress
sense. Only the best for Armand. He wore socks and
underwear once, then threw them away. Shirts he might
wear twice, but that was it. And his hand-tailored suits
never stayed in his closet longer than a month.

The hostesses persevered, for not only was Armand
mega rich, but it was rumored that back in the small
Middle Eastern country he originally hailed from, he
possessed some kind of title.

He never spoke of that.

It took him a couple of months to get Nona to his
penthouse, on the pretext of showing her a rare Picasso
he'd recently acquired. He did not mind the wait; in fact,
he quite enjoyed the anticipation of the conquest.

She arrived at eleven in the morning, an innocent
time of day. She had on a pale pink Chanel suit with a
lacy blouse underneath, and beige Louboutin heels that
clicked on his highly polished marble floor as he led her
around his penthouse, giving her the grand tour. Finally
they ended up in the master bedroom, a masculine room,
all deep burgundy leather couches and black cashmere
throws covering the oversized bed.

"No family photos," Nona said, glancing around his
stark bedroom. She laughed coquettishly. "Armand, you
are *such* a man of mystery. And why do I always see

you with a different girl? Surely you wish to meet a woman you can share your life with."

"Why would I want to do that when I can have a woman like you?" he said, gazing into her eyes as if he meant it.

And just like that, all his hard work paid off. All the compliments and sly attention and flattery, flattery, flattery.

She was his. All his to use and abuse and humiliate.

Because that was his pleasure. That was his kick.

First he kissed her, roughly forcing his lips down on hers, thrusting his tongue into her mouth, giving her no chance to object. Then, without warning, his hand swooped under her skirt, and his thick fingers slid past her panties into the soft mound of flesh that was wet and willing and waiting for discovery.

No foreplay for this one. She was turned on the minute she'd walked into his apartment. Nona Constantine wanted it. And he was about to give it to her. Hard.

Navigating his thick fingers through her wiry pubic hair, he was excited by the furriness. He wound strands of hair tightly around his fingers until she cried out in pain. This pleased him. If he wanted a woman shaved like a child, he would have a child.

"Oh, Armand," she gasped, flushed and breathless. "We shouldn't be doing . . ."

It was a little late for objections. Too late.

He shoved her down onto the bed and thought about Martin Constantine and the concealed camera recording every moment. His thoughts made him as hard as he'd ever been.

Dipping into his bedside table drawer, he withdrew a glassine bag of cocaine and sprinkled some of the white powder on her erect nipples.

She writhed beneath him as he snorted the powder from her breasts. Then, as she begged him to fuck her, he gave it to her hard, ramming his penis into her with considerable force, then turning her over and taking her from behind—ignoring her objections and sudden cries of pain.

Realizing this was not going the way she'd hoped it would, she struggled to escape his relentless attack, but he was having none of it as he rode her hard, punishing her with his penis for being an unfaithful bitch.

He felt invincible and powerful. He was the man, and once again a woman had proved to him that all women were dirty whores.

Except perhaps his wife. But who cared about her? He certainly didn't.

Later, after relentlessly fucking Nona Constantine in every possible way, he informed her that she was a cheating, filthy prostitute, physically dragged her from his bedroom, and threw her out.

The shock on her face was palpable as he hustled her out his front door, flinging her designer clothes after her.

"What? What did I do?" she sobbed, red in the face as he slammed the door on her.

He didn't bother replying.

It was satisfying to know that there was nobody she could complain to, nothing she could do. She was fucked in more ways than one.

Once rid of his conquest, Armand snorted more coke and summoned Fouad, who worked downstairs in a different apartment. "Come up here," Armand commanded. "Right now."

Fouad hurried to the penthouse.

"What's happening with The Keys?" Armand demanded as soon as Fouad walked in.

"There is a half-naked woman crying outside your door," Fouad remarked, noting that the prince wore only a bathrobe, and that there was a telltale residue of white powder under his nose. Armand's use of cocaine was escalating, and it worried Fouad as he watched Armand become even more irrational and moody.

"I trust you ignored her," Armand said, striding purposefully toward his palatial bathroom.

"Who is she?" Fouad asked.

"Martin Constantine's wife," Armand boasted. "I told you I can have any woman I want. They're all whores."

Fouad shrugged and followed him into the bedroom. He was well aware of Armand's predilections when it came to women. Privately, he considered it a sickness, but he would never dare say anything. Although lately Armand's sickness, coupled with his excessive use of drugs, was becoming almost dangerous.

"That crying bitch deserved everything she got," Armand said, dropping his robe. "I took care of her in ways she won't soon forget."

"Does it not worry you that she might tell her husband?"

"Don't be ridiculous, Fouad. She came here of her own free will. She wanted it. She was begging for it. Now remove the DVD from the camera, make two copies, and put them in my safe."

"Yes, Armand," Fouad said. He would make three copies and keep one for himself. Nothing like insurance when dealing with a man like Armand.

"And The Keys?" Armand said, unabashedly naked as he stepped into the all-marble shower. "What's happening?"

"I have several calls in," Fouad said, not wishing to reveal that he'd spoken to the owner's attorney, and that he'd been informed that it was highly unlikely The Keys was for sale.

"What is taking so long?" Armand demanded as four powerful showerheads rained down on his body.

"You only told me you wanted to buy it two days ago," Fouad pointed out. "There are times it is prudent to be patient."

Armand stepped out of the shower dripping wet. "I am not a prudent man, Fouad. You above all people should know that."

Fouad noted the prince's large appendage and attempted to avert his eyes, even though he'd seen it many times before. The prince, like his father the king, was not shy.

"I understand, Armand," he said evenly. "I am on top of it."

"You'd better be," Armand responded, vigorously toweling himself dry. "Whatever the price, I am prepared to pay."

"Of course," Fouad agreed, because agreeing was simpler than arguing.

"How is your wife?" Armand asked, abruptly changing the subject.

Fouad hesitated for only a moment. He had no wish to discuss his wife with Armand. He was well aware that Armand did not approve of his marriage. Armand thought he had made a mistake marrying an American girl. But Fouad adored his wife and two little children, and nothing Armand could say would ever change that.

"Alison is very well," he answered carefully.

"Hasn't cheated on you yet?" Armand said with a spiteful smirk.

Fouad maintained a steely silence.

"All American women cheat on their husbands eventually," Armand stated. "Look at the whore I just threw out. She's a classic example of a rich bitch with an itchy cunt."

Fouad chose to ignore Armand's crass remarks.

Sometimes he found them difficult to understand, considering that Armand's own mother was an American. But then Armand's relationship with his mother had always been something of a problem.

"Go make some phone calls," Armand said, abruptly dismissing his faithful right-hand man. "And before the end of the day, I wish to know that The Keys is mine."

CHAPTER SIX

"What's going on today? Anything I should know about?" Denver asked Leon, a young detective with whom she'd become friendly. It was Leon who had encouraged her to transfer to the drug unit, a move she was excited about.

Leon was African American and quite laid-back. He was excellent at his job, and had helped her get acclimated when she'd first arrived. They had a good buddy thing going on, which she hoped would last because sometimes she had a sneaking suspicion that Leon was on the verge of asking her out.

Please don't, a little voice whispered in her head. *I'm taken. Besides, it would be awkward.*

Not that Leon wasn't attractive. He was. He had a kind of chill Will Smith vibe going for him, and the ladies were always giving him the look. Denver ribbed him a lot. He acted bashful, but she knew he was a stud at heart.

"There's a hostage deal happening," Leon explained. "Some Mexican drug pusher grabbed his baby and barricaded himself in his house with an arsenal of weapons. I'm goin' over there now. They've had to clear the neighborhood an' close the street."

"What else is new?" Denver asked, immediately thinking how blasé she sounded. And well she should, because if it wasn't a hostage situation, it was a random shooting or a gang initiation or a murder or a high-speed car chase. Things were going on all the time, and she could not believe how isolated she'd been working at a top Beverly Hills law firm, where the main excitement of the day was some coked-out Hollywood starlet with two DUIs trying to dodge jail time, or a boring client lunch at Spago.

"Not enough for you, huh?" Leon said with a wide grin. "An' how come you was late this morning?"

"I . . . uh . . ."

"Boyfriend in town?" he asked, leaning his elbows on her desk.

"Yes. Bobby's here," she admitted, a touch sheepishly. "But that has nothing to do with—"

"Morning sex," Leon said, his grin spreading. "Now, *that's* what I'm talkin' about."

"Excuse me?" she said, pretending she had no clue what he was alluding to.

"You got the glow, girl," Leon teased. "Comin' off you in waves."

Damn! She knew she did, and there was nothing she could do about it. Whenever she had sex it was written all over her face for everyone to see. How annoying was *that?*

"I have to work," she said, powering up her computer. "So if you'll—"

"I'm outta here," Leon said, throwing up his arms. "Out. Gone. Good-bye. Adios."

"Be careful," she said.

"Always," he said.

As soon as Leon left, her thoughts drifted to Bobby. It was ridiculous, but whenever she wasn't with him, all she could do was think about him. So juvenile. It was almost as if they were back in high school, and who could forget those days? Bobby Santangelo Stanislopoulos, the most popular boy in school. Football star, major jock, head of his class at everything. All the girls lusted after him, including her. But he'd never noticed her, hadn't even realized she existed. And now, ten years later, she was his actual girlfriend. How weird was that?

Stop thinking about Bobby and get to work.

Okay, okay, I will.

"You're up early," Lucky said, regarding her daughter as Max came wandering outside onto the patio. The girl was all long bronzed legs, with a coltlike body. Her green eyes were still sleep-filled, her dark hair a cloudy mess. "Hard day's night?" Lucky questioned, thinking what a beautiful child she and Lennie had created. Although Max was no longer a child; she was a young woman getting ready to take off.

"What?" Max mumbled.

"A Beatles reference."

"Wow, Mom, you can be so obscure," Max complained, flopping into a chair.

"And good morning to you too," Lucky said dryly.

Yawning, Max reached for a jug of orange juice.

"What were you up to last night?" Lucky inquired.

"You're not gonna question me, are you?" Max said, flashing her a disgusted look. "That would be so lame."

"Why? You got something to hide?" Lucky replied, faintly amused.

"Oh yeah, like anyone could hide shit around you."

"Nice," Lucky said, thinking how much Max reminded her of herself as a teenager. Restless, full of sass, yearning for adventure, determined to do things her way yet still not quite sure of herself.

"Sorry," Max allowed after a few moments of silence. "Crappy night."

"That's okay," Lucky said, taking the understanding route. "By the way, I spoke to your brother yesterday. He sends much love."

"Bobby?" Max said, perking up.

"No, your other brother, Gino Junior. He's loving their trip; so is Leonardo. They're currently in Switzerland, skiing like mad. Apparently they're having a fantastic time."

"Where *is* Bobby?" Max asked, wondering if she should tell him about Frankie. Or not. He'd probably be furious at her for taking Cookie and Harry to River in the first place. But how was *she* supposed to know it was Frankie's club? She wasn't a mind reader.

"Not sure," Lucky said. "However, I do know he'll be at your birthday party in Vegas."

"Mom . . ." Max ventured. "I've been thinking about it, and I'm not certain I want a party."

"Do *not* even attempt to back out," Lucky said firmly. "You're going to be eighteen. It's a big deal. Everyone will be there. Gino, Lennie, Bobby . . ."

"Is Bobby bringing his girlfriend?"

"Which one?"

"You know perfectly well which one. Denver. They're like a major hookup."

"They are?" Lucky said vaguely.

"Oh *please!*" Max said, laughing. "You know it."

"No, actually, I don't."

"Wow! Then you're the only one who doesn't. Why do you think Bobby keeps coming to L.A. when his clubs are in Vegas and New York?"

"How do you know he keeps coming to L.A.?"

" 'Cause I just do."

Lucky was silent for a moment. She hadn't realized that Bobby was getting serious with anyone. She'd always thought that Bobby was the love 'em and leave 'em type, like his grandfather before him. He was still in his twenties, too young to tie himself down. She'd met Denver maybe once, but she hadn't taken much notice of the girl since—like all the others before her she hadn't thought Denver would be around for long. Apparently she was wrong. Therefore if Bobby was bringing her to Max's party, she'd better make some kind of effort to get to know her.

What really surprised her was that Bobby was—according to Max—spending a lot of time in L.A. and not even calling.

Who was this girl? And what kind of hold did she have over Bobby?

It was obviously time to find out.

"So you're gonna have a baby," Bobby said as he and M.J. made their way into the art deco glass elevator that led them upstairs to Mood. "That's really something, Daddy M.J. Never thought the day would come!"

"Yeah," M.J. said ruefully. "Kinda weird, huh?"

"Getting married in Vegas overnight was kinda weird," Bobby pointed out. "Starting a family goes right along with marriage. But what the hell, 's long as you're happy."

"Couldn't be happier," M.J. answered without taking a beat.

"You're sure?" Bobby said, shooting M.J. a quick look and thinking that he didn't seem exactly ecstatic.

"Course I'm sure," M.J. said, hesitating for a moment before adding, "except for maybe one minor detail."

"An' that would be?"

"Cassie doesn't want to have a baby right now," M.J. blurted. "She keeps on threatenin' to get an abortion."

Bobby frowned. "You're screwing with me, right?"

"'Fraid not. An' what the fuck am I supposed t' do about *that*?"

"Shit, man," Bobby said, shaking his head. "How would *I* know?"

"It's a problem," M.J. admitted. "A big fuckin' problem."

"You got plans to solve it?"

M.J. gave a helpless shrug. "I'm playin' it strong. Tellin' her if she goes ahead an' does that—we're over."

"Seriously?"

"I'm dead serious."

"Well," Bobby said, finding himself at a loss for words, "I gotta wish you luck, man. Seems like you're gonna need it."

The elevator came to a stop and they stepped into the reception area of Mood.

Bobby glanced around. It always gave him a feeling of achievement to note what he and M.J. had accomplished. Their club was sleek and sexy; it featured spacious booths with muted gold leather banquettes imported from Italy, Brazilian wood tables, smoky-mirrored walls, and clever lighting supplemented with glowing candles. And in the middle of everything was the pool, surrounded by private dinner cabanas—*the* place to be seated. And of course a state-of-the-art sound system, the best that money could buy. The entire vibe screamed style and class, comfort and fun.

Since its opening, Mood had become *the* club of choice for visiting Hollywood celebrities, high rollers, affluent Vegas locals, and showbiz performers when their shows finished and they were looking for somewhere to hang and relax. Tourists had a hard time getting in. Privacy was the name of the game.

Yes, Mood was banging—the very best.

"Remember Sukie in high school?" M.J. ventured, heading toward the bar. "The girl I knocked up?"

"Turned out to be a false alarm, right?" Bobby said, following him.

"Uh, no," M.J. said. "I didn't tell you 'cause you were taking off to spend the summer in Greece with your other family. Besides, Sukie swore me to secrecy."

"Man, why didn't you say something?" Bobby said

earnestly. "I would've been there for you, you know that."

"Yeah, I know," M.J. said, going behind the bar and opening one of the fridges. "But we had to do something fast, 'cause by that time, Sukie was almost four months."

"What *did* you do?" Bobby asked, perching on a bar stool.

"The janitor at school told us 'bout this midwife downtown," M.J. said, extracting a couple of cans of Diet Coke. "He told us that for five hundred bucks, she'd take care of it. No problem." He slid a can of Diet Coke across the bar to Bobby.

"And?" Bobby said, opening the can.

"We drove to a run-down house in some shit neighborhood, where an old Chinese woman took us inside, bundled Sukie into what she called her 'operation room,' an' demanded the cash."

"Jeez! Did you even have it?"

"Uh-huh. I stole it from my dad's dresser that mornin'. Had no other way of getting the money."

"Then what?"

"For a start, we were both scared shitless."

"I bet you were."

"Anyway, I handed over the cash an' waited. After a while the old crone comes walkin' back into the room where I'm sitting. This time she's carryin' a big bucket, an' in it was the dead baby. She fuckin' *showed* it to me, like it was some kinda prize. 'You see,' she says—like she's proud or somethin'. 'All done.'"

"Oh, *fuck!*"

"Oh fuck is right. I swear to you it was a sight I'll never forget. Jesus, Bobby, I threw my guts up." M.J. shook his head as if he couldn't stand remembering, then after a long beat he said, "I couldn't wait t' get us out of there. I got Sukie into the car, but on the way home she started getting major pains. She was bleeding, so I panicked an' called my dad. He put her in the hospital. I guess he saved her. I'll never forget seein' that baby," M.J. added sadly. "It was a boy. *My* boy. The image burned itself into my eyeballs."

"I can't believe you never told me this before."

"Too painful, Bobby. I was too ashamed of what I did."

"Yeah, I can understand that. But now you gotta tell Cassie, explain how you feel."

"No way. She wouldn't get it," M.J. said, vigorously shaking his head. "An' don't go repeatin' the story to anyone."

"C'mon, man," Bobby said. "You were a kid— sixteen. You didn't know any better. You got nothing to feel guilty about."

"I guess," M.J. said miserably. "Only I still get fuckin' sick when I think about what we did. It wasn't right, it simply wasn't right."

"I get it," Bobby said sympathetically.

"It's somethin' I gotta live with," M.J. said, adding a determined, "But believe this—I'll *never* let it happen again."

"Then you *gotta* tell your wife," Bobby insisted. "She'll do the right thing when she hears your story."

"You don't know Cassie."

"*Make* her listen to you. Seems to me you got no choice."

CHAPTER SEVEN

Lunch was a daily ritual for Armand. He always selected a different restaurant and a different guest, and he always made sure to pick up the check. Armand had no wish to be beholden to anyone. He was in charge, and let nobody doubt it.

Today he was anticipating his luncheon engagement more than usual, because today his guest was Martin Constantine, and how satisfying it would be to sit across the table from Martin and reflect on his morning activities with Martin's lovely, unfaithful, whorelike wife.

Martin and he had come up against each other in various business deals, and usually Armand managed to come out on top. But the last deal they'd both been trying to close had gone in Martin's favor, and that infuriated Armand. Hence the assignation with Martin's wife. A satisfying punishment toward his business rival. And the secret knowledge that he'd had her in every sexual position he could think of.

Martin Constantine was a puffy-faced New Yorker in his sixties, with ruddy cheeks, a weak chin, and red-rimmed eyes. He was also a billionaire, although Armand suspected on paper only.

The two men shook hands and settled into a corner table. Martin had come to the lunch only because he was curious to find out what Armand wanted. It had to be something, for the two of them were hardly best friends—more like polite enemies. Not that Martin considered Armand polite. Actually, he couldn't stand the man. He abhorred the way Armand swaggered around town, always with a different woman on his arm—the way he attempted to give everyone the impression that his real-estate holdings were the cream, and that everyone else's were inferior. As far as Martin was concerned, Constantine Holdings could buy and sell Jordan Developments and not even notice.

Lunch was uneventful. Small talk. Business talk. A derisive chat about Donald Trump's television career, and how neither of them would ever sink that low. Reality television was for peasants, not for men of substance.

Armand was under the distinct impression that Martin would give his left ball for the public recognition of Donald Trump, whom Martin very much admired, but he would never admit it.

Over coffee, Armand contemplated telling his lunch guest about his morning activities. He had an urge to do so, but then he realized it was more prudent to wait until he needed something from Martin.

"How is your beautiful wife?" he asked when they stood up to leave. *I fucked her this morning. I shoved my cock up her tight ass while she screamed like a banshee. I violated her in every way I could. She loved it. I did things to her that you would never dare do.*

"Nona is a fantastic woman," Martin boasted. "I am so fortunate to have found her. She is the light of my life." He paused for a moment before continuing. "You should try marriage sometime. It might surprise you, being with one woman."

"Ah yes," Armand replied, keeping a straight face, because he'd discovered that before Martin had "found" Nona she was working as a call girl in Amsterdam. Armand had his spies. "I am certain that marriage is an honorable institution."

They shook hands and parted company. Armand got into his Mercedes smiling to himself. What an old fool Martin Constantine was. He'd divorced his wife of thirty years and married a call girl.

The satisfaction was in the not telling.

And Armand would not tell. Not until it suited him.

Later in the day, Armand summoned Fouad to his study. "Developments regarding The Keys?" he demanded, leaning back in his leather desk chair, tapping his fingers impatiently on his desktop.

Fouad paused a moment before answering. He knew Armand was preparing to throw one of his screaming fits. With the news he was about to deliver, there was no avoiding it.

"Unfortunately . . ." Fouad began.

Armand glared at him. " 'Unfortunately'?" he questioned, his eyes becoming narrow slits. "Did you say 'unfortunately'?"

"Indeed I did," Fouad said, small beads of sweat decorating his forehead. "Because unfortunately, I have learned that The Keys is not for sale."

There was a long moment of deadly silence before Armand began to yell.

"What do you mean it's not for sale?" he shouted, banging his fist on his desk. "Everything is for sale. Every person, every building, every damn thing in the world."

Fouad remained silent. There was nothing else he could say.

"Who told you it's not for sale?" Armand continued. "What fool uttered those asinine words?"

"The owner's lawyer, Jeffrey Lonsdale."

"What *owner*?" Armand said with a derisive sneer. "The Keys would not have an *owner*. The Keys would belong to a company. And that company should be prepared to sell. To me. I will pay whatever it takes, Fouad. Do you hear me? Whatever it takes."

Typical Armand behavior, Fouad thought. Show him something he can't have, and he will move heaven and earth to get it. Fouad recalled the case of the exquisite baby-faced call girl Armand had used on occasion. One night he required her services, and it turned out she had left the business and married a rock star. Armand was incensed. He wanted her and he would have her, so he'd devised a complicated plan that involved setting the rock star up with a paid-for call girl, making sure baby-face walked in on her cheating husband, and then flying her to New York for a reunion fuck. It had cost him plenty, but to him it was well worth it.

"The Keys is owned by a private company. And the company belongs to a woman, Lucky Santangelo," Fouad said. "I spoke with her lawyer, who informed me that there is no way she is prepared to sell, whatever the price."

"A woman," Armand said disdainfully. "A mere woman." He shook his head in disgust. "I can see I will have to deal with this matter myself. Tomorrow I go to Akramshar for my father's birthday, and upon my return we will travel to Vegas or wherever this Lucky Santangelo woman is, and you will watch me convince her to sell me The Keys. Set up a meeting. And find out everything there is to know. Sometimes, Fouad, I wonder at your ineptitude. It seems there are times that if I don't do it myself, nothing gets done. Perhaps marrying an American woman has blunted your business acumen. Your wife addles your brain—such as it is."

Once again Armand was making disparaging remarks about Fouad's marriage. It infuriated him, and one day in the not-so-distant future, Fouad knew he would have to leave Armand's employ, but until that day came, he would simply be forced to suffer the insults aimed at his wife and his marriage in silence.

"It is done, Armand," Fouad said, always calm, always polite. "I will make sure all arrangements are in place for us to fly to Las Vegas."

"The Presidential Suite at The Keys," Armand stated. "And you will see—soon it will be all mine."

CHAPTER EIGHT

It was noon when Frankie Romano hauled himself out of his oversized bed with the clichéd black satin sheets and regarded himself in the mirror above his bathroom sink. He considered himself a good-looking son of a bitch. Not in the classically handsome sense, but he had an edgy style and plenty of attitude, plus he knew how to present himself. And he certainly knew how to score with the ladies. Oh *yes!* Frankie Romano was a first-class cocksman, and nobody could argue that.

Last night he'd mega scored with Cookie, Gerald M.'s sexy little offspring. A teenager with real tits and real enthusiasm. Not some tired old twenty-something Hollywood blonde who'd had more hot cocks than hot dinners. Oh no, Cookie was something else—a real prize.

Frankie made his way into the living room of his apartment, all chrome and leather furniture, the full-length windows overlooking the Sunset Strip. He laid out a couple of lines of coke on his mirrored coffee table and rolled a twenty-dollar bill.

Was he living the dream or what? After splitting with his longtime live-in Annabelle Maestro, he'd figured he was done for a while. But after watching her shine as a TV personality, he'd gotten pissed and reconnected with Rick Greco, a former teen idol who'd parlayed his dead career into a successful gig as a club promoter. "We gotta open a club together," he'd informed Rick. "We can fuckin' own this town between the two of us. Who do you think got Bobby Santangelo's New York club off the ground? It was fuckin' me, man. All me."

Which was not at all the truth, but what did he care? Frankie could spin a masterful story. The truth was, he'd been a deejay in Bobby's club, and that was about it. He'd also had a lucrative sideline selling overpriced designer drugs, and then there was the very successful business he'd created with Annabelle, running call girls. But eventually everything had crashed and burned. Luckily, he was Frankie Romano, and therefore nothing fazed him.

Rick Greco had taken to the idea of going into business with Frankie. Frankie had a big mouth and a big personality, and that's what the club business needed—a front man who knew everyone and made them feel important.

Frankie didn't know everyone, but he was a fast learner, and he certainly knew the club business. So Rick had put together a group of investors, and River was born. It was a new club, but Frankie was determined to make it as successful as Mood in New York and Vegas. Screw Bobby and M.J. They'd both deserted him just when he'd needed them. Bobby all cozy with his Deputy DA girlfriend, and M.J. with his hot, sexy little wife. Fuck 'em both.

Unfortunately, Rick had not made him a full partner. Rick had come up with the weak excuse that since Frankie wasn't putting up any money, it wasn't possible. So he'd had to settle for a percentage. But he'd soon figured out a way to make his own personal score.

Seeing Max Santangelo had made his night; he'd always had eyes for Bobby's hot little sister. But when he sensed he wasn't about to get anywhere with her, he'd switched his attention to her cute friend, which wasn't a bad thing, because Cookie had a famous father—soul icon Gerald M. And it soon occurred to Frankie that if he started dating Cookie, the tabloids would immediately latch on, and he too could hit the rags.

It was a plan.

Frankie liked having a plan.

"I'm giving you my schedule," Lucky informed Max. "I'll be taking off for Vegas tomorrow, staying there until after your party. I've got a board meeting of investors on Friday, and other business to take care of."

"Sounds like a fun time."

"Don't knock it, Max, 'cause one day you'll understand how much fun it can be running your own business."

"Not me," Max said, vigorously shaking her head.

"What *do* you want to do, then?" Lucky asked, slightly exasperated that Max didn't seem to have much drive.

"Dunno," Max said with a casual shrug. "Gonna live life an' find out."

Sure, Lucky thought. *You'll find out, all right. Things are not always as easy as they seem.*

"Anyway," she continued, "you'll find three e-tickets to Vegas on your computer for you, Cookie, and Harry. The five o'clock flight on Thursday. Are you sure you'll be okay in the house by yourself?"

Will I be okay? Max thought. *Hot shit! This is totally rad. I'm planning my own party. No parents. Lose the housekeepers. It's all one big green light. I cannot wait.*

"Mom," Max said scornfully. "It's only for, like, *one* night. I think I can manage *that*."

"Is Ace coming into town?" Lucky inquired.

Why was Lucky always carrying on about Ace? Did she think he was such a good influence? "Dunno," she muttered. "Maybe."

"You should invite him to your party in Vegas."

"Sure," Max said, checking out a text from Harry on her phone. "I'll do that."

"You could come to Vegas before Thursday if you felt like hanging out," Lucky suggested. "What do you think?"

"That's okay," Max said, thinking she'd like nothing less. "I'm into being by myself. It'll give me a chance to consider my future."

"Ah," Lucky said. "Your future."

"Yeah, Mom, my future. Can we, like, *not* discuss it now?"

"Do you still want to move to New York?"

"Maybe, maybe not," Max answered vaguely. "I told you—I'm gonna decide."

"And you're absolutely certain you have no interest in going to college?"

"*You* didn't do the whole college thing," Max said, irritated that Lucky kept on bringing it up. "Why should I?"

"Those were different times," Lucky pointed out.

"Yeah. The Dark Ages," Max said, rolling her eyes.

Lucky shook her head. No use getting pissed off. Nothing to be gained.

"Strangely enough," she deadpanned, "we had phones during the Dark Ages. Instead of texting, we actually talked. Can you imagine?"

"What a thrill," Max drawled.

Brat, Lucky thought. *Spoiled Beverly Hills brat. But she's my brat, and one of these days she'll grow up, just like I did.*

"I'm off," Lucky said, standing up. Sometimes playing the concerned mom was not for her. She loved her kids, but once they reached a certain age, it was best to let them fly. "Are you home for dinner?"

"Don't think so," Max replied. "Gonna hang with Cookie and Harry."

"Okay, then. We'll see each other in the morning before I leave. Oh, and if you hear from Bobby, tell him to call me."

"Will do."

Max waited until Lucky was out of sight, then she called Harry. "Party time at my house tomorrow night," she announced. "Alert the troops, and grab as much booze as you can from your dad's liquor cabinet. Got it?"

Harry got it.

Once every few months Lucky had lunch with her old friend Alex Woods, the legendary and unpredictable film director. They shared a history, a long friendship, and one night of twisted passion a long time ago when Lennie was missing and Lucky thought he was dead. Alex had never gotten over her, and she knew it, but she wasn't prepared to give him up as a friend. He was loyal and insane and incredibly talented and forceful and sincere when he felt like it. During the time she'd owned Panther Studios they'd produced a movie together, and when she'd embarked on building The Keys, Alex had come in on the project as one of her major investors.

If Lennie weren't around, she would be with Alex, and they were both aware of it, although it was never discussed.

In the meantime, Alex dated Asian women. They came. They went. Sometimes they stayed longer than a few weeks. He didn't care. Like Lennie, he lived to make movies—women and love affairs were secondary. Except for Lucky, who, in his eyes, became even more wildly beautiful as each year passed.

He studied her as she walked into Mr. Chow. She wore white pants, a casual jacket, and plenty of gold gypsy-style jewelry. She strode in like a panther, all sleek movement, her dark eyes flashing, her trademark mass of tumbled jet curls as wild as usual. Alex stood up from the table.

"Such a gentleman," she teased as he moved forward and kissed her on both cheeks, inhaling the exotic fragrance she always wore. "How are you, Alex?" she asked, sitting down. "Working hard?"

"What do *you* think?" he said with a wry smile. "I'm in post on the war movie I recently finished shooting in Morocco, and my editor is driving me nuts. Plus, we're way over budget, and the studio is throwing a shit fit. Fuck 'em."

"Are you pleased with it?" she asked, scanning his face. He looked a little ragged around the edges. Alex drank too much; that and his excessive smoking were not good for him. He was still an enormously attractive man, though, and she loved him dearly—as a friend.

"Am I ever pleased with anything?" Alex said, picking up a tumbler of Jack Daniel's. "You know me, Lucky. You probably know me better than anyone."

"Isn't it a little early for the heavy stuff?" Lucky inquired, indicating his drink.

"Jesus!" Alex said. "Since when did *you* become the AA rep? Whyn't you leave it to my girlfriends to be concerned about my drinking? They're the ones who get off on bitching."

"How sweet."

"Sweet is the last thing I'm looking for."

"Well then," Lucky said briskly, "you should stop picking actresses and try finding a girl—I mean a woman—you can have a decent relationship with. It's about time you gave up the chasing."

"Believe me, honey, it's them who do the chasing," he said dryly.

"Don't call me honey."

"Why not?"

"Save it for your one-nighters."

"You were a one—"

"Alex!" She stopped him with a deadly look. He was venturing into forbidden territory, and she didn't like it one little bit.

"Yeah, yeah, I get it," he said, taking another gulp of Jack.

She ordered a bottle of Evian and leaned across the table. "Tell me about your movie."

"Don't want to bore you."

"Why would I be bored, Alex?"

"'Cause you know exactly what I'm going to say."

"And that would be?"

"I'm gonna regale you with stories about what a bunch of fucking assholes my actors are."

"Then why do you hire them?"

"Got no choice. Unfortunately, I need 'em."

"How inconvenient for you."

"Yeah, robots are more my style," he said with a cynical laugh.

"Imagine that!"

Alex smiled. It didn't matter what kind of a mood he was in, Lucky could always make him feel better.

"Did you hear that Venus is in the process of divorcing Billy?" she asked.

"Should I be surprised? Working with Billy was like slogging up the Himalayas with no Sherpas. That little prick took 'asshole' to new heights."

Lucky laughed. "Billy's major box office. The public seems to love him."

"We all know that the public has no fucking taste."

"That's what I like about you, Alex."

"I knew there was something," he said with a wry grin.

"You tell it the way you see it."

"That's me, Lucky. No bullshit."

"You're unique."

"Takes one to know one," he said, signaling the waiter to bring him another drink. "How's Lennie?"

"Lennie's fine."

"Shame," he said with a resigned shrug. "I was hoping he'd slipped off a cliff."

"Stop!" she said sternly.

"You know that'll never happen," he countered. "And I do mean never."

They stared at each other, a long intent stare that Lucky finally broke.

"Okay," she said, taking a deep breath. "I want you to come to Vegas."

"I fucking hate Vegas," Alex said vehemently. "Especially after what happened there with Ling."

Lucky flashed onto the memory of Alex's former live-in girlfriend, who had been sending her threatening notes and hatching a plan to shoot her. It was all so bizarre, but when Alex caught Ling with his handgun in her purse during the opening festivities of The Keys, he'd gone berserk and thrown Ling out.

"There are two reasons I need you to come to Vegas," Lucky said as persuasively as she could.

"Go ahead," Alex said. "Try to convince me."

"Reason one, it's Max's eighteenth birthday next weekend, and I'm throwing her a party. You know she'd love you to be there. After all, you've known her since she was a baby."

Alex groaned. "Blackmail," he said flatly. "Psychological blackmail."

"No such thing," Lucky said crisply.

"Reason two?"

"A board meeting of all the Keys investors."

"Jesus! I'll send my business manager. He handles that kinda shit."

"I'm sure Max would be thrilled to see him, but I'm expecting *you*."

"Will Lennie be there?" Alex asked, shooting her a meaningful look.

"Of course."

"What kind of incentive is that?"

"Knock it off, Alex. You're doing this for me. Okay?"

"Whatever the Lady Boss says."

"Fuck you, Alex."

"Anytime, Lucky."

"Then you'll come?"

"If only," he said with a lascivious grin.

Lucky ignored his double entendre. "I'll book you a suite. Don't let me down."

"Jesus Christ! You're so fucking bossy," Alex complained. "But I guess I'll be there. For you, I'll always be there."

"Thank you, Alex."

As soon as Max was sure that Lucky had left the house, she began texting friends about the Malibu party she was planning. Never mind Vegas, she'd have her own crazy celebration, and with the house all to herself, it should be a major blast.

To invite Ace or not to invite Ace, that was the question. She wasn't sure what to do about him. Ace could be totally great or, as Cookie and Harry had pointed out, totally controlling. Besides, it wasn't as if she was in love with him.

Max had imagined she was in love only once, and that was in high school with a boy named Donny Leventon, who'd broken her heart and left her crushed and disillusioned.

She'd never told anyone he'd broken her heart. She'd laughed off the fact that she'd caught him in Houston's, of all places, with another girl.

She was sixteen at the time. Donny was seventeen, and they'd never slept together, although they'd done plenty of other things. Experimenting with sex was fun. Going all the way was not an option, not until she found The One.

Discovering that Donny was seeing another girl was a shattering experience. It had driven her to the Internet, where she was determined to hook up and lose her virginity to a suitable candidate—whether he was The One or not. She'd set up a meeting with a twenty-two-year-old boy who'd posted a majorly hunky photo. After arranging to meet him in Big Bear, she'd turned up, only to find that the major hunk was a disgusting, ugly perv, who'd then kidnapped her and locked her up in some deserted cabin in the woods.

She shuddered at the memories. Thank goodness for Ace, who'd come along at exactly the right time and rescued her.

She wasn't in love with Ace. She liked him in small doses, and that was okay because he didn't live in L.A. They hadn't slept together, but as with Donny, she'd done plenty of other things with him.

Yes, she was still a virgin, and it was becoming an embarrassment, especially as Cookie had slept with an army of guys and boasted about them constantly.

But she wasn't Cookie, and she didn't want to be.

She was waiting—for what?

She didn't know, but when it happened she'd be all over it.

CHAPTER NINE

With Bobby in Vegas, Denver decided to have a night at home by herself. She was happy when he was in town. But she was also happy when he wasn't.

I'm confused, she thought. *I love him but I don't want to love him. I don't want to get hurt. I don't want to make myself vulnerable.*

BUT I LOVE HIM!

She thought about calling Carolyn, then remembered that her friend was out on a gay date. How random was *that?* Carolyn had never indicated a yen for the same sex, but everyone had their secrets . . . and if taking the lesbian route was what she wanted, then so be it.

She put on the TV and checked out the news. The standoff with the Mexican man and his baby—the two of them barricaded in a house—was all over the news. Denver hoped that Leon was all right. She'd grown quite fond of him, and everyone knew that a crazy man with a gun was always a dangerous situation. She'd worked with Leon on a couple of cases—both drug-related— and won both of them. They made a good team. He caught the bad guys, she prosecuted them. Currently Leon was tracking a drug trail that he was hoping would lead him to the big guys, and then she would really have an important case to work on.

Throwing open the freezer door, she inspected the contents. Ice cream, frozen pizza, a half-open packet of

596   JACKIE COLLINS

waffles, and some spaghetti sauce in a plastic container
with ice forming a suspicious film on the top.

Damn! Nothing she wanted for dinner, so maybe a
quick walk to the burger place on Santa Monica.

Amy Winehouse was giving her a look as much as
to say, *Are we taking a walk or what? I need some activity.*

"Yes," Denver said out loud, returning Amy's baleful stare. "We're taking a walk."

Amy's tail began to wag. The dog understood English
perfectly.

After quickly changing into jeans, a tartan shirt with
rolled-up sleeves, and sneakers, Denver grabbed Amy's
leash and set off.

Amy was in fine form, dragging her down the street
at a fast pace. By the time they reached the burger
place, Denver was out of breath. She stopped for a
moment, thinking she needed to spend more time at the
gym.

Ah . . . if she only had more time. Work took up most
of it, and Bobby the rest. Not that she was complaining;
spending nights and weekends with Bobby was always
the best. But a weekend in Vegas with his family was
not something she was looking forward to.

"Denver?"

Somebody spoke her name and she spun around.

"Sam?" she countered.

They both grinned and hugged.

"What are *you* doing here?" she questioned, flashing
on the last time she'd seen Sam, her New York screenwriter friend with the lean body, crooked teeth, and dis-
arming sense of humor. He'd been standing outside her
front door in L.A. when she and Bobby had returned
from rescuing Carolyn in D.C. Just standing there with
an overnight bag and an expectant expression, which totally threw her, because it wasn't as if he was her boy-

friend. They'd shared one very pleasant night of passion in his New York apartment and a delicious breakfast the next morning. That was it.

After Bobby had taken off, she'd asked Sam in for a drink and told him she was kind of involved. They hadn't spoken since.

"They're making my movie," Sam said, his wacky smile going full force. "Remember I told you I sold my screenplay?"

"You mean it's actually in production?" she asked, surprised, because she honestly hadn't imagined he was a successful screenwriter.

"Can you believe it?" he said modestly. "And they've made me a creative consultant. Which means I stand around the set making incredibly smart comments, and nobody listens to me, including the actors."

"You're the writer," she said succinctly. "Why would they?"

"You got that right," he said, bending down to pet Amy. "Hey, buddy."

"He's a she," Denver pointed out as Amy basked in the attention.

"That's me," Sam said wryly. "Always confusing the sexes."

Denver smiled. She had fond memories of Sam; he was a really interesting and funny guy.

"What are you doing right now?" Sam asked. "Can I buy you a burger?"

"No," Denver replied. "But I'll buy *you* one. Kindly take into account that L.A. is *my* city. You're merely a visitor."

Sam held up his hand, "My mom taught me that when a beautiful woman wants to buy you *anything,* go for it."

"Your mom's a smart woman," Denver said, liking the "beautiful" comment.

"She is," Sam agreed, ushering her to a seat at a plastic table on the outdoor patio. "She taught me a lot of things."

A waitress, balancing her out-of-work actress body on roller skates, appeared and handed them menus.

Denver hid behind hers for a moment, studying the list of various hamburgers. Mexican, Puerto Rican, Southwestern. She wondered if Bobby would mind her sharing a meal with an old friend.

Hmm . . . an old friend she'd slept with. But only once, and it wasn't as if she was planning on sleeping with him again.

Sam was just a friend. Period.

Now that he was getting a divorce from the Queen of the Divas, Billy was determined to enjoy his newfound freedom. It was about time. He felt like he'd escaped from a gilded cage and was finally able to do whatever he wanted.

And what *did* he want?

To ride his Harley.

Get blow jobs beside his pool.

Wake up late when he wasn't working.

Flirt with anyone and everyone without Venus checking out his every move.

Never wear a tuxedo again.

Fart in bed.

Drink milk from the carton.

Play video games all night long.

Watch wrestling at midnight.

And porn whenever he felt like it.

Yeah, being free was a good thing. He liked it a lot.

His lawyer had recently informed him that Venus was going for the jugular. She was under the misguided impression that he was sleeping with his costar, and nothing could be farther from the truth.

The breakup of their marriage had come about because Venus never trusted anything he said anymore. She'd taken to checking his e-mails, poring over his Tweets, going through his pockets, reading his texts.

He *was* faithful. She simply hadn't believed him.

One divorce, coming up.

He was relieved.

Freedom meant he had his life back.

Max, Cookie, and Harry were working on texting big-time.

"This is gonna be one flat way-out cool rave!" Cookie decided. "We should have In-N-Out burgers come by. I'll organize the truck. I can use my dad's credit card, he'll never notice."

"And we should get pizza," Harry said. "Everyone's always up for pizza. My dad has a charge at Cecconi's. I'll order from there."

"No deadbeats or losers," Max instructed. "It has to be kids we know an' trust. An' I don't want anyone hangin' around in the house—they can only use the patio, the pool, or the beach."

"Whatever," Cookie said, waving her beringed hand in the air. "I'm telling Frankie he can only bring way hot guys."

Max frowned. "You're inviting Frankie?" she said, not happy at the news. "Why are you doing *that?*"

"'Cause why shouldn't I?" Cookie responded, immediately combative. "He's cool. He'll fit right in. Besides," she added succinctly, "he could be my future boyfriend."

"Gimme a fuckin' break," Harry muttered, snorting with disgust.

"What if I wanted to invite Bobby?" Max argued. "You know they kind of fell out."

"Bobby? Here? At our party?" Cookie said, pulling on her dreadlocks. "No way. Bobby's a killjoy. He'd stop the booze an' all kinds of crap. He's like your *way* too protective big brother. Forget 'bout inviting *him*."

"Cookie's right," Harry said, fingering his spiked hair so it stood up even higher. "Bobby's always checking out what you're drinking an' watchin' out for you. It's sick."

"That's 'cause he *cares* about me," Max said, getting all defensive.

"Well, you don't want him *caring* when we're tryin' to have ourselves a time," Cookie remarked. "What fun is *that*?"

"Yeah," Max admitted. "I suppose you're right."

"You askin' Ace?" Harry wanted to know.

Max thought about it for a moment. Should she ask Ace? Or would he do the Bobby thing and prevent her from having fun? And she *really* wanted to have fun, maybe even get a little crazy. Why not? It was about time. "Dunno," she answered vaguely. "Maybe."

"Or maybe not," Cookie said with a knowing smile. "I'd keep it loose if I was you. Who knows what tomorrow night will bring. Let's go for it all the way. Let's PARTEE!"

M.J. and Bobby's Russian investors consisted of two burly men and an exceptionally tall woman in her fifties with yellow vampirelike teeth, thick legs, and an overbearing, critical attitude. Not to mention a hideous fuchsia masculine-style business suit. She spoke in her native tongue to her two companions and practically ignored Bobby and M.J., who were showing them around the premises.

Bobby was getting aggravated. The woman was a rude piece of work, and he couldn't stand her. However, these investors represented major money, so he attempted to stay cool.

M.J. calmed him down. "They've already agreed to

put up all the money for the L.A. and Miami clubs," he said in a low voice. "This is just a courtesy visit. I got the contracts all ready for them to sign."

Fuck 'em, Bobby thought. *I don't need their money. I could finance both clubs with my own money.*

If he wanted to.

Which he didn't.

Long ago he'd made up his mind that his success could not depend on his inheritance. For some insane reason he had it in his head that he had to make it on his own. It was something he felt strongly about.

The Russians finally finished their tour, whereupon M.J. suggested they sit in a booth so they could sign the contracts that both sets of lawyers had already approved.

"We sign, we sign," Vampire-Teeth said, scarlet lipstick caking on her thin lips. "Later. We come back later, see club full."

"Sure," M.J. said, all easy charm as he guided them toward the glass elevator.

"Sure my ass," Bobby grumbled when they'd left. "I'm supposed to be on a plane to New York tonight. I've got meetings."

"Don't sweat it," M.J. said. "I can look after them."

"No," Bobby said. "You've got too much on your mind. I'll take an A.M. flight an' stay here with you. This is too important to screw up."

"Are you sayin' I'd screw it up?"

"No way, man, but we both need to be here. We have to make sure they sign the contracts tonight."

"You're right," M.J. said. "I'll have the office change your flight."

Bobby nodded. The last thing he wanted was to be stuck in Vegas without Denver. But some things had to be done, and this was one of them.

* * *

In between texting and making calls about their upcoming rave, Cookie expected to get a call from Frankie, and when it didn't come, she was pissed.

"I'm callin' *him*," she announced.

"Don't do that," Max warned.

"Why not?"

"'Cause it'll make you look desperate."

"Screw it. I'm doin' it."

The three of them, Cookie, Max, and Harry, were holed up in Harry's room at the top of his father's Bel Air mansion, a sad place since his mom, a born-again Christian, ran off with her pastor. They now resided in Arizona.

Harry's room was all dark and creepy, with heavy purple drapes to keep out the sunlight, and walls painted black. He'd actually painted the room himself, and he was so pleased with it that he'd painted his bathroom black too.

"Your living quarters suck," Max complained, staring around at the gloomy surroundings. "It's so, like, *depressing*. I dunno why we're here."

"To load up on booze," Harry reminded her. "My old man won't be home till midnight, an' I can't move a dozen bottles of tequila an' twelve cases of imported beer by myself."

"Right," Cookie said, distracted, as she was still hoping Frankie would call.

"How come a dozen bottles of tequila?" Max asked.

"Some actor sent them to him to try to score a part on one of his shows. He's always getting suck-up gifts. He won't even notice they're missing."

"Cool," Max said.

"Bribery," Harry responded. "And the douche actor didn't even get the job."

"If Cookie can separate from her phone, we should load up," Max suggested, ready to get going.

"Whose car we gonna put it in?" Harry wanted to know.

"Mine," Max decided. "That way we can unload it all when Lucky's left."

"What time's she going?" Harry asked.

"Early in the A.M., I hope. The sooner she shifts outta L.A., the quicker we can get goin' on the party."

"An' you're certain your old man's not gonna spring a surprise an' come home unexpectedly?" Cookie questioned.

"Who, Lennie?" Max replied. "No way. Once I give the housekeepers the day off, we're free—totally free! And I for one cannot freakin' wait!"

CHAPTER TEN

Armand did not own a plane—too much trouble. He preferred hiring a private plane to fly him wherever he wished to go. On his yearly visit to Akramshar, he enjoyed stopping off for twenty-four hours in London, where he spent all his time at the Dorchester Hotel, ordering in a series of call girls. He insisted that his madam of choice—a titled woman who resided in a mansion in Belgravia and was forever recruiting new girls—send him only the best. Well-bred English girls with clipped upper-class accents, slim bodies, and excellent pedigrees.

Humiliating English women appealed to him. He plied them with drugs and watched them prostitute themselves while doing anything he commanded. It made a pleasant change from dealing with American whores, who sometimes acted as if they were faking it.

Recently, Armand's cocaine habit *had* escalated, just as Fouad suspected. At first Armand had simply enjoyed watching the women lose all their inhibitions on drugs. But after a while he'd found he enjoyed the enhanced sensation of sexual power he felt when high on coke. And why not? He was invincible. He could do anything he wanted.

He especially enjoyed snorting cocaine off the women's bodies—using them, toying with them, debasing them in any new way he could think of.

With his sexual appetite well sated, he was finally

ready to spend forty-eight hours in Akramshar, avoiding Soraya and his four offspring, whom he barely knew. He only made the yearly trek because of his father and their shared business interests.

When King Emir Amin Mohamed Jordan passed on, there would be a huge fortune to be divided between the king's sons (the women of the family would inherit nothing), and Armand had to make certain he received his rightful share. Not that he needed it, but he was damn well going to see that he received it. Plus, the companies he'd formed with the king would be all his.

He was fully aware that his father considered him the favorite among all of his sons, who now totaled eleven. He was the one who got away and made a huge success in America. He was the only one worth shit. And he was the one the king trusted to funnel his money into America in case he ever needed it.

Returning to Akramshar was always a jarring experience. Leaving the Western world and entering a city where men ruled supreme was quite primitive and yet strangely satisfying. Subservient women behaved the way all females should. But try telling the Americans that.

A black Mercedes met him at the airport and ferried him to his palace. Yes, he had a palace, on loan from the king. Sometimes he wondered how the stringy, social-climbing New York hostesses would feel if they knew he was a prince and lived in a palace. They would slit their skinny throats to get a piece of him.

Servants abounded, but Soraya was not there to greet him. As if he cared. The children were confined to their quarters—another plus.

Upon his arrival, he shed his clothes and enjoyed the comfort of the traditional male robe that all men wore. Most of the women in Akramshar were expected to be covered at all times, and rightly so. His mother had told him that under their burqas the women in the harem wore expensive clothes purchased in Rome and Milan, where King Emir sometimes took a select group of his wives for a long weekend. The king especially favored lacy lingerie, and on these trips he encouraged his wives to spend, spend, spend.

Peggy had needed no encouragement to do exactly that. She'd amassed an impressive collection of jewelry during the years she'd spent in Akramshar, and several trunks full of designer clothes.

Armand tried not to think about his mother too much. Sidney Dunn had died a year previously, and it annoyed him that since then Peggy had become quite demanding—phoning him at all hours, claiming that she didn't see enough of him, wondering why he'd never married and given her grandchildren. Since she had no contact with anyone in Akramshar, she knew nothing of his wife and children.

Armand was well aware of what a nightmare it would be if she ever found out that he already had a family. A nightmare he was not prepared to deal with. She would insist on being involved, and when Peggy insisted on something, there was no stopping her.

Fouad was the only person who knew about his family, and he trusted Fouad to keep his silence. Fouad would never betray him; it was in his blood to remain loyal.

After changing into his robe, he retired to a males-only terrace room, far away from Soraya and the children. A manservant immediately brought him a cup of strong black tea and a plate of sweet biscuits. Another servant asked if he required a massage.

Yes, a massage was exactly what he required.

He sipped his tea, then entered a side room where soft music played. Two young women helped him out of his robe and, when he was fully naked, onto a massage table.

These women were not whores, they were servants who treated him like the prince he was. They trickled hot oil over his chest and stomach, moving slowly down to his groin area with their soothing hands. They wore white robes, which after a while he instructed them to remove. They were young—but not too young to service him with their soft lips. He felt aroused, and lay still while they brought him to orgasm. They were too young to humiliate; he couldn't be bothered.

When they were finished, he required nothing except solitude and time to think about the prize he was about to acquire when he returned to America.

The Keys.

His hotel.

A place where he'd decided he would be forever content.

CHAPTER ELEVEN

Spending time with Sam was nice. Denver really appreciated his slightly skewed sense of humor. He was so laid-back and unthreatening, and not overly good-looking, although he was attractive in an Owen Wilson quirky kind of way. Also, he didn't hail from a high-powered family, or at least she didn't think he did, and that was another plus. Her brothers would love him; he was their kind of guy. Bobby—not so much. They'd find Bobby a bit out of their league.

Out of my league too, she thought wryly. *Way out of my league.*

Or not.

Lately she'd found herself trying to talk herself out of being with Bobby. It was almost as if she didn't feel she deserved him, which of course was ridiculous.

Or was it?

He'd never even noticed her in high school, so why was he with her now? She was the same person. Well . . . almost. Minus the braces and bad hair and chubby curves.

Sam had walked her back to her apartment, and she hadn't invited him in.

"Are you still seeing that guy you were with last time I was here?" he'd asked, striving to sound casual.

"Kind of," she'd replied.

Kind of! Bobby would throw a fit if he heard how offhand she sounded about their relationship. Why hadn't she said, "Yes, we're together. Very much so. I love him and he loves me. So sorry, Sam, *that's* why I'm not inviting you in."

"Okay then," Sam had said. "Maybe you'd like to come by the set one day—watch them all ignore me." She laughed. "I can offer you a fine lunch off the catering truck," he added. "Whaddya think?"

"Sounds irresistible. Only please remember I'm a working girl."

"We're shooting all next weekend," he said, determined not to give up. "How about dropping by Saturday or Sunday?"

"I, uh, think I might have to go to Vegas," she said, keeping it vague. "But, uh, I'll call you."

Great, Denver. Getting all friendly with an ex would not go down well with Bobby. What's wrong with you?

Nothing. Or everything.

Suddenly she missed Bobby like crazy.

Finally Frankie returned one of Cookie's seven calls. Max and Harry exchanged a relieved look. Cookie had been driving them nuts with her endless stream of comments about Frankie, all about what a stud he was, and how she could definitely fall for a guy like him, and WHY THE FUCK WASN'T HE CALLING HER BACK?

"He wants me to go to the club," she announced, shooting Max and Harry a triumphant look. "Wanna come?"

"No thanks," they chorused.

"Why not?" Cookie demanded, already trying to decide what to wear.

" 'Cause I have to get everything ready for my party," Max said.

She was excited about the party. It was actually the first time she would have the Malibu house all to herself.

And it was an amazing house, so perfect to throw a fantastic party. As long as she could keep everyone out of the house, what harm could anyone do? She planned on locking all the bedrooms, the screening room, and Lucky's and Lennie's private studies. The enormous patio, the infinity pool, and the sandy beach would be more than enough space for everyone to have a great time. She estimated they'd invited around thirty people, who would probably all bring a friend or two—so maybe they'd end up with seventy or eighty. Just the right number of bodies.

Harry was busy organizing a deejay he knew, and Cookie had already booked the In-N-Out hamburger truck to arrive at ten P.M., so it was all systems go.

Max had still not made up her mind about whether to invite Ace. He'd be a last-minute decision.

Cookie took off, and Max decided an early night wouldn't be a bad idea, so after she and Harry had finished loading up her trunk with as many boxes of beer and tequila as they could fit in, she gave Harry a hug and headed for home.

Tomorrow would be a very busy day indeed.

Bobby was not happy. He'd had to postpone his flight to New York, and now he was sitting in a strip club with M.J., the two male Russian investors, and the lone female, who was obviously a raving lesbian the way she was stuffing hundred-dollar bills into the strippers' almost nonexistent G-strings.

Fuck! He wanted out. But he couldn't leave M.J. to handle them on his own. They were a tricky trio. First they'd requested dinner and a show. Then they'd spent ten minutes in Mood—thank God it was only ten minutes. Finally M.J. had gotten them to sign the papers, at which point they'd insisted on celebrating at a famous Vegas gentleman's strip club to cement the deal.

Bobby had a strong aversion to clubs that featured strippers. He wasn't one of the guys when it came to a bunch of bored, vaguely desperate females taking off their clothes for the public's pleasure. He felt sorry for the girls, and even sorrier for the usually drunk guys who sat there with their mouths hanging open, hoping for a stray tit to come their way.

The strippers immediately gravitated toward Bobby and M.J.—two handsome, apparently sober guys.

"Wanna go private, honey?" a breast-enhanced redhead whispered in Bobby's ear, her tasseled nipple grazing his cheek.

"Uh . . . not tonight," he managed.

"You won't regret it, sweet thing," she purred, licking her lips. "I got moves you ain't gonna see on *Dancing with the Stars*."

"I bet," he said, backing away and indicating Miss Russia, who had shed her jacket and stern expression and was eyeing a small blonde with lustful eyes. "Take *her* private. I'll pay."

"Spoil sport," the redhead whispered, but she moved over to the woman, grabbed her by the hand, and led her back to one of the private champagne rooms.

Bobby leaned over to M.J. "They've signed the papers. You think we can get the hell out of here?"

Before M.J. could answer, Bobby's cell rang. He almost didn't hear it, what with Lady Gaga screaming about paparazzi on the sound system, and the general noise.

It was Denver. He'd tried to reach her earlier to tell her he hadn't left for New York yet, but she hadn't picked up.

"Hey," he said.

"Hey," she responded. "What's all that noise?"

"Long story," he said, delighted to hear her voice.

"Are you in New York?" she asked.

"Got delayed," he answered, waving off a determined

blonde with painful-looking nipple rings enhancing her overly large fake breasts.

"What? I can't hear you."

"I'll call you back."

"No. I'm going to sleep. Call me tomorrow."

"Will do."

He clicked off. Nothing worse than an unsatisfactory end to the evening.

CHAPTER TWELVE

An army of hardworking executives made sure that The Keys ran as smoothly as possible, considering there was a workforce of thousands. From the head of security to the woman in charge of guest relations, everyone pitched in, for Lucky had made sure there were plenty of incentives for every employee—whatever their position—to do their best.

When she'd built the hotel, she'd put together a syndicate of investors, who all held equal shares in the private company she'd created. Very soon, she hoped, her investors would begin receiving money back. The Keys was doing well, but the initial investment was monumental, and the downturn in the economy was not helpful. However, the casino was one of the most successful in Vegas, thanks to a band of casino hosts who were the best in the business. The hotel was usually at 90 percent capacity, plus the apartments had all sold for record-breaking prices.

Lucky was satisfied with the way things were going. The Keys was her child—her love child—created from her desire to build the perfect oasis in Las Vegas, the city where she'd first made her mark when she'd taken over the building of Gino's hotel after he'd been forced to leave the country on a tax exile.

There were good memories and bad ones. Gino's moneymen had refused to deal with a woman, so in the middle of the night she'd paid one of them a visit, held a knife to his balls, and demanded he pay up—otherwise she'd be back to cut 'em off!

Surprise, surprise, he'd paid! Oh yes, that was a fun memory.

Not so funny was remembering Marco, her fiancé, who'd been gunned down next to the hotel swimming pool. And her brother, Dario, murdered and tossed from a moving car.

Lucky refused to dwell on the past. After taking a suitable revenge, she'd moved forward. It was the only way to survive.

The Keys was her tribute to Marco, Dario, and her beautiful mother, Maria, another victim of a brutal crime.

Lucky often wondered if Max had any idea about their family history. Max never asked questions; she didn't seem interested. One day Lucky planned on sitting her down and telling her everything. Max needed to know the battles the Santangelos had gone through, from which they'd emerged triumphant. And she had to be made aware of their famous motto—*Never fuck with a Santangelo*.

So far Lennie had prevented her from filling Max in on the family saga. "Let her grow up first," he'd said. "There's plenty of time."

Lennie Golden. Her husband. The best man on the planet. When she'd first met him, he was a stand-up comedian at her hotel. She'd propositioned him. He'd turned her down. And when they'd next run into each other, she was married to Greek shipping billionaire Dimitri Stanislopoulos, and by some weird coincidence, he was married to Dimitri's spoiled daughter, Olympia. A crazy situation.

But in the end it had all worked out, and she could honestly say that Lennie was the love of her life. They were compatible in every way. True soul mates.

Before setting off for Vegas, she peeked in on Max, who was still asleep. Her child appeared so innocent when she was sleeping. Long-lashed eyelids covering brilliant green eyes, dark curly hair fanning out over the pillow.

Lucky stared at Max for a moment, remembering the day she was born, and Lennie's expression when he'd held his daughter for the first time. They'd named her Maria after Lucky's mother—a name Max changed in her teens because she felt Max was more her. So little Maria had become little Max. The new name suited her style; she'd always been an assertive child and quite a tomboy. Max Santangelo Golden.

Lucky sighed. Soon Max would be out on her own. They all grew up too quickly. Time moved at such a lightning pace.

"Bye, sweetheart," she whispered, bending down to kiss Max on the forehead. "See you soon."

The moment Lucky left her room, Max—who'd been faking sleep—jumped out of bed and ran to the window to witness her mother's departure. She'd pretended to be asleep because she hadn't wanted to get involved in a conversation about what she was going to do while everyone was away. Too risky, considering she was not the world's greatest liar, and unfortunately, Lucky possessed an extraordinarily keen bullshit detector.

Soon enough she observed Lucky striding out of the house and getting into a waiting town car to take her to the airport.

Max immediately reached for her cell and called Harry and Cookie, giving them the all clear. "Get your asses over here, we've got much to do," she said excitedly.

Her next job was getting rid of the two housekeepers, who might present a problem. They were recent hires, sisters from Guatemala. Fortunately, twenty-four hours of freedom suited them just fine. Lucky did not believe in keeping a large staff around—she was very down-to-earth in that respect, preferring to do things for herself. She'd also never cared to raise her children in a pampered environment.

Cookie arrived at the house first, a blissful smile on her pretty face. "No more *boys* for me," she announced with a dismissive wave of her hand. "It's men all the way."

"Oh, for God's sake!" Max responded, rolling her eyes. "It's *Frankie*. Get a grip. He's a major loser."

"He is *so* not," Cookie argued. "You don't know him."

"I've known him longer than you, thankyouvery-much," Max retaliated.

"Not in the way *I* know him," Cookie said with a secretive smile.

"Don't tell me you had sex again?" Max said, hoping she was wrong but sure that she wasn't.

"Wouldn't *you* like to know." Cookie giggled.

"Not really," Max said, hurrying over to the window to make sure the two young housekeepers got into the cab she'd ordered to take them to their families. She'd instructed them not to return until noon the next day, and she'd given them each fifty bucks cash, plus cab fare, to make sure they understood. The older sister had been worried about Lucky finding out, but Max had assured the girl in her best high school Spanish that Lucky would never know.

Once the housekeepers were gone, the three of them hurried downstairs and began unloading the booze from Max's car and lugging it out to the bar by the swimming pool.

"Who's going to make everyone drinks?" Cookie

asked, filling the outdoor fridge with bottles of beer. "Frankie kinda suggested we could borrow one of his bartenders. Whaddya think?"

"So you *did* invite him?" Max said, turning on her accusingly.

"Told you I was," Cookie said.

"But we didn't agree," Max objected. "Seems you're forgetting it's *my* party."

"Get over it," Cookie snapped. "You're just jealous 'cause I'm getting it an' you're not."

"That's crap," Max said, although maybe she was a little bit put out that for Cookie, sex seemed so uncomplicated. "And by the way, you stink of weed."

"Want some?" Cookie offered, digging into her purse.

"I do," Harry said, darting forward with an eager gleam in his eyes.

Max threw him a withering look. "No thanks," she said to Cookie. "And no bartender either. Everyone can help themselves. I'm dropping by the market and buying a ton of plastic glasses we can throw away later."

Cookie yawned, feigning boredom. "Whatever," she muttered. "It's *your* party."

"Okay, girls," Harry said, thinking it was time he butted in. "We've got work to do. Let's get to it."

The hostage situation worked itself out, and Leon was by Denver's desk early in the morning. For several weeks he'd been tracking a dealer who'd been selling his wares to a local high school, and he was close to making an arrest. But they both knew it wasn't the small-time dealer he was out to nail, it was the supplier, so his plan was to not Mirandize the guy, to get him to talk, then set him free.

Denver was in on the plan, and she fully approved.

Getting the big-time supplier into court was their ultimate goal, then, after a triumphant victory, throwing
him into jail, where he belonged. She couldn't wait to
get in on the action.

"What didja do last night?" Leon wanted to know,
hovering by her desk.

"Nothing much," Denver replied. "And you?"

"Went on a date with a Cuban girl who was into having sex in the elevator of her apartment house."

"Excuse me?" Denver said, raising an eyebrow.

Leon laughed. "She was one of those danger freaks.
Y'know, let's see if we can get ourselves caught."

"Lovely."

"I hadda say no, an' then she blew me off."

"In the sexual sense?"

"I wish," he said, laughing again. "Bitch called me
chicken an' told me to get out."

"Because you wouldn't have sex with her in an elevator?"

"You think I wanna get arrested for indecent ex-
posure? I can see myself comin' up in court with *you*
prosecuting my ass."

"If that ever happens, I'll be gentle," she promised,
smiling.

"Bullshit!"

They both laughed.

"Seriously, Denver," Leon said. "I gotta say I like
workin' with you. You're kinda one of the boys."

"I am?" she said, taking it as a compliment.

"Yeah. All the guys think so, an' believe me, that's
high praise."

"Well . . . I'm not sure what to say."

"You don't hav'ta say nothin'."

"Then I won't."

Leon circled her desk. "Y'know, this weekend, my
partner, Phil, an' his wife are throwin' a barbecue.

Nothin' fancy, but a lot of the guys are goin', an' I thought you might wanna tag along. Get t' know everyone."

"That's so nice of you, Leon, but this weekend I'll be in Vegas with my, uh . . . boyfriend." She felt stupid saying the word *boyfriend,* but that's exactly what Bobby was. Anyway, she needed to let Leon know she was taken, even though she was sure he already knew.

"Vegas, huh?" Leon said, hiding his disappointment. "Now, doncha go runnin' off an' sealin' the deal in one of those Elvis impersonator weddin' chapels."

"I promise I won't."

"Then I guess I'm gonna hav'ta let you go."

"I have your permission, do I?" she said, amused.

"Yeah, Denver. Put it all on lucky seven, an' don't come back without a big score."

"Yes *sir!*"

Her cell rang. It was Bobby. Leon took the hint and left.

"Where were you last night?" she asked. "I couldn't hear a word you said."

"Long boring story," Bobby replied, deciding he didn't need to mention the strip club. "Those Russian investors I told you about dragged everything out, and I ended up having to stay in Vegas."

"Poor you."

"Got on a plane early this morning, and just landed in New York." A beat. "But never mind about me. How are *you?*"

"Lonely."

"That's what I like to hear."

"Missing you."

"Even better."

"When will you be back?"

"Thursday night. Then Friday we'll fly to Vegas. Please tell me you're saying yes."

Alternatives: Visiting Sam on a movie set. Attending

a cop barbecue with Leon. Seems like no contest. "I'm saying yes, Bobby," she said softly.

"That's my girl. I'll call you later. Have a good one."

Checking out a couple of gossip sites on his computer, Frankie was delighted to find several shots of himself and Cookie leaning all over each other at River. She looked hot, kind of like a young Janet Jackson.

He quickly scanned the copy:

> *Eighteen-year-old Cookie, daughter of soul icon Gerald M., getting thisclose with her new boyfriend, Frankie Romano, at his club, River.*

Perfect! Exactly what he'd planned. He'd given access to a paparazzo, who'd gotten the shots in the club and then sold them. Of course, Rick Greco would be pissed that they'd called River his club, but hey—he *was* the front man. *He* was the one bringing the crowd in. Yeah! They all loved Frankie Romano. He knew how to satisfy everyone's decadent cravings. Nothing bad about *that*.

Unbeknownst to Rick, Frankie had a secret to assuring happy repeat customers, and that secret was a lucrative drug business he ran on the side. Coke, pills, Ecstasy, crystal meth, pot. You name it, Frankie could supply it. His rich and famous customers loved the convenience of having a virtual pharmacy at their disposal. Frankie had all his connections down, and now he was starting to make real money.

Too bad Rick hadn't made him a full partner; he might've considered sharing.

CHAPTER THIRTEEN

After spending some time with his father, who was resting before the next day's wildly extravagant birthday festivities, Armand returned to his palace and the family he had not yet seen.

This time Soraya was waiting to greet him. They had been married for eleven years, and he had to admit that from the fifteen-year-old girl he'd wed, Soraya had turned into a striking woman. She was tall and slender, with a sweep of long, straight black hair and large sad eyes. Her body was covered by the traditional burqa.

He found himself wondering what this woman he hardly knew would look like in Western clothes, and if, when he wasn't around, she actually wore them. The truth was he didn't care, even though she had given birth to four children—*his* children.

Soraya rarely spoke when she was in his presence, only answered him when he directed a question at her.

"Where is Tariq?" he asked, naming his only son.

"I will fetch him if you wish," Soraya replied.

He'd noticed that she never looked him directly in the eyes; she avoided any kind of contact, including physical. He'd stopped sleeping with her several visits ago. He had no desire for yet another daughter, and it seemed that every time he touched her, she ended up pregnant. Not that sleeping with her gave him any enjoyment. The few times he'd had sex with her, she'd lain beneath him like a stone statue, unmoving and unresponsive.

So be it. There were many women who would do anything he requested—no request too bizarre. Only yesterday in London he'd had two women crawling around his suite on all fours wearing leather dog collars, serving him dinner and then pleasuring each other for his amusement, while he sat back and snorted coke until he got bored and sent the whores away.

Soraya left the room and returned with Tariq, a tall, skinny boy of eleven. The boy was clad in an American Lakers T-shirt, jeans, and sneakers.

Armand was incensed. "Why is Tariq dressed like this?" he demanded. "It is disrespectful to me. Have him change immediately."

"Yes," Soraya murmured, shooing her son from the room.

"When I come here," Armand said, his voice a harsh command, "I expect obedience and respect. Do you understand me?"

Soraya hung her head, still refusing to look at him.

Armand didn't care. When the king died and he inherited what was his, perhaps he would abandon Akramshar and never come back. For it was not his country, not his home. America was his home. And Soraya and her brood were not his family.

King Emir Amin Mohamed Jordan embraced tradition—his own personal tradition. Every year it was the same thing: an elaborate parade put on by his legions of grandchildren, of whom he was extremely proud, followed by a public proclamation to the citizens of Akramshar, who revered their generous king. Then there was a series of more private celebrations. First a massive feast of roasted lamb, goat, and various other animals. The men on one side of the huge tent erected for the festivities, the women and children on the other. For entertainment, a dozen or so plump belly dancers jiggled their wares for several hours, until eventually the women and children were sent away and a parade of exquisite Eastern European women appeared, dressed in tight, low-cut cocktail dresses, with soaring high heels on their bare legs, and an abundance of makeup.

The women formed a line, and the king chose the ones he wished to sit with him and his sons. Later the king would pair off with a woman or three of his choice, and after he had chosen, it was his sons' turns to pick whomever they wanted. Since Armand was not the eldest son, he had to wait. This infuriated him. He felt that because of his business dealings with his father, he should be next. But tradition ruled. When his time came, he selected a sultry honey-blonde from Ukraine. She reminded him of Nona Constantine, and he enjoyed reliving the ravishing of Nona. The high-class call girl didn't complain, but she was paid a small fortune not to, so Armand had his fun with her, humiliating her in every possible way. When he finally dismissed her, he could see the hatred in her eyes. It did not bother him. She was a paid whore; why would he care?

Year after year, the king's celebrations were a repeat performance. And the next morning Armand was on a plane out of there, back to civilization; back to the life he preferred.

Good-bye, Akramshar.

Good-bye, Soraya.

Good-bye to the family he'd never wanted.

CHAPTER FOURTEEN

Driving along Pico on her way home from work, Denver checked in with Carolyn. She was curious to find out what had taken place on Carolyn's date with a woman. It seemed such a random thing for her to do—changing sides for no particular reason.

"Is Bobby in town?" Carolyn asked.

"No. He's in New York," Denver replied, pulling up to a red light. "Why?"

"'Cause I was thinking you might feel like picking up a Chinese chicken salad from Chin Chin and coming over."

"Sounds like a plan," Denver said, happy to do so. She hadn't felt like spending yet another evening home alone, and although she wasn't really into babies, she had to admit that Andy was extremely adorable.

Sam had called and left a message. She hadn't called him back; she didn't want to encourage him. After all, she'd told him she was still involved—sort of. Maybe he hadn't taken her as seriously as he should've.

After stopping by Chin Chin, she headed straight for Carolyn's house.

Carolyn was sitting out in her back garden, Andy balanced on her knee. The two of them made a perfect picture, straight out of *Modern Mother* magazine.

Denver wondered whether her friend was thinking of going back to work anytime soon. Andy's dad, the cheating Senator Stoneman, was certainly not sending her any child support. Who knew if he was even aware that he had a son? And since Carolyn's parents had split up, they were probably not prepared to give financial aid to their daughter forever. Besides, Denver reckoned it would be therapeutic for Carolyn to find a job and put all the Washington trauma behind her.

"Hey," she said lightly. "I left the food in the kitchen. Don't you ever lock your front door? I walked right in."

"Nothing for them to take except me and Andy," Carolyn remarked, completely unconcerned. "And I'm sure nobody wants us."

"How about your TV, your computer, your camera?" Denver pointed out. "All valuable items."

"I'm hardly ripe for a robbery."

"Everyone should take precautions," Denver admonished. "Crime is all around us."

"Spoken like a true DA."

"So," Denver said, throwing herself into the empty lawn chair beside Carolyn's, "I'm dying to know—how was your walk on the wild side?"

"Interesting," Carolyn said as her front doorbell chimed. She stood up and handed Denver the baby. "*Some* people ring before entering," she commented.

"*Some* people haven't known you since you were twelve," Denver replied tartly. "Are you expecting someone?"

"You'll see," Carolyn said, vanishing into the house.

"I only brought enough salad for two," Denver yelled after her. "And I'm starving, so I'm not in the mood for sharing."

Andy let out a big burp, and a dribble of drool slid down the side of his mouth. Awkwardly, Denver tried to wipe it away with the back of her hand. She wasn't used to babies; somehow the maternal gene had yet to kick in.

And then a vision appeared. A gorgeous woman with

soft, naturally curly blond hair, kind eyes, and a boun-
tiful figure.

Carolyn was right behind her. "Denver, meet Vanessa," she said briskly.

Denver was surprised and shocked. Somehow or
other she'd imagined Vanessa to be big and butch with
cropped hair and no makeup, dressed in a manly leather
jacket. This lovely, feminine woman was the complete
opposite.

"Uh, hi," Denver said, embarrassed that she'd had
such a clichéd view of what a lesbian should look like.

"Hello," Vanessa said, proffering a firm handshake
and a friendly smile. "Carolyn talks about you a lot. It's
such a pleasure to finally meet you."

Finally? One date and now Vanessa was acting as if
they were in a relationship. *What the hell?*

"Vanessa works for a TV production company," Carolyn said, smiling blissfully at her new friend. "Docu-
mentaries and the like."

"Really?" Denver said, suddenly feeling as if *she* was
the odd one out.

"Yes," Vanessa said, swooping down to steal Andy
out of Denver's arms. "I'm hoping to convince Carolyn
to come join us. With all her Washington experience,
she'd be such an asset. Will you please talk her into it?"

"I'll try," Denver said with a weak smile.

Carolyn giggled. Carolyn was *so* not a giggler. "I'm
thinking about it," she said coyly. "Nobody has to talk
me into anything."

"Well, think faster," Vanessa chided, and the two exchanged an intimate look.

Oh my God! Denver thought. *They're acting as if
they're already a couple. Who knew?*

Lucky's apartment in The Keys was her dream home.
Not that she didn't love the Malibu house and spending

time with her kids, but her haven in Vegas was her special place. Whenever she was there, she felt at peace. Sometimes she needed to be alone, and sitting in her penthouse above the Strip—looking out at the sparkling lights of the city—gave her immense satisfaction. It also reminded her of so many Vegas memories. Sometimes the memories were overwhelming, good and bad.

Picking up the house phone, she called downstairs to Danny, her personal assistant. Danny was the eyes and ears on everything Vegas when she wasn't in residence. He'd only worked for her a year, but he was quite possibly the best assistant she'd ever had. He was young, twenty-something, gay—in a long-term relationship with Buff, his high school buddy. She trusted him implicitly.

"Did Gino arrive yet?" she asked.

"He's here," Danny responded. "Feisty as ever. I cannot believe how old that man is!"

Lucky smiled, thinking of her ninety-something father, who never slowed down. "Yes, he's remarkable, isn't he?" she said. Gino had his own suite at The Keys, and there was nothing he liked more than sitting in a lounge chair outside his private cabana at the pool, watching all the pretty girls pass by. He had not acquired the nickname Gino the Ram for nothing. Over the years, he'd certainly lived up to his reputation. Now married to his fifth wife, Paige, a woman decades younger than him, Gino seemed to have more energy than anyone.

"Is everything set for the board meeting on Friday?" Lucky asked.

"Of course," Danny replied. "It's all in order."

"I think I've persuaded Alex Woods to come. Make sure he has the right accommodations. And arrange to have cars meet everyone at the airport."

"Got it, Lucky."

"Okay, then," she said, tossing back her long jet-black hair. "I'm on my way to see Gino. We'll talk later."

* * *

The Malibu party started off slowly. A trickle of friends hanging out by the pool drinking beer and Coke from cans, laughing and talking and generally getting loose.

Max glanced around and wished she *had* invited Ace. Maybe this would've been the night they consummated their relationship, shifting it to another level. Since she was about to be eighteen, wasn't it time to do something about taking things all the way?

She took a quick peek at her watch and realized it was only just past eight, so if she called him now he could probably make it in a couple of hours. But then he'd be annoyed that she hadn't told him about it before, so it was best to leave it alone.

Cookie was busy draping herself all over the deejay Harry had gotten. The guy was Latin and a major hottie straight out of a Calvin Klein ad. Maybe Frankie wouldn't show, and Cookie would settle for this guy. He certainly knew his stuff—rocking everything from Usher to Drake to Miley to old eighties soul and Beatles classics.

This is going to be a perfect evening, Max thought. *A mellow way to celebrate turning eighteen. And after I'm eighteen, I'm moving to New York, far away from parental concerns. I'm going to be exactly like Bobby and make my own life.*

Doing what?

I haven't decided.

She darted inside the house to check that she'd locked up all the main rooms. She certainly didn't want anyone coming into the house. Lucky would *so* not appreciate it.

Harry followed her, his spiked hair gelled higher than ever. "You gotta tell Cookie to lay off Paco," he said, sounding flustered. "She's such a greedy bitch. If it's got a dick, she wants it."

"Who's Paco?"

Harry's pale skin reddened. "The deejay."

"Why d'you want her to back off?"

" 'Cause I gotta wild hunch he's gonna be way more into me than her," Harry said.

"Oh crap!" Max exclaimed, getting the message.

"So *do* something about her," Harry pleaded.

"I'll try," Max promised. "But you know Cookie. . . ."

Yes, everyone knew Cookie. If there was a party, she was there. If there was a hot guy, she was there. Cookie had lost her virginity to one of her famous father's friends when she was fourteen, and she'd never looked back.

It kind of irked Max that she lurked so far behind in the sex stakes, but then again, she didn't want to give it up to just anyone. The first time had to be special, and she was making sure that it would be.

Back in New York, Bobby stopped by his apartment, checked his e-mail, took a shower, put on fresh clothes, and headed for Mood.

It was past ten by the time he arrived, and the place was packed, as usual. Wednesday nights were usually extra happening, as it was guest deejay night, and everyone enjoyed the change of pace. His manager, Paulo, a suave Italian, assured him things were going well.

Bobby did the rounds, stopping by tables, buying people drinks, complimenting the women. He wasn't crazy about playing the genial host, but he did it because he knew it was good for business.

Martin Constantine—the real-estate mogul—insisted that he join him and his wife, Nona, for a glass of champagne. At one time Bobby had considered asking Martin if he'd be interested in investing in future clubs, but then he'd decided against it, because Martin wouldn't simply put up the money; he was the kind of man who'd expect to be involved.

Nona, an ex–beauty queen from Slovakia, was not her normal flirty self. Bobby was relieved. He'd never quite figured out how to deal with the horny wives of rich men, and it was surprising how many came on to him. Horny wives were a business hazard he tried to avoid.

After having a quick drink with Martin and Nona, he moved on to sit with Charlie Dollar and Cooper Turner, two old Hollywood stalwarts who still attracted a parade of beautiful girls. There was something about weathered movie stars that prevented them from being perceived as dirty old men. It was the Jack Nicholson/Al Pacino syndrome.

After a while, Paulo approached and whispered discreetly in his ear that the outrageous superstar Zeena was requesting his presence at her table.

Ah, Zeena! They'd had a few run-ins, the last one in Vegas, where she'd unexpectedly appeared in his shower and given him head, later practically announcing it onstage in the middle of her concert, while he was on his first date with Denver. Not easy explaining *that* little incident to Denver. It had gotten them off to a rocky start. But fortunately, everything had worked out, and the last thing he needed was Zeena screwing things up again.

He instructed Paulo to make sure there was no one taking any photos in the club—one had to watch out for cell phones—then reluctantly made his way over to Zeena's table, where she was holding court with her usual entourage of hangers-on and her latest boyfriend, an emaciated English actor famous for playing a blood-crazed vampire on TV.

Zeena was her usual over-the-top self—she was half Brazilian, half Native American, and her exotic beauty could be mesmerizing.

"Bobbee," she purred in her low-down husky voice.

"Zeena hasn't seen you for too long. Where has my Bobbee been?"

He stared into her catlike eyes and realized that the crush he'd once had on her was long gone. "Around," he said casually, shaking the hand of her pale-faced boyfriend.

"Maybe Zeena should come visit you," Zeena suggested. "You like?"

Vampire boyfriend spoke up. "No," he said firmly. "He wouldn't like, and neither would I."

At last! Zeena had finally hooked up with someone who wasn't afraid to stand up to her.

Bobby laughed, easing the sudden tension. "Zeena, always the joker," he said smoothly, patting her boyfriend on the shoulder. "I'm sending your table more champagne. Enjoy."

And before she could respond with another unwelcome come-on, he was on his way to the next booth, where Adrien Brody and his friend Dieter Abt were ensconced with a group of beautiful models, male and female.

A fast escape. The best kind.

"Y'know," Lucky said affectionately, "if I didn't know any better, I would swear you weren't a day over seventy! You're amazing!"

Gino roared with laughter. Remarkably, he still had all his teeth, and although his hair was gray, it was still there. Age had not bowed him. "I'm in my nineties, kiddo," he said. "Outlived 'em all. An' I don't regret a minute of the life I lived. 'Cept maybe when you an' me wasn't talkin'."

"Well, that didn't last, did it?" she said, remembering their many famous fights over the years.

"Naw. Knew it wouldn't," Gino answered, grinning. "You're easy."

"Sure I am," Lucky replied sarcastically.

They were sitting together in Lucky's favorite restaurant at The Keys, a cozy Italian place tucked away in a corner spot, aptly called Gino's. The restaurant served all the food Gino loved. Meatballs with garlic and a rich tomato sauce. Penne pasta. Tasty veal chops with roasted Tuscan potatoes and myriad vegetables. Plus an assortment of pizzas named after various members of the Santangelo family.

Paige had elected not to join them, claiming she was tired, but Lucky knew it was because Paige was smart enough to know they enjoyed spending time together, just the two of them.

"How's little Max?" Gino wanted to know. "Still plannin' her escape?"

"Oh yes," Lucky said ruefully. "There's no stopping that one."

"Just like you, Lucky, huh?" Gino said, nodding at the memories.

"I hope not. I was a wild one."

"You still are, kiddo, you still are."

"Thanks, Gino, but I don't know about that."

"Yeah, well, I do. You inherited the Santangelo balls; that's what makes you such a winner. An' you gotta teach Max how t' deal."

"She's pretty smart, Gino."

"Not as smart as you when you were her—"

"There's plenty of time for her to learn," Lucky interrupted.

"Time goes quickly, kiddo. You'd be surprised."

"Not for you it doesn't."

"Y'know," he said, lowering his gruff voice, "if ya wanna know what goes on in my head, I'm gonna tell ya—I got this thought goin' on that I'm only thirty." A big grin spread across his face. "How's about *that?*"

"Right," Lucky retorted. "And I'm sixteen, getting

my ass married off to some dumb senator's son 'cause my daddy thought it would control me. Lotsa luck with *that*."

"Here she goes," Gino groaned. "Always dredgin' up the past."

"Just f-ing with you, Gino," she said lightly. "Nothing I like better than watching you squirm."

And once again she smiled, realizing there was nothing more satisfying than spending time with her father, for who knew how long he'd be around.

Willow Price and her posse of nubile young women— all various shades of blond and bubbly—decided they would like to go clubbing. And since Billy had nothing better to do after buying them all dinner at an expensive restaurant, he thought he might as well tag along. After all, his image was out of control and he kind of liked it. Leaving BOA with the darling of the tabs, Willow Price, and her blond entourage guaranteed a major media blitz, and since Venus had been seen out and about with her young costar *and* the grizzled director of her current movie, it was only fitting that he do the same.

Also, Venus's lawyer had informed *his* lawyer that she intended to keep their Vegas apartment in The Keys, and since he'd paid for half, that really pissed him off. He'd told his lawyer to fight her on that one. Screw Venus. Screw the big superstar who thought she could get anything she wanted.

Think again, sweetheart. He might be thirteen years younger than his soon-to-be ex, but he was no pushover.

Willow clung on to his arm for the sake of the paparazzi. The photographers descended like a pack of rabid dogs, screaming both their names, while the unknown blondes hovered and giggled, and flashed their tits and long legs emerging from tight micro miniskirts, thrilled to be a part of such mayhem.

"If you're a very, *very* well-behaved boy," Willow whispered in his ear, pouting innocently for the cameras, "I'll let you watch me lick pussy later."

He contemplated the future scenario she had in mind. Watching was not his thing. If he wasn't a participant, he wasn't interested.

"That's all right," he mumbled. "Whyn't we get in the car an' stop by River?"

"Oh yes," Willow purred. "I'd like that."

One last pose for the cameras, and they were on their way.

CHAPTER FIFTEEN

Three hours into what seemed like an under-the-radar, mellow party, chaos reigned. Max couldn't figure out how it had happened. From the maybe seventy or eighty people they'd expected, others were pouring in at an alarming rate. Carloads of teenagers she didn't know, didn't want to know, and could do nothing about. And not only teenagers, but a bunch of dirty old men—probably agents or producers—in their flashy Porsches and Bentleys, not to mention flocks of random girls in tiny backless, almost frontless, outfits.

Several people brought booze with them. A boy in a Batman outfit dragged in a keg. Two girls came armed with a margarita machine. Some people were smoking weed, others snorting cocaine. A whole bunch of naked men and women were frolicking in the pool, while others were making out on the patio. It was insanity. And neither Cookie nor Harry was any help. Harry had affixed himself to Paco, the deejay, and refused to move, while Cookie was snorting and drinking and having herself a fine old time. They were both stoned. Both feeling no pain.

Max rarely drank, and she didn't do drugs. Apparently she was the only one.

People were finding their way into the house. They'd already taken over the living room, and a drunken group of girls was attempting to break the lock on Lucky and Lennie's bedroom door.

Panicked, Max thought about anonymously calling

the cops and complaining about the noise, but that wouldn't help, considering they might file a report of a disturbance, and then Lucky or Lennie would find out. Not a smart move.

What was she supposed to do to stop the invasion?

Lucky would go totally ape shit if she ever found out what was going on. Max knew she'd be grounded for weeks, maybe even months. Life as she knew it would be over.

Although, wait a minute, she thought. *I'm about to turn eighteen; they can't ground me.*

Or can they?

What they *could* do was cut off her allowance and not pay for her ticket to New York and the six months' rent on an apartment Lucky had promised her as a birthday present.

Pulling herself together, she confronted the girls trying to force their way into Lucky's bedroom.

They told her to screw off.

She yelled back at them that it was her house and *they* could screw off or she'd call the cops and accuse them of trespassing.

They retaliated with a few obscene gestures and insults, then staggered off.

Max wished she had invited Ace. He'd know what to do. She didn't. As far as she was concerned, her party had turned into an uncontrollable nightmare, and she was totally helpless to do anything about it.

Lucky would know how to handle it. Lucky knew how to handle anything.

Dammit. Why couldn't she be more like her mom in situations such as this?

The insistent buzz of his doorbell awoke Bobby with a sudden start. Groping for his watch, he noted it was four A.M.

Goddammit! Who was outside his apartment at four in the morning? And what the fuck was his doorman doing that he allowed someone to come up unannounced?

Muttering to himself, he rolled out of bed and headed for the door in nothing but his Calvins.

Then he stopped. Dead still. There was only one person who would have the balls to come calling at this time. Zeena.

Of course!

The doorbell continued to ring, and he stood silently in his hallway trying to figure out his next move.

It suddenly occurred to him that there was only one answer, and that was to do absolutely nothing and hope the predatory superstar would slink away into the night. It wasn't the first time she'd turned up at his apartment at some unearthly hour. She was one hell of a persistent woman, who when she wanted something, expected to get it. And tonight she obviously wanted him.

They had a history. Once upon a time he'd harbored a slight crush. She'd turned up at his New York apartment and they'd gone at it like a couple of wild things. One time was enough. Crush over. But the unfortunate thing was that she'd continued to pursue him, culminating in the embarrassing shower scene on the night of his first date with Denver. That was some memory.

He'd had no contact with her since, and tonight he'd been pleased to note she was with her latest conquest.

Apparently her latest conquest wasn't enough to satisfy Zeena, for now she was on *his* doorstep.

And what was he supposed to do about *that?*

Exactly nothing.

"Who wants to come to a party in Malibu?" Frankie asked Billy, Willow, and their assorted hangers-on.

"Whose party?" Billy wanted to know.

"Does anyone care?" Willow retorted, always up for a fun time. "It'll be *our* party when we get there, no doubt about that."

They'd all been hanging out in the club for a while, during which time Frankie had presented them with primo weed and made sure all their drinks were comped. Willow's crazy girlfriends were dancing on the tables to Katy Perry, while Willow watched them cavort, a secret smile playing around her glossy lips as she anticipated the scene that would take place later.

Billy sat back, downing a vodka or two. He looked bored. He *was* bored. The session with the girl he'd picked up on Melrose had not satisfied him. Momentarily, yes. But somehow he craved more than a fast blow job beside his pool. Lately he'd been thinking that it might be refreshing to find someone he could conduct an actual conversation with.

Willow was certainly not that person, nor were her nubile groupies. But that's what he seemed to be stuck with—for now.

Meanwhile, Frankie was buzzing. Having celebrities in his club was a plus, especially as he got off on spending time with anyone famous. Celebrities validated his existence.

Cookie had phoned several times asking when he was getting to the Malibu party. The last time she'd called he'd assured her he was on his way, and since Cookie was his pathway to bigger and better, he wasn't about to let her down. Arriving with Willow and Billy—two of the hottest stars around—would definitely impress her.

After a while he rounded up Billy, Willow, and the girls. "Got a couple of limos downstairs. Time to bounce," he informed them. "Refreshments in the limos," he added with a knowing wink, wondering if he stood half a chance with Willow—although rumor had it that she was a tried-and-true carpet muncher.

But hey, he was Frankie Romano. Who knew *what* could happen?

Feeling out of her depth, Max grabbed a bottle of beer and fled down to the beach. She didn't know what else to do. Maybe if she stayed away from the chaos, everyone would go home.

Wishful thinking.

Whose dumb idea was it to have a party in the first place?

Mine! Mine! Mine!

As for Cookie and Harry, the two of them were useless. She'd thought they were at least loyal, but they'd turned into party animals, thinking only of themselves. Although she didn't blame Harry so much. He'd finally found a gay dude he could latch onto, and he wasn't about to let the opportunity go to waste.

Why can't I enjoy myself too? she thought. *Just get stoned and drunk like everyone else?*

Because there's no one I can enjoy things with. Besides, I'm a Santangelo—gotta stay alert.

She slumped down on the sand, closed her eyes, and allowed the hypnotic sound of the waves crashing on the sand to wash over her.

After spending an awkward couple of hours with Carolyn and Vanessa, Denver drove home filled with mixed emotions. What was Carolyn thinking? How could she simply decide she was gay and that was it?

They'd been best friends since they were twelve. They'd shared everything—all their thoughts and dreams and problems with the men in their lives. Now Carolyn had taken off down a different road, and Denver couldn't help feeling that somehow she'd been left behind. It wasn't that she didn't like Vanessa; the woman was warm and friendly. Quite lovely, in fact. So what was it?

Am I jealous? she wondered. *Do I feel as if Carolyn is deserting me?*

Or maybe she sensed that their friendship was slipping away, because if Carolyn became a couple with Vanessa, there might not be any room left for her. Sad but true.

She wished Bobby were at home, waiting for her.

But no, Bobby was in New York, so she'd just have to make do without him. And that was one of the problems of having a long-distance relationship: the separations were a bitch.

Once they arrived at the party, Billy soon decided that he wasn't in the mood to mix with a bunch of stoned people he didn't know, who were all busy brownnosing him simply because he had a hit movie. If he weren't a movie star, they wouldn't give a shit. He'd be just another good-looking dude searching for a break. And he knew this because of his experiences when he'd first arrived in Hollywood with no money and no foreseeable future. Countless auditions that had taken him nowhere, sleeping on friends' floors, waitering for a living, until he finally got the big break he'd been praying for—not that he was religious, but a prayer or two in the right direction never hurt. The big break was in an Alex Woods movie, *Seduction,* playing opposite the incredibly famous Venus.

And so it had begun. The crazy career. The road to stardom, marriage to Venus, and all the bullshit that went along with it.

The party and the people were getting on his nerves, so after fifteen minutes of meaningless conversations, he made his way over to the steps that led down to the beach, leaving the party behind.

As he walked along the sand, he noticed a girl curled

up against a rock. He edged toward her. "Hey," he said, gingerly nudging her with the tip of his foot, hoping she wasn't dead or sick or anything overly dramatic. "You okay?"

Max sat up with a start. Wow! She'd downed a beer, closed her eyes, and zoned out. Talk about an escape hatch!

"I'm, uh . . . fine, thank you," she said stiffly, somewhat embarrassed.

He proffered his hand.

She took it, and he pulled her up.

"What're you doing down here by yourself?" he asked.

"Same as you, probably," she said, pushing her clouds of dark hair off her face. "Getting away from all those morons."

Billy laughed, and took a second look at the sexy young girl with the jet-black curls and the exceptionally pretty face. She was clad in rock 'n' roll torn jeans and a midriff-baring white shirt knotted under her breasts, with multiple silver chains and crosses hanging around her slender neck. He narrowed his eyes. "I *know* you," he said, thinking she looked vaguely familiar.

"And *I* know *you*," she responded, staring at the studly tousled-haired movie star with the piercing blue eyes and rippling torso nicely displayed in a tight black T-shirt. Of course she knew him. Everyone did.

"Saw my movie, huh?" Billy said, thinking that his fame was such a useful conversation opener. And this girl was majorly hot—in a very un-bimbo-like way. He'd left the bimbo squad cavorting naked in the pool with Willow, and he couldn't care less about any of them.

"I didn't, actually," Max lied, thinking that he looked way better offscreen, because she'd seen his latest movie. Twice. But she wasn't about to tell *him* that.

"Then where do we know each other from?" Billy asked, realizing that he'd smoked too much weed and downed too many vodka shots, which was another reason he'd headed to the beach to chill out.

"Um . . . you were married to my mom's best friend," Max blurted.

"Who's your mom's best friend?"

"Venus."

Billy's face registered shock. "You're—"

"Yeah, I'm Max. Lucky's daughter."

"You *gotta* be shittin' me," he exclaimed.

"Now, why would I do that?" she asked innocently.

"Jeez!" he said, his mind taking off in many different directions. "Thought I recognized the house. I must've been here a couple of times. Where's Lucky and Lennie?"

"Lucky's in Vegas. Lennie's shooting a movie," Max said, slightly breathless because this was Billy Melina, and along with Johnny Depp and Robert Pattinson, he was one of her favorites. She'd harbored a secret crush for months, ever since seeing his latest movie.

"Don't tell me this is *your* party?" Billy said, gesturing up toward the distant house where music was blaring and lights were flashing. Someone had added fireworks to the mix, so every few minutes the sky lit up and the noise was out of control.

"Unfortunately, yes," she admitted. "It's a total bad scene, right?"

"Let me get this straight," Billy said, somewhat perplexed. "So even though it's your party, you're down on the beach because . . . ?"

"'Cause I just told you—it's a freaking nightmare," she said with a helpless shrug. "I made a daring escape. Can you blame me?"

"Hmm . . ." he said, giving her a long quizzical look. "Do Mommy and Daddy know you're entertaining?"

"What do *you* think?" she replied, gazing directly into his electric blue eyes.

"I'm taking a wild guess an' saying they don't."

"And you're *so* not about to tell them, are you?"

"Hey," he said with a casual shrug. "We're hardly on speaking terms, what with Venus bad-mouthing me big-time."

"Oh yes," Max said tartly. "Auntie Venus."

"Shit!" Billy mock-groaned. "Don't say that, you're makin' me feel old."

"You *are* old, aren't you?" she said boldly.

"Thirty, chicken. An' you?"

"Eighteen," she answered, which wasn't *such* a huge lie, because there were only three more days to go.

They exchanged a long look, one that sent shivers up and down her spine.

Was this really happening?

Yes. Absolutely.

"Hey," he said, breaking the look. "Wanna take a walk?"

She nodded. Like it was Billy Melina; there was no way she'd turn *him* down.

They started strolling along the sand, close to the shoreline, and after a while, Billy began to talk. The more he talked, the more she found herself really liking him. He told her about the movie he was shooting and a whole load of interesting and funny stories to do with the cast and crew. Soon she began telling him about her plans to move to New York and start a new life away from her parents, and the cool thing was that he actually listened to her, told her it sounded like a great move to make and that she should definitely do it.

Yes, he was way hotter offscreen than on. In the past she'd seen him from afar several times with Venus, and she vaguely remembered watching him laughing and joking with Lucky and Lennie at the opening of The

Keys. He'd never taken any notice of her before, but this time was different. This time they were two people with an awesome electric current buzzing between them.

She wondered if he could feel it too.

Suddenly she wanted nothing more than to touch him, feel his skin against hers, experience everything he had to offer.

Oh God! Could this be it? Had she finally met The One?

Billy Melina.

Soon-to-be ex of her mom's best friend.

Red-hot movie star.

What better way to lose her virginity?

Sometimes Frankie got into fights. He had his enemies. A club promoter he'd butted heads with in the past was coming on to Willow and her naked nymphs in the pool, calling them names and generally being obnoxious.

Sitting in a lounge chair with a giggly and very stoned Cookie, Frankie felt perfectly content until Cookie hissed in his ear, "Do something!"

So he did, and almost got coldcocked for his trouble.

"Goddammit!" he exclaimed, nursing his jaw. When had he become the protector of dykes? "That prick could've knocked my fuckin' teeth out."

"Well, he didn't," said an unconcerned Cookie as "that prick" was escorted off the premises by two macho gay guys who worshiped Willow Price and would do anything for her.

"Where were they when I needed them?" Frankie grumbled.

"Never mind," Cookie cooed, getting up and leading him into the house. "Let's go do some more blow. You know that'll make you feel *way* better."

It was almost four A.M. and the party was starting to wind down. There were only a few stragglers left in the living room. Harry was around, helping the deejay pack up.

Cookie had no clue where Max was, and she didn't care. It was time for Frankie to give it up, and not only the cocaine.

Cookie was one very happy camper.

"Maybe we should get back up to the house?" Billy suggested after a while.

"Sure," Max said, totally aware that something powerful was going on between them, an unstoppable attraction.

"Or . . ." He moved toward her, placing his hands on her shoulders. "We could stay here."

Yes, he senses it too! Oh crap!

She leaned a touch closer to him. "Maybe we *should* stay here," she managed.

"Maybe you're right," he countered.

Then, before she could think of anything else to say, his lips descended on hers, insistent and strong.

She kissed him back, shudders of excitement racing through her body, an excitement so intense that she couldn't wait to rip her clothes off, or have him do it for her.

After a few moments he began unknotting her shirt, pulling it off her, then touching her breasts with his fingertips, pushing them together before bending his head to suck ever so slowly on each nipple.

"Billy," she murmured, rubbing her hand between his legs, stroking him the way Ace liked her to do—although he wasn't Ace, with whom she'd only gone so far. He was Billy Melina, movie star, friend of her parents, soon-to-be ex-husband of Venus.

She didn't care. She didn't care about anything except having him close to her.

Hurriedly, he ripped off his T-shirt and threw it down

on the sand, then somehow he maneuvered her on top of it and he lay on top of her. Within minutes they were both naked and enthralled with each other.

Billy was vaguely aware that he shouldn't be making this move with Lucky's daughter. If Venus ever found out, she'd go nuts. But jeez, he hadn't felt this way since the first time he'd had sex with his high school girlfriend. There was something very special about Max. She wasn't just another casual pickup.

Oh yeah, on one hand he knew being with her would cause nothing but trouble.

On the other hand, he didn't give a flying fuck.

Max felt the same way as she gave in to the feelings that were completely overpowering her. This was it. This was the man she'd been saving herself for, and as far as she was concerned, nothing was going to stop the inevitable, and to hell with the consequences.

He began to make love to her, slowly, surely, taking it easy.

She closed her eyes and fell into his rhythm.

He smells so good, she thought. *Like a strong, fragrant soap mixed with his masculine body smell.*

She smells like sweet sin, he thought. *And it's a smell that turns me on to the highest degree.*

He has a body to die for.

She has the kind of body I dream about.

Smooth skin.

Taut surfaces.

Erect nipples.

Hers—deep rose.

His—black like the night.

I think I'm in love.

I think I'm in lust.

First time.

Tactile touches.

A rush of pure sweat.

An avalanche of desire.
Plunging into heaven.
Going all the way.
Feeling his power.
Feeling her acceptance.
Working together.
So gentle.
So soft.
And hard.
Breathless.
Wow!
Amazing.
Forbidden fruit.
Barely ripe.
Heady.
Intoxicating.
Falling into ecstasy.
And finally
Together.

CHAPTER SIXTEEN

Arriving back in New York, Armand was escorted through security by an airport representative, then ushered to a limousine parked at a private entrance where Fouad was waiting. Most times he accompanied Armand to Akramshar, but this time Armand had chosen to go alone.

Before Fouad could say a word, Armand demanded to know what was happening with The Keys.

Typical Armand, thought Fouad. *No time for pleasantries; straight to business.*

"We have a meeting in Vegas tomorrow," Fouad said, clearing his throat. "It was not easy arranging it. As I told you before, according to her lawyer, this Santangelo woman is not interested in selling, so I informed him that we were thinking of perhaps financing future projects she might be open to. Her lawyer seemed to entertain the thought of unlimited investment capitol."

"For God's sake!" Armand snorted derisively. "Why did you say that?"

"It was the only way I could arrange a meeting," Fouad explained.

"Such a fool," Armand muttered.

"In the meantime I had a dossier compiled on Lucky Santangelo," Fouad said, handing Armand a thick manila envelope. "I thought you might find it interesting. I know I did."

" 'Interesting,' " Armand sneered. "Show me an interesting woman and I will show *you* a freak of nature."

"She is not your average woman," Fouad said evenly. "I would read it if I were you."

"Unfortunately for you, you're *not* me," Armand replied with a note of disdain, tossing the envelope on the floor of the limo.

Fouad wasn't surprised. Over the past few months, Armand had become even more arrogant and difficult. Fouad realized that this was due to Armand's escalating use of cocaine, and it worried him. At first Armand had used it as a recreational drug, but lately it seemed he needed it all the time.

Fouad deeply disapproved of any kind of drug use, but when he'd tried to tell Armand that the habit he'd acquired was turning into an out-of-control addiction, Armand had thrown one of his angry screaming fits.

There was a time Fouad had enjoyed working with Armand, but ever since Fouad had gotten married and created a life for himself, Armand had treated him less like an equal and more like an employee. Fouad did not like it. Armand continuously disrespected him, it was as simple as that.

"Your mother wishes to speak with you," Fouad said, keeping his expression impartial, because he knew Peggy, Armand's mother, was the only woman on Earth that Armand felt he could not control.

"Did you not tell her I was away?" Armand said, his voice a hostile missile.

"She knows that," Fouad answered quietly. "She is well aware of the date you visit our country each year."

"Your point?"

"She asked that you call her immediately upon your return."

Armand scowled. But he took out his cell phone and made the call anyway.

* * *

Since the death of her husband, Sidney, Peggy Dunn was beginning to realize that without a rich husband by her side, she was just another lonely Manhattan widow. At first her friends had rallied, making sure that she was still included in dinner dates, events, and parties. But as the months drifted past, she began to notice that the calls became less and less frequent, until she was fortunate to receive one dinner invitation a month. One a month! For a woman who was used to going out five nights a week, this was shocking. She was sixty years old, a decade younger than Raquel Welch, and, like Raquel, she was still an attractive woman. Not as beautiful as the eighteen-year-old girl King Emir Amin Mohamed Jordan had plucked from the chorus of a Vegas show and whisked back to Akramshar to become his fifth wife, but beautiful all the same. Thanks to one of the best colorists in New York, her hair was still flaming red. Her skin, smooth and pampered from weekly facials and twice-a-week massages, was still impeccable. Her body was passable, in spite of an extra ten pounds she couldn't seem to lose.

When Sidney died, she had expected to meet someone else, but that hadn't happened, and being alone did not suit her.

She was angry at her only child, Armand, a man who had made quite a name for himself in business—and only because of the money the king had given him on his twenty-first birthday, plus Sidney's counsel and advice about how to invest it wisely.

Armand was a billionaire simply because of the two men in her life. He had *her* to thank for his good fortune. And how had he repaid her? Not in any way she could see. When Sidney was alive, the three of them had dined together every few weeks, but since Sidney's unfortunate demise she'd hardly seen her son, and every time she called him, he seemed to come up with a work-related excuse. Furthermore, Armand had never married, and therefore had no children. At forty-two years old, he was still single.

Peggy did not think it was right that he had not presented her with grandchildren. For a while she and Sidney had feared he might be gay, but then they'd run into him at various events around town and he'd always had a pretty girl on his arm, so that had assuaged their fears.

"He's merely a late starter," Sidney had assured her. "He doesn't wish to get tied down for now. It's understandable."

Sidney was always so smart about everything. How she missed him!

However, the time had come to do something about Armand, and she fully intended to. If he couldn't pick a wife for himself, *she* would do it for him. As his mother, it was her duty.

When he called, she was ready.

"How was your trip, Armand?" she asked.

"The same as usual," he replied.

"And the king?"

"Nothing changes."

"Any new wives?"

"I do not notice such things."

Of course he doesn't notice such things, Peggy thought, slightly aggravated that her son never had any juicy gossip when he returned from his yearly visit.

"Well anyway," she said. "I wish to see you."

"When I get back," Armand said, wondering what the hell she wanted now.

"You just got back," Peggy said, pointing out the obvious.

"I know," he said impatiently. "But tonight I fly to Vegas for an important meeting."

"What time tonight?"

"Does it matter?"

"Yes, Armand, it does," she said, keeping her tone even. "Because tonight I am coming with you."

CHAPTER SEVENTEEN

Upon awaking early Thursday, Bobby was pleased with himself. He had not answered his door to the four A.M. caller, whom he was positive was Zeena. His only fear was that she might have been accompanied by a bodyguard who would be quite capable of springing the lock on his front door. Fortunately, this had not happened, and after fifteen minutes, the ringing had stopped and he'd gone back to bed. Now it was morning and he was safe.

Man! What an insane situation. Scared of an ego-driven superstar desperate to get in his pants. Who would believe it?

After shaving and showering, he called Denver, who was at work. "I'm hoping to catch a three o'clock flight out of here," he told her. "That means if I don't get delayed, I should be with you around six."

"Uh . . . how do you feel about dinner at my family's house?" she ventured, thinking that the time had come. "Family dinners are a Thursday-night tradition, and since you haven't met them, I thought . . ."

"You mean you're actually going to introduce me to your family?" he teased. "What are you—on drugs?"

She laughed weakly. "Is that a yes?"

"Damn right it's a yes."

"Then consider yourself invited."

"Oh, you bet your ass I will."

Things were looking up. He was finally going to meet Denver's family. He couldn't wait.

* * *

"Morning," Billy said, fit and tanned, tousled dirty-blond hair flopping on his forehead.

Max rolled across the sand and slowly opened her eyes. There he was, Billy Melina, standing over her holding a glass of orange juice. *So it wasn't all a crazy dream! He's here, and so am I.*

"Where . . . where did you get that?" she asked as he passed her the glass.

"From the house," he said calmly. "Hate to be the one to tell you, but it's a freakin' wreck up there. We're gonna need a cleanin' crew."

We; he'd said *we.* How exciting was *that!*

The sun was just coming up and it was chilly. Shivering slightly, she attempted to recall details of the previous night. Getting together with Billy was some kind of wonderful hazy blur. But one thing she knew for sure was that it had been totally great, and she didn't regret one single minute of it.

"You're still here," she murmured, stretching her arms above her head.

"Course I'm still here," he answered cheerfully. "What did you think, that I was gonna run off an' leave you?"

She gazed up into his super-blue eyes and broke into a wide grin. "You wouldn't do that, would you?" she said happily.

He grinned back. "No," he said sincerely. "I wouldn't do that."

"Didn't think so."

"Oh, like you know me so well," he teased, dropping onto the sand next to her and placing his arm around her shoulders.

She snuggled close. "You do know that last night was . . . uh . . . my . . . uh . . . first time," she murmured softly.

"Yeah," he said, nodding. "I kinda realized that."

"And you weren't disappointed?" she asked, dying to hear what he would say.

"Are you kiddin' me?" he said, throwing her a quizzical look. "You made it all the way to eighteen, that's almost a record."

"Uh . . . actually, I won't be eighteen until Saturday," she confessed, deciding that she'd better be honest with him.

"Huh?"

"Yeah, I kinda fudged a little," she admitted.

"Ah, jeez!" he groaned.

"*What?*"

"That means you're not even legal."

"Almost," she said quickly.

"'Almost' doesn't cut it," he said, imagining the headlines if this got out. "You do realize I could get my ass thrown into jail for what we did last night?"

"Who's going to know?"

"You, me, and no one else, right?" he said, swallowing hard.

"Right," she agreed.

"That means you cannot tell anyone—an' I mean *anyone*. Got it?"

"Like who exactly am I gonna tell?" she asked, regaining a little of her composure.

"Lucky, for a start."

"You *have* to be insane!" she exclaimed. "Lucky's the *last* person I'd tell."

"And who'd be the first?"

"Oh, I dunno," she answered vaguely. "*The National Enquirer, Star* magazine, TMZ—"

He lunged on top of her, and they rolled across the sand, laughing. The orange juice spilled, but neither of them cared.

"You're funny," he said.

"I try," she replied, suddenly breathless.

"*And* a nasty little liar," he added, but not in a bad way.

"Sorry," she said, feeling quite exhilarated.

"But I like you," he said quickly.

"And I like you back," she replied, equally fast.

"Jeez, this is crazy, isn't it?" he said, touching her face.

"Way crazy," she replied, marveling at the intense blue of his eyes and the feel of his hard body on top of her.

Actually, it was beyond crazy. Never mind about the party, if Lucky and Lennie found out about her night of lust with Billy, they would totally *freak!* Her losing her virginity probably wouldn't faze them. But her losing it to Billy Melina was a big huge NO!

Anyway, who cared? She'd just experienced the most fantastic, awesome night of her life. Now all she really wanted to do was be by herself so she could relive every magical, fantastic moment.

"I suppose we should drag our asses up to the house," Billy said.

"I guess," she said, worrying about what kind of devastation she'd find.

"I'd better warn you, you're not gonna be thrilled," Billy said, leaping to his feet and helping her up.

"Is anyone still there?"

"A coupla strays."

She hoped the strays were Cookie and Harry, but she doubted it. Knowing them, they'd both taken off and left her to deal.

"Is it a mess?"

"You'd better believe it."

"What am I gonna do?" she groaned. "How am I gonna fix it?"

"Don't sweat it."

"Well," she said, searching for a solution, "at least the housekeepers are coming back at noon."

"Gonna take more than a couple of maids to fix this," Billy said, shaking his head.

"You think?" she asked nervously.

"Come on," he said, pulling her toward the steps that led up to the house. "I've already called my manager. He's gettin' a crew over here."

"You can't do that," she said, frowning. "I've got to keep this under the radar."

"Don't worry, my manager's a cool dude. Nobody's gonna know whose house it is."

"You're *sure?*" she asked, certain that somehow or other she was going to get busted. Oh God! The wrath of Lucky and Lennie didn't bear thinking about.

"Course I'm sure."

Billy's amazing, she thought, gazing up at him. *He won't let me down. He's definitely a take-charge kinda dude, unlike Ace, who's always vacillating about what he's going to do with his life.*

Still . . . Ace had been her on-again, off-again boyfriend for eighteen months, and now she would have to break up with him for sure. She liked him, she'd just never liked him enough for him to be The One. The truth was, even if she never saw Billy again, she was glad he'd turned out to be The One. It was super karma.

As they reached the top of the steps and approached the once immaculate pool area, she let out a gasp of horror. "Oh my *God!*" she yelled, trying to control a sudden rush of panic. "They've trashed my house!"

A trail of destruction surrounded the pool. There were overturned loungers, overflowing ashtrays, cigarette butts stamped out on the marble surround by the pool, and empty firework boxes everywhere, plus scorch marks on some of the sun umbrellas. Not to mention crushed beer cans, broken bottles, half-eaten burgers, cartons of French fries, ketchup spilled everywhere, and trash, trash, trash.

The pool resembled a garbage dump—what hadn't ended up around it was in it. A mass of floating debris.

"Lucky's going to *kill* me," Max wailed. "She'll freaking *murder* me!"

"Stay cool," Billy said, in charge and liking it. "It'll all be taken care of."

Venus had *never* let him take charge; she'd had "people" to do everything. This situation was refreshing, made him feel manly and useful.

"When?" Max demanded, thinking of all the ways she could be punished. "How?"

"They're on their way," Billy assured her.

"*Who's* on their way?"

"I told you, I called my manager. A cleaning crew will be here any minute."

"You think?" she said, forcing herself to calm down because she had no wish for him to perceive her as a hysterical kid. That would really be lame. After all, he was used to being with Venus—who was not only a worldwide superstar, but the epitome of cool, even though she was old. Well, not exactly old, but certainly older than him.

"It's a done deal," he said easily. "So calm down."

"If you say so."

"I do," he said, taking her hand and leading her over to the outside bar, where they perched on two tall bar stools.

"I'm, uh . . . going to Vegas later today," Max blurted. "Lucky's throwing me a birthday party on Saturday."

"No shit?" he said, picking up a half-full bottle of Evian and taking a long swig.

"It's not what I want," she said quickly. "Not at all."

"No more parties for you, huh?" he said, thinking what a knockout she was with her dark curly hair, olive skin, and brilliant green eyes. So different from Venus, who was all seductive blond perfection and toned muscles.

But she was young—too young?

Hell no. He was Billy Melina; he could hook up with anyone he wanted.

"Absolutely not," she said, shaking her head. Then after taking a long beat she added, "I don't suppose . . ." Trailing off, she looked at him expectantly.

He caught her drift and hurriedly said, "Sorry—no. Much as I'd like to be there for you, it ain't gonna happen." *No way, babe. Are you kidding? Lucky would have my balls for breakfast.*

"No?"

"No."

"I get it." She sighed.

And then she thought, *But there's no way I'm giving up on Billy Melina.*

No way at all.

Once a year Lucky planned a board meeting for all her original investors, hopefully a celebration of how well The Keys was doing in such a downward economy. Generally Vegas had taken a big hit, but not The Keys, oh no. Business was on an upward spiral.

The day before the meeting she gathered a group of her key executives, who early on had each received shares in her company. Being part of the process was the biggest incentive of all, and everyone appreciated Lucky's generosity. She'd learned from Gino that making people who worked for her feel like part of a family was a key move. Actually, it was something she enjoyed; personal interaction couldn't be beat for creating a loyal group of executives who were always there for her.

A lunchtime gathering took place on one of the flower-filled outdoor patios, where Lucky made sure to have a one-on-one conversation with each individual. She had a knack for not only remembering everyone's name, but also remembering the names of their spouses, kids, and family pets if they had any. Lucky was adored by the people who worked for her; they were extremely dedicated, and they too strived for The Keys to be the best it could be.

As Lucky moved between groups, stories were exchanged about difficult guests, high rollers who weren't worth the trouble they caused, con artists, stars and their egos, jewelry thieves, card sharks, petty criminals, fake identities, and beautiful women passing themselves off as high society when in fact they were highly expensive call girls. All Vegas hotels and casinos suffered from the same proliferation of scammers, but Lucky liked to think her security team worked at the top of their game. She enjoyed hearing the stories, always interesting, sometimes bizarre, often hard to believe.

Jerrod, her head of security, was the best, formerly a captain in the Israeli army. Nothing and no one got past Jerrod.

Jerrod was Lucky's rock, and like she did Danny, she trusted him implicitly.

Oh my God! What have I done? Denver thought, panicking slightly.

You've invited Bobby to meet the family, her inner voice replied, unruffled and in control.

Why? she asked herself, still panicking.

Because you know it's time.

The problem is, will they like him? And will he like them?

You'll just have to wait and see, won't you?

Fortunately, she was due in court to prosecute a famous actress who was up on a shoplifting charge, so she didn't have much time to think about Bobby and her somewhat eccentric family. But she was anxious all the same. She so wanted them to like him.

And they will.

What if they don't?

Stop obsessing.

On her way into court she got a text from Carolyn asking what she thought of Vanessa.

Hmm . . . interesting question, but she had no time to give her opinion of Vanessa now. She had a high-profile shoplifting case to win, a family dinner to worry about, and an upcoming trip to Vegas.

Briskly she texted back. *Seems nice.* But she didn't add *or not.* Had to keep a positive attitude. It was Carolyn's life.

Then she dived into court with work on her mind.

Now that his slippery Russian investors had finally signed on to put up the money for his L.A. and Miami clubs, Bobby was more than ready to meet with the architects and designers he'd chosen to work with. Mood in L.A. had to be a total winner considering the fierce competition. Clubs in L.A. came and went all the time, so Mood had to stand out as *the* place to be.

Bobby's vision was of a rooftop space with panoramic views of the city, incorporating a sixty-foot pool with underwater speakers, a forty-foot stone bar surrounded by a dozen private party cabanas, a kick-ass restaurant run by a world-class chef, and a major dance space—all with a tropical feel. Simple, stylish, the perfect hang.

The meetings took longer than expected, and he was so caught up in the details that when he checked the time, he realized he'd never make his flight.

Damn! Denver was not going to be happy, but there was nothing he could do about it.

Too bad. He'd been looking forward to finally meeting her family.

CHAPTER EIGHTEEN

The cleaning crew went to work like the well-oiled team of professionals they were.

Billy threw Max a triumphant look and said, "Y'see? They're taking care of business. No worries."

She had to admit he was right; they were fast and thorough. By the time the housekeepers arrived back, things were looking a lot better. Although once the women figured out what had taken place, they threw Max contemptuous looks and muttered under their breath because they knew that if anything important was broken or missing, it was them who would get the blame.

Fortunately, Billy spoke a smattering of Spanish, so he moved into action and charmed them into a hypnotized state, then made them assure him they would not utter a word of this to Max's parents. After he was sure they understood, he handed each of them five hundred bucks as insurance.

Max was impressed. He was protecting her, which is more than she could say for Cookie and Harry—who'd obviously both taken off without a thought about how she was going to put the place back together. Man, they were totally selfish! She had a good mind to rescind their Vegas invitation. How dare they run out on her?

Or . . . maybe they'd tried to find her and couldn't, which was a possibility because she'd been sequestered on the beach with Billy.

But if that was the case, shouldn't they have been worried about her?

On the missing list and nobody gave a rat's ass.

Whatever . . .

At shortly after two, Billy glanced at his watch and muttered, "Shit!"

"What?" Max asked, still basking in the glow of his company. They'd been sitting in the kitchen, where she'd fixed him a tuna fish sandwich while they watched the cleaning crew finish up. It was all good. In fact, it was all totally awesome.

"I've kinda blown off a big interview with *Rolling Stone,*" he announced. "My PR's gonna be so pissed."

"Does that mean you have to go?" Max asked, trying to hide her disappointment.

"Yeah, but I guess I can turn up late—what're they going to do, shoot me?" he said with a wry smile. "Problem is I don't got a ride."

"I'll drive you," she said, quick as a flash.

"Nah," he said, with a casual shrug. "I'll call a cab."

"Why would you do that?" she asked, determined to hang on to him as long as possible, because who knew when she'd ever see him again? "Don't you trust my driving?"

"Course I do, babe. But if I ain't in the driver's seat, then I'm your front-seat passenger from hell. Trust me, you'd hate it."

She was beginning to feel slightly desperate. "How about if *you* drive?" she offered. "That way I'll be the one sitting in the passenger seat."

Too needy, Max. Calm down! Stop sounding like a stalker.

"Wouldn't work out," he said. "I gotta get my ass straight to the interview. It's at the Sunset Towers, an' driving up with you in the car is not an option."

"Okay, then," she said, coming up with a plan that

would assure her of seeing more of him. "You can take Lucky's Ferrari, and I'll pick it up from you later."

"C'*mon*," Billy said disbelievingly. "There's no way Lucky would want me driving her car."

"She wouldn't mind," Max lied, knowing full well that Lucky had a thing about her precious Ferrari, so much so that she wouldn't even leave it with a valet parker. "I drive it all the time," she added. "Believe me, Lucky hardly ever uses it."

Big fat fib, but hey—this was major.

"You're sure about that?" Billy said, still hesitating.

"Dead sure," Max said convincingly.

"Then it's a deal," he said, being a big fan of fast cars ever since Venus had bought him his first Ferrari, which he'd recently sold. "Only how're you gonna pick it up if you're flying to Vegas today?"

Darn it! She'd forgotten all about Vegas and her upcoming party.

"Uh . . . actually, I'm not leaving until tomorrow."

Another lie. But if it meant seeing Billy again, totally worth it.

Prosecuting a famous actress was an easy road. The woman's defense team (and there were three of them) were highly paid and totally inept. Denver listened to their weak excuses for the woman's behavior, then she swooped in with her witnesses—a series of fed-up sales people and store managers who had been putting up with the actress's stealing addiction for years.

The jury was unimpressed with the woman's fame. Too many high-profile people were getting away with— yes—sometimes even murder.

Denver's immediate boss had told her to go for it with all she had. So she did. And her closing argument sealed the deal. The jury took twenty minutes to come back with a guilty verdict.

Her boss informed her that she'd done a stellar job, then asked if she would care to grab a drink with him to celebrate her victory.

Inappropriate, she thought. *Why, if a woman is single and attractive, do all men feel the need to make a move?*

He was fat and fifty *and* married, plus he was her boss, so why would she even think of putting herself in that position?

She mumbled something about next time. But of course there would be no next time, as she was moving on. "Sorry, family commitments," she added, and made it to her car.

Yes. Family commitments. Introducing boyfriend to Mom, Dad, and the rest of the Jones clan.

Anticipation was the name of the game.

Danny gave Lucky the word that Max would not be arriving Thursday night as planned; instead she would be getting there the next day.

Lucky was disappointed. She'd arranged dinner with Gino and Paige, and she knew that Gino was looking forward to spending some time with his feisty granddaughter. Gino got a kick out of joking around with Max.

Family. They were always the ones that felt free to change plans at the last minute, never taking into account that everything had to be shifted. Well, Bobby better be on his way.

Lucky called him to make sure.

"Just getting on a plane," he informed her.

"To Vegas?" she asked, hoping he might make it for dinner.

"No. I'm in New York, on my way to L.A. Heading to Vegas tomorrow."

"So is Max. Maybe you can fly in together."

"Uh . . . I'm using the Stanislopoulos plane," Bobby said, sounding slightly sheepish.

"*Really?*" Lucky said, aware that Bobby only used the plane when it was for something important. "What's the occasion?"

"No occasion," Bobby answered vaguely. "Kinda feel I should use it sometimes, let the relatives know I'm still around."

The relatives Bobby referred to were his late father's two sisters and their respective families, who were all on the board of Stanislopoulos Shipping and resided in Greece. Bobby wasn't exactly close to his Greek relatives. America had always been his home. But he was, after all, along with his niece, Brigette, one of the main heirs to the enormous Stanislopoulos Shipping fortune.

"Okay," Lucky said. "Then you can give Max and her friends a ride."

"Sure," Bobby agreed, albeit reluctantly, because he was so not wanting Max and her cohorts on the plane. He'd planned a romantic trip with Denver, just the two of them. However, saying no to Lucky was never an option.

"I'll tell Max to call you," Lucky said. "And if you get here in time, maybe we'll all have lunch."

"Uh . . . not so sure about that," Bobby said, trying to come up with a fast excuse. He wanted time alone with Denver before the whole family thing took over.

"Okay," Lucky said. "I'll plan on it and hope you can make it. Fly safe."

That settled, Lucky went over her Friday schedule with Danny. An early breakfast with Venus, who was flying in late Thursday, then a meeting with Jeffrey Lonsdale and the people who'd wanted to buy The Keys. Though she refused to ever sell, she'd learned that they were now apparently interested in investing in future projects. Then the board meeting, perhaps a late lunch with Bobby and Max—if they arrived on time—and finally dinner alone with Lennie.

Ah, Lennie . . . They'd been apart for six weeks, way too long, although making up for lost time was always the most exciting.

Friday night was reserved strictly for Lennie. There would be no distractions. No family. Just the two of them.

She couldn't wait.

Billy was totally into taking a ride in Lucky's Ferrari, especially as it was one of the latest models, a Ferrari California—sleek and smooth and definitely kick-ass. He'd recently read up on it, and he couldn't wait to drive a car that had a top speed of 193 miles per hour. In fact, he'd been thinking of buying one, so this would be an excellent test run.

"Sweet!" he said, easing himself behind the wheel.

Max hovered beside the car, nervously biting her lower lip. "Uh . . . when should I pick it up?" she asked.

Billy's attention was on the Ferrari, not her. "C'mon by my house around seven," he said, smoothing his hands lovingly over the steering wheel. "Maybe we'll go grab a bite."

Was that a dinner invitation? Cool!

Billy gave her his address, blew her a distracted kiss and took off at full speed.

Please God, Max thought as she watched her mom's car vanish into the distance. *Let Lucky's precious Ferrari survive the ride. Otherwise I am one dead person.*

"Where's this Bobby character we've heard so much about?" Denver's father, Derek, asked in his loud—some would say booming—voice. He was a maverick lawyer and quite used to intimidating people.

"I told you, Dad," Denver explained patiently. "His plane from New York is delayed. He'll be here later."

"Will he now?" Derek said in a tone that expressed deep disbelief.

"Yes," Denver said confidently. "He will."

"You're sure about that?"

"Oh, for God's sake, Dad. It's no big deal."

"Someone's gettin' edgy," Scott, her favorite brother, singsonged. "What's so special about this dude, anyway?"

"I never said he was special," Denver retaliated, glaring at him.

"You're sure as shit acting as if he is," Scott said, irritating her even more.

"Language!" intoned Autumn, Denver's mother, a tall, imposing woman with gray hair worn in a low ponytail, no makeup, and a penchant for the hippie clothes she'd favored as a teenager. "If you cannot speak properly, then do not speak at all."

As if on cue, Hanna, Scott's five-year-old daughter, raced into the room screaming, "Fuck! Fuck! Fuck!"

Scott scooped up the little girl and shushed her.

"Disgusting!" Autumn shrieked as Hanna's seven-year-old cousin ran in with a fully loaded water pistol, which he proceeded to shoot at Hanna, who immediately began screaming again.

Pandemonium reigned.

Just another normal Thursday-night gathering in the Jones household, Denver thought. *They're all crazy, including the kids.*

And suddenly she wasn't so upset about Bobby not making it.

"What the fuck?" Max yelled over the phone to Cookie. "You are *such* a douche."

"Wassup?" Cookie mumbled in her best innocent

voice—the voice she used when she knew she was in trouble.

"*C'mon*," Max complained, having finally reached Cookie after sending four texts—all ignored. And now, miraculously, Cookie had answered her cell. "You ran out on me, left me to clean up a huge freaking mess. You *know* they trashed my house big-time, how could you not?"

"They did?" Cookie said, maintaining her innocent approach. "I didn't know that. I was busy with Frankie."

"Of course you were," Max said heatedly. "In *my* bedroom. Thanks a lot. You left coke residue all over my bathroom sink. *And* you used my freaking bed. You're gross!"

"What makes you think it was me?"

"Oh, I dunno, maybe 'cause you an' Harry are like the only two who knew where I hid the keys."

"Forgive me!" Cookie said, going all pseudo dramatic. "Can I help it I wanted to get laid by my *boy-friend?*"

"Frankie Romano is *so* not your boyfriend," Max scoffed.

"Yes he is," Cookie argued. "Check out RadarOnline and Perez. Our photo is all over the place."

"You *gotta* be delusional."

"Would I make it up?"

"Your dad's gonna freak."

"My dad doesn't give a shit," Cookie said matter-of-factly. "He's too busy being his famous self."

"Anyway," Max said, deciding it was prudent *not* to tell Cookie about her and Billy. Cookie had a big mouth, and it was definitely best not to trust her. "No Vegas today. We're going tomorrow morning. I changed our flight."

"Hmm . . . about Vegas," Cookie ventured, hesitating for a moment. "Here's the thing—"

"What?" Max said sharply. "Don't you *dare* bail on me. I'll freaking *kill* you."

"Is it cool if I invite Frankie?"

"*Why* would you want to do that?"

" 'Cause, duh, didn't I just tell you? He's my *boyfriend*."

"But didn't *I* just tell *you* Frankie and Bobby aren't talking?"

"Then this would be the perfect opportunity for them to chill," Cookie said, perking up. "Frankie told me that he really misses Bobby. It wasn't as if there was a huge fight. They just kinda drifted apart. After all, they *were* best friends."

"I don't know . . ." Max answered unsurely. "I thought M.J. was his best friend."

"M.J., Frankie . . . they were all kind of a team. An' besides, it's *your* birthday party," Cookie said, turning up the pressure. "Which means that basically it's up to you whether Frankie comes or not."

"You think?"

"Yes, Max. An' it's not as if I ever ask you for anything."

"Yes you do," Max objected. "All the time."

"You *gotta* do this for me," Cookie pleaded. "Do it, an' I'll owe you big-time."

Max weakened. Why not? It wasn't as if she hated Frankie or anything. And since it was Frankie who'd brought Billy to the party . . .

"Fine," she said at last, adding a stern "Only no drugs—save that for your quality time together."

"You're *such* a star!" Cookie squealed. "Frankie will be like majorly psyched, and I promise we'll leave all illegal substances at the door. Deal?"

"Deal," Max agreed, hoping that Bobby wouldn't be too mad.

CHAPTER NINETEEN

Naturally, Armand chose to blame Fouad for his mother wishing to accompany him to Vegas. Someone had to be held responsible for her infuriating request. Not even a request, more a statement of intent—"I am coming with you," she'd said in a take-no-prisoners tone of voice.

Dammit! What did she want from him?

Armand was furious, but he'd acquiesced all the same, since he'd never been able to say no to Peggy. Whenever he was in her presence, he felt less of a man, more of a boy. Unfortunately for him, there was nothing he could do about it, it had always been that way.

His childhood memories were not pleasant. A few weeks after his eleventh birthday, Peggy had caught him torturing the neighbor's cat, whereupon she'd forced him to pull down his pants in front of several of her friends and whipped him on the butt a dozen times with a thick leather belt. He'd barely been able to sit down for a week.

The deep humiliation mixed with the intense pain and the fear of his mother had stayed with him for a very long time. After that, whenever he did anything bad, he made sure she never found out.

On their return trip to the airport, Armand had Fouad alert their driver to stop and pick up Peggy. She sashayed out to the limousine accompanied by five pieces of Louis Vuitton luggage. As usual she was dressed for attention, wearing a yellow Valentino suit and matching

Louboutins, her flaming-red hair setting off her pale skin.

Armand tried not to breathe in her overpowering scent. The familiar smell sickened him; it reminded him of when they'd moved from Akramshar to New York, and she'd insisted that every morning he jumped into her bed for a cuddle. The cuddle had involved the feel of her soft breasts pressed against him while her strong perfume completely enveloped him. He was eight years old, and the smell had lingered in his nostrils all day long. Childhood memories did not please him.

"Peggy," he said, greeting her stiffly, using her name because the moment he'd hit his teenage years she'd requested that he no longer call her Mother, claiming it made her feel old. So Peggy it was.

"Mrs. Dunn," Fouad said, always polite and proper. "It is so nice to see you again. I feel that it's been too long."

Armand shot him a disgusted look. How dare Fouad encourage her, make her feel welcome? She was not welcome at all.

"Nice to see you too, Fouad. Tell me, how is your lovely family?" Peggy inquired, always gracious.

"Very well, thank you for asking," Fouad replied.

"I only wish Armand would find a nice girl and settle down." Peggy sighed. "You are a shining example, Fouad. I admire you."

"Thank you, Mrs. Dunn."

"Why this sudden interest in coming to Vegas?" Armand asked, his tone brusque.

"Why not?" Peggy said, delighted she'd made the decision to accompany her only child to Vegas. "It was once my home, you know," she added, looking forward to revisiting the city she'd been plucked from as an eighteen-year-old girl.

Forty-two years had passed, but Peggy had never forgotten her life back then. As a dancer in one of the most popular shows in town, she'd received more than her share of attention. With her red hair and delicate white skin she'd been quite the standout; men could not get enough of her. And then King Emir Amin Mohamed Jordan had swooped into town and claimed her for himself. He'd plied her with gifts and jewelry, and she'd allowed herself to be swept up in the dazzle. It was mysterious and exciting, like a fairy tale. Without much thought, she'd accepted the king's proposal and gone with him to his country, leaving behind her pit boss boyfriend, Joe Piscarelli, who she'd always suspected was mob connected. When she told Joe she was leaving, he flew into a vile rage, called her a gold-digging cunt, and warned her to never set foot in Vegas again.

She hadn't until now.

Where was Joe Piscarelli forty-two years later?

Probably dead, Peggy thought with a frisson of satisfaction. *Buried in a ditch somewhere in the desert. That would teach him to call her names.*

Back in the day, Vegas was quite the place to be if you were a girl with big dreams. Her dreams had certainly materialized—marriage to a king, an enormously rich second husband, and a billionaire son. Not too shabby for a girl who'd come from nothing.

The flight to Vegas was turbulent. Armand was never bothered by things like that, but since becoming a father to his two children, Fouad hated turbulence. He white-knuckled his way to landing, then set about organizing the luggage to be loaded into the stretch limousine waiting on the tarmac alongside the plane.

Armand was annoyed that Peggy had brought so many suitcases with her. He sat in the back of the limo and fumed. "We're only here for a day or so," he muttered. "Why did you feel the need to bring so much?"

"You never know," she answered, with a vague wave of her hand. "I might stay awhile."

Her statement alarmed Armand, for when he purchased The Keys, the last person he wished to have hanging around was Peggy. His mother belonged in New York, and that's exactly where he expected her to stay.

"What meetings do you have here, Armand?" she asked as the limousine sped away from the airport.

None of your damn business, he would say if Peggy were a normal woman.

But she wasn't normal.

She was his mother.

The only woman he had ever feared.

Armand was situated in the Presidential Suite at The Keys. Four bedrooms, two living rooms, a sauna, a steam shower, five bathrooms, a fully equipped bar, a pool table, a game room, and a private rooftop swimming pool and Jacuzzi. It was more luxurious than his New York apartment, and he decided that when he bought the place, he would use this suite as his own pied-à-terre while he built himself a magnificent mansion on the property.

There was no doubt in his mind that The Keys would be his. No doubt at all.

"Make certain Peggy stays elsewhere," he'd instructed Fouad before arrival. "Book her into another hotel. Tell her The Keys is full."

"Are you sure?" Fouad had asked.

"Of course I'm sure," Armand had replied, annoyed that Fouad would question him.

Fouad had managed to arrange a one-bedroom suite for Peggy at the Cavendish, a neighboring hotel to The Keys. She was surprised when the limousine dropped her off first.

"No room at The Keys," Armand said brusquely,

shooting Fouad a *Why didn't you tell her?* look. Jesus Christ! Did he have to do everything himself?

"The whole point of my coming here was to spend more time with you, Armand," Peggy complained, quite disappointed. "There are things we need to discuss."

"It's unfortunate, but there is a big convention at The Keys," Fouad explained, attempting to smooth things over. "No more suites available. And of course Armand did not wish to put you in a room. He requires only the best for you."

Little did Peggy suspect that Armand would be occupying a suite with four bedrooms. If she'd known that, she would have insisted on staying with him.

"Very well," she said, pursing her lips. "And what time will you be picking me up for dinner?"

Armand had not factored in taking Peggy to dinner. This was Vegas, home of the most expensive and inventive call girls in America. Girls who never balked at any request, however out of line. As long as the money flowed, anything was possible, and he'd been planning on taking full advantage. Armand's line of credit in Vegas was limitless, plus he always travelled with a suitcase full of cash in case of an unforeseen emergency.

Yes, he was ready to indulge himself, and now Peggy expected dinner? Goddammit! This was not the trip he had imagined.

"I thought you would be tired after the flight," he said tersely. "Perhaps room service?"

Peggy threw him a scornful look. "Tired, Armand? Me? How *old* do you think I am? Eighty?"

"I didn't mean—"

"Pick me up at eight," she ordered, cutting him off. "And make sure we go somewhere fancy. I plan on dressing up."

The moment Peggy was out of the limousine, Armand issued more instructions. He handed Fouad an engraved card stamped with the name Yvonne Le Crane, a phone number, and an e-mail address. "Book two women to be in my suite at five. An Asian and a black girl, both under twenty-five," he ordered. "I will keep them for two hours. Then at midnight, three more girls. White, preferably from Texas, with blond hair."

Fouad was almost speechless. Since when had he been appointed head pimp? He was not an assistant, he was a vice president at Jordan Developments, a man who deserved at least a modicum of respect. Now Armand was instructing him to order up hookers? This was a ridiculous situation.

"I suggest you might want to make this phone call yourself," Fouad said, swallowing his anger. "There could be questions I cannot answer. And I wouldn't want you to be disappointed."

Armand considered Fouad's words and, surprisingly, agreed. Yes, he was specific when it came to the women he paid. *He* would call Yvonne Le Crane; that way he would get exactly what he required. No mistakes.

After all, he was a prince among men, and he expected only the best.

CHAPTER TWENTY

A text from Bobby informed Max that she and her friends should meet in the private sector of LAX at noon the next day to take the Stanislopoulos plane to Vegas.

She was excited to go on Bobby's plane, and even more excited to spend time with her big brother, whom she adored.

As luck would have it, after she'd agreed that Cookie could bring Frankie to Vegas, Cookie had announced that they would be driving, since Frankie wanted to have his car there. Max considered this to be perfect, because turning up to meet Bobby with Frankie in tow might've been majorly awkward.

Harry was delighted about being invited on the private plane, and asked if Paco, who had a gig in Vegas, could hitch a ride too.

Max agreed, and then she thought, *Oh, great. Everyone will have someone in Vegas except me.*

No time to think about that; her main concern was planning the perfect outfit to wear to Billy's house. Her closet contained a ton of options, none of them quite right. After rummaging through everything she possessed, she finally settled on skinny black jeans, a simple white tank top, and a black cashmere dance hoodie. Tough but cute. It was her look, especially when she added a dozen thin studded bangles, big earrings, a long leather necklace with crosses and shark teeth hanging from it, and a low-slung belt.

Staring at her reflection in the mirror, she wondered if she looked any different.

Would anyone be able to tell that she'd finally done the deed?

No way.

"But I can tell," she whispered to herself. "And it feels so right."

Then Ace ruined everything by texting that he was driving into L.A. so that they could celebrate her birthday together.

Crap! She hadn't told him about Vegas. And she certainly wasn't planning on telling him about Billy. What was a girl supposed to do?

She quickly texted him back, hoping that he wasn't already on the road. *My mom wants me in Vegas,* she tapped out, keeping it vague. *Call you when I get back.*

That should stop him. And when she did get back, she would give him the news that it was over between them.

Sorry, Ace. Too bad. It was fun while it lasted.

Meanwhile, she had Billy on her mind. She couldn't stop reliving their night together: their long conversations, the feel of his body next to hers. It was like some kind of awesome dream, a dream she never, ever wanted to stop.

Billy Melina. Who would believe it?

"Billy Melina. Who would believe it?" the reporter said as Billy slid into the booth beside her. The girl was in her late twenties, pretty in an aggressive way, with big boobs and an ultra-short skirt. She was on assignment from *Rolling Stone*, and she didn't seem to care that he was three hours late for their sit-down interview.

Bambi, his personal publicist, cared. So did the studio publicist. So did the groomer—hired for the day to make sure Billy looked his best at all times. They all hovered anxiously by the table, until Billy waved them away and told them to come back in an hour.

Girl reporter, whose name was Melba, repeated her words.

"Sorry I'm late," Billy said, leaning back and ordering a Diet Coke. "Got hung up at the beach."

"Were you getting laid?" Melba asked, licking her lips and giving him a flinty stare, as if she knew everything about him, or was about to.

"'Scuse me?" Billy said, narrowing his blue eyes. This one was determined to be confrontational, and he didn't like it. Dealing with female reporters could sometimes be tricky.

"I always like to start an interview off with a bang," Melba said with a half smirk.

"Really?"

"Yes, I like to get down early on. Move in real close to my subject. The closer, the better."

Was she propositioning him? Probably. Now that he was a big star, all the girls did. And the guys too, because naturally gay rumors abounded—as they did with every other young male star. He wasn't gay. Never tried it. Never had any desire to do so. Not that there was anything wrong with it.

Normally he might've contemplated taking this girl back to his house for the old blow-job-by-the-pool routine. But after being with Max, he wasn't feeling it. There was something about Max that was incredibly fresh and appealing, and he'd begun to think that it might be nice to get to know her. But there was a big problem—she was Lucky and Lennie's kid, and with the whole Venus divorce drama going on, dating Max was hardly about to fly.

He decided that he'd have to let her down easy. She was young and vulnerable, and seemed to like him a lot. He didn't want to hurt her, so he decided that when she came to pick up Lucky's Ferrari, he'd tell her he had another PR gig to go to and send her home.

"What's on your mind, Billy Melina?" Melba asked, licking her lips yet again. "You're not concentrating."

"What's on yours?" he countered. Sit-down interviews were not his strong suit, and he had a bad feeling about this one.

"Your divorce," Melba said, anticipating a juicy reply. "How nasty will it get?"

"Not at all on my part," he said nonchalantly. "I'm fine with it."

"No gory details?" Melba pressed. "Some salacious tidbit that nobody else knows?"

"Sorry to disappoint—no."

"Shame. I would've thought being married to a controlling older woman would've produced all kinds of problems."

"You heard it here first," Billy said, keeping his cool and wishing he hadn't sent the PRs away. "No problems. And, uh . . . shouldn't we be talking about my movie?"

Sometimes Denver felt that she could cheerfully murder her family. They never let up on her all night with questions about Bobby.

When's he coming?

Why is he so late?

Who is this guy?

What exactly does he do?

You like him, you really like him.

She'd received a series of texts from Bobby full of excuses about cancelled and delayed flights, but she was disappointed by the time she headed home. Couldn't he have made more of an effort to meet her family for the first time? It pissed her off that he hadn't done so.

Amy Winehouse greeted her as if she'd been gone a year. A rush of happy barking, followed by wet doggy

licks and kisses all over her face. It was comforting to
feel wanted.

She took Amy for a walk around the block, and returned to find that Sam had left another message. He
was certainly persistent.

And normal.

And attractive.

Why not go for him instead of the dazzlingly rich,
too-handsome-for-his-own-good Bobby Santangelo
Stanislopoulos?

Interesting question.

Easy answer.

I love Bobby, and that's all there is to it.

Prowling around Kennedy Airport was giving Bobby
the distinct feeling that he was trapped in a maze of
bars, fast-food restaurants, and donut and magazine
stands, plus a hundred other useless stores. The flight
he was supposed to be on had been canceled at the last
minute, while the current flight he was booked onto kept
getting delayed.

It occurred to him that he was an idiot not to have
had the Stanislopoulos plane pick him up in New York.
Such a dumb move. What was he thinking?

After trying to get on an earlier flight—fully booked—
he made his way back to the lounge with the latest Har-
lan Coben thriller and attempted to read and chill out.
But he soon found it impossible to concentrate—too
much going on in his head. The new clubs he was planning to build were a real challenge. Exciting, but at the
same time quite daunting. He'd conquered New York
and Vegas with Mood, so bring on L.A. and Miami.
After that, who knew?

His big ambition was to create an empire. *His* empire. And maybe, like Gino and Lucky before him, he
would eventually move into the hotel business. He had

in mind small boutique hotels that would cater to a distinct clientele, people who were looking for somewhere special and private.

"Bobby?"

He glanced up, and there stood Annabelle Maestro, Frankie's ex-girlfriend, now a minor TV personality since the murder of her movie-star mother and the arrest of her action-star father. Annabelle was a true child of Hollywood. She had written a book about growing up in L.A. with famous parents, and then all about the year she'd spent running call girls in New York. Like most people who became stars of reality television, she'd made a career out of simply being seen around, appearing on talk shows, and doing nothing much at all.

"Annabelle Maestro," Bobby exclaimed, putting down his book. "How're *you,* stranger?"

Annabelle immediately sat down next to him without being invited to do so. "I'm doing so well it's ridiculous," she gushed, pretty and powdered in a slightly plastic way, with her very long pale-golden-red hair, high cheekbones, and suspiciously plump lips.

Bobby had known her way before she'd hooked up with Frankie, along with M.J., Denver, and Carolyn; they'd all attended the same Beverly Hills high school.

"My schedule is completely insane," Annabelle continued. "Ever since the success of my book."

What book? Bobby was tempted to say, but then he vaguely remembered Denver mentioning something about it.

"My Life: A Hollywood Princess Tells All," Annabelle said, reminding him of the title. "Currently out in trade paperback, which is why I'm in New York doing publicity. I was on *Watch What Happens Live* this week with the adorable Andy Cohen. Did you see it?"

Was she kidding?

" 'Fraid not," he said, opening a courtesy packet of nuts. "This has been a quick trip for me."

"Trip?" she questioned, fluffing back her long hair. "I thought you lived in the city."

"Uh . . . yeah, but now I kinda spend most of my time on the West Coast."

"Hmm," Annabelle said, giving him a piercing look. "Don't tell me you're still seeing Denver? That's a surprise."

"Why is that a surprise?" Bobby asked, sensing that a bitchy response was headed in his direction.

"You know," Annabelle said with a dismissive shrug. "Denver's hardly the girl I see by your side."

"Yeah?" Bobby said, not about to put up with her crap. "And who *would* you see by my side?"

A coy giggle. "Someone like me."

Jesus Christ, did she honestly imagine he would ever go for someone like her? All fake—from her hair extensions to her obviously enhanced cheekbones. No freaking way.

"The thing is," Annabelle continued, unfazed by his lack of response. "You and I come from the same background. We're pedigrees, while I guess you would have to call Denver some kind of mutt."

"Jesus, you're a real bitch!" Bobby exclaimed. "Are you listening to what you're saying?"

Annabelle shrugged. "The truth can be a harsh pill to swallow," she said. And then, "Where's your plane? Shouldn't we be taking *that* to L.A.?"

Bobby abruptly stood up. "Go fuck yourself," he said, loud and clear. And then he walked off.

Dinner with Gino again, not such a bad thing. This time, Paige, his third wife, was with him. And Jeffrey Lonsdale joined them, along with the owners of the Cavendish

Hotel—a lesbian couple, Renee and Susie, whom Lucky liked very much. Renee was a ballsy old broad, and her partner, Susie, was an ex–Hollywood wife. They both had plenty to say for themselves, and Gino always enjoyed their company.

Lucky had organized a window table at François, the best French restaurant in Vegas. Since it was located at the top of The Keys, the view of the sparkling Las Vegas lights was breathtaking.

Sitting across the table from Gino, Lucky couldn't help staring at him and wondering what the hell she'd do without him. They had such a rocky history, but she loved him with every bone in her body, and she was fiercely protective of him, as he was of her. Over the years, they'd fought off many enemies from Gino's past, but in the end they'd reigned victorious, although it had not been an easy ride.

Lucky smiled thinking of the family motto, *Never fuck with a Santangelo*. They were words to live by.

Earlier, she'd called Max at the house to see how she was doing. No answer there. No answer on her cell. Lucky wasn't worried; Max could take care of herself. She'd thwarted that crazy pervert who'd attempted to kidnap her a year ago, and she'd come out a winner.

In her heart Lucky knew that Max was a true Santangelo and could protect herself come what may.

Max took a cab to Billy's house. Like most L.A. cab-drivers, her driver barely spoke English and drove as if he were involved in a high-speed car chase with cops inches behind him. The cab stunk of garlic, and the driver kept on muttering under his breath in a foreign language. Several times he applied the brakes so hard that she almost fell on the floor. Lovely!

By the time they reached Billy's, she was nervous and flustered, a combination of the out-of-control ride and the thought of seeing Billy again. She hadn't mentioned what had taken place between her and Billy to anyone, not even Harry, who at times could be relied upon to be fairly discreet. Harry had dropped by her house earlier, apologized for running out on the chaos and mess, then proceeded to smoke a joint and rave about Paco for one full hour. Eventually she'd told him he'd better leave because she had to get ready for a hot date. Interest piqued, Harry wanted to know who her date was. She'd managed not to tell him, even though she was dying to confide in someone.

Arriving at Billy's house, she was horrified to observe a bunch of paparazzi milling around outside the gates. Hurriedly, she instructed the driver not to stop, and had him take her around the corner, where she pulled out her cell and called Billy.

"There's an alley behind the house," he informed her. "Take that, an' I'll make sure the back gate is open."

Her heart was beating fast. She had a date with Billy Melina. She'd actually *screwed* Billy Melina. Or he'd screwed her. Whatever. She'd done the deed, and that was all that mattered.

Man, this was totally surreal.

Over coffee and dessert, Lucky grilled Jeffrey about their morning appointment. "Exactly *why* do you feel it's necessary for me to meet with these people from Jordan Developments?" she asked.

"Because they have plenty of money to invest in future projects, and in my opinion it's always prudent to keep that money close," Jeffrey explained. "Who knows what you'll decide to do next, Lucky. And in this economy, investors with actual cash are gold." Jeffrey had worked with Lucky for several years, and he always tried to keep a step or two ahead of her. Knowing the way her mind worked, he was sure she would eventually want to expand, so he was merely putting everything in place should this happen. "I checked out the company," he continued. "It's solid. Armand Jordan is legitimate. He's a billionaire and a useful man for us to know. Fouad Khan is his right-hand man."

"Isn't this the company you told me wanted to buy The Keys?" Lucky asked, sipping a *limoncello.*

"Initially, yes. But they know it's not an option. No harm in seeing what they have to offer."

"I suppose you definitely want me to be there?" Lucky questioned.

"It's a meeting," Jeffrey said firmly. "What's to lose?"

"Fine," she said, downing the rest of her *limoncello* in one quick gulp. "And now it's time to get personal. What's all this about you getting a divorce?"

Jeffrey fidgeted uncomfortably; he hadn't been expecting this.

"Tell me everything," Lucky continued. "Don't hold anything back."

Reluctantly Jeffrey began to reveal every little detail. Lucky had a knack for getting people to talk. She would have made an excellent interrogator.

"Enough," Gino said at last, intervening with a hoarse chuckle. "Give the poor bastard a break. You're makin' him sweat."

"Sure," Lucky said with a half smile. "I'll let Jeffrey off the hook. Only you have to agree that I would've made a great shrink. Oh, and Jeffrey, after the board meeting tomorrow, I expect plenty more info on your marital woes, so be prepared."

"Yeah, and you'd better come up with somethin' juicy," Gino added with a crafty grin. "You know my Lucky, she always goes straight for the goods."

"Ah yes, and guess who I learned it from?" Lucky replied with a wink.

"I do believe a toast is in order," Gino's wife, Paige, announced, lifting her glass of champagne. "To the Santangelos. May they never stop bickering!"

Everyone laughed and clinked glasses.

CHAPTER TWENTY-ONE

"Hey," Billy said, greeting Max at the back gate, barefoot and casual in jeans and a faded denim work shirt.

"Hey," she replied, thinking he truly was so majorly hot that it almost hurt.

Leonardo, Taylor, Rob, take a backseat. Billy Melina is the hottest dude in town—any town.

"Wassup?" Billy asked, heading toward the living room.

"Had a cabdriver from hell," she complained, trailing behind him. "He drove the freeway like a maniac. Thought I'd be, like, *dead* before I even got here."

"That sucks."

"Totally," she said, her eyes darting around his living room, which was all sparse concrete curves and modern furniture. "This is different," she remarked.

"I'm renting," he explained. "Not my style, really."

"Nice pool," she said, moving toward the glass doors that led outside.

For a brief moment he was tempted to take her out to the pool, have her blow him the way he enjoyed, then send her on her way.

But no. Max wasn't that kind of girl.

"I guess when the divorce is finalized I'll be lookin' to buy," he said. "Maybe at the beach. I kinda love Malibu."

"When's that gonna be?" she said, thinking how cool it would be if Billy was her neighbor.

He gave a casual shrug. "Dunno. Soon, I hope."

"Uh . . . how was your interview?" she asked, wondering if she should sit down, or were they going straight out?

"Some pissy uptight girl with attitude. All she wanted to talk about was Venus an' the divorce. After ten minutes of her crap, I cut the interview short."

"What did your PR say? She must've been pissed."

"Who gives a shit," he said, moving to the open-plan kitchen. "Want somethin' to drink?"

"Yes please," she said, testing him. "I'll have a double vodka on the rocks with a twist."

"Very funny."

"You asked."

"A Coke? 7-UP? Sprite?"

"What makes you think I don't drink?"

"Do you?"

"Not much."

He gave her a quizzical look. "So what's it like being Lucky's kid?"

"Don't call me that."

"You get along, don't you?"

"I take after my brother Bobby," she explained. "Of course, I love Lucky, *and* my dad. But I gotta forge my own identity. That's why I'm moving to New York." She hesitated for a second, then added, "Uh . . . maybe." Because now that she'd met Billy, she wasn't so sure she still wanted to make the move east.

"I get it," Billy said, nodding. "That's exactly how I felt being married to Venus. It was a total downer. I was never my own person. However famous *I* got, she was always more famous. It's a drag tryin' to live up to somebody else's success."

"Don't I know it."

"Uh-huh. You got it comin' at you from both sides. Your mom, an' then Lennie."

"That is *so* true," Max agreed, thrilled that he seemed to understand. "Being the daughter of two famous parents is no joke."

Billy opened the fridge, took out a can of 7-UP, and handed it to her. "I'm guessing," he said.

"Good guess," she answered, opening it and gulping down a few blasts.

Billy decided that now was the time to tell her he had something else to do, but somehow he wasn't feeling it. He *liked* having her in his house. He liked spending time with her.

"So . . . are we going out or what?" she asked, immediately regretting her words because God forbid she come across as pushy.

"It's kinda not a cool idea," he replied. "Y'know, what with the paparazzi an' all. They're doggin' my every move 'cause of the divorce."

"Oh yes," she said quickly. "I totally get it."

"But," he added, noting her disappointment, "that doesn't mean we can't send out for food. What d'you feel like?"

I feel like you kissing me, and telling me that last night meant something to you. That I'm not just another notch on your movie-star belt. That you want to see more of me. Much, much more.

"Uh, pizza," she said.

Billy grinned. She noted that he had amazing dimples and extremely white teeth. "Cheap date," he remarked. "Thought you were gonna ask for caviar."

"Caviar's not for me," she said, wrinkling her nose. "It's gross and tastes all fishy."

"Right on!" Billy said, heartily agreeing. "Venus was always trying to get me to like it. 'Caviar's an acquired taste,' she would say. Too bad for her I never acquired it."

Max giggled, wished that she hadn't, wished that he wouldn't keep mentioning Venus, wondered if they were going to do it again, and hoped that he would make a move.

He didn't. He picked up the phone and ordered two large Margherita pizzas from Mulberry Street.

"Uh . . . how was driving the Ferrari?" she ventured.

"Some freakin' car!" he enthused, thinking it was best not to mention that he'd gotten pulled over on San Vicente and that a dozen paparazzi had materialized from nowhere, capturing the whole thing with a thousand intrusive flashes. "Nearly got me a speeding ticket, but the cop recognized me an' let me take off."

Max was relieved that he hadn't gotten a ticket, which would have automatically been sent to the owner of the car. Or maybe not. Was a speeding ticket the same deal as a parking ticket? She didn't know and she didn't care, as long as Lucky's Ferrari was in one piece. That was all that mattered.

"Must be a kick getting recognized," she said, wondering if she'd ever be famous. Not that she wanted to be. Her plan was to succeed in business just like Bobby. Although what business that would be she hadn't quite figured out.

"At first, yeah," Billy said, with a casual yawn. "Then it gets old, *real* old. Fame comes with plenty of downside."

"And plenty of money," she blurted, hoping the yawn wasn't a hint that she should go.

Why did I say such a stupid thing? I don't care if he has any money or not.

"Gotta pay my agent, manager, PR, accountant, business manager, and the tax man. It's not as much as everyone thinks," Billy said. "At least I don't hav'ta pay Venus alimony, an' I want nothin' from her. Our only fight is over a couple of properties."

Once again Max wished he would stop mentioning Venus. Every time he did, it brought her back to reality with a nasty jolt.

"Wanna talk about what happened last night?" Billy asked, startling her.

No! She did not want to talk about last night. Too embarrassing. Did he honestly think they were going to have a casual chat about him taking her virginity? *No thank you!*

She wished she'd never told him it was her first time going all the way. After all, it wasn't as if she was inexperienced with guys. She'd gotten down and dirty with a few of them. Oral sex was nothing new—although Billy hadn't asked her to do that. She and Ace had definitely taken it to the brink on many occasions, stopping just in time.

Anyway, it was no big deal. She was glad she'd waited. And she was thrilled that Billy had turned out to be The One.

When and if she ever confided in Cookie, her friend would say "What the hell were you waitin' for, girl? It's not just the boys who can have fun!"

"Uh . . . last night was great," she mumbled. "What time's the pizza coming?"

He arched an amused eyebrow. "Starving hungry or in a hurry?"

"Both," she answered in a rush.

"Didn't you say you had time to go to dinner?" he said, crinkling his blue eyes.

"Well, we're not doing that, are we?" she said, a touch truculently.

"Disappointed?"

"Why would I be?"

He shrugged, somewhat perplexed that she seemed to be veering toward a bad mood. Had he said something? Done something?

Females. Mercurial creatures, always changing. They were all the same, whether they were seventeen or forty.

"I'll call back an' put a rush on it," he volunteered.

"You don't have to do that."

"Hey, if you're in a hurry—"

"I'm not," she said, feeling like an idiot. Why was she giving him a hard time? It wasn't as if she meant to.

"Then whyn't we go outside, sit by the pool, put on some sounds an' relax," he suggested.

And just when she was thinking how perfect that would be, his doorbell rang.

It was past midnight and, finally back in L.A., Bobby used the stealth move to get into Denver's apartment. He made his way in very quietly, but Amy Winehouse heard him at the door and came bounding out of the bedroom, tail wagging.

Hurriedly, he quieted the dog, then began stripping off his clothes before heading for the bedroom.

Just as he thought: Denver was asleep, *au naturel* as usual, with only a sheet covering her.

He slid into bed beside her, edging up against her smooth body. Man, she had skin like satin.

Screw Annabelle Maestro for daring to call her a mutt. What a jealous bitch, because not only was Denver gorgeous, she was smart, thoughtful, and dedicated to her job, but most of all she was real in every way. Every one of her qualities added up to one hell of a lethal combination. Annabelle Maestro should be so lucky.

"I'm home," he whispered in Denver's ear, feeling a familiar stirring.

"Mmm," she murmured, slowly turning over so that she faced him. "It's about time. . . . Why'd it take you so long?"

"Didn't mean to wake you, sleepyhead."

"That's okay," she said softly, all thoughts of being pissed at him vanishing as she reached down under the sheet and began caressing his burgeoning hard-on.

"I really didn't want you to wake up," he repeated.

"Sure you didn't," she drawled, still caressing him. "This fine upstanding member of society wouldn't wake me at all."

"I've been saving up," he quipped, loving the feel of her hands on him.

"How very thoughtful of you," she replied, experiencing a fervent rush of desire. Her man was home, and that was all she cared about.

"Missed you," he said, moving even closer. "*Really* missed you."

"You did?"

"Of course I did."

"Missed you too," she responded, reveling in the feel of him hard and strong against her thigh.

And without any further conversation, his hands began exploring her body, touching her in all the places he knew she liked to be touched. Kissing her breasts, fondling her nipples, kicking off the sheet and moving down her body with his tongue, licking her skin every inch of the way.

Then he was between her legs, slowly parting her thighs, plunging his tongue into her wetness, causing her to throw her arms across her face and groan with pleasure.

After a few minutes, he surfaced for air.

"*Sooo* good." She sighed, feeling the joy. "More, please. I think I've been deprived."

"Is that an order?" he said with a knowing laugh.

Another sigh. "You'd better believe it."

And with no more doubts about whether she should be with Bobby or not, she gave herself up to the moment, luxuriating in his touch.

On Billy's doorstep stood his best friend, Kev, a total stoner, fresh from New York with luggage to prove it.

Kev was short, with wiry brown hair and a cocky expression.

"Fuck!" Billy yelled, happy to see him because Kev was his friend from way back—before the fame, the adulation, and the high-profile marriage. In fact, when he first arrived in Hollywood, he'd slept on the floor of Kev's one-room apartment, and later—when he'd finally made it—Kev had acted as his chief gofer. They'd been inseparable until they'd both gotten married. Billy's marriage had lasted a lot longer than Kev's. "Why didn't you tell me you were comin'?" he said, giving Kev a manly hug.

"Didn't want you gettin' too excited," Kev joked, making his way into the living room, stopping short when he spotted Max. "Oh, shit!" he exclaimed. "Am I interrupting something?"

"No, man," Billy said. "Say hello to Max."

"Hello, pretty girl with the boy's name," Kev said.

Max rolled her eyes. "Like I haven't heard *that* before."

Billy laughed. "This is my buddy Kev, an' I can see you two are gonna get along just fine."

Max hurriedly checked Kev out. From the two duffel bags by the front door, it seemed Kev had arrived to stay. He reminded her of E from *Entourage,* one of her favorite TV shows.

"We just ordered pizza," Billy announced. "Max is starving and in a hurry."

Max felt her cheeks burn red. Was Billy now dismissing her because his friend had arrived? What a bummer!

"Pizza an' a beer sounds like it's gonna hit the spot," Kev said, flopping down on the couch as if he lived there. And if his luggage was anything to go by—he was about to move in any second.

"So, Max," Kev said as Billy handed him a can of beer, "how come a boy's name?"

What an asshole question, but she answered it anyway, because if he was Billy's friend, she supposed she'd better get him to like her.

"My given name is Maria," she answered lightly. "You go figure why I changed it."

Kev looked at Billy as if to say *What the fuck? Maria seems like an okay name to me.*

"Too *Sound of Music*," she explained, thinking they would get it. But from their blank expressions it appeared that neither of them was a movie buff. Lucky and Lennie had organized movie nights since she was a little kid. From *Grease* to *Saturday Night Fever* and *Flashdance*, she'd been exposed to all the popular classics on DVD.

"How long you here for?" Billy asked, turning his attention back to Kev.

"'S long as you'll have me," Kev replied with a jaunty wink.

Max felt her stomach dip. This was not a good turn of events. Not good at all.

CHAPTER TWENTY-TWO

Las Vegas. City of lights. City of sin. A magical mystery town where anything could happen, and usually did.

Take call girls—they were obliging creatures, ready for action at all times. So when Armand called Yvonne Le Crane, a woman he'd dealt with several times before, she immediately sent two of her best girls. Tia, a petite Asian, and Fantasy, a slightly more robust black beauty who'd been told she resembled a young Naomi Campbell.

They arrived at Armand's hotel suite prepared to do whatever it took to make the client happy, armed with a selection of sex toys, handcuffs, whips, rubber bikinis, rolled joints, lotions, Viagra and Cialis, and a bunch of condoms. Between them they had everything that might be needed crammed into their oversized Gucci purses. The expensive purses were a gift from a Malaysian prince who'd been more than satisfied with their performances. So satisfied that on top of their normal fee, the purses had come stuffed with hundred dollar bills.

Little did they know they were about to service another prince. Not such a generous one, though.

Fantasy had been a working girl for almost two years, while Tia was newer to the game. They'd both come to Vegas hoping to score a gig as a dancer in one of the big shows, only it hadn't happened for either of them. Then along came Yvonne Le Crane, a middle-aged madam always on the search for new girls, and they'd both decided that making plenty of money doing something they usually did for free was a far better prospect than hoofing in a show six nights a week.

So far they'd had no complaints. However, so far they had not encountered Armand.

"Strip," he ordered the moment they entered his suite.

"Where's the bedroom, honey?" Fantasy inquired, in the special sexy voice she reserved for clients. Obviously this was a man who wanted to get straight to business, and that was no problem. The sooner he came, the sooner they'd be out of there.

"Refrain from speaking, and do not call me 'honey,'" Armand said, his voice a sharp command. "Remove your clothes, leave your shoes on, and climb on top of the pool table."

Fantasy and Tia exchanged glances. Apparently this was not about to be the sexy little scene they'd choreographed so many times. They'd got themselves a freaky one, the worst kind.

"Sure, hon—" Fantasy began to say. Then she caught a glimpse of his hard, cold stare, and hurriedly shut up.

Tia was already divesting herself of her clothes. A simple silk dress and a red thong—that was it. She kept her strappy high-heeled sandals on, as requested. Armand's eyes flicked over her nakedness. Too thin for his liking, and her jutting breasts were obviously fake and oversized for her body. He reminded himself to request women with real breasts in the future.

Fantasy, on the other hand, was the kind of nasty bitch he enjoyed humiliating. She would fight back when he instructed her to do certain things. She would entertain him.

As Fantasy stripped off her clothes, a short skirt and a low-cut top, no underwear, he couldn't help admiring her body. Gleaming ebony skin, long legs, a pierced navel, and one pierced nipple. Normally he would watch and instruct—touching hookers was not always for him; he was far too fastidious. But for this one he might make an exception.

"On the pool table," he commanded.

The girls obliged.

"Now get on all fours and play doggie."

"'Scuse me?" Fantasy said.

"Do you have a problem with your hearing?" Armand said. "Lick each other's asses and try to look as if you're enjoying it."

"Fucking perv," Fantasy whispered under her breath. But she did as he asked, like all professionals. The money was waiting at the end of the gig, so did it really matter how she got there?

Two hours later, Armand was picking up his mother. Meanwhile, Fantasy was waiting for her car, and bitching to her friend, a valet parker at The Keys, about the kinky customer in the Presidential Suite, a man who'd demanded all kinds of lewd acts *and* anal sex from her and Tia, then refused to pay extra.

"Cheap mothafucker," Fantasy muttered as she got in her car. "Who the fuck he think he is?"

Soon word started filtering up via the staff grapevine about the perverted cheapo in the Presidential Suite. It didn't take long before the gossip reached the ears of Jerrod.

Call girls were not encouraged at The Keys, but since high-end call girls were a fact of life in Vegas, their existence was tolerated. However, Jerrod had certain standards, and if they came to do a job at the hotel where *he* was the head of security, then they should be paid for their services.

Jerrod decided to do some discreet investigating.

* * *

Armand chose to take Peggy, along with Fouad, to François, a select and expensive restaurant he knew she'd approve of. He needed to make Peggy happy, and preferably drunk. His dear mother was very fond of a bottle of wine. Give her enough, drop her off at her hotel, and she'd sleep it off.

How many times had he watched her do that when he was a kid? Too many to count. His mother, the drunk. Thank God for Sidney Dunn, who'd come along, married her, and taken the pressure off.

Now that Sidney was gone, did she honestly expect to latch onto him again?

Earlier, he'd enjoyed himself with the whores, especially the black one. Women would do anything for money—he'd established that time and time again, and he had the videos to prove it. Two little whores at play. Another shining example to add to his extensive collection.

He stored his videos under certain categories:

Married Women
Whores
Single Women
Famous Women

Yes, he'd had a few famous women sniffing around, all set to land their own personal billionaire—something they imagined would up their pathetic profiles in the tawdry entertainment magazines.

The blonde with the penchant for jocks.

The anorexic brunette who swore she wasn't anorexic.

The girl who'd written about her life as a Hollywood princess.

The stupid blonde with the big boobs.

The drugged-out singing star with a major crack problem.

All one-nighters—his choice, not theirs. There wasn't one of them that he'd care to conduct a repeat performance with.

The restaurant was full. His casino host had arranged the reservation.

Later he would gamble before being entertained by the three Texan blondes he'd ordered up for his midnight entertainment, for when it came to sex, Armand was a true voyeur, a connoisseur of the raw and raunchy.

"I do not like this table," Peggy complained in a high voice. "Why are we not seated at a window table? I would prefer to sit somewhere with a view."

Armand dispatched Fouad to deal with the situation. The restaurant was full, but a five-hundred-dollar tip to the maître d' should certainly make the right table available.

After a few minutes, a group at a well-situated window table got up to leave.

The maître d' had probably told them to get the hell out, Armand thought, satisfied that money could get him anything he required.

"You see," he informed his mother, with a triumphant gleam in his eyes. "Your wish, and it is done."

But Peggy wasn't listening, her attention was fixed on the group making its way out.

"What are you staring at?" Armand demanded.

"That old man," Peggy said, agitated. "I think I know him. Find out his name."

Armand couldn't help himself. "For God's sake," he snapped, curling his lip. "You're ridiculous."

Peggy honored him with an icy stare. "Too much trouble?"

Frowning, Armand turned to Fouad. "Do as she asks."

It was at that exact moment that Fouad decided the

time had come to move on and extract himself from the toxic environment Armand had created. He had money, plenty of it. He had copies of most of Armand's explicit sex tapes. And he'd had it being treated like some kind of gofer expected to jump at his master's bidding.

This was not Akramshar, this was America, and as soon as they returned to New York, he was out.

"Certainly, Armand," he said, getting up from the table. "I will deal with it immediately."

The three blondes suited Armand just fine. Lithe and lovely with real breasts and mounds of pale pubic hair, they were exactly what he needed after a stupefyingly boring dinner with his mother. Peggy always put him on edge. She was the gift that kept on giving. Lately she'd started lecturing him about getting married and having children. Little did she know . . .

Exhibiting a rare flash of generosity, he'd invited Fouad to join him and the women. It infuriated him when Fouad declined. How stupid that Fouad remained faithful to his dreary American wife. What a fool.

The blondes did everything he asked. They fucked and sucked, did not object when he ordered them to stick old-fashioned Coke bottles up their asses, licked each other, and complied with his every request.

Fully sated from the two skanks he'd entertained earlier, he mainly watched, snorted a mountain of coke, and issued instructions.

When he was finally ready, he had all three of them take turns going down on him. Then he dismissed them, sending them on their way, never realizing that one of them was a transsexual. If he'd known that, it would have sent him into a royal fury.

After the women were gone, he slept the night through, once again content in the knowledge that tomorrow The Keys would be all his.

CHAPTER TWENTY-THREE

Friday morning, Denver awoke early. She turned her head and there was Bobby sprawled out next to her, lying on his stomach, his lean back exposed. She ran her fingers lightly down his spine, but he didn't stir. For a few seconds she reverted to her teenage years, remembering how she'd crushed on Bobby from afar. Now he was in *her* apartment, in *her* bed, and he was all hers.

Their late-night sex session had been something else. So passionate and emotional in its intensity. The connection they had was unbelievably strong, and it wasn't just the sex. It was more than that. It was love and like with a healthy dose of respect. She only hoped he felt the same way about her.

She jumped out of bed, grabbed a loose T-shirt, went into the kitchen, and put on the coffee. Personally she preferred green tea, but Bobby was a coffee freak—he had to have it strong and black before he was ready to face the day.

Today they were flying to Vegas, apparently on the Stanislopoulos plane.

Denver sighed as she filled the coffeepot. Sometimes she found it odd that Bobby never spoke of his deceased father, or of the huge fortune he'd inherited. She knew he didn't want to touch the money, that it was important for him to make it on his own. She also knew he'd set certain goals for himself, and that he was intent on achieving them.

So why use the plane? It didn't seem to fit into his overall plan.

One day she'd ask him, but not today.

A few moments later Bobby strolled into the kitchen wearing the white terry-cloth robe she'd bought him when he'd first started staying over. He looked so sexy and macho in it with his black curly hair and deep olive skin. Man, he was so damn handsome, he gave her goose bumps.

"Morning, beautiful," he said, grabbing her around the waist.

"Morning, handsome," she responded. "I was just about to bring you coffee in bed."

"Forget about the coffee, how about bringing me *you* in bed," he said, taking her hand and pulling her back toward the bedroom.

"You're insatiable," she said with a dreamy smile, allowing herself to go with him.

"And *you're* irresistible," he replied, tumbling her onto the bed and starting to make love to her again.

His touch was too good to resist. Firm yet gentle. Warm and encompassing. Hard and, this time, fast.

Fact of life: she couldn't get enough of him.

After making out, they headed for the shower together, which led to even more making out, while Amy stood by the glass door attempting to force her way into the shower and under the streaming water. Eventually Amy was successful.

Giggling, they finally emerged, along with a soaking-wet Amy, who, after shaking her fur all over both of them, proceeded to race around the room like a dog possessed.

"Time to get dressed, 'cause it's wheels up at noon," Bobby said, reaching for his pants. "Oh yeah, and I forgot to tell you—little sis is comin' on the plane."

"She is?" Denver questioned, not thrilled at the prospect.

"No avoiding it," Bobby said, buttoning up his shirt. "Besides, you like Max, don't you?"

"Actually, I hardly know her," Denver said, opening up her closet and throwing some things into an overnight bag.

"To know Max is to love her," Bobby said. "She's a wild one."

"Hmm," Denver said, wondering if the party would be dressy and if she should take her one and only Diane von Furstenberg cocktail dress. What was she thinking? Of course she should. It was Vegas and the Santangelo/ Golden clan. Whoopee!

"What's with the *hmm*?" Bobby said, his still damp hair curling over the collar of his shirt.

"Well," Denver said tentatively, "I've only met Max a couple of times and she wasn't exactly talkative."

"Max can be shy. Don't forget, she's only a kid."

"Really?" Denver said, loathe to point out that Max had gone out of her way to practically ignore her. And about to hit eighteen was hardly a kid. But maybe Max would lighten up now that she and Bobby had been together a while.

Maybe being the operative word.

"Why's your mom's Ferrari all over the Internet with, like, Billy Melina behind the wheel?" Cookie demanded over the phone.

"Huh?" Max said, a sudden chill coursing through her body. "What're you *talking* about?"

"Check it out, girl," Cookie said, unaware of the panic she was causing. "Do you think Lucky *lent* it to him? And why'd she'd do that with his divorce deal goin' on? Isn't Venus like her BFF?"

"I've no idea," Max said, already racing to her laptop and checking out the gossip sites. And there it was: a video of Billy climbing out of Lucky's distinctive customized red Ferrari at a gas station in Pacific Palisades.

He'd stopped for gas! Why would he *do* that?!

And if that wasn't enough, there were numerous photos of him getting pulled over by a traffic cop!

"Seems strange t' me," Cookie continued. "Maybe I'll ask Lucky what's up."

"No!" Max said, totally panicking. "Don't do that."

"Why not?"

"'Cause, uh, maybe she doesn't want Venus to know."

"Ohhh!" Cookie squealed. "D'you think she's hookin' up with Billy? It's always the best friend you gotta look out for. Wouldn't *that* be something."

"You are *so* gross."

"What's gross about it? Billy Melina is a total stud muffin. *I'd* do him in a flash."

I bet you would, Max thought, totally mortified that Cookie was even thinking about Billy in such a fashion.

"Anyway," Cookie continued, "didja know Frankie brought Billy to the party? We think he left with Willow Price. Frankie says she's a raving lesbo. Only *I* think she and Billy are totally doin' it. I got to meet both of 'em."

"Awesome," Max said distractedly, thinking that if Cookie knew the truth, she'd go totally nuts.

"Yeah," Cookie said casually, pleased with herself. "You could've met 'em too if you'd been around. Where *were* you all night?"

"*Now* you're asking. Where were *you* when it was time to clean up?"

"Okay, okay," Cookie said impatiently. "So I flaked on you. Let's not get carried away about it."

"'Carried away'?" Max said indignantly. "Screw you!"

"We're takin' off for Vegas soon," Cookie said, completely unfazed that Max was pissed. "What time are *you* planning on arrivin'?"

"This afternoon," Max said, swallowing hard while attempting to stay calm, for if Lucky saw these pix of Billy with her Ferrari, Max would be in deep shit. "Oh, and Cookie," she added quickly, "do *not* say anything to Lucky about her car."

"Why not?"

"'Cause it wouldn't be cool."

After getting rid of Cookie, Max attempted to think of a brilliant excuse should Lucky come across the video. Not that she was likely to on her own; Lucky was totally uninterested in trolling the gossip sites.

But what if someone showed the video to her? What if *Venus* saw it?

Throw up time!

Wasn't it enough that Billy's best friend had turned up and ruined what was about to be a perfect evening? Kev, with his inane remarks and stupid face. She'd automatically hated him, so after gulping down a slice of pizza, she'd taken off, and to her chagrin, Billy hadn't even tried to stop her. And when he'd walked her out to the car, Kev had come too! What an insensitive *jerk*.

Billy had given her a brief peck on the cheek, warned her to drive carefully, and that was it. No *When can I see you again?* Not even *I'll call you.*

She was furious and hurt and felt like a total idiot. It was apparent that Billy had used her for a quick bang. Just because he was a big freaking movie star, he obviously felt that was acceptable behavior.

Well, screw him. Screw him *big-time.*

Now she was left knowing that Lucky could easily discover that Billy had driven her car. And how exactly would she explain that?

Her dream evening had somehow turned into a disastrous nightmare.

She *hated* Billy Melina.

Danny got off on filling Lucky in on all the hotel gossip, scurrilous and otherwise. Danny collected information without even trying; it came to him whether he wanted to hear it or not. Yes, Danny was a magnet for all things juicy. He culled all the latest information over a very early coffee with some of the staff before everyone reported for duty.

It amused Lucky to hear everything that was going on in her hotel, and Danny was always a great source.

Friday morning the news was all about the pit boss caught cheating with a married woman who worked in the catering department. Then there was the delectable and extremely young PR engaged to a croupier, but busy having an affair with a teenage singing sensation who visited Vegas a lot. And lastly the perverted pig in the Presidential Suite who'd refused to pay hookers for extra services rendered.

"Men!" Danny exclaimed, rolling his eyes at his boss. "Why order in if you're not prepared to pay?"

"Ah," Lucky sighed as they made their way onto the terrace of her magnificent penthouse, where a virtual breakfast feast was laid out on a marble side table. "Men can be mysterious creatures, exactly like women."

"You're too kind," Danny said with a snippy edge. "But believe me, most men are nasty little piggies."

"Do you really think that?" Lucky asked mildly.

"Oh, yes indeedy," Danny responded. "I could tell you a thing or two about men. You know, before Buff and I got together—"

Lucky cut him short. "Much as I would love to hear your life stories, Danny, I'd prefer you go pick up Venus and escort her here."

"One day," Danny said, slightly put out that Lucky didn't want to hear what he had to say, "you should listen to my stories."

"One day I will," Lucky assured him. "But not today."

"You're such a machine," Danny said with a knowing nod. "Everything and everyone has to be on time—no room for error."

"And fortunately for you, Danny, you never make errors," Lucky said briskly. "So I suggest you move your tight little ass and go fetch Venus."

"In some circles that remark might be construed as sexual harassment," Danny sniffed. "Besides, you know Venus will keep me waiting. She's such a diva."

"Good-bye," Lucky said, thinking that one of the reasons she got along with Danny so well was that he wasn't scared of her. Because of everything she'd achieved, some people viewed her as intimidating. Danny was never intimidated; he had a sweet but sometimes perverse nature, plus he was efficient and full of energy. He was the perfect assistant for her.

Danny reappeared fifteen minutes later with Venus, a vision in an all-white workout outfit trimmed with gold braid, her platinum-blond hair piled on top of her head.

Danny escorted her onto the terrace to join Lucky, then left. The two women shared a warm hug. "I'm so glad you made it," Lucky said. "Wasn't sure you would."

"You know I love Vegas," Venus remarked. "And I was thinking we could work out after breakfast." She did an elaborate twirl. "You see, I dressed the part. This is from my new clothing line, Body by Venus. You like?"

"Sensational, but I can't get sweaty today," Lucky said, wishing she had the time. "Got a meeting, followed by the board meeting with potential investors you promised to show your face at. Remember?"

"I did?" Venus said innocently.

"You did," Lucky assured her.

"Damn!"

"Suck it up, superstar," Lucky said, laughing. "You know you get off when everyone's creaming all over you. You're an attention junkie, and it shows."

Venus smiled. It was true; she never tired of being in the spotlight. "I guess Danny can work out with me," she said, checking out the table of food. "Right, Danny?"

"Sorry to disappoint you," Lucky said, helping herself to a plate of scrambled eggs and bacon. "But Danny will be with me, taking notes."

"You're no fun," Venus said, opting for a dish of yogurt and blueberries. "At least you could lend me Danny."

"Don't tell me you flew in by yourself?" Lucky questioned as they sat down. "No entourage to attend to your every need?"

"Do I need one?" Venus questioned, lowering her Dolce & Gabbana sunglasses.

"Apparently yes. You can't go wandering around on your own. Where's your stylist? Your hair person? Your usual glam squad?"

"I thought this weekend was all about family, so I came alone."

"How adult of you."

"Actually," Venus admitted, "got me a surprise package who's even now on his way here."

"Ah!" Lucky exclaimed. "I knew it!"

"Of course you did."

"And who might it be?"

"Well . . ." Venus said, an evil smile hovering on her luscious lips. "Yesterday at the shoot for my new clothing line, they hired a very buff stud to be in the shot."

She paused for effect, then continued, "I couldn't let the poor guy go to waste, now could I?"

"You're incorrigible," Lucky said, laughing.

"Oh, like *you* weren't when you were single?" Venus shot back. "I seem to recall you would fuck 'em an' leave 'em quicker than any guy."

"Single," Lucky protested. "I was single. And please, don't *ever* mention that to Max."

"Well, now *I'm* single," Venus said, "which means I will not be wasting a minute of my time."

"As if you ever do," Lucky said dryly.

"By the way," Venus added, "he's twenty, Brazilian, and hardly speaks a word of English." Once again she paused for effect. "I think I'm in love!"

"Does that mean I'll hear no more moaning and groaning about Billy?" Lucky said hopefully.

Venus gave another deliciously evil smile. "Billy who?"

Frankie drove his Grand Sport convertible Corvette like a maniac, all the while speaking on his BlackBerry, reaching over to change a CD, texting, and maneuvering in and out of traffic lanes like he was playing dodgem cars.

Cookie didn't care; she was down with a touch of danger, and Frankie offered her all that and then some. When he picked her up they'd done a couple of lines of coke to prep themselves for the four-hour drive, then she'd gone down on him, and promised that when they hit the desert, she'd do it again.

"While I'm driving," he'd said, salivating at the thought.

"What do I get in return?" she'd demanded.

"Depends on how you do it."

"Ha!" Cookie exclaimed. "Who d'you think won the blow job competition at school when she was fourteen?"

Frankie was intrigued. Teenagers indulging in blow job competitions—he'd thought it was an urban legend. Satisfying to know it was true, and that *his* girl was the champ. How about that?

His girl. His first steady since Annabelle Maestro, who in the end had treated him like a piece of shit. He would never forgive her for that. Annabelle had even written about him in her dumb book, and not in a flattering way. He'd thought about suing, but everyone had warned him against it. Not worth the time, money for lawyers, and pure frustration it would entail, so eventually he'd decided against it.

If only he'd had the foresight to make a sex tape while he and Annabelle were together. What a financial bonanza *that* would've been.

But no, he hadn't done that, he'd blown a major opportunity to score. Vivid Entertainment would've paid big. They'd forked out millions for Paris Hilton and the Kardashian broad with the big ass. He could have made a killing. Colin Farrell, here I come!

Too late now.

Then the thought occurred to him—how about a sex tape with Cookie? She was certainly adventurous enough. And if he assured her they were making it just for their own private viewing pleasure . . .

Yeah. Like Annabelle—whose dad was action movie star Ralph Maestro—Cookie had a famous father: Gerald M., soul singer supreme. Although since rap and hip-hop had taken over the airwaves, Gerald M. was not exactly at the top of his game. However, he was still a huge star in Europe. They loved all that Lionel Richie–, Barry White–style of sexual healing.

First order of business when they hit Vegas: buy himself a Flip video and get to work.

Yeah, it was a plan.

* * *

"Let's work out plan B," Bobby said as they sat in the back of a town car on their way to the airport and his plane. He was feeling bad about letting Denver down and wanted to make it up to her. "When do I get to meet the family?"

"There is no plan B," Denver responded. "You had your chance."

"Not my fault," Bobby objected. "If there's one thing I can't control it's the airlines."

"Apparently you can," Denver argued. And then she couldn't help going there. "Where was *your* plane when you needed it? And how come we're using it today? Isn't it a somewhat extravagant move?"

"Questions, questions," Bobby teased, trying to get her to lighten up. "My girlfriend the DA gets off on asking questions."

"Deputy DA," Denver corrected. "And your *girlfriend* is extremely disappointed you didn't show."

"But sweetheart, I tried," he said artlessly. "My intentions were good."

"Sometimes the best of intentions don't cut it," Denver pointed out, deciding that in spite of the great morning sex, she was still somewhat annoyed that he hadn't made it in time to meet her family. "I really wanted you to be there, and everyone was expecting you. You not turning up made me look stupid."

"C'mon, babe," he said, throwing her a quick glance. "*You* could never look stupid. You're the smartest girl I know."

"Says you."

"You *gotta* stop breaking my balls," he insisted. "This is supposed to be the start of a romantic weekend, so don't go ruining it."

Very romantic, Denver thought. *Surrounded by your entire family, who will be judging me to see if I'm suitable girlfriend material for the heir to—who the fuck knows what?*

She let out a long deep sigh. "Whatever," she murmured.

Bobby couldn't help laughing. "Now you sound as if you're twelve," he remarked.

"Sometimes," she said wistfully, "I wish I were."

CHAPTER
TWENTY-FOUR

"Good afternoon!" Bright-eyed and full of good cheer, the two flight attendants, Hani and Gitta, welcomed Bobby and Denver aboard the Stanislopoulos plane.

Denver had flown on it a couple of times before, but not when she'd been Bobby's actual girlfriend. She wondered if Hani or Gitta knew that she and Bobby were now a couple, then she decided that they probably did, because they looked like the kind of women who made it their business to know everything.

Max, Harry, and Paco were already on board. Harry was in a state of delight to be sharing the pleasures of a private jet with his new friend, while Paco was somewhat in awe. Meanwhile, Max had fallen into a depression about the way Billy had ended up treating her. How dare he! She wasn't a one-night conquest. She wasn't some random girl he could screw and walk away from. *And* he'd taken her virginity. Snatched it from her like a thief in the night. She was mortified.

Lurid thoughts of punishment crossed her mind. She could tell Lucky and Lennie that Billy had forced himself on her. Ha! If Lucky thought he'd done that, she'd blow his balls off. Her mom took no prisoners; everyone knew that about Lucky.

Or . . . she could mention it to Bobby, who was practically ignoring her now that he had a steady girlfriend.

Crap! She hated the fact that Bobby seemed really into this Denver person. Why couldn't he have just gone on being a player? Girls were always chasing after Bobby. With his dark good looks and appealing personality, he could take his pick. So why had *he* picked Denver?

After a while she decided it was time to assert her authority, show Denver who really mattered in Bobby's life. "Big brother!" she squealed, dashing toward him and flinging her arms around his neck. "I haven't seen you in *ages!* I've missed you *soooo* much!"

A startled Bobby extracted himself from her cling. "You remember Denver," he said pointedly.

"Oh yeah, sure," Max said, purposely making it sound like she didn't.

"Hello, Max," Denver said, already sensing trouble ahead. "It's nice to see you again."

"Hey," Max said, with a vague wave in her direction.

Dammit, Denver thought. *Now I've got to deal with a truculent teenager who is not at all thrilled I've hooked up with her brother, whom she obviously adores. Great start to a weekend trip I didn't want to come on in the first place.*

"Everyone please take their seats, turn off their cell phones, and buckle up," Gitta announced. "We are preparing for takeoff."

Denver fastened her seat belt.

Bobby reached for her hand. "Happy flying, sweetheart. We're about to set off on a memorable weekend. Prepare yourself for plenty of fun."

The plane roared down the runway, and soon they were on their way to Vegas.

"Wassup with you, man?" Kev inquired. "Your mind's like on a trip somewhere in space."

"Yeah," Billy answered distractedly. "I'm thinkin' we might wanna make a Vegas pit stop."

"Vegas!" Kev snapped to attention. Vegas was his

kind of town. "I'm *way* down with that. When we gonna do it, bro?"

"Today," Billy said, making a decision on the spot.

He'd been thinking about Max all morning. Truth was, he'd been thinking about her ever since Kev had dragged him out to a club the previous night. As usual there'd been dozens of girls draping themselves all over him, but he simply wasn't into any of them. He'd promised Max dinner, but somehow with Kev arriving unexpectedly, he'd allowed her to slip off, and that wasn't what he'd wanted at all.

It was his own fault. She was so young that he'd gotten kind of scared and guilty; he hadn't quite figured out how to handle the situation. Then Kev arriving had given him a convenient out. But after thinking about it, he hadn't wanted a convenient out. What he'd really wanted was to spend more time with Max. Yes, she was young, but she was special and fresh, and maybe it was too soon to know, but he had this weird feeling that she was his soul mate, the girl he was supposed to be with.

And yet . . . he'd let her go, and now she was probably pissed at him. Girls were sensitive in that way. Especially as the sex they'd had together was her first time.

He was mad at himself. And how to make it up to her?

Vegas. Her birthday. Show her that he cared.

Not that he could simply turn up unannounced at her birthday party; that wouldn't fly at all. He could imagine Lucky's face if she got even a tiny hint that he was screwing her daughter. And Lennie's too.

But . . . he could be in Vegas and meet up with Max on the sly. Lucky didn't have to know.

It seemed like a way to go. He'd do it, and he'd take Kev along for the ride.

*   *   *

After breakfast with Venus, Lucky set off for her meeting with Jeffrey Lonsdale and the people from Jordan Developments. Since she didn't have any current projects in mind, she wasn't at all sure why she'd agreed to meet with them. Raising money was never a problem, but Jeffrey seemed to think that they might be useful if, for instance, she decided to build a version of The Keys in Atlantic City or any other big American city where gambling was legal. Jeffrey never allowed her to invest a dime of her own money. Not that he was in control, but she always listened to his sage advice. Jeffrey was smart.

Danny arrived to escort her to her office.

"News flash," Danny announced, looking all pleased with himself.

"What?" Lucky asked, striding to the elevator, chic in black leather pants, boots, and a cashmere shell, her long hair wild and falling around her shoulders, large yellow diamond studs affixed to her earlobes.

"It's juicy," Danny exclaimed, hopping to keep up with her.

"Give it up, Danny, or shut it up," Lucky said.

"The perv in the Presidential Suite I was telling you about earlier is the man you're on your way to meet."

"Huh?"

"Armand Jordan. Jordan Developments."

"You're kidding."

"One and the same."

"Remind me again what the story was."

"Apparently," Danny said, savoring every morsel, "Mr. Jordan hired a couple of expensive call girls, made them do all kinds of unspeakable acts, then refused to pay extra for, ah . . . certain things that require more money."

"Nice."

"Are you sure you should meet with him?"

"Why not?" Lucky replied with a casual shrug. "It's quite likely I can embarrass him into paying up. Wouldn't *that* be fun."

"And you'd do that, wouldn't you?" Danny said, delighted at the prospect of watching his boss in action.

Lucky grinned. "Working girls deserve every red cent they make. Maybe I should consider it my good deed for the day. Whaddya think, Danny?"

"Oh yes, I think definitely yes!"

Cruising down the highway with Cookie's head in his lap, and his cock in her mouth, Frankie couldn't have felt more on top of the world.

What could be better than this? Drake loud and sexy on the sound system. The hot sun burning down on them. The smooth thrust of his Corvette as the speedometer hit 80. Plus the insane sensation of holding back what he knew was about to be a mind-shattering orgasm.

Man, Frankie was flying and then some.

Until . . . the goddamn siren. The cop car drawing alongside them. And a red-faced motherfucker of a cop frantically signaling for him to pull over.

He did so, and the cop marched up to his window.

"Sorry, Officer," Frankie said, attempting to seem contrite. "Music too loud?"

"License and registration," Angry Cop said. "And get out the car." He peered suspiciously over at Cookie. "You too."

Cookie, who was busy applying a fresh layer of sticky lip gloss, frowned. "What did *I* do?" she asked petulantly.

"Lewd behavior in a moving vehicle," Angry Cop announced. "I'm thinking of booking both of you."

Frankie tried to remember where he'd stashed the coke and the grass and the pills he'd brought along on the trip—the main reason he hadn't wanted to fly. Then he remembered that all his drugs were in his overnight bag, along with his shaving kit.

Oh shit, this could still be bad.

As Cookie climbed out of the car, Angry Cop gave her a hard piercing look. "How old are you?" he demanded. "And have you been drinking?"

Once they were in the air, Denver decided to make an effort to be nice to Bobby's truculent little sister. She moved over to sit next to her. "Bobby tells me you're planning on relocating to New York," she said. "Sounds like an exciting thing to do."

Max grunted.

"Any idea what you want to do when you get there?" Denver asked, persevering.

Another grunt.

"Well, anyway," she continued, "I bet your mom'll miss you. I know my mom was very upset when I moved out, and *we* were living in the same city, so you can imagine."

No reaction at all.

Denver gave up. Screw it. What did she care if Bobby's sister approved of her or not? It was quite obvious that Max felt she had dibs on her brother, and woe betide any girl who came too close.

Bobby was sitting up front talking music with Paco, while Harry sat listening to them, his pale face full of rapt attention.

"If you want, while we're in Vegas, you can spin at my club for a couple of hours," Bobby offered. "I'm always searching out new talent, and a happening deejay makes all the difference."

Harry nodded enthusiastically. "Paco's the best," he announced proudly. "You'll definitely want to hear what he can do."

"I already got a gig in Vegas," Paco said, polite and nervous at the same time. "But spinnin' at your club would be an honor."

"We'll figure something out," Bobby said, grabbing Denver's arm as she came over and settled into the seat next to him. "This girl's into Adele, Winehouse, Mayer. Not me—I'm into everything," he added, squeezing her hand.

"Ah yes, that's me," Denver said wryly. "The girl who's into mellow."

"Nothing wrong with that," Paco said earnestly, trying to hide his excitement at actually sitting with these people on a private plane. His family, who all resided in the Bronx, would never believe him. "The mix is what matters. Rap, Cuban, rock, mellow—it all works together. That's the way you get people on the floor."

"You see," Denver said, shooting Bobby a look. "This guy knows what he's talking about."

"Yeah, yeah, I see," Bobby said, still grinning.

Hani came by carrying mimosas in tall glasses. Bobby handed one to Denver, then took one for himself.

"Here's to the weekend, babe," he said, clinking glasses. "We're gonna have a great time."

She smiled and realized that she was hopelessly, happily, deeply, in love.

"I'll drink to that," she said softly.

And suddenly she was delighted she'd agreed to come on this weekend.

Once more they were on the move, Frankie's Corvette roaring down the highway at full speed. Somehow or other Cookie had convinced Angry Cop they were on their way to get married, and that the sex thing he thought he'd seen wasn't what it looked like, and that her daddy, Gerald M.—yes, *the* Gerald M.—was waiting to greet them, along with several camera crews and a shit-load of paparazzi. Only she didn't say *shitload;* she cooled it with the language.

At first Angry Cop didn't believe she was Gerald M.'s daughter, but she had proof—several photos of them together on her iPad, and his latest CD in her purse. She carried it with her at all times for just such an occasion.

Angry Cop's wife was a fan, so Angry Cop wasn't so angry anymore, and after a short lecture on road safety, he sent them on their way with a warning to be more careful in the future.

"You should be a freakin' actress," Frankie exclaimed, full of genuine admiration. "That little performance you just put on was insane!"

"I know," Cookie said with a less-than-modest giggle. "I'm the real shit, right?"

"You bet your ass," Frankie agreed.

"My dad taught me t' use his name whenever it would get me outta trouble. There's gotta be *some* perks to being his kid."

"Your dad sounds like a smart dude."

"Not so much. When it comes to pussy, he's a total douche."

"I'd still like to meet him," Frankie said, thinking of the possibilities.

"One of these days," Cookie answered vaguely.

"Well anyway, I'm impressed," Frankie said. "I thought we were definitely gettin' busted."

Cookie giggled again. "That's the fifth CD I've used as payoff. It works every time."

"Yeah?" Frankie said. "So tell me, how many dudes you been caught givin' head to in a movin' vehicle?"

"Wouldn't *you* like to know," she murmured mysteriously.

No, actually, he wouldn't. Some things were best left unsaid.

* * *

Feeling sorry for herself, Max decided a mimosa was a fine idea. So even though she didn't usually drink, she downed two, and immediately felt light-headed.

Nobody cared. Bobby was too busy with his girlfriend to notice, while Harry was totally locked into Paco, who didn't seem at all gay—so what was *that* about? Was Harry delusional? Or had something actually taken place? She hadn't bothered to ask him; she was too caught up with all the drama in her own life.

Tears threatened to flow. *Snap out of it*, she warned herself. *Get a grip and stop acting like a girl. You're a Santangelo. Suck it up. So you had a one-nighter with Billy Melina. Big freaking deal.*

They hadn't used protection.

Dumb.

Super dumb.

What if she was pregnant?

The very thought shocked her sober, and she moved as far away from everyone as possible, strapped herself into a seat, closed her eyes, and attempted to shut out the world.

"I must say, you certainly know how to put me together with the classiest of people," Lucky complained to Jeffrey when they met up in her office adjacent to the conference room.

"What are you talking about?" Jeffrey asked, looking puzzled.

"These Jordan Development people," Lucky said, tossing back her hair.

"Yes?" Jeffrey said, clearing his throat.

"Apparently they're into hooker paradise and not paying."

Jeffrey adjusted the heavy old-fashioned horn-rimmed glasses he always wore to business meetings.

"Is there some information I should know about?" he asked, uncomfortable that Lucky apparently knew things he didn't.

"Yes," Lucky said, moving behind her oversized art deco desk and sitting down. "If I know it, so should you."

Jeffrey pulled up a leather chair opposite her desk. "And how do we know this?" he inquired.

"We know," Lucky replied, tapping her fingers on the desk. "Because Danny is the eyes and ears of everything that goes on in my hotel. Right, Danny?"

Danny, who was busy setting up his laptop at a side table so he could recount every detail of the upcoming meeting, nodded.

"What exactly did you hear?" Jeffrey asked.

Danny repeated his story. He really enjoyed being the center of attention; it made a welcome change from hovering in the background.

Jeffrey frowned. This did not bode well for the upcoming meeting. If he knew Lucky, she couldn't care less that the man they were meeting with had entertained hookers. But the fact that he'd stiffed them would definitely irk her.

Before Jeffrey had time to think it through, the receptionist announced that the people from Jordan Developments had arrived.

Lucky smiled a slow, dangerous smile, her black eyes sparkling.

"Let the show begin," she drawled. "This could turn out to be quite interesting."

CHAPTER TWENTY-FIVE

Armand often reflected on what his life would have been like if he'd been raised as a normal boy in America. He wasn't normal; he knew that. He was special. He was a prince. His childhood in Akramshar had been anything but normal. He'd been born in a palace, nursed by women in long black robes who'd barely talked to him. And it wasn't until he and his mother moved to New York when he was eight that he'd finally gotten to spend time with her. Up until then he'd had very little to do with Peggy; she was merely this dazzling redheaded woman who'd occasionally swooped into the nursery wearing low-cut silk gowns and magnificent jewelry.

The king had different rules for the women in his country. Poor females were not allowed to be educated and wore long body-covering robes at all times. Rich females could do whatever they wanted. Most girls from affluent families were schooled in Europe, and many of them chose not to come back, for arranged marriages at the king's request were quite normal. Soraya, Armand's wife, was one of the girls who'd come back.

Armand never gave much thought to Soraya. She was the mother of his children, that pleased the king, and pleasing the great man was all that mattered.

Returning to Akramshar once a year had shaped Armand's life. He was a tried-and-true prince, and one day he might be tempted to let the world know, for he was well aware how impressed Westerners were with titles.

But not today. Today he was buying a hotel, soon to be the jewel in his property empire, the crème de la crème of Vegas.

Armand believed in pampering himself. After doing several lines of coke, he thoroughly showered before applying various lotions to his body, spending an inordinate amount of time massaging his balls and fine shaft of manhood. Thinking of the whores from the night before caused him to become so hard that he had no choice but to attend to his needs. Inconvenient, but far more enjoyable than being with any woman.

When he was finished, he took another shower, applied more lotions, stared at his reflection for a while, and finally got dressed. First a silk Turnbull & Asser shirt made especially for him in London, a $350 tie from Neiman Marcus in Beverly Hills, and finally an $8,000 pinstriped custom suit in pearl gray.

Admiring himself once again in the mirror, he had to admit that he made a dashing figure. It was no wonder women pursued him. The *New Yorker* magazine had recently listed him as one of the city's most eligible bachelors.

New York indeed. How about the world?

Peggy did not sleep well at all. She couldn't relax. Her mind was buzzing, filled with memories of the young girl who was once the toast of Vegas.

Ah . . . she remembered those times so well. And she also remembered Gino Santangelo. When Fouad had told her the old man's name, she'd been filled with excitement. She'd thought it was him, but she hadn't been sure. Now she knew.

Seeing Gino again after so many years was quite a

surprise. It had brought every long-distance memory crashing back.

LAS VEGAS 1968

Peggy Lindquest. A young, ambitious girl from Ohio. A girl with legs up to here, translucent skin, and fiery red hair. A girl who captured every man's attention.

Peggy hit town like the proverbial firecracker, filled with ambition and the desire to make a career for herself, or at least snag a rich man. She was eighteen and hot to tango.

It wasn't long before she landed a job at Caesar's Palace, dancing in the chorus of a big flashy show. Dancing, and sometimes showing her breasts while attired in a fantastic showgirl costume of sequins and feathers. Her breasts were real and quite something. A 36C with rosebud nipples. Men lusted after her perfect breasts.

Peggy was no virgin. She'd been having sex with boys since she was thirteen. She knew what men wanted, and she was prepared to let them beg for it.

She met Joe Piscarelli at a party. Twelve years older than her and dashingly handsome in a gangster kind of way. Girls swooned over Joe, but not Peggy. She played hard to get until he was begging her to move in with him. Eventually she did so, and it was blissful for a while, until she discovered that Joe possessed a vile temper, which sometimes exploded into violent rage. When that happened, Peggy ran away to stay with one of her girlfriends.

It was on just such an occasion that she'd

*encountered Gino Santangelo. Gino was an older
man, but he was full of charisma and powerful
vibes. Everyone knew Gino in Vegas; he was kind
of a legend. And quite a ladies man.*

*Peggy slept with him. Once. It was a night to
remember.*

*The next day she was back in Joe's bed. And
two weeks after that she was on her way to Akramshar with the king.*

*But Peggy had never forgotten her one night of
lust with Gino Santangelo. And seeing him again
all these years later—even though he was now an
old man—she couldn't stop remembering their
night of unbridled passion.*

It was a memory she cherished.

Satisfied with his image, Armand added solid-gold cuff
links, an onyx and diamond masculine-style bracelet,
and on his other wrist a $250,000 diamond-encrusted
watch.

At last he was ready for his meeting. A meeting that
would change his life. He was sick of New York, the
clubs, the women, the social events. He needed a change.

Vegas had so much to offer. It was his kind of town.

And soon he would own it.

CHAPTER TWENTY-SIX

"I'm starving," Max whined to Bobby as he exited the bathroom on the plane.

She knew she sounded needy, but she simply couldn't help herself; she had a strong urge to take her frustration out on someone.

"How can you be hungry?" Bobby questioned, eager to get back to Denver. "There's a whole buffet laid out."

"I feel like a hamburger," Max insisted. "Can we go to the Hard Rock when we land?"

"Sorry, kiddo," Bobby said. "I'm busy. Gino's in town; call him when we get there, he'll take you."

"Oh," she said scornfully. "I really want to go get a burger with my *grandfather*."

"Might I remind you, your *grandfather* is one of the greatest men you'll ever come across," Bobby said, frowning. "He practically invented Vegas, so you should try listening to his stories sometime. Maybe you'd learn something."

"Why are you being so mean to me?" Max asked, her eyes filling with tears.

"Who's being mean? Not me."

"Yes you are," she said fiercely. "You're, like, *ignoring* me."

Bobby shook his head in exasperation. "What's up with you today? How come you're acting like a spoiled little kid?"

"I am *so* not," she said crossly. "It's *you* and what'sher-name."

"Her *name* is Denver," Bobby said sternly. "And you might try being a bit nicer to her."

"Why's that?" Max demanded, narrowing her eyes. "Are you planning on *marrying* her or something?"

As soon as she said it, she wished she hadn't. The last person she wanted to alienate was Bobby. She was hoping he'd forget what she'd just said, hug her, and act all big brotherly. Why couldn't he do that?

Instead he threw her a hard-ass look and returned to his seat, whereupon Gitta made the announcement that they would be landing in fifteen minutes, and everyone should please buckle up.

Max slunk back to her seat, her mind racing. What was Billy doing? Was he out and about shagging some other unsuspecting female simply because he could?

Being a movie star meant getting laid anytime you wanted. And she should've known that. Coming from such a high-profile family, she was hardly naïve.

But no, she'd so fallen for his nice-guy shtick. *Stupid! Stupid! Stupid!*

Ace, where are you when I need you?

Ace was actually behind the wheel of his truck, heading full speed toward Vegas. He was feeling pretty upbeat about surprising Max on her birthday. There was no way she'd expect him to leave the construction job he was working on in Big Bear; it would be a real shocker, especially as she was always urging him to loosen up and be more spontaneous.

The two of them had a long-distance relationship, which seemed to work, although one day he hoped to save enough money to make the move to L.A. Then they could see how things panned out when they were living in the same city.

Max was his addiction. One moment she was the vulnerable, thoughtful girl he'd first met. The next, she was some kind of tough party animal who liked spending all her time dancing on tables in L.A. clubs with her somewhat sketchy group of friends. Harry was a weirdo, with his dyed black hair and white face. And Ace especially couldn't stand Cookie; she was definitely a negative influence, with her flashy lifestyle and obvious coke habit.

The problem with Max was that she hadn't figured out what she wanted her life to be. But at least she didn't sleep around like Cookie; she had that under control.

As far as sex was concerned, he'd never pushed her to go further than she felt she was comfortable with, although now that she was about to turn eighteen . . .

Ace was almost twenty-one, and he wasn't about to wait forever for them to take it to the next level. He had his needs, and if Max didn't meet them, then maybe it was time to rethink their situation.

Striding through the airport, Billy attracted major attention. Paparazzi dogged his every step, girls excitedly texted about spotting him, airport personnel treated him like royalty, ushering him and Kev to the front of every line. Of course, Kev loved it; why wouldn't he?

"We should do something together," Kev suggested, fully basking in the attention.

"Like what?" Billy said, signing autographs for three overweight security women who'd all abandoned their posts and were gazing at him adoringly.

"I dunno," Kev answered vaguely. "Maybe I could produce your next movie. Like I'm a real winner at dealing with actors an' shit. I could totally nail it."

Billy knew full well that Kev's social skills were non-existent, but Kev was a loyal friend, who unfortunately couldn't seem to keep a job, even though he'd tried and failed countless times.

"Producing's not for you, Kev," Billy said as he was hustled through a private security door with an officious airport escort.

"Then how about I write a script?" Kev said, trailing behind them. "Like, y'know, kinda a buddy-style comedy. Somethin' like *The Hangover*. An' here's the kicker—*you* can star in it."

"Hate to break it to you," Billy said briskly, "but I'm booked solid for the next five years."

Kev's eyebrows shot up. "Holy jeez! Are you shittin' me?"

"'Fraid not. Signed, sealed, an' delivered."

"I could be your manager, then," Kev ventured, not prepared to give up. "That'd work. I'd be a kick-ass manager."

"Got one of those," Billy said, wondering where this was going.

"I need a job, Billy," Kev said, suddenly becoming serious. "Gotta pay alimony to that cooze I was married to for five minutes. An' I got debts up the wazoo in New York. I figured if I came back to L.A., you'd be able to hook me up. . . ."

"No worries," Billy said, remembering the days he'd slept on Kev's floor when he was stone-cold broke with no future prospects. "I'll come up with something."

"You will?" Kev said, his face brightening.

"Leave it t' me," Billy assured him. "There's no way I'd ever leave you hangin'."

And with that they entered the VIP lounge, where Billy was besieged by even more autograph requests and adoring females.

And while Billy was catching a plane, Venus was catching up with her Brazilian stud from her photo shoot. His name was Jorge, and he was quite a specimen.

The moment he sauntered into her apartment, macho strut going full force, smoky eyes sending out major sex signals, she was ready for action. Venus had never been slow about coming forward.

Jorge wasn't quite sure what had hit him. One moment he was a penniless wannabe model working as a busboy at Cecconi's who'd been in L.A. less than a month, and the next he was plucked from obscurity by a randy old agent who'd gotten him the gig on the Venus photo shoot. And before he knew it, Venus had invited him to Vegas for the weekend, and now here he was.

Venus greeted him with kisses on each cheek as she led him into her sumptuous apartment at The Keys. It was quite a place—all white leather furniture and luxurious throws. A giant Buddha sitting in the hallway welcomed guests. Low lighting cast a magical glow, for Venus had all the shades drawn shut. Incense-infused candles wafted scent into the atmosphere.

They hadn't made love yet, but they both knew it was inevitable.

Venus didn't believe in wasting time. After Jorge had been in her apartment for a few minutes, she said, "Come with me. I'll show you the bedroom." Taking his hand, she led him to her bed, and without words they both began stripping off their clothes. Jorge took a moment to catch his breath when he saw Venus naked. She was magnificent.

"Do something!" she commanded.

Jorge jumped to attention, manhandling her breasts before pushing her onto the bed in a take-charge kind of way, a move she was definitely into. His nude body hovered over her like a falcon trapping its prey before he plunged into her, keeping up a mind-blowing series of thrusts for a full twenty minutes.

Their sexual encounter was a marathon of tongues and wetness and acrobatic positions. It was all that she'd hoped for and more, for what Jorge lacked in technique, he made up for with pure brute strength, and a staggeringly beautiful uncircumcised cock. Jorge was a stud and then some, plus his lack of English only heightened the excitement she experienced.

When they were finally done, Venus decided she was perfectly delighted with her new plaything. He far surpassed her two previous conquests. She couldn't wait to put him on parade.

Screw you, Billy Melina. I have officially moved on.

The landing in Vegas was extremely bumpy. Tightly strapped into her seat, Max seriously considered the possibility of the plane crashing and them all facing a fiery death. Or maybe only Denver would suffer a fiery death, and she and Bobby would be miraculously saved.

Yes, that was a way cool scenario. Billy would hear about the crash and rush to her side, full of apologies for the shitty way he'd treated her. Then they'd immediately run off and get married at one of those crazy wedding chapels with an Elvis Presley look-alike officiating.

Cool. Bobby would be their best man. And Harry's deejay friend would come up with a majorly badass sound track for the occasion.

She giggled at the thought.

The plane touched down, skidded along the runway, and finally shuddered to a stop. No fiery death for anyone today.

Bobby unclicked his seat belt and came over to her. "Glad to see you're smiling," he said, bending over her seat. "It's going to be a great weekend. No fighting, right, sis?"

Little did he know the reason she was smiling. Denver was dead. Billy was back on the scene. And all was well in the world.

"Sorry, Bobby," she said, meekly. "You're right, it's gonna be a way cool weekend. And I promise I'll behave." Her smile widened. *Not!*

CHAPTER
TWENTY-SEVEN

Lucky took the power position behind her desk, with Danny somewhere behind her, getting ready to take notes on his computer. Jeffrey was seated across from her.

She gave Armand a long cool stare as he entered her office. What she saw was an arrogant man, impeccably dressed, not bad-looking, with a small, neat mustache and cold, hard eyes. The man accompanying him was much more low-key, and seemed slightly uncomfortable. Lucky considered herself an expert at reading body language, and she immediately got it—Armand Jordan was the boss, and Fouad Khan his faithful lackey.

After announcing the names of the two men, Jeffrey said, "May I present Ms. Lucky Santangelo."

Armand did not proffer his hand; instead he gave her a dismissive nod of his head, making no eye contact.

Fouad spoke up. "It is a pleasure to meet such an accomplished businesswoman," he said, causing Armand to shoot him a furious glare.

Lucky did not miss the energy passing between the two men. It seemed that Fouad was happy to be present, while Armand was certainly not.

"Thank you," she said, picking up a silver letter opener with the inscription *Never fuck with a Santangelo.* Bobby had given it to her last Christmas, a reminder of the family motto. "Gentlemen," she said coolly, "kindly take a seat."

"We should get down to business," Armand said, addressing Jeffrey as he sat stiffly in a high-backed leather chair. "I have no time to waste. I am sure neither do you."

Lucky was amused by this man's obvious difficulty in dealing with a strong female presence. She'd encountered men like him before. Men who were basically scared shitless by powerful women. Men whose balls shriveled at the mere hint of a female being in charge. Men who always had to pay for it, otherwise they were incapable of getting it up.

Ah yes, she'd come across men like Armand Jordan many times. They were unemotional, pathetic creatures who obviously needed help.

It occurred to her that Jeffrey should never have requested that she attend this meeting, for she had no intention of venturing into any deals at all with the arrogant asshole who sat before her. First of all, she didn't need his money, and second, she certainly didn't need his sexist attitude.

"There is really nothing concrete to discuss," Jeffrey said, instantly realizing that there was no way Lucky would ever enter into business with Armand Jordan. This meeting was useless, and he'd better wind it up as quickly as possible, because knowing Lucky, there was no doubt she would bring up the hooker incident if she felt in the mood to embarrass Armand. "Mr. Khan requested a meeting regarding future financing of any major projects that Ms. Santangelo might want to proceed with," Jeffrey continued. "He thought it prudent that the principles get together, and I agreed. However—"

"Fouad must have given you the wrong impression," Armand said, rudely interrupting, while still not addressing Lucky directly. "I am not here to talk about future financing. I am here today to purchase The Keys. And furthermore, I am prepared to pay whatever it takes to do so."

Lucky flashed Jeffrey a look that said, *Are you fucking kidding me?*

Fouad sunk deeper into his chair.

Danny glanced up from his laptop, well aware that there was about to be trouble. He knew better than anyone how Lucky hated to waste time, and this meeting was definitely a huge time-waster.

"There has no doubt been a big misunderstanding," Jeffrey said, adjusting his glasses. "I made it perfectly clear when Mr. Khan visited my offices in New York that The Keys was not in any way for sale." Jeffrey turned to Fouad. "Isn't that so?"

Fouad fidgeted uncomfortably and opened his mouth to say something, but Armand silenced him with a shake of his head.

"I'm not sure that you are hearing what I am saying," Armand said, speaking very slowly, as if dealing with a backward child. "I wish to buy The Keys, and I will pay whatever it takes. This is not a negotiation, it is an offer you cannot refuse."

Finally Lucky spoke up. "Really?" she questioned, her voice dripping with sarcasm.

Armand made the mistake of continuing to ignore her, once more addressing Jeffrey. "I have no time to waste," he said abruptly. "This deal has to take place immediately."

"Why the urgency?" Lucky asked, playing with him.

"My lawyers in New York are waiting for your call," Armand said to Jeffrey. "I expect you to make that call today."

"Mr. Jordan," Lucky said, willing him to look at her. "Although I realize that you are totally delusional, I think it's about time I set you straight."

"Excuse me?" Armand said coldly. "Are you addressing me?"

"The Keys is not on the market for you or anyone else," Lucky said, her tone as sharp as an ice pick. "Whatever the offer."

Armand threw her a severe look. His lip curled, exhibiting his distaste at having to speak to a woman about business. It was quite obvious to him that she was merely a figurehead, and that Jeffrey Lonsdale was running the show.

"Excuse me?" he repeated, annoyed that a mere female would have the audacity to address him in such a brazen fashion. "We're wasting valuable time," he added, making a controlled effort not to lose his temper. "Surely you realize that my offer is too good for you to turn down. I am telling you to name your price." *So do it, bitch. Do it now.*

Lucky raised a cynical eyebrow. *"Telling* me?"

Here it comes, Danny thought. *And I for one cannot wait!*

Armand refused to back down. Finally locking eyes with Lucky, he repeated his words. "Yes," he said harshly. "Telling you."

"Hmm," Lucky said, remaining surprisingly calm. "Let me give you a piece of valuable advice." She picked up the *Never fuck with a Santangelo* letter opener, balancing it in the palm of her hand. For one wild moment Danny thought she might stab the man. But she didn't, she continued talking. "This is the deal, Mr. Jordan. If you wish to keep doing business, then I suggest you make a supreme attempt to conquer your extremely obvious and very intense fear of women. It makes you seem impotent and weak, and you wouldn't want that, would you?"

Armand glared at her, trying to imagine her naked, crawling around on all fours while he pissed all over her, for that's exactly the kind of treatment the cunt deserved.

"You make it clear why women should be seen and not heard," he said at last. "How *dare* you presume to know me. You know *nothing* about me."

"Ah, but I do know that you're an asshole," Lucky said, rapidly losing patience with the game that was taking place.

"And you," Armand replied, his words laced with venom, "are nothing but a foolish, impudent woman with an extreme lack of brain power."

Jeffrey began to speak, but Lucky silenced him with a wave of her hand.

"As I said before," Lucky said, directly addressing Armand, her blacker-than-night eyes feline and deadly. "You're an asshole with both feet planted firmly in the Dark Ages. So I strongly suggest we end this ridiculous conversation right now. I repeat for the last time: The Keys is not for sale. Get that into your hooker-riddled head and then get the hell out of my hotel. Oh yes, and finally," she added fiercely. "Those two working women you fucked last night want the money you owe them. So be a man for once and pay up."

Danny felt like applauding. Who else had a boss as feisty and perfect as Lucky Santangelo? She was unique.

Filled with unmitigated rage, Armand abruptly stood up and marched to the door. Once there he stopped and turned, in spite of Fouad trying to maneuver him out. Glaring at Lucky, he spat his final words. "I can assure you, *bitch,* this is not the end, it is merely the beginning of a battle you will eventually lose. So get off your high horse and back into the bedroom where you belong. The Keys will be mine; there is nothing and no one who will stop me from owning it. Be warned, because I will do anything to get it. And when I say anything, I do mean anything. And that, my dear, is not a threat, it's a cold hard fact."

Lucky rose to her feet, her dark eyes flashing danger

signals. She'd had it with this expensively clad douche bag. "Get the fuck out of my hotel, moron. And never bother coming back. Because if you ever do, I promise you'll regret it."

Before Armand could reply, Fouad managed to hustle him out the door.

As far as Fouad was concerned, this was one deal that would never happen.

CHAPTER TWENTY-EIGHT

Arriving at The Keys, Max felt as if she was coming home, for she knew the place as well as their Malibu house. She'd swum in every pool, availed herself of all the spa facilities, eaten in every restaurant, shopped in every high-end shop, and explored the lush gardens countless times. She had her own suite in the hotel, on a special floor reserved strictly for family and friends.

Lucky's apartment was off-limits. "It's my haven of peace and quiet," Lucky had explained when she'd started spending time in Vegas. "It's a no-kid zone unless you're invited."

At first Max was furious when her mom had informed everyone of the rule. But then again, her mom was Lucky Santangelo, and everyone knew that Lucky did things her way. Now Max was totally into the fact that she could come and go as she pleased, *and* have her friends to stay whenever she wanted. It was a way cool situation, except when brother Gino Junior and her half brother, Leonardo, were around. Fortunately, the two boys were gone for the entire summer, traveling around Europe with a guardian. It was Lennie's idea that they get a view of life beyond Beverly Hills and Vegas. Max was psyched to be rid of them; they were both younger than her and majorly annoying, especially when they all ended up having to spend time together in Vegas.

Bobby had arranged to have his Lamborghini waiting for him at the airport, so the moment they arrived, he and Denver took off. A chauffeured SUV collected Max, Harry, and Paco and headed straight to the hotel.

"Are you *sure* Paco is gay?" Max whispered to Harry on the drive to The Keys. "He doesn't seem as if he is to me."

"Shh," Harry scolded, his pale face turning bright red. "That's such a random thing to say."

"Only asking," Max said irritably, thinking that Harry should be a little nicer to her, considering she'd gotten his new friend a ride on Bobby's plane. "No need to throw a fit."

"He's sitting two feet away," Harry hissed. "For crap's sake—shut it!"

Oh great. What a birthday *this* was going to be. Bobby in a mood, Harry acting like a dick, and no boyfriend, plus Cookie would be all over Mister Cokeaholic when they arrived.

Fantastic fun. She might as well drown herself in one of the pools.

"How very thoughtful of you to bring my favorite car," Denver said dryly as she gingerly lowered herself into the passenger seat of the Lamborghini. "I love it because it's *so* low-key."

"Hey," Bobby said, with a quick grin, "a boy's gotta have *some* toys."

"And you are *such* a boy," she responded. She couldn't help laughing, because it was true. At times Bobby could be quite serious, but it was his playful streak she couldn't resist. The private plane, the fancy car—all big-boy toys. He'd never admit it, but he had very expensive tastes.

"By the way," Bobby said, revving the engine. "Guess who I ran into at the airport in New York?"

"Hmm, let me see . . . the pope? The president?"

"Very amusing."

"I try."

"Annabelle Maestro."

"Oh my God! Not Annabelle," Denver said, flashing onto her old school friend, who'd always treated her like a poor relation—even though they weren't related. And when Annabelle's movie-star mother had been murdered, and Denver was involved with defending Annabelle's famous dad, she'd *still* been treated like the poor relative, even though she was a respected attorney with a top Beverly Hills law firm. "How is she?"

"The same entitled bitch on wheels, minus Frankie."

Now Denver flashed onto Annabelle's ex—the coke-addicted Frankie Romano, who used to be one of Bobby's best friends. "Well," she said, remembering Annabelle's annoying sense of self-importance, "I hardly think it's likely she'll ever change. What did she have to say?"

Bobby decided it was prudent not to mention that Annabelle had referred to Denver as "some kind of mutt."

"Not much," he said, sliding into traffic. "Carrying on about that book she got published."

"Oh yes, *My Life: A Hollywood Princess Tells All.* What a crock of shit!"

"I take it you're not a fan?" Bobby said, amused.

"Hell, no," Denver said, shaking her head. "Annabelle was always a piece of work. Surely you remember her in high school."

Oh yes, he remembered Annabelle, all right, and it was a memory he'd sooner forget. He and M.J. had double-teamed her—with her consent—on a drunken prom night. Something to never mention, especially to Denver, who he was sure would not appreciate hearing about it.

"I guess Frankie had a welcome escape," Bobby ventured, zipping in front of a Cadillac.

"I think they both did," Denver said, briskly closing the subject. The last person she wished to talk about was

Annabelle Maestro. And as for Frankie Romano—a total loser.

"When we get to the hotel," Bobby said, "unpack, an' put on something casual."

"Why's that?"

He grinned. "You'll see," he said, barely missing a jaywalking pedestrian.

"Mystery Man," she murmured, loving that he had such a strong romantic streak.

"Yeah," he said, still grinning. "An' doncha love it!"

Yes, Bobby, I do.

"We're here, an' I'm, like, so into it!" Cookie sing-songed, sliding her long brown legs out of Frankie's car, flashing the valet parker with her miniskirt, under which she wore no panties.

Frankie hadn't bothered to book a room, because Cookie had informed him they would be well taken care of. He hadn't realized they would be staying on what Max referred to as the Santangelo floor. When they got off the elevator, he was already feeling horny again, in spite of Cookie servicing him in the car. A little sex, a little gambling—Vegas had that effect on him.

A stern-looking older black woman armed with a lengthy guest list sat at the reception desk facing the elevator.

"Hiya, Betty," Cookie said, swooping in for a friendly hug. "Are we in my usual room?"

Betty gave Frankie a disapproving once-over.

"'S okay," Cookie said gaily. "He's my boyfriend."

Betty reached for her glasses and consulted her list. "And his name is?"

Frankie bristled. "Frankie Romano," he said shortly. "An' you can forget about a room; we need a suite. An' make sure any calls get put directly through to me. Romano. R-O-M—"

"I know how to spell, Mr. Romano," Betty said caustically. "And I do believe all the suites are reserved."

"Well, unreserve one," Frankie said, giving her a sharp look. "Lucky would want me to be comfortable."

Frankie and Betty locked eyes. It was not a friendly interaction.

"I'll see what I can do," Betty said at last, shuffling papers.

Frankie reached into his pocket and flipped a hundred-dollar bill onto her desk. "You do that, hon."

Betty picked up the bill and gave it back to him. "Not necessary," she said.

"Take it," Frankie insisted, thrusting it toward her.

"No thank you," Betty said, ignoring him as she calmly handed Cookie her door card.

Cookie grabbed it, and pulled Frankie away from the desk. "Let's go," she singsonged. "Don't mess with Betty, she can be fierce!"

He threw Betty another look. "Suite," he said shortly. "Deal with it."

Betty continued to ignore him.

"Max and me—we come here all the time," Cookie announced, flouncing into a large blue bedroom with a balcony overlooking the main swimming pool. "This is usually my room."

"I hope you heard me," Frankie said, not pleased. "We need a suite. When Max gets here, *you* deal with it."

"Take no notice of Betty," Cookie said. "She's only doing her job. I'll score us a suite. Don't go gettin' your balls in a spasm."

"You'd better," Frankie said, grabbing her ass and squeezing hard. "I do not appreciate slummin' it."

"Here's the good news," Cookie said. "Everything's comped. Spa, restaurants, pool, shows. You name it—we get it for free." She fished from her purse a black-and-gold credit card with her name engraved on it. "*This* is my ticket to ride," she boasted. "Lucky handed them out to special people when The Keys opened. Bangin', huh?"

Frankie decided he wanted one of those. How come Bobby had never offered him one?

The porter entered with their bags. Frankie tossed him the hundred-dollar bill the douche at reception had refused to accept. Always good to get out the word that there was a big spender in town.

He wondered if Cookie's magic credit card covered gambling, then smirked at the thought of losing Lucky Santangelo's money in *her* casino. What a coup that would be.

Thinking about Bobby's foxy mom, he realized he hadn't seen her in a while, ever since he and Bobby had lost touch. Lucky and Lennie had always been laid-back with him, always friendly. They were a major power couple, and a kick to be around. He decided that he should try to see more of them, invite them to his club, get reacquainted.

Yeah. This was going to be some weekend, and Frankie Romano was expecting to take full advantage of whatever Vegas had to offer.

"Where we gonna stay?" Kev asked as they boarded the plane.

Billy had been so intent on getting to Vegas that he hadn't bothered to work out the details. Obviously it would not be wise to stay at The Keys. He called Bambi, his publicist, and told her to book him into the Cavendish.

"Why exactly are you on your way to Vegas?" Bambi was curious to know. "Are you going for the big fight?"

"You know I'm not a boxing fan."

"Well, then," Bambi said. "Is something happening that I'm missing out on?"

"Nothing but a twenty-four-hour crazy gamble with my friend Kev," Billy assured her.

"Okay," Bambi said, somewhat put out. "Only please don't forget that you have a cover shoot for *Vanity Fair* on Monday."

"Wouldn't miss it, Bamb."

"You say that now, Billy," Bambi lectured, worried that her star client was up to no good. "However, you kept the reporter from *Rolling Stone* waiting for three hours, *then* you proceeded to cut the interview short. She wasn't happy, and I can't say I blame her."

"The she who wasn't happy was aiming to talk her way into my pants," Billy explained. "You know how it is with some female reporters; they're only around for the perks."

"You're a big boy, Billy," Bambi admonished. "Surely you can handle that sort of thing."

"Hey, Bamb," Billy said, deftly switching subjects. "I got a question."

"Yes?"

"When your parents named you Bambi, did they expect you to be a porn star or a stripper?"

"Billy! That's so inappropriate."

"Just askin'."

"I'll arrange a comped villa at the Cavendish," Bambi said snippily. "Good-bye." And she cut him off with a determined click.

"What's she look like?" Kev immediately wanted to know, conjuring up a vision of a juicy blonde in hot pants and a nipple-revealing tank.

"Think about her name, and then imagine the exact opposite," Billy said. "She's a dragon lady with teeth that could bite your cock off in one fell swoop. So fuhgedaboudit."

"Copy that," Kev said, shuddering at the graphic image.

* * *

Ace had spent time at The Keys with Max on several occasions, which meant he was aware of the routine. There was a reserved underground parking section for the Santangelo/Golden family and their guests, so he drove his truck right to it. The valet parker greeted him like an old friend. After exchanging pleasantries, he grabbed his overnight bag and headed upstairs in a private elevator that deposited him on the Santangelo/Golden floor. There he was met by Betty, the middle-aged concierge. Betty was armed with a list of expected guests. Fortunately, he knew her, and he quickly informed her that he was Max's birthday surprise, so not a word that he was here.

Betty nodded agreeably. After Cookie and her obnoxious boyfriend, Ace was a delight, a nice-looking young man, tall and lanky, and always polite.

"Any idea what time Max is getting here?" he asked.

"Soon," Betty replied. "The Stanislopoulos plane landed twenty minutes ago."

"The what?"

"Bobby's plane."

"Oh, yeah," Ace said, suddenly remembering who he was dealing with. Max's brother had the use of a plane, and Max was obviously on it. "I'll wait," he said, groping in his pocket to make sure the box with the present he'd purchased for Max was still there. He'd spent $250 on a gold heart pendant, and he was hoping she'd love it. She'd better; it was the most expensive gift he'd ever bought anyone.

"I'm curious," Denver said when they were finally settled in Bobby's suite at The Keys. "What's your mom's fascination with Vegas?"

Bobby moved over to the window and stared out at the staggering view, which never failed to thrill him.

"My grandfather on Lucky's side built one of the first hotels here, way back in the forties," he explained. "Gino. You've met him."

"I have?" Denver said, unpacking her bag.

"Maybe not," Bobby said, turning back to look at her. "But you will this weekend. He's some colorful character, my granddad. He used to hang out with Meyer Lansky, Jake the boy, Lucky Luciano—a whole slew of those old-time gangsters. Back in the day, those guys ruled everything, and Gino was right up there. He named Lucky after Lucky Luciano—kind of an homage."

Denver stopped what she was doing. "No way."

"Yeah. Kinda wild, huh?"

"I would say so."

"Anyway, Gino was in the hotel business, and decades later, when he fled America on a tax evasion thing, Lucky moved right in an' took over the building of his latest hotel. She was like twenty or something."

"That's quite an achievement."

"It sure is. But hey, that's my mom. Balls of steel." He chuckled. "Rumor has it she threatened some poor slob in the middle of the night that she'd cut off his dick if he didn't put up the building costs he'd signed on for."

"And did he?"

"What do *you* think?"

Denver was half impressed and half horrified. She'd always admired strong women, but maybe Lucky Santangelo took strength to a new level.

"What about you, Bobby?" she ventured. "How tough was it when you lost your father?"

"I was too young to remember much about it."

"And was Lucky a good mother? Was she always around?"

"What's with all the questions, babe? I feel like I'm on the stand."

"I'd just like to know more about you. Is that okay?"

"Lucky is Lucky. She's the greatest," Bobby said, moving toward her. "Anyway, I'm here, and I ain't doin' badly, so no more questions an' let's get going. You're in for a big surprise."

"And what would that be?"

"Now, if I told you," he said lightly, "it wouldn't be a surprise, would it?"

"Well, if you put it that way."

And Denver realized that he'd completely steered her off track. No more Lucky revelations today. Bobby was closing ranks on *that* conversation.

After Armand left, Jeffrey expected that Lucky would have plenty to say, and quite frankly he wouldn't have blamed her. Instead she was silent, and the moment he started to apologize she abruptly cut him off.

"Forget about it," she said coolly. "We all make mistakes."

Although outwardly she appeared calm, inwardly she was seething. Armand Jordan was the kind of man she abhorred—a self-absorbed, egotistical, chauvinistic pig. It infuriated her that Jeffrey had actually put her in the same room with the creep. Perhaps her lawyer was not as smart as she'd thought, or maybe his divorce was addling his brain.

"Danny," she said, all business, "inform the desk that I want Armand Jordan out of my hotel before noon. I don't care how it's done, but I want him out."

Danny snapped to attention. "Yes, Lucky," he said. "I'll make sure it's taken care of."

"And Danny, as soon as you've done that, get me a full dossier on Armand Jordan." She turned to Jeffrey. "Something I probably should have seen *before* the meeting."

Jeffrey looked uncomfortable. He knew he'd let Lucky down, and that wasn't good, considering she was his most important client. "His company is top-rate," he began to say. "Armand Jordan is on the Forbes list. I wouldn't bring you—"

"For my own interest," Lucky interrupted, not wishing to listen to Jeffrey's excuses. "I need to know who I'm dealing with. *Especially* when they threaten me."

"Lucky, once again, I'm so sorry—"

"Time for the board meeting," she said, her beautiful face expressionless, only her deep black eyes revealing her annoyance. "Let's go. I don't intend to keep anyone waiting."

Danny shut his laptop and trotted after them, wondering how Lucky was able to keep her cool. Armand might be a chauvinistic billionaire, but if he, Danny, was in Lucky's place, he would've slapped the man's face, a resounding slap heard for miles.

Ah yes, Danny thought dreamily. *One of those old-fashioned slaps that used to take place when Diva Queens ruled the movies. Bette Davis, Ava Gardner, Joan Crawford.*

Danny had rented and avidly watched all their movies; their outfits alone had sent him into a euphoric state.

"Danny," Lucky said sharply, turning her head. "Stop following us and go deal with getting that person tossed from my hotel. I want you to personally make sure he leaves the premises, and be sure to tell Jerrod to alert everyone that he is not allowed back. *Comprende?*"

"I'm on it," Danny said, once again jumping to attention. "Although surely you need me at the board meeting?"

"Send one of the assistants to cover it."

"Really?" Danny said, disappointed because he hated missing anything.

"Yes, really," Lucky said briskly. "And don't forget that Lennie is arriving at five. Make sure he knows I'm at the apartment. And once he gets here, we do not expect to be disturbed under *any* circumstances. Got it?"

"Got it," Danny repeated.

"Tell Bobby and Max we'll see them for breakfast tomorrow. And organize anything they or their friends might need for tonight. I'm picking up the tab."

Danny nodded. He understood. Whenever Lennie reappeared, Lucky carved out alone time with her husband. And that, Danny decided, was the reason they had such a happy and successful marriage.

Lucky had her priorities straight. Nothing and no one came between her and her man.

CHAPTER TWENTY-NINE

Armand was burning up. He had never—repeat, *never*—been spoken to in such a fashion, and by a woman! He was enraged. He felt as if his head was going to explode with sheer fury. Black spots danced in front of his eyes. He was sick sick sick with anger.

The moment they left Lucky's office he turned on Fouad and began screaming a litany of expletives, as if Fouad were personally responsible for the unfortunate meeting. "Fuck that whore bitch. And fuck you," Armand yelled, the veins standing out in his forehead. "Motherfucking *cunt*."

Fouad wasn't quite sure whether the "motherfucking cunt" insult was directed at him or Lucky Santangelo. It didn't matter. He'd made up his mind about moving on, and as soon as he had all his affairs in order, it would be *sayonara* to Armand Jordan and everything he represented. He couldn't wait to return to New York.

However, in spite of Armand's loathsome anger, he managed to remain stony-faced. He'd warned Armand that The Keys was not for sale, but Armand had insisted on meeting the owner anyway. Had he read the research that Fouad's assistant had gathered on Lucky Santangelo, he would have realized that she was no ordinary woman. Lucky Santangelo was a lethal force. A woman with a dangerous and powerful past. A strong, intelligent woman who seemed able to achieve anything she set her mind to. And a beauty too. Fouad was quite struck by her looks and composure.

"What now?" Fouad asked when Armand finally stopped yelling. "Should I arrange for a plane?"

"A plane?" Armand snarled, clenching his fists. "For what? You think I'm running away? You actually imagine I would leave here without getting my prize?"

Why was Armand still thinking he could gain ownership of a property that was not for sale? Surely, as a businessman, he realized there was no deal to be made. Especially after his confrontation with Lucky Santangelo.

This situation was becoming ridiculous. Armand was behaving like an out-of-control child who'd failed to get a new bike for Christmas. Could anyone respect a man who behaved like that? Lucky Santangelo and her lawyer were probably laughing at them. Armand had made a mockery of the meeting. A mockery of Jordan Developments.

"She's not going to sell, Armand," Fouad said patiently. "You heard her. Not to you or anyone else."

"Fuck the cunt. I want this hotel, Fouad. And it's time you got it into your useless head that we are not leaving Vegas until I get it."

Peggy enjoyed a leisurely breakfast out by the pool at the Cavendish. Earlier, she'd phoned her son to see if he would care to join her, but there was no answer from either Armand's cell or his suite. She didn't mind; she was sure that she presented a mysterious and glamorous figure clad in a white sundress, a large straw hat, and Chanel sunglasses, sitting at a table by herself watching the passing parade of tourists and young couples with kids. It was still early; the serious gamblers and bachelor-party groups had yet to emerge.

A middle-aged man in a Hawaiian shirt who was sprawled at a nearby table with his overweight wife couldn't take his eyes off her. Lust was in the air. Peggy could smell lust a mile off.

She smiled to herself. Vegas agreed with her. Being back there was almost like re-visiting her youth. Ah yes, as one of the most desirable and sought-after girls in town, she'd created quite a stir. Many a man had fallen for her obvious charms. She treasured the memory of those times.

Seeing Gino Santangelo had given her a jolt. The fact that he was still alive was a big surprise. She realized that he must be at least ninety-something, because on the one memorable night she'd spent with him, he was in his fifties. Even so, he'd been a vigorous lover, such a power-house.

At eighteen she'd considered herself experienced, but Gino Santangelo had given new meaning to the act of making love.

LAS VEGAS 1968

Peggy Lindquest and Joe Piscarelli made quite the dashing couple around town. Peggy was a stunner, and Joe was no slouch in the handsome stakes, with his wannabe gangster movie-star looks. Their relationship was volatile due to major jealousy issues on both sides. Joe, at the age of thirty, had been around and then some, which meant there were quite a few exes in his world. One-nighters, two-nighters, and so on.

Peggy claimed she had been with only one other man—her high school boyfriend. She was lying, of course, but since she was new to Vegas, there was no way for Joe to prove otherwise.

They fought like wildcats. And then they made up as if they were starring in a porno movie.

It was their pattern.

The one thing that scared Peggy was Joe's violent temper, and when it got too bad, she usually spent the night at a girlfriend's house. Joe always arrived to collect her the next morning, and all was quiet on the Western front. But Peggy's girlfriends kept on warning her that Joe's vile outbursts could easily escalate and become physical. Peggy refused to believe he would ever hit her.

One night he did act out, shoving her violently across the room. Shocked, she fled to her girlfriend Veronica's apartment in a panic, tears and everything.

Veronica, a statuesque black beauty who was a dancer in the Folies Bergere show at the Tropicana, was on her way to an exclusive party at Caesar's Palace. She insisted that Peggy dry her tears and come with her. Peggy declined, until Veronica whispered in her ear, "There's a rumor Sinatra may show up."

Frank Sinatra. Every Vegas showgirl's dream.

Peggy rapidly changed her mind, and the two girls set off to join the party, dressed to conquer.

Sinatra never appeared, but Gino Santangelo was there, and Gino Santangelo was a legendary figure in Vegas.

Peggy set her charm on high beam and went for it. She'd had no idea it would turn out to be such a heavenly experience. The man was not nicknamed Gino the Ram for nothing.

After a short conversation at the party, he invited her upstairs to a sumptuous suite and asked if her breasts were real. When she said they were, he slowly proceeded to strip her, garment by garment, until she stood before him in her high heels and nothing else.

She wasn't shy. She was almost naked onstage every night.

He admired her body, slowly fingering her in the most intimate of places, and when he decided she was ready, he took her into the bedroom and laid her on the bed with her legs spread. Then he went down on her, slowly, surely, until she was in such a state of ecstasy she was begging him to fuck her.

But he didn't. He forced her to wait until he was ready to make her come with his tongue.

She lay on the bed writhing with passion, desperate for him to ravish her, all thoughts of Joe set aside.

But Gino took his time, exciting her all the more. He pulled her off the bed and led her to the shower, and only then did he divest himself of his clothes and climb in with her, whereupon he proceeded to soap her body until she reached orgasm again, screaming aloud with pleasure.

Finally they returned to the bedroom, where he made love to her for what seemed like hours. At dawn, he sent her home in a chauffeured sedan, and she never heard from him again.

Peggy had something on her mind, something she'd conveniently never faced up to but always secretly wondered about.

In the space of one week in 1968 she'd slept with Joe Piscarelli, Gino Santangelo, and King Emir Amin Mohamed Jordan. A month later she'd discovered she was pregnant.

So who was Armand's real father?

Was it Joe Piscarelli, her would-be gangster boyfriend?

Gino Santangelo, her one-night stand?

Or her ex-husband, King Emir Amin Mohamed Jordan?

Surely it was about time she found out . . .

CHAPTER THIRTY

The board meeting was about to start, and after her un-settling and annoying morning, Lucky was pleased to be in a room with her investors—all of whom were full of positive vibes.

Alex Woods was standing in a corner drinking a cup of coffee.

She headed in his direction. "Thanks for coming," she said, touching his arm. "I wasn't sure you would, but I'm glad you did."

"You think I'd miss little Max's birthday?" he replied, giving her a long steady look.

"It's nice of you to make the effort."

"And she's so formal," he remarked, giving her an-other long look, a look that said *We could be making beautiful love together, but you're still hung up on your goddamn husband.*

"Well . . . I know how busy you are."

"Never too busy for you, Lucky," he replied, his eyes never leaving hers.

"Okay," she said, attempting to lighten things up. "Let's not get carried away."

He fished a packet of cigarettes from his pocket, and went to light one up.

"No smoking!" she admonished.

His look turned quizzical. "Are you fucking kidding me?"

"Please, Alex, for me. I gave it up, and I don't want to be tempted."

"You don't, huh?"

"No thank you."

He put the cigarette back in its packet. "When's Lennie getting here?" he inquired.

"Didn't you just ask me that in L.A.?"

"Is it a crime to ask you again?"

"Knock it off, Alex," she said, suddenly becoming impatient. "I know what you're doing."

"Huh?"

"Why didn't you bring a girlfriend with you?"

"What now?"

"A girlfriend, Alex," she said, repeating herself. "A gorgeous young thing to keep you occupied so Lennie doesn't get the impression that you're still lusting after me."

"Oh, I see," Alex said, squinting slightly. "Is *that* what you think?"

"Actually, it's not what I think, it's what I know."

"Well," he said with a sardonic edge, "glad to note your ego is alive and well and living happily in fantasy land."

"Cut the crap, Alex," she said, shaking her head. "Why don't you do yourself a big favor and send for one of your many women?"

"Why would I do that?"

"Because the last thing I need is any tension between you and Lennie, who incidentally arrives later this afternoon, which I do believe I already told you."

"Screw you, Santangelo," Alex said, scowling.

"And wouldn't you like to," she fired back.

"Jesus!" he complained. "You're out of control."

"Well that makes two of us, doesn't it?"

Before Alex could reply, Gino strolled over. "Y'know,

I'm kinda surprised you two never got together," Gino remarked. "You're always at each other's throats. Makes for a combative mix."

"Do I *look* Asian?" Lucky drawled.

"I get it," Gino said, chuckling loudly. "Alex only raises the flag for—"

"Don't even go there!" Lucky warned, well aware of the politically incorrect word Gino was about to use.

"Let him say it," Alex said with a throaty laugh. "He's old, it doesn't matter."

"Who're *you* callin' old?" Gino griped. "It takes balls t' reach my age an' still be standin' on two fuckin' feet."

"And I give you kudos for that," Alex said. "You're my idol, Gino. I want to be just like you when I grow up."

"For God's sake!" Lucky exclaimed. "Why don't the two of you go form a circle jerk and be done with it."

"She's *your* daughter," Alex pointed out.

"Yeah," Gino agreed, with another wicked chuckle. "She's the son I never had."

"You *had* a son. Dario," Lucky reminded him sharply. "And just because he was gay there's no reason for you to disrespect him."

"Kiddo, I didn't mean—"

"You know what, screw both of you," she said, shaking her head. "You're a couple of little big boys, so go ahead—get your kicks playing with each other. That's just about the level of your style."

"Hey," Gino objected. "Is that any way t' talk to your old man?"

Lucky shook her head again. Sometimes dealing with Gino was like dealing with a little kid. "Where's Paige?" she asked. "Shouldn't she be taking care of you?"

"That'll be the day, when I need takin' care of." Gino snorted. "I might be gettin' up there, but I'm not fuckin' dead. Anyway, she's over at the Cavendish dealin' with beauty shit."

"What's wrong with the salon here?"

"She's got her special girl over at the Cavendish. Do *I* know?"

"Okay, I get it. So I suggest you and Alex take your seats and let's get this show on the road."

And so they did, and the meeting took place, and went extremely well. Everyone was enthusiastic about how successful The Keys was in spite of such a flat economy. The hotel was operating at capacity. The casino couldn't be busier. And there was a long waiting list to purchase one of the multimillion-dollar apartments.

Halfway through the meeting, Venus dutifully put in an appearance, beguiling everyone with her radiant blond beauty and dazzling star power. Venus certainly knew how to captivate a room.

Afterward there was a buffet lunch, during which Lucky managed to avoid another one-on-one with Alex. Too uncomfortable. She wished he'd get married or start living with someone again. Having Alex on the loose was too dangerous. Unfortunately, there was still a deep connection between them. And if Lennie weren't around . . .

No! she told herself sternly. *Don't even think it.*

Jorge didn't gamble, but Venus did, and after her appearance at the board meeting she felt like some action. Gambling was always a turn-on, especially when she ended up a winner.

Entering the casino at The Keys, Jorge went into semi-shock. Such opulence. Such a huge number of people throwing their money around. Not to mention such beautiful cocktail waiters and waitresses attending to the customers' every need.

He immediately wondered if he could get a job here, for he was street-smart enough to know that this thing

with Venus wouldn't last, and when she tired of him—
which he knew she would—what then? Was he supposed to run back to L.A. and the sex-crazed fat agent
he'd been forced to service simply to score a job on
Venus's photo shoot?

No, Jorge had not fled Rio and the favelas, where
he'd almost raised himself, to become the plaything of
a series of horny American women.

Venus was exquisite, but she was too famous for him,
and at forty-something, too old—even though she was in
impeccable shape, with her perfect body and muscled
thighs. Earlier, while he was going down on her, she'd
almost strangled him with those thighs. Lost in her juices,
he'd had to splutter and grunt to get her to release him.

Jorge hung back as two security guards accompanied
Venus around the casino. Soon he noticed a crowd beginning to form, and he wondered what it must be like
to be so famous.

One day . . . one day somewhere in the future, he
vowed to find out.

"Remember that time you got a dose of the crabs from
some piece a stray you banged, then you hadda 'splain
it to Venus with some bullshit story?" Kev said with a
raucous chuckle. "Good times, buddy, good times."

"For you, maybe," Billy responded, cracking a slight
smile. "I hadda tell Venus I caught 'em from a crapper.
Don't think she believed me."

Kev snorted with mirth. "Yeah, those were the badass
days. God, I miss 'em."

They were now settled in a luxury villa at the Cavendish, and Kev was hot to hit the tables. He kept on
encouraging Billy to do the same.

"I gotta coupla biz calls to make," Billy said, thrusting
a few hundred-dollar bills at Kev. "Go put this on seven
for me. An' try to make sure I'm a winner."

"Like when're you ever not?" Kev grumbled, grabbing the money and taking off. "See you in the casino."

"Ten minutes," Billy promised. "Don't forget—number seven."

As soon as Kev left, Billy paced up and down for a minute or two, then he called Max on her cell. No reply. He hesitated about leaving a message, then decided against it. He'd sooner talk to her personally.

Unusual for him, but he was feeling slightly apprehensive about what she'd have to say. Would she be pleased he'd followed her to Vegas? Or would she blow him off?

For now he'd just have to wait and see.

CHAPTER THIRTY-ONE

"You ever thought of dumpin' the dreads?" Frankie inquired as he and Cookie lay side by side on top of the bed in their hotel room, casually sharing a joint.

"Huh?" Cookie replied, immediately tugging on the Caribbean dreadlocks that she considered her trademark. "Never had any complaints before."

"I was kinda thinkin' you might wanna go for a softer look," Frankie suggested.

"You sound like my dad," Cookie said, dragging on the weed. "I'm totally into my dreads. Who wants to look like every other girl in L.A.?"

"*You,* never," Frankie insisted, extracting the joint from her fingers and taking a deep hit. "You're an original."

"Why you even askin'?" Cookie demanded, thinking that for an older guy, Frankie sure had his shit together. He was okay in the sack. He came up with a steady assortment of drugs, and he was a kick to be around. Not boring, like Max's boyfriend, Ace. And not a weirdo like Harry—because even though Harry was one of her best friends, she had to admit he was kind of eccentric at times.

"'Cause every time you give me a b.j., your dreads keep hittin' my balls," Frankie said, exhaling a thin line of smoke.

"Ew!" Cookie giggled. "Wouldn't wanna damage your precious *cojones.*"

"You wouldn't, huh?" Frankie said.

"No, 'cause then you couldn't get it up."

"You got a dirty mouth."

"An' doncha love it," Cookie responded, rolling over and climbing astride him. "Anyway," she added, "who'd you want me to look like?"

"Janet Jackson at her peak," Frankie said with a wink. "You're as pretty as her."

Cookie giggled again and snatched the joint back from him. "A *thin* Janet Jackson," she said pointedly. "With way better tits."

"Now, hold on," Frankie objected, pushing her off him. "You gotta admit the woman's got a dynamite pair. We all saw 'em at the Super Bowl."

"An' I don't?" Cookie said, pouting.

"That goes without sayin', honeytits."

"Honeytits!" she squealed. "Where'd you come up with *that?*"

"Mel Gibson, I think."

"Screw Mel Gibson. An' anyway, he called that cop sugartits."

"Same thing."

"No way."

"I got an idea."

"What?"

"Whyn't you blow me, sugartits, an' shut the fuck up."

Cookie so appreciated being treated like an adult.

Bobby's surprise was a private boat on Lake Mead, with a gourmet late lunch and an attentive waiter. Denver could've done without the lunch and the waiter, but she didn't say anything because she was fully aware that Bobby meant well, and it was a very thoughtful gesture.

However, she couldn't help sneaking a peek at her BlackBerry to see what was going on back in L.A. Taking Friday off was not a career-enhancing move, but

Bobby had been so insistent, and since she was moving on to the drug unit, did it really matter? She'd won her final case and avoided her horny boss, and Monday she would start fresh.

"What are you doing?" Bobby wanted to know, leaning over her shoulder.

"Just checking on work."

"No," he said firmly.

"No, what?"

"Not while we're on our first vacation."

"Bobby," she reminded him gently, "this is not a vacation, it's a weekend."

"And our first one away together," he pointed out, kissing her neck.

"Okay," she said, clicking her phone off. "Whatever my Lord and Master wants."

"Easy!" he laughed. "I'm not *that* bad."

"Well, you *are* being kind of overbearing."

"Thought I was being romantic."

"You're right." She sighed. "I'll leave work alone until later."

"Later I might have more surprises."

"Hmm . . . something to look forward to?"

"You'll just have to wait and see."

"I appeared at the Maracanã Stadium in Rio once," Venus informed Jorge, who was now massaging her feet after their stint in the casino. She'd won $25,000 at blackjack, so she was on a high. "Thousands of people, and little old me," she reminisced. "It was a fantastic night. Very memorable."

"Ah, Maracanã," Jorge murmured. He spoke more English than Venus thought, and he understood plenty, but he'd decided it was prudent to pretend he had yet to master English. It was also prudent not to mention that he was ten years old when he and some friends had sneaked into the famous Maracanã Stadium and watched her perform. He could still remember the hard-on she'd given him that night.

Growing up in a two-room shack with seven brothers and sisters, no father, and a mother who lived only for Carnival, Jorge had been forced to take care of himself. At the age of ten he'd started stealing from tourists in Rio, and from fourteen on he'd been robbing and fucking them, picking up a smattering of English along the way. The moment he'd stashed enough money, he'd gotten himself a passport and purchased a one-way ticket to Los Angeles. At least he had ambition.

Now what? He might be only nineteen (Venus thought he was twenty), but he was smart enough to know that being with this platinum-blond superstar might be his only opportunity to score big.

He didn't know what, but this weekend he was determined to do *something* to cement their connection.

Determined not to feel sorry for herself, Max entered the elevator, which zoomed her upstairs. Harry and Paco had stopped off at the drugstore to pick up God only knew what. Harry was acting totally lovesick; she could hardly stand it.

Betty was sitting in her usual place. Max gave her a quick hug. "Is Cookie here yet?" she asked.

Betty nodded, a disapproving glint in her watchful eyes. "Indeed she is. With that new boyfriend of hers."

"Oh yes, Frankie," Max said, with a knowing grin. "Cookie hit the jackpot, right?"

"Seems too old for her," Betty remarked. "And smarmy, with a smart mouth."

"Hey, we all know Cookie," Max said, grabbing a handful of M&M's from Betty's desk. "This is *way* better than her dragging random dudes up here every night."

"I have never approved of that girl's behavior," Betty said, tight-lipped. "She needs discipline. Where are her parents?"

"You *know* where they are. We've had this conversation before," Max said. "By the way, be prepared. Harry has a, uh . . . boyfriend too. They'll be checking in any minute."

Betty's eyebrows shot up. "A boyfriend?"

"Oh c'mon, Bets." Max giggled. "You *know* Harry's gay."

"He is?" Betty said dryly.

"Please don't tease me. It's almost my birthday and *they've* both got boyfriends, while *I'm* all alone. Charming isn't it?"

"Don't worry, dear," Betty assured her, thinking of the boyfriend all set to surprise her. "You'll still have a lovely time."

"Thanks, Bets," she said as she headed down the corridor to her suite.

Slipping her entry card into the door, she walked inside.

"Hey," Ace said, jumping up to greet her with a big smile on his face. "Happy birthday, sweet eighteen!"

CHAPTER THIRTY-TWO

Getting thrown out of The Keys was without doubt the most insulting thing that had ever happened to Armand—an offensive affront to his dignity. When Fouad had informed him that they were being forced to leave, Armand had refused to believe him. In his mind it was not possible that this could happen. But happen it did, and when four burly security men arrived to escort him off the premises, he finally understood that it was for real.

Armand did not go silently. He threatened every staff member in the vicinity with expulsion the moment he owned the hotel. He had Fouad take down names, and he let everyone know that they would soon all have no jobs. He radiated a dark, cold fury.

Danny, hovering on the sidelines, was startled by the man's level of lethal anger. He'd never witnessed such frightening rage.

Fouad had a limousine waiting downstairs. Once again he had assumed they would head straight to the airport—he'd even left a message for Peggy that they would be picking her up very shortly.

Armand had other ideas.

"Do you honestly believe that I would run from here like a whipped dog with its tail between its legs?" Armand said, enraged. "How many times do I have to tell you? Are you brain-dead, Fouad? Do you not listen? Are you a complete fool?"

Yes, Fouad thought, *I am a fool for continuing to put up with your verbal abuse. You contaminate everything you touch.*

"Get me the best they have at the Cavendish," Armand instructed. "And attempt to listen to me for once, Fouad." An ominous pause. "We are not leaving Las Vegas until I own The Keys. That whore bitch will not win. I will see her die before she gets the better of me. Do you understand me? I WILL SEE HER DIE."

Many years ago Peggy had decided that if she did discover who Armand's real father was, she would never tell her son. Armand considered himself royal born, and she refused to dispel the myth—if indeed it was a myth. If it turned out that he wasn't the king's son, the ramifications would be disastrous. And were the king to find out, who knew *what* he would do? The punishments in Akramshar were harsh, especially toward women. They included the ancient custom of stoning, and long spells in prison for nothing more than disrespecting a male.

Not that Peggy would ever consider going back, not under any circumstances. She'd made her life in America, and that's exactly where she was staying. Maybe even in Vegas if she met the right man.

For a woman in her sixties—however great she looked—the pickings in New York were lackluster. Old men with Viagra hard-ons required women in their thirties, and in a pinch, in their forties. So where did that leave her? In Vegas, with casinos full of rich gamblers who might appreciate an attractive redhead in her prime.

Well . . . maybe a tad past her prime, but so what?

After a leisurely breakfast, she visited the spa, where she allowed herself to be primped and pampered while she wondered how she could get close enough to Gino Santangelo to obtain a DNA sample. She'd watched enough *CSI*'s on TV to know that determining paternity was not difficult. A scrap of hair, a cigarette stub—and there were labs advertised on the Internet where you could simply mail in your sample. She'd even found one in Vegas, which (for a price) promised twenty-four-hour turnaround service.

Peggy was excited. She'd always wondered, and now it might be possible to find out.

"Have you ever heard of a man called Gino Santangelo?" she asked the tall brunette who was giving her a facial.

The girl almost choked. "Gino Santangelo is one of the most famous characters in Vegas," she said, lowering her voice. "His daughter built The Keys. The Santangelos are Vegas royalty."

"Shh," hissed the bleached blonde who was busy giving Peggy a pedicure. "His wife's over there getting her nails done."

"His wife," Peggy said, her eyes darting across the room. She observed a short woman with a mass of frizzy copper-colored hair and a compact body. The woman was well preserved, but Peggy—an expert at such things—decided she was in her late sixties.

Mrs. Gino Santangelo. Perhaps this was the opportunity Peggy had been looking for.

Yes, an opportunity to get closer to the truth, and she was about to take it.

Settled into a private and secluded luxury villa at the Cavendish, Armand continued to rant and rave about how sickened and angry he was at the outcome of his meeting with Lucky Santangelo. That a woman could get away with speaking to him in such a crude and vile way was unthinkable. His skin crawled at the thought. Her words reverberated in his head and filled him with even more hate.

"In my country she would be stoned to death for her

disrespect," he screamed, pacing up and down. "I am a prince. You hear me, Fouad? A royal man. She is noth-ing but a whore peasant, and she *must* be punished!"

Fouad stared at Armand and realized that he was no longer a man in control. It seemed he had lost any sense of reality. Had Armand honestly believed that just like that he could fly into Vegas and purchase a property such as The Keys? Was he becoming so convinced of his own importance and power that he'd thought it was possible?

Ever since the incident with Martin Constantine's wife, Fouad had sensed that there was something basically wrong with Armand. He appeared to be unrav-eling, caught up in a fantasy power trip of huge propor-tions. Now he was proclaiming himself a prince—which of course he was, but his title meant nothing in America.

"You do know," Armand shouted, fixing Fouad with a manic glare, "that one day I will rule Akramshar. *I* will be king."

"I thought your plan was to stay in America," Fouad said, shocked by Armand's announcement.

"My father will expect me to take over," Armand said, a feverish look in his eyes. "Do you think I would disappoint him? Because if you think that, you're an id-iot. A *useless* idiot." He paused, then added, "Lately, Fouad, I have been thinking I should rid myself of your useless existence."

Once again Fouad was shocked. He'd grown up in Akramshar, the son of a palace guard, and he'd heard these slurs many times coming from the king. The word *useless* was one of the king's favorite insults. He used it on wives, workers, his children—anyone he felt deserved the wrath of his tongue. He spat it out like a snake's venom, making it sound worse than any expletive.

Was Armand turning into his father?

Was he suffering from delusions of grandeur?

Did he honestly believe that when King Emir Amin Mohamed Jordan died he could become ruler of Akramshar?

Impossible. The king's other sons would never allow that to happen. Armand might have been born in Akramshar and lived there for all of eight years, but he had left the land of his birth and become a high-powered American business tycoon. He would never be accepted back. Fouad happened to know that the only reason the king paid Armand so much attention was that through Armand's various holdings and companies, he was able to filter money for the king, legitimize it. In America they called it laundering.

"Get me everything you know about Lucky Santangelo," Armand suddenly ordered. "That file you had. Where is it? Give it to me at once."

"Do you mean the file you refused to pay attention to?" Fouad said, unable to resist a small dig.

"I want it *now,*" Armand said brusquely. "Immediately."

"I will have it sent up."

"Disrespectful whore," Armand muttered. "She will pay dearly for daring to challenge me."

Fouad couldn't quite figure out how Armand had reached the conclusion that Lucky Santangelo had challenged him. She'd merely turned down his offer to buy The Keys. That was it. But obviously she'd triggered something in Armand that had set him on a revengeful path.

"I should go," Fouad said evenly. "You need time alone."

"No. What I *need* is a couple of whores while I think about what to do," Armand raged, his face dark with anger. "Arrange it. I want them here immediately."

Was this what things had come to—ordering up prostitutes for Armand's perverse pleasure?

No. Enough was enough. Once again he refused to do it.

Moving over to the desk, he picked up a hotel notepad and wrote down a number.

"Here," he said, handing the notepad to Armand. "It's best if you call yourself."

And before Armand could object, he made a swift exit.

Fouad is a pathetic excuse for a man, Armand thought. *Why do I continue to put up with his inadequacies, his American wife and his stupid children?*

Not that he'd ever met Fouad's children. Truth was, he'd only encountered the wife on two occasions. A blonde from Tennessee, she was boring and bland and not even that pretty. She'd ruined Fouad, turned him into a sheep incapable of functioning properly in the world of business. *That's* why the meeting to buy The Keys had failed. Fouad's wife had cut off his balls, rendering him weak and ineffectual. Lucky Santangelo had sensed weakness and used it against him. Conniving whore.

Yes, Armand was sure of it. Now it was up to him to make certain the sale happened.

He paced around the living room of the villa, which was not nearly as luxurious as the Presidential Suite he had occupied at The Keys.

After a while he laid out several lines of coke and soon did all of it. Fortunately, he always traveled with a full supply—courtesy of his New York dealer, who took care of keeping him well stocked.

By the time Fouad sent up the information on Lucky Santangelo, Armand felt ready to rule not only Akramshar, but the rest of the world too. He was flying high, angry and resentful. He needed to vent his frustration at not getting what he wanted.

Picking up the phone, he called Yvonne Le Crane.

Yvonne was not pleased to hear from him. She did not appreciate her girls being stiffed. If they failed to receive the full amount of money they were due, it meant less commission to tuck into her latest Prada purse—Prada being her current obsession. When Armand Jordan got on the phone and demanded more girls, she was less than friendly, especially since a certain important person in Vegas had been asking questions about him.

"You didn't pay my girls everything they were due," she accused.

"The two women whom I did not pay extra were inexperienced and unprofessional," Armand stated coldly. "It does not reflect well on your services."

"My services are the best in Vegas," Yvonne retorted, quite insulted. "My girls are clean, beautiful, and honest."

"Your girls are filthy whores," Armand sneered.

"If that's what you think, then I suggest we cease doing business and end this conversation."

"No. We will not end it," Armand said sharply, his anger building as he leaned over the coffee table to snort another line of coke. "You will send me two girls. Big breasts. Thirty thousand. Cash. Have them here at six. I am now at the Cavendish."

Yvonne was silent for a moment. She didn't trust Armand Jordan, and even though she'd never met him, there was something off about him, something she didn't like. Several of the girls she'd sent to him before had complained that he was a crass pervert, and for them to complain was unusual.

However, it occurred to her that she didn't have to send him her girls. There were other places she could obtain talent. Armand Jordan was a sicko; he wouldn't know the difference, since all he chose to do was debase and humiliate them, so what the hell? Above all else, she was a businesswoman, and $30,000 was a tempting amount of cash.

Yes, Yvonne decided, she would send Armand Jordan exactly the type of girls he deserved.

CHAPTER THIRTY-THREE

After the board meeting, Lucky met with Danny, who filled her in on Armand's furious exit. "What a misogynistic asshole!" she exclaimed. "He's demented. A crazy man. Who *is* he, anyway?"

Danny had printed out everything he could find about Jordan Developments, but as Lucky flicked through the thick file, she discovered there were no personal details about Armand at all. Wikipedia supplied scant information; there was nothing about where he was born, just a brief mention that he'd come to America at the age of eight, the schools and college he attended, and that his socialite mother, Peggy, had remarried an investment banker—since deceased. Who was her first husband? Obviously Armand's father. There was no mention of Armand having a wife or children or any other family members.

It seemed Armand Jordan only existed as the CEO of Jordan Developments, along with several other subsidiary companies.

Because of his far-fetched threat about some kind of future battle, Lucky felt she should find out more about him.

Danny clicked onto various gossip sites and came up with a few photos of Armand at New York City social events—always with a different woman on his arm.

While Danny was doing that, Lucky went straight to the WireImage site on her Mac and typed in Armand

Jordan, and up he popped—once again photographed with a series of attractive young women.

The man was a serial dater, although his dates were never named. Odd. A couple of B-list actresses appeared in photos, but they only accompanied him to one event each.

Studying the photos of the girls with no names, Lucky figured they had to be high-class call girls or professional escorts. She recognized the look—sleek, expensive, and bland.

Sure enough, when Danny checked out one of the most exclusive and private escort sites—with a $10,000 entry fee, which Lucky agreed he could put on her credit card—they came across photos of several of the girls Armand had been seen with.

"He's a hooker hound!" Danny exclaimed, deciding that this little investigation certainly made up for missing the board meeting. Danny was so into a bit of intrigue, it made his day.

"He certainly is," Lucky agreed. "Obviously one of their best customers."

"Not a huge surprise," Danny sniffed. "After all, he ordered up girls here, so it's his pattern."

"Do we know which madam he used?" Lucky asked, her curiosity on full alert.

"I'll find out," Danny said, deciding not to mention that during his adventures on the Internet, he'd come across Lucky's Ferrari being driven by Billy Melina. What was *that* about?

"Do it," Lucky said briskly. "And get me in touch with the New York madam. I think I want to find out more about Mr. Jordan."

"I gotta go see M.J. before dinner," Bobby said when they finally arrived back at the hotel. "You okay for an hour?"

"Bobby," Denver assured him, "you do not have to

babysit me. I'm perfectly fine on my own. Actually, it'll give me some time to work on my laptop."

"Anybody ever told you you're a workaholic?"

"And you're not?" she responded lightly.

"Touché," he said, grabbing his jacket. "I'll see you later. Dinner. Just you and me. We'll make it even more romantic than lunch."

"I thought we were getting together with your family?"

"Not tonight, sweetheart. Tonight is all ours."

"How come?"

"'Cause I reserved tonight for us."

"I like it," she said, secretly delighted that she wouldn't have to deal with the Santangelo/Golden clan until tomorrow.

"So . . . beautiful," he said, bending down to kiss her. "Wear something sexy."

"Only if you do the same," she teased, affectionately touching his cheek.

"A black thong do it for you?" he joked.

"Get *out* of here," she said, the thought of Bobby in a black thong putting a smile on her face.

As soon as he was gone, she pulled out her Black-Berry and scrolled through her messages. Among them was a text from Sam. It was apparent that he now considered himself back in her life, and he was not giving up easily.

Having a fine time on set being ignored by actors and director alike, except when they need an instant rewrite on a line. Then I'm king of the hill and they kiss my skinny ass. As an observer of the human race, you would enjoy every second. How's Vegas? Do u miss my eggs?

Denver grinned. The *Do u miss my eggs?* line was a reference to the delicious scrambled eggs he'd made for her in New York the time she'd ended up spending the night in his apartment. It was his not-so-subtle way of reminding her that they had shared a bed. And had sex.

She quickly texted him back.

Vegas fun. Given up scrambled, moved on to poached. Good luck with being ignored.

Then she clicked Send before she changed her mind. They were friends, nothing more, and Bobby wouldn't mind a touch of banter between friends. Or would he?

Too bad if he did. It wasn't as if they were married or anything.

Wow! she thought. *Where does marriage enter into this equation? It's certainly not on my mind.*

Leon had also texted her, but his text was all about work. She appreciated him giving her a heads-up on what she'd be getting involved with the following week. Leon was dedicated to getting drugs off the streets— especially the small-time dealers who set up shop near high schools, targeting kids as young as ten and eleven. Leon was a solid guy, and after working at a top level Beverly Hills law firm defending the probably guilty, it was refreshing to know she was finally getting into something that really mattered.

So there he was. Ace. Her boyfriend. Standing in front of her with a big proud grin on his face, which meant she wasn't about to be alone on her birthday. Ace had apparently skipped out on his job and driven all the way to Vegas to be with her. Ace was fully present. Ace loved her. *Yippee!*

Then why wasn't she happy? Why was she suddenly suffused with guilt? Why was she wishing he hadn't made the trip?

"Wow!" Max exclaimed as he moved forward to hug her. "This is crazy. What are you *doing* here?"

"What do you *think* I'm doing here?" he responded. "Making sure I'm with you for your birthday. Wouldn't miss it."

"That's so cool," she managed, extracting herself from his hug.

"Yeah," he said, still grinning. "Had a feeling you'd want me to be here."

"I do," she insisted. "Only we're not alone. Harry's downstairs with some new friend. And Cookie's hanging out somewhere, and I know you're not wild about being around either of them."

"Thanks for the heads-up," Ace said. "But we can sneak off somewhere by ourselves, right?"

"Can't do that," she said. "They're here for me, so it wouldn't be cool to desert them. Anyway, you *know* they're my best friends."

"And what does that make me?"

"Uh . . . my boyfriend," she said, almost choking on the word.

"That's exactly why I'm not into getting caught up with the crowd," he said restlessly. "Haven't seen you in weeks; don't wanna share you."

Thoughts were flying through her head. Thoughts of Billy, and the offhand way he'd treated her. Thoughts of their one night together on the sand. The way he'd touched her, the blue of his eyes, his kind of half-crazy laugh, and his hard abs.

How could she tell Ace that she wasn't a virgin anymore? Oh man! He'd be so bummed that she'd done the deed with someone else after he'd waited forever.

Bad girlfriend.

Cheating girlfriend.

She wanted to cry.

"Look," Ace said, touching her arm. "Dump the miserable face. If it means that much to you, we'll hang with Cookie and Harry, 's long as they don't start doing drugs in front of me. You know I'm not into that crap."

Her boyfriend, Mister Straight. He wouldn't fit in with Frankie for sure.

"You know what?" she said. "Since we're gonna see them all tomorrow night at my party, I guess we can escape an' do something on our own."

"Now *that's* my girl," Ace said. "Knew you'd see it my way."

Lying on the bed, smoking yet another joint while thumbing through a Vegas magazine, Frankie was startled to see that Gerald M.—Cookie's dad—had a one-night engagement at the Cavendish that very evening. "Shit!" he exclaimed, sitting up, wondering why Cookie hadn't told him.

"What?" Cookie asked, entering the room with her key card, fresh from a four-hour session at the hair salon, where she'd had them remove her dreadlocks. A lengthy process but hopefully worth it.

Frankie barely glanced up. "Didja know your old man's appearing at the Cavendish tonight?" he demanded. "A one-off sold-out performance."

She marched over to the bed, stood in front of him with hair that curled softly around her pretty face, and said, "Screw my old man. Whaddya think of my new hairstyle?"

"Oh yeah, your hair," he said vaguely, giving her a cursory once-over. "It's lovely, doll. Told you, no regrets."

"It took *forever,*" she complained, flopping down on the end of the bed.

"I bet it did."

"Do you really love it? Are you wild about it? Do I look awesome?"

"Course you do," Frankie lied, because he wasn't sure he liked it. Now she looked like every other pretty young black girl instead of standing out as one of a kind. But at least it had given him a free afternoon to play the tables. He'd taken a beating at craps, although he was confident that tonight he'd win it all back.

After all, he was Frankie Romano. He always came out on top.

"So about the concert?" he said. "I think we should go."

"Seriously?"

"Yeah, seriously."

"I'll see what I can do."

CHAPTER THIRTY-FOUR

Lucky had major connections. She could pick up a phone and get through to almost anyone, and if she couldn't, Gino certainly could. After she'd talked to the New York madam who supplied girls for Armand Jordan, and the Vegas madam, Yvonne Le Crane, a pattern emerged. He booked girls to be seen with, and if sex was involved, his preference was to humiliate and debase them.

I knew he was an asshole, Lucky thought. *Probably can't get it up.*

Then she suddenly decided that she was wasting too much time investigating Armand Jordan's dumb ass; it was getting boring. He was a sick joke, not someone to be concerned about. She informed Danny to cut off any further digging, adding a terse "Just make sure he never gets into my hotel again. Okay?"

"Got it, Lucky," Danny agreed. "I'll have Jerrod circulate his photo."

"Good plan. Did you hear if Max and Bobby got here yet?"

"They've both arrived. And according to Betty, Max's boyfriend, Ace, turned up unexpectedly."

"Nice surprise for her," Lucky said, pleased, because she liked Ace a lot, and he seemed to be a good influence on Max. "Any of them requesting reservations tonight?"

"I'll check with everyone shortly."

"Thanks, Danny. You're always on top of it. I know you'll make sure they're all taken care of."

Danny appreciated getting praise for a job he knew he handled well.

"Well," Lucky continued. "I'm about to throw myself into a sauna, so I'll see you in the morning."

"You certainly will," Danny said, still unsure about whether he should mention Billy Melina being spotted in her car.

Best not to, he decided. His boss was getting ready to greet Lennie. Why ruin her evening?

Being a star, in Vegas, with nobody around to protect him except Kev—who was about as helpful as a teenager on crack—was turning out to be a bad idea. Everywhere Billy went, fans surrounded him. Girls with longing and hero worship in their eyes. Couples from middle America who requested he pose for a photo with them because their granddaughter was his biggest fan. Gay guys who simply gazed adoringly. Autograph hounds. And predatory middle-aged women who thought that since he'd been married to Venus, he must be into older women.

Kev got off on every fan-filled minute. He was even collecting digits from the fans with the biggest attributes. "Didn't realize you was *this* popular, dude," he announced, happily taking advantage of it all. "They're treatin' you as if you're Johnny Depp or Brad Pitt."

Billy was aware that Kev did not understand the price of fame. The loss of privacy, the way people treated him as if he were simply there for their viewing pleasure, the demands they made. It was all too much.

And then there was the touching. Billy loathed the touching. Random strangers throwing their arms around him as if it was their right to do so. Girls trying to feel his hair. Clammy handshakes. Every personal interaction turned him off. It was an intimacy issue he could well do without.

Venus had always surrounded them with bodyguards when they were out in public, and now he realized why. When it came to the PR game, Venus was way more savvy than he was.

After attempting to play blackjack at the casino in the Cavendish, he finally gave up and went back to the suite, where he played with the remote until he found a sports channel on TV, settled on the couch, and attempted to recover from the fan-fest.

Kev stayed in the casino, basking in Billy's fame.

After fifteen minutes of college football, Billy tried Max's cell again. His call went straight to voice mail.

This street was turning out to be a dead end.

"So?" Bobby said, joining M.J. in the coffee shop.

"So?" M.J. retaliated, stirring his coffee, a blank expression on his face.

"You know what I'm asking," Bobby said, signaling the waitress, who came hurrying over.

"Yeah," M.J. agreed. "But I don't got an answer yet."

"Are you telling me you haven't talked to Cassie about keeping the baby?" Bobby said as the waitress filled his cup with strong black coffee. "You *know* you gotta do it."

"Uh . . . you could say we're kinda at an impasse," M.J. admitted, staring miserably at the table.

"Impasse not good," Bobby stated.

M.J. gave a weary sigh. "Tell me about it."

"You gotta grow a pair," Bobby insisted. "It's time."

"Comin' from you, that's sweet."

"What does *that* mean?" Bobby said, a frown creasing his forehead.

"Since you hooked up with Denver, the clubs have

taken second place," M.J. complained. "You're never here. An' you're sure as crap not in New York."

Bobby could not believe what he was hearing. "You *gotta* be shittin' me," he said, still frowning.

"Just tellin' it like it is," M.J. responded.

"Goddammit, M.J. I was here three days ago jerking off the Russians. You got a short memory."

"Big of you to drop in."

"Fuck *you*. What's with the attitude?"

"So now I got *attitude?*" M.J. said, losing his cool. "I'm here every night bustin' my stones, while you're camped out in L.A. cozyin' up with your girlfriend. We're supposed to be partners."

"Jesus," Bobby said, annoyed that M.J. was taking his problems out on him. "Where the fuck is this coming from?"

"I dunno," M.J. admitted, shrugging helplessly. "I'm gettin' buried here. Don't mean to rag on you."

"Look," Bobby said understandingly. "I get it. You're under pressure, you need a break."

"What I'd like to do is take Cassie on vacation, get into her head an' convince her to do the right thing."

"Then you gotta do it."

"I want this baby, Bobby, an' I know I hav'ta tell her exactly how I feel before it's too late."

"Then like I said—do it."

"I was thinking we could take off after Max's party. Maybe hit the Bahamas."

"Cool with me."

"You'll handle things here?"

"Sure," Bobby said, mentally canceling all his next week's plans. "And as a bonus, you can even use my plane."

"Shit!" M.J. said. "You certainly know how to throw it back."

"Oh yeah," Bobby said, with a wry grin. "I certainly do."

"Thanks, man," M.J. said, relieved. "I've been going crazy."

"Once again, I get it."

"How about dinner tonight?" M.J. suggested. "Just you, me, Cassie, an' Denver."

Bobby hesitated for only a second. M.J. was going through a personal crisis, and when a friend was in any kind of trouble, he was there.

"Sure," he said, wondering how Denver would react to this sudden change of plans. "How about eight o'clock at the steak house?"

"We'll be there."

Enjoying another brief casino visit, still closely followed by her bodyguards, Venus ran into Alex on the casino floor. They had worked together in the past and enjoyed a cordial relationship, even though they'd fought like lions on the set of the movie Alex had directed her in.

"Alex," Venus said, throwing him one of her cultivated sultry looks. "Meet my friend Jorge. He's from Brazil."

"Your what?" Alex said rudely, his eyes raking over the studly young Brazilian. "Who is he—your son?"

"Alex!" Venus scolded, mock cross. "Behave yourself!"

"I would if I could, but you always bring out the bad in me."

"Do I now?" Venus replied, flirting slightly because Alex was such a brilliant director and she wouldn't mind working with him again.

"You know damn well you do. Remember our fight-a-minute movie?"

"How could I ever forget?" She sighed, playing with a lock of her platinum-blond hair. "You cast Billy in it. Thanks a lot."

Alex gave a twisted grin. "Sorry about that."

"Well," she said, with a half smile, "I suppose you weren't to know I'd be foolish enough to turn around and marry him."

"Jesus Christ!" Alex said, shaking his head at the many memories he had of dealing with Billy. "That kid was a pain in the ass to work with, but I gotta say—a talented little prick."

" 'Little prick' is about the right description," Venus murmured succinctly.

Why is it that whenever a woman gets mad at a man, Alex thought, *the first thing she goes for is the size of his dick?*

Growing impatient, he glanced across the packed casino. "What's your game of choice tonight?" he asked.

"I was thinking roulette," she said as her bodyguards blocked a steady stream of excited autograph seekers.

"Of course you were," he replied. "Nothing like a game of chance to get the juices flowing."

"Hmm . . . don't think I need a round of roulette to do that," Venus replied, with an almost imperceptible nod toward Jorge.

Alex gave a low chuckle.

"I think the three of us should have dinner tonight," Venus said, fluttering her hand on his arm. "Since Lucky is all tied up with Lennie, the least we can do is try to amuse ourselves, don't you agree?"

"What about the boy from Ipanema," Alex asked, motioning toward Jorge. "Does he speak?"

"Not a lot," Venus replied. "But then again, he doesn't have to."

"Will he be joining us?"

"I promise you he'll sit quietly."

"Okay, Venus, we'll dine. I got nothing better to do."

"Where?" she asked, delighted she'd convinced him.

"Asian."

Venus smiled knowingly. "Naturally."

CHAPTER THIRTY-FIVE

Peggy was big on charm. She'd used it all her life to get her own way. The king had fallen under her spell, and then poor old Sidney Dunn, who'd given her the lifestyle she'd desired. Sidney had worshipped her. Peggy's little secret? Lots of flattery and charm mixed with excellent oral sex could keep a man very happy indeed. Sidney had never had cause to complain or look at another woman, Peggy had made damn sure of that.

Sometimes, during her years with Sidney, she'd yearned for the days and nights of her youth. Wild sex with Joe Piscarelli. Parties. Recreational drugs. Her one night with the infamous Gino Santangelo. Not to mention the fervent admiration of so many men as she'd paraded across the stage half naked.

The king had sometimes enjoyed the company of two or three women at a time. Since they were all his wives, it never really bothered Peggy. She'd quite enjoyed the softness of another woman's lips and the silkiness of their skin.

She had never revealed any of this to Armand; he would be shocked. Her son was quite a mystery, not the warm and nurturing man she had hoped he would turn out to be. Armand had a cold personality, and a certain disregard for women she could not understand. Surely she was the perfect role model. She's always been an elegant presence, always available for him.

But no, Armand did not appreciate all that she'd done for him over the years.

Earlier, Fouad had called and informed her of their move, and that they might be staying in Vegas longer than expected. He'd also wanted to know why she'd asked about Gino Santangelo. "I thought it was someone I knew," she'd lied, keeping it casual. "But I was mistaken. Wrong name."

Fortunately for Peggy, her charm worked on everyone but Armand, and after starting up a conversation with Paige Santangelo in the beauty salon, she soon had Paige's attention as she chatted about New York and what an exciting and vibrant city it was to live in.

"We had an apartment in New York once," Paige mused, a tad wistfully. "However, my husband, who's quite a bit older than me, decided we should live in Palm Springs, so that's where we've stayed. It's a little boring."

"You're fortunate your husband is still alive," Peggy said, playing the sympathy card. "I lost my dear Sidney a year ago. He was twenty years older than me. I have to say it's been quite hard being by myself, but with the help of my son and dear friends, I manage. I do not mean financially; Sidney left me set for life. But women of our age, alone—it's not easy."

Before long, the two women found they had plenty in common. After a while Paige asked Peggy if she would care to join her and Gino for dinner.

"I'd be delighted," Peggy responded. "Tell me where and when, and I will be there."

Armand flicked through the dossier Fouad had sent him on Lucky Santangelo. The only thing he found interesting was that she had children—two sons and a daughter.

Ah . . . children. A weakness he could use against her if he had to. But unfortunately, they were not little children; two were teenagers, and one a grown man.

But still, children made a person vulnerable. And yes, most people would do anything to protect their offspring. It was a basic human instinct.

Peggy phoned, interrupting his train of thought. He'd forgotten about his mother; she was the furthest thing from his mind.

"What?" he said curtly.

Peggy did not appreciate his tone of voice, but she chose to ignore his gruffness.

"Fouad told me you have moved to a villa at my hotel," she said. "I hear the villas are lovely."

Armand was immediately furious. What was wrong with Fouad? Couldn't he keep his stupid mouth shut about anything? Now he'd have Peggy turning up, infuriating him even further.

"Yes," he said flatly. "However, I cannot take you to dinner tonight. I have business to attend to."

"Not to worry, dear," Peggy said, sounding surprisingly mellow. "I wasn't asking you. I already have plans."

"You do?" he said, quite surprised. "With whom?"

"Old friends from my past have invited me to dine with them." She paused, then said, "Perhaps I can come by for breakfast tomorrow?"

"We'll see," Armand replied, relieved that he didn't have to bother getting rid of Peggy tonight. It seemed she could look after herself.

"I'll phone you in the morning," Peggy said. "Fouad told me we may be staying longer than anticipated, and I'm open to that. Are your meetings going well?"

"I have to go," he said abruptly. "I'm running late."

"Very well, Armand. Tomorrow."

"If I can," he said, banging down the phone.

Peggy. His mother. Why had she insisted on coming to Vegas? She brought him nothing but aggravation and bad luck. She and Fouad were bringing him down. He hated them both. The two of them reeked of bad karma.

If it weren't for them The Keys would already be his.

Armand Jordan had requested big breasts, and Yvonne Le Crane decided she would find him big breasts. And while she was at it, how about enormous breasts? Breasts of a ludicrous size? Fake shockers?

She'd informed Armand she would accommodate him, and dispatched a messenger to pick up the cash. Soon the two women she'd booked would be on their way to his hotel.

She'd ordered them from a strip club in town called Dirty Den's. Yvonne was on cordial terms with the owner, a former boxer. She'd called him up and offered him a thousand apiece for two of his freaks, and he was more than happy to oblige.

It was a done deal.

This would teach Armand Jordan for calling her girls filthy whores when they were the crème de la crème of Vegas talent.

Now she was about to walk away with a $28,000 profit, so Armand Jordan could go piss in the wind.

Once again it gave her extreme satisfaction to know that Mister Sicko was about to get exactly the kind of girls he deserved.

CHAPTER THIRTY-SIX

The secret to a sensual, sexy marriage is knowing when to leave children, pets, family commitments, and business affairs at the door.

Lucky had a knack for being able to do just that. She and Lennie shared a bond that dated back to the first time they'd met, a true bond that neither of them had ever allowed to slip away. Sex was sex, and they'd both decided early on that if they expected their marriage to stay hot, then they had to work at keeping the passion on permanent sizzle. They both knew how to do that. Sometimes it involved role-playing. Sometimes it didn't. But whatever it took, they were into it one hundred percent.

Rule number one: Leave any family problems outside the bedroom.

Rule number two: Remember the first time.

Rule number three: No inhibitions.

And rule number four—the most important rule of all: Absolutely no interruptions.

Anticipating Lennie's arrival, Lucky felt the old familiar excitement. They were never together long enough for either of them to get bored with each other. Their reunions were always going to be something special, she made sure of that. So even though family and invited guests were in Vegas for Max's party the following night, Lucky had decided that tonight family and friends were on their own, for tonight belonged to Lennie. He was her number one priority. Always. That would never change.

By the time he arrived, she was ready to greet him, a stunning vision in a soft black leather dress, slit thigh high, her jet hair framing her oval face, the drop emerald earrings Lennie had presented her with last Christmas her only adornment.

Tonight she was nobody's mommy. She was Lucky Santangelo at her wildest.

The moment Lennie entered the apartment, she strode toward him and handed him his favorite drink—a black Russian.

Lennie smiled. His smile was one of the things she loved most about him. It crinkled his eyes—ocean green, paler than Max's brilliant emerald. And she loved his mouth, and his longish dirty-blond hair. But most of all she loved his warmth, his talent as a filmmaker, and his soul. They truly were soul mates.

"Who are you tonight?" he asked, throwing down his bag.

Lucky gave an enigmatic smile. "Whoever you want me to be."

"You know exactly who I want you to be," he said, moving purposefully toward her.

"Tell me," she whispered as he reached her and began peeling down the spaghetti-thin straps of her dress.

"My wife," he muttered, crushing her to him so tightly that she could barely breathe. "My life, my love, my everything."

"You *gotta* come with us," Cookie pleaded over the phone to Max. "Frankie's *insistin*' that we go see my dad's concert. There's no way I can do it without you."

"Ace is here," Max stated, sitting on the edge of the couch in her usual suite, trying to figure out what to do about Ace.

"What's up with that?" Cookie said, sounding surprised. "Thought you weren't inviting him."

"Well, he's here, and I promised we'd hang out by ourselves."

"No freakin' way," Cookie wailed. "I need help, an' Harry's goin' to some shitty gig with his Mexican pal."

"Paco," Max said patiently. "The dude's name is Paco."

"Oh, get you—Miss all Politically Correct."

"Where's your dad's concert?"

"At the Cavendish. Can you freakin' believe it? An' Frankie has to find out about it. *Then* he tells me he's always wanted to meet him."

"That's Frankie—the original star fucker."

"He's so not," Cookie argued.

"Then why's he so desperate to get together with your old man?"

"How would I know?" Cookie said irritably. "Maybe he's into that retro soul shit."

"Really?" Max said unbelievingly.

"Yes, *really*. You gonna do this for me or not?"

"I suppose so," Max said, kind of relieved in a way, because spending the night alone with Ace could've been majorly awkward, considering the circumstances of what had recently taken place between her and Billy.

"You're a star!" Cookie exclaimed. "Can you have Danny score us tickets, an' meet us by the elevator in half an hour? Oh, an' turn your cell on. I was tryin' forever to reach you until I thought of callin' your actual room."

Max hung up and dug in her purse for her cell, which she'd forgotten to take off plane mode. Just as she was about to turn it back on, Ace emerged from the bedroom. He'd taken a shower and put on his usual outfit of jeans and a denim work shirt. He looked hot, but not as hot as Billy.

What was she going to do? He obviously expected to stay in her suite, but as far as she was concerned, everything was different now.

"Here's the thing," she said, waves of guilt washing over her. "I totally forgot. Cookie's dad has a show at the Cavendish, and I promised to go. Sorry—can't bail."

Ace shook his head as if he didn't quite believe her. "That's a drag," he said, scratching his chin.

"I know," she apologized, realizing that she was acting like such a phony. "But what can I do?"

"You could say you're busy," he suggested.

"Can't do that," she said, jumping up.

"Why not?"

"'Cause I just can't, that's why," she said stubbornly. "Cookie's my friend. Gotta help her out."

"There goes our one night alone together."

"Yeah, bummer," she said, trying desperately to sound as if she cared. "Only since I didn't know you were coming, I made plans. Big deal."

"You an' your plans," he said, throwing her a look.

"Gotta go get changed," she said quickly. "We're leaving soon."

"You're expecting me to come too?"

"Well, yeah. Unless you wanna sit around here on your own."

"No thanks."

"I'll be right out," she said, heading for the bedroom.

Dammit! Ace knew her pretty well; did he sense that things were different? That she'd changed? That she'd given it up to someone else?

Oh man! She hoped not.

But she couldn't worry about it now. Later would do.

By the time Bobby got back to the hotel, Denver had closed her laptop and was preparing for the romantic evening Bobby had promised her. Just the two of them, no distractions. She was looking forward to it, because maybe it was time to have The Talk, figure out where they were headed. He'd spoken about buying a house in L.A. for them to move into together. Was it the right time to say yes? Had they reached that stage in their relationship?

It was an exciting and scary thought, especially as he still hadn't met her family.

And yet . . . they were so close, and she knew that she loved him, so why wait?

Or was she mistaking love for lust?

They certainly hit it off in the bedroom. The sex was incredible. *He* was incredible.

Stop holding back, she told herself. *You do love him, and it's time to let go and trust that he loves you too. So go for it.*

Yes. Tonight was the night. No more insecurities.

When Bobby arrived back, she ran over to greet him, threw her arms around his neck, and whispered in his ear, "Guess what? I really missed you."

"You did?" he responded. "Thought you didn't need babysitting."

"I don't. Only that doesn't mean I didn't miss you. *And*, I can't wait for dinner—where are you taking me?"

"Yeah," he said hesitantly. "About our romantic dinner for two . . ."

"What about it?"

"It's, uh . . . kinda turned into dinner for four."

"You're kidding?"

"Sorry, babe, but M.J. really needs us, and there's no way I can let him down."

"Seriously?" she said, disappointed.

"M.J. has a problem."

"What kind of problem?"

"I didn't tell you before 'cause I figured he and Cassie would work it out, but it's big."

"Didn't they just get married?"

"Almost a year ago, and here's the deal—she's pregnant and wants to get an abortion, but M.J.'s against it all the way."

Bobby then proceeded to tell her the full story about M.J. and the girl he'd knocked up in high school.

Denver listened in silence, then finally said, "I don't see how having dinner with us is going to help their situation."

"It's a support thing," Bobby explained. "He's trying to tell Cassie that if she gets rid of the baby, their marriage is over."

"That's pretty harsh."

"Maybe, but it's the way he feels."

"And is the way *he* feels the only thing that matters?"

"No, but—"

"How old is Cassie?" Denver interrupted.

"I dunno. Maybe a year or so older than Max."

"Maybe *that's* the reason she isn't ready to have a baby now. It's frightening for her. She's so young—and having a baby is a huge responsibility."

"I understand. But M.J. is entitled to feel the way he does."

"Of course he is. But surely he's prepared to listen to what *she* wants. Her needs are just as important as his."

"Like I told you, sweetheart, M.J. had a life-changing experience that turned him against abortion. He doesn't believe in it."

"Do you?" she asked, suddenly realizing that she didn't know as much about Bobby as she thought she did.

He shrugged. "Dunno," he answered carefully, because it struck him as a loaded question. "Never really thought about it. Unless you find yourself in that situation, it's difficult to say."

"Interesting," Denver said, giving him a long hard look.

"Interesting how?" he said, knowing they were venturing onto dangerous ground.

"Well, I'm assuming you believe in a woman's right to choose?"

"Huh?"

"You heard."

"Look," he said, sensing a fight looming if they continued with this line of conversation. "They're taking a trip right after Max's party. Hopefully they'll work it out."

"You think?" she said, a tad sarcastic. "A trip'll solve everything, right?"

"Who knows?" he said, deciding it was definitely time to change the subject. "What I *do* know is that I'm having to stay in Vegas to keep an eye on things."

"Well, I can't stay. You know I have to get back."

"I wasn't expecting you to, sweetheart. I'll be putting you on a plane to L.A., and we'll speak every day. It's only for a week."

Denver nodded. It looked like The Talk would have to wait, along with their romantic dinner for two.

Suddenly she wasn't so sure about anything anymore.

CHAPTER THIRTY-SEVEN

"What've you done to your hair?" Max gasped when they all met by the elevator.

Self-consciously, Cookie reached up and patted her newfound curls. "Felt like a change," she mumbled.

"It's, like, a way big change," Max exclaimed, thinking how weird it was seeing Cookie without her trademark dreadlocks.

"My idea," Frankie boasted.

"I bet," Max retorted, flashing him a look.

"What? You don't like?" Frankie said, a touch aggressively.

"It's . . . different," Max said as the elevator arrived and they all piled in.

Danny had booked them a limo, even though the Cavendish was within walking distance.

Now it was Ace's turn to look at Max, as if to say, *A limo on top of everything else. What a joke.* But they all got in, and five minutes later they were there.

The Cavendish was nowhere near as luxurious or glamorous as The Keys. But its two owners, Renee Falcon Esposito and Susie Rae Young, made sure the hotel was a fun alternative. When Lucky built The Keys there'd been bad blood between them—at least on Renee's part. Renee had imagined The Keys was her competition, but it had turned out to be quite the opposite. Being located next to such a magnificent new hotel complex had revitalized the Cavendish, and business was booming. Renee and Susie adored Lucky, and would do anything for her. Lucky often came to their hotel and hung out, especially since they'd adopted a five-year-old Vietnamese orphan who was the light of their lives.

When Danny had called to get front-row seats for Max and her friends to attend the sold-out Gerald M. concert, Renee was happy to oblige, although why she was supposed to do it when one of Max's friends was Gerald M.'s daughter, she wasn't quite sure.

Gerald M. was quite a draw with middle America. The ladies were all agog—he represented old-fashioned sexy. Quite a few of them stashed an extra pair of panties in their purse, for when the opportunity arose they planned on tossing them onto the stage in the hope of attracting his attention, at least for a second or two.

Max and her group arrived at the theater in the hotel with minutes to spare. They were led to their seats by an enthusiastic attendant, also a big Gerald M. fan.

"I want to go backstage after," Frankie said to Cookie as they took their seats. "He does know we're here, doesn't he?"

"Uh . . . yeah," Cookie lied. She was hoping that by the time the concert was over and if they took their time getting backstage, her dad would've taken off to the airport and the private plane he always had waiting. She was not thrilled about the prospect of Gerald M. meeting Frankie. Not that her dad would object to her having an older boyfriend, but she knew it was quite possible the two of them would bond—smoke a joint together, snort a little coke. And that thought horrified her.

Once they were settled in their seats, Ace reached for Max's hand. She held his reluctantly, still struggling about what to do. Should she tell him about her and Billy? Or just carry on as if nothing had changed?

It was a dilemma she couldn't quite work out. Eventually she would, because it wasn't as if Billy was still in the picture, and Ace *was* a major hunk.

However, Lucky had always taught her to be honest. Tell the truth. Accept the consequences.

What to do? It was a difficult decision.

"Who's this dude Cookie's hooked up with?" Ace asked in a low, disapproving voice. "I've seen him somewhere before."

"He's an . . . uh . . . ex-friend of Bobby's," Max replied. "You probably ran into him at the opening of The Keys. He used to go out with Annabelle Maestro."

"Who?"

"It's not important."

"I'm not getting a good vibe from him," Ace said.

"You're not?"

"He's got that rich dude sleaze factor goin' on. Not to mention that he's too old for her."

"Whatever." Max sighed. "You know Cookie. It won't last."

"After the concert we're taking off on our own, yes?"

Saved by the announcer, who planted himself center stage and instructed everyone to turn off their cell phones, which reminded Max that she had yet to turn hers on since the plane ride.

Then, to thunderous applause and plenty of screaming fans, Gerald M. sauntered onstage, resplendent in tight purple leather pants and a blowsy white shirt unbuttoned to his waist, diamond medallions vying for space on his exposed chest. More Tom Jones than Usher, he immediately launched into a medley of his many hits—albeit most of them a decade or two old.

The mostly female audience erupted into hysterical sighs of joy as they leapt to their feet. Soon the panties would start flying.

Cookie shot Max a look that said *Kill me now!* while Ace groaned, and Max giggled.

Frankie wondered if he could sell Gerald M. a supply of pharmaceuticals. Why not? Had to invite him to River. Make him a regular customer. Get him to hang out there with some of the gorgeous girls he was always photographed with. Cookie could arrange it; it was about time she made herself useful. Sometimes a man required more than just an enthusiastic blow job.

"You didn't tell me we were gonna have *this* much fun," Ace whispered in Max's ear. "This dude's got one foot firmly planted in the eighties. Does he know he's a relic?"

"Shh," Max scolded. "He's Cookie's dad. Be nice."

Ace squeezed her hand. "You really are a loyal friend, aren't you?"

Suddenly Max remembered why she liked Ace. He always had her back, and he was always kind. The last thing Ace was into was being Mister Hollywood. He would never dump a girl after taking her virginity. No way.

She squeezed his hand back. "Glad you're here," she whispered. "Wouldn't want to go through this slow torture without you."

"Right back atcha, birthday girl."

"Holy shit!" Kev exclaimed, sitting bolt upright at the table he shared with Billy in the Asian Fusion restaurant at the Cavendish Hotel. "You are *not* gonna believe who just jiggled her ass in here."

Billy started to turn around.

"Don't do that!" Kev warned. "It's your friggin' ex with that director you were always bitchin' about."

"Alex Woods?" Billy said, forcing himself not to turn and stare.

"The very same."

"Just the two of them?"

"Some young dude is taggin' along."

"That's just fuckin' great," Billy said grimly. He was pissed off enough that he couldn't reach Max; now his annoying ex was in town. Why was *she* in Vegas? And why was she with the sadistic Alex Woods, the mother-fucker who'd forced him to do every stunt known to man on the movie they'd made together? Alex had almost killed him with his insane demands.

"My luck," he muttered. "Can they see us?"

"No," Kev answered, busily watching. "They're being seated in a booth across the room."

"Then let's get the fuck outta here while we can," Billy said, starting to stand up.

"We just ordered," Kev pointed out. "An' I don't know 'bout you, but *I'm* starvin'. Reminder—we never had lunch."

"Jeez! Is your stomach more important than my comfort zone?"

"Guess so."

"'S long as you're sure they can't see us," Billy grumbled, slouching back into his seat.

"No way, man," Kev assured him. "We're invisible."

"Hmm . . . you give great homecoming," Lennie said, lazily stroking Lucky's thigh as they lay on the bed post-lovemaking, sated and at peace after a passionate two hours. Having been involved with a documentary about tantric sex, Lennie was totally into it. Lucky had no objections. Tantric wasn't all about the climax, it was about the slow, steady climb, and the bliss that awaited at the top of the mountain.

When Lennie had first started practicing it a couple of years earlier, she'd been highly suspicious that he'd hooked up with some twenty-year-old yoga fanatic who was teaching him all the moves. But after experiencing it herself, she was into it too. What woman could resist endless foreplay with a man who knew how to do everything right?

She often thought how far Lennie had come from the brash stand-up comedian she'd first met. Age and a series of traumatic experiences had mellowed him into a special and extraordinary man.

She loved him so much that sometimes it scared her. It was always somewhere in the back of her mind that the three people she'd loved the most had all been taken from her. Her gentle mother, Maria. Her brother, Dario. And the love of her life before Lennie—her fiancé, Marco. Each of them murdered on the orders of one man, her godfather, Enzio Bonnatti.

She'd shot and killed Enzio in what was seen as an act of self-defense.

Self-defense. Sure. If that's what everyone believed.

The truth was, she'd set up the appropriate scenario and blown the motherfucker away. He'd deserved it.

True Santangelo justice. And she didn't regret it. Not for one single minute.

"How's little Max?" Lennie asked. "Excited about her party?"

"She's a teenager, Lennie. The only thing that excites teenagers is getting away from their parents or a night of lust with Ian Somerhalder."

"Who's Ian Somerhalder?"

"*The Vampire Diaries* on TV. Sex and vampires. Guaranteed to get any teenager hot."

"I'm in the movie biz—it's a different scene."

"Really?" Lucky drawled.

"Yes, really."

"I'd never have guessed."

"Shut the fuck up."

"Here's what I love about you, Lennie," Lucky murmured softly. "You do exactly what you want to do, and so do I."

"Which is the reason our marriage works so well," he responded. "No ties. No petty jealousies."

"Amen," Lucky agreed.

"*And* we have a daughter who takes after both of us," Lennie said with a grin. "Little Max. She's a maverick. Gotta let her go do her thing."

"Are you intimating that *I'm* stopping her?"

"Well, sweetheart, you *can* be kind of controlling when the mood hits you."

"Ha!" Lucky exclaimed.

"Ha what?" Lennie retaliated.

"Ha! It's amazing that I still love you after all these years."

"All what years?" Lennie questioned. "Seems to me like we've only been together a couple of months."

"Sweet-talker."

"An' doncha love it!"

"Sometimes."

" 'Sometimes,' she says," Lennie said affectionately, pulling her close.

"Okay." She sighed. "I'll admit it. All times."

"That's my Lucky."

She smiled, dark eyes flashing. "Always."

At the same time as Billy was contemplating leaving the restaurant, Venus was enjoying her time with Alex and Jorge. Two extremely attractive men, generations apart. Jorge was a young stud bursting with testosterone, while Alex was world-weary but filled with stories and life experiences Venus was dying to hear about.

Out of nowhere she suddenly found herself crazily attracted to Alex. He had a Jack Nicholson kind of vibe going, and even though he was getting up there, he was still wildly sexy in a dissolute kind of way.

Of course it was a well-known fact around Hollywood that Alex only went for Asian women. He'd already started hitting on the waitress, a petite girl from Thailand with appealing slanted eyes and a sheet of black hair that hung halfway down her back. But Venus was privy to the information that he'd always had a thing about Lucky. And since Lucky was forever faithful to Lennie, what would be wrong with her taking a shot?

After two extra-strong lychee martinis, she felt the need to share. Jorge was busy stuffing his face with spareribs and seaweed. Young, handsome, and dumb. Why was she even bothering?

Oh yes, sex with a studly stranger. Always a kick.

"You know, Alex," she murmured, leaning toward him, her tone low and seductive. "I never understood why you and I didn't get together when we were making our movie."

"Could it be that you were too busy fucking Billy?" Alex said, arching one of his thick eyebrows.

"Or that *you* had a crush on our producer?" Venus countered, not willing to be outdone. "You know you did."

"If you mean Lucky," Alex said, speaking slowly, "we've always been best friends."

"Hmm . . ."

"What does *that* mean?" Alex said with a deep frown. "Has Lucky ever said anything to you about me?"

"Wouldn't *you* like to know," Venus teased.

"If you've got something to tell me, dear, spit it out," Alex said, his tone tense.

"Why would I have anything to tell you?" Venus replied, delighted that she'd hit on Alex's weak spot. Oh yes, he definitely still lusted after Lucky—the woman he could never have. Typical behavior. Show a power-ful man an unobtainable woman, and he wanted her.

"Don't screw with me, Venus," Alex said, still frown-ing. "I do not appreciate being played."

The edge in Alex's voice attracted Jorge's attention. The young Brazilian put down the sparerib he was nib-bling on, turned to Venus, and said, "Everything good?"

"Ah, he speaks!" Alex mocked.

"Yes, Jorge, everything's fine," Venus said, ignoring Alex, while placating her boy toy with a firm pat on his finely muscled arm. "Alex is a major director," she added, speaking slowly as she pantomimed operating a movie camera. "Very important."

"Jesus Christ!" Alex scoffed. "The boy probably speaks perfect English, an' you're treating him like a dummy."

"He's not a boy," Venus said, annoyed that Alex was getting on her case.

"What is he, then?" Alex questioned, raising a cyni-cal eyebrow.

Before Venus could answer, a plump woman in a flowered dress managed to circumvent Venus's body-guards, who were sitting at a table by the door, and presented herself in front of their table.

"You're just so pretty," the woman cooed, fluttering her hands. "I simply had to tell you. I'm from Kansas, and I seen you on tee-vee, but you are *much* prettier in person." The woman took a deep breath. "And yes, I have to say it—years younger."

"Thank you," Venus said graciously. *And where the hell are my bodyguards when I need them?* She quickly glanced over at their table. The morons were actually eating, and had not noticed she was under attack. Secu-rity. What a crock.

"You must get a ton of attention," the woman gushed. "What with your divorce an' all, an' your husband—or

should I say your ex—sittin' over there. An' him bein'
a young man still. An'—oh." She looked directly at
Jorge. "Is this your son?"

Alex burst out laughing.

Venus was speechless with fury. At this point one of
her bodyguards stumbled over—red in the face—placed
a controlling arm on the woman's shoulder, and moved
her swiftly away.

Alex was still chuckling. Jorge looked casual, as if
he didn't know what was going on, although of course
he did.

"I think it's time to leave," Venus said, cold as ice.

Was Billy really here? In this restaurant?

Damn him. What exactly was he doing in Vegas?

CHAPTER THIRTY-EIGHT

Hyped up on too much coke and ready for action, Armand took a stroll through the casino while he waited for the prostitutes he'd ordered. He was in need of some kind of sexual release while he decided how he was going to deal with the Santangelo bitch.

His surroundings did not please him. The Cavendish was a shit-hole compared to The Keys.

And why was he staying in a shit-hole?

Because of Fouad and Mother Peggy—the whore mother of all time.

It all made sense to him now. Peggy might dress in fancy clothes and stink of expensive perfume, but when the king had discovered her she was probably a prostitute like all the rest of them.

After a while he approached a roulette table and threw down several thousand dollars. In exchange he received a stack of high-denomination chips from an eager croupier.

A steely-eyed pit boss stepped forward and offered to open a private table for his pleasure.

Armand nodded. No need to mix with the sweaty masses. He abhorred crowds.

Roulette was not his usual game of choice, but tonight he felt like playing a different game. Tonight he had a strong feeling that one way or another, he would force Lucky Santangelo's hand. He didn't know how, but it *would* happen, because *he* was all-powerful. Lucky

Santangelo might think she had won, but what she didn't realize was that Armand Jordan was invincible.

The more he thought about her, the more he hated her. She was a witch with her dark hair and evil blacker-than-night eyes. The words that had spewed forth from her mouth were unacceptable. She was the devil incarnate. A morally corrupt whore with a black heart.

And then it suddenly came to him like a blinding flash of lightning. SHE DID NOT DESERVE TO LIVE.

The thought struck him like a meteor—a fast-moving meteor that illuminated his mind and told him what he had to do.

Lucky Santangelo had to die. There was no doubt about it.

Peggy immediately realized that Gino Santangelo did not remember her, and even though he was quite spry for a ninety-something old man, she was quite surprised that he managed to remember anything at all. She felt sorry for Paige, who was decades younger than her husband. At least Sidney had died before she'd been stuck with nursemaid duties. What a nightmare that would've been. Nurse Peggy. Not her calling in life.

Actually, she hadn't expected Gino to remember her. Why would he? According to his reputation, he'd had thousands of girls. And such as the circumstances were now, it was better that he didn't recall their one night of fevered lovemaking. As far as Gino Santangelo was concerned, she was a friend of his wife's. Paige had kindly invited her to join them for a quiet dinner at François, and she'd been delighted to accept.

Peggy was embarking on an exciting mission; it gave her mundane existence new meaning. She'd dressed for the occasion. A Valentino cocktail dress. Black Louboutins. Tasteful jewelry. And a large Hermès purse, in which she hoped to stash the evidence she was about to procure. A strand of his hair, his cocktail glass, anything she could get her hands on.

Gino made it easy for her. Fifteen minutes into the dinner, he experienced a major sneezing fit and blew his nose into a napkin. Usually Peggy considered men who did that social outcasts, but tonight she was thrilled.

However, there was a problem—how to maneuver the soiled napkin into her purse before the waiter came over and spirited it away?

Like a true amateur detective, the answer came to her. Without even thinking about it, she nudged her martini glass so that its contents spilled across the table and onto Gino's lap. Confusion ensued, during which Peggy managed to stuff the napkin into her purse. Mission accomplished!

Peggy experienced a moment of deep satisfaction, and even deeper excitement. After all these years wondering who Armand's real father was, soon the suspense would be over.

Earlier that evening she'd visited the computer center at her hotel and Googled Joe Piscarelli. He too was still alive, and had obviously prospered, for he owned a chain of car dealerships and several gentlemen's clubs. Joe was not as old as Gino Santangelo—nor was he buried in the desert as she'd imagined. Obviously he'd gotten over his criminal tendencies and gone legitimate. He was now a married man with two grown children and two successful businesses.

Peggy had not yet decided how she would approach him and obtain a DNA sample. Right now, Gino was all she could manage.

The girl's name was Luscious. She was twenty-two and well jaded for one so young. She'd been around the block countless times, and it showed. Once the prettiest girl in high school in spite of a pronounced overbite, she was now a strung-out erotic dancer and sometime hooker with a criminal boyfriend and her own rap sheet for a variety of offenses ranging from shoplifting to prostitution and two DUIs. Luscious (formerly Sara Smitton from Oklahoma) could care less that she had a rap sheet. Her main concern was keeping the attention of her boyfriend, Randy—a former pro wrestler, con man, petty thug, and porn star. Unfortunately for Luscious, Randy possessed a wandering cock—which she didn't mind when he was using his impressive instrument for work. But she got royally pissed off when she suspected said impressive cock was going elsewhere.

Luscious and Randy. A true Vegas couple, always trying to wriggle out of debt and better themselves, only getting nowhere in a hurry.

Recently things had been looking up. Randy had gone into business with his ex-con older brother, Mikey, and started dealing drugs. Mikey procured the product, and Randy was the deliveryman, which suited him fine. Deliver the order, collect the cash, split it with Mikey, and voilà—money in his pocket.

But all was not so fine as far as Luscious was concerned. She suspected that Randy had a hard-on for Mikey's wife—a fellow dancer who went by the name of Seducta Sinn (formerly Norma Wilkas from Chicago). Luscious considered Seducta major white trash with her enormous fake tits and out-of-control big ass. They performed alongside each other at Dirty Den's, and often vied to see who could score the biggest tips. Even though they were banging brothers, in Luscious's eyes that did not make them friends. However, when Dirty Den himself offered her five hundred bucks to service a john at the Cavendish Hotel, and another five hundred to take along a "friend," Luscious immediately thought of Seducta. Why not? Fantastic money and a chance to see what tricks Seducta possessed that she didn't.

Naturally, Seducta was up for the gig; she was always complaining that she and Mikey were one step away from the poorhouse.

Lying douche, Luscious thought. She was sure that Mikey was cheating Randy out of his fair share of the drug money. Mikey was a slippery character, and Luscious didn't trust him at all. Nor did she trust Seducta, but Randy insisted that Mikey was family and would never cheat him.

Luscious knew a thing or two about family. A mother strung out on crack, a stepfather who was always trying to slip her his limp cock, and an uncle who'd raped her repeatedly when she was twelve.

Family indeed. Luscious knew more about family than anyone. They'd stab you in the back and bury the corpse if they thought they could get away with it.

Armand placed a $10,000 bet on number 11. The roulette wheel spun around and 11 came up. He let his original bet ride, and 11 came up a second time.

He'd won $340,000 in less than ten minutes. Time to walk away.

Or stay.

It didn't matter. The money wasn't important; it meant nothing to him. His mind was racing. How could he go about hiring a hit man? Was it like in the movies?

No. Of course it wasn't. He had to be careful and think this through.

He was in Vegas. Anything could be arranged in Vegas.

How much for a hit?

The money was of no consequence. Finding the right person to take care of it was all that mattered.

Where was Fouad? Not that Fouad would approve; he was no longer the loyal lackey Armand depended on. Fouad was a weakling who couldn't arrange anything.

Armand needed another hit of coke. After taking a gulp of scotch from the glass a scantily clad cocktail waitress handed him, he threw a large tip at the croupier and got up. Just as he was about to leave, a girl approached him, a pretty girl in an all-American way. She had long golden-red hair and exceptionally high cheekbones, and acted extremely confident as she slid onto the seat next to him. "Armand," she said, greeting him as if they were old friends. "Long time no see. Are you here for the fights?"

"What fights?" he mumbled.

"Oh please!" The girl gave a tinkly laugh. "I'm sure you have the best seats in the house."

He had no idea who she was, but she obviously knew him.

"Not here for the fights," he said, getting up from the roulette table.

"You know," the girl said, lowering her voice and leaning toward him, "I thought we had a good time together, and yet you never called."

"Ah . . ." he said, trying to recall through a haze of too much coke where it was he'd had her—New York? London? Vegas? Or maybe she was one of the imported call girls who'd been flown in for the king's birthday in Akramshar. "Did I pay you?"

"Pay me?" she said, an uncomfortable expression crossing her face. "Why would you pay me?"

"Remind me," he said gruffly. "What's your name?"

Instead of being insulted, she seemed relieved. "Ah, so many women, such a short memory," she trilled. "Annabelle. Annabelle Maestro."

And then it came to him. Annabelle, the daughter of Hollywood movie stars, one of them brutally murdered. She'd written a book about it, and how—for a time—she'd acted as a madam in New York, and for the right price sold herself on occasion.

Sure, he remembered her now. They'd met at a dinner party in New York and he'd had her in the bathroom between courses. She hadn't minded when he'd ravished her against the cold marble of the vanity. And the next night he'd taken her to the opening of a play, then back to his apartment, where once again the somewhat raunchy sex was consensual.

As far as he could recall, she was up for anything, so of course he hadn't called her. Where was the kick if he couldn't humiliate her? He hadn't paid her either. She was obviously under the impression that he didn't know about her past.

The woman was a reformed whore. The best kind. Maybe she could help him find what he was looking for.

"Would you care to join me for a drink, Annabelle?" he asked, turning to her with a plastered-on smile.

She nodded eagerly.

He had plans for this one.

CHAPTER THIRTY-NINE

Although Denver liked M.J., she wasn't that comfortable with his young, overly ambitious wife, Cassie. The girl couldn't stop talking about herself and her burgeoning career—which as far as Denver could decipher, had failed to take off. She'd had one shot at making a record and a few singing gigs in hotel lounges, but Cassie kept on boasting about how she was about to sign with a new agent, a man who'd promised he could jump-start a fabulous career, making her into the next Rihanna.

This girl has no intention of staying pregnant, Denver thought. *This girl has major ambition on her mind, certainly not babies.*

"I'm younger than Katy Perry," Cassie mused. "*Way* prettier than Ke$ha. And way hotter than Taylor Swift. Which means my chance of making it to the top is *huge*. Right, baby?" she said, turning to M.J., finally acknowledging his existence.

M.J. nodded, although he didn't look too happy about his young wife's enthusiasm for a career that had yet to happen.

Denver could understand why. Surely he knew that there was no way he could persuade Cassie to change her mind about getting an abortion. She shot a quick glance at Bobby. His expression was impartial. One thing about Bobby—he was not into confrontations unless there was no other way. "I'm going to the ladies' room," she said, rising from the table.

"Me too!" Cassie squeaked, jumping to her feet.

"Talk to her," Bobby mouthed to Denver.

Right, so *that's* why she was in Vegas, to induce a would-be pop star into giving up her dreams and having a baby.

Cassie beat her to it. As soon as they reached the powder room, she threw her sparkly purse on the counter, turned to Denver, and said, "Can you keep a secret?"

Oh no! Denver thought. *Please don't make me your confidante.*

But Cassie was determined. "Can you?" she repeated.

"Uh, not so hot with secrets," Denver managed, quickly ducking into a stall to escape.

Cassie was waiting when she emerged, standing at the counter applying cherry-red lip gloss with her finger. "You're so lucky to be with a dude like Bobby." Cassie sighed. "All the girls in the club are crazy for him."

"Good to know," Denver said, washing her hands while wondering who "all the girls in the club" were. Customers? Staff? What the hell?

"My friend Lindy, well, she says Bobby's into you 'cause you're so smart."

"Also good to know," Denver said dryly.

"I bet he's a total stud in bed."

"Excuse me?"

"Is he?"

"I don't think that's anyone's business except mine."

Cassie giggled. "You're such a lady! I guess that's another reason Bobby likes you. Y'know, he has a big rep for lovin' an' leavin', but you're hangin' in there."

Jesus Christ! Denver thought. *Why do I have to stand here listening to some young girl telling me what a stud Bobby is and how lucky I am to have him. How about he's lucky to have me?*

"I'll see you back inside," Denver said, preparing for a quick exit.

"Wait!" Cassie implored. "I need your help."

"Help?"

"Well, kinda. Y'see, it's like this . . ."

And the story of her pregnancy came tumbling out—all about how there was no way she could have the baby, and M.J. was being stubborn, and what was she supposed to do?

"Look, I'm not a marriage counselor," Denver said patiently. "However, it seems to me you've got a choice here—have the baby and keep M.J., or go the career route."

"I know," Cassie agreed. "But all I want is for M.J. to get it. I can have a baby anytime—the career thing is right now. *Why* doesn't he get it?"

"You should speak to your mom," Denver suggested. "I'm sure she'll advise you."

"Done that," Cassie replied with a careless shrug. "My mom doesn't care."

"Come *on*. I'm sure she does."

"No," Cassie said, shaking her head. "She'd like me *not* to have a kid. She's only thirty-five an' isn't ready to be a grandma."

"Well," Denver said briskly. "I wish I could help you, but unfortunately I can't. All I can say is follow your inner self and work out what you want most."

"Got it!" Cassie said cheerfully. "Knew you could solve it for me."

Denver frowned.

As far as she was concerned, she hadn't solved anything.

"I think we gotta hit a strip club," Kev announced as they exited Asian Fusion.

"No way," Billy replied, standing still for a minute. "You think I wanna be all over TMZ with a bunch of strippers tellin' everyone how much I tipped?"

"Where's TMZ?" Kev said, playing dumb. "Don't see 'em hidin' under a palm tree waitin' to pounce, do you?"

"Trust me. They're everywhere," Billy assured him, itching to try to reach Max again. The fact that she wasn't picking up her phone was becoming an obsession. He'd flown to Vegas, for crissakes, screwed up his entire weekend, and now she wasn't answering her damn cell. Could it be that she was purposely blowing him off?

"What're you so edgy about?" Kev questioned. "*I'll* protect you from the paps. I'm an expert at runnin' interference."

"Yeah?" Billy said shortly. "Then where were you when I was gettin' attacked in the casino earlier?"

"Those were *fans*," Kev said, as if that explained everything. "Fuckin' fans who worship at your cock."

"Knock it off, Kev."

"You could've had any one of 'em. You know it, and so do I."

"Thanks," Billy said caustically. "I think my tastes run a little higher than that."

"Not the Billy I know," Kev said with a knowing leer. "Back in the day you would've fucked a log if it winked at you."

Kev was starting to get on his nerves. "Back in the day," indeed. Didn't Kev get it? Things had changed. He'd forgotten how jarring his old friend could be.

They lingered outside Asian Fusion too long, because before he could even think of escaping, Venus stalked out in full star glory, trailed by Jorge and her two bodyguards. Alex had lingered behind, attempting to hook up with the waitress.

Billy realized there was no way they could avoid a face-to-face. "Hey," he managed, caught off guard.

For a moment he thought Venus was about to blank

him. But she didn't. She rallied, hung on to Jorge's arm, and threw him an icy "Hello."

So much for remaining friends, which is what she'd said in a recent interview. *"Billy and I are, and always will be, the closest of friends. I wish him nothing but the best."*

Knowing Venus, what she actually meant to say was *"Fuck that son of a bitch. I hope his career implodes and I never have to see him again."*

"You're lookin' good," Billy muttered. It was all he could think of to say. One thing about Venus, she was always in spectacular shape. Too much for any one man to handle.

The dude she was clinging onto was young—young enough to not know what he was getting himself into. At thirty, Billy felt like a veteran of the star wars. Maybe he should warn the poor bastard, help him out.

"Hey, Venus," Kev piped up. "Long time no see."

Venus gave Kev an imperious wave of her hand—her signature move when dealing with an annoying presence. She and Kev had never gotten along. When Kev was Billy's assistant she'd insisted that Billy fire him. He hadn't done so, which had made her resent Kev even more.

Suddenly the theater next door to the restaurant began hemorrhaging crowds of people. The Gerald M. concert was over, and hundreds of excited fans were on the loose.

Venus's bodyguards closed ranks around their precious star and immediately began moving her off.

Billy decided he'd better get going before he was spotted.

Too late. A gaggle of delirious women descended on him, yelling his name. Soon he was surrounded by screaming fans.

Where was Kev when he needed him?

* * *

"I get edgy in crowds," Ace said as they fought their way out of the theater. "This is a freakin' nightmare."

"Stay cool," Max whispered as a fat woman inadvertently shoved her in the back. "It'll soon be over. Then we'll go find an In-N-Out Burger. That'll put a smile on your face."

"You got that right," Ace said, grabbing her hand.

"Shouldn't we be heading backstage?" Frankie said, stopping and indicating a side door where select VIPs were being assembled to be escorted back to pay homage to Gerald M.

"Yeah, right," Cookie answered vaguely. She'd hoped he wouldn't notice, but obviously he knew the routine. Major stars always had their assistants gather the people who merited a pass, then bring them back to the luxurious private bar, where they patiently waited their turn for an audience with the star. Such bullshit.

Frankie changed direction and headed for the side door, while Cookie pulled on Max's arm and hissed, "You gotta come with us. *Puh-leeze!*"

"Oh for crap's sake!" Max complained. "This entire night is turning out to be all about you."

"Ten minutes," Cookie pleaded. "Then we'll go wherever you an' Ace want."

"What *he* wants is for us to be by ourselves," Max said, wishing she was anywhere but here.

"You can do that anytime."

"Not really, considering Ace doesn't live anywhere near me."

"He should move," Cookie sniffed.

"Maybe he will. But tonight I have to do what *he* wants. He drove all this way just to be with me. That has to count for something."

"Okay, okay," Cookie said impatiently. "Ten minutes, that's all I ask."

"Fine." Max sighed. "After that, you're totally on your own."

It didn't thrill Venus running into Billy. She supposed he must be in Vegas for the fights. He was with his horrible friend Kev—a bone of contention in their marriage. She'd always suspected Kev was a bad influence, therefore she'd never trusted him. She was sure he'd always been trying to hook Billy up with random girls on the side.

Well, at least Billy wasn't with that little tramp, his most recent costar, Willow Price—famous for flashing her snatch at every photographer in town.

Her bodyguards hustled her through the casino and into a waiting limo hovering curbside. Jorge trotted behind them and jumped onto the seat next to her.

"Where to, Miss Venus?" the driver inquired.

"Back to The Keys," she said to the driver, removing Jorge's hand from her thigh. "Stop at the private entrance to Mood." She turned to Jorge. "Do you dance?"

He nodded.

"Excellent, 'cause I feel like letting loose."

"You told Cassie about the Bahamas yet?" Bobby asked.

"I'm gonna surprise her," M.J. replied. "Kinda zip her out to the airport from Max's party. She'll never know what hit her."

"Girls don't like surprises," Bobby warned. "They're into preparing and all that crap."

"Preparing *what?*" M.J. said. "I'll buy her anything she needs when we get there."

"If you really think that's the way to go."

"Yeah. She'll love it."

"Okay, she'll love it," Bobby said, although he didn't believe it for a moment.

"Cassie wants me to meet up with some superagent who's considering representing her," M.J. said, signaling for the check. "We're having a drink with him at the Cavendish, then we'll swing by Mood. Okay with you?"

"Sure. I'll hold things down."

"We've got a lot of VIP reservations tonight," M.J. said. "Everyone's in town for the fights on Sunday."

"And you're not staying," Bobby stated. "What's up with that?"

"Yeah, bad timing," M.J. said. "But here's the good news—I'm givin' you my tickets."

"Jeez," Bobby exclaimed. "True love rules."

"Ringside, my man," M.J. boasted. "Primo position. Cannot be beat."

"Problem is, I don't think I can use 'em," Bobby said, watching Denver and Cassie as they walked back to the table.

"Why not?" M.J. asked. "Aren't you listening? Ringside, man."

"I'm not so sure it's something Denver's into."

"Exactly what am I not into?" Denver asked, sliding into the booth.

"Boxing," Bobby said. "Not your thing, right?"

"How did you guess?" she said coolly. "Two grown men beating each other's brains out is hardly my idea of a brilliant time."

"Yeah," Bobby said. "I had a hunch you'd feel that way."

"I'm crazy for the fights," Cassie piped up. "We're goin' Sunday night, right, hon?"

M.J. exchanged a glance with Bobby and nodded. "Course we are. Wouldn't miss it."

Denver wondered what was happening back in L.A. She missed her apartment, her dog, and her work.

So far Vegas was not doing it for her. She couldn't wait to get home.

CHAPTER FORTY

Luscious and Seducta set off in Seducta's 1998 shocking-pink Pontiac, her pride and joy—a wedding present from Mikey after they'd gotten hitched by a Lady Gaga look-alike six months ago after indulging in a drunken orgy with several Scottish footballers. Seducta harbored such fond memories of that special day, she'd even had the date tattooed on her ass.

"How come Mikey bought you an *old* car?" Luscious sneered as she settled in to the passenger seat and attempted to fasten the broken seat belt across her skinny waist.

"Better than that piece of garbage *you* drive," Seducta sneered back, referring to Luscious's used 2008 Toyota. "My Pontiac is vintage."

Luscious wasn't quite sure what vintage meant, so she kept quiet.

"Who *is* this john we're seeing?" Seducta inquired, weaving in and out of traffic with a total lack of concern for other drivers on the road. "What's his deal? Girl on girl? 'Cause if it is, I'm warnin' you—don't go stickin' your tongue in my cooze. You gotta fake it. We clear on that?"

"How the fuck I know who he is?" Luscious said irritably. "It's a job. The jerkoff's payin' top dollar. An' might I remind you to get a life—'cause the last place my tongue wants t' go is anywhere near your fat cooze."

"Fat?" Seducta hissed, tapping the steering wheel

with long fake nails—several of them chipped. "If anythin's fat it's your big mouth. Since you had that shit injected in your lips, they remind me of two gnarly worms."

"You're bein' jealous again," Luscious said, refusing to get into a war of words. "Randy gets off on my lips."

"Not what he told *me,*" Seducta replied with a knowing smirk.

"Since when did *you* get to talkin' to *my* boyfriend?" Luscious demanded.

"Like I'm not allowed to speak to my own *brother-in-law,*" Seducta jeered. "You seem to forget we're related. Randy an' me—we're *family.*"

Luscious narrowed her squinty eyes. Seducta was dumb as a sheep, and she wasn't about to take the bait, because that's what Seducta was doing—baiting her into losing her cool. She wished she hadn't thrown this well-paid gig Seducta's way; the fat cow didn't deserve it. She should've picked one of the other girls.

Too late now. The best thing she could do was grit her teeth and put a smile on it.

CHAPTER FORTY-ONE

"I have a yen to surprise everyone," Lucky murmured, sliding seductively out of bed. "I know I said we wouldn't emerge until tomorrow, but it's only eleven and I'm sure they'll all end up at Bobby's club. What do you think? Shall we put in an appearance?"

"My wife," Lennie said, leaning back with a benevolent smile on his face. "Always ready for action."

"Hmm," she said, also smiling. "Tonight I've had enough action to last me until your next visit."

"Jesus," Lennie burst out laughing. "You're making me sound like some kind of randy sailor on shore leave."

"Yeah, that's it," Lucky teased. "My sexy sailor husband—the man with all the right moves."

"If you say so," he said, pulling her back to bed. "Although I'm thinking there could be a few moves we haven't explored yet."

"You think?"

"I do."

"When's your next visit?" she asked, snuggling up close and idly stroking his chest.

"Stop with the visiting crap," he scolded. "I'm away on location making a movie. I'll be home permanently in a few weeks."

"Nothing about you is ever permanent, Lennie."

"Isn't that exactly the way you like it?"

"How well he knows me," she drawled.

"Yeah," he said, scratching his head. "If anyone knows you at all."

"I had a strange meeting this morning," she ventured. "Actually, it was verging on creepy."

"What kind of strange?" Lennie asked.

"I'm not sure, really—it was with some moronic asshole who figured he could waltz right in and buy The Keys. Can you imagine?"

"No shit," Lennie said, his interest piqued. "Who was he?"

"A man called Armand Jordan. Jeffrey set the meeting up; he was under the impression that Armand's company was interested in investing in future projects."

"And I'm guessing that wasn't the case."

"Not at all. This Armand character seemed fixated on buying The Keys for any price. He had this weird vibe about him—it was almost as if he had a vendetta against women."

"Oh yeah, babe," Lennie said dryly. "Just your type. Did you hang his balls on a post?"

"No," Lucky said, smiling because Lennie knew her so well. "But I did have him bounced from the hotel."

"Poor bastard," Lennie said, laughing. "He had no idea who he was messing with."

"I guess not," she said thoughtfully.

"Anyway, you threw him out and he's now history. Right?"

"Exactly."

"So end of that story, and on to other more important things. How's Max doing?"

"The same as ever. Desperate to make a break for it, and get out there on her own."

"You've got to accept that our girl is a free spirit. All she wants is her space."

"She gets all the space she needs, thankyouvery-much. *And* we're throwing her a fantastic party. By the way, Ace drove here to be with her."

"He seems like a good kid."

"Don't you think she's too young to stick with one person?" Lucky questioned.

"Not if he's the right one."

"Oh, you mean like you and me?"

"You got it, sweetheart," Lennie said, laughing.

"I bet you don't remember our first date," Lucky said, deciding to challenge him.

"Is this a test?" Lennie asked, propping himself up on one elbow and giving her a quizzical look.

"Maybe," she teased. "Perhaps I want to see if you can pass."

"Come *on*. As if I could ever forget our first date."

"Go ahead, then," she said, continuing to bait him. "I expect details."

"New York. Chinese restaurant. We killed a bottle of vodka."

"I'm impressed," Lucky said. "You really do remember."

"Did you honestly believe I wouldn't?"

"Well . . . I thought you'd close in on the first time we made love on that raft in the South of France. Now *that* was unforgettable."

"You got that right. We should take a look at reenacting that scene sometime soon. Like as soon as I've wrapped my movie."

"I'm up for it."

"Me too."

They exchanged a long intimate look.

"But hey, I gotta admit—our first date was hot too," Lennie said. "After killing the vodka you dragged me off to some Greenwich Village jazz joint until four in the morning."

"Then *you* dragged *me* to some after-hours dive

where we stayed forever, drinking endless cups of coffee and talking about everything."

"And you, my little Lucky, loved every minute of it."

"I'm not denying it. But even better," she added softly, "we fell in love that night."

"We did?" he said, feigning surprise. "Now, that I don't recall."

"Don't mess with me, Lennie Golden," she said, narrowing her eyes in a threatening fashion. "You know you won't appreciate the consequences."

"Okay, okay," he said, grinning. "I guess we did, an' now look at us—an old married couple with kids."

"Easy on the 'old,' mister," Lucky said, throwing him a playful punch.

"However, Mrs. Golden, you're still as beautiful now as you were then. Besides, I like a woman with a little seasoning on her."

" 'Seasoning,' huh?"

"Oh yeah."

"Fuck you, Lennie Golden!"

With one swift move he rolled on top of her, pinning her beneath him. "Sure, love of my life. I live to oblige."

Most stars conduct a meet and greet after their concerts. Sometimes Gerald M. couldn't be bothered, but in Vegas he was never sure what celebrity could be lurking in the audience, so tonight he hung around to see who might appear. Besides, he was staying in town for the fights, and since he'd recently broken it off with his latest conquest—an ambitious actress (weren't they all?)— he'd decided to sample the local talent.

The last person he expected to see was his almost unrecognizable daughter. Without her trademark dreads, Cookie looked quite different.

"What's up with your hair, chicken?" he asked as she

and her group were ushered into his large but crowded dressing room adjacent to the hospitality bar.

"Don't *call* me that," she said, rolling her eyes in horror. "It's *so* uncool."

"This girl is my little chicken," Gerald M. crooned to the assorted gathering. "Hatched her myself. Now look at her—she's all grown up." A lackey handed him a rum and Coke, which he downed in two big gulps. "What you doin' here, sweet thing? How'd ya like the show?"

I hated the show, Cookie was tempted to say. *I hated seeing my father up on stage thrusting his leather-clad dick at a screaming audience of middle-aged loser women desperate to get laid.*

"Your show was phenomenal," Frankie announced, maneuvering himself in front of Cookie and shaking Gerald M.'s hand. "You are the consummate artist. You always rock their fuckin' world—'scuse my language."

"And you are?" Gerald M. said, backing off.

"Frankie Romano, Cookie's friend. Pleasure to meet you, sir."

"'Sir'!" Gerald M. spluttered with laughter. "How the fuck old d'you think I am?"

Oh crap, Cookie thought. *This is so bad. They're bonding already.*

Max hung back. She figured she'd fulfilled her obligation as a friend, and now it was time for her and Ace to duck out.

Cookie was not having it. "You've gotta stay with us," she begged. "Otherwise Frankie's gonna want to hang with my dad, an' there's *no way* I can handle it!"

"But Cookie—" Max objected.

"*Puh-leeze!* I'll never ask you for anything again!"

And so it was that they stayed.

* * *

Bobby and Denver were sitting at a table in a candlelit poolside cabana at Mood with people swirling all around them. It was almost midnight, the music was loud, and the club was packed. Beautiful girls abounded—even the cocktail waitresses were great-looking in their skimpy uniforms. Denver was feeling out of place and inadequate. Club scenes were not her favorite venues.

"What's with the attitude?" Bobby asked, catching her mood.

"What attitude?" Denver shot back, unable to help herself from taking her frustration out on him.

"You just seem"—he shrugged—"I dunno—kinda uptight."

"As opposed to *not* uptight, like all the girls that keep coming over and talking to you?" she retorted, wishing she didn't sound so damn jealous.

"Hey Denv, you *know* it's only work," Bobby said, stroking her arm. "Since it's my club, what do you expect me to do—ignore them?"

"That's an idea."

"C'*mon*. Drink your wine, loosen up."

"I thought tonight was going to be all about us. Instead it's me trying to talk Cassie out of getting an abortion, and you working the room. Not my idea of a romantic evening."

"Sorry you feel like that. But surely y'know I've only got eyes for you?"

He gave her the look—a look she couldn't resist.

The trouble with Bobby was that he was so damn good-looking, and on top of that, genuinely nice. Then of course there was the rich factor—so naturally women were going to be chasing him. If he was indeed her future, she realized that she'd just have to get used to it.

"Well," she said, softening her tone, "if you put it like that . . ."

"You know where I want to put it," he whispered in her ear.

"Bobby!"

"Half an hour, then we're taking off. That's a promise."

"You mean it?"

"Course I do," he said, leaning in and kissing her.

She kissed him back. "I know I'm behaving like a jealous girlfriend and I don't understand why," she murmured. "It's so not me, you know that."

"I get it," Bobby reassured her.

"You do?"

"I sure do."

"Well then—perhaps you can enlighten me."

He grinned at her again. What a smile. Dazzling.

" 'Cause you love me," he singsonged.

She sat up straight, her heart pounding. Had he just mentioned the L word? And why was he putting it on her? Wasn't it up to him to say it first?

"Excuse me?" she said, slightly breathless.

"L-O-V-E," Bobby said, spelling it out. "And since you're not about to be the first to say it, I'm saying it for you, 'cause I love you too, Miz Jones, and I'm through with holding back. So deal with it. Okay?"

Somehow or other Kev managed to lure Billy to a strip club, where the manager—a big fan with caterpillar eyebrows and a smarmy leer—spotted him and immediately sequestered him in a deluxe VIP suite with champagne on the house and two of the club's most popular girls.

Kev was in heaven. If he were by himself he would've been sitting next to the stage staring up at an array of tempting pussy with all the other nobodies. Hanging with Billy was the best. First-class service all the way.

A baby-faced blonde was busily trying to tempt Billy with her wares—shiny new tits, flat stomach, long legs, and shaved pussy. But Billy wasn't buying. "Got a girlfriend," he informed her. Which was news to Kev, because wasn't Billy in the middle of a divorce?

"Sorry about that," Baby-face cooed, adding a cheeky "But just because your dick is occupied, doesn't mean you can't let it out for a run!"

Billy laughed, fleetingly thought about going for it, then hurriedly excused himself, walked outside the club, and tried Max again.

Once again there was no answer, so this time he decided to text her.

"Hey, it's me—Billy. Where r u? Been trying to reach u. I'm in Vegas. Want to c u. Call me."

It was done. He'd contacted her; now all she had to do was respond.

Everyone ended up piling into the restaurant area of Mood. Gerald M. and entourage consisted of his two backup singers and his assistant/procurer of female talent.

Then there were Cookie and Frankie (so up Gerald M.'s ass there was no room for anyone else), Max, and a reluctant Ace.

"What happened to ducking out on our own?" Ace said in a low voice to Max as they settled in at the table. He was becoming resigned to the fact that it seemed like he was never getting her to himself.

"This is Vegas, things happen," she answered restlessly. "Besides, we can't be here and *not* see Bobby. He's sitting in a cabana by the pool. Let's go visit."

Before Ace could object, she grabbed him by the hand and began pulling him across the restaurant to the outside club area.

Bobby spotted them approaching. "How to ruin a special moment," he muttered to Denver. "Trust Max to have the worst timing in town."

"She doesn't know," Denver said, feeling light-headed. "Besides, I really would like to get to know her."

"You're sure about that?" Bobby said, standing up as Max descended.

"Hey, big bro," Max said, flinging her arms around him in her usual proprietary fashion. "Remember Ace?"

"Absolutely," Bobby said, giving Ace an amiable nod. "And you all know Denver."

Max threw her a perfunctory nod, while Ace said a polite "Nice to meet you."

"Likewise," Denver replied, thinking that if this was Max's boyfriend, she'd done well for herself.

"Ace drove all the way from Big Bear just to be with me," Max said, hovering by the table.

"How nice," Denver said. "I bet you were thrilled to see him."

As usual Max ignored her. "Guess who's here?" she said to Bobby.

"You know I'm not good at guessing games."

"Your old BFF Frankie Romano."

"Where?" Bobby said. He hadn't seen Frankie in quite a while, not since they'd parted ways after a falling-out about Frankie's addictions.

"We're sitting with him at Cookie's dad's table in the restaurant. You should come over. I know he'd love to see you."

"Maybe later," Bobby said. Once, he and Frankie, along with M.J., had been best friends, but those days were over. "You know," he added sternly, "you're not supposed to be in this area of the club."

"How come?" Max shot back.

"'Cause you're not twenty-one. And that means we could lose our license."

"As if!" Max scoffed. "Besides, we've all got fake ID's."

"Great," Bobby said sarcastically. "That makes me feel so much better."

Then, to his relief, he spotted Lucky and Lennie walking in. Great timing, because it meant that Max was no longer his problem. Let Lucky deal.

"Here come your mom and dad," he warned. "Better skip back to your table, little girl, or Mommy might give you a smack on your bottom."

"You are *so* mean," Max said, making a face. "I hate you!"

"Not mean, just protective."

"Anyway, what are *they* doing here?" Max said, twisting her head to take a look as Lucky and Lennie approached. "I thought they wanted alone time. So gross!"

"Nice way to talk about your parents," Bobby said.

"They're yours too," Max pointed out.

"Half mine," Bobby said, correcting her.

"Whatever."

Moments later Lucky and Lennie were upon them, and Lennie was giving Max a hug while Lucky was checking out Denver and Bobby was thinking, *Half an hour later and we could've been safely out of here.*

In the club business, the night was only just beginning.

CHAPTER FORTY-TWO

Annabelle Maestro was a talker. She didn't shut up for a minute. Armand had no idea what or who she was talking about. He didn't know and he didn't care. Names came and went as they sat in one of the open lounges drinking tequila on the rocks with *limoncello* chasers—a lethal combination thought up by Annabelle. He liked the buzz the liquor was giving him. He liked the fact that there was no Fouad around keeping a watchful eye on him.

"If you're not here for the fights, what *are* you doing in Vegas?" she asked, rubbing her index finger around the rim of her glass and staring at him expectantly.

"I am buying The Keys hotel and casino," Armand announced. *Yes, that's what I'm doing. Damn you, Lucky Santangelo. You'll soon learn that when Armand Jordan wants something, he gets it. I am unstoppable. And if I say something is going to happen, it will, whether you think you can stop it or not. But how can you stop it if you're dead? Impossible.*

"You're kidding!" Annabelle exclaimed, her eyes widening. This guy wasn't just rich; he was mega rich. Ever since their one date a few months ago, she'd had her eye on him. Although they'd experienced one long wild night of sex, he'd never called. Annabelle did not appreciate rejection, especially as she considered herself semifamous, and he should've been thrilled to date her.

Armand had quite a reputation in New York as being aloof and difficult to pin down. But Annabelle was well aware that he was a major catch, and she craved a steady boyfriend; there'd been nobody permanent since she'd broken up with that sad sack druggie Frankie Romano.

Earlier in the evening she'd had a big fight with her latest boyfriend, Eddie Falcon, the superagent. They'd only been seeing each other a few weeks, but tonight she'd discovered, by scrolling through his texts, that Eddie was cheating on her with not one but three other girls. Apparently he was the Tiger Woods of superagents. What an asshole! She'd been planning on dumping him and flying back to New York, but then, walking through the casino to cool off, she'd run into Armand.

When opportunity beckoned, Annabelle was not about to turn it down.

"I never thought Lucky would sell," Annabelle said. "When's this happening?"

"Soon," Armand replied, feeling the need to get to his villa and indulge in a few more lines of coke before the hookers got there. He'd informed the concierge to alert him when they arrived, and to have them wait in his villa. For a thousand-dollar tip, Armand figured the concierge would fuck them himself.

"Then you must be going to the party tomorrow night," Annabelle ventured.

"What party?" Armand asked, thinking he would invite her back to his villa to see if he could get her to interact with the prostitutes. Now *that* might be worth watching.

"Lucky's daughter, Max, is turning eighteen. There's a big blowout at The Keys," Annabelle said. "Since I told my boyfriend to take a hike, I could go with you. I know the Santangelos; I'm sure they'd be delighted to see me. Bobby and I went to high school together."

"Who is Bobby?"

"Lucky's son. He runs the club Mood in The Keys. We're tight. Maybe we should stop by for a drink."

Tight. What did that mean? This girl spoke a language he didn't understand and certainly didn't want to. However, since she knew the Santangelo family, she could turn out to be useful.

"What do you think?" Annabelle asked, tilting her head to one side.

"I think we should go to my villa first. Spend some private time."

Annabelle considered his offer. She didn't want sex—followed by no phone call. Oh, no, that wouldn't do at all.

On the other hand, Armand *was* one of the most eligible bachelors in New York, and perhaps the timing was right to give him another chance. What did she have to lose?

"One drink," she said brightly. "Then on to Mood. Is that a plan?"

Armand nodded.

Why did God give women the ability to speak? Why couldn't they just keep their stupid mouths shut?

Once Peggy captured her prize—Gino's sneezed-in napkin—she was anxious to end the dinner and get back to her suite.

But Paige was having none of it. She was enjoying Peggy's company, and suggested they move on to the Cavendish club for a nightcap.

"I'm a little past nightclubs," Peggy demurred.

"If I can do it, so can you," Gino wheezed. "I'm two hundred years old, hon. You're a spring chicken."

For a moment Peggy was tempted to remind him of their one-night fling all those years ago. But good sense prevailed and she said nothing.

844   JACKIE COLLINS

"You see what I have to put up with," Paige said with a complacent smile. "The man is tireless. He hardly ever sleeps."

"What? I should sleep my friggin' life away?" Gino interrupted. "When I go, it won't be quietly in the night, it'll be in the middle of a fuckin' party."

Paige shook her head. "Energy to burn," she said. "If we could bottle it we'd make a fortune."

For a split second Peggy flashed onto a memory of Gino making love to her. Energy to burn indeed. He'd been an insatiable lover. Other men had paled in comparison, especially King Emir, who after a while had suffered from premature ejaculation—something that didn't seem to bother him because he was a king, so who would dare to criticize?

"I suppose one drink wouldn't hurt," Peggy said, removing her powder compact from her purse and checking her appearance.

"Not bad for an old broad," Gino said with a lecherous chuckle.

"I thought I was a spring chicken," Peggy retorted. And for one quick moment she thought she spied a hint of recognition in his dark, all-knowing elderly eyes.

Carlos, the chief concierge at the Cavendish, a well-put-together Latin man, personally escorted Luscious and Seducta to Armand Jordan's villa. The two women smelled of cheap perfume, musty sweat, cigarettes, and booze. Hardly a winning combination.

Carlos was surprised to observe such low-rent women. Surely a man such as Armand Jordan expected better than these two?

Luscious pranced around the living room on her cheap six-inch red hooker heels, a cigarette dangling from her overplumped lips. Her legs were bare, and on her left calf was a tattoo of a bodybuilder winking at no one in particular.

"Where's the . . . uh . . . mister?" she asked.

"He'll be here shortly," Carlos replied, deciding it would not be wise to leave them alone in the villa. They looked like the type of women who—if left to their own devices—would steal anything that wasn't locked down. "And this is a no-smoking room," he added. "So if you'd refrain—"

"Fuck that shit," Luscious said, boldly blowing a smoke ring in his face. "If I get cancer an' die I promise not to blame you."

Seducta guffawed as she threw herself down on the couch, one streaky fake-tanned leg casually flung over the side. Her large breasts threatened to fall out of the flimsy top she was wearing, while her red, white, and blue G-string was fully on show. "I could go for a drink while we're waitin'," she said, winking meaningfully at Carlos.

He glanced at his watch. Was he supposed to serve these two creatures drinks? Armand Jordan might be an excellent tipper, but he, Carlos, was nobody's lackey. "Mr. Jordan will be here shortly," he said. "It's up to him if he wishes you to drink."

"For crissakes," Luscious whined. "Lighten up. You're a workin' stiff, just like us. Get the stick out your ass and pour us a fuckin' drink."

"Yeah, I'm parched," Seducta agreed, sitting up. "One drink, an' if you promise to behave, I'll show you my titties."

"I don't—"

"Oh yeah, you do!" Seducta said, peeling down her top and revealing the largest fake boobs Carlos had ever seen.

The women were disgustingly vulgar, but he was a

man, after all, and the sudden stirring in his pants reminded him of that fact. He realized that he had to leave immediately before he did something to dishonor his lovely wife of six months. Let them steal; whatever they took, he would simply add onto Mr. Jordan's bill.

"The drinks cupboard is behind the bar," he said, hurriedly backing toward the door. "Help yourselves."

"Bye, honey," Seducta crooned, shaking her enormous bare breasts at him. "See you around!"

"What took place between you and the man you came to Vegas with?" Armand asked as he and Annabelle walked through the casino on their way outside to his villa. He wasn't at all interested in anything she had to say, but faking it socially was a talent he'd cultivated over the years. Make them like you, then stick it to them—hard.

"He was one of those hotshot Hollywood jerks," Annabelle complained. "A lying prick who had me figured as a money machine for him to milk. Promised me my own reality show, then when we got here I discovered he'd not only pitched another celeb, but he was sleeping with her too."

Armand made a sympathetic sound in the back of his throat. As if he cared. He didn't. Not one bit.

"Tell me about the party tomorrow night—you say it's for Lucky Santangelo's daughter?"

"That's right," Annabelle said. "Lucky dotes on Max. It's all about ego—Max is like a little version of her mom." She paused for a breath. "Surely you're invited, considering you're buying The Keys? I can't imagine they wouldn't invite you."

"I keep business separate from social occasions," Armand stated. "And since you are one of the few people who know about my imminent purchase of such a prestigious property, I would appreciate your discretion, and trust that you will not mention it to anyone."

"Naturally," Annabelle agreed, quite flattered that she was in the know, although disappointed that Armand obviously didn't have an invite to the party.

She threw him a sideways glance. He was an attractive man—not movie-star handsome like her dad, who was a well-established movie star, but not bad-looking, in a buttoned-down way.

The mustache would have to go, a new haircut might help, and the way he dressed was old-fashioned and too formal. But she could get him into shape. He'd be quite a prize to return to New York with.

Yes. Tonight she would seal this deal. No doubt about it.

CHAPTER FORTY-THREE

If there was one thing that turned Gerald M. on, it was holding court with an attentive audience hanging on to his every word. He reveled in the spotlight—it shored up his escalating fear that his kind of music was becoming irrelevant. Diddy, Jay-Z, and Akon ruled. Plus, every week a new rap sensation hit the street.

Gerald M.'s manager had not so subtly suggested that he might like to try taking a different direction—maybe make a CD of old standards like Rod Stewart had, or perhaps invite some happening rapper to join him on a track or two. But Gerald adamantly refused to even consider the idea. Soul was his thing. Good old-fashioned soul, which got the women hot and horny and the men laid.

In Europe he was still an enormous star. In America— not so much. Although tonight his fans had come out in force and his assistant had collected an array of panties thrown onstage to prove it.

Gerald M. was feeling on top of everything.

Cookie wasn't. Max was so right: Frankie Romano was a major star fuck. He was all over her dad as if Gerald M. was the second coming. She was being ignored, and it was pissing her off big-time.

Max—who was now back at the table—bit her tongue so as not to blurt out *I told you so. Frankie's always been this way. He's a major loser.*

"What's up with his crap?" Cookie complained. "He's all actin' like a freakin' fan. I can't even watch it!"

"Most people get like that around stars," Max offered matter-of-factly. "When Lucky owned Panther Studios, kissing ass was a daily occurrence."

"He's, like, so ignorin' me," Cookie said, her eyes flashing daggers.

Although Max was trying to concentrate on what Cookie was saying, to her horror she suddenly observed Venus making a grand entrance.

Ohmigod. Lucky's best friend. Billy's soon-to-be ex. Ohmigod!

Quickly turning to Cookie, she said, "Y'know what? We should take off, teach your boyfriend to pay you more attention. Besides, Bobby's getting all uptight 'cause he doesn't want us in the club on account of his precious license, so we can't even dance or score a drink, plus my parents are all over me, so whyn't we hit one of those clubs where we can do what we like an' not be under constant scrutiny."

"Yeah," Cookie agreed, still shooting Frankie dirty looks. "Let's go. I'll show Frankie Romano who he's screwing with!"

Sitting next to Lucky Santangelo, Denver felt all her insecurities come rushing back. Bobby had just told her he loved her, followed by the instant intrusion of the irritating and rude Max, and now Lucky and Lennie Golden had joined them. She was overwhelmed, even more so because Lucky was extremely friendly and nice, not to mention totally stunning.

Likewise Lennie.

It was all too much.

"So . . ." Lucky said to Bobby, smiling warmly across at Denver. "*This* is the woman you've been keeping a big secret."

"No secret," Bobby replied with a sheepish grin. "You've met, haven't you?"

"Maybe once," Lucky said, sipping a martini. "Very briefly."

"Well, *we* certainly haven't met," Lennie said, extending his hand to Denver. "It's a real pleasure. Where has Bobby been hiding you?"

If she was intimidated before, Denver now felt completely out of her depth. Lennie Golden was a force unto himself. She was a longtime fan of his movies, which only made things worse. How embarrassing to find herself trapped in this situation. Wasn't it enough that they would all be together the following night?

Oh God! Why hadn't she pursued a relationship with laid-back, uncomplicated Sam? Why had she picked Bobby?

Or had *he* picked *her?*

She didn't know. She wasn't sure. She was confused.

"Bobby tells me you're a DA," Lucky said, leaning toward Denver as if she were really interested in hearing her reply.

"Uh, Deputy DA, actually. That's what they, uh, call us."

Oh great, I sound like the idiot girlfriend who comes to Vegas with one dress. And now what am I supposed to wear tomorrow night? And Bobby's mom is too gorgeous for words—slim and sexy in a sliver of a top and black leather pants, with numerous diamond bracelets stacked up her toned and tanned arm, and a huge emerald ring on her engagement finger. She looks like some kind of exotic supermodel.

"You should meet my brother Steven," Lucky said. "He's living in Rio at the moment, but when he visits, we must all get together."

What the hell—was Lucky trying to fix her up? *Please, no!*

"Steven was a DA," Bobby hurriedly explained, noting her confusion.

"Really?" Denver murmured.

"Yeah," Bobby said. "You two probably do have a lot in common. Steven started out as a defense attorney, then felt it wasn't right for him—just like you."

"You were a defense attorney?" Lennie asked, and he too seemed genuinely interested.

"Yes," she managed. "With Saunders, Fields, Simmons and Johnson in Beverly Hills."

"And you switched because?"

"I was, uh, one of the defense attorneys for Ralph Maestro. It became . . . complicated."

God, she was actually sitting in a nightclub in Vegas chatting away to *the* Lennie Golden.

"I can imagine," Lennie said, reaching for Lucky's hand and squeezing it.

Apparently they are the perfect couple, Denver thought. *Still in love and don't care who knows it.*

Could she and Bobby ever achieve that kind of closeness?

Yes! Stop wimping out and embrace what we have together.

Before she could give herself more of a pep talk, here came a test in the form of a curvy brunette poured into an equally curvy outfit. The girl approached Bobby from behind, covered his eyes with her well-manicured hands, and cooed, "Guess who?"

To his credit, Bobby didn't panic. He stayed calm, removed the girl's hands, and glanced up at her. "Hey, Gia," he said, without taking a beat. "Have you met my girlfriend, Denver?"

Gia's smile froze. Denver could almost see the thoughts flying through the girl's head. *Girlfriend? What's that about? Bobby's a player. No fun to be had here.*

"No," Gia said at last. "I wasn't aware that you—"

Not allowing Gia to finish her sentence, Bobby was on his feet, walking her away from their cabana.

"Hazard of the business," Lucky remarked dryly, noting Denver's discomfort.

"Excuse me?" Denver said, trying to sound light-hearted.

"Girls throwing themselves at the good-looking boss," Lucky said.

"It doesn't bother me," Denver said, attempting to sound breezy and unconcerned. The last thing she wanted was Lucky feeling sorry for her.

"It doesn't bother me either," Lucky replied. "Girls are always coming on to Lennie. Or at least they used to."

"Hold up," Lennie interrupted, shaking his head. "Whaddya mean, used to? I gotta fight 'em off with a stick."

"Sure, baby," Lucky crooned. "And you better make sure that stick stays in your pants or else!"

"Or else what?"

"You know what."

The two of them giggled like a couple of in-heat teenagers. Denver felt like an intruder on their intimacy; she'd never witnessed two people so into each other.

Bobby returned to the table. Handsome Bobby, so damn hot in a black shirt and pants. Dark hair, intense eyes, strong jawline. Yes, he was a babe magnet, no doubt about it.

"Sorry, sweetie," he said, sitting down.

"Old girlfriend?" Denver questioned, although *old girlfriend* sounded all wrong—shouldn't it be *young sexy girlfriend, who looks like she recently stepped out of a Victoria's Secret catalogue?*

"We went out a coupla times," Bobby admitted. "Nothing serious. And I can assure you it was way before you and me."

"You and I," Denver murmured, adding a succinct, "I have ex-boyfriends too, you know."

"I do know that," Bobby said, playing along. "And I've got the urge to smash 'em in the face if they ever put in an appearance."

"You do?"

"If I have to."

They exchanged a knowing smile.

"So what am I supposed to do about *your* exes?" she asked, feeling better already.

"Ignore 'em," Bobby said. "It's you I'm with, and that's the way it's meant to be." He put his arm around her and pulled her close. "I'm hoping you feel the same way."

"Yes," she murmured. "You know I do."

Giggling hysterically, Cookie and Max piled into a cab, a dour-faced Ace along for the ride. He wasn't happy about getting stuck with Cookie, but he was pleased enough to escape from Gerald M. and his adoring entourage. Hanging with those kinds of people was not his ideal. "Where we going?" he asked.

"There's this club for under twenty-ones. No alcohol served, but awesome sounds," Max offered, thinking that a riotous time on the dance floor was exactly what they all needed. "Harry's new friend Paco is deejaying there sometime tonight. We gotta go check him out."

"What're we waitin' for?" Cookie said, scrolling through the messages on her cell to see if Frankie had missed her yet.

He hadn't.

Well, he wouldn't, would he? Too busy paying homage to Gerald M.

"Who wants a joint?" she asked, digging in her purse.

Ace shook his head as Cookie found what she was looking for and lit up.

"In a cab? Really?" Ace said to Max in a disgusted tone.

"She's upset," Max whispered. "Besides, it's only one little joint. Nobody's going to throw us in jail for *that*."

"You're unbelievable," Ace grouched. "I drive all this way, and this is what we end up doing."

"Sorry," Max retorted. "But you know I wasn't expecting you."

"Thanks a lot," he said restlessly. "You're making me feel so frigging welcome."

Ace's bad mood was getting to her. Wasn't it enough that she'd gotten dumped by Billy? Now she had to put up with Ace and his complaints.

Why couldn't he relax and simply go with it?

CHAPTER FORTY-FOUR

"Did I just see little Max running out of here?" Venus asked as she joined Bobby's fast-expanding table in his poolside cabana at Mood.

"Don't tell me she left," Lennie said, frowning. "That damn kid—I hardly got to see her."

"Ah, the doting daddy." Venus sighed as she slid into the booth beside him. "And might I say that you, Mr. Golden, are looking great as usual. In all the time I've known you, you *never* change."

"I could say the same for you, Venus."

"Then say it."

"You look incredible for an old—"

"Lennie!" Lucky warned.

"I'm teasing her," Lennie said with a big grin. "She knows it."

"Of course I do," Venus said, smiling. "Lennie and me—we've got a special relationship."

"Not too special, I hope," Lucky said.

"What do *you* think?" Venus said. Turning back to Lennie, she added, "How's your movie going?"

"Two more weeks of hard labor and I'm back in L.A.," Lennie said, picking up his drink.

"For about five minutes," Lucky quipped, joining in. "We all know Lennie—he'll be off again soon. It's impossible for him to stay in one place for long. That's how he rolls."

"And that's how you like it," Lennie retorted.

"My husband the workaholic." Lucky sighed. "But that doesn't mean I don't miss you."

"I know, babe," Lennie said. "But if we were together all the time we'd tear each other apart."

"True," Lucky agreed.

"I wish you'd think of writing something for me," Venus said wistfully. "You know how much I'd love to work with you, Lennie."

"As if I'd trust you and your 'special relationship' alone on location with my old man," Lucky said jokingly. "Surely you're aware what they say about best friends?"

Listening to their banter, Denver was in awe. Not only was she sitting with Bobby's illustrious parents, but superstar Venus was now in the house and had joined them too! It was all becoming a little bit surreal. It wasn't as if she hadn't encountered quite a few stars when she'd worked at Saunders, Fields, Simmons & Johnson—after all, it was a major Beverly Hills law firm, and she'd represented some big names. However, this was different. This was up close and extremely personal.

"We'll leave as soon as M.J. gets here," Bobby said, leaning over and whispering in her ear.

"Can I count on that?" she whispered back.

"Yeah. Sit tight. I just gotta go deal with a couple of things." And he was gone—lost in the heady mix of loud music, strobing lights, and clinking glasses.

"Hello," a voice said.

She turned to the man who'd moved in next to her. He was model-boy perfect and quite young.

"I am Jorge," he said, with a strong accent. "I am here with Venus."

"Oh, hi," she said, sensing that he felt as out of place as she did. "I'm Denver. I'm with Bobby."

"Bobby?" he said blankly.

"Uh . . . do you know Lucky?"

"Lucky?" He shook his head. His soulful brown eyes had the look of a lost puppy's.

"Lucky, Venus's friend," Denver explained. "She's Bobby's mom, and, uh, Bobby is my boyfriend."

The word *boyfriend* immediately made her feel uncomfortable. It was so straight out of high school. But he *was* her boyfriend—or maybe *lover* would be a better description.

"Ah," Jorge muttered vaguely.

It would be nice, Denver thought, *if Venus introduced her escort to everyone instead of getting all cozy with Lennie Golden.*

Watching Lennie in person, she'd already decided that he did not disappoint. He might be an older man, but he exuded a George Clooney under-the-radar kind of sex appeal. Lucky did indeed have it all. A mega-successful hotel and casino, a great family, and a smart, talented husband. What more could any woman want?

"We go dance?" Jorge suggested in a surprisingly deep voice.

Was he asking her? Was it inappropriate if she said yes?

He was already up and ready to go; she couldn't just leave him standing there.

"Sure," she said, glancing at Venus, whom she hadn't even met. The platinum-blond star was busy talking to Lucky and Lennie. Would Venus even notice her boyfriend was missing?

Probably not.

Without thinking more about it, she got to her feet and followed Jorge onto the crowded dance floor. Bobby didn't dance—early on in their relationship he'd announced it wasn't his thing. At least there was *something* he didn't excel at.

On the other hand, she loved to dance, and since Jorge was no slouch either, the two of them were soon enjoying themselves to the sounds of Bruno Mars and Alicia Keys.

The Wonderball was one of the most popular clubs on the strip on account of its no-alcohol, no-drugs policy. For a twenty-five-dollar entry fee, all the under twenty-ones could rave until it was time for a total collapse. The Wonderball featured live bands and guest deejays. It was a major mob scene, and naturally plenty of booze and drugs got smuggled in.

When Max, Cookie, and Ace arrived, the club was filled to capacity. They barely made it through before the fire marshal turned up and posted a NO MORE GUESTS sign at the door.

"This ain't too bad," Cookie allowed, gazing around the cavernous space crammed with writhing sweating bodies, the music so loud conversation was an impossibility. "I could get into this," she yelled, heading for the dance floor. "It's like my kinda crazy."

"We're gonna try to find Harry and Paco," Max shouted above the noise. "If Paco's playing, we can hang out in the booth. See you there."

"Right on," Cookie agreed, dancing and checking her phone at the same time, which reminded Max she still hadn't taken her phone off plane mode.

She quickly did so, and immediately saw that she had several text messages.

The first one was from her two younger brothers on their European tour wishing her a happy birthday. The second was from Bobby's niece, Brigette. And the third was from Billy.

YES, BILLY!

Her heart jumped. When had Billy texted her? How come she'd missed it?

WHAT THE FUCK?!

Her hands began shaking as she started to read his message.

Hey, it's me—Billy. Where r u?

I'M HERE. RIGHT HERE!

Been trying to reach u.

REALLY?

I'm in Vegas.

OMG!

Want to c u. Call me.

"What're you doin'?" Ace shouted, making himself heard above the noise.

"Nothing," she said, hurriedly clicking her phone off.

"Are we gonna find Harry or what?" Ace asked.

"Yeah, sure," she yelled back, wondering exactly how she was supposed to make a clean getaway. Billy was in town, and seeing him was her number one priority.

Bobby met M.J. and Cassie at the door. They were with a man in an expensive suit and tinted aviator glasses. He had slicked-back hair and acted as if he and Bobby were old friends.

"Eddie Falcon," he said to Bobby, proffering his hand. "You and I hung out at Brett Ratner's house. You were diddling with two Playboy Bunnies, an' I was flyin' solo."

Playboy Bunnies were not Bobby's style. He had no idea who this Eddie Falcon was, and he didn't much care.

M.J. filled him in as Cassie and Eddie headed off to a table.

"Eddie's the agent Cassie wants to sign with," M.J. explained. "She says he's hot shit."

"More bad timing, huh?" Bobby remarked.

"I figure if she lands herself an agent, it'll make her happy," M.J. reasoned. "Then she can work on her music stuff while she's sittin' around pregnant. You know she's into writing her own songs, so this could be a way t' go."

Sometimes it amazed Bobby that M.J. could be so dense when it came to his wife. She didn't want to have a baby right now. All she wanted was a career. And Bobby had a strong suspicion that nothing M.J. said or did would change her mind. Signing with a smooth, fast-talking agent would only make Cassie more determined to put her career first.

Not my problem, Bobby thought. *I need to get the hell out of here so that Denver and I can spend some special alone time together.*

And just as he was thinking of exactly how he would take his girlfriend on a sweet ride to ecstasy, a hand clapped him on the shoulder and a familiar voice boomed, "Hey, guys. It's me, Frankie. I'm back in town!"

CHAPTER FORTY-FIVE

Having drinks with Paige and Gino was not where Peggy wished to be. In full detective mode, she was primed to seek action regarding her first DNA sample. Then it occurred to her that she needed something from Armand. He'd told her he was busy with important meetings, so if she could just get into his bedroom and take a few strands of hair from his hairbrush . . .

She already knew where the villas were located, and the sooner she got there, the better. But Gino, at his advanced age, did not seem to be slowing down at all. The man was a freak of nature. And was it her imagination, or as Paige imbibed her fourth glass of wine, was Gino's wife becoming a little *too* friendly?

Peggy feigned a yawn and murmured, "You really must excuse me. I'm still on New York time, and I'm afraid it's catching up with me."

"We're gonna let you go on one condition," Gino said gruffly, winking at her.

"And that would be?" Peggy asked politely.

"Dinner again tomorrow night."

"Gino," Paige said, reminding him. "Tomorrow night is Max's party."

"So Peggy'll come t' the party," Gino said magnanimously, once again giving Peggy the wink.

Was it possible that he *did* remember their one night of lust? It was so long ago, and yet . . .

"I think I'd enjoy that," Peggy replied, getting to her feet.

"I'll call you in the morning, then," Paige said, and just like that, before Peggy could react, Paige kissed her full on the lips. After which Peggy beat a hasty retreat.

Carlos the concierge was right about Luscious and Seducta: If it wasn't nailed down, they had an urge to collect.

Seducta carried an oversized fake leather purse she'd recently swiped from K-Mart. It was roomy enough to hold all her favorite things for a rip-roaring night of paid-for sex. Condoms, a double-headed black dildo, and enough lubricant to please an elephant. However, as she flitted around the villa, she still had room to throw in several bars of expensive hotel soap, a couple of crystal shot glasses from behind the bar, and various snacks and several miniature bottles of booze from the mini-bar, plus two marble ashtrays and a couple of rolls of toilet paper. Every little bit helped. Besides, what was wrong with bringing home gifts for Mikey?

Luscious was more discerning. She raided the bedroom and rifled through Armand's personal possessions, grabbing a silk tie still in its cellophane wrap, and two pairs of what looked like solid-gold cuff links. The dude would never notice; he had a shitload of stuff. Too much.

Luscious wondered who he was. Obviously loaded. Probably wanted a show since he'd requested two girls.

Another night, another pervert.

Luscious was up for it as long as Seducta knew how to behave. They'd never worked together in front of a john. There was a rhythm to making sure the client ended up with a satisfactory happy ending.

Luscious knew exactly how to do it. The question was, did Seducta?

* * *

When the Cavendish Hotel was built, the team of architects had created a series of on-the-property luxury villas meant for high rollers only, private and discreet—a golf-cart ride away from the main hotel or, if the guests were so inclined, a walk along a series of leafy pathways.

Armand chose to walk, Annabelle by his side.

"How far is it?" she asked after a few minutes of uncomfortable tottering. "These Jimmy Choos are not made for walking."

Armand ignored her; he had many other things on his mind. The concierge had texted him that the women he'd ordered were waiting in his villa. Perhaps sex would clear his head.

He couldn't wait to see Annabelle's expression when she realized they were not alone.

Would she run out on him?

Or would she stay?

He needed her to stay. She knew the Santangelo family, so that made her useful. Perhaps ignoring her was not in his best interest.

What *was* in his best interest?

His mind was filled with raging thoughts of seeing Lucky Santangelo dead. Shot. The bullet hitting her directly in her loud mouth, the mouth that had dared to insult him.

But how to arrange it?

Fouad would not help. Fouad was a sniveling lackey who thought only about himself. It infuriated Armand that after all these years he could not depend on Fouad.

Enough money would buy him the right person to do the deed, but how to find that person? Would the Internet be of any help? No, probably not.

"I said my feet are killing me," Annabelle repeated, wishing he was a little more attentive.

"Take your shoes off," he suggested, stopping for a moment. "Bare feet can be quite sexual."

"Oh no," Annabelle mock-groaned, hoping to get at least a smile out of him. "Don't tell me you have a foot fetish?"

"Would that bother you?" he asked, testing her.

Annabelle thought for a moment, then leaned up against him while she removed her spike heels. Foot fetish or not, she had him in her sights, and this time she was hanging in there.

Armand seized the opportunity to forcefully kiss her, his tongue darting into her mouth while his hand reached down, making its way roughly up her skirt—heading for ground zero.

She was startled but still game. At least he was interested. This was her shot, and this time she had to make sure it worked out, for unfortunately she had big financial problems. After her somewhat scandalous book was published, her father cut her off, so now money was not exactly falling out of the trees, which meant she needed a man like Armand Jordan to support her and give her credibility. Armand had everything she wanted. Money. Power. Status. And when he became the new owner of The Keys, she would have her own personal playground to entertain her friends. What could be better?

"Easy," she whispered as his thick fingers negotiated a passage past her thong and into her pussy, which was not exactly wet and willing. But she could rally.

Armand Jordan was her major catch of the day.

Peggy elicited the help of a willing desk clerk, who for fifty bucks was only too happy to escort her on a golf-cart ride to Armand's villa and then let her in with a passkey. For who would suspect that this well-groomed woman—loaded with expensive jewelry—was anything other than the person she claimed to be. She'd told him she was Armand Jordan's mother, and that she had to pick up some important papers from her son's villa. He had no reason to doubt her.

"Should I wait for you?" the desk clerk asked.

"That would be lovely," Peggy replied, not relishing the long walk back to the main hotel. "I'll only be a minute or two."

She entered the villa and was shocked to encounter two women of extremely dubious appearance. They were lolling around on high stools by the bar, drinking cocktails and smoking.

Luscious and Seducta were equally shocked to see Peggy.

"Where is Armand?" were the first words out of Peggy's mouth.

"Who?" questioned Seducta, adjusting her mammoth breasts, which were fighting to escape from a lime-green halter top that was several sizes too small.

Luscious, slightly quicker on the draw, said a fast "He's on his way. Who're you?"

Peggy stood tall, trying to hide her dismay that this was the type of women her son was associating with. These women were certainly not ladies; they resembled cheap street hookers, the kind she'd observed acting the part on *Law & Order*.

"I am Armand's mother," Peggy said grandly, walking toward what she assumed was the bedroom.

"Kinky," Seducta muttered.

"Shh," Luscious admonished in a hoarse whisper. "Wouldn't think the old bag's here to stay."

"Then what've we got ourselves stuck with?" Seducta said, gulping down her cocktail. "Some sexed-out freaky momma's boy?"

Luscious shrugged. She wasn't sure herself.

After a few moments, Peggy emerged from the bedroom and hurried to the door. She'd gotten what she'd come for, and she had no desire to run into Armand, not with these two dreadful women present. Her disgust was so palpable that she didn't even bother saying anything as she slipped out the door. Tomorrow she vowed that she would sit down with Armand and discuss with him his choice of female companions. He might be a grown man, but it was blatantly obvious that it was time someone gave him guidance.

She was his mother.

She was entitled.

CHAPTER FORTY-SIX

"We could hit another club," Kev suggested.

"Why'd we wanna do that?" Billy responded.

"What the fuck's t' matter with you, dude?" Kev asked, squinting. "You're acting like you don't wanna do nothin'."

"Maybe I don't," Billy replied. He simply wasn't feeling it, and the more time he spent with Kev, the more his old friend was getting on his nerves. Some people you eventually outgrew. Kev was one of them.

"This is Vegas, man. Freakin' Vegas!" Kev said, venting his frustration. "Land of pussy an' cream."

"So go get yourself some," Billy suggested. "Me, I'm headin' back to the hotel."

"Why'd you wanna do that?" Kev complained. "We should be out there rippin' up this town, tearing it to shreds."

"Like I said, you're on your own. You don't need me."

"Why not?" Kev said, sensing that a fun evening of debauchery was slipping away from him. "You're a pussy magnet. The girls cream their panties just lookin' at you."

"Thanks, Kev," Billy said grimly. "Exactly the description of my talent I was jonesing to hear."

"It's a freakin' compliment, man," Kev insisted.

"Yeah, yeah. Pussy catnip," Billy said, getting more irritated by the minute. "Just the compliment I was hoping for."

"Don't take it the wrong way," Kev said, finally realizing he was pissing Billy off and that it was time to backpedal.

"What way should I take it, Kev?"

"Okay, okay, I get it. We're on our way back to the hotel."

"You can stay here an' do your thing. It's not like I need an escort."

"Yeah, I think you do. All those bachelorette parties goin' on in the hotel lobby. You need me t' run interference."

Billy's cell buzzed. Turning his back on Kev, he fished it out of his pocket and answered.

"Hey," said Max, sounding very young and very excited. "It's me. What are you *doing* here?"

Although Jorge was quite a dancer, after a while Denver could tell he was dying to talk. She was very adept at reading people, and this poor guy seemed so damn desperate, as if he was in way over his head and didn't quite know what to do.

"How long have you and Venus been together?" she asked, not really interested but making conversation anyway.

"Today. Tonight," Jorge said with a helpless shrug. "Not sure about tomorrow."

"Well, if Venus invited you to Vegas with her, then she must really like you," Denver said encouragingly.

"She ignore me," Jorge said glumly. "In front of people, she treat me like pet. Like little dog."

"Oh dear," Denver said sympathetically. "That's not okay."

"She not even introduce me," Jorge complained. "Like I no matter."

"Venus is a big star. I'm sure she doesn't mean it."

"We see," Jorge said resignedly. "I come long way to
be in America, to make success here."

Then, whether she wanted to hear it or not, Jorge
launched into the story of his life.

Denver realized she was trapped, but at the same time
she felt sorry for him, so she remained on the dance
floor and listened.

Frankie Romano in all his boastful glory was quite a
show.

"What up?" he said to Bobby and M.J., happy to see
them.

"Same old," M.J. replied, exchanging a quick fist
pump with his old friend.

"Hey," Bobby said, repeating the gesture. "Long time
no see."

"You two guys, you never change," Frankie said, his
left eye twitching. "Son of a bitch! You both smash it
out the park. A coupla studs."

"You're looking good too," Bobby offered, although
he didn't think so.

"Didja hear?" Frankie said. "I opened my place in
L.A. River. Course, it's nothin' like this setup. Mood
is spectacular, with the pool an' the lights an' the view.
But you gotta gimme kudos 'cause I finally got my
shit together, an' now I'm runnin' my own club, an' it's
flyin'."

Bobby had heard all about River. It was the go-to club
for any drug you desired. Coke, meth, quaaludes, E,
weed, pills. Yeah, sure it was doing okay. L.A. was
an easy town in which to acquire customers for your
wares. Everyone had their secret little addictions—
some of them not so secret.

Jokingly, Bobby had once suggested to M.J. that
they'd be better off opening up luxury rehab centers

than opening clubs. It seemed celebrities were willing to pay thousands of dollars a week just to give the impression that they were clean. More hooking up and illicit pill popping went on in rehab than anywhere else. Then a week out, everyone was back using.

"It's great seein' you guys," Frankie said. "Missed your smilin' faces."

"Glad to hear you're doing well," Bobby said, keeping it neutral. Just because Frankie was in his club didn't mean they had to become close buddies again. Those days were over. In a way, he missed Frankie, but in another way he didn't. Frankie's coke habit had gotten out of control, and from the looks of him, scarey-eyed and emaciated, nothing much had changed.

"You here for the fights?" M.J. asked.

"If I can score me some ringside seats," Frankie said. "Any connections?"

"As a matter of fact," M.J. said, always Mister Nice, "I might be able to help you out."

"That's my main man," Frankie said, clapping M.J. on the back. "You always did have your finger on what's goin' down. An' speakin' of goin' down—you still married?"

"You bet I am," M.J. replied. "Marriage rocks, man."

"How 'bout you, Bobby?" Frankie asked, taking a swig from the glass of vodka he was holding onto. "You still with that little lawyer piece of ass?"

"If you mean Denver," Bobby said, annoyed that Frankie would be so disrespectful, "we're very much together."

"Hey, that's cool. Me, I can never stick with one of 'em for too long. Annabelle was my last big mistake." Another swig of vodka, and a quick glance back at his table to see if he was missing any action. "Right now my thing is movin' on. Lately I'm hangin' with Gerald M.'s daughter, Cookie. You might've seen our pix online. Cookie's young, hot, an' boy, is she ready to *par-tee*—if you get my drift."

"Max's friend?" Bobby said, aghast. What the hell was Frankie doing with a teenager? Corrupting her, no doubt.

"'S right. But believe me, she's one horny little tamale. On the ride here she was—"

"Gotta go," Bobby said, itching to move on for two reasons. One, he remembered why he and Frankie had ceased hanging out. And two, what was Denver doing out on the dance floor with some random dude? He'd just noticed, and he wasn't pleased.

Screw it. Was she trying to prove something?

If so, it certainly didn't fly.

Eddie Falcon wasted no time in making the move over to Bobby's table and concentrating on Venus, which did not sit well with Cassie, who fell into a major sulk. *She* was supposed to be the center of attention. This was *her* night.

Venus was enjoying the attention. Lately she'd been thinking of seeking new representation, and Eddie's timing couldn't be better. She knew of Eddie's reputation, and it was stellar. He was a comer and hungry, the best kind of agent to have working for you.

"I can get you anything you want," Eddie boasted to Venus. "Any*one* you want. Director, star—Clooney, DiCaprio, Depp—you name who you'd like to work with, and I can make it happen."

"Can you, now?" Venus said, not actually falling for it—she'd been in the business too long to believe everything an agent on the make had to say, but she was liking his enthusiasm. Her current representatives were doing nothing for her moviewise, and she was tired of always having to embark on a world tour every time she put out a new CD. With her divorce almost behind her, she was ready to concentrate on her film career, and Eddie Falcon might be just the man to make it happen. Besides, Billy was huge in movies. It was about time she reclaimed her throne.

"What's going on?" Lucky said, inserting herself into the conversation. She'd known Eddie since he'd worked in the mailroom at Panther Studios. He'd always had big ambitions, and she was glad to see he was working it. "Is Eddie promising you the moon?" she asked with an amused grin.

"And the stars," Venus responded with a smile. "Should I believe him?"

"Well," Lucky said, still grinning, "the day you believe a Hollywood agent is the day you should pack your bags and scoot your fine ass out of town."

"Thanks, Lucky," Eddie said. "Nice to have your full support."

The three of them laughed.

"Ah, show business." Lucky sighed. "I do not miss it. Not one little bit."

"I need your help," Max said, cornering Cookie in the ladies' room, where a crowd of underdressed and overmade-up girls jostled for space at the mirrors. The room was smoke-filled even though smoking was not allowed, and the smell of cheap perfume and musty sweat overpowered everything.

"Can you believe the a-hole, like, hasn't even texted me to find out where I am?" Cookie griped, once again checking her phone. "He probably hasn't even noticed I'm missing. What a douche!"

"I could've told you that," Max said, grabbing Cookie's arm, attempting to get her full attention. "But this is about *me*."

"No," Cookie argued, applying blush. "It's about *me* havin' to put up with a dumb-ass famous freakin' dad who gets everyone fallin' all over him. You are so right about Frankie. He's a major star-fucker."

"Listen, I have to get outta here," Max said, wishing Cookie would concentrate for once. "It's totally urgent."

"Why? Where're we goin?" Cookie asked, guilelessly.

"*We* are not going anywhere, that's the whole point. *I* have to get out of here and, uh, meet someone."

"Someone like who?" Cookie asked, her curiosity finally aroused.

"Someone I don't want Ace to know about."

"Woo-hoo! *Now* it's gettin' interesting," Cookie said, her brown eyes lighting up.

"The thing is," Max continued, "there's no way I can pull it off without your help. So you've got to tell Ace that I got an important call from Lucky, and that I had to take off. Okay?"

"You're kiddin', right?" Cookie said, curling her lip. "Like what makes you think I'm gonna do this for you an' you're not givin' me the lowdown on who you're meetin'?"

"It's just a boy," Max said, feeling desperate.

"What boy?" Cookie demanded. "Who is he? Is he hot? Hotter than Ace?"

"Please do this for me, Cookie," Max said, her voice rising. "Tomorrow I'll tell you everything."

"I dunno—" Cookie started to say.

"Screw you!" Max yelled, suddenly losing it. "I've been doing what you want all evening—so get it together and do this one thing for me. Tell Ace I'll see him back at the hotel later, and don't make it seem shady."

And with that she stormed off, leaving an openmouthed Cookie in her wake.

CHAPTER FORTY-SEVEN

As they reached Armand's villa, Annabelle was more or less sure that tonight she would be able to cement herself firmly into his life. This time she was not letting him slip away; he was too valuable a prospect.

She'd allowed him to finger-fuck her on the walk to his villa, and now it was time for her to exhibit her considerable bedroom skills. When she was living with Frankie Romano, he'd often told her that her blow jobs were superlative—the best he'd ever had. Now she had the opportunity to show off her technique (learned from a gay friend when she was fifteen) to Armand. Men loved nothing better than a woman going down on them. Annabelle knew that they considered it the ultimate power trip—a beautiful woman on her knees servicing them, his hand pressed firmly on her head. It was the best.

She recalled that when she and Frankie were running their call girl business in New York, the girls were always full of outrageous stories about their clients and the things they were into. Blow jobs were the number one topic. It seemed that once a man got married, the blow jobs ground to a sudden halt. Too bad, because there were always plenty of working girls ready and able to pick up the slack.

These were the thoughts running through Annabelle's head as they entered the villa, but they came to an abrupt halt when she saw the two half-dressed women lounging on stools by the bar.

"Good evening, ladies," Armand said, not at all surprised that he had company.

"Ladies"! Was he kidding? These two were straight
off Forty-second Street on a bad night.

"Hello there," Luscious said, greeting the client in what
she considered a suitable manner. "Nice t' meet you."

Seducta, who'd imbibed a little too much free vodka,
burped discreetly.

Armand gave Annabelle a sly look. The expression on
her face was all that he needed to fuel his sexual desire.
He walked behind the bar and opened a bottle of champagne. Had to celebrate, for this was about to be an evening to remember. It was his personal celebration of what
he knew was destined to happen to Lucky Santangelo.

Eventually.

It was a done deal.

All he had to do was arrange it.

The phone rang in Peggy's suite. She immediately
thought it was the messenger service she'd ordered to
transport her samples to the DNA testing lab, which, for
a price, had agreed to work on a weekend, enabling her
to get fast results. Only in Vegas.

However, it was not the messenger service, it was
Paige Santangelo.

"I wanted to make sure you got back to your room
safely," Paige said, her voice husky and intimate.

"I did," Peggy replied. "And thank you so much for
a delightful dinner."

"I'm glad you were able to join us," Paige said. "It's
always nice to have new company. Spending time with
Gino can sometimes be . . . difficult."

"Difficult how?"

"Gino is old, he's set in his ways. When he was younger
he was quite a dynamo."

Oh yes, I know! Peggy thought.

"Anyway," Paige continued with a deep sigh, "Gino's not the man he used to be—if you understand where I'm going."

Where are you going? Peggy wondered.

"Can I be frank?" Paige said after a long pause.

"Certainly," Peggy replied, wondering if the messenger was on his way.

"The sad fact of life is that sexually, Gino no longer satisfies me."

And here it comes, Peggy thought. *She's been heading in this direction all night, and I was too preoccupied to get it.*

"I see," Peggy said calmly.

"Do you?" Paige asked, sounding anxious.

"Do I what?"

"Do you understand that I have needs that are not being fulfilled? I'm getting the feeling that you might be in the same position."

Peggy realized that she was being propositioned, and although it was not by a man, it was flattering all the same. Her sex life had been dead on arrival since Sidney's passing, so what would be wrong with indulging in a little Sapphic lovemaking? It wasn't as if she hadn't experienced another woman before, albeit a long time ago—during her fantasy life in the king's palace. Paige might be older, but so was she. And they were both attractive, well-preserved women.

"Your silence is making me uneasy," Paige said. "So why don't we forget I said anything. I will—"

"No," Peggy interrupted, a sudden recklessness flooding her senses. "I . . . I understand exactly what you're saying." She paused. "If you care to drop by for a nightcap, I would be delighted to see you."

"I didn't know you were expecting company," Annabelle said, pointedly waving a stream of smoke away from her face as Seducta blew a series of smoke rings into the air.

"These women are not company," Armand replied, drinking champagne. "They are paid-for whores, here to entertain us. They will do whatever we want. Does that excite you, Annabelle?"

She thought for a moment, realizing that she was heading onto dangerous ground. This was not what she'd expected, not at all. However, if she planned on nailing Armand, it seemed as if she would have to join the party or make a fast exit.

"'Scuse me," Luscious said, hopping off her bar stool with an indignant expression. "We're paid-for, but that don't mean you gotta ignore us. We're people too . . ."

"Take your clothes off and keep your mouths shut," Armand ordered. "Do it now."

And without waiting for a reply, he turned to Annabelle and once again stuck his hand roughly up her skirt.

She automatically pushed his hand away. This was all happening too fast.

"More champagne, please," she said, trying to appear cool in the face of such disturbing circumstances.

"I'll offer you better than that," he said, marching into the bedroom and returning with several small glassine bags of cocaine.

"Shall we?" he said, walking toward the glass-topped coffee table.

Damn! Annabelle thought. *Another Frankie Romano scene. I sure can pick 'em.*

Meanwhile, the two hookers were disrobing in a desultory fashion across the room, flinging their clothes in a corner until they were bare-assed naked except for their shoes. Then they hovered, waiting for instructions.

By this time Armand was alternating swigging champagne and snorting lines, feeling no pain, feeling as if he could take control of the entire world. And he would.

When he'd disposed of Lucky Santangelo, there would be no one to stop him.

On his alcohol- and cocaine-fueled high, Armand was becoming more and more determined that Lucky had to be . . . what was the word that lingered in his mind? Ah yes—*assassinated*.

The word thrilled him; it revolved in his brain like a mantra. The whore bitch deserved to die. And he would be the one to make it happen.

If they were in Akramshar he could arrange to have her stoned to death. Buried in the ground up to her neck while big jagged rocks were thrown at her until she died a painful and slow death. Unfortunately, that wasn't possible in America. What a shame, because Lucky Santangelo was the slut whore of all women. She deserved many punishments.

Lucky was his dear mother pushing her breasts up against him when he was a child, before beating him with a leather strap while her friends looked on.

Lucky was all the whores he'd ever had sex with, the dirty, filthy, disgusting, money-hungry whores.

Lucky was his dumb wife, who'd given birth to children he'd never wanted.

Oh yes, Lucky Santangelo was the woman who deserved to be punished for all of them.

It was only fitting.

And when she was gone, The Keys would be all his, and life would finally be perfect.

CHAPTER FORTY-EIGHT

The moment Lucky spotted Alex entering the club with an attractive Asian girl on his arm was the moment she decided it was time for her and Lennie to split. By this late hour she knew that Alex would've had quite a few drinks, and when Alex had been drinking, anything could happen, so she figured it was wise to get out while the going was good.

But Lennie had other ideas. He wanted to stay.

Lucky knew better than to try to change his mind. Like herself, Lennie did what he wanted, and he wouldn't budge until he was ready to leave.

He and Alex had an edgy relationship filled with macho posturing, for not only did they both have a thing for Lucky, but they were both director/producer/writers. Not that they were in competition with each other. Lennie made low-budget independent movies, while Alex went the studio route and put together big, high-profile movies—usually controversial and generally critically savaged or acclaimed, depending on the critic. The fact that they both did the same thing always made it interesting. They argued all the time, about other people's movies, politics, books, sports—anything they could think of.

Lennie was well aware of how Alex felt about his wife, but he did not possess the knowledge that once—long ago, during the time he'd been kidnapped and Lucky had thought he was dead—she'd actually slept

with Alex. One time. One time only. Alex had never forgotten their one night together. Lucky had tried to put it
behind her. In her mind, it was a regrettable mistake.

"There you all are," Alex said, walking straight over
to their cabana, the pretty Asian girl trotting behind
him. "Can we join?"

"Sit right down," Lennie said, making a magnanimous gesture. "Room for everyone."

Prowling around the edge of the dance floor, Bobby was
experiencing an emotion that was new to him. Jealousy.
He was actually jealous! He could hardly believe it
himself. There was Denver, the woman he loved—the
woman who professed to love him—and she was dancing closely with another man. A handsome and muscular
man.

The deejay was playing some kind of slow smoochy
sound, and the dude on the dance floor was taking full
advantage. He had Denver pulled in close, and it looked
like she was enjoying it.

Fuck it! Bobby was livid. He hit the deejay stand in
a hurry.

"What's this slow-assed shit you're playing?" he demanded. "Change it to something fast, now! You're
turning this place into a morgue!"

Startled, the deejay switched to Pitbull, and Bobby
nodded his approval. He glanced over at the dance floor
to watch them separate, but they didn't.

What the fuck? Was the dude deaf? He still had Denver pulled in close, and she was making no move to get
away.

Bobby felt a jealous burn he'd never felt before, and
he didn't like it. The burn was mixed with a slow-rising
anger, an anger that was telling him to do something.
But what? He'd never found himself in this position be-

fore. Ever since he could remember, girls were always fighting over him. Girls in high school, girls in Greece (where he'd spent the summers with his father's family), girls in college, girls in clubs. Girls, girls, girls. Bobby Santangelo Stanislopoulos. He was always the prize, always the guy they wanted.

So no, he had never actually found himself in this position, and it was a pisser.

He circled the floor, hoping that Denver would notice him. But she didn't, because the dude she was dancing with was talking into her ear while pressing up against her. Meanwhile, everyone else on the floor had split apart.

"What's up, Bobby?" Gia asked, appearing beside him. Sexy Gia, with whom he'd once spent several memorable nights.

"Nothing much," he said.

Gia got it immediately. "Your girlfriend looks like she's having a good time," she murmured with a spiteful gleam in her eye. "Who's the guy? He's cute."

Bobby narrowed his eyes. "Do you know him?" he asked.

"No," Gia replied with a low laugh. "But I'd like to."

In a fit of pure frustration, Bobby took Gia's arm and pulled her onto the dance floor.

Let's see how Denver would like *this* turn of events.

Max took a cab to the Cavendish, where Billy had informed her he was staying in one of the high-roller villas. Of course he was—he was a movie star, and movie stars always scored the best accommodations.

She was beyond excited. Billy had come to Vegas especially to see her, and after the gloom and despondency she'd been feeling about their short time together, this was totally unexpected and more than awesome. She couldn't have wished for a better present.

Billy Melina is my birthday present, she thought. *He flew to Vegas just for me.*

OH . . . MY . . . GOD!

Then she remembered that Ace had also made the trek to Vegas to see her, and she started feeling pretty guilty about the way she was treating him. Ace was a cool guy.

But Billy was cooler.

Shivering at the thought of seeing him again, she wished she'd worn a better outfit. She had on leggings, high boots, a cut-off top, and a slouchy sweater. Cute enough, but nothing spectacular.

Thank God Billy hadn't booked into The Keys. Awkward. She could just imagine Lucky's face if she spotted her darling daughter with the soon-to-be ex of her best friend. Even more awkward, Venus was in town and was obviously going to be at Max's birthday party.

Max felt a twinge of guilt, but only a twinge. It wasn't as if she had come between Billy and Venus. Their divorce was well under way when she and Billy got together.

After the cab dropped her off at the front of the hotel, she made her way through the casino and out the back to the leafy paths that led to the villas.

Billy had sounded totally psyched to hear from her, and if he was telling the truth, he'd come to Vegas only to see her. How great was that?

Okay, Billy, I'm on my way! she thought, and once again she shivered with anticipation.

Frankie did a line or two with Gerald M. in the men's room. They were bonding big-time.

Frankie had no idea where Cookie was, but he figured she was off doing her thing somewhere, and that didn't bother him because he'd already got what he'd wanted out of the relationship—a strong connection with her famous father. He liked Gerald M. The man was a star, and even better, he acted like one.

If Frankie had to make a choice, it would be daddy every time—girls were crawling all over Gerald M. Pretty girls, sexy girls, girls willing to do anything to get up close and personal.

Cookie was cute, but if he really thought about it, she was just a kid, and he was way out of her league.

He was Frankie Romano, after all. He had to reach higher.

Jorge had almost finished his stories of woe—an impoverished childhood, a lack of any adult supervision, begging for food, robbing tourists, sleeping with tourists, and finally his arrival in America and his meeting with Venus.

"She use me," he said vehemently, his handsome face darkening. "I know that."

How about you're using her too, Denver wanted to say. But she didn't, because the more Jorge talked, the more upset he seemed to get.

"Look," Jorge said, gesturing toward their table. "She ignore me. She treat me like ship."

"Shit," Denver murmured, correcting him while thinking that it was time to find Bobby and leave, as he'd promised they would as soon as he'd finished taking care of whatever it was he had to take care of.

Then she spotted him dancing with Gia, and she was rendered speechless.

First of all, Bobby was actually dancing! And not very well at that. Second, why was he on the dance floor with a girl who he'd admitted was one of his exes?

This was unacceptable.

"Excuse me," she said, hurriedly breaking away from Jorge. "There's something I have to deal with."

"I come too?" Jorge asked, a look of dependence in his puppy-dog eyes.

"No," Denver said. "You go back to Venus. I'm sure she misses you."

And she headed toward Bobby and Gia, a determined look on her face.

CHAPTER FORTY-NINE

When Paige knocked on the door to her suite, Peggy couldn't help feeling slightly anxious. Was Paige simply there to talk? Or were matters of sexual gratification on her mind?

Either way, Peggy had decided she would go with it. Why not? She was lonely. She hadn't had sex since Sidney's demise, and she wasn't getting any younger. She also had a son who obviously consorted with prostitutes, a lackluster social life, and no male partners. Besides, she'd never forgotten the softness of the women's lips when they'd exchanged kisses and more in the sanctuary of the king's harem. It was a fond memory.

Although it was late, Paige had changed outfits, and instead of the pale-blue cocktail dress she'd worn earlier, she was clad in leather pants, a black turtleneck, and a brown leather jacket. With her lack of height, pocket Venus body, and cropped copper hair, from a distance she could almost be mistaken for a male. It was obvious Paige was into this. Peggy felt like a novice, and yet at the same time extremely feminine.

She fixed Paige a drink, and they sat on the couch, where Paige proceeded to tell her the story of the time Gino had walked in on her pleasuring his previous wife, Susan Martino. And how, after that, threesomes were quite the norm.

"Gino used to be an amazing lover," Paige confided.

Then she gave Peggy a penetrating look and added, "But you already know that, don't you?"

Peggy felt a blush rise on her cheeks. So Gino *had* remembered. "I . . . I didn't think he would recall that night so long ago," she said. "It was only one time, but yes, I have to admit—he *was* an amazing lover."

"Gino might be old, but he has a steel-trap memory," Paige said, toying with a gold bracelet. "As soon as he saw you, he knew."

"That wasn't why I introduced myself to you," Peggy quickly explained. "It was pure coincidence that it turned out you were married to Gino."

"I'm sure," Paige replied. "But what does it matter? It brought you and me together, and here we are, cozy and alone with no one to bother us."

"Doesn't Gino mind?"

"Gino doesn't know. I tucked him up in bed with a couple of Ambien, and he'll sleep through until morning."

"Oh," Peggy responded as Paige leaned toward her and touched her lightly on the cheek. "Then I guess—"

"You guessed right," Paige purred, her hands moving toward Peggy's still very nice breasts.

Peggy closed her eyes and thought of how pleasant it was to once again be the object of someone's desire.

Luscious was getting fed up. The dude with the snake eyes and snotty attitude might be paying them a shitload of money, but what was the deal leaving them shivering and naked in the corner while he drank champagne and snorted lines with the girl she'd seen on TV a couple of times? What was that?

The only good thing about it was that she'd had the opportunity to check out Seducta's body—the body she figured Randy might possibly be lusting after. Seducta's tits were ridiculous.

Luscious couldn't help smirking to herself. Why would Randy want to go with that when he had her to come home to? She might not have giant fake tits, but at least hers were the real thing.

Although she would never admit it, Luscious was mad that Seducta had gotten Mikey to marry her. She'd been with Randy for almost a year, and he'd never mentioned the word *marriage*. She waited on him hand and foot, never nagged him, and sucked his dick whenever he wanted. Goddammit, Luscious considered herself the perfect girlfriend.

She glanced over at Seducta, who'd now gotten several miniature bottles of scotch from behind the bar and was going through them at an alarming rate.

Drunken twat. Luscious preferred to stay sober, just in case. A girl never knew when a john could go postal and beat the crap out of her. It had happened to her once, and she carried the scars to prove it. Some old rocker dude with a penchant for girls crapping on his face had beaten her up when she'd refused to do what he'd wanted. She'd ended up in the emergency room getting sixteen stitches under her chin, and several on her forehead. Ever since then she'd worn bangs and plenty of makeup so no one noticed, but she knew the scars were there, and that was enough for her to make sure she stayed alert.

She took another quick peek at the john, still hunched over the coffee table snorting coke with his girlfriend— although the girlfriend didn't seem to be as into it as he was. The girlfriend was definitely hanging back.

Luscious felt like laughing out loud. These rich assholes with their delicate little coke habits didn't know dog shit. The real thrill and a way quicker high was smoking crack cocaine. Yeah. That was the shit, and Luscious should know, for she'd been doing it on and off since she was sixteen.

Randy, on the other hand, was into speedballs; he swore they gave him the best high ever. A line of coke followed by a powerful snort of heroin—Randy called it his dream combination, and it certainly put him in a euphoric state.

Luscious had tried it a couple of times. It frightened her, so she was canny enough to stick to the drug she was used to.

Speedballing led her to another planet.

Planet out-of-your-fucking-mind.

"Not for me, thank you," Annabelle said politely as Armand laid out even more lines. She was not a coke freak like Frankie Romano, who'd become so totally dependant on it that it had put her off him. "I would prefer another glass of champagne."

"You would, would you?" Armand replied, slurring his words slightly.

"If it's not a problem," Annabelle said, getting the distinct feeling that maybe Armand wasn't the man of her dreams after all. This entire situation was surreal. The naked hookers in the corner. The mounds of cocaine on the table. Eddie Falcon might have cheated on her, but as far as she could tell, he wasn't into prostitutes and drugs.

She wondered where Eddie was. They'd had a knock-down, drag-out fight and she'd walked out on him, but there was nothing to stop her from walking right back in. It wasn't too late.

Armand was making no move to pour her another glass of Cristal. She could tell the hookers were getting restless, especially the little one with the bad dye job and various tattoos on her skinny body. Where on Earth had Armand found these two freaks? And what were his plans for them?

Annabelle made a quick decision: whatever his plans,

she did not wish to be included. A fast exit was in her future.

"Excuse me," she said, getting up. "Just using the little girls' room."

As she walked by the two hookers, she attempted to avert her eyes. But she knew they were staring at her, checking her out, wondering what the scene was.

Her skin crawled.

She made it to the bathroom, locked the door, took out her cell, and called Eddie. Fortunately, he picked up, although she could barely hear him, as there was a cacophony of noise in the background.

"Where are you?" she asked.

"You calmed down yet?" he questioned.

"Have *you?*" she countered.

"I'm at Mood with an interesting group," he said. "You wanna join me?"

"You know what, I think I do," she replied, relieved that he didn't seem to be holding a grudge. She'd yelled some vile names at him, but that's what she liked about Eddie, he was basically a smart guy with a red-hot future. If she could wean him off cheating, they might make it as a couple. "I'll be there soon."

Back in the living room, Armand had finally decided to utilize the services of the two prostitutes. They were not exactly what he'd required—not the usual high-end call girls he was used to—but he was too drunk and coked-out to care.

"The whores are going to dance for us," he announced to Annabelle, patting a place beside him on the couch. "That's before I fuck the life out of them."

Wonderful, Annabelle thought, perching on the edge. *This is exactly where I don't want to be.*

Armand raised his arm, snapping his fingers at Luscious and Seducta. "Over here," he commanded. "Now!"

CHAPTER FIFTY

There were times Denver discovered a boldness within her that usually only came out when she was in full control in the courtroom, a place she loved to be. She considered herself a low-key kind of girl, not prone to outbursts of any kind. However, the sight of Bobby dancing with a vaguely triumphant Gia was enough to spur her into action. After dumping Jorge—who was getting on her nerves anyway—she made it over to Bobby, who pretended not to see her approaching.

"Hey," she said, tapping Bobby firmly on the shoulder. "I thought we were leaving."

"Yeah," he answered, barely looking at her. "We will. Just catching up with Gia. See you back at the table."

"Really?" Denver said coolly. "Is that what you'd like me to do? Go back to the table?"

"Sure, hon," he said, determined not to fold. "Maybe your, uh, friend'll walk you there."

"Friend?" she questioned.

"The dude you were locked on the dance floor with all night."

Oh wow, so that's what this is all about. How dumb.

"I guess you must mean Venus's sad-sack boyfriend," she said sharply.

"I don't give a fuck who he is," Bobby responded, completely out of character for him. "You were with him all night."

Gia, in all her Victoria's Secret sexiness, tugged on Bobby's arm and said, "Are we dancing or not?"

Bobby was torn. Should he stay on the dance floor with Gia, or show Denver that she couldn't get away with dissing him?

Before he could decide, Denver took off.

Shit! He'd called the wrong shot. Denver wasn't into playing games; he should've known that.

Ace was not happy about Max running out on him, and Cookie wasn't happy being the one who had to tell him. She was also livid that Frankie had made no attempt to contact her. He was probably so far up her daddy's ass that there was no room for thought. What a major dick. She should've listened to Max.

As soon as she gave Ace the bad news, he told her he was leaving.

"Where're you goin'?" she asked, thinking that it might be a good idea to tag along.

Ace shrugged. He wasn't in the mood for company, especially Cookie's. "I'm taking a walk," he said shortly.

Cookie nodded. Walking wasn't her thing. "See you back at the hotel, then," she called after him as he strode away.

"Yeah," Ace said over his shoulder. "Later."

Cookie wondered who Max was hooking up with. It had to be someone special for her to dump Ace in such a brutal way. After all, the poor guy had driven all the way to Vegas just to spend time with her.

Still thinking about it, Cookie made it to the deejay booth, where Harry was rocking out with Paco. She thoroughly questioned Harry, but he didn't know anything either, so once again she checked her phone for messages. Nothing. Nada.

Screw Frankie Romano. He was now number one on

her shit list. If he thought he was sharing a bed with her tonight, he had another thought coming.

Getting rid of Kev was not easy. He was determined to visit more strip clubs and generally party, but the problem was that he didn't want to do it without Billy's movie-star presence. So when Billy said he was heading back to the villa, Kev announced that he would come too.

"No," Billy said resolutely.

"No what?" Kev said, his eyebrows shooting up.

"Change of plans," Billy said, walking to the curb and hailing a cab. "You can't come back to the villa with me."

"Why?" Kev asked, a blank expression on his face as he tried to figure out what was going on.

"It's not cool. I'm expecting someone an' I don't want you around."

"You *gotta* be shittin' me," Kev said, dumbstruck.

"I'm not."

"C'mon, man," Kev pleaded. "There's two friggin' bedrooms. I'll shut myself in mine, an' whoever you got comin' over won't even know I'm there."

"It ain't gonna happen," Billy said. He'd made up his mind that this time everything would go smoothly; no Kev around to screw things up. "Go book yourself a room at the hotel. Tell 'em to charge it t' me."

"Seriously?" Kev said, shocked that he was getting dumped.

"Sorry, Kev," Billy said, getting in the cab. "That's the way it's gotta be."

Furious at Bobby, Denver decided against going back to the table. Bobby had made her so mad; what kind of childish game did he think they were playing? He knew she was insecure about the legions of women he'd probably slept with, and just because she'd felt sorry for Venus's young stud, he'd deemed it necessary to hit the dance floor with one of his many exes. A drop-dead gorgeous ex at that.

He'd made a stupid move, and she wasn't playing.

Besides, she was not thrilled with the way their so-called romantic weekend was progressing. Whatever happened to their intimate dinner for two? Not only had it failed to take place, but instead she'd been stuck with M.J.'s young wife, trying to talk her out of getting an abortion. After that she'd had to sit at a table in Mood, surrounded by Lucky and her famous husband and friends, while Bobby was off somewhere attending to club business. It was all too much.

After confronting him, she'd needed breathing space, so she'd simply taken off.

Now she was adrift in the middle of the Keys casino and she had no idea what to do next.

"I like your girlfriend," Lennie remarked when Bobby finally returned to the table. "She's a smart one, and beautiful too. You should hang on to her. How come I haven't met her before?"

"Could be 'cause you're always away on location," Bobby replied, checking the group out and not seeing Denver. Where was she now? The dude she'd been dancing with was sitting beside Venus, who seemed more interested in talking to Eddie Falcon. "Uh . . . have you seen her?" Bobby said to Lennie, his eyes still searching.

"You're asking *me?*" Lennie said, raising a caustic eyebrow. "She's *your* girlfriend. Gotta keep tabs on this one. She's a keeper."

"*Who's* his girlfriend?" Lucky inquired, leaning

over Alex, who'd decided to sit himself down right next to her.

"The smart one," Lennie said. "She gets my seal of approval. How about you?"

"Whatever Bobby wants, Bobby gets," Lucky said with a warm smile at her son.

"Just like you, Lucky," Alex said, nursing a large tumbler of scotch.

"And you know that, do you?" Lennie retorted, putting a proprietary arm around Lucky's shoulder.

"I know it 'cause we're best friends," Alex said, refusing to back down.

Here we go, Lucky thought. *The two bulls are about to go at it. Why couldn't we have left when I wanted to?*

"Y'know, Alex, you're so full of crap," Lennie said. "What makes you think Lucky's your best friend?"

"Does it bother you?" Alex taunted. "Make you anxious that while you're away—"

Lucky stood up. "Both of you, shut the fuck up," she said, her tone brooking no argument. "What's wrong with you, Alex? I told you earlier, you're out of line, so zip it with the childish comments. I gave up having best friends in seventh grade."

Alex scowled and turned to the Asian girl sitting on his other side.

Lennie looked amused.

Bobby left the table, deciding that Denver must be in the ladies' room.

"Can we go now?" Lucky asked, turning to Lennie. "I think this evening has just about peaked."

"You do?" Lennie said calmly. " 'Cause I think it's only just beginning."

Damn Lennie. He could be the most stubborn man on the planet. And maybe that's why she loved him so much, because he never jumped at her command.

Well, if he was set on getting into it with Alex, that was his problem.

Lennie could be infuriating, but Lucky knew that she wouldn't want him any other way.

CHAPTER FIFTY-ONE

"Dance," Armand commanded, glaring with unfocused eyes at the two naked creatures who stood before him. The images he had of them were not quite clear.

Were these two what he'd ordered? He vaguely remembered requesting big breasts, but this fat sow was not up to the usual standard of girls Yvonne Le Crane sent over, nor was the thin one.

It didn't matter. Putting Annabelle together with these two would be enough to amuse him; they were only whores, after all. And when he had them all exactly where he wanted them, perhaps he'd join the party.

Right now his mind was taking him on a trip. He was imagining ejaculating all over Annabelle's pert face. He'd pretend she was Lucky Santangelo and defile her in every possible way he could think of. Then he'd make the whores defile her too.

Yes, he'd do all the things to Annabelle that he really wanted to do to Lucky Santangelo, the whore bitch of them all. He'd fuck them over until they begged for mercy.

It was their destiny.

It was his destiny too.

After all, he was Prince Armand Mohamed Jordan, soon to be king of Akramshar. No woman would ever disrespect him again. THEY WOULDN'T DARE!

Armand had his plans, and he was sticking with them.

* * *

Luscious did not appreciate the john barking orders at them like they were his slaves. They were performing a service, so surely he should treat them better. But he was a man, and early on she'd learned that all men were pigs—there were simply different degrees of piggery.

Seducta didn't give a damn, because by the time Armand summoned them she was so drunk that she couldn't care less how she was treated as long as she got her money at the end of the gig. Dirty Den had informed them that he would hold on to their money until the job was completed, which was okay with Luscious. That way they wouldn't have to wrangle it out of the client, and maybe the john would hand over a fat tip when he was finished with them, which she hoped would be soon, because they'd already been there for over an hour, and it was almost midnight.

She wondered what Randy was doing. At least he wasn't getting the opportunity to go chasing after Seducta and her giant tits. A drunken Seducta was safely here with her, and boy, could she put it away. Luscious hadn't realized what a lush Seducta was. It sort of gave her a stab of satisfaction to know that *she* was the sober one, she was the one in charge.

"We gotta have music if you want us t' dance," she said to Armand, determined to move this show along.

He grunted.

Without waiting for permission, she went over to the music system and activated the sound. Loud sound. Eminem and Rihanna together on "Love the Way You Lie."

Oh yeah, her kind of song. She admired the way the sexy singer who'd gotten herself beaten up had bitch-slapped Chris Brown with this track. It fuckin' rocked.

Seducta was standing in front of Armand and Annabelle like a dumb sack of shit, gazing longingly at the mounds of coke.

"You want some of this?" Armand offered, his blood-shot eyes raking her over. "You want some, come and get it."

Seducta didn't need asking twice. She rushed forward and knelt on the other side of the coffee table to take a snort, and before she knew it, Armand was on his feet, his hand was on the back of her head, and he was shoving her face down onto the table and into the white powder.

Instinctively, Luscious jumped forward and pushed him off her. He spun around and slapped her hard across the cheek.

Seducta surfaced, spluttering and choking, her face a mess of white powder.

"You bastard!" Luscious yelled. "You could've suf-focated her."

Armand laughed, an evil laugh. He felt powerful and invincible. He *was* powerful and invincible.

"I'm ready now," he said, sitting back down. "Dance for me, ladies, before I'm forced to punish you even more."

Annabelle watched what was going on in horrified si-lence. She was shocked by Armand's behavior. He was a crazy man, and there was no doubt in her mind that she had to get the hell out. Fast. Armand Jordan was a definite sicko, and things could only get worse.

It occurred to her that she should've escaped on her first trip to the bathroom, but something had held her back. She'd honestly thought that since he was with her, he would have sent the two women away, but it hadn't happened.

Now he was manhandling them, and forcing them to dance.

It was a horrible, disgusting scene. She wanted out. She wanted to get back with Eddie.

*   *   *

To go or stay? That was the quandary Luscious found herself faced with. Her cheek stung where the john had slapped her, and Seducta was a sloppy mess. But the money was too good to risk getting stiffed. Dirty Den might have to give it back if they ran out on this jerk. So since he seemed to have settled back on the couch, Luscious reluctantly started with a few lackluster stripper moves, encouraging Seducta to do the same.

Suddenly his girlfriend rose to her feet, mumbled something about having left her phone in the bathroom, and hurried past them.

Luscious had a hunch that she wasn't coming back, and Luscious's hunches never let her down. At the age of fifteen, while she was blowing a preacher, he'd stopped her mid-blow and informed her she had psychic powers and that what she was doing to him was God's work. "You must visit me every day," he'd insisted. "It is God's will."

So she'd done so, until eventually he'd moved away.

To this day she still believed in her psychic abilities. After all, wasn't it her who'd told Randy he was going to do better this year? And sure enough, Mikey had given him a job. Okay, so delivering drugs wasn't the greatest job in the world, but it was a whole lot better than the lowdown crap he'd been into before.

Yes, she was definitely psychic, and if she knew anything at all, it was that the stuck-up bitch wasn't coming back.

After rushing past the dancing hookers, Annabelle made it into the bathroom, where she quickly locked the door and leaned against it, catching her breath. What a nightmare scene. She had to get out now.

Earlier, she'd noticed a large window above the Jacuzzi tub, and rather than get into a fight with Armand—for she suspected that if she told him she was leaving, he would not let her go quietly—she decided the window was the perfect way out.

Removing her high heels and stuffing them in her purse, she gingerly stepped into the tub, and from there she scrambled onto the surrounding marble ledge, opened the window, and, since it was higher than she'd anticipated, tumbled out onto the damp grass outside and into an arrangement of small palms.

Cursing softly to herself, she jumped up, got herself together, and set off down the path toward the main hotel.

The thought of getting back together with Eddie Falcon was looking more appealing every minute.

Unable to sleep, Fouad tried, but the tossing and turning would not allow him to fall into a peaceful slumber. He realized that he was so used to being at Armand's beck and call that not hearing from him for at least twelve hours was disturbing.

Armand's words kept playing in his head: *I will see Lucky Santangelo die before she gets the better of me.*

Empty threats, of course, but Armand was definitely veering out of control with his excessive drug use. An intervention was needed, and it had to happen soon.

Then it came to Fouad. He decided that in the morning he would tell Armand's mother everything: the drugs, the prostitutes. He might even tell her about Armand's family in Akramshar, although he knew if he did that, Armand would never speak to him again.

Perhaps it was wise just to inform her about the drugs. Not too much information all at once.

Armand Jordan desperately needed help, and as far as Fouad was concerned, Peggy was the only person he would listen to.

Now Fouad could sleep, for with tomorrow would come the solution.

CHAPTER FIFTY-TWO

Annabelle Maestro was the last person Max expected to run into as she made her way down the leafy pathway heading to Billy's private villa.

Annabelle seemed equally taken aback to see her.

They both stopped, both tried to think of a quick excuse as to why they were there at midnight.

"Hi," Annabelle said at last.

"Uh . . . hi," Max said, thinking that Annabelle did not look like her usually sleek self. She was somewhat disheveled, and for some unknown reason she was carrying her shoes.

"Aren't you at the wrong hotel?" Annabelle asked. "Isn't The Keys where you should be?"

"Just, uh, visiting friends," Max said vaguely.

"Me too," Annabelle replied, equally vague.

"Why are you barefoot?"

"'Cause my shoes are killing me."

"Oh yes, I know the feeling."

There was an awkward pause.

"You've got a birthday coming up," Annabelle remarked. "That's exciting."

"Tomorrow, actually."

"Happy birthday."

"Thanks."

"I hear Lucky's throwing you a big party."

"That's right," Max said, wondering if Annabelle was fishing for an invite, because if she was it couldn't happen on account of Cookie being with Annabelle's ex now.

"How nice," Annabelle said.

"It is," Max agreed.

"Well, uh, have a good one."

"You too."

They both scuttled off in different directions, happy to make their respective escapes.

After waiting around outside the ladies' room for a good ten minutes, Bobby tracked down M.J. and told him he was leaving.

"What happened to Denver?" M.J. asked.

"Think she's mad at me. She took off."

"Don't tell me the great Bobby S. got himself dumped," M.J. said, laughing. "Finally! There is a God!"

"Go fuck yourself," Bobby said, shaking his head. "She's probably waiting for me in the room."

"You hope."

"I *know,* man. She's got nowhere else to go."

"She could hop a plane back to L.A. Denver's not one to put up with your crap."

"What crap?"

"Half the club saw you dancing with Gia. She's on the cover of *Sports Illustrated;* she's kinda high-profile."

"C'mon, man, it was nothing."

"Yeah, tell *that* to your girlfriend."

Bobby hurried from the club and out into the main hotel, where he took the private elevator up to their floor.

To his chagrin, their room was empty. No Denver. But the good news was, her clothes were still there, along with her laptop and her phone. It was no wonder he'd never got an answer when he'd tried to reach her on her cell.

Dammit! Was she going to make him sit and wait for her?

Apparently so.

* * *

Grabbing a cab outside the Cavendish, Annabelle set off for The Keys. She couldn't believe what she'd almost got herself into. Drunken dancing hookers. An excessive amount of cocaine. A crazy sex fiend with cold, hard eyes and a definite cruel streak. What was she thinking?

Oh yeah, right. She was thinking that Armand Jordan might be the catch of the day. How wrong she'd been about *that*.

Then on top of everything else, she'd run into Lucky's daughter. Where was Max going at such a late hour?

Not her concern.

After paying off the cab, she entered The Keys and headed straight for the ladies' room, where she attempted to clean herself up. Her white Chanel skirt had a few streaks of mud on it, and she realized she should've stopped off and changed. Too late now. She didn't want to miss meeting up with Eddie, so after touching up her makeup and brushing her hair, she headed for Mood.

Armand Jordan was just a distant creepy memory.

Lennie and Alex were embroiled in one of their favorite arguments—about the death penalty. Alex was for it, Lennie against, and neither of them was prepared to give an inch. Lucky had heard it all before, and since she wasn't prepared to take sides, she moved over to sit with Venus, Eddie, M.J., and Cassie. Jorge was perched uncomfortably at the end of the table.

"So *that's* your little plaything," Lucky observed, checking out Jorge.

"Not so little," Venus replied with a wicked grin.

"You do know you're ignoring him."

"He'll get plenty of attention later," Venus said, fluffing out her platinum hair. "Besides, Bobby's girlfriend was entertaining him."

"She was?" Lucky said, surprised. "How did Bobby feel about *that*?"

"How would *I* know? *You're* his mother. And if you weren't, believe me, he'd be next on my list of things I have to do."

"Calm down, he's way too young for you," Lucky said with a low chuckle.

"Sorry to disappoint, only the way I'm going, Bobby is exactly the right age."

"Yes, I seem to remember that you've always had a crush on him."

"This is true," Venus confessed with an unabashed grin.

"At least you admit it."

"And *you* have to admit that your son is one hot catch."

Lucky nodded. "You got that right, which is why he has to be careful to avoid any girls who happen to be on the make. He's rich, he's handsome, and he's available. What do you think of Denver?"

"Didn't get a chance to talk to her."

"She seems to be making Bobby happy," Lucky mused. "I think I might like her."

"How nice," Venus drawled. "Maybe they'll get married and give you a bunch of sweet little grandbabies."

"Get the fuck outta here," Lucky said good-naturedly. "Bobby's got a lot of living to do before he even *thinks* about settling down."

"Ohhh . . . Momma Bear's *veree* protective," Venus said, laughing, before adding a succinct "And here comes trouble."

Lucky glanced up to observe Annabelle Maestro approaching their table. They all knew Annabelle from her days with Frankie, her famous parents, and her very public confessional book.

"Remember what the late great Andy Warhol said

about fifteen minutes of fame?" Venus remarked, slow-ing sipping a cocktail. "Well, this one is milking it for the number one prize. I feel sorry for her father."

"You feel sorry for Ralph Maestro?" Lucky said, aghast. "Why would you feel sorry for him? He mur-dered his wife, for God's sake. He should be sitting in jail alongside O.J."

"He *arranged* her murder," Venus pointed out. "It's not the same."

"Damn!" Lucky said, shaking her head in amaze-ment. "You should go sit with Lennie. The two of you can discuss the advantages of having murderers walk the streets. What fun you can have."

"Excuse me, everyone," Eddie said, standing up as Annabelle arrived at the table. "I'd like you all to meet my girlfriend, Annabelle Maestro."

"Hey," Billy said.

"Hey," Max responded, standing at the door to his villa, feeling a tad shy.

Loud music was blaring from the villa across from them, a lizard darted in front of her, and there was a brisk night breeze. She shivered, Billy smiled, and all was well in Max's world.

"Can I get a hug?" he said, his intense blue eyes draw-ing her in.

You can get anything you want, Billy Melina.

"Of course you can," she said, falling into his arms, immediately forgetting how much she'd been hating him.

He hugged her, then led her inside. "Someone's hav-ing a party over there," he remarked.

"Sounds like it," she said, breathless at the sight of him.

He shut the door and they stared at each other.

"Sorry about L.A.," he said at last.

"What about it?" she said, keeping it casual.

"Well, y'know," he explained. "I kinda let you get away."

"From what?" she asked, going for the flippant approach.

"Then you took off."

"I told you I was coming to Vegas."

"Why d'you think I'm here?"

"Really? Just to see me?"

"Yeah, really." And he moved in for a kiss that dispelled any doubt that she was doing the right thing.

"We're going," Venus announced, standing up and signaling Jorge that it was time to leave. He had a resentful scowl on his boyishly handsome face. She'd ignored him all night, and now she was summoning him to come with her like a pet dog.

He got up anyway, and stood stiffly beside her. He had no alternative.

"I'll be in touch," Eddie said to Venus, jumping to his feet and bowing and scraping a little. Landing Venus as a client would be a huge coup. "We can do great things together."

"I'm sure," Venus murmured. "All you have to do is prove it to me."

"I can do that, all right," Eddie said with a boastful smirk. "You won't be disappointed."

"We'll talk."

"We certainly will."

He sat back down, a satisfied expression on his face.

"Did you just poach Venus from her agent?" Annabelle asked, quite impressed.

"Not yet, but I will," Eddie said, full of confidence, and quite unaware of where his girlfriend had spent the last few hours.

"Congrats," Annabelle said. "I'm proud of you."

"That's a change from calling me a cheating asshole."

"You know I didn't mean it."

"How about I get that in writing?"

"Spoken like a true agent," she giggled.

God! she thought. *It's so nice to be back among normal people.*

She turned to Lucky. "I understand I should be congratulating you too," she said, delighted to have the opportunity to hang out with Lucky Santangelo.

"Why's that?" Lucky asked, looking around to see where Bobby was.

Annabelle lowered her voice. "I know it's supposed to be a big secret and all, but I heard that you're selling The Keys."

"*Excuse* me?" Lucky said, startled.

"Please don't worry. I won't say a word."

"I'm not worried, I'm confused. Who told you this?"

Annabelle glanced quickly at Eddie. He was busy talking to Lennie and Alex. "Uh . . . Armand Jordan. I ran into him at the casino."

"*My* casino?"

"No. Over at the Cavendish. He's staying in a villa there." She paused. "I'm so sorry. I guess I shouldn't have said anything. Armand swore me to secrecy."

"About what?"

"That he's buying The Keys, and the deal will be set tomorrow."

"You *are* kidding me, aren't you?"

"No, I'm not," Annabelle said, feeling a slight shiver of apprehension because the deep anger in Lucky's eyes was unmistakable. "I'm simply repeating what Armand told me."

"Where do you know this man from?"

"New York. We, uh, went out a couple of times."

"How *well* do you know him?" Lucky asked, her dark eyes glowing.

"Not . . . uh, not that well. He's more of an acquaintance than a friend," Annabelle stammered, realizing that she had probably said the wrong thing. Lucky did not seem at all happy about it.

"Then if you know him at all, you know he's a misogynistic, lying, delusional scumbag."

Alex leaned in for the end of Lucky's speech. "Talking about me again," he said with a wry grin.

"You wish," Lucky said, abruptly standing. She beckoned M.J. "I need to make a private call. Take me to the office."

"Certainly," M.J. said, jumping to his feet. "Follow me."

"I think I just pissed Lucky off," Annabelle said to Eddie.

"Well, darlin'," he replied. "Seems you're an expert at doing that. C'mon, let's dance. I'm in a celebrating mood."

CHAPTER FIFTY-THREE

It was a while before Armand realized Annabelle wasn't coming back. By this time he was blurry-eyed from too much cocaine, too much booze, too much of everything.

"Where is she?" he demanded of Luscious, who was using a tall potted palm as a makeshift stripper pole.

Luscious stopped what she was doing and said a ladylike "We gonna fuck or what?"

By this time Seducta had almost passed out. She was slumped on the floor, her eyes half closed.

It was a sorry scene, but Armand was too high to even notice.

"Where is she?" he repeated, rising from the couch, swaying slightly, almost losing his balance altogether.

"Your girlfriend took off an hour ago," Luscious offered, leaving her potted palm and moving over to him. "Least I *think* she did. Either that or she's dead in the bathroom." Luscious snickered. Wouldn't *that* be something. Another psychic revelation. Although if the girlfriend was dead, best not to hang around.

"Bathroom?" Armand questioned. He wasn't thinking straight at all. His heart was pounding, and he felt nauseous.

"Yeah," Luscious said. "She went in there. Want I should take a look?"

"Why?" Armand said, giving her a hard stare.

"See if she's there."

"Do you have a gun?"

"'Scuse me?"

Armand threw her a disdainful look. "A gun?"

Luscious wrinkled her nose. This motherfucker was sicker than she'd thought. Although she preferred him in this state than the way he was when he'd slapped her and Seducta around. "Whaddya want a gun for?" she inquired, thinking it might be smart to humor him.

"Because," Armand stated mysteriously.

"'Cause what?"

"Because I have time to kill," he answered grandly.

Shit! He was off his rocker—something her mom used to say when the old cow was sober enough to say anything at all. What the hell. He was either a stark raving loony or a dangerous psycho.

"You're not lookin' so hot," she ventured. "You'd better sit your ass down."

"Are you aware that I have more money than you'll ever see in your lifetime?" Armand boasted, reaching into his pocket and pulling out a stack of hundred-dollar bills. "You're a whore, you should appreciate money," he added, tossing a handful of bills at her.

The money fluttered around her naked, skinny, tattooed body before falling to the ground.

This nut job with the snake eyes was definitely crazy.

She squashed the urge to bend down and snatch the money up.

Seducta wasn't so patient. After watching the money fall, she began crawling over on all fours to collect.

Luscious wasn't having it. Before Seducta could get there, she quickly bent down and scooped up as much money as she could. *Holy fuck!* she thought, cramming the bills together. *There has to be a coupla thou here. This asshole is loco for sure.*

"A gun," Armand said. "I wish to obtain a hired gun. Do you know where I might find such a service?"

"Why?" Luscious said boldly. "You gonna shoot your girlfriend?"

"What makes you think that you can speak to me in such a fashion?" Armand said, glaring at her, a disdainful look on his face. "Do you not *know* who you are addressing?"

"You di'n't give me your name," Luscious said, noticing a couple of hundred-dollar bills she'd failed to pick up.

"Not a name," he announced with another grand gesture. "A title. Prince Armand Mohamed Jordan, soon to be king of Akramshar."

"Sure, honey," Luscious said, carrying on humoring him while grabbing her purse and stuffing the money inside. "Whyn't I just call you Arnie?"

"A hired gun," Armand continued, nodding to himself. "To kill an enemy of the people. Get me that, and money is no object."

"No object, huh?" Luscious said, a thousand jumbled thoughts running through her head. "Y'know what, Arnie? I gotta hunch you might have yourself a deal."

Randy Sorrentino lay back on a lounger (a couch that was about to fall off the back of a truck was being delivered next week), abstractedly stroking his cock and balls while a *Real Housewives* of somewhere episode played on the TV in front of him. Rich pieces of ass with tight faces, plastic bazooms, and stupid fuckhead husbands made it a trip to watch. Plus, he liked checking out their over-the-top houses to see how easy it would be to break in and relieve them of some of their stuff. They all had too much stuff. A little sharing wouldn't hurt.

Randy was done for the day. He'd taken care of business, and now he could relax until Luscious got home.

His girlfriend of almost a year was a piece of work. She catered to him like no other woman ever had before, and that was saying something, because there had been a lot of women. Oh yeah, too many to remember, especially when he'd been into making porn flicks and there'd been an assembly line of fresh gash every week—each girl desperate to make it as the next Jenna Jameson.

Yeah, Luscious was different, and if it weren't for her crazy jealous streak, he might have even considered making it legal between them. But the jealousy thing turned him off. He couldn't help that he'd been endowed with a huge piece of meat. It wasn't his fault that plenty of women wanted to give it a good old chewing.

For instance, Seducta was always coming on to him, rubbing her big tits up against him, whispering dirty messages in his ear, trying to grab a quick feel, suggesting that they'd make a fine team.

No way. She was married to his older brother, and Mikey, like Luscious, was jealous as shit. So Randy attempted to steer clear, but Seducta was relentless. She kept pushing, and lately Luscious seemed to think that it was *him* coming on to Seducta.

It was a fucked-up situation, and if Mikey got wind of it, he'd beat the crap out of him. Which would be a shame, because over the past couple of months he and Mikey had patched up their differences and were getting along fine, which hadn't always been the case. Right now they had a lucrative drug business going, which suited both of them. It was steady money, which made a pleasant change.

Randy was considering whether or not to whack off, when his cell phone buzzed.

It was Luscious.

"What?" he said impatiently.

"Get your ass over here," she said in a hoarse whisper, her voice rising with excitement. "We got ourselves a live one. An' bring the crack pipe, your piece, an' your big old self. We're about to make us some *real* money."

CHAPTER FIFTY-FOUR

Son of a bitch! Lucky thought. *Son of a motherfucking bitch!* What kind of balls did Armand Jordan possess, going around telling people that he was buying The Keys? No fucking way was she letting the asshole get away with it. He was dealing with the wrong woman.

She'd known he was trouble the moment he'd set foot in her office with his "women are inferior" attitude and smug expression. What a dumb prick! And in Lucky's world, if a prick had the temerity to challenge her, she was up for it. Oh yes, nobody got away with this kind of shit. To think that he had the nerve to go around saying that tomorrow The Keys would be his. This was something she had to put a stop to immediately. She didn't care that it was way past midnight, this was too infuriating to wait. It had to be dealt with *now*.

She didn't tell Lennie where she was going, because Lennie—always the voice of reason—would've tried to stop her. And right now she was in unstoppable mode.

Instead she tried calling Danny. But Danny wasn't home—Danny was at a gay club with Buff, dancing the night away. She sent a text message to his cell.

Next she called Jeffrey Lonsdale, who also failed to answer. Jeffrey was in bed with an attractive divorcée he'd met at the blackjack table, and he'd put his phone on vibrate. She didn't bother leaving him a message.

Finally she called Fouad Khan, whom she presumed was at the Cavendish also.

The phone rang in his room and no one picked up. Fouad was standing outside on his terrace smoking a cigarette—a habit he did not often indulge in, but he was hoping it might help him get to sleep. He did not hear the phone because he had the glass door shut lest the smoke make its way into his room and bother him.

Frustrated, Lucky made an on-the-spot decision. She would deal with it herself.

M.J. was waiting outside the office for her to emerge. "Tell Lennie I had to go take care of an urgent problem," she said briskly. "Okay?"

"Is it anything I can help out with?" M.J. asked.

She shook her head. "Nope. It's something I have to do personally. And since I don't want Lennie coming with me, just say that I'll see him back at the apartment."

"Right," M.J. said, wondering what was going on.

"Is Bobby around?"

"I think he left. You want me to double-check?"

"No problem," she said, thinking, *Mr. Armand Jordan, you are about to get a visit from your worst fucking nightmare. A woman—who's going to kick your sorry ass.*

Denver soon observed that a woman on her own walking around a casino was fair game. Every man appeared to think he had the right to talk to her.

"Where you from, honey?"

"Here on vacation?"

"How about I buy you a drink?"

These comments came from men traveling alone. However, men traveling in packs were far bolder.

"Nice rack. How much for a night?"

"Wanna go to a slumber party?"

"You got an ass that would stop traffic."

After a while she'd had enough. She probably did look as if she were selling it, wandering around in circles.

Still, she wasn't ready to go upstairs. If Bobby was there, they'd probably get embroiled in a dumb fight, and if he wasn't . . . well, she didn't want to think about him *not* being there.

Then her imagination launched into overdrive, and she pictured him in bed with Gia, kissing Gia, going down on Gia . . .

Oh my God! I'm turning into one of those too-much-in-love pathetic idiots!

She determined to do something positive, and spotting an open seat at a blackjack table, she slid onto the vacant stool.

It wasn't what Max had intended to happen, but it was inevitable—falling into bed with Billy. He was so sexy and strong, and downright gorgeous, and he smelled so good.

Mister Movie Star—the man who just that afternoon she'd thought she hated—was once again making mad love to her, and this time it was even better than the first.

If that was possible.

Yes, it was possible.

The way he touched her was electrifying. She'd had no idea that actually doing it could feel this good. Wow! If only she'd known, she would've been into it a lot sooner.

Or maybe not. There was a reason she'd waited, and the reason was Billy.

"Couldn't get you off my mind," Billy said in a low voice, gently running his fingers down her back as they lay on top of the bed. "Kept on remembering the beach, an' finding you there like a social outcast all by yourself."

"Social outcast!" she objected, stretching languorously. "It was *my* party."

"And you weren't enjoying it one bit. Not until I came along. Admit it, Green Eyes, you were hiding out."

"True."

"But if you hadn't been hiding, I wouldn't've stumbled across you, and we wouldn't be here together. Right?"

"So right," she murmured, thinking about how happy she was to be with him.

"You do know it's way past midnight, so today's your birthday," he stated. "Makes me pissed that I'm not going to be spending it with you."

"I wish you could," she responded. "But can you imagine everyone's face if I turned up with *you* by my side?"

"I get it," Billy said. "Lucky an' Lennie would throw a shit fit."

"You're not wrong about that. And . . ." She hesitated for a moment. "Venus is in town. I saw her earlier at Mood. She'll probably be at my party."

"I saw her too. Ran into her outside the restaurant where Kev an' I were eating."

"Kev's with you?"

"He came along for the ride. Don't worry, he's not gonna bother us. He's got his instructions."

"It's not that I don't like him . . ." she said tentatively.

"Listen, Kev can be a big pain at times, but the thing about Kev is that he means well."

"Did you *speak* to Venus?" Max asked curiously.

"Briefly. She hates me now."

"She does?"

"Divorce brings out the bitch in everyone."

"Y'know," Max mused, turning over, "Venus has been my mom's best friend since I was a little kid."

"You're *still* a little kid," he teased, lazily tickling her stomach, thinking how luminous and pretty she was with her olive skin and brilliant green eyes. She wasn't just pretty, she was a beauty.

She squealed and rolled away from him.

He laughed and came after her, lowering his lean, bronzed body on top of her, slowly moving inside her until she sighed with pleasure.

Now she realized what Cookie meant when she carried on about how great it was doing the deed instead of holding back the main event.

Once again she realized she was glad she'd waited. Billy Melina was perfect, the birthday present of her dreams.

"Where's my little girl?" Gerald M. suddenly demanded, glancing around the crowded table at Mood. He was drinking Jack Daniel's and feeling no pain.

Frankie, who'd managed to insert himself between two buxom blondes, gave a casual shrug. "Dancin' her ass off," he replied, although he had no idea where Cookie had vanished to, and he didn't much care. The blondes had already invited him to their suite, and he had plans to go, maybe take along Gerald M. if he was so inclined.

"Aren't you supposed to be *with* my little girl?" Gerald M. inquired, a belligerent look in his eyes. "She told me you drove here together."

Cancel the blondes, Frankie thought. *The dude's just remembered he has a daughter.*

"That's right," Frankie said, keeping it casual. "Only you know Cookie—she's a girl who likes t' do her own thing. I wouldn't want to hold her back."

"Go find her," Gerald M. said, scowling. "It's late. I don't like the idea of her wandering around on her own."

"I'm sure she's fine," Frankie said, left eye twitching.

Gerald M. gave him the Big Star look, a look that said *When I want something done—do it.*

"Yeah," Frankie said, reluctantly getting up. "Think I'll go find her now."

* * *

When Lucky was intent on doing something, there was nothing and no one capable of stopping her. She lived by her own rules, and her rules were stringent. *Never fuck with a Santangelo* said it all.

Armand Jordan was fucking with her, and she would not have it. Oh no, shooting his mouth off that he was buying The Keys might be a minor infraction to some people, but to Lucky it was out-and-out war. She would not allow the fool to go around saying such things. She would put a stop to it instantly.

She made her way down to the private Santangelo parking basement, where she discovered that the attendant was asleep on the job. Instead of waking him, she reached her arm inside his cubicle to the board of keys and collected the ignition key for her Vegas car, a silver blue Aston Martin, making a mental note to have the attendant fired the next morning, unless of course he had a wife and family—in which case she might reconsider.

It felt invigorating to be doing something about Armand Jordan. She hadn't liked the man from the moment he'd set foot in her office that morning. Bad vibes. Very bad vibes.

Damn Jeffrey—he should've known better than to put her in the same room with him. But Jeffrey was going through a divorce, so he probably wasn't thinking straight. Divorces seemed to do that to people, even lawyers.

She drove her car up from the underground garage, adrenaline surging.

It didn't matter that it was almost one in the morning. In fact, it added to the drama.

Armand Jordan was about to find out that nobody fucked with a Santangelo. Nobody.

CHAPTER FIFTY-FIVE

Randy Sorrentino clumsily hauled his big muscled body off the lounger and tried to get his brain around what he should wear. His drug delivery uniform—a light sports jacket over a maroon shirt and pants? Or should he go for more casual wear, such as his prized Guns N' Roses sweatshirt from way back and torn jeans?

Randy Sorrentino did not believe in rushing; he believed in taking his time. His mind worked slowly, so rushing didn't do it for him. He liked to think things through before he left the safety of his apartment.

Earlier in the evening, Luscious had informed him that she wouldn't be dancing at Dirty Den's tonight. Instead she had a high-paying gig at the Cavendish Hotel, and she was taking along Seducta. Randy wasn't sure whether the high-paying gig was for stripping or hooking. He hadn't asked; he didn't need the details. If his girlfriend wanted to open her legs and invite strangers in for money, it was all right with him. As long as she didn't come trotting home with some other dude's stink on her. In the porn business he'd learned a lot about protection and personal hygiene, and thoughtfully he'd passed all the info along to Luscious, who swore she always made the john use a condom.

The money she brought in helped. Eventually they might want to buy a house, or maybe get hitched and start a family. But that was way off in their future. Right now it was all about enjoying themselves, and if there was one thing Randy excelled at, it was enjoying himself.

He considered Luscious's hurried words over the phone. *Get your ass over here. We got ourselves a live one.*

That could mean anything.

An' bring the crack pipe, your piece, an' your big old self.

Was this for a party? Or was he supposed to make a sale?

Randy didn't like it when she called him old. He was only twenty-eight, and yeah, some people might consider him big—230 pounds of pure muscle—but he was also big in all the right places, something that had always helped him on his journey through life. It was the one thing he had over Mikey.

Thinking of Mikey, he considered whether he should bring him in on this. He had to admit that Mikey was the brains of the family, and he was the brawn. So if—as Luscious had said—they were about to make some real money, wasn't including Mikey the right thing to do?

Yeah, Mikey was the man.

Randy pulled up his pants and reached for the phone to summon his big brother.

Armand was slumped on the couch, his mind veering off in all different directions. He'd never combined alcohol and cocaine before, so he was feeling quite disoriented.

The whores weren't dancing, although the music continued, loud and raucous, the harsh beat throbbing through Armand's brain. One of the whores had fallen into a naked, drunken stupor on the couch. She was snoring, her mouth open.

"What's wrong with her?" he muttered to the skinny whore, who for some unknown reason was standing by the bar holding a phone, her scrawny tattooed body nude.

"Got someone on the way," she informed him. "Someone who's gonna do whatever you need done." After a crafty pause, she added, "For a price, of course."

For a price. Armand digested her words. *For a price.*

What was this someone supposed to do for a price?

Then he remembered. They were going to blow Lucky Santangelo's brains out.

Yes, that was it.

And he would pay whatever it took.

Randy picked his brother up in his super-charged gold Dodge.

Mikey was standing outside his house, a sinister figure clad all in black, including oblique tinted sunglasses, which he wore day and night.

Mikey and Randy shared a mother, not a father. Mikey's dad, a hardened criminal, was doing life in prison, while Randy's dad—a former bodybuilder—sat at home picking up a disability pension.

Mikey was not big and tall like his younger brother; he was slight of build and less than five feet eight. To compensate, he wore black snakeskin cowboy boots with three-inch semi concealed heels and a secret compartment where he stashed a six-inch hunting knife.

"What's this shit all about?" Mikey asked as he climbed into the passenger seat.

"Sounds like it's somethin'," Randy said, revving the engine. "Luscious wouldn't steer us wrong."

"She'd better not," Mikey responded. "'Cause if she's wasting my time, I'm gonna slap her sideways till she can't see straight."

CHAPTER FIFTY-SIX

"Is this seat taken?"

Denver didn't bother looking at the man who'd seated himself next to her at the blackjack table. She was fed up with being hit on—enough was enough. Besides, she was doing very nicely, accumulating a tidy pile of chips. Gambling was actually fun, although if she was truthful with herself, she knew she would sooner be with Bobby.

She placed her next bet and waited patiently for the dealer to slide the cards.

The dealer did so—and blackjack! She'd scored again.

"Nice one," said the man seated beside her. She gave him a quick glance and realized it was Bobby.

"Thank you," she said politely, acting as if they were total strangers.

"You're welcome," he said, playing along.

A paunchy man in a Hawaiian shirt sitting two seats away made a triumphant gesture with his thumb and mumbled something about her killing them. "This little lady is picking all my cards," he complained good-naturedly. "But she's way too pretty to get mad at." He nodded at Bobby. "Maybe you'll change the balance."

"I'll try," Bobby said.

They played for fifteen more minutes, until Denver finally lost a bet.

Without looking at Bobby, she gathered up her chips

and stood up. "Cashing out," she said, tossing the dealer a generous tip.

"We'll miss you," said Mister Hawaiian Shirt.

Bobby stood too. "Can I buy you a drink?" he asked, addressing Denver.

"Well . . ." she demurred.

"He's not a bad-looking guy; I say go for it," Hawaiian Shirt encouraged. "That's unless he's married. You got to take a look-see at his ring finger. It's always a sure giveaway—you'll see the tan mark."

Denver gave Bobby a solemn look. "*Are* you married?" she asked.

"Nope," Bobby replied, equally serious. "Are you?"

"I recently divorced my third husband," she said.

"Dangerous!" Hawaiian Shirt exclaimed.

"Thanks for all the encouragement," Denver said, smiling at him. "I'll let you know how it turns out."

Hawaiian Shirt nodded eagerly. He loved Vegas—there was always something going on.

"So," Bobby said, still playing along as they walked toward a nearby lounge. "What brings you to Vegas?"

"Like I said, I recently divorced my third husband."

"Did he do something to piss you off?"

"Danced with an ex."

"Really?"

"It didn't sit well with me."

"I guess it wouldn't. Although I'm sure it was perfectly innocent."

"Maybe," she said, shrugging. "Or maybe not."

They reached the lounge and settled in at a corner table.

"What'll you have?" Bobby asked as a pretty waitress came over to take their order.

"A vodka martini," Denver said, getting into their unexpected game. "Make it a dirty double."

"A dirty double, huh?" Bobby said, raising an eyebrow. The Denver he knew was a white wine girl. But this wasn't Denver he was sitting with—this was a stranger, and he found himself getting quite turned on. "Okay then, make it a double vodka martini for the lady, and I'll have a beer," he told the waitress.

"And why are *you* in Vegas?" Denver asked as the waitress moved away.

"Came here for a romantic weekend with my girlfriend, but we kinda got off track."

"You did?"

"Shit happens."

"How true."

The drinks came and Denver downed her martini as if she were celebrating at a Russian wedding.

"Hey," Bobby said, trying not to laugh. "Easy."

"Some men think I am," she murmured provocatively.

"What kind of men would they be?"

She gave a casual shrug. "Oh, I don't know . . . the adventurous kind."

"I'm adventurous."

"You are?"

"Certainly. Uh . . . how about coming upstairs to my room and I'll prove it to you."

"Will your girlfriend be there?"

"My girlfriend's long gone."

"You're sure?"

"Oh yeah, I'm dead sure."

She gave him a bold look. "Then what are we waiting for?"

He threw money on the table, stood up, and offered her his hand. "Nothing I can think of," he said.

Lucky did not want Armand Jordan to be forewarned that she was on her way to pay him a visit. Surprise was the name of the game. A nice big fat surprise.

It wouldn't be a physical confrontation, not like the time she'd visited an investor in one of the Santangelo hotels who'd refused to pay up. Ah yes, she'd visited him in the middle of the night while he was sleeping and held the cold steel of a knife next to his balls. The following day, the money was forthcoming.

Lucky smiled at the memory. God, she'd been a wild one—and even though she was now a happily married woman with grown kids, deep down she was still a wild one.

Armand Jordan would soon find out. She'd warn him to stop shooting his mouth off about something that would never happen, and if he didn't comply and she heard any more stories about him supposedly buying her hotel, then he too might experience the touch of cold steel on his precious balls.

The instant they hit the elevator, it was on. Throwing Denver up against the wall, Bobby inserted his knee between her legs, rendering her helpless, then began kissing her. Wild, hungry kisses that she immediately responded to.

He had her pinned; she couldn't escape, and since she had no desire to do so, it was fine with her. She kissed him back, loving the taste of his mouth, loving the feel of his body pressed tightly up against her. God! She loved everything about this man.

After a few moments he reached up, roughly ripped the top of her dress, exposing her breasts, then bent to suck and bite her fully erect nipples.

The unexpected excitement of what was happening filled her with fire. His mouth on her breasts, his hard penis jammed against her. Completely forgetting where they were, and that a security camera was probably recording their every move, she quickly unzipped his pants and started caressing him. He felt so damn good.

The elevator was on the move, but neither of them cared.

Bobby's hand crept up her thigh, reached her thong, and tore it off. Then he lifted her so that her long legs were clasped around his waist, and without stopping, he began thrusting inside her.

Sex between them was usually passionate enough, but this was different. This was a sweaty, hot, crazy, out-of-body carnal experience.

The elevator stopped, and the doors opened at a floor. Both of them heard the shocked gasp of a woman before Bobby leaned over and pressed the Close Door button.

"Maybe we shouldn't be—" Denver managed before Bobby pressed his hand over her mouth to stop her from talking. Then he fondled her breasts again, pushing them together, tweaking her nipples, all the while still thrusting into her.

She moaned with pleasure as the thrilling climb began. Nothing mattered except being there with Bobby. He was her soul mate. He was everything she'd ever wanted. She loved him desperately.

"Oh . . . my . . . God!" she cried out as she felt herself approaching orgasm. "This . . . is—"

"Insane!" Bobby yelled, finishing the sentence for her as he shuddered to a mind-blowing climax at exactly the same moment.

The elevator stopped again, the doors opened, and a group of elderly tourists from Florida peered in at them in stunned silence.

Quick as a flash, Bobby zipped up, took off his jacket and threw it around Denver's shoulders, grabbed her hand, and exited the elevator.

"Honeymoon," he explained to the dumbstruck tourists. "Sometimes you just gotta do what you gotta do."

* * *

Without Billy by his side, Kev was getting nowhere fast. Every time he tried to chat up a girl, her eyes wandered, searching the room for a more likely prospect.

Until Ellie.

Ellie wasn't his dream girl, although she was cute enough in her torn jeans and blue T-shirt, a hooded sweatshirt tied around her waist. She was sitting at a bar he'd stopped at, drinking a beer and doodling on a notepad. Not the type of girl he usually went for, but this was Vegas, so spending the night by himself was not an option.

"Pretty girls should never drink alone," he said, settling himself on the stool next to her.

After giving him a cursory glance, she went back to her scribbling.

"Writing a book?" he joked.

"Working," she snapped, not in a friendly fashion.

Kev did what he did best: he played his trump card. "Me too," he said. "Just left my boss, Billy Melina. What a guy! What a slave driver! Can you believe it's past midnight an' I'm only now off the clock. Movie stars! They dance to their own tune."

Oh yes, surprise, surprise, he had her interest now. Billy's name scored points every time.

"Billy Melina is here?" she said, tapping her pen on the bar. "In Vegas?"

Kev nodded. "'S right," he said. "In all his movie-star bullshit."

She gave him an intent look. "How do I know you're not making this up?"

"Why'd I do that?"

"'Cause."

"'Cause here's the proof," he said, pulling out his phone and clicking on a few choice photos of him and Billy at play. "Take a look at me an' my master."

Ellie scrolled through the photos, then snapped her

notebook shut. "How'd you like to make a couple of thousand bucks?" she said.

"Doing what?" Kev asked, his curiosity aroused.

"Nothing illegal."

"Then what?"

"Come with me, and I'll tell you what."

"It's not that I *want* to go, but I guess I have to," Max said reluctantly, her head cradled on Billy's bronzed chest.

"How's that?" Billy said, gently brushing a lock of hair off her face. "There's nobody waiting up for you—right?"

WRONG! Ace will definitely be waiting up for me, and what am I supposed to say to him?

"Uh . . . no," she lied. "Only I don't think my mom would be thrilled if she heard about me staying out all night."

"You're eighteen now," he pointed out. "She's got no say anymore, you can do anything you want."

"Yeah," Max said unsurely. "But, uh, being with you is definitely going to create waves."

"More like a tsunami," Billy said, laughing.

"It's no joke," she admonished, sitting up. "You were *married* to my mom's best friend."

"Shit!" he quipped. "How did *that* happen?"

"It's not funny," Max said. "Actually, it's kind of creepy."

"Are you callin' me creepy?" Billy said, mock serious.

"Not *you*," she said quickly. "The situation. I mean, I can't tell them we're seeing each other. You're not even divorced yet."

"Almost."

"Doesn't cut it."

"You're a tough little piece of work."

"*I'm* a piece of work?" she said, indignantly. "*You're* the movie star."

"How does that make *me* a piece of work?"

" 'Cause that's how movie stars roll. They're catered to by everyone, and it stops them from acting like normal people. Believe me, I saw it all when my mom owned Panther Studios."

"So now you're tellin' me I'm not normal?" he said, amused.

"You're Billy Melina. How could you be?"

He laughed again and grabbed her leg. "*You're* not normal," he said. "You're too freakin' pretty an' sexy an' hot to even *think* about bein' normal."

"You calling me sexy?" she asked, secretly thrilled.

"Yeah, Green Eyes, I'm callin' you sexy. So forget about runnin' out on me, an' let's see what tricks I can teach you next."

"Don't bother. I got tricks of my own that'll blow you away," she said confidently. "You might've taken my virginity, but I'm not exactly Miss Innocent, so there, Mister Movie Star."

"Feisty. I like it."

"Do you?" She sighed, wondering if this was what falling in love felt like.

"You bet your ass, Little Miss Green Eyes," Billy replied enthusiastically. "I like you a whole damn lot. So we're gonna have to figure out a plan, 'cause I'm not givin' up on you. Okay?"

"Okay," she said. And her heart skipped a beat, because maybe, just maybe, this could be the real deal.

CHAPTER FIFTY-SEVEN

Loud music was emanating from the villa at the Cavendish. Too loud for comfort.

"Sounds like a party," Randy said, standing outside the door, not at all disappointed. One thing about Randy, he was always up for a party.

"No party," Mike growled, narrow eyes behind dark shades checking out his surroundings. "We're here for business. Got it?"

"I got it," Randy said. It was never a wise idea to argue with Mikey. The last time he and Mikey had gotten into a physical altercation, he'd ended up losing two teeth, a painful memory.

Even though Randy was younger, bigger, and stronger, Mikey had moves that came out of nowhere, moves that could flatten a man in less than five seconds, which was why Randy refused to fuck with him. Mikey was the Man.

Randy hammered on the door, and it fell open.

Automatically Mikey reached for his piece. One thing about Mikey, he was always cautious, always alert.

Gingerly, Randy stepped into the room, Mikey right behind him.

The scene that greeted them was quite something. Seducta was sprawled naked and out for the count on the couch. Armand sat next to her in a shirt and tie, no pants, his legs akimbo. Luscious was positioned on her knees in front of him, her mouth and slightly buck teeth enveloping his engorged manhood, her head bobbing up and down.

Loud rap blared on the sound system. Mounds of coke were piled on the coffee table, while empty bottles of champagne, along with miniatures of scotch and vodka, littered the floor.

"This is some shit-hole," Mikey stated grimly, still fingering his piece. "Someone turn the fuckin' noise off."

Luscious stopped what she was doing, turned off the music, and jumped to her feet. She hadn't expected Randy to bring Mikey—with Mikey involved it meant less money for them. She was pissed. Why share when they didn't have to?

Blurry-eyed, Armand took in the new arrivals. Had he invited them? Who were they?

He shook his head, trying to think straight, and stood up.

"For crissakes, put your junk away," Mikey snarled.

Randy was glad Mikey had said it; he was embarrassed by the sight of another man's equipment. Jeez! Some people had no sense of modesty. This wasn't a porno shoot, this was real life.

Luscious wiped her hand across her mouth and snatched up Armand's pants, which she then handed to him.

He put them on and regarded his visitors. "Who are these people?" he demanded of Luscious. "Why are they here?"

"It's only my boyfriend, Randy, an' his brother, Mikey," she said, retrieving her skimpy tank top and short skirt from the corner and slipping them on. "They're gonna take care of that stuff you wanted done. Remember?"

"What stuff?" Armand asked, realizing that if the room didn't stop spinning, he was likely to lose his balance.

"You *know*," Luscious said, nudging him. "Money's-no-object stuff."

"Ah . . ." Armand said, stumbling slightly.

Then it occurred to him that he'd actually done it; he'd hired himself a hit man. Or two.

While they were talking, Randy edged closer to Luscious.

"Why you gotta bring Mikey with you?" she whined.

"'Cause Mikey knows what he's doin'."

"An' you don't?"

"Who d'you need takin' care of?" Mikey said, stepping toward Armand. "An' be aware, it's gonna cost you, friend. Plenty. I don't work cheap."

Once again, Armand attempted to gather his thoughts. This was not the usual way he conducted business. And this *was* business. Urgent business.

Where was Fouad when he needed him? Fouad always took care of the details.

"I have the money," he said. "Whatever the price for your services."

Mikey gave a hollow laugh. "Twenty-five grand for the job. Cash. You got that kinda moola sittin' around?"

"Of course," Armand said with a lofty nod.

"Half up front. The rest when it's done," Mikey said. "Who's the target? You got a picture? And I'll need t' know where to find 'em."

Armand stared at him blankly.

Mikey was beginning to tense up as he waited for an answer. His body language screamed that he was about to do someone harm for dragging him out of his house and away from his big-screen TV, where he'd been watching a program about killer whales.

He noticed Seducta, moved closer to her, and kicked her off the couch with the tip of his snakeskin boot.

She bounced to the floor and surfaced in a groggy stupor.

"Put your clothes on," he ordered. "We're outta here."

"Huh?" she muttered.

Luscious suppressed a triumphant smirk. Randy could see for himself what a piece of trash his brother had married. Maybe he'd stop coming on to Seducta now that he'd observed what a skank she really was.

"We're goin'," Mikey repeated.

"You can't leave," Luscious said quickly. "Arnie here wants t' make a deal. Doncha, Arnie?"

"A non fuckin' disclosure agreement," Mikey grumbled. "What the fuck. This shit's not for me. This is a handshake deal, or I'm out."

Luscious tugged on Armand's arm. "You told me you wanted somethin' done," she whined. "I got these guys here special. Which means you gotta tell 'em what you want, an' work it out, otherwise they're leavin'. An' you don't want that, do you?"

No, Armand decided, he didn't want that. There was a job to be done, and he understood that money had to exchange hands.

He was a businessman.

A prince.

This could all be settled to everyone's satisfaction.

CHAPTER FIFTY-EIGHT

Emerging from the shower with a towel wrapped around her sarong style and a smile on her face, Denver walked right into Bobby as he let himself into their suite.

"Hey," he said, feigning surprise. "I was hoping I'd find you here."

"That's perfect," she answered brightly. "'Cause I was hoping the same thing."

"Were you now?"

"Yes indeed."

They grinned knowingly at each other.

"So . . ." Denver continued. "Where were you?"

"Well, I finished up at the club," Bobby said, scratching his head. "Then I came directly here."

"Directly?"

"Kinda. Had a little detour on the way."

"A detour?"

"Met this beautiful woman at the blackjack table."

"Really? And who might she be?"

"I think her name was . . ." He thought for a moment. "Uh . . . Chicago."

"Chicago, huh?"

"Right. Gorgeous woman, with real breasts, long silky hair, fantastic legs, and best of all, a taste for adventure."

"Should I be jealous?"

"I dunno. It depends. Where were *you*?"

"Ah," Denver answered mysteriously. "I ran into a tall

dark stranger with mad sexy moves and a hard . . . body."

"Sounds exciting."

"It was. We had sex in the elevator."

"Hmm," Bobby said lustfully. "Tell me something—did he make you come the way I'm about to make you come?" And with a deft flick of his wrist, he removed her towel.

They both burst out laughing as the towel dropped to the floor.

"Oh my God!" Denver exclaimed, still laughing. "You're insatiable."

"You bet I am, and don't you just love it," Bobby said, steering her into the bedroom and onto the bed.

She smiled up at him as he began to kiss her very deliberately. Then, at a slow pace, his tongue started moving down her body until he gently spread her legs and began going down on her.

Throwing her head back, she luxuriated in his touch. His hands were on her thighs, holding them apart. Once again she felt deliciously trapped.

After a few minutes, he came up for air. "You're making me forget about Chicago," he said. "That woman is becoming just another distant memory."

"And that's exactly the way it should be," Denver murmured dreamily, thinking that this was definitely turning out to be a weekend to remember.

On the one hand, Kev felt guilty; on the other hand, he thought—screw it—he was entitled to make some decent money. Billy was rolling in it, bathing in it. Billy was a friggin' movie star, and who was he? Poor old Kev who tagged along for the ride, and then got kicked to the curb like some beaten-up old dog, without even a decent explanation. Oh yeah—*So long, Kev. Book yourself a room, Kev. Charge it to me, Kev.*

Was Billy forgetting the months he'd camped out in Kev's apartment when he'd first made it to Hollywood? Billy Melina had not had a pot to piss in, and he, Kev, was the one who'd been paying all the bills, putting food on the table and supporting Billy all the way.

So fuck it. He had a chance of making some real money, and who could blame him for taking it?

It turned out that Ellie was more than just a pretty girl sitting at a bar scribbling in a notebook. Ellie was a freelance photojournalist who was in Vegas to dig up as much dirt as she could on the many famous celebrities flocking into Vegas for the big fight.

"Y'know," she informed Kev after they'd shared a couple of beers, "the right photo of a hot celeb can fetch up to a hundred grand. And with your boss going through such a public divorce, well . . . if I can get an exclusive photo of him with someone new—bingo! We're in the money. You arrange it, and you're in for half."

Who was he to turn down such a lucrative offer?

Screw loyalty. It didn't seem to matter to Billy.

Frankie frowned. Where was he supposed to start looking for Cookie? She wasn't on the dance floor, she wasn't in the damn club, so where the hell was she? He had no idea, but he did know that if he wanted to stay on Gerald M.'s good side, he'd better make an attempt to start searching for the little minx.

Gerald M. was the kind of dude he was desperate to hang with. Yeah, Gerald M. might be older, but he was a tried-and-true star—like a Smokey Robinson or a Lionel Richie. Old-school. And Frankie would like nothing better than for Gerald M. to plant his ass in River every night, give the place some star power. He'd even supply him with free drugs for the pleasure of his company.

However, this wasn't going to happen until he produced Gerald M.'s precious daughter.

How precious would Daddy think Cookie was if he'd seen her sucking Frankie's cock on the drive up? Not so precious anymore.

Frankie approached M.J. and was taken aback to observe his ex Annabelle Maestro sitting at the table, right next to Lennie Golden and the red-hot agent everyone was talking about—Eddie Falcon. He and Annabelle hadn't spoken in months, not since he'd threatened to sue her for publishing a libelous, untruthful book, painting him as some kind of dissolute, lowlife drug addict.

He knew Eddie—the agent had stopped by River on several occasions—so he said a brusque "Hi" and attempted to ignore Annabelle.

Eddie wasn't having it. "You know my girlfriend, Annabelle Maestro," Eddie said. He paused, then added, "Wait a minute, didn't the two of you used to go out?"

"Briefly," Annabelle said, refusing to look at Frankie.

"Way back," Frankie said, turning to M.J. "You seen Cookie?" he asked.

"Dating juveniles now," Annabelle murmured. "How appropriate."

Frankie pretended not to hear her.

"She and Max were goin' over to Wonderball," Cassie offered.

"Wonder *what?*" Frankie said, wishing he was anywhere but standing in front of this group.

"It's a kids' club on the strip," Cassie said. "Wonderball. Everyone knows it."

Great. His teenage girlfriend had run out on him to go party with the kiddies. Well, at least he could tell Gerald M. where she was.

"Thanks," he said to Cassie.

"No prob," Cassie responded.

Back to his table he went with his newfound information on Cookie's whereabouts.

The table was empty. Gerald M. and his entourage—including the two blondes Frankie had lined up for later—had taken off. All that was left was the check.

His freakin' luck. What the hell was he supposed to do now?

Max loved the fact that Billy didn't want her to go; it meant that he really liked her.

"When am I gonna see you again?" he asked, sitting on the edge of the bed watching her as she pulled on her leggings and boots. " 'Cause if I'm *not* gonna see you, I may as well hop a flight back to L.A."

"Well . . ." she said, thinking about how she could work it out. "I've got lunch with my family, but after that I don't see why I couldn't come by. Maybe we could do something, go somewhere."

"Sweet dreams, babe," Billy said with a rueful laugh. "If I set one foot outta here, the paps'll be all over me, an' you'll be labeled my new mystery woman."

"Is it *that* bad?" she asked, thinking what a drag it must be to lose your privacy.

"Believe me," Billy assured her, "it's that bad. Even without the divorce thing it was full-on. Now multiply that, an' the situation escalates. I hate it."

"But surely they don't even know you're in Vegas?" she questioned.

"Oh, they know. They just haven't found me yet."

"Does this mean we can't go anywhere together? Even in L.A.?"

"Not unless you're prepared for everyone to find out about us."

Max considered Lucky and Lennie's reaction and shuddered. They would totally *freak*.

"Okay," she said hesitantly. "Then why don't I come back here later and we'll watch TV or something."

"I'm liking the 'or something,'" he said with a lascivious grin. "Your education shall continue."

"Ha!" she said scornfully. "Stop imagining that I'm, like, some innocent little flower you're teaching how to grow. Honestly, I'm not that girl."

"Do not shatter my illusions," he said. "I'm happy that I'm your first. It makes everything very special between us."

"Hmm," she said, trying not to let him see how thrilled his words made her. She had to play it a little bit cool, couldn't let him see how hooked she already was. "Well anyway, I gotta get out of here," she added, standing up.

"Call me when you get to your room," he said. "I want to be sure you got back safely. I'd escort you, but—"

"Yeah, I know, I know, those freakin' paps."

"Right," he said, grinning. "You catch on fast."

"You'll find out soon enough."

"Lookin' forward to it, Green Eyes."

"So am I!"

Lucky knew the Cavendish as well as she knew her own hotel. During the time she was building The Keys, she'd stayed in the villas many times. She was aware of exactly where Armand's villa was located, having gotten the number from the switchboard.

As she drove to the hotel, she decided she'd park in a special spot near the villas. No need to walk through the lobby or the casino. Later, at a decent hour, she'd call Renee, the owner of the Cavendish, and ask her to arrange for Armand Jordan to be thrown out.

But right now she was looking forward to having him exactly where she wanted him. It was a game. A game she excelled at.

CHAPTER FIFTY-NINE

If he hadn't been so stoned, Armand would have been well aware that what he was doing was reckless and beyond stupid. He would have known that he should summon Fouad to make sure that the details were handled properly. And he would also have known that Fouad would put an immediate stop to what he had planned.

Ah, yes . . . Fouad would caution him that he was behaving in an impossible and dangerous fashion. That he was putting himself in distinct jeopardy for dealing with such bad people. Whores and thugs who would do anything for money.

WHORES AND THUGS.

Armand laughed. He didn't care. He had his mind made up.

He walked unsteadily into his bedroom, pulled out the money suitcase and unlocked it. Twenty-five thousand to get rid of an enemy was a cheap price to pay. Twenty-five thousand and good-bye, Lucky Santangelo.

He stared at the neat stacks of bills, organized into bundles of twenty thousand. Cash. There was nothing like it. No paper trails to catch a man out.

Before he knew it, Luscious was standing beside him, her mouth gaping open as she gazed down at the suitcase stuffed full of money. "You rob a bank or somethin'?" she asked, her eyes wide with greed.

"My bank. My money," he replied, vaguely annoyed that she'd followed him into the bedroom.

"You're a rich mothafucker, ain't'cha?" she said, hanging onto his arm. "Rich an' sexy."

"You think I'm sexy?" Armand said, quite pleased that she would say so. He'd never given a woman the opportunity to call him sexy before—he'd always been too busy humiliating them, or telling them they weren't fit to speak.

"Sure you is," Luscious said, still clinging onto him. "An' . . . I got a treat for you all set up in the other room. Somethin' real special."

"What would that be?"

"You ever done crack, Arnie? 'Cause if you never did, then I'm gonna take you somewhere you ain't *never* gonna forget." She pulled on his arm, dragging him away from the suitcase stuffed full of money. Leaving it unlocked and open. "Let's go, big boy. This'll be a night t' remember."

Crouching in the bushes near Billy's villa alongside Ellie and her long-lens camera, Kev experienced a pang of guilt. He and Billy went way back. They were long-time friends, and now he was about to sell him out.

But hey—it was all Billy's fault. Billy had decided not to trust him, and that was okay. No trust between friends meant all was fair.

"We could be stuck here all night," Kev muttered, not relishing the thought.

"Okay with me," Ellie replied, perfectly cheerful. "Whoever is in there with him has to come out eventually, and when they do, I've got the shot."

"You've done this before, haven't you?" Kev said, wondering when he should make his move. After all, this was Vegas, and tonight he was definitely getting laid.

"A few times," Ellie replied, a tad sarcastic. "Learned from my dad. Now *he* was one of the greats. He shad-

owed Jackie O. Captured Elvis fat and thin. Michael
Jackson in his pj's. O.J. on the run. Diana and Dodi. Oh
yes, my dad nailed it every time. He taught me that the
trick is to lie dormant until the exact right moment, then
go for it. Kinda like bird-watching. The subject doesn't
even know. Night-vision camera, sweet lens. It's a trip."

"I dunno who he's with in there," Kev said for the
third time. "Could be Venus for all I know. We ran into
her earlier."

"What a shot *that'd* be," Ellie said, adjusting her camera position. "Front page everywhere. Oh my!"

"He's been seeing Willow Price," Kev offered.

"Old news. Besides, everyone knows she's a pussy
hound."

"Then there was this young girl in L.A. Max something or other."

"Young is good," Ellie said matter-of-factly. "Or
black. Or a porn star. The best would be if he pulled a
Charlie Sheen. Always a winner."

"Not Billy," Kev said with conviction. "That's not his
scene."

"No? One thing I've learned in this business, anything is possible."

"I really don't wanna let you go," Billy said, walking
Max to the door, his arm around her waist.

"And *I* really don't want to go," she responded, reaching up to playfully touch the dimple in his chin.

He opened the door, and they stood there, bathed in
the moonlight, not ready to part company.

Billy leaned forward and kissed her on the lips, a long
sexy kiss. "Night, Green Eyes," he said. "See you tomorrow."

"I guess I should make up a nickname for *you*," she
said, reluctant to leave. "How about Dimples?"

"How about that sounds like somebody's pet monkey,"

Billy said, snorting with mirth. "Dimples, my ass. Think of something macho."

Giggling, Max wrapped her arms around his neck. "What, then?"

"You'll come up with something," he said, hugging her affectionately.

"Oh yes I will."

"Oh yes you will."

And neither of them heard the steady click of the camera lens hidden in the bushes.

The euphoria that overcame Armand was like nothing he'd ever experienced before. Sharing hits from a crack pipe with these people—his new best friends—was magical. They *were* his friends.

No. Better than that. They were his loyal subjects, here to do his bidding. Here to help him achieve greatness.

Yes. Greatness. FOR ARMAND JORDAN WAS THE MAN WHO WOULD BE KING.

And when he was the ruler, he would transport everyone to Akramshar, where they would all live in harmony and peace.

He stared at the two women—Luscious and Seducta. These women were not whores, they were beautiful creatures. Exquisite. He wanted to fuck them. He wanted to fuck them both. He wanted to fuck them forever.

They would all float together in a sea of happiness. Their bodies would be filled with wonderment. It was the way it was supposed to be.

His heart was on a crazy trip of its own. It was beating so fast he could hardly keep up. And yet the rhythm was comforting; it made him feel warm and safe.

He could do anything.

Being alive was such a pleasure.

It was heavenly.

He was heavenly.

"Do you recognize her?" Ellie asked, keeping her voice low.

"Think it might be the one from L.A.," Kev said, squinting to get a better view. "Max somethin' or other."

"She looks young," Ellie observed.

"She *is* young."

"All the better," Ellie said, clicking away with her long lens as Billy and Max continued to hug and kiss.

Kev wondered if when Ellie had taken enough photos he was going to get laid.

Laid *and* paid. It was a win-win situation.

"Seems to me your wife is on the missing list," Alex said, making digs at Lennie as he'd been doing all night.

"My *wife* is at home in bed waiting for me," Lennie responded.

"You mean she leaves you in a club without so much as a good-bye?" Alex taunted, swigging more scotch.

Lennie gave a dry laugh. "Just goes to show how well you know Lucky. She does her thing, I do mine. We never feel the need to check in."

"A modern marriage, huh?"

"Modern, not open."

"Just asking."

"Ask away, Alex. But I think I should tell you— Lucky will *never* be yours. Never. And that's something you can take to the bank." He paused to let that sink in, then added, "Do we understand each other?"

"I'm tellin' you," Luscious whispered in Randy's ear. "We gotta forget about the hit. There's a shitload of money in a suitcase in the bedroom—could be more than a hundred thou."

Randy had just taken a solid drag on the crack pipe and he wasn't concentrating, which infuriated Luscious. So did the fact that Seducta was lolling all over him, and he wasn't shoving her off. Her tits were in his face, and he didn't seem to mind.

Sometimes Randy didn't get the bigger picture, but Luscious was sure that Mikey certainly would. She was starting to think that it was time for her to move on.

Mikey was standing by the window smoking a long thin cheroot. He'd pocketed the $12,500 deposit, now he was waiting for the client to tell him who the subject was.

It had crossed Mikey's mind that he could take the money he already had, stick it in his safe deposit box, and do nothing. This visiting prick was so out of it he wouldn't know the difference. And if he did that, there was nothing the john could do. The asshole would be fucked, screwed, caught on a freeway without a ride and no pants.

Mikey gave a grim smile. He didn't do drugs. He smoked. He drank—never to excess. Mikey was a man intent on staying in control.

As he watched them all getting wasted, he felt sorry for them. No willpower. No backbone. Truth was, they were nothing but a bunch of losers.

He observed his wife sucking on the pipe. Dumb as shit. The puzzle was, why had he married her?

Could it be that in a weak moment he'd succumbed to the power of pussy and the lure of big tits? Foolish. Even Luscious—who was no prize herself—was smarter than Seducta.

As if reading his mind, Luscious sidled up to him. "We gotta move fast," she said in a low voice.

"Move fast why?" Mikey said, flicking ash on the rug.

"There's a suitcase in the bedroom stuffed fulla money. I saw it." She indicated Armand. "He's too fucked-up to know anything. What we gotta do is take it an' get the shit out."

"How much money?" Mikey questioned, his interest piqued.

"Go look for yourself," Luscious insisted. "I'm tellin' you—it's worth runnin'."

Mikey didn't need asking twice. He headed purposefully toward the bedroom.

CHAPTER SIXTY

"The time has come," Bobby said. "For us to move in together."

"Don't you ever sleep?" Denver groaned, rolling over in bed. "What's the time?"

"A house, I'm buying us a house," he said decisively. "Half yours, half mine. I'll decorate my half, you can go for it on yours."

"Oh," she said, yawning. "So now you're a decorator."

"I know what I like. I worked with my design team on Mood."

"You're something else, Bobby Santangelo Stanislopoulos." She sighed. "A man of many talents."

"What's your favorite?" he asked, reaching his arms around her.

"Right now my favorite is sleep, plenty of it."

"Then we're agreed?" he said, spooning up against her. "I can buy us a house?"

"I didn't say—"

His hands slid under the oversized T-shirt she wore to bed and began caressing her breasts. "*What* didn't you say?"

"No sex. Sleep," she begged. "You're turning into a horn dog."

"Only if we got a deal."

"Okay, okay, we got a deal," she agreed.

"Is that a promise?"

"Yes, it's a promise."

"Are you a woman of your word?"

"Yes! Yes! Yes!"

"Okay, then," he said, grinning. "You can go to sleep now."

"You're sure?"

"Well . . ." he said, his hands on the move. "Maybe we should—"

"Bobby!"

"Hey—third time for luck."

"Oh my God! Has anyone ever told you you're turning into a sex maniac?"

He grinned again. "Only you."

"Was I right or was I right?" Luscious said, addressing Mikey, a triumphant gleam in her eyes.

Mikey, standing in front of Armand's open suitcase filled with nothing but money, let out a long, low whistle. "Yeah," he said at last. "You was right."

Praise from the inscrutable Mikey was praise indeed. Luscious preened.

Mikey began tapping his right foot on the plush carpet, a sure sign that he was thinking. By his quick calculations there had to be at least $300,000 in the suitcase. Maybe more. He'd *never* seen that much money in one place, and he'd been around drug dealers and criminals all his life. This was big-time.

"Who is this prick?" he muttered.

"Dunno," Luscious said, making a helpless gesture. "Just another john with a shitload of cash."

Mikey knew he had to tread carefully as he considered their options. Was it drug money? He didn't think so, for he was familiar with most of the players in town.

Gambling money? Most likely. The john was probably a rich degenerate gambler who came to Vegas for the gambling and the prostitutes.

Luscious was all hyped up and anxious for action.

"We gonna take it or what?" she asked, licking her lips in anticipation.

"Yeah," Mikey said slowly. "We're gonna take it. Leave it t' me to work out how."

Lucky was not having second thoughts, not at all. It had been a while since she'd had to deal with a situation such as this, and it had her adrenaline pumping.

Mr. Armand Jordan boasting to people that he was buying her hotel. The nerve of him was unbelievable. And she was about to set him straight in no uncertain fashion.

She hoped she was about to catch him asleep in bed so that she could scare the shit out of him. Yes, that would be fun.

She drove her car into the parking section reserved for the villa guests. It was late, no valet on duty, which was good for her, but not so good for the Cavendish. Lucky considered it lax security; she would never allow it to happen at her hotel. Security for the protection of hotel guests was always a priority.

Why are you doing this? she asked herself. *Isn't it beneath you? Calling out some jerk in the middle of the night?*

No. It's a kick. He's a moron who hates women, and I'm about to show him who's boss.

Actually, she was loving it. Kicking butt—her favorite thing to do.

"Okay." Max sighed, extracting herself from Billy and his tempting lips. "This is it. I've *really* got to go."

"Really?" he said, teasing her, grabbing her, kissing her.

"Yes, really," she giggled, enjoying every minute. *I love you, Billy Melina!*

"Okay then, go. Leave me wanting more."

"I'll call you when I get to my room."

"You'd better."

"Oh, I will," she said, finally pulling away.

Billy watched her leave, a smile on his lips. She made him feel as if he was back in high school. She washed away all the random girls who'd been giving him blow jobs beside his pool. She obliterated the Venus years and all the crap that went along with being married to a world-class superstar. When he was with Max, he wasn't movie star Billy Melina, he was just a guy having fun with his girl.

Suddenly Max doubled back, rushed past him, and darted into the villa. "Close the door," she gasped, a frantic expression on her face. "I think I just saw my mom!"

"Here's what we're gonna do," Mikey decided. "You an' Seducta gonna keep the prick busy while Randy an' me get the suitcase outta here."

"You mean you expect *me* an' your stoned wife t' stay here while you take off?" Luscious said indignantly. "No fuckin' way, Mikey. That's not how it's goin' down."

"Do *you* wanna carry the goddamn suitcase outta here?" he said, stony-faced. "Is that it?"

"No," Luscious said, determined to do things her way. "Randy can take the suitcase while *you* stay here keepin' the mark busy. Me an' Randy'll take it to a safe place."

"An' what's your idea of a safe place?" Mikey said scornfully. "Hidin' it under your fuckin' bed? 'Cause when this prick emerges from his drug haze tomorrow, he's gonna come lookin' for you big time."

"Why'll he be lookin' for me?"

"'Cause you're the slut who was in his room blowin' him."

"I'm not a slut, Mikey," Luscious said, her eyes

unexpectedly filling with tears. "You shouldn't call me that. It's your wife who's the slut."

Mikey didn't answer. He was thinking. He was coming up with a plan.

"Got it," he said at last. "You an' me take the suitcase. We leave Randy an' Seducta here. They stay until the john passes out, or whatever the fuck he's gonna do."

"What if he starts lookin' for his suitcase?"

"If that happens, Randy'll deal with it."

"How?"

"How d'you think?"

Luscious preferred not to think. It was one thing to steal the money, but she didn't condone violence.

"I'll fill Randy in on the plan," Mikey said. "You go shut the suitcase, 'cause any minute now we're gettin' outta here."

"What about Seducta?"

"What about her?"

"Are you just gonna leave her?"

"Don't go worryin' about Seducta. She's a big girl. She can look after herself."

"But she's your wife," Luscious felt obliged to point out.

"That don't mean nothin' t' me," Mikey said coldly.

Luscious nodded. Who was she to argue?

Besides, her loyalty was now firmly with the money.

"What're you *talkin'* about?" Billy said, quickly closing the door and following Max back inside.

"It's Lucky. I saw her," Max said, almost hyperventilating. "She's walking down the path on her way here. She *knows* about us. What're we going to *do?*"

"First of all, we're going to calm down," Billy said, hiding his own panic. Nobody relished the thought of messing with the infamous Lucky Santangelo. "And second, you're going to think about who knows you're here."

"Nobody. I didn't tell anyone."

"Does anybody know about us?"

"I just told you," Max wailed. "I haven't mentioned you to anyone."

"Did she see you?"

"I don't think so."

"Let's hope she didn't," Billy said, thinking fast. "So here's what we're gonna do. You go hide in the bathroom, an' when she knocks on the door I'll say I don't know what she's talkin' about."

"Oh my God! You don't understand. She's gonna *kill* me. *And* you."

"You're *sure* it was her?"

"For God's sake, Billy, it's my *mom*. Of course I'm sure."

"Then where is she?"

"I dunno," Max said blankly. "Where is she?"

They both rushed over to the window and peered out.

Lucky was there, all right. She was just about to enter the opposite villa.

Their plan was in action. While Luscious was blocking Armand's view, Mikey was lugging the money suitcase to the door. It was heavier than he'd expected, too heavy for him to make it to the car. He needed help from Randy, the ox with no brains who was currently in la-la land along with Seducta and the john. But Luscious didn't want that. Luscious wasn't having him and Randy skip out with the money, because Luscious was just about smart enough to know that once they had the money, they weren't hanging around. Well, he wasn't anyway. Randy could do what the fuck he liked. If Randy wanted to stay in Vegas with a crackhead he

could do just that. But Mikey had no intention of staying. Once he had the suitcase in the car, he was hitting
the road. Too bad about Seducta and Randy; they were
on their own.

Luscious was something else. She could be useful.
But would she leave without Randy?

Mikey wasn't sure.

He had the money suitcase by the door. Luscious had
turned the music back on so that the john wouldn't hear
when he opened it. The moment he got it outside the
villa, he and Luscious would get it to Randy's car.

Money.

Freedom.

Fuck Vegas.

He opened the door and came face-to-face with a
woman. A beautiful woman with deep olive skin and
clouds of black hair.

For a second or two Mikey was confused. Was she a
late-night call girl the john had ordered?

No. Couldn't be. She didn't look like a hooker. She
looked like a fucking movie star.

They stared at each other for a long silent moment.
Lucky and Mikey.

Finally Lucky broke the silence. She was cool and
collected. Nothing threw Lucky, she always expected
the unexpected.

"And who are you?" she questioned, staring down a
sinister-looking man with blackout shades covering his
eyes and a vicious scowl.

Mikey was not one bit intimidated. "Who the fuck
are *you?*" he retaliated.

"I'm here to see Armand Jordan. Where can I find
him?"

Mikey indicated the room behind him as he dragged
the money suitcase past her. "In there," he said. "Go join
the party. You'll fit right in."

CHAPTER SIXTY-ONE

Things were winding down at Mood; it was late, and the music was becoming mellower, while most of the clientele were getting ready to call it a night.

Lennie was mad at himself. He should've left when Lucky wanted to go, but Alex and his attitude pissed him off, so he'd stayed—kind of like a screw-you gesture toward Alex. Yes, Alex Woods was one of the few people who managed to annoy him with his superior ways, and his constant lusting after Lucky.

Ah . . . Lucky. His beautiful, unpredictable wife. Later she would laugh at him, tease him about his ongoing feud with Alex. And they would make love as they always did before sleeping. Lucky was the woman of his dreams. She completed him, she always had.

He sought out M.J. and told him he was leaving.

"Did Lucky solve that problem?" M.J. asked.

"What problem?"

"I'm not sure," M.J. said, realizing he probably shouldn't have said anything. "She made a call, told me she had to take care of something urgent, then left. She wanted me to tell you that she'd see you back at the apartment."

"Thanks for the information," Lennie said, frowning. "How come you didn't wait until tomorrow to tell me?"

"Sorry," M.J. said, a tad sheepishly. "I kinda forgot."

Lennie shook his head. If Lucky had a problem to solve, why hadn't she come to him?

Then again, why would she? Lucky always took care of things on her own terms. She copied Gino in that respect.

The Santangelos. Father and daughter. Two tough birds.

Lennie wouldn't have them any other way. He was proud to be part of the Santangelo family, just as Lucky was proud to be Mrs. Golden.

He wondered if the problem had anything to do with Max. His daughter hadn't seemed too happy earlier. And she should've been ecstatic, considering she was about to turn eighteen. Now it was way past midnight, so she was already eighteen.

He had a surprise present for her, a present he hadn't even told Lucky about because she would accuse him of spoiling Max. But hey, he *wanted* to spoil her. What the hell—eighteen only came along once in a lifetime; why not enjoy it with a brand-new silver BMW?

Lucky would kill him, but death would be worth it when he saw the look on Max's face.

"You are *not* coming in!" Cookie shrieked as Frankie tried in vain to get her to open the door of their room.

"Why not?" he demanded. "If I'm correct, it was *you* who ran out on *me*. I'm the innocent party."

"Innocent my ass!" Cookie yelled through the closed door. "You were so far up my dad's butt that you didn't even notice I was gone."

"Sure I did," Frankie answered soothingly. "I missed you like crazy."

"No you *didn't*. If you had, you would've called or texted."

"Maybe you should let me in so we can discuss this like two adults."

"No!"

"You're behavin' like a child."

"Screw *you*."

"Is that all you got to say?"

"Here's somethin' else. Good-bye."

"For crissakes, Cookie, at least let me get my bags."

"No!" she shouted, still steaming. "You made me ruin my hair, and I hate you."

Frankie could not believe he was getting the boot, and from a teenager, no less.

And what had he done?

Nothing.

Scowling, he turned around and headed for the elevator.

Peggy had never considered herself a lesbian, but then neither had Paige. They were merely two heterosexual women who found they could enjoy an occasional walk on the wild side. And wild it was.

Peggy could not recall Sidney making her come the way Paige had. In fact, Paige took her back to the early Vegas days, when sex really mattered and orgasms were a daily occurrence.

Paige knew her way around the female anatomy. She'd taken control, and Peggy had enjoyed every second.

When they were finished, Paige dressed and murmured that she had to get back to Gino before he awoke.

"I wish you could stay the night," Peggy found herself saying.

"So do I," Paige said. "I don't like leaving Gino for too long. He's old; one never knows. However, you'll come to his granddaughter's party tomorrow, and maybe after that . . ."

"I'll look forward to it," Peggy murmured.

And then Paige was gone, and once again Peggy found herself alone with her thoughts. Soon she would have to confront Armand about his choice of female companions.

She was his mother, it was her duty.

Ellie was clicking away. "Plenty of activity going on here," she remarked, almost to herself. "I'm just taking pictures, we'll see what we've got later. I think we have a definite bonanza."

"You think?" Kev said, attempting to stretch his aching legs. Crouching in the bushes was not for him, although it didn't seem to bother Ellie. She was into all the comings and goings, and there were plenty. It seemed there was a party taking place in the villa across from Billy's, and Ellie was capturing plenty of images as people came and went.

"We need to know who the girl is with Billy," Ellie said. "Think you can find out?"

"I'll do my best," Kev replied. "It shouldn't be a problem."

After a while, Ace realized it didn't look like Max was getting back to the hotel anytime soon. Cookie had told him she'd had to meet Lucky, but he wasn't sure he believed her. Now it was past one in the morning and he'd had it. He hadn't driven all the way to Vegas to be treated like this. After all, it wasn't as if Max had acted like she was thrilled to see him. No. He'd had to hang out with her crazy friends all night, sit through a painful concert, and then she'd taken off. To do what?

He didn't know, and he didn't care anymore. She was treating him as if he didn't matter, and he wanted out.

He took the present he'd brought her and placed the box on the bed. Then he wrote "Happy Birthday" on a piece of hotel stationery and left it on top.

After that, he grabbed his overnight bag and took off.

Max was no longer his problem.

* * *

And still Fouad found it impossible to sleep. He'd tried everything: watching a movie on TV, ordering a hot drink from room service, lying perfectly still and allowing his mind to go blank.

Nothing worked.

Somehow he couldn't shake the thought that something was going on with Armand, something bad.

Over the past few weeks, Armand's drug use had escalated to the point where he did not seem to be in control of his actions anymore. Sleeping with Martin Constantine's wife, then throwing her out of his apartment was a prime example of behavior gone wild. And then there was the embarrassing scene with Lucky Santangelo and the empty threats Armand had hurled at her. Not to mention his ongoing addiction to prostitutes.

Armand was in a bad place, and although Fouad resented the way he'd been treated lately, he still felt a certain responsibility toward Armand. Perhaps this was not the right time to desert him.

On a whim, Fouad decided to get dressed and take a walk.

What harm would it do to stroll past Armand's villa and make sure everything was all right?

CHAPTER SIXTY-TWO

Always expect the unexpected was one of Lucky's mottos, along with *Never fuck with a Santangelo.* So she wasn't surprised to observe the tableau that greeted her when she entered Armand's villa. A man awash in cocaine, a crack pipe, and champagne. That would be Armand. Another man, big and brawny—perhaps a bodyguard—joining in the activities. And a naked woman.

It occurred to Lucky that this was not the perfect moment to tear him a new asshole. He wouldn't understand, he wouldn't get it. Armand Jordan was completely trashed. If asked, he probably wouldn't even remember his own name.

What a shame; she'd been so looking forward to putting him straight.

She stood stock-still, staring at the scene that greeted her. The woman with mammoth breasts noticed her first. "Wanna join?" the woman slurred, waving her over. "Plenny fer everyone."

Lucky shook her head and thought how pathetic Armand Jordan was. He didn't deserve her wrath. Who would believe anything he said anyway? He was a nothing, a nobody. He wasn't worth her time.

She turned around and started to leave, only to find the man she'd first encountered blocking her way at the door.

He wasn't wasted like the others. He was stone-cold

sober, and he wanted to know who she was and what exactly she wanted.

"You first," she said, unable to stare him down because of his dark glasses, which she found most irritating.

"I asked what you want here," Mikey repeated. "This is a private party."

"Didn't you just tell me that I'd fit right in?" Lucky said, noticing the bulge of a gun at his waist.

"Don't get cutesy with me," Mikey said, signaling Luscious. "What'd you come here for?"

Luscious rushed to his side, gave Lucky a filthy look, and said, "Who's this?"

"That's what I'm tryin' t' find out," Mikey said, fast losing patience. "'Cause she don't belong here."

"You're so right I don't," Lucky agreed amicably. "Only I'm beginning to think that neither do you."

"Why're you takin' photos of other people?" Kev asked Ellie, who was snapping away. "You've got what we came for; time to split."

"I'm liking this other stuff," Ellie said, concentrating on catching images. "The dude with the sunglasses is classic. And there's some hot woman who just went inside the house."

"Jesus," Kev grumbled. "You're such a voyeur."

"Don't you know that's what real photographers do? They take pictures of interesting people. It's not all about dumb celebs and who they're sleeping with. Those are my money shots. It's the unexpected shots of real people that turn me on."

"I could think of somethin' else that'd turn you on," Kev said, realizing it was time he climbed out of the bushes and got some action going. He put his hand on the back of her neck, and gave her a little rub.

"I'm not sleeping with you," Ellie announced, still clicking away. "So don't go getting any ideas."

"You're not?" Kev said, deflated. "Why not?"

"Because," Ellie answered. "In case you don't get it, I don't play on your team."

For a moment Kev was not sure what she meant. Then it sunk in, and he couldn't believe his lousy luck. Only he would hit on a dyke! Dammit, why hadn't she told him before?

"Don't sweat it," Ellie assured him. "You might not be getting laid tonight, but at least you're making money."

"Thanks a lot," Kev said, wondering if it was too late to score a replacement.

"We're takin' care of Arnie," Luscious said, swiping her hand across her nose. "He's havin' himself a good ole' time. I don't remember nobody invitin' you."

"May I ask what's in the suitcase?" Lucky said, pointedly staring at the case Mikey had managed to drag outside the door.

"That wouldn't be your concern, now would it?" Mikey said flatly.

"Maybe I should ask . . . Arnie," Lucky said, her face betraying no emotion. "What do you think?"

"I think you should get t' fuck outta here if y'know what's healthy f' you," Mikey said. "An' forget 'bout anythin' you seen here."

"Is that what you think?" Lucky said, wondering exactly what was going on. "Really?"

Mikey hated the fact that he didn't seem to be getting through to this cunt. She was standing in front of him chill as a fuckin' tall glass of lemonade. She should be running her ass for the hills, not sassing him with her rich-bitch demeanor.

He stepped aside to let her pass through the door. Best to get rid of her; she reeked of trouble.

"Like I told you—get the fuck outta here," he said in his most menacing voice.

"I'm not sure I'm planning on doing that," Lucky replied, cool as an ice cube, still standing in the doorway.

Mikey stepped close to her, so close she could smell his vile breath. "Listen, bitch. Go," he said, adding a threatening "While you still can."

Lucky gave him an implacable look and didn't budge.

This infuriated Mikey, who was shocked that she possessed the gall not to run for the hills—which is exactly what she should be doing. He frightened people; they were supposed to be scared. But not this one. Oh no, fuckin' Miss Movie Star was unafraid.

"I'll go when I've talked to Arnie," she said.

"What're you, his fuckin' wife?" Mikey exploded.

"Would that be a problem if I was?"

Mikey didn't know what to say. If she *were* the john's wife, she'd know about the money—or would she? And if she knew about it, that wouldn't be good, for in Mikey's mind the money was already his, and nobody else was getting their hands on it.

"I don't wanna hurt you," Mikey threatened. "But hear this: if you don't haul your ass outta here, you're likely t' make it happen, an' it'd be a shame t' mess up your pretty face."

Lucky felt her adrenaline rise. Nothing and no one frightened her; she'd been through too much in her life. She'd discovered her mother's brutalized body floating in the family swimming pool when she was five. She'd seen her brother's dead body thrown from a moving car. She'd watched her fiancé, Marco, shot to death in front of her. Did this two-bit punk and his scrawny girlfriend honestly think they were scaring her? No way.

It wasn't that she gave a damn about Armand Jordan and what he'd gotten himself into. But the situation intrigued her. And it had been a while since she'd been faced with an element of danger. She felt invigorated and ready for anything.

"I don't know what scam you're pulling—and believe me I don't particularly care," she said evenly. "Only I'm not leaving until I talk to Armand, so if you'll excuse me, I'm going back inside."

Mikey put his hand on her arm to stop her.

She shook it off and gave him a look that clearly said, *Do not touch me. Or you will regret it.*

There was something in her dark eyes that made him think twice about messing with her. Fuck it. If she wanted to go back inside, let her. He had the money; why hang around? This bitch was about to cause nothing but trouble, so the smart thing would be to get out while things were relatively calm.

"Let's go," he said to Luscious as Lucky moved past them back into the house.

"Huh?" Luscious responded. "You're gonna let her—"

"I told you," Mikey snarled. "We're outta here. Now help me with the goddamn suitcase."

Billy and Max stayed by the window, observing the goings-on at the villa across from them. They'd watched as Lucky marched up to the front door and encountered a man dragging a suitcase out. They'd both assumed that once she realized she was at the wrong villa and that Billy wasn't there, she would leave. But that hadn't happened. She'd gone inside, then reappeared at the door and was now involved in some sort of animated discussion with the suitcase man and a woman. Unfortunately, neither Billy nor Max could hear anything except the blaring music.

"What is she *doing?*" Max said, peering to get a better look.

"Beats me," Billy replied.

And then they saw her vanish back inside the villa.

"Where do you think Lennie is?" Max said. "This is, like, so weird."

"Hey," Billy replied. "It's kinda obvious she's not on to us. It looks as if she's got her own thing goin' on."

"What do you mean by *that?*" Max asked, wide-eyed.

"I mean it's a coincidence that we happen to be in the next villa. There's some all-night party goin' on over there, an', uh, Lucky's obviously into it."

"Are you crazy?" Max exclaimed. "Why would my mom be at a party without Lennie?"

Billy shrugged. "Sometimes married couples do things on their own. I dunno, Green Eyes, you just gotta be thankful she's not stalkin' us."

But Max wasn't thankful, not at all. Something was going on, and she was determined to figure out what it was.

CHAPTER SIXTY-THREE

Martin Constantine was not a violent man. Ruthless, perhaps, but when building a business empire one had to be uncompromising and tough. And since he'd come up the hard way, those were two qualities Martin possessed in abundance.

Business, making deals, and accumulating a fortune was Martin's life. That and his exquisite wife, Nona.

Nona and he had been introduced by a mutual acquaintance in New York, and Martin was immediately smitten with the exotic-looking Slovakian beauty queen. So much so that it didn't take long before he'd divorced his wife of thirty years and promptly married the delectable Nona. Martin was sixty-five and Nona was twenty-five. The discrepancy in their ages made no difference to Martin. What was forty years between soul mates?

Eight months into their marriage, Nona had given birth to Martin's one and only son. Since his first wife had only managed to pop out girls—three in a row—Martin was ecstatic. He doted on his wife and his young son. They, along with his business empire, were his life.

Yes, life was very good until the confession.

The confession came one day as they sat at the breakfast table. Nona suddenly broke down in floods of tears. Concerned, Martin asked her what was wrong. In between wracking sobs, Nona told him.

She'd made a mistake. A terrible mistake.

Martin informed her that there was no mistake that could not be rectified.

Secure in the knowledge that he worshipped her, Nona began telling him the story. She told him that she'd gone to Armand Jordan's apartment to view a rare Picasso he'd recently purchased, and that once she was there, Armand had suddenly gone berserk, and viciously raped her in every possible way. Now she suspected that she might be pregnant.

At first Martin had not believed this could happen, that Armand Jordan would dare to commit such a vile act. But once she got talking, Nona insisted on reliving every disgusting detail, including the way Armand had tossed her out of his apartment when he was finished with her as if she were a sack of garbage.

Martin's fury grew. He was not angry at his wife, for she was merely the victim of a perverted monster who had taken out on her his frustration at not getting a building they were vying for. His rage was directed toward Armand.

But Martin Constantine had ways of dealing with rage. And it wasn't long before he took steps to alleviate his anger and his wife's pain.

Nobody messed with Martin Constantine's family and got away with it. Nobody.

Martin knew exactly what he had to do.

CHAPTER SIXTY-FOUR

There was no Lucky waiting for him in their apartment, which right away made Lennie uneasy. It was his first night back, and usually when they'd been separated for a while, they didn't leave each other's side. He blamed himself. Lucky had wanted to depart Mood earlier, and because he was being obtuse about Alex Woods, he'd insisted on staying. Now where was his beautiful stubborn wife, and what problem was she dealing with in the early hours of the morning?

Knowing Lucky, she was probably doing this purposely to get his attention. Not that she needed to do that, she'd always had his attention from the very first moment they'd met. Ah yes, their lives were filled with memories . . . making mad crazy love on a raft in the South of France, falling insanely in love while they were both married to other people, enjoying all kinds of challenging adventures.

So where was she?

He paced around the apartment for a few minutes before picking up the phone and calling Danny.

Danny was at a gay club with his partner, Buff. They were contemplating whether to ask a handsome young barman if he would care to come home with them and spend the night.

Buff was all for it, but Danny was not so sure. He wasn't that fond of sharing Buff with anyone. Why should he?

On the other hand, if it was what Buff wanted, who was he to deprive him?

Danny's phone buzzed. For a moment he panicked. Phone calls in the middle of the night could only mean bad news. His needy mom? His disapproving stepdad? His straight brother who could never hold a job for more than two minutes?

He'd imbibed three cosmos, and decided that he wasn't ready to deal with any kind of a crisis, but he rallied anyway, and answered the phone.

It was Lennie, wanting to know where Lucky was.

"I'm off the clock," Danny sniffed.

"Does that mean you don't give a shit?" Lennie responded, sounding pissed off.

Danny gathered his thoughts. He was speaking to his boss's husband, so maybe he should make out as if he cared. Which of course he did, but he couldn't help noticing that Buff was whispering in the bartender's ear, and that wasn't right, that wasn't sharing. A threesome meant three people, not two.

"Uh, sorry, Mr. Golden," Danny said, throwing Buff a dirty look. "I thought Mrs. Golden was with you."

"She was. But apparently something came up that she had to deal with. Any idea what it could be?"

"No."

"Okay then." He waited a moment, then said, "You're sure?"

"Quite sure, Mr. Golden."

Lennie put down the phone.

Danny clicked off his cell, failing to notice that he had a text message waiting.

Frankie could not believe he was out in the cold with his dick in his hand. Cookie had turned out to be a tough little minx. She hadn't even opened the door for him to collect his stuff. Juvie cunt. She had his clothes and, even more upsetting, his drug stash.

And what exactly had he done? Nothing earth-shattering. He'd been polite to her old man, something that should've pleased her. But oh no, nothing was good enough for Gerald M.'s daughter. She was a spoiled brat, although he had to admit she gave great head.

And thinking of head, what was Annabelle doing with Eddie Falcon? Or rather, what was Eddie Falcon doing with her? Strange bedfellows. Eddie Falcon was a comer; he didn't have to settle for used goods.

Frankie made his way back to the casino in the hope that he might find Gerald M. at one of the tables. They could resume their friendship, especially when he was able to tell Gerald M. that his lovely daughter was safely tucked in for the night.

Frankie felt like doing a couple of lines, but he was fresh out and Cookie wasn't opening her door anytime soon.

He had a name and a number. Randy—the delivery-man.

Frankie decided to give him a call.

"I dunno what," Max said. "But something shady is going on."

"Hey," Billy said. "Your mom's at a party. No biggie."

"You don't understand," Max said, trying not to lose patience with Billy, who was starting to annoy her. "Lennie came home today. There's *no way* she'd go to a party without him."

"Like I said—in marriages certain events happen. Lucky's doin' her own thing. I know she's your mom, but she's one helluva sexy lady, an' maybe Lennie just doesn't do it for her anymore."

"You are so full of crap, Billy," Max said, suddenly

furious. "You don't know anything about my parents, nothing at all, so kindly shut your face."

"*And* she has a temper," Billy said.

"Yes," Max said, shooting him a daggers look. "She has a temper."

"Sorry, babe."

"About what?" Max said, still angry. "Being rude about my parents?"

"I wasn't being rude, I was simply trying to tell you the way it is in some marriages."

"And what makes *you* an expert?"

"C'mon, Green Eyes," he groaned. "I don't wanna fight about this."

"I'm going over there," she said, making up her mind.

"You're doing *what?*" Billy said, frowning.

"I'm seeing for myself what's going on."

"Big mistake."

"Why?"

"'Cause first she's gonna want to know what you're doin' here," Billy explained. "An' second, if she's havin' herself a good time, you're only gonna embarrass her."

"It's a party, Billy. I'll sneak in; she won't even see me."

"Then I'm comin' with you."

"Not a plan."

"Why?"

"'Cause if she spots me an' then you, well, you know Lucky—she's not stupid."

"And if she *does* see you, what're you gonna say?"

"I dunno. I'll think of something."

"It's not a good idea," Billy warned.

"Well, it's *my* idea, and *I'm* doing it."

CHAPTER SIXTY-FIVE

The pain hit Armand in the pit of his stomach. It startled him, almost made him gag. Not quite, for he had no time to give in to pain. He was enjoying himself too much. He had never experienced such joyous feelings. He was wrapped in a warm cloak of bliss, which might have had a little something to do with the speedball Randy had shared with him—the lethal combination of heroin and cocaine.

Randy and Seducta were his best friends in the world. They cared about him in ways that were so endearing. Seducta had taken her top off again, and he snuggled his face against her mammoth breasts. She reminded him of his mother—dear, sweet Peggy.

Randy snorted coke off her nipples.

Armand smiled. They were sharing. This was exactly the way it should be.

And then suddenly, there was Lucky Santangelo staring down at him. Words were coming out of her mouth, but he couldn't hear them.

He decided that Lucky was beautiful too. She was his friend. He didn't want her dead, he didn't want anyone dead. They would own The Keys together and exist in perfect harmony.

The pain hit Armand again. He screamed and doubled over. Then everything faded to black.

* * *

"For God's sake, someone call 911!" Lucky yelled, wondering how she'd gotten caught up in this situation. She was supposed to be reaming Armand a new asshole, not saving his sorry life. How had this happened?

Randy staggered to his feet. He was almost as out of it as Armand, but self-preservation kicked in, and it occurred to him that he'd better get out. He looked around for Luscious.

"Jesus Christ!" Lucky exclaimed, reaching for her cell. "This man could be dying and you can't even make a phone call. What kind of people are you?"

Seducta giggled hysterically. "Fun people," she said, her voice a drowsy slur, white powder decorating her nose. "Arnie loves us."

"While Arnie might love you, he could be dying, you stupid cow," Lucky said, calling 911 and requesting an ambulance.

"Where's Mikey?" Seducta asked, her face crumbling, mascara smudged under her eyes.

Randy flexed his considerable muscles. "Where's the fuckin' money?" he wanted to know.

"You people are the dregs," Lucky said, feeling Armand's wrist to see if he had a pulse. He did.

"We gotta get t' fuck away from this shit," Randy said, suddenly realizing that trouble was looming.

"That's right, run," Lucky said. "You pathetic pieces of crap."

"Where's Mikey?" Seducta whined for the second time. "I want my Mikey."

Ten minutes after speaking to Lennie, Danny checked his messages. Sure enough, there was one from Lucky.

He could've kicked himself, for Danny prided himself on always being available to his boss. He quickly scanned her text and experienced a sinking feeling in his stomach.

Armand Jordan is going around boasting that The Keys is his. Off to Cavendish to confront. Care to join?

Yes, he would love to have joined if only he'd known. It was all Buff's fault, flirting with the bartender, taking his mind off work. Threesomes. Ha! Who needed them?

He called Lennie and filled him in on the situation, telling him about the unfortunate morning meeting and what a chauvinistic pig Armand was.

"And you let Lucky go over there alone?" Lennie said, his voice heated.

"I didn't know!" Danny replied, duly chastised. "Besides, have you ever tried stopping Lucky from doing anything? You know it's impossible."

"I'm on my way to the Cavendish," Lennie said.

"I'll meet you there," Danny said.

To hell with Buff and the bartender. Lucky was his priority.

"So!" Ellie exclaimed. "Lots of activity at the party house."

"Aren't you supposed to be concentrating on Billy an' the girl?"

"I've got more than enough pix of them together. Anyway, they're back in the villa. Whaddya want me to do, crawl through the keyhole?"

"Don't be facetious."

"Big words coming from a little guy."

"I might be on the short side, but haven't you heard about large surprises comin' in small packages?"

"Lost on me, Kev," Ellie said, shaking her head. "I told you—I'm gay."

"I could turn you."

"Confident, aren't we?"

"Wanna give it a go?"

"No thank you."

"Can't blame a dude for tryin'."

"However," Ellie said with a wicked smile, "if you were to suddenly change into Billy Melina . . ."

"Fuck *you!*" Kev said. Why was everything always about Billy?

"No chance," Ellie said, laughing. "Not unless you cut off your dick and call yourself Daisy!"

Danny met Lennie at the top of the pathway that led to the villas. "Villa number four," he said, all business. "Apparently there've been complaints about the noise coming from there."

"Noise?"

"Music. My friend at the desk says there must be a party going on. One more complaint and they're sending security."

"Why haven't they done so already?"

"They don't like messing with the high rollers," Danny explained. "Bad for business."

"So you think Lucky walked in on a party?" Lennie said.

Danny shrugged. "I don't know. Armand Jordan didn't strike me as a party animal, unless it involves hookers."

"Why does Lucky do this?" Lennie questioned.

"Do what?"

"Walk herself into situations she can't control."

"She's *your* wife."

"Thanks, Danny," Lennie said dryly. "I think I know that."

"I'm sure she's fine," Danny said.

Fouad hurried down the pathway toward the villas. He had a bad feeling in his gut. Something wasn't right, he knew it. Leaving Armand alone to do whatever he felt like doing was not wise. Armand was too volatile a personality—he had to have some restraints. Fouad had always been the voice of reason, a calming influence. The truth was, Armand needed him.

It was cold out and quite dark, but Fouad could hear loud music ahead of him, and he was sure it must be coming from Armand's villa.

As he got nearer, he suddenly encountered two people, a man wearing sunglasses at night and a skinny, raggedy-looking woman. Fouad might have passed them with a polite nod of acknowledgement, except for one thing. Between the two of them they were lugging one of Armand's distinctive Louis Vuitton suitcases—his initials on the handle.

Immediately, Fouad knew. It had to be the suitcase packed with money that Armand always insisted on bringing to Vegas. Over $750,000 in cash.

"Excuse me," Fouad said.

Mikey stopped for a moment. "What?" he snarled.

"I think you have something that doesn't belong to you."

CHAPTER SIXTY-SIX

On the stroke of midnight, Mr. O arrived in Las Vegas by private plane. A rented town car waited for him at a prearranged spot, the keys under the floor mat as he'd requested.

Mr. O could have been a *GQ* model or a famous actor. He was black and beautiful, a cross between Denzel Washington and Blair Underwood. However, Mr. O had chosen a different profession—a profession that would last as long as he wanted. A profession that paid him top dollar, because he was the best at what he did.

Mr. O was a mechanic. A hit man. A solver of anyone's problem—as long as the price was right.

Mr. O was the best at what he did. And only the best hired him.

This was not the first job he was about to do for Martin Constantine, and it would not be the last.

Mr. O always took care of business.

CHAPTER SIXTY-SEVEN

Mikey was not about to accept shit from anyone. He'd had a trying evening, and now he was all set to take off with the prize—a suitcase stuffed full of Benjamins. The last thing Mikey needed was some random ass wipe stopping him and telling him that the suitcase was not his.

Luscious hovered next to him, a shivery presence in her tiny skirt and top. She wouldn't be any help in an argument; she was already a hindrance.

Mikey had decided that when they reached Randy's car, he'd send her back, ostensibly to get the others, then he'd drive off into the night, leaving them all behind. They were a worthless crew—including his big ox of a brother. The truth was, he had no use for any of them.

Mikey took a long steady look at the man confronting him. He did not seem like a threat; he seemed nervous, which was good, because Mikey enjoyed making people nervous.

"You wanna get outta my way, sport?" he said, standing very still. "I won this suitcase legitimate, so back t' fuck off."

"Yeah," Luscious said, joining in, her tinny little voice getting on his nerves. "Back t' fuck off."

Mikey shot her a scathing glare. What were they—a comedy duo?

"I'm afraid I shall have to confirm that with the prince," Fouad said, asserting his authority, although his hands were trembling and he wasn't sure if he could handle this.

"Prince?" Luscious squeaked.

"This is a gamblin' town," Mikey said flatly. "I won this fair an' square. You don't hav'ta check with no one."

"I'm afraid I do," Fouad said, standing his ground.

There was a long moment of silence, then, in a sudden fit of temper, Mikey reached down into his boot and slid out the six-inch hunting knife. He'd had enough jacking around; it was time to go. "Is this what you're lookin' for?" he yelled at Fouad. "You wanna get yourself cut, mothafucker? Is that what ya want?"

"The suitcase does not belong to you," Fouad said, his throat so dry that he could barely speak. "Kindly leave it and get away from here."

"You dumb *fuck*," Mikey snarled, plunging the knife into Fouad's chest. "You dumb, cocksuckin' fuck!"

Fouad staggered slightly, thought about his wife and children for a brief second, then fell to the ground.

Standing at the window, Max and Billy watched in horror as the man with the suitcase produced a knife and began stabbing the other man.

"Oh my God!" Max yelled, panicking. "We've got to do something."

"I'll call security," Billy said quickly.

"No, no it'll be too late," Max urged. "We have to help now."

Lucky decided there was nothing she could do for Armand except wait for the paramedics. Then she heard yelling, so she ran outside in time to observe Mikey, in a frenzy, stabbing Fouad, who was now on the ground.

She didn't hesitate. Grabbing Mikey's right arm, she twisted it back until she forced him to drop the knife.

Mikey turned on her in a deadly fury. "You fuckin'

bitch," he screamed, kicking and punching her. "I'll fuckin' kill you."

"Oh my God!" Max cried out, still by the window. "It's my mom. We've got to help her!" She ran outside and, without thinking, pounced on Mikey's back, clinging tightly around his neck and scratching his face, while Lucky attempted to pick herself up and reach the knife.

With a roar of anger, Mikey sent Max flying, then swooped down and grabbed the knife before Lucky could get to it. At which point Billy joined the fray, springing into action-hero mode, a role he'd played many times on the big screen. He'd had a few fights in his time, and he knew that the best line of defense was attack, so he directed a vicious kick at Mikey's balls.

Mikey doubled over for a few seconds before letting out another powerful yell and striking out with the knife, catching Billy down the side of his cheek.

Blood flowed.

By this time, Lucky was up, and only thinking of protecting her daughter. She had no idea where Max had come from or what she was doing here, but it didn't matter. All Lucky wanted was to get Max away from the violence, somewhere safe.

"Get out of here!" she yelled at Max. "Run! Go get help!"

"I can't leave Billy," Max cried, sinking to the ground and cradling Billy's head in her lap, attempting to staunch the flow of blood. "He's hurt. Oh my God! He's bleeding."

Fouad was also on the ground, moaning, while Luscious stood to one side—transfixed. Was it? Could it be? Was she looking at Billy Melina, the movie star?

Mikey possessed the strength of a bull. His adrenaline was running strong. Three down. All that was left was the woman, and she wasn't backing away. Oh no.

She was staring at him like a black widow spider waiting to pounce.

He had a strong urge to cut the bitch, cut her good. But even more important was taking off with the suitcase.

Where the fuck was Randy?

"Randy!" He roared his brother's name, and the big oaf came lumbering out of the villa, buttoning up his pants.

"What the fuck," Randy mumbled, taking in the chaos.

"We're gettin' outta here," Mikey commanded. "Pick up the fuckin' suitcase, an' let's go."

Lucky stood back and watched them, savvy enough to realize there was nothing she could do, although if she'd had a gun she would not have hesitated to use it. They were the dregs. Criminal dregs. And they were stupid too. She knew without a doubt that they'd be caught within twenty-four hours.

"So long, bitch," Mikey said, throwing her a triumphant look. "Whoever t' fuck you are."

The fight was over. The Sorrentino brothers were on their way, Luscious trailing behind them, Seducta left snoring on the couch inside the villa.

As soon as they were gone, Lucky took stock of the situation. The sudden violence was over. In spite of everything, Max seemed to be okay. Fouad was not so good, and Billy was still bleeding.

"The paramedics will be here any minute," she said, gazing intently at her daughter. "Are you okay?"

Max nodded, a lone tear trickling down her cheek. "I was so scared for you, Mom. I tried to help. *We* tried to help."

"Yes," Lucky said gravely. "I know you did." Then she added with the hint of a smile, "We make quite a team. Where did *you* learn to kick ass?"

Max gave a wan smile. "From my amazing mom, where else?"

And they exchanged a warm look.

Minutes later Lennie and Danny arrived, followed by the paramedics.

Lucky knew that this was not the right time to ask Max what was going on. There was always another day. And eventually she would find out everything.

CHAPTER SIXTY-EIGHT

Mysteries take place, and sometimes they are never solved.

Take the case of Armand Jordan. The man lost consciousness due to an overindulgence of liquor, heroin, and cocaine. The paramedics arrived in time to save him, but it was not to be, because no one was able to save him from the precise bullet hole right between his eyes.

Prince Armand Mohamed Jordan had been shot execution style, and only two men knew why.

To everyone else it was a mystery that would never be solved.

EPILOGUE
Three Months Later

Everyone was questioned about Armand Jordan's murder, even Lucky. It became quite clear to the investigating detectives that while the melee was taking place in front of the villa, a lone assassin had managed to somehow slip inside the villa and finish Armand off.

It was a professional hit, no doubt about it. The only witness was an exotic dancer commonly known as Seducta Sinn. But Seducta claimed to have been asleep (passed out) at the time, and saw and heard nothing.

Within days, Mikey and Randy Sorrentino were arrested outside of Nashville and charged with grand theft and aggravated assault.

They both lawyered up and instantly turned against each other.

Mikey ended up back in jail, while Randy found himself facing ten months' probation.

The money suitcase was eventually returned to Fouad, minus $15,000.

Seducta Sinn reveled in a few weeks of minor celebrity. She was the woman in the same hotel room as a murder victim—a well-known New York businessman. She was an exotic dancer, and all the TV shows clamored for an interview.

Her newfound fame did not last long, and eventually she resumed her job at Dirty Den's. A few weeks later she filed for divorce from Mikey, and shortly after that she moved in with Randy.

The two of them decided they'd found true happiness at last, even though Randy didn't have a job, and some nights Seducta was too drunk to make it to Dirty Den's.

But true happiness comes in all different forms, and they were content.

Luscious vanished with the $10,000 she'd persuaded Mikey to give her from the infamous suitcase. The moment they'd left Vegas, she'd decided she wanted out. Mikey scared her, and she'd finally decided that Randy was an idiot.

She'd worked on Mikey until he'd agreed to give her some money, then she'd taken it and fled. She hadn't wanted any involvement in what she thought of as the Cavendish Hotel incident. She'd changed her name and taken a bus cross-country to Chicago, where she got a job as a waitress and faded into the background of a mundane life. For the time being, living a mundane life suited her just fine.

Paco informed Harry, after one brief awkward encounter in the men's room at Wonderball, that he wasn't (just as Max had suspected) gay after all.

A very disappointed Harry continued searching for the right one.

Annabelle and Eddie got married at The Beverly Hills Hotel. It was the first time for both of them, and each of them had their reasons.

Eddie figured marrying Annabelle was somehow or other getting himself attached to Hollywood royalty. After all, her parents were movie stars, even though her dad, the very famous Ralph Maestro, had probably arranged the murder of her very famous mother, Gemma Summer Maestro.

Who cared? This was a Hollywood murder. Ralph Maestro walked free.

And Annabelle decided that marrying Eddie was a good thing because he was a comer with clout and an A-list cluster of clients.

One day Eddie would run a studio, Annabelle was sure of it. And she'd be Mrs. Eddie Falcon, with power up the wazoo. Not such a bad thing.

She never spoke of her evening with Armand Jordan. It was best forgotten.

Alex Woods still had lust in his heart for the unobtainable Lucky Santangelo. He moved yet another Asian beauty in with him, and bided his time.

Alex was not a man who gave up easily.

Remaining Venus's resident stud for almost three months garnered Jorge a huge amount of publicity. The two of them were all over the Internet, a staple of gossip columns, and of magazines that loved nothing better than putting them on the cover. Together, they made a stunning couple.

The publicity benefited them both. Women were envious of Venus, but they also admired the fact that at forty-something, she was able to attract and keep the attention of such a virile young man.

Jorge became a known name in his own right. So much so that Calvin Klein hired him to be the face and body of the next big underwear campaign.

Jorge was on his way to getting exactly what he wanted.

Fame.

Money.

Recognition.

Love would come later.

Meanwhile, Venus met a Venezuelan avant-garde film director who saw her as more than just a blond and beautiful superstar sex symbol who happened to sing, dance, and act. He saw her as everywoman, an earthy creature whose incredible potential had yet to be unleashed on the world.

She saw him as the intellectual savior she had been searching for.

Together they had big plans.

Danny and Buff got married in Oregon. The trip was a wedding present from Lucky, who felt Danny deserved some time off.

Danny complained all the way about how ridiculous it was that gay marriage was not legal in California, the most laid-back state of all.

Buff heartily agreed.

And after five wonderful days, they returned to Vegas in full wedded bliss.

M.J. never did get to take Cassie on the trip he'd planned, for the night of Armand Jordan's murder was the night she lost their baby, solving all their problems. Although deep down, M.J. couldn't help feeling that maybe she'd done something to facilitate the miscarriage.

He desperately tried to put it out of his mind, but somehow it lingered.

Fouad recovered nicely. His wife and children flew to Las Vegas to be by his side, and later, back in New York, they all shared in the surprise that Armand Jordan had split his estate fifty-fifty. Half to his mother, and the other half to Fouad.

It made Fouad sad that Armand had come to such an unfortunate end, for although Armand had been an extremely difficult and challenging man, they had indeed shared many interesting times before the drugs had taken hold.

Strangely enough, Fouad missed him.

To celebrate his newfound position as head of Jordan Developments, Fouad collected all of Armand's sex DVDs and promptly destroyed them.

He determined that Armand's legacy would be pristine, and that his reputation would remain untarnished.

Peggy Dunn was all set to organize a spectacular New York funeral for her only son. She had Fouad contact the king and tell him the sad news in case he wanted to attend. The king responded by saying that he wished the funeral to take place in Akramshar. It would be a state funeral, and his people would make all the arrangements.

Peggy agreed, and it was then that Fouad revealed that Armand had a wife and four children in Akramshar.

At first Peggy was horrified and shocked. How could Armand have a family she knew nothing about? Why had he never told her? It was unbelievable.

But as the news settled in, she experienced a strong feeling of excitement and anticipation.

She had grandchildren. Four of them. She was not alone, she had a family.

Peggy couldn't wait to meet them.

On the plane to Akramshar, sitting beside Fouad and his lovely wife, Alison, she reached into her purse and took out the envelope from the DNA sample lab. She had not opened it, and now she decided she never would.

In her mind, Armand was a prince. May he rest in peace.

* * *

Ace returned to Big Bear, where he hooked up with a young, pretty waitress who came from a similar background to his. He tried to forget Max Santangelo. She wasn't for him; why had he been fooling himself? They lived in two different worlds, and much as he'd tried to fit in, he'd finally realized it was never going to happen.

Kev became rich, or relatively so, for Ellie's pictures caused a bidding war among the tabloids, and true to her word, Ellie cut him in for half.

But Kev wasn't happy. He'd betrayed his friend, and not only that, he'd stayed hidden in the bushes like a coward as the dude with the knife had started attacking everyone. He hadn't even emerged to help Billy, and the guilt was killing him.

He took his money and slunk off to New York.

Ellie sold her pictures to the tabloids before talking to the police. As a potential material witness she was sternly warned that she should have come forward instead of concealing evidence. She never mentioned that there was someone with her. Kev had begged her not to say he was present, so she'd complied.

Eventually she'd hired a lawyer, pleaded innocence, and handed over all her photos.

All except one.

She'd captured the image of a tall African American man in a black suit, slipping quietly into the villa as Randy emerged.

Was she the only one to see him?

Apparently so.

She placed the photo in a safe-deposit box and wrote a note to her significant other that if anything happened to her it should be given to the police.

Ellie was nothing if not street-smart.

* * *

Sam's movie came out and was a big hit. Hollywood wanted him, and was prepared to pay for the privilege.

He still sent Denver the occasional text, but she had yet to visit him on the set.

In Sam's mind, there was always tomorrow.

Gerald M. took off on a European tour with a Swedish blonde he'd met in Vegas. He was proud to have her accompany him to London, Paris, and Berlin, countries where he was still a certified superstar. The fans appreciated the smooth soul that was the sound of Gerald M. They worshipped at his feet.

He asked Cookie if she'd like to accompany them.

She declined. Having the run of the Bel Air house all to herself was a far more tempting prospect.

Since moving on from Frankie, and hitting the street with a sexy new hairstyle, Cookie had discovered there were far more interesting prospects out there than a coked-out old loser like Frankie.

Cookie decided she wanted to be an actress, and enrolled in acting class.

Young, hot would-be actors were everywhere.

Soon Cookie was having herself a fine old time.

Dumped by a truculent, spoiled teenager, Frankie Romano drove back to L.A. determined not to sleep with any girl under twenty-one. He was part of the Hollywood club scene, for crissakes. Pussy abounded. He was a star in his own world.

His drug business was out of control. Supply could not keep up with demand. He'd partnered up with a young Colombian, Alejandro Diego, who had big family connections back in Colombia, and who assured him he could keep the supply coming. Now the money was really rolling in.

Frankie loved his life. He wouldn't have it any other way.

Max and Billy. Caught on camera for all to see. Cover of the tabloids along with MURDER AT VEGAS HOTEL—as most headlines screamed. Billy came across as the hero of everyone's dreams. This super-hot movie star had gotten his handsome face cut defending his young girlfriend. Although his PR team immediately denied that Max was his girlfriend—in spite of the intimate photos that appeared everywhere. According to his reps, she was merely a family friend he'd been protecting.

Billy was rushed to the emergency room, and the finest plastic surgeon in Beverly Hills was flown in to consult on his damaged face. The cut on his cheek turned out to be a surface wound, and within weeks Billy was back to his handsome self, a handsome self whose advisers (lawyers, PR people, the studio, etc.) had warned him to stay under the radar until his divorce from Venus was finalized, and not to see Max.

Reluctantly he'd agreed it was for the best. After all, he was getting a divorce from an icon, and already carrying on with a teenage girl was not the image his people wished him to project. "The public can turn on you like a dime," they warned him. "Do not screw with a brilliant career. Not at this time."

He spoke to Max on the phone and told her they should cool it for a few weeks. She wasn't heartbroken; too much was going on and she needed to get her head straight. She was a big girl now. Eighteen. And although Lucky had decided the right thing to do was cancel the Vegas party, she'd been okay with it. Especially when Lucky suggested that they take a family trip to the South of France instead.

Her mom had turned out to be way cooler than she'd ever thought. Lucky didn't berate her about Billy, she merely shrugged and said, "We can't help who we fall for. But maybe Billy wasn't the best choice."

Max still thought about Billy.

She thought about Ace too.

Ace had left her such a thoughtful gift and a sad little note. She knew he had to have seen the photos of her and Billy, and it tore her up imagining his reaction.

Ace had always been her rock, and she'd let him down, but as Lucky said—"We can't help who we fall for."

After giving in to the L word, Denver and Bobby returned to L.A. and settled in to the new house Bobby purchased. "No huge megamansions," Denver had warned him. "Something manageable, please. And not in any fancy area. I like normal."

"Normal" turned out to be a one-story house in the Hollywood hills with three bedrooms and a panoramic view of the city. It had a reasonably sized garden and a simple lap pool. Amy Winehouse was in dog heaven!

Denver finally introduced Bobby to her family, not without a great deal of trepidation. Surprise, they all loved him. And as her mom said, "What's not to love? He's a great guy."

Yes, Bobby was a great guy, and she was happy they'd moved in together. She was also happy with her new position in the drug unit. Working closely with Leon was a kick, and they had a lot going on. Leon had been tracking a Colombian drug lord, Pablo Diego, for months, and they were near to closing in on his U.S. connections. Pablo's son, Alejandro, was one of their main targets, along with all the dealers he supplied. A series of arrests was imminent.

Denver was well aware that one of their upcoming arrests would be Frankie Romano. Ethics prevented her from mentioning this to Bobby. What he didn't know, he couldn't do anything about, and even though Frankie was no longer his close friend, Bobby had an innate sense of loyalty, and could try to warn Frankie, enabling him to skip town.

This could not happen, so silence ruled.

Denver loved Bobby so much. She'd even attended a few of *his* family events, and managed to forge a warm relationship with Lucky—who was not as intimidating as she'd imagined. She also adored Lennie, who was so smart and acerbic in a delightfully clever way. And she and Max were warming up to each other slowly but surely.

All in all, Denver felt nothing but positive thoughts about her future with Bobby.

Things were going so well that Bobby had a plan. He'd pulled off buying a house and moving into it with Denver, and now he was thinking he wanted more. Denver was so damn special. Beautiful, smart, sexy, his best friend. What more could he look for in a woman?

He wanted to ask her to marry him, but instinctively he had a feeling she'd turn him down. It had taken him forever to get her to move into a house with him—marriage could send her running.

Or not.

He didn't know.

Help was needed, so he secretly met up with her best friend, Carolyn, who was now part of an extremely content lesbian couple, and asked her advice. Carolyn's advice was sound. "Do not rush her," she said. "When the time is right for both of you, you'll know it."

In the meantime, Bobby went to Tiffany's to purchase a seven-carat engagement ring, which Denver would probably think was way too flashy. But what the hell—it was his prerogative to spoil her.

He put the ring away, and waited patiently for the right time.

Lucky Santangelo Golden and Lennie Golden. True soul mates. Who said marriages in Hollywood didn't last?

They dealt with the Max/Billy situation in the only way they knew how, and that was with understanding, love, and a nonjudgmental attitude.

The South of France trip turned out to be exactly what everyone needed. They stayed with friends in a magnificent villa above Cannes, and Max hit it off with the son of the family, a twenty-two-year-old French aspiring screenwriter. Nothing serious, just fun. Lucky realized that was exactly what Max needed right now, some mindless fun.

Meanwhile, Lennie had plans of his own. "We're driving to Saint-Tropez for the day," he informed his wife. "Just you and me."

"Let's go," Lucky said, for she knew exactly what he had in mind.

And so it was that they relived the first time they'd made love. They went to the same beach and swam out to the same raft. Making love on it was just as amazing—if not better—than the first time.

Lucky still reveled in Lennie's touch. The excitement between them was still as passionate and intense. But everything had to come to a crashing halt when a couple of kids swam toward the raft and hauled themselves aboard.

Giggling as if they were teenagers themselves, Lucky and Lennie took off, plunging in the sea and swimming back to shore, where they collapsed on the sand, still giggling hysterically.

"Love you," Lennie muttered when they calmed down.

"I know," Lucky replied, her black-as-night eyes gazing into his.

They were two people who had found each other, and nothing and no one would ever split them apart.

Two reckless, passionate people, filled with sensual zest and a hearty thirst for living that would take them wherever they wished to go.

Lucky and Lennie. Two of a kind.

Read on to find a sneak peek
at extracts from

THE SANTANGELOS

Jackie Collins's dynamic new novel
in hardcover and eBook
in June 2015 from St. Martin's Press

PROLOGUE

The King of Akramshar—a small but wealthy Middle Eastern country located between Syria and Lebanon— ruled his oil-rich country with an iron fist. King Emir Amin Mohamed Jordan embraced many old-fashioned values, traditions, and rules. He had countless wives and over thirty children. In his mind they were all useless. Women were only good for two things—giving birth and being at his sexual beck and call. As for his offspring—some of them grown men—they were all disappointments. The only son who'd given him any pleasure at all was his dear departed son, Armand—a worthy successor to the King's coveted crown. And Armand was gone. Murdered by the American infidels. A bullet to the head in a degenerate American city called Las Vegas.

The King's fury was boundless. How could this have happened? And why?

The King had given Armand a royal funeral fit for his favorite son. His people had lined the streets, heads bowed, showing their respect as they should. Several of his many sons carried the gold casket on their shoulders. Peggy, Armand's American mother, his widow, Soraya, and his four children walked behind. The women, including Peggy, wore traditional robes covering their entire bodies. The King rode on a white stallion, resplendent in a gold-trimmed uniform, waving to his people.

King Emir was a man who believed in revenge. And who exactly was to blame for the unfortunate demise of his favorite son, shot to death like a dog?

King Emir had his own ideas. Armand had been trying to buy the very hotel he was murdered in—The Keys—a hotel owned by a woman. That a woman could actually own a hotel was ridiculous, but even more ridiculous—according to Peggy—the woman had refused to sell her property to Armand, and on top of that she had insulted him to his face, and the King had no doubt that it was she who had arranged for Armand's brutal murder.

King Emir simmered with fury, while dark thoughts of revenge filled his head. Justice had to be done.

But how?

Kill the woman? Take her life exactly as she had taken Armand's?

No. That was not punishment enough. The woman had to suffer, her family had to suffer.

This was a given.

King Emir was busy putting plans in place—for his rage would rain down on the offensive American mongrels. And they too would feel the pain.

LUCKY

The Keys was Lucky Santangelo Golden's dream hotel, but sometimes one can dream bigger, and Lucky had decided that she should create something even more special. She was at a place in her life where she felt that it was time for a new challenge. Everything was running smoothly, her kids were all doing well. Bobby, with his chain of successful clubs. Max, busy making a name for herself in London as an up-and-coming model. Young Gino Junior and Leonardo (Lennie's son she'd adopted) were ensconced in summer camp. And her father, Gino, was happily living out his days in Palm Springs with his fourth wife, Paige.

So Lucky had decided it was time to shake things up, and she'd come up with the idea of building a hotel/casino/apartment complex plus a movie studio. This was something nobody had done before. And why not? It was a brilliant idea.

When she'd told her filmmaker husband, Lennie, he'd thought it was crazy but certainly doable. The movie community would love it. Everything in one place. And it wasn't as if Lucky were a newcomer to making movies; she'd owned and run Panther Studios for several years. She *was* the Lady Boss. Lucky Santangelo could do anything she chose to do.

Today she was lunching with a team of architects that she was considering hiring. One of her favorite moves was testing people, observing their strengths and weaknesses, deciding if working with them would be calm or stressful.

Danny, her trusty assistant, accompanied her on the way to The Asian, an elegant Chinese restaurant in her hotel.

Danny was one of the few privy to the fact that she was plotting and planning on building yet another fantastic Vegas complex. Danny got it; he understood that The Keys—a truly amazing combination of grand hotel, luxurious apartments, and one of the best casinos in Vegas—was simply not enough for her. As usual, his dynamic boss wanted more.

The moment Lucky entered the restaurant conversation stopped and people stared. They couldn't help themselves, Lucky had a magnetic, charismatic quality about her.

She radiated a presence full of beauty, power, passion, and strength. A lethal combination.

Danny relished every minute of the way people reacted when they saw Lucky. She deserved the attention. She was a true star, an incredibly smart businesswoman who could achieve anything she set her mind to. The thing about Lucky was that she needed to be collaborative, but she also needed to be in control. Nobody told Lucky Santangelo what to do. Her motto was: "If I'm going to fail, I'll fail on my own mistakes, not on someone else's." Her other motto was: "Never fuck with a Santangelo."

Danny had both mottos engraved on two coffee mugs that sat in the kitchen of his L.A. apartment along with his somewhat mangy cat, Ethel.

BOBBY

It pissed Bobby Santangelo Stanislopoulos off that his live-in girlfriend, Denver Jones, was never available to travel with him. Even with texting, sexting, and Skype, long separations were no damn good. Oh sure, he understood that Denver was fixated on her job as a high-powered assistant district attorney, but surely— just sometimes—she could put him first?

Lately she'd been so into the drug case she was working on that even when he was home at their house in L.A., he barely saw her. She was intent to prosecute, and he'd never seen her so determined.

This too shall pass, he told himself. *And when it's over, I will finally give her the seven-carat Tiffany diamond engagement ring I purchased months ago, and ask her to marry me.*

He had to tread carefully with Denver, she wasn't like the other girls he'd been with. She was exceptionally smart, beautiful, and a self-achiever. She didn't want anything from him other than his love, and that suited him just fine, because as the heir to a great shipping fortune, most women looked at him with dollar signs flashing in their eyes.

Bobby Santangelo Stanislopoulos, son of the infamous Lucky Santangelo and the late Greek shipping tycoon Dimitri Stanislopoulos. Drop-dead handsome with longish dark hair, intense eyes, and olive skin— all inherited from the Santangelo side of the family. Six feet three, with his father's strong features and steely business acumen, plus Lucky's street smarts. An interesting mix of skills.

Without touching his massive inheritance, Bobby had gone into business for himself. Along with his partner M.J., they'd opened a chain of highly successful nightclubs called Mood. From New York to Las Vegas Mood was the place to see and be seen.

Currently they were in the process of opening Mood in Chicago and later in the year, Miami, which meant Bobby had a full agenda.

Pacing up and down in his Chicago hotel room, he missed Denver, although at the same time he was also kind of mad at her. In the course of pursuing a notorious drug cartel, she'd been part of a sting operation that had ended with the arrest of Frankie Romano. Poor old Frankie—who happened to be a long-time pal of Bobby's. Unfortunately, Frankie had gotten himself caught up in the so-called glamor of the Hollywood high life. A druggie, who'd once been Annabelle Maestro's boyfriend, Frankie had ended up partnering in a sleazy Hollywood club with the son of a Colombian drug lord, then gotten himself taken down for illegally peddling drugs. The charges against him were distribution and possession—charges that could get him a twenty-year prison sentence. It seemed his operation was connected to a notorious Colombian drug cartel—and Denver was making it her business to find out exactly how. She was relentless in her pursuit.

MAX

"More?" Athena Hyton-Smythe inquired, leaning over to her friend, Max Golden Santangelo. Athena was tall and ultra-skinny—six feet *without* her five-inch Louboutins. She had flame-colored, frizzed-out hair, cut-glass cheekbones, cat-eyes, and a permanent but super-sexy scowl. At twenty Athena was the current "It" girl of the modeling world, and Max was her sidekick, and on the way to making a name for herself as well. The London gossip columns had nicknamed them "The Terrible Two." They had a reputation for all-night partying and always being the leaders of the pack.

"More what?" Max replied, sucking a long, tall Mojito through a straw.

"Whatever turns you on," Athena said with a casual shrug of her glistening bare shoulders randomly scattered with gold glitter. "Coke, grass, tequila shots, Molly, pills, you name it." She indicated a heavyset man sitting in their booth downing shots of straight vodka. "This Russian dude is like a freakin' pharmacy. He's offering, so we should take advantage while we can. You know I don't get off on paying for my drugs."

Max leaned back on the plush leather banquette in the London club and considered her options. She was a very pretty girl with full pouty lips, emerald green eyes, and long dark hair. Tonight she wore a cut-off top, multiple gold chains, ridiculous heels, and tight black leather pants.

Max was eighteen, almost nineteen, and delighted that in London she could get away with drinking in clubs. Her brother, Bobby, who owned a string of successful nightclubs around the world, wouldn't allow her to drink in his Vegas and New York clubs. "You're underage," he'd informed her. "Go get someone else's license pulled."

"Screw you, Bobby," she'd always responded.

The truth was that since moving to London, she really missed Bobby—along with the rest of her family. Mom, Lucky. Dad, Lennie. Little bro, Gino Junior, half brother Leonardo, and Grandpa Gino. What a family. What a close-knit group. She loved them all, but she'd had to get away after everything that had taken place.

Athena was pushing her for an answer. Drake was pounding it over the sound system.

"What?" Max said irritably. "You go for it, 'cause I'm not in the mood for getting high."

Athena widened her eyes like she couldn't quite believe anyone would be dumb enough to turn down free drugs. "Oh, please," she said impatiently. "Make a decision."

"Actually, I'm about to head out," Max announced, reaching for her phone and texting for an Uber cab to pick her up.

"You're leaving me?" Athena said with a put-upon frown.

"You're a big girl, you'll manage," Max said, sliding out of the booth past the heavyset man and several other rich men only too happy to pick up the check for two delectable young females.

DENVER

"Long-distance relationships suck," Denver Jones complained to her friend, Carolyn Henderson, as they sat on the back patio of Carolyn's small house in West Hollywood eating breakfast, while Carolyn's infant son, Andy, slept nearby in a wicker carry-cot.

"Then maybe you should break up with him," Carolyn responded with a casual shrug, tearing at a warm croissant and smothering it with butter.

"I didn't *say* I wanted to break up with him," Denver said, throwing her a stony look, wondering why Carolyn was always so negative. "I'm merely bitching about Bobby traveling all over the place while I'm stuck in L.A. 'cause of my job."

"Ah, but it's a job that you live, breathe, and totally love," Carolyn pointed out.

"Oh, yeah," Denver drawled sarcastically. "I so *love* trying to nail sleazebags who sell drugs to children and murder people when they get in their way. It's *so* rewarding, not to mention major exciting."

"Although, as a very competent assistant D.A., you *do* love it when you hear the magic word—guilty," Carolyn said matter-of-factly. "You're the one who gets to lock the bad guys away."

"And how often does *that* happen?" Denver said, reflecting on how screwed up the justice system could be. Nothing was ever a sure thing. "These guys hire the most expensive and canny lawyers, men in five-thousand-dollar suits who are paid fortunes to get those criminal assholes off the hook. And most times they succeed."

"Unfortunately that's the system," Carolyn said, adding jam to her croissant.

"Yeah," Denver said glumly. "The system blows, and I should know since I was once part of it. I am *so* much happier being on the other side."

"I can tell," Carolyn said. "And you *did* get Frankie Romano arrested and thrown into jail."

"True," Denver said thoughtfully. "In spite of Bobby urging me to go easy on him."

"Bobby gave you a hard time, right?"

"He certainly did, Frankie being an old friend of his. I mean, what did he *expect* me to do? It's my *job*, for God's sake, there's no way I can call in favors. Frankie's apartment was drug city. *And* he was dealing big-time."

Since leaving the law firm of Saunders, Fields, Simmons, and Johnson, where she had been one of their youngest defense attorneys, Denver was thrilled that she no longer had to defend scuzzy celebrities who were obviously guilty—including action movie star Ralph Maestro. It was all a big relief, she was so glad she'd switched sides to become an assistant D.A. Now she was currently part of a drug task force—a tight-knit group of people, all with the same endgame in mind—valiantly attempting to stop the endless flow of illegal drugs into America. The stories that she saw and heard devastated her. Babies born addicted to crack; teenagers overdosing at parties; young girls forced into addiction and prostitution. And who profited from all this misery? The dealers, of course. From the kids on the street who peddled pot and pills, to the drug lords like Pablo Fernandez Diego—an unprincipled Colombian drug lord who funneled drugs from his country into the U.S. at an alarming rate. The Diego cartel was notorious for supplying large shipments of cocaine, marijuana, heroin, methamphetamine. It seemed his drug operation was unstoppable, and although it would be more or less impossible to nail Pablo in Colombia, if they could nab his lowlife son, Alejandro, it would be a major coup. Alejandro owned Club Luna, a Hollywood hangout which everyone knew was a front for drug running—but so far nothing could be proved. Arresting Frankie Romano was a positive, and Denver had high hopes that eventually Frankie would start hemorrhaging information, for as Alejandro's former close friend he had to know plenty.

Leon, one of Denver's colleagues, had been working undercover, which was how they'd managed to nail Frankie. Now, getting him to talk was the key to maybe indicting Alejandro, but so far Frankie was refusing to cooperate.

"Have you ever thought that Bobby might fool around on you?" Carolyn asked.

"Are you kidding me?" Denver said, surprised that Carolyn would even suggest it. "Why would you say that?"

"It's never crossed your mind that he could cheat?"

"No, it never has."

"Then you're more naïve than I thought," Carolyn said, taking a gulp of hot coffee. "*All* men cheat."

ALEJANDRO

"That fuckin' D.A. is a fuckin' bitch cunt," Alejandro Diego fumed, pacing up and down the polished white marble floor of his luxury penthouse located on the Wilshire Corridor in L.A. "I got people telling me she's trying to get Frankie fucking Romano to spill on me. You know what my father would say? That they both got to be dealt with, an' my papi is always right."

"Pablo's not here," Rafael, Alejandro's right-hand man, pointed out. "Pablo's in Colombia."

Alejandro's nostrils flared, indicating his sour anger. "You think I don't know that?" he steamed. "You think I'm a fool?"

"You should never have become involved with Frankie," Rafael said in his best I-told-you-so voice. "I tried to warn you he was bad news. The problem is that you never listen."

"Shut the fuck up," Alejandro spat. "How come you're always the voice of doom? What is it with you?"

"Your lawyer says you're safe for now," Rafael said, remaining calm, even though he had an urge to smash Alejandro in his dumbass face.

"My lawyer doesn't know shit," Alejandro muttered. "It's *my* opinion that matters, and *I* say that Frankie needs taking care of before he opens his big mouth. As for that attorney bitch, take care of her, too. You *know* she's trying to get me indicted, so why aren't you doing something?"

"I am," Rafael said quietly.

"What?" Alejandro demanded.

"You'll see. There is a plan in motion."

Alejandro turned on Rafael with a vicious expression. "It better be good," he threatened.

"It will be."

Alejandro was the privileged son of Pablo Fernandez Diego, a feared Columbian drug lord, who ruled an empire. And Rafael was the lowly son of Eugenia, Pablo's housekeeper. The two men had grown up together.

Eugenia, a comely woman, had cared for both boys as if they were brothers, and many people suspected that they were, for Eugenia had no husband or significant other. The only man in her life was Pablo, whom she doted upon.

Pablo Fernandez Diego was not only a major drug lord, he was also a notorious womanizer. Married three times to a trio of beauty queens, he entertained an endless parade of mistresses. After business, sex was his favorite pastime.

Alejandro's mother had died in a tragic car accident when he was a baby, so the only mother figure he'd known was Eugenia. He had no siblings—maybe Rafael, although neither Eugenia nor Pablo would admit that Rafael *was* his actual brother, which suited him fine. Alejandro took pride in the fact that *he* was the chosen one who would eventually inherit Pablo's huge drug empire. Rafael had no inheritance rights.

At twenty-nine the two of them were a month apart in age—Rafael being the oldest. They'd attended school together, hung out together, screwed the same girls, and finally completed their education at UCLA in California, where Rafael had spent most of his time clearing up Alejandro's messes. Over time there were many—from several girls Alejandro had gotten pregnant to a major cheating scandal.

Alejandro had fallen in love with the American way of life, and after returning to Pablo's ranch in Bogotá for a couple of years, working in the family business, he'd persuaded his father that there was more money to be made if Pablo appointed him in charge of trafficking cocaine and other illegal shipments to California.

"I already have people in place who are taking care of that," Pablo had informed him. "Everything's running smoothly."

"I know," Alejandro had replied, working on Pablo as only he could. "But do not forget, Papi, that *I* am family, so who better to trust?"

After a while Pablo had agreed that it wasn't such a terrible idea. If his son wanted power, perhaps it would be prudent to give him a small taste. Eventually he'd arranged for Alejandro to make the move to the U.S.—as long as Rafael accompanied him, and the two of them worked with the people Pablo already had in place.

Rafael had balked at the thought of leaving. He now had a young girlfriend, Elizabetta, who'd recently given birth to a baby boy, and he had no wish to leave them. However, Pablo insisted—and when Pablo insisted, nobody dared to argue, not if they valued their life.